The Columbia Anthology of Chinese Folk and Popular Literature

TRANSLATIONS FROM THE

ASIAN CLASSICS

Translations from the Asian Classics

The Columbia Anthology of Chinese Folk and Popular Literature

Edited by Victor H. Mair and Mark Bender

COLUMBIA UNIVERSITY PRESS
NEW YORK

Columbia University Press
Publishers Since 1893
New York Chichester, West Sussex

Library of Congress Cataloging-in-Publication Data
The Columbia anthology of Chinese folk and popular literature / edited by Victor H. Mair and Mark Bender.
p. cm— (Translations from the Asian classics)
Includes bibliographical references.
ISBN 978-0-231-15312-6 (cloth : alk. paper)
ISBN 978-0-231-15313-3 (pbk. : alk. paper)
ISBN 978-0-231-52673-9 (ebk.)
1. Folk literature, Chinese—Translations into English. 2. Folklore—China.
3. Ethnic folklore—China. I. Mair, Victor H., 1943– II. Bender, Mark.
GR335.c64 2011
398.20951—dc22
2010045027

Columbia University Press books are printed on permanent and durable acid-free paper.
This book is printed on paper with recycled content.

Printed in the United States of America

c 10 9 8 7 6 5 4 3 2 1
p 10 9 8 7 6 5 4 3 2

References to Internet Web sites (URLs) were accurate at the time of writing. Neither the editors nor Columbia University Press is responsible for URLs that may have expired or changed since the manuscript was prepared.

CONTENTS

PREFACE

This is a book with a long gestation. In teaching courses on Chinese literature at the University of Pennsylvania back in the early 1980s, I constantly felt the lack of a comprehensive collection of folk and popular genres. With the 1990s, the abundant coverage of mainstream poetry, prose, fiction, and drama in several superb anthologies and reference works published just before and during that decade only made me feel all the more keenly the need for a comparable gathering of texts that not only would introduce the folk and popular literature of the main ethnic group, the Han, but also would present the oral and written literature of the so-called minority groups. Even the availability of materials for the study of literature belonging to the Han ethnic group was skewed by overemphasis on works written in Literary Sinitic (classical Chinese) or Mandarin, with almost no attention whatsoever paid to topolectal literature in Cantonese, Taiwanese, Wu, and many other languages with rich performance traditions.

By the mid-1980s, if not before, I already had begun to contact colleagues at various institutions, asking them to send me contributions for what—in an inchoate fashion—I envisaged as an anthology that would remedy the absence of a suitable textbook for courses on Chinese folk and popular literature.

The contributions came in, but ever so slowly, making me realize that although the students who would benefit from such an anthology were numerous, colleagues who were interested in and able to provide competent translations of this type of literature were scattered far and wide. One such person, about whom I had come to know while he was still a graduate student, was Mark Bender, at The Ohio State University.

Mark Bender was, and still is, one of the few scholars in the West (not to mention the whole world) who focus exclusively on Chinese oral and performing arts. Much of his research is based on extensive experience in the field. One aspect of Professor Bender's work that I most appreciate is his recording and transcription of stories, ballads, and so forth directly from the performers. This is particularly important, since so much of what had passed for Chinese (writ large) folk and popular literature in the past was badly bowdlerized by researchers who converted everything into sanitized, homogenized, bland pabulum that could not help but disappoint even the most enthusiastic reader. One of the principles of this collection is that, as much as possible for non-Sinitic and non-Mandarin literature, we avoid passing everything through a Modern Standard Mandarin filter.

Even after Mark Bender joined me as coeditor, however, the compilation went slowly. There are a number of reasons for this dilatoriness. First of all, it was difficult to find suitable materials from the many different groups and genres that we wished to have represented. Second, even when we were able to identify appropriate materials, it was hard to locate specialists capable of dealing with them in a competent fashion. Third, the sheer scale of the volume meant that it was bound to take a considerable amount of time to assemble the relevant texts, to arrange them in a logical order, and to provide useful introductions for them. Finally, however, by sheer dint of stubborn persistence, and with the encouragement of our editors, colleagues, and students, we have somehow managed to bring this volume to completion. It is our earnest expectation that our labors will not have been in vain.

The Columbia Anthology of Chinese Folk and Popular Literature is meant to serve as a companion to *The Columbia Anthology of Traditional Chinese Literature* and *The Columbia History of Chinese Literature*, as well as to other related publications on premodern and modern Chinese literature from Columbia University Press. Together they constitute the most complete and comprehensive set of textbooks for the study of Chinese literature in all its manifestations that has ever been presented to the public. It is our hope that, through these works, those interested in Chinese literature will come to know it better and in a more thorough way than heretofore has been possible. In this endeavor, *The Columbia Anthology of Chinese Folk and Popular Literature* is perhaps the most crucial link, since it offers the reader a broad range of material that has never before been made available in English, material that is essential for a complete understanding of the literature of China from the most diverse levels, groups, and periods of Chinese society and history.

Victor H. Mair

ACKNOWLEDGMENTS

The editors of this volume wish to extend heartfelt thanks to everyone involved in this project. Over the course of many years, a great number of people from several continents have participated by submitting manuscripts, supplying background information, helping with formatting and editing tasks, arranging access to archives and cultural sites, and offering encouragement.

Paula Roberts, associate director of the Center for East Asian Studies at the University of Pennsylvania, was a major force in shaping the final book manuscript and we deeply appreciate her contributions.

A number of Mark Bender's students at Ohio State—including Sarah White, Jon Noble, Max Bohnenkamp, Yu Li, Shan Wu, Bao Ying, Rachel Kou, Peace Lee, Brian Bare, Zhang Yunxin, Anne Henochowicz, Levi Gibbs, Pai Yi-fan, Tim Thurston, and You Ziying—helped in many ways over a period of years. Several of these and other students contributed selections to this volume based on projects in Bender's seminars on the translation of Chinese oral literature.

On behalf of the contributors, we would like to thank the many singers, storytellers, actors, and other local participants who gave generously from their stores of memory, talent, and heritage to make this collection possible.

The editors would also like to acknowledge the various presses and journals for allowing the use of previously published material, as noted in "Sources of Previously Published Selections," which appears at the end of the volume.

Victor Mair is grateful to his students and colleagues, as well as to the staff of the Department of East Asian Languages and Civilizations and the librarians of the University of Pennsylvania, all of whom have assisted him in various ways during the making of this volume. Mark Bender takes delight in acknowledging the many people who have influenced or aided him in his career. Although this list can only be partial, it includes Eugene Ching, Frank Hsueh, Royall Tyler, Zha Ruqiang, Zhong Jingwen, Duan Baolin, Sun Jingyao, Wang Jiaxiang, Hou Depeng, John Deeney, Li Zixian, Li Shizhong, Jin Dan, Che Xilun, Ivan Wolffers, Larry Tyler, Anthony Walker, Timothy Wong, Gary Snyder, Susan Blader, Wu Zongxi, Bamo Qubumo, Chao Gejin (Chogjin), Huang Jianming, John Miles Foley, and Luo Qingchun. His thanks extend to his supportive colleagues at Ohio State in the Department of East Asian Languages and Literatures, the OSU Center for Folklore Studies, and the OSU Libraries.

Finally, both editors wish to acknowledge the support of their family members. As always, Victor Mair is grateful to Li-ching Chang Mair for her sagely observations and saintly patience. Mark Bender thanks his parents, the Reverend George E. Bender and Pauline Ella (Pike) Bender. He owes the greatest debt of thanks to Wei Fu Bender and Marston Arwine Bender, who endured living rooms invaded by trails of manuscript pages and numerous other indignities over the life of the project.

CHINESE UNITS OF MEASURE

chi (usually translated as "foot")	1.09 feet (0.33 m)
cun (usually translated as "inch")	1.3 inches (3.3 cm)
li (usually translated as "tricent")	0.31 mile (about 500 m)
liang (usually translated as "ounce")	1.75 ounces (about 50 g)
mu (usually translated as "one-sixth acre")	about 0.16 acre (667.5 sq m)
zhang (usually translated as "ten feet")	3.6 yards (3.3 m)

The Columbia Anthology of Chinese Folk and Popular Literature

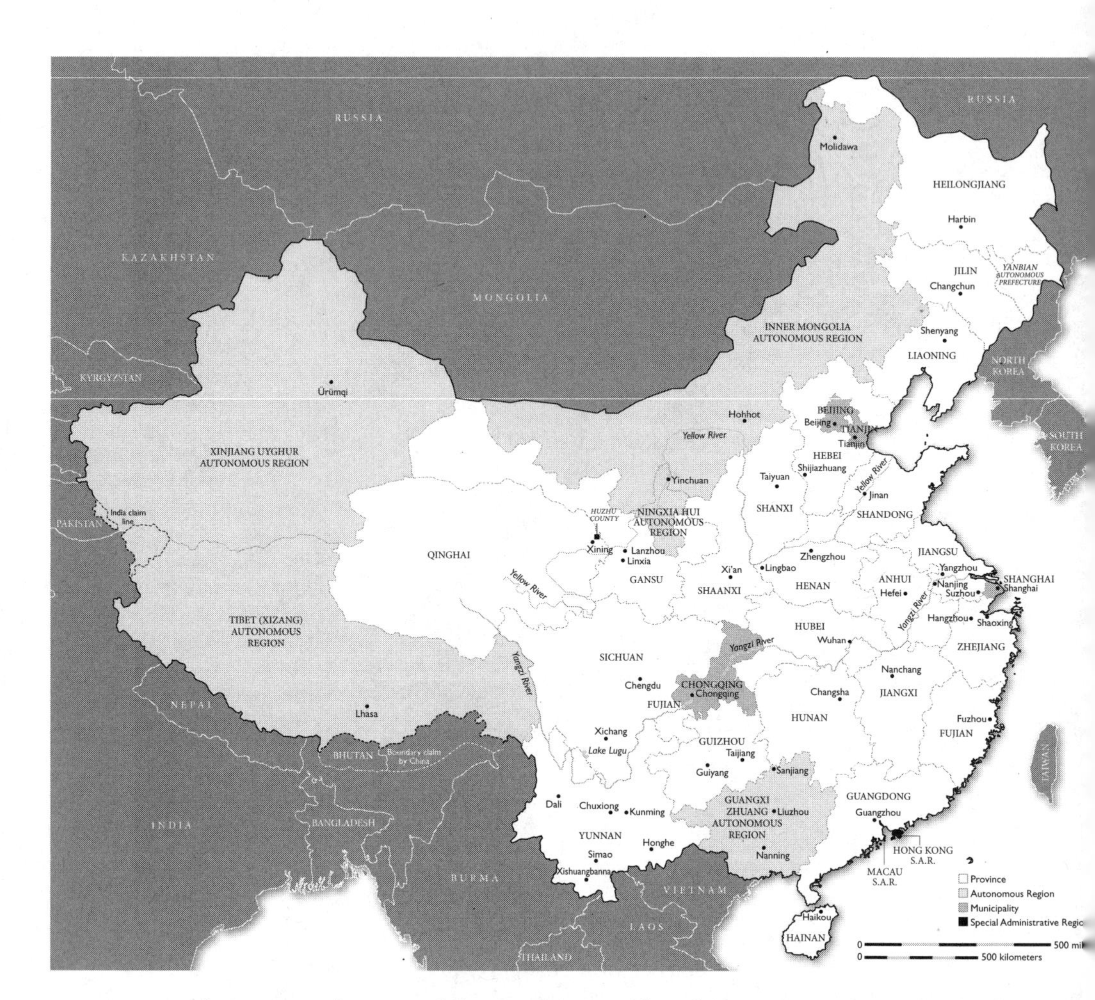

Administrative divisions of the People's Republic of China. (Map drawn by Carol Zuber-Mallison)

"I SIT HERE AND SING FOR YOU"

The Oral Literature of China

MARK BENDER AND VICTOR MAIR

"I sit here and sing for you"—appropriate as a distillation of all the works collected here—is but one line in a folk song from an ethnic minority group in south-central China: one line in a collection of translations drawn from a massive body of oral literature accumulated by Chinese and non-Chinese scholars over a period of several hundred years. To get an idea of the scale of the available corpus, envision this: between 1949 and the early 1990s, Chinese researchers, in a series of nationwide "intangible culture" investigation projects, collected approximately 3 million folk songs and nearly 2 million folk narratives from the many ethnic groups in China—not to mention 7 million proverbs![1]

These vast collections are, of course, only the most recent additions to the substantial body of oral-based materials that have been passed down in written form, beginning in the fifth century B.C.E. with the *Book of Odes* (*Shi jing*), followed by the Music Bureau (Yue Fu) ballads of the Han dynasty (206 B.C.E.–220 C.E.); the numerous dramatic forms of the Yuan (1271–1368) and later dynasties; the many narratives combining speaking and singing of the Tang (618–907), Ming (1368–1644), and Qing (1644–1911) dynasties; the folk song collections of the Ming and Qing; and the great number of songs and stories collected during

1. Delegation of the People's Republic of China, "Current Status of the Protection and Legislation of National Folklore in China" (paper presented at the World Intellectual Property Organization, Geneva, June 14, 2002), 2.

the Folk Song Movement of the May Fourth era of the 1920s and 1930s, when young intellectuals like Gu Jiegang and Zhong Jingwen helped stimulate modern scholarly interest in the oral literature of the local and ethnic cultures in China. And then there are the substantial collections made by missionaries and scholars in the nineteenth and early twentieth centuries. Since the early 1980s, as the mainland reopened after years of isolation between the 1950s and the 1970s, opportunities for recording oral literature in media other than writing have been enhanced first by the widespread availability of tape recorders and then by the influx of digital video and recording equipment in the late 1990s and early twenty-first century.

Our goal is to present in this volume a multivoiced selection of works from this vast array of oral literature that will draw well-deserved attention to rich but often unfamiliar material. In creating this collection, we have been able to introduce only a fraction of the available pieces. Since many of the earliest examples of oral literature and major dramatic traditions have found their way into anthologies of Chinese literature, we have focused our selections on works recorded or written in the past four hundred or so years. Many of our major categories (which we discuss in this introduction) are filled with selections drawn from living local traditions and collected over the past few decades.

The selections range from a detailed version of the story of the woman warrior Hua Mulan that was recorded in a collection of oral literature compiled by an important Mongol official in nineteenth-century northern China to performances of professional storytellers in the highly populated urban centers of the Yangtze (Yangzi) delta, whose art was nurtured for centuries in the land of "fish and rice"; the selections also include Manchu (Manzu) shaman rituals and a tale of a trickster-hero of the Daur people from the forests of the northeast; the antiphonal folk songs of the Zhuang people living among the fantastic limestone hills of the Guangxi Zhuang Autonomous Region, of the mountain-dwelling She of Fujian province, and of the Cantonese-speaking boat people of Hong Kong; epic poems of the heroes Geser Khan and Jangar from the endless steppes and stony deserts of Inner Mongolia; a tale about the sad marital fate of Sister Qeo from the Mongghul people of Gansu and Qinghai in the arid northwest; and a local drama (rice-planting song) from the alluvial plains of Hebei province.

As is made clear in the introductions to the individual selections, many once-living traditions of oral literature now survive only as "oral-connected" written texts, while others are still performed for local audiences, despite pressures created by social shifts and upheavals over the past century and competition from increasingly varied and alluring electronic media in a rapidly changing, consumption-driven environment. In some cases, we were fortunate enough to have material translated directly from local Chinese or ethnic minority languages. In other instances, it was necessary to work from texts already translated into Mandarin Chinese (Putonghua). In all cases, we have relied on the efforts of reliable translators with deep knowledge of the original languages, cultures, and processes of collection.

LOCAL CULTURES AND ETHNIC MINORITIES

Before discussing the generic categories and terms used to organize and describe the selections, a few words are needed about local cultures and ethnic diversity in China. By "China," we mean a pluralistic China—a nation of many differing peoples whose more than 1.3 billion citizens live within the borders of a land as culturally varied as it is geographically diverse. The government of China officially recognizes fifty-six major ethnic groups. In the 1950s, these groups were identified as "nationalities" (*minzu*), following the model of the former Soviet Union, though in recent years the term "ethnic groups" has often been used in official translations. The largest of these groups, constituting about 90 percent of the population of China, is called the Han. The Han majority is actually a mixture of many local and regional cultures tied together by tradition and relationships to the imperial governments of the past. Its name is derived from China's first long-lasting imperial dynasty, the Han, which perfected a bureaucratic structure that set the pattern for most of the dynasties to follow, until the end of the imperial system in 1911. This huge majority ethnic group, however, is a modern construction and can be divided into many smaller regional subgroups. Particular markers of difference, still prominent in some rural areas, include foodways, folk costumes, customs, lineage descent patterns, architecture, farming practices, and—not least—linguistic features.

Language is one of the most obvious markers of these Han local cultures, which include speakers of Yue (Cantonese), Min, Gan, Wu, Xiang, Hakka, Mandarin (spoken varieties in northern, northwestern, and southwestern parts of the country), and so forth. Although all the respective local Han languages (which we here call topolects) are in the Sinitic branch of the Sino-Tibetan language family, and the common medium of written Chinese has tied the Han local cultures together for millennia, many of the languages are mutually difficult to understand or even unintelligible. This feature directly affects the performance of oral literature in terms of the language register of performance and audience reception. If an audience cannot understand what is going on, its attention will be difficult to hold. A performer must adapt to the local situation or move on. For example, professional storytellers in the Suzhou chantefable tradition perform in a complex and conservative linguistic register that is now difficult for younger audience members even in the home region to understand. When invited to perform in Beijing or other venues outside Jiangsu province, they face audiences who find it virtually impossible to follow what is being said or sung in their performances. This intelligibility problem is to a degree mitigated by performing parts of the engagement in Mandarin (or, in some cases, displaying a translation on a screen), though the performers (and knowing audience members) rightly feel that such performances lack the flavor of the original language.

The situation with China's fifty-five official minority (that is, non-Han) ethnic groups is even more complex. Although the largest percentage of ethnic minority citizens live in specially designated autonomous regions, prefectures, counties, and townships, many also live in urban centers all over the nation. Among the present ethnic minorities are the descendants of those who conquered and ruled China in the past or who established strong, competing kingdoms on its shifting borders. These include Mongols, whose ancestors ruled the entire country during the thirteenth and fourteenth centuries; Tibetan groups, who live on and to the east of the Tibetan Plateau and whose powerful kingdoms competed with the Tang dynasty; and Uyghurs, who, by the ninth century, held sway over the oasis cities of the northwestern deserts and basins. During the expansive Qing dynasty, the Manchus—who now number over 14 million—integrated territories populated by a number of these groups into the borders of an already vast land. Other officially recognized ethnic groups include the She, Miao, Yao, Dong (Gaem), Zhuang, Yi, Lahu, Bai, Mosuo (a subgroup of the Naxi), and Wa (Va) of the south and southwest; the Tu of the northwest; the Daur and Chaoxian (ethnic Koreans) of the northeast; and the Hui (a Muslim people) of the west and other parts of the country. Many of the larger ethnic minority groups have dozens of subgroups, all going by different names. The Yi of southwestern China, for instance, have around seventy subgroups with names including Nuosu, Nasu, Lipo, Lolopo, Azhe, Sani, and Gni in a total population of more than 7 million.

Like the Han local cultures, these ethnic minority groups and their subgroups all have traditions of oral literature. Because of the complex interactions between the various cultures over the centuries, there are many cases of mutual influence between the traditions. These influences can sometimes be seen in specific plots and characters, tropes, motifs, imagery, and performance style. For example, figures from Han popular literature such as the Monkey King (a main character in the romance *Journey to the West* [*Xiyou ji*]), the ill-fated lovers in the gender-bending tale of Liang Shanbo and Zhu Yingtai, and the tiger-killing hero Wu Song (a figure from the prose narrative *Outlaws of the Marsh* [*Water Margin* (*Shuihu zhuan*)]) appear in many local traditions of oral performance across the Han subgroups and have historically been adopted into the traditions of some minority ethnic groups. In other cases, the motifs of heroes with flying horses, mortal combat with fearsome monsters and evil khans, and privations on long journeys to rescue captured family members or brides are common in folk stories, ballads, and epics among many of the steppe- and forest-dwelling peoples in the north and northwest. Likewise, the use of local flora and fauna imagery—especially flowers and insects—is pervasive in the banter-filled song duels of antiphonal singers all across the multiethnic regions of southern and southwestern China.

GENERIC CATEGORIES

Throughout nineteenth-century Europe, emerging nation-states sought to collect and organize distinctive items of their respective national heritages, resulting in collections of folklore such as *Children's and Household Tales*, more commonly known as *Grimm's Fairy Tales*. The generic categories that were established in that era included folk songs, folk stories, epic poetry, folk ritual, and folk drama. In the late nineteenth and early twentieth centuries, these categories, with some modifications, were introduced into Japan by folklorists such as Yanagita Kunio and were eventually adopted in China during the era of cultural enlightenment that began with the May Fourth Movement of 1919 and continued into the 1930s. In this volume, most of the selections are grouped under these general categories, which, though not culturally specific, are useful in organizing the diverse materials in our collection. It should be understood, however, that each culture represented in the volume has its own, native terms and system of classification for its verbal art genres.

The terms "folk" and "popular" in connection with literature appear throughout this volume. Our use of both words refers to broad classifications of oral-based literature. By the 1920s, Chinese scholars who would become the first generation of modern Chinese folklorists had begun to adopt certain Western terms (often via Japanese scholarship) and to coin some of their own terminology to describe traditional forms of verbal art. The term "folk literature" (*minjian wenxue*) is regarded by Chinese scholars such as Duan Baolin as describing creations of verbal art circulating orally among the common people. These include stories told around the hearth, songs sung by young people courting under the village tree, and other forms of expression such as proverbs. Most of the examples in this collection were gathered in rural contexts, though modern scholars also recognize the existence of urban folklore and folklore of various classes and groups in society. The word *suwenxue*, which can be translated as "popular, or vernacular, literature," is an umbrella term used by Chinese scholars to group various sorts of written texts that tend to have many "oral" features and, in some cases, are directly related to or mimic local oral-performance traditions. Many such texts were circulated by dealers or hand to hand among urban audiences, often in complex commercial networks extending into remote inland cities and towns.

The category of oral literature known as speaking and singing literature (*shuochang wenxue* or *jiangchang wenxue*) is well represented in many cultures in East Asia. Such traditions are most likely linked, at a remove of some distance, to ancient styles of performance once used for propagating Buddhism, that alternate between passages of prose and those of verse. While only written texts remain of the older forms, some of the more recent manifestations of this style are still performed. In China, the written forms of this tradition are also categorized as "speaking and singing literature" (*shuochang wenxue*)—close in meaning to the term "prosimetric," which we have adopted in this volume to describe such works. The vast body of these works includes the "transformation texts" (*bianwen*) of the Tang dynasty and a plethora of largely under-studied forms (several represented in our selections) that had their heydays of popularity in the eighteenth and nineteenth centuries, often as written forms of popular literature.

Since the late 1940s, the general term "art of melodies" (*quyi*) has been used to categorize the living (or recently moribund) prosimetric traditions, some with histories of hundreds of years. Such traditional forms are performed by professional or semiprofessional storytellers at teahouses, special storytelling houses, banquets, variety shows, old folks' homes, and other venues that continue to emerge as the traditions struggle to remain viable in a rapidly changing society. Examples of these living traditions are chantefables (*Suzhou tanci*), bamboo clapper tales (*kuaibanshu*), and Shandong fast tales (*kuaishu*).

In the West, the word "epic" has traditionally been used to describe long poems filled with ethnic spirit conjured by deeds of battling heroes enacted in vast and dangerous spaces on land and sea far from home. It was once believed that China had no epics. While long poems featuring martial heroes are hard to find in Han Chinese repertoires, some of the prosimetric works with what Lauri Honko has called exemplary characters (who might be scholar-officials or talented, beautiful women) could be described by the term.[2] Works in the more classic pattern of martial heroes are not uncommon in the oral literature of some minority ethnic groups, however. The great Tibetan epic of King Gesar and its Mongol counterparts featuring Geser Khan, the Mongol epic *Jangar*, and the Kazakh epic *Manas* are among the longest poems in the world.

There are also many myths in the form of epics recounting the creation of the sky and earth. Since the 1950s, a large number of long poems (some in antiphonal style) describing the creation of just about everything have been collected among many ethnic groups in the southwest. These narratives often contain motifs of the separation of the sky and the earth, a hero who shoots down extra suns and moons to end global overheating, several generations of protohumans, a great flood, and the consequent repopulation of the earth by survivors (often a brother and sister) who escape the rising waters in a calabash or similar vehicle. At some point, the ensuing children learn to speak the languages of the locale and then divide and spread out to populate the various ecological niches. These themes are repeated and combined in many ways in epics among ethnic groups such as the Miao, Yi, Lahu, Yao, and Dong and, as recent studies have shown, even among some Han in the south-central region.

Prominent among the folk song traditions in the collection are those sung in antiphonal style. Possibly of very early origin, they have been documented in many areas all over China and in contiguous regions in Asia. The basic pattern is that of a sort of conversation or contest in song. Typically, one or more singers (often a pair singing as one voice) sing several lines, to which response is made by one or more other singers. This dynamic may continue for only a few minutes, or it can extend for hours. Such songs are commonly part of courting rituals, and the imagery may at times be sexually suggestive. Tunes, structural patterns, imagery, and performance situations vary locally and regionally. Although

---

2. Lauri Honko, *Textualising the Siri Epic*, Folklore Fellows Communications, no. 264 (Helsinki: Suomalainen Tiedeakatemia, Academia Scientiarum Fennica, 1998), 28.

in general decline, antiphonal singing is still viable in some rural areas of the south, southwest, and northwest.

TYPES OF ORAL LITERATURE

Throughout this volume, we employ several general terms that describe various types of oral literature that we have categorized under the words "folk" and "popular." Scholars of the epic John Miles Foley and Lauri Honko have both, in somewhat different ways, suggested that oral literature falls into several typological categories.[3] Foley, in particular, has argued for a definition of what he calls oral poetry that goes beyond the idea of the mutually exclusive realms of orality and writing, maintaining that many traditional written texts share sufficient connections with oral performance that they have a place within the large tent of oral literature. Although we employ somewhat different terms, Foley's idea that oral literature encompasses a range of verbal art wider than pure "oral tradition" is useful in approaching the situation in China, especially in regard to the many written prosimetric traditions. Inspired by these theorists, we describe the works of folk and popular literature in this volume using the terms "oral performance," "oral connected," and "tradition oriented."

ORAL-PERFORMANCE TRADITIONS

In our usage, the term "oral performance" covers traditions of live performance—whether telling a folk story, singing a ballad, or enacting a ritual or folk drama. In the ideal of pure "oral tradition," a text has no identifiable connection to writing or written traditions and is handed down and performed wholly by oral means, which may include not only the spoken or sung word but also conventionalized paralinguistic sounds and gestures. In this conception, oral tradition consists of those works of verbal art that exist (at least before someone records them) as ephemeral performances, recast from memory and made meaningful in each act of performance. From a scholarly perspective, these oral texts typically show variation among performances (sometimes quite radical) but still involve the re-creation of part of a certain set of consistent elements in each performance. In some situations, such as in the antiphonal folk song traditions, the folk audiences expect competent innovation in the combination and recombination of traditional images, rhyme schemes, and sometimes even schemes of linguistic pitch tones (many languages in China are tonal, employing several distinct tones, as in the four tones of Mandarin). In other cases, as with some folk rituals, a greater degree of sameness (or at least a perceived degree of sameness)

3. John Miles Foley, *How to Read an Oral Poem* (Urbana: University of Illinois Press, 2002), 38–53; Lauri Honko, *Textualization of Oral Epics* (Berlin: Mouton de Gruyter, 2000), 4–9.

is expected among recitations of lyrics and accompanying actions. Examples in this volume of oral traditions that historically have existed without the factor of writing include most of the folk song traditions, folk stories, and some of the epic, ritual, and dramatic texts.

In many situations, however, a range of influences from written traditions and other media may come to bear on orally performed material. For instance, memory aids in the form of complete written scripts, skeletal plotlines, or notes are reviewed, rehearsed, or meditated on by many professional storytellers in China before taking the stage or storytelling platform—helping to refresh already internalized plots and circumstances. This situation may exist even with storytellers who were initially taught the elements of their craft by listening to and imitating a master's live performances without access to notes or a script. Unless a song or story has intentionally been memorized word for word from a script, writing-enhanced performances are still subject to creative modification in the act of performance and may exhibit considerable variation among performances. In other cases, printed matter may be consulted for ideas, images, or plots. For example, in the early 1980s a popular series of volumes of short love songs, categorized as the steps involved in the antiphonal song courting process, made thousands of song motifs readily available to singers throughout the rural areas of Guangxi, in the southwest. Because of such differing situations, we employ the term "oral performance" to cover both "uncontaminated" oral tradition and other types of enacted, orally delivered traditions of performance.

A complicating element in the discussion about what extra-performance factors affect oral-performance traditions is the recent exponential growth in access to media by way of an array of digital recording devices. Today it is normal in many areas for rural folk to watch—and even shoot—locally produced digital video recordings of themselves or others engaged in folk-singing events, rituals, and local festival activities. A more urban phenomenon is the increasing number of online folk song and storytelling sites that have been created by storytelling aficionados or troupes, which sometimes feature whole archives of videotaped performances in a variety of styles, available to any interested party.

This sudden and wide availability of technology has raised new questions about the nature of "orality" in China. How will scholars regard performances by singers who have been exposed to the "frozen in time" recordings of performances by themselves or other singers, available for memorization much as written texts are utilized but with the whole range of auditory and paralinguistic gestures that can never be fully represented in a written transcription? How will this sort of engagement with static elements of a tradition, lacking the creative potential for variation at the core of live performances, affect the tradition in the long run? From another angle, does technology in some ways help sustain or revive interest in traditions that increasingly lack performers and audiences, or form or synthesize new traditions?

ORAL-CONNECTED TEXTS

The term "oral connected" refers to written texts that have certain connections to oral-performance traditions. A number of selections in this volume are written remnants of what are now lost performance traditions. Several of the prosimetric narratives fall into this category. Many works of traditional popular fiction (in both prose and prosimetric form) employ a convention sometimes called the storyteller's manner. Such narratives are related in styles that, to varying degrees, suggest oral-storytelling sessions of professional storytellers. Many of these vernacular texts, however, seem to be more suited for reading (silently or aloud) rather than as scripts for any sort of staged performance. An example is "Suitable Attire," a selection from "women's chantefable" (*nü tanci*) that is part of a much longer prosimetric tale written by and circulated among elite women in the Yangtze delta in the late eighteenth and nineteenth centuries.

Most of the oral-connected works seem to have been written especially for literate audiences, but there is evidence that some were adapted for use by professional storytellers, in a circular, interpenetrating dynamic between oral performance and writing. Although many traditions were typically handed down by word of mouth from master to student (as in the case of the "Wu Song" storytellers from Yangzhou), sometimes scholars or other literate storytelling aficionados (or even the storytellers themselves) wrote lyrics or reworked episodes from written texts for delivery in performance. Thus the category of oral connected is a complicated one, suggesting that each work has its own, unique story.

TRADITION-ORIENTED TEXTS

A subset of the oral-connected category is what Lauri Honko termed tradition-oriented texts.[4] Such texts are semiliterary written works that simulate or mimic a particular oral-performance tradition or that draw on existing versions of stories or songs to create written works, such as the *Kalevala*, a pastiche of Finnish oral literature composed by Elias Lönnrot in the nineteenth century.[5] In a similar vein, a large number of composite versions of ethnic minority oral narratives were published in the 1950s and again in the 1980s in China. In many cases, a number of variants were collected, and in a process involving selection, deletion, reassembly, and polishing, "complete" and definitive versions of a story or an epic cycle were created for a reading public. According to Huang Jianming, a folklorist of the Sani ethnic group, such exercises sometimes have involved negotiations between the performers of different versions over what constitutes the most authentic version. In this volume, one example of such a text is the Yao

4. Honko, *Textualization of Oral Epics*, 6–9.

5. Honko, *Textualising the Siri Epic*, 37.

epic poem *Miluotuo*, which is based on several versions collected and edited by local scholars and then recast in Chinese by a local poet of the Zhuang ethnic group.

An issue that has received attention in both modern China and abroad is the reliability of such texts. Virtually all oral literature texts released for public consumption before the mid-1980s were edited under guidelines (varyingly enforced, construed, or skirted) to remove or veil content deemed "unhealthy," "crude," "feudal," "superstitious," "damaging to ethnic unity," "not part of the ethnic culture," or otherwise "politically incorrect." In some instances, content was simply omitted, sometimes on-site in the field, or it was deleted or bowdlerized at an editor's desk. Collecting was complicated by linguistic, translation, and cultural problems, as well as by varying degrees of collector competence and the limitations of technology (much material was recorded by hand, word for word). More interesting was the publication of some ethnic minority texts whose content had deeper meanings for cultural insiders than for others (for example, an innocuous song might actually have been part of a ritual tradition). Despite the strictures (which affected some works more than others), a number of valuable collections were made under the guidance of well-trained researchers, the best produced by cooperation between trained researchers and local tradition bearers. In approaching texts of this era, it should be understood that many irreplaceable transcriptions and texts were destroyed during the dark days of the Cultural Revolution (1966–1976). Thus each surviving work must be assessed on an individual level, with input (when still possible) from participants familiar with the original collection activities.

CONSIDERATIONS OF TEXTUALITY

The wide definition of oral literature described in the preceding section raises questions about the relation of the works in this collection to original folk contexts and traditions. Many of the texts in this volume originally existed in oral form or were written in non-Chinese scripts. Whether a folk song that was sung and recorded, or an oral-connected prosimetric story translated from one language into another, one mode of expression often was replaced by another. As many theorists have noted, while certain aspects of a song or story's content are often fairly easily expressed in other media (say, in the movement from an oral performance to a written text), many features of the original mode of expression are lost in the acts of translation and writing. Although we have attempted to utilize original language texts when possible, in some instances we have selected a work that was originally communicated in one of the minority languages or topolects and then translated into Modern Standard Mandarin rather than forgo the work entirely. In such cases, we have been careful to choose reliably collected and translated texts (which sometimes appeared in bilingual formats), and, if possible, we actually conferred with the persons involved in these processes. The final steps for the works selected here involved translation into English, placement among other texts that did not share a folk context, and presentation to nontraditional audiences across the globe.

APPRECIATING THE SELECTIONS

An important motivation for compiling this volume is its potential for classroom use. Aside from this general introduction addressing the diversity and nature of the Chinese traditions of oral literature, we attempt to facilitate the practical use of this book by providing a brief introduction at the beginning of each chapter and selection, all the while making an effort to keep notes to a minimum. Some instructors may find it useful to observe that versions of several "classic" or more familiar works of Chinese literature and drama appear toward the end of the volume. These include a passage from the vernacular romance *Journey to the West* in bamboo clapper–tale form, a local drama version of the widespread Mulian story, and a Manchu bannermen's tale version of the now global Hua Mulan story. The sources in the bibliography are provided as a guide to those interested in further exploring the topic of oral literature in China.

In the classroom, the texts can be dealt with in a variety of ways. Aside from use as traditional assignments read silently and discussed in class, there is room for actual enactment of many of the songs, stories, and dramas. One goal of the ethnopoetics movement of the 1970s was to increase the awareness of oral literature by voicing translations of underrepresented traditions at public readings. In terms of the selections in this volume, enough contextual information is provided in the individual introductions and bibliography for a simplified reconstruction of performance situations that will allow students to momentarily experience voicing and even embodying the texts. Although the integrity of ritual texts should be respected, many particular traditions invite creativity in the act of performance—with the understanding that in native contexts, certain bounds may be set. It is notable that during the 1950s and 1960s in China, countless experiments were made on the form and content of the *quyi* storytelling arts in the spirit of giving a new face to old traditions. Some of these experiments yielded lasting results, such as the many new styles of storytelling music and creative borrowings between traditions of storytelling and those of drama (a dynamic with deep historical roots).

One format practical for classroom use is an adaptation of the Suzhou chantefable tradition. Normally, one or two professional storytellers sing and speak while playing stringed instruments—a performance style that is hard to duplicate without the instruments (though imaginary "air" lutes and three-stringed banjos might be a possibility!). On some rare occasions, however, portions of stories are told without instrumental accompaniment. In other cases, three or more storytellers cooperate in a performance, dividing roles among themselves. Of course, portions of the professionally told stories from Yangzhou in our collection are normally told by a single performer without instruments. In this and other situations, several students might perform passages in succession, divide the roles by character type, or even adapt the text into more dramatic styles involving several actors and a narrator to create a new pattern of performance.

Other possibilities exist with the antiphonal folk song traditions. In the tradition of Guangxi love songs, two or more pairs of singers make "song talk," members of each pair voicing the same lyrics simultaneously. Thus a song exchange representing a dialogue between two lovers may actually involve four people, two on each side of the exchange. As the selection of Guangxi love songs demonstrates, with the inclusion of two matchmakers, the total count comes to six singers in the exchange! In the case of epic performances, it is not uncommon for a series of singers to participate in a long recital. Depending on the tradition, some may act as relief singers to a major singer, or several singers may cooperate by singing the sections in which each is individually most competent. In some epic traditions from southwestern China, antiphonal styles involving pairs of singers are also used. Such flexibility in some of the traditions offers creative opportunities in the classroom that not only enliven the texts but also allow for maximum experiential participation.

From another perspective, story plots, motifs, and performance conventions have been borrowed—and often modified—in countless ways among individual performers and groups. Students can be asked not only to compare the various items to traditions they are familiar with but also to attempt to provide "the next episode" in a selection or create a series of songs or a story inspired by a particular tradition. Students can also be encouraged to create their own ethnopoetic recastings of particular pieces, taking inspiration from the format of Mareile Flitsch's northeastern ginseng collector's story "The Mother's Brother and His Sister's Son." Further possibilities can be explored by delving into the bibliography for more thorough treatments of individual traditions. For example, Vibeke Børdahl and Jette Ross's *Chinese Storytellers: Life and Art in the Yangzhou Tradition* includes detailed descriptions of performance conventions and is illustrated by an accompanying DVD.[6] Other virtual examples of performances can be found at online sites. In the editors' experience, once students are inspired, they readily engage in the dynamics of experimental re-creative performance.

6. Vibeke Børdahl and Jette Ross, *Chinese Storytellers: Life and Art in the Yangzhou Tradition* (Boston: Cheng and Tsui, 2002).

Chapter 1

FOLK STORIES AND OTHER SPOKEN TRADITIONS

Folk stories constitute a special category of oral narrative that has received a great deal of attention from scholars worldwide since the 1840s, when the Grimm brothers began to publish collections of stories gathered from rural inhabitants in Germany. From that time on, tales such as "Cinderella," "Hansel and Gretel," "Jack and the Beanstalk," "The Princess and the Pea," "Little Red Riding Hood," and many others appeared in print form in many languages, often in versions censored to appeal to prevailing sensibilities about sex and violence. As the nineteenth century progressed, many scholars worldwide extensively collected large bodies of similar folk narratives, often weaving the stories into the fabric of the nationalistic movements of emerging nations. Folk stories were thought to embody the collective character of a given people, and, like canons of written literature, were seen as necessary parts of a mature nation's heritage. The study of folktales had become a national project in Finland by the end of the century, and a major intellectual school of folktale studies developed there that still has influence worldwide.

By the early twentieth century, scholars in China had begun to systematically examine China's folk literature, drawing on historical records and literary works, and by the May Fourth Movement of 1919, they were collecting stories from urban and rural areas all over the country. Stimulated by the efforts of Russian and Finnish folklorists, Yanagita Kunio in Japan, and Stith Thompson in America (who compiled a massive index of common folktale motifs), Chinese researchers such as Zhong Jingwen, Gu Jiegang, and many others took on the project of collecting and analyzing folktales and other types of oral literature not only from Han Chinese areas but also, to some extent, from ethnic minority areas that were often still "foreign" to the Chinese of the large coastal and northern cities. These collecting activities often involved a large number of students who would spend time in rural areas interviewing local tradition bearers and writing down their stories, which would later appear in modern literary and folklore journals.

In the course of the 1930s and 1940s, some folktales (along with folk songs and music) were appropriated by both Nationalist and Communist forces for use in their respective social education and propaganda efforts. After 1949, even larger and more organized folk literature collection projects were carried out nationwide, covering virtually all the fifty-plus ethnic groups in China (which were only then being given official recognition), and huge numbers of folk stories were recorded, edited, and published, often in altered form to appeal to prevailing currents in the political wind. During the period from 1950 until the early 1980s, stories were regularly bowdlerized to put the proper spin on gender and class issues and to eliminate crude, pornographic, or "feudal" references in the interests of creating a "new China." Between 1966 and 1976, most stories that appeared had overt political content and in many cases were fabricated or distorted beyond recognition. By the early 1980s, however, more reliable collections had reappeared, though for a number of years editorial policies continued to be conservative.

Yet, as with many folk stories that have been collected elsewhere in the world, folk stories published today in China tend to appear in a more or less idealized and rather literary format that does not attempt to represent many of the stylistic features of actual storytelling situations. In recent years, however, a few scholars, influenced by folklorists outside the country, have begun to experiment with new models of collecting and editing that may open new avenues for appreciating China's rich heritage of folktales. The following stories are a few examples from the vast store of these folktales, presented in a variety of editorial formats. Probably the most unfamiliar to readers is the "ethnopoetic" style of presentation of "The Mother's Brother and His Sister's Son," a ginseng tale from northeastern China. The words are printed in a manner that allows the reader to get a sense of the stresses and pauses of the original language. The other stories are presented in more traditional formats that were developed in part to facilitate easy reading.

While whole volumes could be devoted to the topic, only a few stories can be presented here. They were translated from their original languages or, when that was not possible, chosen from among especially interesting tales that had been translated into Chinese and were felt to widen our understanding of the range of styles and topics. For instance, the Daur tale "Mengongnenbo" has imagery and situations found in stories of other northern ethnic minority groups as well as features of trickster tales that resonate with stories from many parts of the world. Stories of a human-eating "wild woman" of the mountains comparable to "Cannibal Grandmother," a Nuosu tale about Coqo Ama, have been collected from other ethnic groups in China (including the Han), as well as from Japan, North America, Africa, and other places. The dragon tales represent a common theme found in many parts of China and, like "Goddess Gemu," a Mosuo tale from Lake Lugu (on the border of Yunnan and Sichuan provinces), are also examples of the seemingly endless number of stories about local places in this vast land. The Dai tales not only are a part of traditional Tai Lue lore but also are closely related to Buddhist stories rooted in India, directly illustrating the cross-cultural nature of some stories circulating in ethnic groups in China. An unusual selection is "The Red Silk-Cotton Tree," a Luo folk story from Yunnan province embedded in a funeral chant. This story could easily have been placed in chapter 3, on folk ritual, as could the stories about the origin of rituals from the Tu ethnic group in Qinghai province, in northwestern China.

This chapter also includes two examples of other forms of spoken verbal art. There are "flirting words" and tongue twisters from Tibetans in Qinghai province and riddles from the Namzi, a small Tibetan subgroup in Sichuan province. These selections are included to suggest the many minor styles of spoken oral literature in China.

A GINSENG TALE FROM JILIN

Collected, translated, and introduced by Mareile Flitsch

"The Mother's Brother and His Sister's Son" is a common tale in the folklore of the Changbai Mountain area of northeastern China, of a type concerning the practices of searching for wild ginseng plants. The root of the wild medicinal herb ginseng (*Panax ginseng*) has for centuries been collected as a cash commodity by Han Chinese peasants during seasonal migrations from central China to the northeast. The ginseng hunters (who are called guardians of the mountains or those making their way into the mountains) have their own lore (which includes a guildlike mountain god cult). It provides cultural background for understanding the tales about the collecting of the ginseng plants. The collectors venerate the first ginseng hunter, "Old Chief" (Lao Baotou), who is said to have died alone in the mountains, his grave remaining a place for ginseng collectors to visit and affirm their occupational identity.

Specific rules and secret jargon surround the hunting and digging of the rare plant. Men go out in hierarchical groups led by a chief (*baotou*). In the mountains, the men erect a small hut that is guarded by the lowest rank of the diggers, the cook, who remains in camp while the collectors search the mountainsides. Near the hut, a small altar dedicated to the mountain god is set up for daily sacrifices and obeisances. The hut represents the realm of men and civilization, while the surrounding forest is the realm of the mountain god.

Each day as the collectors go out in search of ginseng plants, they must follow certain customs and taboos. The group has to strictly obey the chief, since any mistake may be severely punished. Speaking loudly is prohibited, and secret names are used for certain objects and animals. The collectors carry large wooden sticks called *suobogun*. When a ginseng plant is found, it is secured first by calling to it loudly, using its secret name and speaking the number of its leaves (or leaf stems, called prongs by American ginseng collectors in Appalachia), that number increasing as the plant ages. The plant stem is then bound to a small wooden stick using red thread, to which two old coins are attached. Then begins the laborious task of digging out the root without damaging any of its fine root hairs. Only bone or wooden instruments may be used; no metal is permitted to touch the root. When released from the soil, the ginseng root is packed into a simple container made from the bark of a nearby tree and filled with forest soil. A message (*zhaotou*) indicating the number and age of the plants at that spot is recorded on the gash where the bark has been peeled from the tree.

Most of the ginseng tales, like the one translated here, concern the initiation of a young hunter into the traditions of the ginseng-hunting cult. A motif is the child who is abandoned in the forest, dies, and is revived by supernatural powers that include snakes, ginseng spirits, the mountain god, or the patron chief of the ginseng diggers. Through his initiation, the young man establishes contacts with such powers of the mountains that enable him to become a successful ginseng collector later in life.

In the ginseng-producing areas of northeastern China, these stories are told in family and village contexts as a part of everyday entertainment, and they are a medium by which knowledge about ginseng hunting is spread. The initiation of young men into the art of ginseng collecting occurs against the background of this knowledge. Another important motif in ginseng folktales is the dreams of diggers that reveal the location of the elusive plants.

The folktale "The Mother's Brother and His Sister's Son" (which in Western terms would concern an uncle and his nephew) was told on the afternoon of June 21, 1985, at the home of the ginseng hunter Diao Xihou, a farmer living in Chenghou village, Ji'an district, Jilin province. The storyteller was Li Yongbao, then sixty years old. A ginseng hunter himself, Li was a disciple of Diao Xihou. The translator visited Diao Xihou with a group of Chinese folklorists from Tonghua and Ji'an during fieldwork on ginseng folklore in the Changbai Mountains. Among the listeners were also members of Diao's family (his wife, son, and grandchildren). Li Yongbao calls his stories lies (*xiahuar*) or legends (*chuanshuo*).

The general plot of the story, which (like all folktales) exists in many versions, is as follows. A greedy maternal uncle takes his (often unwilling) nephew along on a search for ginseng. After a long and fruitless trip, they discover a patch of ginseng at the base of a huge rock. The uncle lowers the nephew down with a rope. The boy digs out the roots and sends them up in a basket. The uncle, unwilling to share the precious roots, steals away, leaving the boy to starve. The nephew is aided by a supernatural being, in this story a protector animal of the ginseng plant, which happens to be a huge snake. The serpent shows the boy how to survive by licking the Lingzhi mushroom (*Ganoderma lucidum*), highly valued for its medicinal potency, which allows the boy to survive the winter in a dormant state in a cave. In the spring, the nephew is helped out of the cave by the snake and returns home, whereupon his uncle is punished.

The translation is based on the transcription of a tape-recorded performance of the folktale. The translation is ethnopoetic in that it strives to present a text that, when recited aloud, gives some sense of what an actual oral telling would be like.[1] In order to maintain the spoken manner in the written form, the text is transcribed in lines, divided by pauses the speaker makes while speaking. A new line indicates a long pause. A line continuing under the last word of the foregoing line indicates a short pause. Gestures, laughter, and other paralinguistic features are presented parenthetically like stage directions. Exclamations are written

1. This tale, represented in a format unlike most others in this volume, presents readers with certain challenges related to comprehension. The so-called ethnopoetic approach (which has been used among certain poets and folklorists dealing with native poetics worldwide) allows special insights into the unfolding of a folktale in a live performance context. Readers are encouraged to attempt an oral recitation of the text.

in capital letters. The English translation follows the Chinese transcription as closely as possible.

THE MOTHER'S BROTHER AND HIS SISTER'S SON

Told by Li Yongbao (Han)

Lies—
Didn't we hear legends told, *ha*?!
From the home in Shandong came
That mother's brother and his sister's son the two
to dig for ginseng
. . .
Didn't the mother's brother and his sister's son
See a patch of ginseng below that rock
His uncle
his nephew went down and dug all
When he had just dug out he of their family
he first sent the ginseng up
He[2] left his sister's son back there
He went back
after he had sold the ginseng for money he went home
Coming home he talked to the wife of his sister's son and said
Said his sister's son of their family had died
Had gone half the way
had fallen ill and died
(*Laughs*)
. . .
That—
Later their family
This
This sister's son of their family
he didn't manage to come up
With this
Rope he had been let down
When he had gone he[3] had been left alone
Soon it would be the Feast of the Eighth Month,[4] HA!
Wasn't there this snake this python or whatever
There was a big cave, *ah*!

---

2. The mother's brother.

3. The sister's son.

4. The Feast of the Eighth Month is a midautumn festival on the fifteenth day of the eighth month of the traditional Chinese luni-solar calendar.

He entered that cave
In order to winter at it
And it was there that he went to lick that Lingzhi
Went to lick this Lingzhi wasn't it in order to be able to winter
He[5] had gone back to their home but he had no way
it also went into that grotto
When he saw that it licked the Lingzhi he also went to lick it
This is how he passed one winter
When he had passed one winter and spring came and flowers opened
He that sister's son of their family and it this python
this big snake then
Carried him somehow on the back
Carried him out
After it had carried him out his sister's son then went back
When he had come back—
When the wife of his sister's son saw it
When his uncle saw that his sister's son had come back
It shamed him so much that he couldn't do anything else
He went to hang (himself)
Aren't these all lies?
(*Laughs*)
These are all lies.

5. The mother's brother.

A FOLK STORY OF THE DAUR

Translated and introduced by Mark Bender and Su Huana (Daur)

Most of the Daur ethnic group, who number more than one hundred thousand, live in the forest and steppe land of eastern Inner Mongolia and Heilongjiang province in northeastern China. Several thousand also live farther west, near the terminus of the Great Wall in the Xinjiang Uyghur Autonomous Region, where they were sent as border guards during the Qing dynasty (1644–1911). The Daur speak an Altaic language closely related to Mongolian, though many borrowings have been incorporated from Tungus–Manchu languages. Some Daur scholars believe that the Daur are descendants of the Qidan (Khitan) tribes, who built the Liao nation in the tenth century. Originally located along the upper reaches of the Heilong River (Amur River), the Daur were forced south to the banks of the Nen River in the seventeenth century by the Manchus in response to incursions by Russian expeditionary forces.

The traditional Daur economy combined herding sheep and horses, raising grains and vegetables, and hunting deer, black bear, and sable for meat or hides. Tobacco, smoked in longstemmed brass pipes, was one of the few cash crops. Extended families lived in isolated settlements consisting of several walled courtyards containing a rectangular log and adobe house that was divided into an inner and an outer room. Much of the inner room was taken up by an adobe *kang* (heated brick platform), which served as sleeping quarters for the entire family as well as a place for eating, receiving guests, and afterdinner storytelling and singing. The outer room was used as a kitchen and storage area. Men hunted and farmed, while women kept to homebound tasks such as cooking, child rearing, vegetable gardening, and finely tailoring deer hide or silk tunics. A headman was elected to solve village disputes and deal with Manchu authorities. Although modernization is making inroads, some older ways continue.

In the traditional worldview, the cosmos is divided into an Upper World of good spirits, the human realm of Earth, and an Underworld of bad spirits. The gods (*barkan*) include native ones, most important the heavenly godhead Tenger Barkan, and Chinese deities such as the Jade Emperor, head of the Daoist pantheon of gods. Shamans (*yadegen*) once led sacrifices to various gods in times of cultural stress and otherwise served as a link between the world of men and the spirits. A common figure in Daur folktales and narrative poems is the mountain god and protector of animals, Bainaaqaa, who often appears as an old man with a white beard offering advice or otherwise helping respectful hunters.

Heroic hunters are the central characters in much of Daur oral narrative. The *mergen*, a hunter figure similar to his heroic counterparts in other repertoires of North Asian folklore, is characterized by reckless energy, bravery, and prowess in the hunt and war. Some female warriors such as the Pine Tree Maiden, who wields two snow-bright swords, fit this mold. Positive women figures are usually cast, however, as bullied, but often capable, damsels in distress, sometimes with supernatural powers. Their evil counterparts are often in the roles of elder sisters, stepmothers, nasty aunts, and cowives. The ultimate bogeyman in Daur folklore is the multiheaded *mangie*, who eats human flesh. In many stories, *mangie* (the Daur version of the *manggus* of Mongol epic lore) and other monsters and demons clash with mighty *mergen*, who wield spears, swords, and bows and arrows as they soar across the steppes on flying, talking horses.

Rich in cultural color, the earthy tale "Mengongnenbo" consists of the tricksterlike antics of an orphaned young hunter who is rescued from death by the daughter of the celestial Jade Emperor. The story was collected in *Molidawa Banner* by Meng Zhidong (Mergendi), a Daur folklorist who has translated and edited several collections of folk stories and written numerous articles on Daur culture.

MENGONGNENBO

Collected by Meng Zhidong (Daur)

Once upon a time there was an old couple who had seven daughters, two of whom were blind.

The old man thought to himself, "Who would be willing to marry those two? They are unable to do any sort of work because of their blindness."

One day, when he went to the mountains for firewood, he asked all his daughters to accompany him and gave them each a birch bark bucket.

"Yesterday," the old man said, "when I was cutting wood in the mountains, I found a place full of wild grapes; it will be easy for you to get a good bucketful."

It was a long hard ride in the oxcart to the mountains. At noon, the old man left the two blind daughters in the mountains and slipped quietly away with the other five daughters.

Though there were grapes everywhere, and though the abandoned sisters worked until sweat ran down their faces, they were unable to fill their buckets before the sun had set. They sat down together for a rest. Suddenly, as if she had noticed something was wrong, the elder sister exclaimed, "Why, these birch buckets have no bottoms! That's why we couldn't fill them!"

"It is plain that our father wished us to die on the mountain," said the younger sister.

At nightfall the sisters cried themselves to sleep under a big tree.

In the morning, they were awakened by a sparrow chirping in the tree. As soon as she awoke, the elder sister began to grope along the trunk of the tree and discovered something soft and round. She thought it might be a bit of tasty food, so she shared it with her sister. After a short while, both sisters began to regain their sight.

That night the sisters again slept under the big tree, but they dreamed too much to sleep soundly.

As dawn was brightening, the elder sister said, "Dear sister, you dreamed some sweet dreams, didn't you?"

"How did you know?" she asked in surprise. Then she told her sister all about her dream.

"It's strange—my dream was just like yours," said the elder sister as they prepared to go.

After walking several miles they came to a clear stream, where they rolled up their sleeves and rinsed their eyes. Immediately, they began to see a bit more clearly than the day before.

They kept on walking till they came to a gold well and a silver well. Each sister took the gold and silver buckets they found there and drew gold and silver water from each of the wells and drank it. Strange as it may seem, both sisters' sight was perfectly restored. Happy, they continued on their way until they came to a gold and a silver tree. In the gold tree were two ripe gold fruits, and in the silver tree were two ripe silver fruits. Each of the sisters ate one of each of the fruits and soon after discovered they were both pregnant.

Not far from the trees they saw a wooden house. Inside they found cupboards filled with dresses on the southern and northern *kangs* in the inner room. All the cooking utensils in the outer room were in pairs and everything inside and out was tidy and clean. The storeroom was fully stocked with food, and there was rice, flour, oil, and salt aplenty. In such fine circumstances, the sisters decided to live there.

It sounds strange, but one day when the elder sister entered the room, she gave birth to a baby boy, and as her younger sister was preparing to get off the *kang*, she also gave birth to a boy. The elder sister named her baby Aletannenbo, while the younger sister named her baby Mengongnenbo.

By the time the cousins were seven years old, they were able to shoot geese, pheasants, and rabbits. The years passed quickly, and the boys were soon young men twenty years old.

One day on their way to hunt in the mountains, they came upon an old white-haired man leaning on a dragon-headed walking stick.

"Hello, where are you going?" the old man asked.

"We are going hunting," they answered.

"Why don't you ride your horses?"

"We have none!"

The old man nodded his head and told them, "My poor children, three hundred *li* from here there is a sparkling lake. Beside the lake, under a big pine tree, is an iron cupboard. Every noon, two claret-colored horses come to bathe in the lake. You should find a way to catch them." So saying, the old man disappeared.

Two days later Aletannenbo and Mengongnenbo arrived at the place the old man had described to them and, hiding themselves behind the pine tree, anxiously waited for the two claret-colored horses to appear.

Sure enough, precisely at noon, two claret-colored horses flew down into the lake to bathe. Soundlessly, the two young men dove in and climbed onto the horses' backs. Startled, the horses jumped out of the water and, kicking up their hooves, ran wildly over the plains, after which they jumped back into the water and rolled madly from side to side. But try as they might, they were unable to throw the young men.

At last the horses docilely climbed out of the water and said, "Please tell us your names."

"My name is Aletannenbo."

"My name is Mengongnenbo."

"When you were born we trembled with fear!" said the horses. "Now, if you can open the iron cupboard, you may become our masters."

Both cousins jumped off their horses. Each struck the door once with his bare fist, and the door opened. Inside were saddles, halters, bows, and golden arrows, all laid out neatly in pairs.

Aletannenbo's and Mengongnenbo's mothers were frightened when they saw two men on flying horses rushing toward them from the east. They hurried back inside and hid behind the *kang* cupboards. The cousins got off their horses and went inside. To their surprise, their mothers were nowhere in sight.

"Where are our mothers?"

"Why have they disappeared?"

Listening carefully, the sisters recognized their son's voices and came out of hiding to greet them. From then on, the cousins took their horses out hunting every day with their new bows and arrows slung on their backs. Unfortunately, only a few years later, Mengongnenbo's mother died.

One day when both cousins were out hunting, Aletannenbo's mother, who was sewing on the *kang*, suddenly found that the ground beside her was gradually rising inch by inch. As it rose above the side of the *kang*, a demon with a head like an egg, an iron belly, legs like hemp stalks, and long, black, skinny fingers reared up out of the ground.

"I am going to eat you," the demon roared.

Aletannenbo's mother was so frightened that she could only gasp, "Why do you want to eat me? There is plenty of meat in the storeroom."

"Who wants to eat meat from your storeroom? If you want to live, you must promise me one thing. From now on, you must regard Mengongnenbo as a thorn in your flesh. Otherwise, I shall come back and eat you!" The demon disappeared, and the ground returned to its original level.

From then on Aletannenbo's mother gave her son fresh meat and white bread to eat, but gave Mengongnenbo only scraps. Each day after eating, Mengongnenbo vomited his meals into a hollow tree behind the house. This went on for ninety-nine days. At last, Mengongnenbo could bear it no longer.

The next noon, Mengongnenbo challenged Aletannenbo to a shooting match in the backyard, with the old tree serving as a target. Aletannenbo agreed to the contest.

Both of them stood one hundred paces from the tree. Mengongnenbo said, "Elder Brother, you shoot first."

"You are the younger brother, you should shoot first," replied Aletannenbo.

So the contest began. Mengongnenbo drew back his bow, but shot away only a chip of tree bark.

Aletannenbo shook his head and said, "What's wrong with you today? That was a lousy shot!"

Then he stood with his legs firmly braced. An arrow whizzed right through the trunk of the tree, which soon began oozing rotten liquid like a man shot in the belly. Aletannenbo hurried over to see what it was. It smelled like rotten vomit!

When he returned his brother said to him, "Brother, that is what remains of the food my aunt gives me to eat. Today is the one hundredth day, and the tree is full. Now I must part with you!" Without another word, he mounted his horse and rode toward the southeast.

As he rode away he glanced back and saw his brother had fainted. Turning his horse back, he rode up to his side and did his best to revive him with cold water.

Then Mengongnenbo said, "Dear brother, I cannot stand my aunt's ill treatment any longer."

No matter how hard Aletannenbo tried to persuade him to stay, he insisted on leaving. Aletannenbo had no choice, so at last he took out an arrow to give to him. "Take this with you! When the shaft is completely rusted, you will know I am no longer in this world."

Mengongnenbo also gave his brother an arrow and repeated the same words. Then they reluctantly parted. Aletannenbo went home and saw his mother was busy preparing a meal.

"Mother, to whom will you serve this buttered gruel?"

"It is for you, of course."

"What will Mengongnenbo eat?" he asked with a solemn face.

"I'll give him a little crusty rice; it's quite enough!"

The *kang* was soon wet with Aletannenbo's tears. He was too sad to do anything except think about Mengongnenbo from morning to night.

As for Mengongnenbo, he lost track of the days as he rode away on the claret horse. When he was hungry he ate wild fruits and vegetables. When thirsty, he drank river water.

One day, he came upon a mountain as high as the sky blocking his path. The claret horse reared up on its hind legs and cried, "Master, oh Master, there is danger ahead!"

"What sort of danger?" Mengongnenbo asked.

"At the foot of the mountain stands a demon with an egg head, an iron belly, legs like hemp stalks, and long, thin, black fingers. It is waiting there to eat you! When I rush by, no matter what happens, you must shatter its head. Otherwise, it will be hard for us to escape with our lives."

Mengongnenbo prepared to shoot and ordered his horse to charge. As the steed rushed past the demon at lightning speed, Mengongnenbo loosed an arrow behind him. The demon's head was shattered to bits.

Crossing the mountain, Mengongnenbo saw a great river, beside which were countless sheep. He led his horse down beside the flock.

"Hello, where are you going?" the shepherd asked.

"I'm trying to find a way to make a living! Whose sheep are these?"

"They belong to Rich Man Su."

"What is your name? Are you from these parts?"

"My name is Tuoku. I am not from this area. Since my family is poor, I have been herding sheep ever since I was eight. This year I'll be forty."

Mengongnenbo decided to take the old shepherd's place herding the sheep and sent him home, along with four hundred of the sheep.

The old shepherd told him, "Rich Man Su's house is on the opposite bank of the river. The flock of sheep must cross the river each day. When crossing the river, you must cry, 'If the river stops flowing for a second, I will not become angry,' which is the magic incantation for dividing the water. Since my childhood, I have worked as a shepherd for Rich Man Su. Every night, I was forced to clean the soles of his wife's feet with my tongue, and I got only cakes of cow dung to eat." Then the old man drove four hundred of the sheep to his home.

Mengongnenbo dressed up as the shepherd and said to his horse, "Starting from today, your name is Hany, and I shall call myself Tuoku! Whenever I call 'Hany' twice, fly to me at once!" Hany nodded and flew away.

It was nearly noon when Mengongnenbo drove the flock of sheep to the river crossing. He pretended to forget the river-dividing incantation and began throwing the sheep into the water by twos and threes. Lady Su, who was taking a stroll on the opposite bank, saw what he was doing and quickly cried out, "If the river stops flowing for a second, I will not become angry." The water parted at her cry, and the sheep were able to cross the river. Lady Su angrily scolded Mengongnenbo, still disguised as old Tuoku, "Tuoku, why did you throw the sheep into the river?"

"Oh, I got a little muddleheaded and forgot the magic words."

At dusk, Lady Su, lying on the *kang*, shouted, "Tuoku, have you eaten your cake of cow dung yet?"

"I'm eating it now," said Mengongnenbo from the outer room. Actually, he had already thrown it onto the rubbish heap.

After a moment, she asked again, "Have you finished yet?" And she went on to ask, "You haven't forgotten to clean the soles of my feet with your tongue, have you?"

"I've almost finished," said Mengongnenbo. Going out of the house, he cut out the tongue of a cow and quickly entered Lady Su's room.

Then he used the cow's tongue to clean her feet. Lady Su felt as if her feet were being filed away and asked, "Why is your tongue so rough?"

"Today I ate some wild vegetables."

"Well, if that's the case, go to the outer room and drink some of the oil that I use to rub my feet."

Mengongnenbo had no intention of drinking the oil, so he stole quietly out and cut out a dog's tongue. Coming back inside, he rubbed Lady Su's feet with it.

"Oh, my! Your tongue is much smoother this time. Now you may go to sleep!"

So Mengongnenbo took the poor man's place and lived a hard life.

Rich Man Su had seven daughters, six of whom had already married rich men, leaving only the seventh sister at home. That year the youngest daughter was seventeen, and Rich Man Su intended to marry her off to a man of great strength. One day Rich Man Su promised the hand of his daughter to anyone who could twist in two a huge iron chain he had made.

Soon, scores of tents sprung up outside the village, each filled with men come to try their luck. Rich Man Su and his wife laid the chain, which was as big as a shoulder pole, in front of them. For two days men from far and wide tried to twist the chain in half, but none succeeded. On the third day, Mengongnenbo came to try his luck.

"You haven't the strength to truss a chicken! What are you doing here?" the people sneered. "So, you'll have the good fortune to marry Rich Man Su's daughter, will you?"

Mengongnenbo paid no attention to their taunts. He picked up the chain and, with a sudden surge of strength, twisted it in two. The assembled people were astonished. Rich Man Su, afraid of being cursed for breaking his promise, had no choice but to allow Mengongnenbo to marry his daughter.

One day Rich Man Su fell ill. He declared he could be cured only by eating the gallbladder and flesh of a bear. So his six rich sons-in-law went into the mountains on horseback with bows and arrows to hunt for bear. Meanwhile, Mengongnenbo changed into his own clothes. Going to the outskirts of the village he called twice, "Hany, Hany, I'm waiting for you!" A moment later, Hany appeared. Together they flew above the trees and through the clouds into the mountains. Mengongnenbo soon hunted down a black bear, which he killed with a single arrow, and removed its gallbladder, which he replaced with a rabbit's gallbladder. Dragging the bear up beside a tree, he made a campfire and sat down to rest. Soon, the six brothers-in-law found the bear beside the tree and began quarreling, each claiming to have seen it first.

"Who are you?" asked Mengongnenbo suddenly. The brothers-in-law came near the fire and saw it was Mengongnenbo.

"Will you sell us the bear?" they asked.

"Yes."

"How much?"

"I don't want any money."

"Well, then how can you sell it?"

"I have a copper pipe bowl. After heating it in this fire, I will use it to brand your hind ends. Is that a deal?"

Preferring being branded to facing their parents-in-law empty-handed, the men reluctantly agreed.

Afterward, Mengongnenbo dressed up again as Tuoku and, setting Hany free, went into the village. A while later his six brothers-in-law returned with the dead bear.

Again in disguise, Mengongnenbo held out his hands to beg, "Oh, such a fat bear; please give me a bit of the intestines."

The six brothers-in-law threw the intestines to him and said, "All right, poor man; take them away!"

"How sweet, how delicious these intestines are," said Mengongnenbo as he recited an incantation, "and how stinking and rotten is the meat!"

"What's that you're saying?" asked his brothers-in-law.

"I said, 'How can I thank you for your kindness?' " he answered calmly.

Although Rich Man Su ate the false bear gallbladder presented by the six brothers-in-law, he didn't recover. The cooked bear meat was so rotten, not even a dog would touch it. One day, Mengongnenbo cooked a bowl of soup with the bear's gallbladder that he had kept and sent it to the sick man. When his parents-in-law smelled the sweet soup, they fought each other to drink it to the last drop. Soon Rich Man Su recovered from his illness.

From then on the six brothers-in-law hated Mengongnenbo with a passion, and they spent twenty nights digging a pitfall ninety feet deep in the eastern part of the village.

One day they said to Mengongnenbo, "Today, we seven will have a horse race."

Mengongnenbo nodded his head silently.

The six brothers-in-law arrived at the racecourse on horseback. A little later came Mengongnenbo riding Hany. From the start Mengongnenbo's horse held the lead. Racing along, horse and rider suddenly tumbled right into the trap.

Mengongnenbo's fall left him unable to move. Hany said to itself, "The Jade Emperor's daughter has braids ninety feet long. Only she can save my master!" The horse leaped out of the trap and flew into the sky.

It so happened that the Jade Emperor's daughter was right in the midst of choosing a first-class horse for her wedding. Hany ran agilely among the horses and was chosen by the Jade Emperor's youngest daughter. Riding the horse in circles around the palace, she embroidered a pillow cover as it completed the first circle. As she flew around the palace again, Hany suddenly descended from the skies and landed beside the trap. Looking inside the trap and finding a dying man, she knew right away why the horse had brought her there.

She said to Hany, "You must fly into the sky and bring back my magic medicine that I keep in my red jewel case."

Hany immediately flew back to the palace, changed into a white cat, and began to mew. When the maids heard the Jade Emperor's daughter's cat crying, they opened the door of the palace to let it in. Hany went right in, picked up the jewel case in its mouth, and flew back down to earth.

After taking the magic cure, Mengongnenbo recovered. He thanked the Jade Emperor's daughter for saving his life and instructed Hany to carry her to her palace.

The six brothers-in-law were terrified when they saw Mengongnenbo return. They were so afraid he would take revenge on them that they fled.

A few days later, Mengongnenbo took out the arrow given him by his cousin Aletannenbo and was horrified to discover that more than half its shaft was covered in rust. He and his wife at once left her parents and flew away on Hany. On the way, tears suddenly began falling from the sky.

Hany stopped and said, "Look there, who is that up in the sky?"

"Please come down, please come down, my savior!" cried Mengongnenbo.

Hearing his cries, the Jade Emperor's daughter descended slowly and said, "Alas! My father told me that I committed a crime two days ago by saving a mortal, so he drove me out of the palace. Now, I must live on earth forever!"

After many days' travel, the three of them arrived at Aletannenbo's house. Mengongnenbo saw that his cousin was on his deathbed. The daughter of the Jade Emperor placed her magic cure in his mouth, and in a twinkling Aletannenbo sat up in perfect health. With tears rolling down his face, he said to Mengongnenbo, "I fell ill not long after you left, and your aunt passed away last year . . ."

A few days later, the Jade Emperor's youngest daughter married Aletannenbo, and they shared a courtyard with Mengongnenbo and his wife, living happily ever after.

FOLK STORIES FROM THE TAI LUE OF SIPSONGPANNA

Collected, translated, and introduced by Ngampit Jagacinski

The Tai Lue of Xishuangbanna, or Sipsongpanna, as it is pronounced in the Tai language, is one branch of the Dai (as transcribed according to Mandarin pronunciation) ethnic group in Yunnan province. The Tai Lue constitute roughly one-quarter of the Dai population in the province. Their area is in the southernmost part of Yunnan, which borders Burma to the southwest and Laos to the southeast. The Tai Lue are close kin to the Tai Yuan of northern Thailand, the Tai Khuen of the eastern Shan state in Burma, and the Tai in Laos. All these groups share language and cultural roots in the thirteenth-century Lanna kingdom, one of the oldest and most highly developed Tai states.

The oral folk story tradition is a shared heritage among various Tai groups, and themes in many of their tales overlap. The themes reflect the intertwining of the indigenous lifestyles and beliefs of the Tais and the Indian influence of Brahmanism and Buddhism. The most obvious Indian influences are the references to places and people in northern India—for example, the city of Benares and its king and the mythic Himmaphan Forest, which is mentioned in many Tai folk stories and is believed to be located in northern India. Less obvious is the hidden message encouraging people to regard certain moral standards as the norm of social behavior. The Theravada Buddhist teachings are a dominant force in both religious and nonreligious tales.

The common theme of virtue versus vice is represented in the two didactic tales "Two Friends" and "The Cow and the Tiger." The hidden message is that of being kind to others. Generosity and gratitude, no matter how mild and remote they may be, are considered to be good deeds and will be rewarded. Dishonest intentions or plots against others, on the contrary, can lead to devastation and the destruction of oneself. The other common theme is the emphasis on cleverness to handle a difficult situation, whether it is a straightforward encounter with danger, as in "Two Friends," or a challenge of a bullying authority, as in "Obtaining Milk from the Deities."

Two nondidactic tales are also included. One is an explanatory story, "Tale of the Two Rivers, Khong and Khorng," relating how the Mae Khong River separates from the Khorng River when it enters Sipsongpanna. The other is "Unclear Sight, but Skillful Hands," a tale reflecting the Lue's sense of humor and entertainment. Stories that laugh at failure caused by stupidity or carelessness are especially popular.

Stylistically, the rhythm of these stories does not build up to a definite climactic point. Instead, they have a relatively even, steady pace, and the ending may seem abrupt. The message and the entertainment value depend on a storyteller's creativity in presenting his material with his own additional personal touch. Two of the following stories were recorded from live tellings, while three were translated from Lue versions that appeared in the journal *Panna* in the early 1980s.

UNCLEAR SIGHT, BUT SKILLFUL HANDS

Told by Aai Khamping and his wife (Tai Lue)

Once there was a young man whose eyesight was not clear.[6] One day, he overheard a father making a suggestion to his daughter that if she were to look for a husband, she would be better off finding one with fluidly vigorous hands.[7] Hearing this, the man then put cooked, sticky, sweet rice on his hands and went out to meet the girl. The girl happened to touch his hands. She felt that they were rough to the touch but fluid in movement. She then told her father that she had found a man with appropriate hands. The father said, "Go ahead and marry him. We can use another helper in the rice field."

The day of the wedding, the man came to the girl's house. Because his eyesight was not clear, he had to feel his way around by touching the fences of the houses along the road. The father saw the man walking along the side of the road in this unusual manner and was puzzled. He asked, "Why don't you walk straight in the middle of the road to my house?" The man told the father of the girl that he wanted to know how far it was from his house to their house. The father said, "Oh, is that why?"

The next day, the man was called upon to help rake the field. He had to ride on a water buffalo to the field. He attempted to get on the buffalo by way of its backside, and he fell down. The father told him that in getting on a buffalo, one must go by way of its stomach. The man replied that it was a custom in his village to do it the man's way. The father said, "Well, if that's the case . . ."

The man then went out and helped the family in the field. When he finished raking, the father was surprised about the unevenness of the work in each plot. The man told him that this was a better method for cultivation. The father said, "Oh, is that so?"

That evening, everyone went back from the rice field to the house, except the young man. The father went back to look for the son-in-law. He found the man moving around in the bottom of the well. The father said, "How terrible that you fell down! I'll help you up." The man told the father that he did not fall down. He, in fact, intentionally went down there to catch a frog. The father then put down a ladder to get the man out of the well. The man climbed up but didn't know that he had reached the top of the ladder and didn't get off. The father called to him to come down. The man then told the father that he was

6. The Tai Lue word is *taa bort sai* (literally, "eyes blind clear"). Perhaps this refers to amaurosis, a serious eye ailment that causes near blindness.

7. The word *mue tsaa* literally means "rugged," but it also implies "strong but agile," in the sense of being fluid and skillful in doing things.

just checking out the rice field. The father said, "Oh, how conscientious!" They then went home.

At dinner, the man clumsily knocked down some dishes. In order to cover up his accident, he pretended to be angry and said, "What kind of food is this! I worked so hard today, I should have a better meal than this."

During the dinner, the father started to notice that the son-in-law had a problem with his eyesight. He told the daughter to get rid of him and find another husband. The daughter then remarried.

At dinner, the new son-in-law did not pay attention to the food. His hands were all over the daughter. She was annoyed and tried to push him away. The father, seeing this, said, "Oh, this son-in-law is not like the other one. He does have good eyesight."

OBTAINING MILK FROM THE DEITIES

Written by Aai Nguen (Tai Lue)

Once, after he had finished his meal, a king, who had nothing much to do that day, thought of a way to challenge a wise man.[8] The king sent a messenger to bring the wise man to his palace. The wise man came. He put his hands together toward his chest and lowered his head to make a gesture of respect toward the king. He asked, "My Lord, you who are highly recognized, you called me here today. Is there anything urgent you would like to tell me?"

The king rose and asked the wise man, "Wise man, look at me and tell me, what do you think I am?" The wise man said, "My Lord, all beings on earth, animal, man, woman, high and low, all know you. If you are a bad king, you would have already lost your kingdom." The wise man, after having said that, made another gesture of respect. The king was very pleased, descended from the throne, walked around proudly among his ministers, and announced very loudly to all his men, "Now, everyone of you heard that, right? It is so true what the wise man said. I am born to be king in this life. But that's not all. I am not only royal, I am also born as a virtuous immortal.[9] Don't you all think I am?"

Upon hearing this, all the ministers made a gesture of respect to the king and answered in unison, "Yes, of course. You are a virtuous and immortal one." Only the wise man didn't make any gesture of respect. The wise man, instead, looked up at the king and snickered. Seeing this, the king was not pleased. He asked the wise man, "What's the matter? You didn't make any gesture of respect and even dare to laugh at me. Do you want to die?"

The wise man stopped laughing and answered, "My Lord, the honorable ministers were paying respect to you, the virtuous immortal. I am just a lowly

8. *Mahoosot* is the word for "scholar" or "wise man."

9. The word *bun* in *tunbun* (virtuous person) refers to the collective merits that a person has accumulated through previous lives.

man from the countryside who was born ignorant. I have walked amid the excrement of pigs and dogs.[10] I didn't dare to make any gesture to an immortal of great virtue. It would be wasting your greatness if a person in my position made a gesture to an immortal like you. The reason I laughed was because of my satisfaction to hear that you are an immortal."

The ministers were frightened to hear this. They all thought, "The wise man is a dead man. His tongue is sharp like a needle." The king was in shock for a while. After he thought about it, he was not pleased. He stormily got up and came face-to-face with the wise man, flushing with indignation to project his authority, and said, "Wise man, listen carefully. I called you here today not just for you to come to laugh. I am sending you to accomplish an errand for me. At the moment I am ill with a certain disease. However, since I am an immortal, I can't take medicines that are for humans in this world. I have to take medicines that are used among the immortals. People say you are a clever man who knows and can do anything. That's why I sent for you. I now order you to go find the deities in the woods. Ask them for their milk and bring it back to me. The milk will cure my disease if I drink it. Do you understand?"

The wise man knew that the king was putting pressure on him. No matter how much he didn't like the idea, he pretended not to be disturbed. He covered up his feelings and politely answered, "My Lord, there is nothing to it. I know the deities. I can go and see whether they will give me the milk." The wise man then went home to rest. When the dry season came, the wise man came back to see the king. After making a gesture of respect, he said, "I just came from the Himmaphan Forest. I asked the deities for the milk. The deities didn't think I was in a high enough position to bring the milk to an immortal. The deities sent me to tell you that you should ask your household gods to go fetch the milk.[11] It will be more appropriate that way. You should be the one to inform your household gods."

After he said that, the wise man walked out with head high. He left to go about wherever he pleased. The king could only try to compose himself. He was at a loss for words.

TWO FRIENDS

Written by Aai Untaan (Tai Lue)

A long, long time ago, in the town called Kaasii, there were two friends. One was a poor man. The other was a rich man. The two had grown up together and had been close friends since they were children. When the time came for the poor

10. The literal translation of the phrase describing the life experience of a destitute person, *yam khii muu khii maa,* is "stomping excrement pig excrement dog."

11. The Tai Lue believe that each household has spirits whose duty is to protect and see to the well-being of the people in the house.

man to get married, he enthusiastically invited the rich man to his wedding celebration. On his wedding day, the poor man even went out of his house to welcome his friend. A feast of food and plenty of wine were all brought out for his friend. When the ritual of welcoming back one's spirit started during the wedding, the poor man invited his friend to take part in the ritual with him.[12] As the ritual proceeded, the rich man saw the bride. He instantly wanted to take her for himself. From that day on, his thoughts turned to finding a way to kill the poor man.

One day, the rich man went hunting. In the woods, he saw a mother tiger and her cubs. He thought, "I have a desire to take that man's wife. I should bring that man out here to be eaten by these tigers." With such a thought, he went home.

That night, he couldn't sleep at all. He kept thinking of his friend's wife. The next day, he went to his friend's house to put his plan into action. He said, "My good friend, a few days ago when I went hunting in the woods, I saw a whole flock of wild chickens. Why don't we go hunt them together tomorrow?" The poor man, unaware of the danger, was pleased to go.

The next day, in the very early morning, when there was still no light in the sky, the two friends went on their hunting trip. When they got close to the place where the tigers lived, the rich man said to his friend, "You just go on ahead of me. I will slow down a little bit." The poor man then went on ahead of his friend. The rich man, however, retreated and went back home.

The poor man roamed around for a while before he encountered the tigers. The mother tiger, upon seeing him, asked, "What are you doing here?" The poor man saw that some of the tigers had no stripes.[13] He then cleverly made up an answer. He said, "I have heard that you, Sister, just had babies. I thought of you, so I brought you a chicken." The mother tiger said, "What's your sister's name? What's your brother-in-law's name? What's your name?" The poor man answered, "My sister's name is The One with Stripes. My brother-in-law's name is The Hunter. My name is The One with Bitter Stinky Tough Flesh."[14]

---

12. The ritual of welcoming or calling back one's spirit is a common practice among certain Tai groups, such as the Tai Lue of Sipsongpanna and the Tai Yuan of northern Thailand. The ritual is based on belief in the three-part composition of the human entity—body, soul, and *khworn* (here loosely translated as "spirit"). *Khworn* is an element that creates and coordinates the well-balanced existence of a person. *Khworn* can be lost during a time of distress or in a disturbing surrounding. A peaceful and contented state of being can be achieved after the *khworn* has been properly recalled through the ritual that welcomes its return to the owner.

13. Tiger cubs do not develop stripes until they are much older.

14. The literal translation of the three names is

ii nang lai: female title woman stripes (The One with Stripes)
aai tsang yum: male title capable grab (The Hunter)
aai phe khum lae tsin yaap: male title urine bitter and flesh tough (The One with Bitter Stinky Tough Flesh)

Notice that the poor man cleverly gives the tigers names denoting respect but gives himself a humble name, implying that he would not be a good source of food for them.

Hearing that the mother tiger said, "My good man, rest for a while. Your brother-in-law went out to get some deer and hasn't come back yet. I haven't got a thing to offer you to eat. Why don't you just climb up on one of the branches and wait there for now." The poor man then climbed up and stayed in the tree.

After a while, the male tiger came back with a deer. As he approached, he asked, "Why is there human smell around here?" The mother tiger answered, "It is the brother who came for a visit. He heard that I just had given birth to these cubs, so he came. He also brought us a chicken. He is on a branch of that tree." The male tiger then said, "Good! Come down and join us. Eat whatever you want here." The poor man then came down and roasted the deer for the tigers. When the deer meat was almost done, the cubs, who smelled the roasted meat, scurried around to find food. The poor man cut the meat and fed the cubs. He let them eat as much as they wanted.

By the time the sun was setting, the poor man bid farewell to the tigers. He said, "Brother and Sister, it is getting very late and there is still a lot of work to be done at home. I would like to say goodbye and head back home now." The tigers agreed. When the poor man was about to leave, the tigers gave him one *haap* each of gold and silver.[15] The male tiger even helped the poor man carry the gold and silver to his house. Before the tiger went back to the woods, the poor man grabbed a small pig that was roaming nearby the house and gave it to the tiger. The tiger left happily. From then on, the poor man was no longer poor. He even became richer than his friend.

Upon hearing about the poor man's fortune, the rich man came to ask him, "Friend, what did you do that brought you so much wealth as this?" The poor man told the rich man all about his encounter with the tigers. After hearing that, the rich man imitated the actions of his friend. He went to the woods with a chicken to see the tigers exactly as the poor man had told him.

That day, the male tiger also returned home with a deer. The tigers, as had happened before, told the man to roast the deer meat. When the meat was almost done, the cubs all came out looking for food. Seeing the tiger cubs making such a commotion over the meat, the rich man said with a sneer, "A buffalo can't help growing rice; a tiger can't change its stripes."[16] He then hit their heads and tried to shoo them away from the meat. Upon being hurt, the cubs noisily cried out. The two older tigers, seeing the rich man hit the cubs, were angry. They said, "This brother is not the same as the previous one." They then jumped on the rich man and mauled him to death.

---

15. The *haap* is a traditional unit of weight commonly used among various Tai groups. It is approximately the weight that one man can carry by suspending two loads of goods on a pole across his shoulders.

16. The phrase is *tsuea suea bau see lai tsuea khwaai bau see khaau*, and its literal translation is "race tiger not waste stripe race buffalo not waste rice." The saying refers to the enduring characteristics of these two animals: the predatory nature of tigers and the usefulness of buffalo in rice cultivation.

THE COW AND THE TIGER

Written by Aai Tsorm (Tai Lue)

Long, long ago, there were two officers; one was a cow and one was a tiger.[17] They both lived in the same woods. One day, they met at a watering hole. The tiger was very hungry. He turned to the cow and told him that he would like to eat him. The cow replied, "We are both officers having equal status. Neither of us can consume the other. Let's not say harmful words to each other. Let's be friends." The tiger thought about it for a while and then said, "All right. Let us make a living together. But we are really hungry; what should we do?" The cow said, "Friend, let's get out of these woods and go to town. I heard that in Benares there's a skillful potter who sells her pottery at the market. We can stay with her and ask her to teach us how to make pottery so we can sell it at the market, too. What do you think?" The tiger was pleased. They both went to see the potter.

After staying there for a while, the cow and the tiger thoroughly learned the potter's skill. Their pottery was much better than that of the old potter, and they sold it in the market. One market day, the king of Benares came. He noticed that the pottery looked better than any he had seen before. He asked, "Who made this pottery? It looks well made and beautiful." The old potter answered, "My Lord, it was the cow and the tiger, the two friends who came from the woods to learn how to make pottery." After hearing that, the king said, "Make a big basin for me by the next market day.[18] I will use it to hold water for bathing."

At the end of the market day, the old potter told the cow and the tiger to make a big basin. When the next market day arrived, the old potter brought the big basin to the king. The king of Benares was very pleased, and he announced, "The two are skillful. I will appoint them to be my ministers in Benares." The king sent a messenger to call the cow and the tiger to his house. The king then appointed the cow to be his right-hand man and the tiger his left-hand man.

After he was appointed, the cow diligently mastered his job. Whatever tasks he faced, he did them very well. Everyone praised him as a good minister. The tiger was unhappy to hear this. He then incited feelings in the king. He said to the king, "My Lord, a person like the cow is not really a good man. The cow is in fact secretly trying to revolt against you." Upon hearing this, the king didn't think carefully, and he asked the tiger, "So how do I punish the cow?" The tiger offered a plan: "Send the cow to find the Pankaap lotuses for you.[19] If he can't find them, then either kill him or chase him out of the kingdom." The king followed the tiger's advice. He sent the cow to find the Pankaap lotuses. Within

17. The cow and the tiger in the story each hold the rank of *seenaa*, referring to a lower-level official who serves the king.

18. The *aang* (basin) is a large container that holds water for indoor use.

19. The Pankaap lotus is probably a subspecies of the *Nymphaea* lotus, which is soft and has no prickly stems or leaves.

seven days, the cow was to bring the Pankaap lotuses to the king. If he didn't succeed, the cow would have to die. The cow had no choice but to go look for the Pankaap lotuses.

The cow was in tears when he went to the king of ants. He said, "My Lord, I am a minister of the king of Benares, who ordered me to find the Pankaap lotuses. If I can't find the flowers, I will have to die. I am in trouble. Could you tell me what place would have the flowers?" The king of ants stuck his wobbly head out and answered, "The ant kingdom doesn't have any. Why don't you go ask the king of birds? If you find the flowers, please give my kingdom one."

The cow left the ant kingdom and went up to the bird kingdom. The king of birds, flapping his wings, said, "Honorable cow, who has a golden complexion like honey, we in this humble bird kingdom don't have any of those flowers. You should go to the boar kingdom. If you get the lotuses, spare one for me."

The cow left for the boar kingdom. The king of boars said the same thing: "My golden cow with branching horns, we in this wild kingdom with cold weather wouldn't have any of the fragrant Pankaap lotuses. You should roam around in the woods of the spirit kingdom. Try it. I don't know whether you will find them."

The cow went to the spirit kingdom, where he found many beautiful Pankaap lotuses. The flowers were just opening and floating in the middle of a pond. The cow collected a number of them and brought them back to Benares. When he passed the boar kingdom on the way back, the cow gave the king of boars one of the Pankaap lotuses. The king of boars in return gave him his daughter. After that, the cow came to the bird kingdom, and he gave the king of birds one of the flowers. The bird king also gave him his daughter. From there, he came to the ant kingdom and gave the king of ants one of the lotuses. The king of ants was pleased, and he, too, gave the cow his daughter. The cow then brought back with him the daughters of the wild boar, the birds, and the ants.

After arriving in Benares, the cow gave the Pankaap lotuses to the king. The king, upon seeing the flowers, said nothing. The tiger then plotted again: "My Lord, these lotuses look beautiful in bloom when they are in a pond. Here there's no pond, and the flowers are wilting. You should order the cow to dig a pond and plant these flowers within seven days. If he can't finish the task in time, then expel him from the kingdom." The king then put out the order. The cow was very worried, and he told the daughter of the boar king about it. Upon hearing that, she said, "Brother, don't you worry. I will dig the pond for you." She then went to the boar kingdom. The king of boars called upon tens of thousands of boars to help. Not quite three days had passed when the boars finished digging the pond. The boars then continued to dig a way for water to flow in to fill the pond. The cow then planted the flowers. When the seventh day arrived, the pond was filled with blooming Pankaap lotuses.

The king of Benares saw the pond and the Pankaap lotuses. He was disappointed but couldn't say anything. The king himself didn't want to test the cow any further at this point, but the tiger came up with another idea: "My Lord, why don't you order three *haap* of sesame seeds to be scattered around the kingdom. Then order the cow to collect them. The cow must collect them all to fill exactly the containers to their original weight. This time the cow will surely fail."

Upon hearing this plan, the king felt confident. He then put out the order for the sesame seeds to be scattered. He laughed derisively while he ordered the cow, "Collect them all in three days."

Seeing that the cow was very sad, the daughters of the king of birds and the king of ants said, "Brother, don't you worry about it. Three *haap* of sesame is nothing. We can collect them all in a short time." They then went to each of their kingdoms. They both brought back many of their fellows. The whole city of Benares was blackened with the enormous number of ants and birds. They all collected the sesame. They retrieved the sesame in full. The cow then called the king and the tiger to witness the accomplishment. The king and the tiger saw thousands upon thousands of birds and ants surrounding the city. They were so frightened that their gullets exploded and they died.

TALE OF THE TWO RIVERS, KHONG AND KHORNG

Told by Aai Kham (Tai Lue)

Once upon a time in the land of Sipsongpanna, Khong and Khorng were brothers of one and the same river. Khong was the upper part of the river and Khorng the lower. The two swore brotherly love and promised to share everything they got. Khong always happily sent over food for his brother downriver. Even a small mouse was equally shared between them. Khong, the older brother, and Khorng, the younger, enjoyed life together.

One day a big flood came, and a bee floated down the high current. Khong, of the upper river, got the bee and saw that the creature was too small to be divided. Khong thought, "Hmm—this bee is not even bite-size for me. Let me not send Brother Khorng his share this time. The water is still rising, and many more creatures will come along. I'll eat up the bee all by myself this round."

In the meantime, the younger brother, Khorng, went through seven days and seven nights without any food. He was very hungry and started to get suspicious that his older brother wasn't sharing food with him. "I've had nothing to eat so long—my upriver brother must have eaten all the food."

Then the following day, there was a porcupine floating down. After eating his share, Khong, the older brother, let the rest of the porcupine float down to his younger brother. Khorng, the younger brother, looked at what was left of the porcupine and thought, "Heh—this was a large porcupine, but what I see here is such a tiny bit. It doesn't add up to a meal. Brother Khong must have gotten a whole lot first. Why didn't he share it with me? Why did he leave me such a small piece? How could he do such a thing? I'm starving, and he still doesn't share what he has."

By now, Khorng was furious with his older brother. He felt belittled. "This is an unfair share. Brother Khong always gets everything first anyway. I just have his leftovers all the time." They then quarreled and were filled with hatred toward each other. Khong then split off from his brother Khorng. They severed their ties and no longer were a part of each other. The river goes two separate ways when it enters the Sipsongpanna area.

A FOLK STORY IN "FUNERAL LAMENT LYRICS" OF THE LUO PEOPLE, YUNNAN

Collected, translated, and introduced by Yu Ming (Yi)

The Luo are a little-known people classified as a subgroup of the Yi ethnic group. They number about ten thousand and live in the border areas of Yunnan, Guangxi, and Vietnam. Legends and historical evidence suggest that at one time the Luo lived in the vicinity of Dianchi Lake, near present-day Kunming (the capital of Yunnan province), migrating south long ago because of regional military conflicts. Traditional customs include the use of ancient cast-bronze drums in rituals, bamboo pole architecture, and batik-patterned clothing (sometimes featuring bronze-drum motifs). A number of clans constitute the social structure. As the people have no native writing system, rituals are important vehicles for passing on traditions.

"The Red Silk-Cotton Tree" is from the repertoire of a funeral lament singer in one Luo village. After a death, the family members assemble in the home, and a singer is called to sing songs to comfort the dead—in a total of forty-eight different tunes. Besides songs intended to placate the soul, the ritual singer tells many stories and myths that reveal Luo values and traditional customs to the living audience. In the folktale, the storyteller reflects on the differences in values between the generations of today and those of the past. Even the ritual specialists (*bimo*) cannot live up to the previous standards. The story seems to be a very old one, however, and may refer to the perennial problems in perceptions between generations as well as an implicit reminder that the forces of change are always present and that people should take care to honor the old ways.

The story was collected from a middle-aged male ritual singer named Huang Jinsi in the village of Longtanshu, Funing county, Yunnan province, in 2003 and 2004. The collector, Yu Ming, who translated it line by line with Huang from Luo into Chinese, and then into English, is a researcher on ethnic costume, material culture, and Luo folklore at the Yunnan Ethnic Minorities Museum (Yunnan Minzu Bowuguan), in Kunming.

THE RED SILK-COTTON TREE

Told by Huang Jinsi (Luo)

Once there was a tree;[20] its fruit was red and attractive, and it had green leaves. Someone went and invited some bees and hornets to sample the tree blossoms. The tree said, "It doesn't matter if you sample them or don't sample them—you are all invited to sample the blossoms."

---

20. The botanical name corresponding to silk-cotton tree is *Gossampinus malabarica*.

Two people who came to help decided to catch a wild horse. Upon finding a wild horse, the first person went to sweet-talk the horse. He first extended the rope halter, but only scared the horse away. The second person went to sweet-talk the wild horse. He first extended some grass, and slowly used the rope to capture it. As the horse extended its head to eat the grass, it was roped. The horse was haltered and was tied to the root of a tree. People brought a rooster and tied it on the horse's back, then brought a ladle of cold water and fastened it to the rooster's wings. They waited until the rooster crowed. As the rooster flapped its wings, the cold water spilled all over the horse's body, and the horse began bucking in fright, shaking against the tree. The fruit fell down. The fruit that fell on the horse's mane made the mane shiny; the fruit that fell on its body made the horse fat; those that fell on the horse's hooves made the hooves very round—completely changed in shape.

But each day the tree grew more withered, and finally it fell down. It fell into a mountain cave and changed into a person. People brought him up out of the cave, and in bringing him out discovered that he had no eyes and no mouth. So people went to find thorns to prick open his eyes and mouth. With eyes and a mouth, he finally looked like a human being. They let him live among the roots of the cogon grass, but he was unwilling to stay, feeling that cogon grass roots had too many sprouts and were too thick; so they also let him live among the bananas [*bajiao*], but he felt it was too damp and cold there. So they let him live among the wild taro roots, but this was also unsuitable. So he decided to build his own house.

He dug out a very flat foundation and planted the house posts as straight as banana stalks. The cogon grass he used [for the roof] seemed like a billowing cloud. Once his house was made, he prepared to invite guests, but there were not many guests, only two types of birds. One type was a thrush, and one type was a sparrow. He was a little angry, so he took his crossbow and shot the two birds, and the birds died. So he ate the bird meat, and when the meat was all eaten, he discovered that the bird bones were too tough and could not be eaten. So he threw them in the fire to roast, but they would not roast properly. So he threw them in the river, but the river would not wash them away. So he took them to feed the dogs, but the dogs would not eat them. So he used them to feed the chickens, but the chickens would not ingest them.

So he broke apart the skeletons and discovered that inside were three cotton seedpods. So he dug three mounds of earth and buried the cotton seeds. After the cotton seeds grew, he gathered three baskets and invited four people to help with the work. But the four people were all unwilling, so he had to undertake the whole business of making thread from growing the cotton seedpods to making thread and weaving cloth from them. Once the cloth was woven, he invited four people to help sew; but the four were unwilling to help, so he had to sew shirts and sew pants by himself.

As it was, no one came to wear the clothes. So he invited four people to come wear them, but the four were not willing to wear them. Finally, there was a young woman who heard about the clothes, and she was willing to wear them. After she put them on, everyone came to look and discovered that the clothing was very well made and that the young woman looked extremely beautiful. Many people began to pursue her. She took up with a young man, but her parents did not agree [to the match], feeling that the gifts he brought were too few; so the poor young man went home. The young woman was angry and thought to herself: "Everyone else agreed; it was only my parents who disagreed with the marriage. From now on I will not listen to their words." The next day, she got up to pound rice by herself. A few birds came to eat the rice, so when she went to scare off the birds, the rice was not completely pounded. She went out in the fields to cut grass. When she was finished with one place, she did not have the strength to cut another one. When she returned to go to sleep, she [tried to] follow her mother and father to sleep. Once they were asleep, she [tried to] follow her brother's wife to sleep, but she still could not sleep. So she decided to go find that young man. On the first day and the second day, she did not find him; on the third day and the fourth day, she did not find him; on the tenth day, she found a young man, but it was not her lover. The young woman said, "Have you seen my friend?" The young man answered, "Because your father and mother's requirements are too high, he has already died from a broken heart." The young woman cried, cried for the couple's lost love that could never be found again.

The young woman's lover had a younger brother, whose name was Mapo. He wanted to go find his brother. Other people had said to him, "You originally had an elder brother, but because he could not raise the young woman's bride-price, he died of a broken heart." The younger brother wept as he went to find the footprints of his elder brother. He came to the place with Orchid Bamboo, thinking it was his elder brother. But he discovered it was not, so he cried. He came to the place with Boar Grass, thinking it was [his elder brother], but it was not; and so he cried once more. He came to a mountain valley, and saw Vine Basket and thought it was [his elder brother], but it was not: so he cried again. He came to the Cliff area and saw Cliff, and [because of like circumstances] cried again.

Passing a village, he walked by some old folks raising a herd of pigs and dogs. The pigs cried out, and the dogs cried out. The old men asked, "Is it in fact a thief on the road or a regular person on the road?" Walking on to the dwelling place of the young woman, he still did not find his brother, but recalled that it was the young woman's family who had killed his brother, so he went to the old people's place to report: "Originally, all you needed was wild grass and wild vegetables to make an engagement, but in my brother's generation, you can kill a pig or kill a cow and still not make the engagement. Originally, it was the elders who taught the young; now the elders every day scold the children. Originally, old women taught the young women to sew and embroider, but now the older women simply scold the young women. In the last generation, the *bimo* conducted the people's ancestral rites. This later generation of *bimo* scold their sons every day, not even allowing people to eat [in peace]. In the past, the craftsmen made hammers, made the bronze drums, doing everything just right. Now, when making a knife, craftsmen cannot even put an edge on it. When making a bronze drum, they cannot even form it so it has ears on it—so it can't be hung up. In the past, the young people did things so honestly, even when sitting it was as if they were walking; when walking, it seemed like they were running; when running, it seemed like they were flying. But today's youth, when flying it seems like they are running; when running, it seems like they are walking; when walking, it seems like they are sitting; when sitting, it seems like they are sleeping. Originally, when called to embroider and sew, a young woman would come with a smile. If she was said to lack virtue, she would cry. If today's young women are called to come embroider and sew, they weep. If they are said to lack virtue, they laugh."

A STORY FROM THE NUOSU OF SICHUAN

Translated by Aku Wuwu, Mark Bender, and Jjiepa Ayi and introduced by Mark Bender

The story "Cannibal Grandmother" is from a large subgroup of the Yi ethnic group known as the Nuosu. The Nuosu live in two large autonomous prefectures in the Liangshan Mountains of Sichuan and Yunnan provinces, numbering over 2 million people. Goats, pigs, cows, chickens, and the occasional yak are raised for meat, felt, and leather, while buckwheat, oats, and potatoes are basic vegetable food sources. Social relations are based on patrilineal clans, and bloodlines are of vital importance in all social interactions. Nuosu society tends to be conservative and inner directed, and many customs reflect strict adherence to social protocol. Traditional beliefs include nature spirits and ghosts. Among the Nuosu ritual specialists is a type of shaman called *sunyi* who deals specifically with ghosts, often when in trance states. Beliefs about ghosts are many, and there are many types.[21] In some cases, as in the following story, it is believed that one dimension of a person can be transformed into a ghost while still in the form of a living human.

Oral lore, including folk stories, songs, and epics, still thrives in parts of the Liangshan Mountains. A popular story form (either mixed in with oral epic performances or told separately) is called *bbudde.* One figure in these oral stories is the wild cannibal woman known as Coqo Ama (Cannibal Grandmother [Coqot Amat, including the linguistic tone markers]). Varying in details by region, stories about her are told informally by anyone who knows them in any number of situations where stories might be recounted. In this version, an incident occurs when a *sunyi* is called to the house to perform a ritual. Sitting in the special place reserved for guests, he accidentally passes gas while going into a trance. Two little sisters, who are grinding grain nearby, break out in laughter. In Nuosu society, it is considered shameful to pass gas in public—young women have been known to commit suicide after doing so in the presence of a male elder. (Also, the euphemism "going outside to have a look" is used when one wants to go to the "restroom.") Thus events are set in motion that result in the girls' being expelled from the family and eventually falling into the clutches of the horrid Coqo Ama.

On one level, "Cannibal Grandmother" reinforces Nuosu ideas about proper protocol and family relations. On another, it encourages perseverance against the forces of nature in a difficult environment—personified in the relation between the girls and Coqo Ama. The tale also lends insight into the still important role of the *sunyi* as a transmitter of ideas about certain supernatural forces—such as ghosts—and ways of dealing with them. Rhetorical features from Nuosu oral art include the phrase "seven days and seven nights," indicating a long period of time. Certain details are specific to Nuosu local culture. These include

---

21. See "The Origin of Ghosts" (chap. 3).

hunting and keeping hunting dogs, which are still common pastimes among some Nuosu men. Prey animals include small deer, like the muntjac and water deer. Typical male clothing is a long felt cloak and a black turban wrapped so that a distinctive cloth "horn" sticks out from the forehead. Women wear ankle-length skirts in color patterns that indicate marital status.

The storyteller, Aku Wuwu (Luo Qingchun), is a well-known Yi poet and a professor of Yi literature who grew up in the Liangshan Mountains of southern Sichuan. The oral story was translated directly from Nuosu into English.

CANNIBAL GRANDMOTHER

Told by Aku Wuwu (Yi)

Long ago, there was an age when all the living things on earth could speak. There was a family with three children: two elder daughters and a little son. They led a happy life in a mountain village.

One day the son became terribly ill. The father invited a famous *sunyi* from another village to cure him. The *sunyi* sat in the guest's place and began his doctoring. Then he stood up, continuing to doctor. At the very moment when his guardian god was coming into him, he passed gas, with a *zhy* sound. Hearing the sound, the two little sisters standing by the millstone, grinding away, couldn't help but burst into laughter. The *sunyi* became very angry when he found that the sisters were laughing at him. After the doctoring was done, he reported the result to the father secretly, "Your boy's illness was caused by none other than the ghosts that were transformed from your two daughters. You'd better split your daughters from the family and rid your home of them; otherwise your little boy won't recover." He then told the father how to get rid of them.

Early the next morning, the father woke the sisters and said, "My daughters, we're going to pick wild greens in the mountains today." So the two little girls followed their father and headed into the mountains. When they came to a place where a lot of wild greens grew, the older sister asked, "Dad, is it okay to pick here?" "No, dear, the wild greens that grow on the top of mountains are the best. My dear daughters, I'm too old to climb anymore; I'll sit and wait for you here. Go and pick the wild greens at the top of the mountain." The sisters followed his instructions and kept on climbing. After climbing for some time, they stopped and turned around: "Dad, now can we pick the wild greens here?" The father answered, "No, keep climbing." So they climbed further and then turned around again and asked, "Dad, can we pick them here now?" "No, not yet."

What the poor sisters didn't know was that this was a trick of the *sunyi*'s. The "father" who answered each time was a tree trunk bewitched by the *sunyi*, covered by their father's cloak and turban. Finally, they went so far that they could no longer hear any answers from the "father," nor could they see "his" likeness.

Night fell and they met Coqo Ama. She said, "Poor little girls, since it's so dark now, why don't you come and stay at my home?" The two little girls had no choice but to follow her.

When they got to Coqo Ama's home, she said, "You two must be very tired; come and go to bed early. The one who has fleas must sleep behind me. The one without fleas must sleep in front of me." The clever elder sister slipped a handful of oat seeds into her pocket. When Coqo Ama asked them to shake their cloaks over the fireplace, the elder sister did so. The seeds in her pocket fell into the fire and crackled. But when it was the younger sister's turn, nothing happened. So Coqo Ama thought the elder one had fleas, and asked her to sleep behind her.

At midnight, the elder sister heard Coqo Ama grinding her teeth. Alerted, she woke up her younger sister. As they were about to escape, Coqo Ama woke up and said, "What are you doing?"

"Ama, I want to go and have a look outside."

"Go ahead if you really want to."

"But I'm afraid of the darkness outside; I need my sister's company."

So Coqo Ama tied a string to the girl's big toe and, holding the other end of the string, let the girls out. As soon as the sisters got out of the house, they tied the string to a small tree and ran away. Coqo Ama waited for a long time, but the sisters didn't return. She tugged on the string, but it was too hard to pull in. When she ran out of the house and saw nothing except the small tree, she became extremely angry. She followed their tracks until dusk, when she found the girls sitting in a big tree.

Coqo Ama tried to climb the tree several times, but failed because the trunk was so slippery and thick.

"Ama, Ama, if you can't climb up, why don't you go and get some cow dung to slather on the trunk. It may help." Coqo Ama did what they said, but the trunk became even more slippery to climb.

"Ama, Ama, if it's still hard for you to climb, try and slather some lard on the trunk." Coqo Ama did so, but the same thing happened.

"Ama, Ama, please go borrow a spear from my maternal uncle. Since you really can't climb up here, as a treat for you we'll pick out our boogers." When she heard the word "boogers"—to her a delicious food—she completely forgot how the girls had fooled her.

Coqo Ama ran and borrowed a spear from their uncle, warning them before she handed over the spear, "You two little girls, don't play any more tricks on me. If you kill me with this spear, I swear my blood will turn into rivers, my flesh will turn into cliffs, my hair will turn into forests, my nails will turn into thorns, and my sinews and muscle will turn into snakes, which will surround you so you can never return home."

"Well, we won't kill you. But please give us the spear to dig out our boogers, or you'll never know how tasty they are." When they got the spear, the girls dug out their boogers and smeared them on the tip of the spear. The moment Coqo Ama eagerly opened her mouth, they drove the spear inside with all their strength.

Coqo Ama died on the spot. As Coqo Ama had predicted, her blood turned into rivers, her flesh turned into cliffs, her hair turned into forests, and her sinews and muscle turned into snakes. Facing all this, the sisters became frightened and worried. Suddenly they saw a prey animal running toward them. They cried, "Prey, prey, please come and help us down. If you do that, we'll marry you."

But the prey animal paid no attention to what they said, running away and crying, "How can I have time to help you when the hunting dog is chasing me?" Then a hunting dog ran up from the distance. So the sisters cried, "Hunting dog, hunting dog, if you rescue us, we will be your wives." The hunting dog looked at them and then ran off, saying, "How can I have time when I'm chasing my prey?"

The sisters were very disappointed and helpless. Then they saw a hunter running from the same direction from which the prey and the hunting dog had come. "Hunter, hunter, please help us down. If you rescue us, we promise to marry you." The hunter glanced up and said breathlessly, "If I can catch my prey, I'll come back and rescue you. But if I can't get my prey, I won't be able to." Anyhow, it gave the sisters hope; so the poor sisters kept praying:

"Successfully hunt the prey;
Successfully hunt the prey;
Successfully hunt the prey . . ."

Luckily, the hunter actually caught the prey animal, came back, and helped them down from the tree. The sisters didn't want to go back on their word, but it was hard for them to choose between the hunter and the hunting dog for their husbands. The elder sister, who was very clever, said that she wanted to get married with a "black house with a tile roof," which indicated a man. But the younger sister, who was vain, said that she wanted to marry a "white house made of bamboo," though she didn't realize this meant a dog. Thus the elder sister married the hunter, and her younger sister married the hunting dog.

One day, a few months later, when the hunter went hunting with the hunting dog, the younger sister gave birth to a litter of puppies. The sisters were so astonished that they burned the puppies to death in the fire and ran away. When the hunter and the hunting dog came back, they found the dead puppies, which made the hunting dog very angry. The hunting dog followed the girls' tracks, trying to catch them.

When the hunting dog had almost caught up with the sisters, they happened to meet a wild boar. "Please help us, wild boar, a hunting dog is chasing us. We are in great danger." The kind wild boar quickly dug a hole in the ground. As they hid in the hole, the boar covered it with a stone slab. In their haste, a corner of the younger sister's skirt had caught under the stone slab. When the hunting dog got to where the girls were hidden, he immediately saw the skirt corner and barked crazily as he smelled it. The clever elder sister drew out a needle and pricked the dog's nose. This hurt the dog, and he ran off howling in pain. The sisters then crawled out of the hole, thanked the kind wild boar, and ran away.

The sisters walked for seven days and seven nights. One day, they came across an old woman who was herding pigs. The old woman asked the girls to look for fleas on her head. While the elder sister was searching, she found a birthmark on the old woman's head. She remembered that in the past she used to search for fleas on her mother's head, and told this to the old woman. The old woman then told of how she once had two daughters who used to search her head for fleas. This was a real coincidence, and they all felt strange. But the old lady wouldn't admit that she was their mother. So the elder sister said, "Ama, if you don't believe us, please go home and check my things. You'll find a bamboo mouth harp beside the millstone and a part of my broken comb is in the bamboo basket that hangs next to another bamboo basket holding my wooden soup spoon." The old woman still doubted what she was told, but she went home and found that the things were right in the places that the girl had said. She then staggered toward her daughters and hugged them, crying sorrowfully and telling them the terrible news that, soon after they left, their little brother had died of illness, though their father was still alive. Once the father heard the news, he acknowledged the two girls as his daughters, with tears in his eyes.

TALES OF DRAGONS

Translated and introduced by Qiguang Zhao (Han)

The dragon has embodied the aspirations and fears of the Chinese people over thousands of years, and this mythical creature has left its mark on many aspects of Chinese culture. Chinese dragons resemble one another but suggest different symbolic meanings in different contexts. The dragon as the symbol of China is the dragon of Chinese orthodox myth and classics. But there are other dragons, such as the Dragon King, whose control of ardently desired rains made him an ambiguous god in Chinese folk religion, or the dragons in folktales, who often manifest themselves as menacing obstacles, just like the evil Western dragons who were born for just one purpose—to be slain by a handsome and spirited hero. The Dragon King's daughter in folktales, however, always loves the poor and lonely young man and repays his favor with her heart and hand. The tales "February 2, the Dragon Raises His Head" and "Dragon-Print Stone of the West Mountains"—the first from local Han cultures in Shaanxi province and the second from Beijing—illustrate some of the various features of these most-beloved creatures of the Chinese imagination.

FEBRUARY 2, THE DRAGON RAISES HIS HEAD

Collected by Fu Kuang (Han) and Jin Shoushen (Han)

The Jade Emperor in the heavens was angry when Empress Wu Zetian ruled China. He asked Taibai Jinxing[22] to send a message to the Dragon Kings of the Four Oceans to say that, as a punishment, the world should get no rain for three years.

The people suffered greatly from this edict. Crops died of drought, ponds dried up, and it became hard to find drinking water. It seemed that everyone would soon die. People cried until they had no tears and until their voices were hoarse. The rain gods heard the cry and felt sad, but they did not dare to disobey the edict of the Jade Emperor.

One day, a cloud floated over and became larger and larger, until it covered the whole sky. After a soft wind blew, *hua-hua-hua*, the rain pelted down. People were so happy for the welcome rain after the long drought that they all knelt down and expressed their thanks to heaven.

The rain was sent by the Jade Dragon, who was in charge of the Heavenly River. He had been banished to the human world to suffer because he had earlier sent down rain to rescue the people. Later he became a white horse and

---

22. Taibai Jinxing (Great White Metal Star) is a reference to Venus, or the Vesper star, who is associated with the Jade Emperor as his deputy. Later in the story, he is called Old Taibai.

followed the monk Tripitaka to bring back Buddhist sutras from India.[23] Scaling mountains and fording streams, he experienced all sorts of trials. He was called back to the Heavenly River to resume his old position because of the merit he had won for helping Tripitaka. He now heard the sounds of crying and saw the scenes of death. He sucked a great deal of water from the Heavenly River and, regardless of the risk he ran of being banished from heaven, spat the heavy rain through his great mouth. The Jade Emperor was mad at this and crushed the Jade Dragon under a mountain in the human world. Then the Jade Emperor set up a stone tablet with the following words:

> The Jade Dragon violated the Heavenly Decree by sending down a rain. He will have to endure a thousand years of hardships in the human world. He cannot return to the heavenly palace until golden beans bloom.

When everyone learned that the Jade Dragon had offended the Jade Emperor for the sake of the common people, they began to look for blooming golden beans in order to save the dragon and pay their debt of gratitude. They also hoped that he could return to the sky and send more rains down. They searched and searched, but they could not find any blooming beans.

February 1 of the next year was a market day. An old woman carried a sack of corn for sale. She did not tie the sack well, and the golden corn fell out on the ground. An idea struck the people: Aren't the grains of corn like golden beans? Won't they bloom when popped? So the idea spread everywhere, and all the local people knew it. They decided that everybody should make popcorn the next day.

On February 2, all families held pans with popcorn and displayed them outside, some even in front of the Jade Dragon. Seeing the kindness of the people, the Jade Dragon could not help yelling, "Old Taibai, the golden beans have bloomed. Why don't you let me go!" Old and weak-sighted, Taibai could not see clearly. He waved his hand and took back his duster, which had been transformed into the mountain over the Jade Dragon. No sooner did the duster arise than the Jade Dragon roared and flew to the sky. With all his strength, he spat water toward the scorched land. *Hua-hua-hua*, in the twinkling of an eye, the rivers and ditches were all filled with water and the earth was soaked.

The Jade Emperor was watching fairy maidens singing and dancing in his Cloud Palace. The god on duty entered to report that, against the imperial edict, the Jade Dragon had again sent down a rain. Immediately the Jade Emperor called Taibai Jinxing to account. Taibai Jinxing knew that he was to blame, but he said, "Didn't you say that he could be released when the golden beans bloom? This morning I saw the golden beans bloom in the human world, so I took back the duster." The Jade Emperor trembled with anger and said, "That was popcorn!" After waiting until the anger of the Jade Emperor had cooled,

23. This is the famous story of *Journey to the West* (*Xiyou ji*).

Taibai Jinxing sounded him out: "I think that all of our incense smoke is that offered by the people on earth. If they all die of hunger, what will happen?" The Jade Emperor thought a moment, and feeling there was no alternative, he called the Jade Dragon back.

Although the Jade Dragon has been in the heavens for many years now, the people are accustomed to making popcorn on the morning of February 2, singing, "February 2, the dragon raises his head. The granary is bursting with grain." This custom of making popcorn on February 2 is still observed in some places.

DRAGON-PRINT STONE OF THE WEST MOUNTAINS

Collected by Fu Kuang (Han) and Jin Shoushen (Han)

There is a temple in the West Mountains, and there is a big stone in front of the temple. On the stone, there is a dragon print. People in Beijing call it Dragon-Print Stone.

It is said that there once was a small mountain village there. An old woman and her son lived in the village. The son was as strong as a tiger, and he was born in the year of the tiger, so people called him Tiger Cub. He could cut firewood and grass, climb mountains, and jump over ravines. A boy of great strength, he could move a stone of several hundred *jin*.[24]

Every day, he cut firewood on the top of the mountains and rested there when he was tired. The weather was changeable there. Sometimes the sky was blue and cloudless, but in a moment, clouds gathered with thunder and lightning. When it rained, Tiger Cub would hide in a cave.

One day, Tiger Cub went to the mountains to cut firewood. It seemed to be a sunny day. With ax in hand, he jumped from one mountain to another and soon cut a few bundles of firewood. A sudden blast of wind brought a black cloud, and it floated over the West Mountains. After a tremendous clap of thunder, the whole sky became as dark as pitch. Then hailstones as big as eggs fell everywhere, and sheep and cattle fled in all directions. Crops were ruined. Then there was spatter of cold rain. Fierce mountain water accompanied by hailstones rushed downhill and flattened the walls and houses of the small village.

Seeing all this, Tiger Cub was panting with rage, thinking, "Who could have been so fierce? He just wanted everybody to die. If he dares to tell me his name, I will chop him three times with my ax, even if he is Grandpa Heaven himself." Thus thinking, Tiger Cub saw a dragon tail swing out of the dark cloud, rolling, spreading, and proudly swaying left and right. Then the dragon with his fierce head appeared, bared his fangs, and brandished his claws. His body then entered the cloud, leaving only the head outside. He rolled his feel-

24. One *jin* is a little over a pound (about half a kilo).

ers, put out his tongue, and inhaled water from the ground. Water columns stood over mountains, ditches, and springs. He absorbed all the water.

Tiger Cub saw everything with his own eyes and murmured, "Aha, it is you! If only you were in my hand, I would knock you into eight pieces." Saying this, he went downhill. He got to the foot of a mountain and saw the ruined village. The old and young alike were weeping. His mother wept more bitterly when she saw him coming back. "You have come back after all," she said. "Do something to save the villagers."

Tiger Cub looked at the villagers. "Don't worry," he said. "I saw everything from the top of the mountain. It was an evil dragon who did it. We will settle with him one of these days. Let us first rebuild our village." Having said this, Tiger Cub instructed everybody to build houses with rocks. They had no food, so they ate wild grass; they had no water, so they licked dew in caves. After some busy days, the villagers settled down. They began once again to farm the fields.

Tiger Cub worked every day, but he was upset. With a worried frown, he thought, "Although we have houses, we can't live in peace with the existence of the evil dragon. I will do everything I can to get rid of him." He told his mother what he was thinking. His mother praised him: "Go, child." Thus Tiger Cub went to the mountains with his ax. Up in the mountains, he cut firewood while paying attention to the situation in the sky. But he found nothing for the first few days.

One day, he went to the mountains again. Halfway up a hill, he met a young man in a black shirt and black pants. With his black beard, the black young man looked evil. He was lying on a stone to get some sunshine. Tiger Cub was puzzled because he came to the mountains every day but he had never seen this man.

"Where are you from? What is your name?"

"I am from Cloud and Fog Village. My name is Dragon Cub. What is your name?" the black lad asked.

"I live just at the foot of the mountains. My name is Tiger Cub. What do you want down here?"

"I have come to check the mountains," the black lad rolled his eyes.

"What for?"

"To find springs."

Hearing the word "springs," Tiger Cub became angry. "Yes, there were springs and an evil dragon inhaled all the water from them. The villagers want to skin the dragon."

"So what? The sky is mine, the mountains are mine. I can do what I want!"

Tiger Cub heard these words and knew that this was the evil dragon he sought. Without a word, Tiger Cub stepped forward, caught the black lad, and chopped at him with his ax. The black lad stepped back, and the ax fell on a stone with a shower of sparks. Tiger Cub would not let him go and knocked him down. With a piece of string used for bundling firewood, Tiger Cub tied him and led him toward the village. At the foot of the mountains, Tiger Cub was going to call the villagers, but the black lad jumped up and broke the string that bound him. In the twinkling of an eye, he turned into a dragon and floated up into the air.

In a flash, Tiger Cub also jumped up, and he grabbed the dragon's tail. Pulling the tail down, Tiger Cub shouted, "You evil dragon. Let us see what more tricks you have!" He then swung the dragon and threw him onto a stone with all his strength. The black dragon opened his eyes round and stretched out his claws, scratching a piece of flesh from Tiger Cub. Blood streamed down. In spite of the pain, Tiger Cub held the dragon's horns and again threw the dragon on the big stone. "Ohh," the dragon cried and a column of water poured out from his mouth. The black dragon was worn out. Tiger Cub swung the dragon in the air and again threw him on the stone. The black dragon opened his mouth and could not move. Thus a deep dragon figure was printed on the stone.

The black dragon was dead; neither drought nor flood, neither storms nor hail would again attack the West Mountains. Streams flowed at the foot of the mountains, and flowers bloomed up in the hills. This place became a well-known area for sightseeing. People say, "The dragon fell on the West Mountains. Tiger Cub took his revenge. Dragon stone and dragon print have scared heaven." Since then, the Dragon-Print Stone has been famous.

A MOSUO STORY FROM LAKE LUGU

Collected by Lamu Gatusa (Mosuo) and translated and introduced by An Xiaoke (Yi)

"Goddess Gemu" is a well-known story of the Mosuo (Moso, or Na) people of northern Yunnan province. The Mosuo number about thirty thousand and live mostly around scenic Lake Lugu in Yongning township in the Ninglang Yi Autonomous County. Although strongly influenced by Tibetan and Naxi cultures, the Mosuo have distinct customs and beliefs. They are famous in China for their so-called walking-marriage system, in which most people take a series of lovers during their lives. Homes typically include several generations of women and their children. An adult male lives in his mother's or sister's home but often spends nights in a lover's residence. The Mosuo retain their own language but have used both Chinese and Tibetan scripts for writing. Traditional beliefs are a mixture of animism, shamanism, and Lamaism. Shamans are known as *daba*.

Most Mosuo are farmers or fishermen, growing crops that include oats, corn, potatoes, buckwheat, and soybeans. They also raise pigs, goats, horses, chickens, and cattle. In recent years, many have become involved in the tourist trade and other money-producing activities. Like the Naxi and Yi, the Mosuo are said to be related to the ancient Qiang peoples who long ago came from farther north. Like the Pumi, the Mosuo have a special rite of passage held on New Year's Day in which children at age thirteen exchange their long gowns for adult clothing and present themselves in the area of the home designated for the maternal grandmother. Mosuo women wear their hair long and tied into a bun. They wear red, green, or black tunics with white pleated skirts and colorful sashes tied around their waists. Mosuo men usually wear short linen jackets, loose trousers, and felted vests, and they carry short knives at their waists. In recent years, the tourist trade has been accompanied by the emergence of new costumes and cultural activities along traditional lines.

The goddess Gemu is the most famous supernatural being in the Lugu area. Many stories about her are told informally in any number of situations. The Going Around the Mountain Festival is the most important festival for worshipping the goddess, and activities include singing, dancing, burning incense, picnicking, and staying overnight in tents at the foot of Gemu Mountain. It is also a good time for Mosuo people to find their lovers. People call their lovers by the term *axia* (though, strictly, the term *axia* refers to female lovers, while *azhu* is used for males). In the walking-marriage system, some lovers are regarded as "long term," while others are regarded as "short term." A conflict between the two sorts of lovers (in the relations between the gods) is part of the story "Goddess Gemu" and may reflect certain tensions in this aspect of the culture. In the Yongning area, lama priests are allowed to take lovers, as suggested in the tale.

Rhetorical features in the story include the phrases "as beautiful as winter jasmine," which refers to the heroine's beauty; "nine mountains and eighteen villages," which signifies many places; and "the proposal songs were like flowing water, and the proposal gifts piled up like hills," which indicates that many young men proposed to her.

The storyteller, Wengjima Luruo, is a Mosuo from the Lake Lugu area. The story was collected in 1990 by Lamu Gatusa, a well-known Mosuo scholar. It was published first in Chinese and then translated into this English version.

GODDESS GEMU

Told by Wengjima Luruo (Mosuo)

Long, long ago, there was a beautiful girl who lived in Zabo Village by Lake Lugu in Yongning county. Seven days after her birth, she could speak as well as sing pleasant songs. Three months after her birth, she knew everything about the world. By the age of three, she was as beautiful as winter jasmine. Her beauty spread over nine mountains and eighteen villages. Many people came around to see how beautiful she was. When she was eighteen years old, all the young men came to propose to her. The proposal songs were like flowing water, and the proposal gifts piled up like hills. But the girl didn't promise herself to anyone. Her name was Gemu.

One day, when she was helping her mother work the fields, the heavenly spirit took a fancy to her. He turned into a whirlwind and swept Gemu away. Gemu shouted from the sky, but the god held her tightly in his grip.

Everyone in Yongning county saw her and heard her voice. People cried out. The voice sounded like thunder. The spirit heard the voice and became flustered. He suddenly dropped Gemu. Gemu fell on top of Lion Mountain and could not get down. From then on, she rode a white horse, holding a pearl tree in her left hand and a flute in her right hand. Gemu strolled about the hills of Yongning county, guarding the people's safety. When storms or whirlwinds came, Gemu became a white cloud over the mountains, warning people to be prepared. The local people were very thankful. On the twenty-fifth day of the seventh month of the lunar calendar, people celebrated the Mountain Worshipping Festival. During the festival, people sang and danced around the mountain, recalling her good deeds.

Like mortals, Goddess Gemu had her own *axia* lovers. Her long-term *axia* was the god Warubura. Her temporary *axias* were the gods Zeji and Gosa. Once Warubura went on an outing and Gemu made a date with the god Zeji. At midnight, Warubura came back. He happened to see the two together. Warubura was so angry that he pulled out his sword and cut off the god Zeji's genitals. Down to today, the god Zeji still lacks genitals.

Another time, the god Gosa made a secret tryst with Gemu while Warubura was out. But they became at odds with each other. The god Gosa wanted to leave Gemu and stay with another lover—Lady Changshan. Gemu hated to lose Gosa, and she pulled him by a sleeve. In this way, one pulled one way while the one pulled the other way until dawn. When the roosters crowed, they had to stop. Since then, with one sleeve belonging to Gosa in Gemu's hand, they stay close by each other's side.

A STORY OF THE PUMI OF YUNNAN

Collected by Yang Zhaohui (Pumi) and translated and introduced by An Xiaoke (Yi)

"The Story of Zerijamu and Cuziluyi" is a traditional folk tale about the genesis of the Pumi ethnic group. The Pumi, formerly known as the Xifan, have a population of roughly thirty thousand. More than 90 percent live in northwestern Yunnan province, in areas that include Lanping county, in Nujiang prefecture; Ninglang, Lijiang, and Yongshen counties, in Lijiang prefecture; and Weixi county, in Diqing prefecture. Their ancestors are the ancient Qiang people, a nomadic tribe on the Qinghai–Tibet Plateau. In the thirteenth century, they fought southward to Yunnan under the order of Kublai Khan. They have called themselves Pumiying, Pumiri, and Peimi, all containing the meaning "white people" in the Han language, for they worship the color white. In 1960, they were collectively named the Pumi ethnic group.

The Pumi language belongs to the Tibeto-Burman branch of the Sino-Tibetan language family. Most Pumi can speak Mandarin, as well as the Bai and Naxi languages. They have adopted the Chinese and the Tibetan writing systems. Their beliefs are animistic, and they regard the white tiger as their totem. Although the Pumi once had their own shamans, today they invite ritual specialists (*daba*) of the Mosuo to aid in holding their ceremonies. Principal festivals are the New Year, planting, and harvest celebrations. The Spring Festival lasts for three to fifteen days, depending on the area. On New Year's Eve, a rite of passage ceremony called Putting on Trousers or Putting on Skirts (depending on gender) is held in families with a thirteen-year-old child.

Most Pumi are farmers, raising crops that include wheat, oats, buckwheat, potatoes, and soybeans as well as fruits and vegetables. Goats, pigs, cows, and chickens are raised for meat, felt, and leather. Dogs are used as watchdogs and for hunting. The Pumi neither eat nor sell dogs.

Pumi oral tradition includes folk stories, songs, and epics. "The Story of Zerijamu and Cuziluyi" is one of many tales about the genesis of humans, centering on a sister and brother named Zerijamu and Cuziluyi. Such stories are usually told by elderly local people anywhere and anytime that circumstances permit. In this version, a supreme deity allows the brother and the sister to marry. Later, the brother and the sister become ashamed of this marriage. So the deity lets the brother become the moon and the sister become the sun. Like many Western mythologists, Chinese researchers have regarded the tale (and others like it) as negating the incest taboo, but they also regard it as evidence of an earlier state of social evolution before marriage became the norm.

Among the symbols in "The Story of Zerijamu and Cuziluyi" is the image of "the two millstones joined together," which also appears in Miao epic lore farther east, in Guizhou province. Like this image, two others, "the sheep flocked together" and "the two puffs of smoke entwined together," indicate that the marriage is the will of heaven. Other aspects of the story are also found in the myths of other peoples of southwestern China as well as in the creation myths of Japan.

The storyteller, Ma Guangjin, is a Pumi from Ninglang county. The story was collected by a well-known Pumi scholar, Yang Zhaohui, in 1999. It was published in Chinese and then translated into this English version.

THE STORY OF ZERIJAMU AND CUZILUYI

Told by Ma Guangjin (Pumi)

In ancient times, the forefather of the Pumi people was called Cuziluyi and the foremother was named Zerijamu. They lived in a cave in a mountain. There were no humans on the earth at that time. They lived alone. Cuziluyi was the brother, and Zerijamu was the sister. They lived with each other, but couldn't get married. So they had to go out and find their own companions.

The brother went toward the east, and the sister went toward the west. After many years, they met each other. The brother went toward the south, and the sister went toward the north. After many days, they met each other again. So the brother and the sister didn't want to seek for companions again. The brother said, "Let's get married." The sister didn't agree. She said, "We are family members, how can we get married?" So they asked the supreme deity. The deity asked each of them to carry a millstone to the mountaintop and roll it down to the foot of the mountain. If the two millstones joined together, they could get married. They did so according to the deity's request. The two millstones joined together tightly. But the sister still didn't agree to the marriage.

They had to consult the deity again. The deity asked them to herd sheep in different directions. If the sheep flocked together, they could get married. The brother and the sister went in opposite directions until they were far apart. But finally the sheep flocked together. The sister still didn't agree to the marriage.

They inquired of the deity again. The deity asked them to climb the mountain, and each of them made a bonfire. If the two puffs of the bonfires entwined together, they could get married. They did so according the deity's requirement. The two puffs of smoke entwined together. So the sister had to marry her brother.

After they got married, the brother and the sister gave birth to many children. They were ashamed of this. They prayed to the deity again. They wanted the deity to change them into the moon and the sun. The god turned the sister into the moon. But the sister said she was afraid of the darkness of night. So the god changed her into the sun. The sister said she was too shy to come out in the daytime. So the deity gave a fire needle to the sister and let her stab the eyes of the persons who looked at her. In this way, the sister, Zerijamu, became the sun, and the brother, Cuziluyi, became the moon.

FOLK STORIES OF THE UYGHUR

Translated and introduced by Cuiyi Wei and Karl W. Luckert

The Uyghur (Uygur) live mostly in the Xinjiang Uyghur Autonomous Region, in northwestern China. Xinjiang (literally, "new borders," an appropriate name for a territory incorporated into the Chinese empire only in the late nineteenth century, by the Manchus) occupies fully one-sixth of the People's Republic of China. It is mostly desert, but there are many large and small oases scattered along the foothills of the mountain ranges that surround and bisect the region.

An ancient people associated with the old Silk Road, the Uyghur have many religious and cultural connections to Central Asia and the Middle East. The Uyghur number over 7 million, of whom many are involved in trade and handicrafts. They speak a Turkic language and possess rich traditions of oral and written literature.

Among the most famous of Uyghur folk heroes is Ephendi, a figure who also appears in folklore in other parts of the Muslim world. The name Ephendi, which means "master" or "sir," ultimately derives from the Greek *authentēs* (lord, master, doer, perpetrator) and is found in Arabic, Persian, and many other Central Asian and Middle Eastern language sources. He is also well known to the Chinese as Afanti.

The stories about Ephendi, including the four presented here—"Growing Gold," "Jingling Coins," "Three Wise Maxims," and "Two Brothers Meet"—are usually full of wit and irreverence toward wealth and authority. Hence the Ephendi figure is a trickster or joker who speaks for the common man.

The story "Afrat Khan and His Nine Daughters" offers a fascinating glimpse into the cultural and geopolitical past of the Uyghur people. Positioned since the Tang dynasty (618–907) between China and the West, they have survived through a combination of skillful diplomacy and valiant determination. The story also shows the resourcefulness and ability of women among the Uyghur and other northwestern peoples. The lesson taught by this legend is clear: defend your homeland, as these women do, but do not hastily engage in foreign wars, as the unfortunate men do.

GROWING GOLD

One day, Ephendi borrowed a few ounces of gold. Riding on a donkey, he soon arrived at a river, where, sitting on the bank, he pretended to sift for the gold.

After a while, the king passed along the riverbank on his way to go hunting.

"Ephendi, what are you doing here?" asked the king.

"Oh, Your Majesty, I am busy growing gold," answered Ephendi.

The king was surprised: "Ephendi, you are indeed clever. Tell me what happens when you grow it."

"Do you not understand what growing means?" asked Ephendi. "Look, the gold that is planted today can be expected to be ready for harvest on Friday. The first ten ounces will be ready for harvesting at that time."

The king became very greedy when he heard this. Certainly there would be great profit for him if he seized this opportunity immediately. So, trying to flatter him, the king consulted with Ephendi in mock seriousness:

"Good, Ephendi. But you will not harvest much by planting such a small amount of gold. If you need seed, come to my palace. I can provide you with as much gold seed as you need. Let us be partners in growing it. When you harvest the gold, give me eighty percent."

"That is excellent, Your Majesty," said Ephendi.

The next day, Ephendi went to the palace to get two pounds of gold. After a week, he sent the king ten pounds of gold. When the king opened the bag and found the shiny gold, he was wild with joy.

Unable to control himself, the king immediately summoned his officials, whom he told to give Ephendi several boxes of gold from the royal treasury so that he could grow more.

When Ephendi received the gold, he distributed it to the poor.

One week later, putting on a long face, Ephendi went to the king with empty hands. Seeing Ephendi, the king narrowed his eyes into a greedy smile.

"Aha, you have returned! You must have come with animals and carts loaded with gold."

"Unfortunately, we have had really bad luck," cried Ephendi, as he wept loudly. "Your Majesty must know that it has not rained recently and all our gold dried out. As a result, we not only lost the harvest but our gold seeds as well."

Instantly the king, who was boiling with rage, rushed up to Ephendi and made a great fuss.

"What a vicious lie! I do not believe any of your nonsense. Liar! Do not dream that you can cheat me. How can gold dry out?"

"How strange!" said Ephendi. "If Your Majesty does not believe that gold can dry out, why did he believe that gold can be grown?"

Upon hearing this, the king became speechless; he could not reply.

JINGLING COINS

One day, Ephendi went to a restaurant where the owner was beating a poor man. Ephendi pulled the owner away from the beggar and asked what was happening.

"This man wants to leave without paying. I am teaching him a lesson," said the owner.

"Why should he pay?" asked Ephendi.

"Because he sat on my doorstep and smelled my savory food. Of course he should pay for that," said the owner, who was very angry.

"Is that the case?" Ephendi asked the poor man.

"Yes, I did want to eat a meal," admitted the beggar. "But I have only a handful of coins left in my pocket. They are not enough for a meal. So I sat on the threshold, waiting for someone to give me some leftovers. While I sat there, I received nothing, and I ate my own bread. Then when I was ready to leave, the owner caught me and began beating me," he explained.

"Aha, I see," said Ephendi. "Where are your coins, then?"

Feeling deeply wronged, the poor man unwillingly picked several coins from his pocket and handed them to Ephendi, who, holding the copper coins in his hands, said to the owner:

"Come over here."

The owner, extremely happy, walked triumphantly toward Ephendi. The latter raised his closed hands in which he held the coins to the owner's ear. He shook them. When the owner heard the coins jingle, his face broadened to a grin. Once again, Ephendi shook the coins and made them jingle. Then he gave them back to the poor man:

"Now you may go," said Ephendi.

The owner became furious: "What are you doing? How can he leave without paying?"

"Look!" said Ephendi calmly. "He smelled your appetizing food, and you heard his coins jingle. That makes you even. Neither of you now owes the other anything."

THREE WISE MAXIMS

One day when Ephendi went to the bazaar to find a job to earn some money, he met a man who said: "I have a box of porcelain bowls and plates that needs to be taken to my house. But instead of paying someone money, I will give him three pieces of good advice."

Not surprisingly, there was no response from the people at the market, except: "Empty words never sound beautiful."

But Ephendi said, "While money can always be found, wisdom cannot."

So he carefully lifted the heavy wooden box filled with porcelain onto his shoulder and began following the man to his house.

After a while, Ephendi said to him: "Please tell me the first wise maxim now."

The owner of the box then gave him advice: "If someone ever tells you that being hungry is better than being full, never believe him."

"Aha, that is quite wise advice," Ephendi said.

Farther down the road, he asked to hear the second wise maxim.

"If somebody tells you that walking is better than riding a horse, never believe him," the owner of the box responded.

"Aha," said Ephendi, "that, too, is a wise observation."

After having gone even farther, Ephendi asked to hear the last of the three maxims.

This time, the other man answered: "If anyone ever tells you there is another worker more foolish than you, please never believe him."

This time, all of a sudden, Ephendi dropped the box onto the ground, where it landed with a crash of breaking porcelain. And looking at the owner, Ephendi gave his own advice, for free:

"And if someone says, 'The porcelain bowls in this box are not broken,' never believe him!" And with that he walked away.

TWO BROTHERS MEET

One day, Ephendi (with his donkey) was on his way downtown when a rich man from the village saw him.

"Hello, Ephendi," he said, as he began to tease him, mockingly. "I see you two friends are having an intimate conversation. Where are you going with your friend?"

Ephendi looked at his donkey and then nodded toward the rich man: "Oh, Your Excellency, you have arrived at the most opportune moment. My donkey has just been bothering me with his complaint that he very much misses his brother. So I was going to take him to your home. Now that the two brothers have met here, so coincidentally, it saves me a trip. Go ahead now, greet your brother!"

AFRAT KHAN AND HIS NINE DAUGHTERS

It is said that in China there once lived a khan of great renown. His name was Afrat Khan. He was very wise, able, and valiant, as well as skilled in battle. He called himself the Khan of the World from East to West.

Whenever the khan waged war, he always charged the enemy lines riding ahead of his troops, with the ferociousness of an angry lion. His two battle steeds could complete a three hundred sixty–day journey in a single day. As a rule, the khan rode his black horse in the morning and his white horse in the evening. He worked hard, day and night, to defend his territory and his people. Whenever he learned that enemies threatened, he rode off galloping to destroy them completely—even if it meant traveling for forty days. As a result, his people lived safe, prosperous, and happy lives. His country became strong, mighty, and famous throughout the world.

The khan was created by heaven. Heaven used the water that was between the blue sky and the earth, blended it with earth, and then mixed and kneaded the dough before letting it dry in the sun. On that account, he was created extraordinarily handsome and perfect.

One day, this great khan of China dreamed that the prime minister of the Roman Empire gave the following advice to this emperor: "Far, far away, there exists a powerful country that has many people and rich resources, the khan of which is brave and mighty. It is a journey of three hundred sixty days and nights from here. The khan has nine sons who always ride on horses, shoot arrows, and duel with swords. It appears that in the near future they are going on a campaign in several directions at once. We should move against them first, and now, while they are not yet fully prepared. Let us seize and kill the khan. Capture his people, and teach them a lesson."

Upon hearing this, the khan of China immediately arose from his bed, fully appreciating the importance of his dream. He hastily made preparations to leave. Wearing his bow-shaped sword and putting on his armor and helmet, he mounted his white horse. At the same time, he woke up his nine sons and instructed them to mobilize their soldiers. Very quickly seven thousand soldiers on white horses were lined up and led out, so that the cavalry would not get lost in the darkness.

Behind these followed seven thousand cavalrymen riding on dark-red horses. Then came another seven thousand cavalry soldiers on brown horses, followed by others on dark-gray ones. Behind these followed still another seven thousand men on black horses.

The great khan raised his head toward the moon and prayed: "Please support us with your power, as well as with the might of the stars."

Then he turned to the thick forest: "Please! May you save us from severe storms and strong winds."

Then he prayed toward the mountain: "Oh, my blessed mountain. We believe that you are our heaven! Please, bless us with life—you, who are mighty forever."

Then he called together his nine daughters. First he urged his youngest daughter, Ayhan [Moon Maiden]: "Now, all the men in the country are going to war. It will be a long journey, and we will not come back soon. So you must lead all the women here to defend our country. Do not mistreat the people. Neither spoil nor destroy their property."

He gave his order to his oldest daughter, whose name was Kan Kiz [Blood Maiden]: "Because you are a girl as courageous as blood, I named you Kan Kiz. Be the khan of this country, temporarily. You are not as skillful in fighting as your sisters, so let your sisters do battle while you stay in the palace to rule the country."

Next he called before him his seventh daughter, Kaz, whom he appointed to be prime minister. Four of the remaining daughters were ordered to guard the four directions. Two girls were commissioned to be officers of the palace guard.

Then he began his journey—a three hundred sixty–day journey from Kashgar.

After traveling for seven days and nights, Afrat arrived near Baghdad, where another khan lived, whose power was unchallenged. This khan also had had a dream, in which he clearly saw that Afrat Khan was coming with his ninety thousand soldiers. So he mobilized his army.

Although Afrat Khan had no quarrel with the khan in Baghdad, their two armies met with swords drawn and bows bent, in an extremely fierce battle that lasted seven days and seven nights. In the end, the soldiers of Afrat Khan were victorious. The fighting had been so violent that the sky became murky—enough blood had been shed to sail in it. The battlefield was piled high with so many corpses that one could not make his way through them without a ladder.

Afrat Khan's troops pursued the fleeing enemy until they came to a pass between two mountains. But there they disappeared from sight. Suddenly, a flash flood swept through the pass, drowning thousands, including Afrat Kan.

Back in China, his nine daughters fell into deep sorrow when they heard the lamentable news. The second daughter suggested that she would avenge herself on the murderers of her father and brothers by leading an army against them. Another said she wanted to burn down the palace of the Baghdad khan. However, the youngest girl had a different idea:

"Our duty now is to defend our country. Our father died because he hastily fought in foreign countries. The lesson we must learn from this is that we should strengthen our defenses at home."

Soon the khan of Yaka, a neighboring land, became jealous of the nine girls and prepared his troops for battle against them.

The nine princesses realized that their women fighters would probably be defeated, so they decided to meet their enemy with wit.

First they asked a witch for advice. She told them:

"If you build a great wall, the enemy will tear it down. If you hide your gold and silver by burying it, your descendants may never find it. The best way to save your property and yourself is by using sand from the desert."

Hearing this, the girls went out to seek sand. In the end, they decided to move the sandy desert to their country. They packed the sand and loaded it on horses and camels, even on their own backs. This task took months and years.

The old witch, who was also the queen of the sandy desert, was very impressed by the enthusiastic hard work of the girls. Therefore, she used an incantation that moved all the sand in a manner so that it covered everything in the realm of these princesses.

Once all the sand had been moved, the battle began. With Ayhan, the youngest princess, in command, the nine thousand female warriors defended their country against the Yaka khan for seventy-two days and nights. He originally had come from a land of devils, but for the purpose of battle had changed into human form. All the same, flames spewed from his mouth that would burn all animals and people for a distance of a six-month journey. He could blow such a vicious storm that it would transform a mountain into a plain. He would cause floods that drowned entire towns. But the princess and her soldiers had been well tempered by heaven—as they had been created from a mixture of earth and water, and inasmuch as they were supported by mountains and forests. Consequently, these girls were not afraid of fire, flood, or storm. The battle was so fierce that every time the sound of Ayhan's clashing swords could be heard echoing through the seven layers of sky, earthquakes could be felt.

The Yaka khan had fought forty-one wars in his life, and he had defeated forty-one heroes. But he had never encountered such a brave warrior as Ayhan. Knowing that he was unable to win the battle, the Yaka khan schemed with his ministers:

"It appears we cannot burn this country out of existence, because our fire cannot travel the distance of a forty years' journey. Neither can we destroy it by wind, because the mountains block our path. So we can use only the sea. Let us flood the entire country."

When Ayhan heard this, she decided to block the floodwaters and save her country and family. For seventy-two days, her soldiers struggled against the flood, until the waters were finally under control.

After this victory, Ayhan and her soldiers built their cities along the edge of the desert, so that they could better defend their motherland. Wailing and crying, she often prayed to heaven that her family and country be blessed. From that time on, many towns were built along the edge of the sandy desert.

Nowadays, if you go to this desert, you can still hear Ayhan's sad wailing and crying. People who live in towns around the desert often go to the great desert to bury themselves in the sand, as though they enjoyed embracing their ancestors. The people do not know how Ayhan finally died. But deep in their hearts, Ayhan will live forever.

A TU FOLK STORY

Collected by Jugui (Tu) and translated and introduced by Limusishiden (Tu) and Kevin Stuart

People of the Tu ethnic group live primarily in Qinghai and Gansu provinces, in northwestern China. Most (but not all) speak a language similar to Mongolian. While Tu is the official name for the group in Chinese, there are different names for the various subgroups, including Monguor, Mangghuer, and Mongghul. Among the Mongghul of Huzhu county, Qinghai, it is mostly older people who speak the language, as the trend among younger ones is to speak Chinese, with the exception of a few students in schools where Tibetan is taught. Aspects of Tibetan Buddhism are prominent in Tu religious beliefs, and there is an element of shamanism. Most members of the ethnic group, which numbers about 240,000, lead lives characterized by subsistence farming on small plots of land, often supplemented by raising a few head of livestock. Traditional Tu clothing is still worn in some areas, especially by women, but, like certain other customs, is becoming increasingly rare.

A folk tale called "The Qeo Family Girl" is widely known among the Mongghul subgroup and reflects traditional, complex relationships between family members, particularly the conflict between mother-in-law and daughter-in-law. According to custom, a mother-in-law directs a daughter-in-law's daily work and strictly regulates her visits to her parents' home. When her in-laws mistreat her, a daughter-in-law might mention this story and say that her life is as miserable as that of the Qeo family girl. The mention of burning earth refers to a custom in which dirt is dug up and piled, dried, and burned to produce a sort of fertilizer.

The teller of the following version of "The Qeo Family Girl," Changminjii, was born in 1960 in Tangraa village, Donggou township, Huzhu Tu Autonomous County. She has two sons and is illiterate. The story was collected in September 1998, in her home. By her account, such stories were often told among women who gathered to do embroidery, during breaks in the cycle of village chores, when visitors came to the home, and to younger children.

THE QEO FAMILY GIRL

Told by Changminjii (Tu)

There was a mother whose daughter married and then went to live with her husband's family in a distant village. The mother missed her daughter very much after she left her home and finally asked her youngest son to bring her daughter back home as soon as possible for a visit.

The youngest son went to the mother-in-law's home with a white horse and a piece of white felt draped over the back of the horse. The youngest son said to his sister's mother-in-law, "I've come to bring my sister to visit my mother. Please let my sister visit my home."

The mother-in-law replied, "She cannot go home to visit her mother because the piles of manure in our twelve *mu* of fields have not been leveled. Once they are leveled, she will have time to visit." The youngest son disappointedly returned home.

Some days later, the youngest son visited the mother-in-law's home again and said, "Today I have come on a white horse with a piece of white felt across its back to take my sister home. My mother desperately wants to see her, and she promises to let her return to your home as soon as possible. Please let her come visit."

The mother-in-law said, "Yes, she has finished leveling manure on the twelve *mu* of fields, but we did not dig the lumps of earth from the twelve *mu* of fields. She can go visit when she finishes digging all of them."

In low spirits, the youngest son returned home.

One month later, the youngest son came again and said to the mother-in-law, "Today I come again with a white horse and a piece of white felt draped over the horse's back to take my sister home. I beg you to please allow my sister to visit my home and see my mother. We will ensure she returns soon."

The mother-in-law said, "She cannot go today for she has not burned the lumps of soil on the twelve *mu* of land. We are going to use the burned lumps of dirt as fertilizer on our twelve *mu* of land. If we don't burn them, we'll have no food to eat next year. Once she finishes burning them, she can visit your home."

The youngest son returned home again.

A month later, the youngest son came again, bringing the white horse with a piece of white felt draped over its back. He said to the mother-in-law, "I have come to take my sister."

The mother-in-law said, "She has not finished leveling the burned piles of dirt. She can go visit her mother once she finishes this work."

The youngest brother was filled with indignation but could only, again, return home without his sister.

Another month passed, and the youngest brother came again, leading the white horse with a piece of white felt draped over its back. He said again that he had come to take his sister home.

The mother-in-law said, "She has not finished spreading the pulverized dirt over the twelve *mu* of land. Once she finishes this, I will let her visit your home."

Without any success, the youngest brother returned home again.

Some days later, the youngest brother came again and said, "She has spread the burned earth in the fields, so may she come visit her mother now?"

The mother-in-law said, "We did not finish planting rapeseed on the twelve *mu* of land. Once that is done, I will let her visit her parents' home."

The youngest brother sorrowfully returned home once again.

The daughter-in-law went to the fields, and in a short time she easily scattered rapeseeds on the twelve *mu* of fields. Afterward, the sown seed sprouted.

Later the youngest brother came to take his sister, leading his white horse.

The mother-in-law said, "She cannot visit her parents' home now for she has not harvested the rapeseed from the twelve *mu* of fields. Once she does that, I will allow her to visit."

The youngest brother despairingly returned home as before.

The Qeo family girl went to the fields to harvest the rapeseed, crying sadly. Magpies and pigeons noticed this, flew close to her, and said, "You need not cry, we have come to help you now." They very soon helped her collect all the seed, and then they flew away.

Then the youngest brother came to take his sister to see her mother, again bringing the white horse with a piece of white felt draped over its back. This time, the mother-in-law agreed that she could visit but stipulated, "It's all right, you can go home, but you have to return tomorrow. And you have to come back with three pairs of shoes sewn for each member of our family during the time you are at your parents' home." The Qeo family girl had to promise that she would do this.

When she reached her parents' home, she immediately started sewing shoes. The time flew by so fast that she wished she could tie the sun with a thread to hold it in the sky. After a day and a night, she finally finished making three pairs of shoes for each of the members of her mother-in-law's home. The next day, she delayed a little before she reached her mother-in-law's home.

This angered the mother-in-law, who ferociously scolded her, and the father-in-law and her husband's younger brother beat her. Finally, her husband's younger brother's wife beat her to death with a broom.

Later, the Qeo family girl's husband returned home accompanied by a large mounted retinue, for he was returning home in triumph after passing the examination to become a Number One Scholar. When he rode near the rear of his parents' home, a bird flew very near him. He then wondered if disaster had befallen his wife.

The retinue reached the front gate, but no one dismounted. The young man's father came to receive him, but he did not dismount. Instead, he said, "Please ask the Qeo family girl to come receive me. Only she can make me dismount at once."

Then his mother came to receive him. Her son said, "I do not want to dismount unless the Qeo family girl receives me."

His younger brother came to receive him, and he told him the same thing.

Then his younger brother's wife came to receive him, and he told her the same thing.

Finally, his younger sister came to receive him and said, "Older Brother, Older Brother, now your younger sister has come to receive you, so please dismount."

The Qeo family girl's husband said, "Ah, I won't dismount if you come to receive me. I want only the Qeo family girl to receive me. Once she receives me, I will dismount immediately."

His younger sister said, "Older Brother, Older Brother, how can we let the

Qeo family girl come here? Mother scolded her, father and elder brother beat her, and finally sister-in-law beat her to death with a broom soon after she returned from her parents' home. Then she was buried in the plow furrows in the field behind the house over there. Please go see."

The young man then pulled his wife's corpse out from the plow furrows in the piles of dirt in the field behind his home. He sorrowfully cremated the corpse and collected her ash and bones in a small wooden box. He then turned his horse and slowly rode away.

A TALE OF THE AMIS

Recorded by Tian Zhongshan (Han) and translated and introduced by Victor H. Mair

Taiwan is home to numerous aboriginal peoples who inhabited the island long before the Sinitic-speaking Han Chinese began to settle there in large numbers beginning around the seventeenth century. Indeed, through a combination of genetic, linguistic, and archaeological studies, Taiwan in recent years has come to be viewed as the possible homeland of the Austronesian language family and a major staging ground for the peopling of the Philippines, Polynesia, Micronesia, and Melanesia. Their roots on the island go back about eight thousand years.

Altogether, there were over two dozen known Austronesian languages on Taiwan, about half of which are extinct or nearly extinct. One of the Austronesian groups that is still doing fairly well is that commonly called Amis, which—like most of the other groups—has numerous alternative names. In 2002, according to the Council of Indigenous Peoples, there were 137,651 Amis speakers, down more than 10,000 from the previous count in the year 2000, when they constituted more than 37 percent of the total indigenous populations of Taiwan. The latter, in turn, amount to roughly 2 percent (around 500,000) of the entire population of Taiwan.

The Amis live primarily in the intramontane valley between Hualian and Taidong, and on the east coast near the sea in the same area. These are relatively remote and inaccessible places that the Han settlers reached rather late and in small numbers compared with the northern, western, and southern parts of the island. The fact that Amis means "north" is indicative of the pressures that must have led to their relocation in the southeast. (Note, though, that the Amis usually refer to themselves as Pangcah, which means "human" or something like "people of our kind," a typical usage among many ethnic groups.) The vast majority of Taiwan's indigenous people were pushed off the northern, western, and southern plains and into the mountains, and hence they have come to be called *gaoshanzu* (high-mountain tribes) in Mandarin. This usage is parallel to that for the montagnards of mainland Southeast Asia, and their existence as mountain dwellers is due to similar historical factors. In Taiwanese, they are more respectfully referred to as *goan-chu-bin* or *peh-oe-ji* (original inhabitants).

The folklore of the Amis and other Austronesian aborigines of Taiwan is starkly dissimilar to that of the Sinitic-speaking peoples who displaced them across most of the island. The same is true of the forms of their folktales. The story "The Egg Boy" offers a good example of the content and ideology of the aboriginal peoples of Taiwan. It also reveals much about the daily life of the pre-Sinitic inhabitants of Taiwan and their consanguinity with other non-Sinitic peoples of the region. Among the indigenous groups of Taiwan, the Amis were unusual for the comparatively large size of their villages, typically ranging between five hundred and a thousand individuals.

A revival of ethnic pride among Taiwan's aboriginal groups is expressed in diverse ways, including the incorporation of cultural elements into current pop music, some of which has become commercially successful. For instance, an Amis chant was used by the musical group Enigma in their hit song "Return to Innocence," and this was also the theme song of the 1996 Atlanta Olympics.

THE EGG BOY

Once upon a time, there was a couple that was already advanced in age, but they had not yet had a child. They hoped very much to have a son. One day, someone told them that if they prayed to the gods every evening, the gods would certainly give them a son. So the old couple prayed every day that the gods would bestow on them a son. Before a year had passed, the wife finally became pregnant. Ten months later, a child was born, but they never would have imagined that the wife bore not a human being but a round, smooth egg. The wife felt terrible about this and thought to herself, "It was hard enough for me to give birth to a child. How disappointing that it turned out to be an egg! If I had known before that things would turn out like this, it would have been better not to beseech the gods."

Whereupon her husband chimed in, "If it's an egg, then let it be an egg! It wasn't easy to produce this child, so let's take good care of it." As he spoke, the husband placed the egg in a wicker ladle. Every day, after the old couple returned from working the land, they would always feel comforted when they took a look at their little egg boy.

The days passed, one after another, until three months had gone by and other children born at the same time as the egg boy were almost all starting to prattle and babble, and the egg boy also began to prattle and babble, which afforded great joy to the old couple. After the sixth or seventh month, when other children were beginning to crawl around on the ground, the egg boy rolled around in his wicker ladle. After a full year, when other children had almost all learned to take a few steps, the egg surprisingly rolled out of his wicker ladle and went outside to play with the other children. Because the egg boy had no legs, he couldn't walk but rolled around on the ground, so that he would be completely covered with dirt. After he had had his fill of playing, he would return home and let his mother wipe him clean with a towel then put him back into the wicker ladle.

One year followed another, until the egg boy was seven and saw that other little boys were going out into the countryside to pasture their water buffalo, which filled him with envy. So he begged his father to let him pasture their buffalo, to which the father replied, "How can you pasture the buffalo? Can you catch up with them?" The egg boy said, "Sure I can. But if you're afraid that I can't keep up with them, you can stick me inside the ear of one of the buffalo. From inside the ear, I'll tell the buffalo where to go, and it will listen to me."

The father could not refuse him, so he put the egg boy inside the ear of one of the buffalo. Once he was settled inside the buffalo's ear, the egg boy began to sing happily, and his singing was very beautiful. Nobody could see the egg boy, but the buffalo obediently followed his commands and went to the pasture to eat grass.

Just as other children grew up, so did the egg boy. One day, the egg boy saw that children from other families went out into the countryside to cut firewood, so he told his father that he also wanted to go out and cut firewood. "You have no hands for holding a knife," said his father. "How can you chop firewood? And you have no shoulders. So how could you carry the firewood back? Aren't you afraid that you'd be crushed by the firewood?"

"What are you talking about?" replied the egg boy. "Just strap a machete on my body, and naturally I'll be able to go and cut firewood."

The father had no choice but to strap a machete on the egg boy's body. Sure enough, the egg boy went rolling off until he rolled all the way to the mountain for cutting firewood. When the father saw the image of his son with the machete strapped to his body flashing and slashing, he felt sad.

After the egg boy had gone halfway and looked around to make sure that no one was watching, he rolled over to the side of the road. Then he gave a shake to his shell, and a handsome young man emerged from the egg. He hid the eggshell, and then he ran quickly to the woods beside his family's fields to cut firewood.

The wood that he cut was all crape myrtle. By noon, he had cut a big pile that he stacked up next to the field. Then he returned to eat lunch. When he was halfway home, he stealthily put the eggshell back on and went rolling merrily along. He sang loudly all the way, rolling slowly until he reached home. "Dad!" he shouted. "I've cut a lot of firewood, and it is all piled up next to the field. You can take a bullock and oxcart and bring it back."

The father was doubtful. Since he didn't have any hands, how could the egg boy cut firewood? Even though he really didn't believe that the egg boy had cut the firewood, he led the oxcart toward the mountain for gathering firewood to have a look. When the father got there, sure enough he saw a pile of firewood. Thereupon, the father happily loaded the firewood onto the cart and brought it back to the house; it took two trips.

The next day, the egg boy went to the fields to work. When he had rolled halfway there, he saw a beautiful girl who also just happened to be going to the fields to work. The egg boy waited until no one was watching him, and then he rolled off to the side of the road, where he shook himself out of the eggshell and hid it off to the side. Racing to catch up with the girl, he beckoned to her and said, "Hello! Where are you going?"

The beautiful girl turned to look at him and saw a very handsome young man, whereupon she blushed deeply, lowered her head, and replied, "I'm going to the fields to pull out weeds."

The egg boy said, "Oh, where are your family's fields?"

The girl pointed to a plot that was adjacent to the fields of the egg boy's family's and said, "My family's land is right next to those fields."

"Ah!" the egg boy exclaimed elatedly. "So the fields next to my family's fields belong to your family! Let's go together." They laughed and talked as they walked along, and before long they had reached the fields.

The two of them pulled weeds out of the fields, singing while they worked. Their songs were very moving, and through them they expressed their mutual admiration. After they had finished weeding, they returned home together. When they had gone halfway, to the place where the egg boy had taken off his shell, he tricked the girl, saying, "You go back first. I have to go off to the side to relieve myself." The girl believed him and went on ahead by herself. Only after the girl had gone quite a distance did the boy put on his eggshell and roll back home.

That evening, after the egg boy had reached home, he said to his parents, "A pretty girl has fallen in love with me."

"*Aiya!*" said his mother and father. "Who could fall in love with you this way? Aren't you afraid that people would laugh themselves silly? You really have no shame!"

One day, the village had an athletic meet in which there were races, wrestling, and so on. All the youths took part. The egg boy told his mother and father, "Mom, Dad! I'm going to the exercise grounds to watch the competitions."

"Aren't you afraid you'll get crushed if you mingle in the crowds?" asked his mother.

"I'll be careful," answered the egg boy. "You don't have to worry." Then he rolled along to the exercise grounds. The crowds there were so numerous that it was almost impossible for him to squeeze in among them. As the egg rolled this way and that way in the spaces between all the people, he would shout loudly when someone was about to trample on him, "Careful not to step on me!" Finally he managed to roll out in front of the crowd, whereupon everyone was startled by the sight of a talking egg.

While all the spectators' eyes were glued to the competitions, the egg boy stealthily rolled off to one side and hid himself. When no one was watching, he shook himself out of his eggshell and then ran onto the field to race with the others. At the beginning of the race, he was at the very rear, in the last position. The others had already run one stage of the race before he had started to move. But once the egg boy got going, he ran at a very fast clip. So fast did he run that his feet barely touched the ground, and each step covered an enormous stretch of ground. In a flash, he overtook the head runner and left all the others far behind. When they saw what was happening, the spectators roared in support and surged forward to gawk at the fine young lad who had taken the championship. The beautiful girl, who was in the crowd, clapped her hands and jumped for joy when she recognized him. After the competitions were over, the two of them walked back together holding hands. When they were halfway home, the egg boy tricked her again, saying, "You go back first. I have to relieve myself." The egg boy waited until no one else was around and then put on his shell and, rolling along, went back. When he reached home, he called out to his parents,

"Today I ran the fastest, leaving all the big guys—every one of them—in the dust."

Since his parents hadn't gone to see the race, naturally they didn't believe what he was saying.

As the days went on, the boy and girl became increasingly intimate, and they told each other everything. Once, after the egg boy had told the girl where he lived, she came to his home to play with him. Not seeing the handsome youth, she asked his parents, "Where did your son go?"

"We don't have a son," said the mother. "There must be some mistake."

"What do you mean you don't have a son?" exclaimed the egg from inside the wicker ladle. "Am I not your son?"

The parents felt awful, because they were unwilling to tell others that their son was an egg. "Aren't you ashamed to speak to others like that?" asked the father.

"What's there to be ashamed of?" asked the egg boy. "This is just the way I am. If nobody loves me, then I won't go look for others to love me."

When the girl heard them conversing like this, she thought that it was very strange. At the same time, she felt awkward asking too many questions, so the only thing she could do was leave.

The next day, the boy and the girl met each other on their way to work in the fields. "Tell me," she said, "where your house really is. Last night I went to the address that you had given me to pay you a visit. How come I didn't see you?"

"Huh?" said the egg boy. "What do you mean you didn't see me? I was sitting right there at home, and I saw you."

The girl had a vague inkling of the truth, so she didn't pursue the matter further with him. That evening when it came time to return, they walked back home together. When they had gone halfway, the egg boy again tricked the girl, saying, "You go ahead first. I have to relieve myself."

The girl took advantage of a moment when he wasn't paying attention to her movements and hid in a distant place, from which she saw clearly that the young man put on his eggshell and went rolling back home. The girl quietly followed the egg boy and went straight to the door of his home.

That evening, she again went to the house of the egg boy to play. She called the egg boy's father outside and told him everything that she had seen that day. The next day, when the egg boy went to work in the fields, his father quietly followed behind him. When the egg boy had rolled halfway to the fields, he hid in a declivity beside the road and took off his shell and then hid it by the wayside. At that moment, as the father clearly saw a handsome young man go off to work in the fields, his heart was filled with ineffable joy. All those years, the old couple had looked after an egg, never imagining that today they would at last see their true son!

After his son had walked away, the father rushed up and secretly took the eggshell back home, where he hid it away. At the same time, he told his wife what had happened.

That evening, after he had finished working, the egg boy walked back to the place where he had taken off his shell, but he couldn't find it. He sat down disconsolate, and even when it became dark he wouldn't go home. Waiting at home, the parents became anxious when they realized that their son was not coming back. The old couple went out to search for him. When they had gone halfway, they spied a handsome young man seated by the side of the road. The old couple hastened forward, and, tugging at the young man, the father said, "Who are you waiting for here all alone? Today I secretly took that eggshell and have put it at home. Every day, we have been longing to see our son's true form." The mother joyfully wrapped her son in a tight embrace. "Let's go," the old couple said. "Let's go home now." The three of them happily returned home together.

After that day, the girl often went to their home to play in the evening. The old couple liked the diligent, beautiful girl very much, and they never again felt awkward in front of others because their child was an egg. After several years, the young man and the girl were married. The young couple was hardworking, but whenever they had some free time, the young man would go fishing in the ocean, and his young wife would gather mussels to bring back as filial presents for his old parents. Their life was filled with good fortune.

STORIES OF TU RITUAL

Translated and introduced by Wen Xiangcheng (Tu) and Kevin Stuart

The Tu ethnic group, of northwestern China, has stories about folk and ritual performances.[25] Two of these tales were told by Wen Xiangcheng (b. 1981), of Wen Family Village, in Qinghai, whose great-grandfather (ca. 1850–1949) was a *yinyang* ritualist, mentioned in the second story.

The first story, "The Origin of the God of Riches," is related to a large-scale ritual performance called *yangguo* held in honor of a local deity called the God of Riches (Caibao Shen).[26] The story is unique in that it merges legends about an actual historical figure with the tales of ogres that are quite common on the northern steppes and contiguous areas. The historical figure is the legendary beauty Wang Zhaojun, from Hubei province, who lived late in the Western Han dynasty (206 B.C.E.–24 C.E.). She was sent by the Chinese emperor as a consort for a ruler of the Xiongnu, a group of nomadic tribes who lived to the north of the Han dynasty territories. In the Tu folk story, elements of her legend merge with a tale of a wild, dull-witted, hairy ogress, or yeti—the local version of the Abominable Snow(wo)man, or Bigfoot.

As of 2008, the ritual connected with the God of Riches was performed only among a subgroup of the Tu ethnic group, called the Mangghuer, in a small village called Guo Family Village. However, the all-male local performance group sometimes enacts the rituals for other area villages. When preparing to visit another village, the participants gather in the home of one group member to light lamps, burn incense, and prostrate themselves before a container of corn or wheat, believed to be the seat of the God of Riches. These actions mark their departure from their village and include wishes of peace for the other village. On their return, they reassemble in the same home and again give thanks to the god.

The trip to the host village is marked by visits of the performance group to all temples and monasteries en route. Such visits may be punctuated by short stops at individual households, which offer the group food, tea, and liquor in return for singing. When the group reaches the host village, the various participants perform on the threshing grounds. The ritual begins about three or four o'clock in the afternoon and ends around midnight. Typically, the lantern holders sing, and then the entire group marches around the threshing field, which is followed by songs from another of the groups, and so on until all the groups have performed.

---

25. See "The Qeo Family Girl."

26. The term *yangguo* may be a local version of *yang'ge* (rice-planting song), a style of ritual dance drama once popular in peasant communities in northern China and now enjoying a revival in more secular forms in both rural and urban areas. See "A Worthy Sister-in-Law" (chap. 5).

Several dozen people participate in the various roles and groups making up the God of Riches ritual performances, which are held in the winter months. The mix of distinct roles, costumes, and accoutrements creates an exciting spectacle. The participants include a man dressed as the God of Riches; the god is accompanied by a host of groups that include a pair of lantern holders dressed in black shirts (worn with the arms tucked inside), long white robes, and sheepskin vests worn inside out (showing the fleece); two fishermen holding oars, dressed in white robes and straw hats with the tops cut out; and the fishermen's wives, who are inside boat-shaped props. Four to eight children—dressed in white shirts, black vests, and dark trousers, with white towels wrapped around their heads—hold sticks in each hand and beat bamboo canisters. Then there are four to eight people dressed in Tibetan-style robes, six to ten drummers in white shirts and sheepskin vests (also turned inside out), six to ten gong beaters, and six to ten cymbal players, all in black hats. About fifteen young couples hold fans in their right hands: the men are dressed like the lantern holders, except that they wear dark cloth vests; the women (who are actually men) wear light-colored silk shirts, long pleated skirts, and long hair with three flowers, and they carry small lanterns. There is also a blind fortune-teller dressed in a sheepskin vest turned inside out, who carries an *erhu* (two-stringed fiddle) slung on his back and who holds a small bell in each hand. Finally, there is a man made up as a woman, who carries a doll representing a baby. All the performers wear a sash and dark sunglasses.

The second story, "A Snake Beats a Drum, a Donkey Rides a Person," relates the origin of local Daoist practitioners, known as *yinyang*. These ritualists read scriptures written in Chinese to determine the time a coffin should leave a home for the graveyard, the compatibility between prospective marriage partners, the best time for weddings, and the way to treat illnesses. In 2008, there were still about twenty active *yinyang* among the Mangghuer.

THE ORIGIN OF THE GOD OF RICHES

Told by Wen Xiangcheng (Tu)

Long ago in China, during the Han dynasty, there was an emperor known as Liu. One night, he dreamed of a very beautiful girl and was eager for her to be his concubine. The next morning, the palace painter, Mao Yanshou, was asked to draw the girl according to the emperor's description. The emperor then sent two generals to search everywhere for the girl portrayed in the portrait.

Several months later, the two generals found the girl, Wang Zhaojun, in Zigui county in Nanjun, Hubei province. She was gifted at playing the lutelike *pipa*. When the generals left with Zhaojun, her impoverished parents were unable to offer anything to the generals. When they got back to the palace, the generals told the emperor that although the girl was truly beautiful, she had a red mole on her left cheek and a blue one on her right cheek. At that time, it was believed that a red mole on a woman's cheek meant that her sons would come to an untimely end and that a blue mole had the same meaning for her husband.

The disappointed emperor then asked the two generals to hide Wang Zhaojun in a loft in an outlying part of the palace. She was then forbidden to meet anyone other than the person who brought her food.

Three years passed, and she was still imprisoned in the loft. She wept every day and played the *pipa* to dispel her distress. One day, the emperor went near where she was kept and heard the sound of the *pipa*. Infatuated, he followed the sound and thus found Zhaojun in the loft. She was the girl he had dreamed of three years ago, but there were no moles on her cheeks. The emperor understood at once that he had been cheated by the two generals and decided to have them executed.

One night, the terrified generals fled to a Mongol area with Wang Zhaojun's portrait and gave it to the Mongol khan, urging him to attack the Han kingdom and seize Wang Zhaojun.

The khan had never seen such a beauty before and was immediately infatuated. He quickly sent two envoys to the Han kingdom to ask for Wang Zhaojun and say that they [the Mongols] would flatten the Han emperor's kingdom with millions of horses if they were not given Wang Zhaojun.

The emperor was shocked, and, in the interests of peace, he decided to give Wang Zhaojun to the Mongols. Su Wu, a minister who was skilled in diplomacy, was ordered to accompany Wang Zhaojun. When they reached the Mongol areas, the Mongol khan was attracted to Su Wu's brilliance and asked him to stay and serve him. Su Wu refused, which angered the khan, who then ordered him to herd three hundred rams on Lianglang Mountain, not allowing him to return to his country until the herd had increased to three thousand. Su Wu then spent more than a decade on Lianglang Mountain, but the sheep steadily became fewer and fewer, because they were all male.

One day, a female yeti limped toward Su Wu. She sat in front of him with a pained expression and stretched out her bloody left foot. Su Wu was very frightened but knew that he could not flee. He plucked up his courage and went nearer to the yeti. He found a big thorn in the sole of her foot, which he removed with a knife.

Greatly appreciating his help, the yeti waved her hand and left. Not long after, however, she returned and pulled Su Wu by the arm to Swallow Cave, on Lianglang Mountain. There, she trapped him by covering the entrance with a boulder. At night, she brought raw meat for Su Wu to eat, and then forced him to sleep with her. This happened every day. In time, the yeti gave birth to a son, known as Su Jin. He was very clever, and his body was covered with hair because his mother was a yeti.

Su Wu had no choice but to stay in the cave with his son and the yeti. When their son was three years old, the yeti decided that Su Wu would probably not run away, and she allowed Su Jin and Su Wu to walk outside the cave every day. In the beginning, the yeti pretended to go hunting in the forests, but instead hid near the cave to see if Su Wu would try to escape. Several months later, the yeti was satisfied and decided that Su Wu would not escape and relaxed her guard by leaving the cave open all day while she hunted far and wide, returning home only at dusk.

Meanwhile, Su Wu never gave up hope of returning home, planning to escape once he gained the trust of the yeti. The opportunity finally came. One morning when the yeti went out to hunt, Su Wu left his son in the cave. He collected a handful of sticks, which were the yeti's favorite toys, and then began his escape.

In the late afternoon, when the yeti returned to the cave, she immediately realized that Su Wu had escaped, and set off in pursuit as fast as the wind blows. Although Su Wu had run a great distance without stopping, the yeti soon caught up with him. Just when the yeti was about to grab him, Su Wu took out a stick and threw it behind. The yeti was very fond of the sticks—she played with them ceaselessly in her spare time. When she saw Su Wu fling the stick, she stopped chasing him and ran to pick it up. She stupidly ran back to the cave, put the stick in a safe place, and then resumed chasing Su Wu.

This happened again and again, until Su Wu had no more sticks. Fortunately, when the yeti appeared again, he had just swum across the river between the Mongol areas and the Han kingdom. This time, the yeti stopped because she could not swim. She shook her breasts and waved her hands at him, signaling that he should return to the cave and their son. Although Su Wu was sad to leave his son with the yeti, he knew that he could not return to the Han kingdom with a boy covered with body hair. He thus moved his hand to the right and left, signaling that he meant he would not return. The heartbroken yeti bellowed in anger and ran back to the cave. She soon returned to the river. Holding Su Jin's legs, she ripped the little boy into two pieces. She threw one half of the body to Su Wu. She then left, holding the other half of the body.

The soul of Su Jin felt that he [his body] had been brutally killed because his father had disowned him, and thus he created awful difficulties for the Han dynasty. The emperor summoned all the Daoist practitioners and ordered them to pacify the spirit causing the disturbances. The powerful Daoists tried their best and, in the end, decided to cover Su Jin's soul with the emperor's golden bell. It was believed that any ghost or soul would vanish in a year once it was covered by this golden bell. Three years later, the emperor decided that Su Jin's soul must have vanished and ordered the golden bell removed. But his soul had instead collected great power from the golden bell in three years, because his soul was actually the Iron Bucket Star—and iron and gold strengthen each other. Su Jin's soul then brought even more problems to the Han dynasty, for now his power was so great that nobody could subdue him.

Fortunately, the emperor had the right to bestow titles, and he therefore bestowed the title "God of Riches" on the spirit, giving it the responsibility of managing money and valuables to ensure that people enjoy a peaceful, rich life. Today, the *yangguo* performances in Wen Family Village are known as God of

Riches rituals. And the most important character in the *yangguo* is the God of Riches. Because the God of Riches' mother was a yeti, his body was covered with hair and he had a long mane. Therefore, the God of Riches performer wears a sheepskin robe inside out, with a chicken-feather duster sticking out of his collar, suggesting a mane.

A SNAKE BEATS A DRUM, A DONKEY RIDES A PERSON

Told by Wen Xiangcheng (Tu)

My great-grandfather, the Wang Family Yinyang, was a very famous Daoist practitioner, or *yinyang*, in a long line of such practitioners in Sanchuan. My mother's father was the youngest of seven sons. All the local people knew the Wang Family Yinyang and his accomplishments; his reputation continued after his death, owing to his unusual abilities with prognostication.

One cold winter morning when the Wang Family Yinyang was very old, he found that he could not get up by himself. When his wife helped him get up from bed and go outside, he found that it was snowing and there was a strong wind. Worse still, several crows were cawing from tall walnut trees outside the gate—a bad omen. He walked to the gate and looked at the trees around his home that he had planted when he was young, and the livestock in the stable. Then he started back inside. At the courtyard gate, he felt dizzy and gripped the gate pole. He shouted to his wife, who was cooking breakfast with the daughter-in-law. She ran to her husband on her tiny bound feet and helped him back to bed.

"I'm afraid I have no time for breakfast. The omens are very bad these days. I divined this morning and found I have lived long enough. It's time to leave. Please call our sons here. I want to tell them something," said the Wang Family Yinyang.

His wife called the sons, and they soon assembled [to hear their father speak]: "All of our forefathers were *yinyang*. We help the local people by treating their illnesses using necromancy and herbal medicine. But the world will soon change, which is why I taught you how to read and write Chinese but never taught you necromancy. Do not become *yinyang*, because monks and *yinyang* alike will be purged in this new world. The day after tomorrow is my burial day, and on that day put a drum near the courtyard gate. Don't take my coffin out through the gate until a snake comes to beat the drum. Only then may you carry my coffin to the graveyard. When you see a donkey riding a person, then you may bury me. Don't forget what I said just now. You'll prosper if you comply, and evil will befall you if you do not!" So said the Wang Family Yinyang, who then died. The villagers, relatives, and many other people who had been helped by the Wang Family Yinyang came to arrange his funeral.

Two days passed quickly, and on the third day, a drum was brought from the village temple and put near the gate. It was very cold and snowy. They waited and waited. Nothing happened. Late in the afternoon, the village leader stood and said, "I think the Wang Family Yinyang lied. Snakes hibernate in winter. Even if a snake is awake, how can it beat a drum? Let's not wait any longer. Let's take the coffin outside."

The Wang Family Yinyang's sons thought this was reasonable—for how is it possible for a snake to beat a drum in cold winter? They agreed, and the villagers took the coffin out through the courtyard gate. Just as they were tying the thick carrying poles to the coffin, a boy shouted, "Hey! Everybody! Look! A magpie holding a snake is flying toward us!" Everyone looked up. A magpie was holding a dead snake in its claws. It flew above the drum and loosened its grip. The snake fell, hitting the drum with a "bang!"

The Wang Family Yinyang's sons then understood that they had taken their father's coffin outside too early. The villagers also thought that they had made a mistake, for it was clear that the Wang Family Yinyang had not lied. They then finished tying the carrying poles to the coffin and took it to the graveyard. They waited, watching for a donkey riding a person.

The weather was becoming colder and colder. No donkey or person passed by. Sunset came. Villagers and relatives ran out of patience and said, "A snake did beat the drum with a magpie's help, but it's impossible for a donkey to ride a person. We're stupid to wait for a person to come by, ridden by a donkey." The Wang Family Yinyang's sons wanted to wait longer, but they had to agree. Then the coffin was lowered into the grave. Just at that moment, a man passed by carrying a newborn donkey on his back.

"Why do you carry that donkey?" they asked.

"My donkey just gave birth. I'm carrying the baby home," answered the man.

Everyone at the graveyard realized that they had made a second mistake. "We didn't obey Father. I'm afraid evil will befall us," one of the sons said when they returned home. In the following six years, one son died each year. Only the Wang Family Yinyang's youngest son survived.

Because the Wang Family Yinyang had not taught his sons necromancy, my grandfather never became a *yinyang* and was not punished or killed during the time of great social turbulence after China was liberated in 1949.

A NAMZI TALE

Collected by Libu Lakhi (Li Jianfu) (Namzi) and translated and introduced by Libu Lhaki and Kevin Stuart

The five thousand Namzi (Namuyi) reside in the southwestern areas of Sichuan province and are officially classified as Tibetan, though their cultural features are distinctive in terms of beliefs, language, costume, and so on. Religious specialists known as *phatse* chant during times of illness and at funerals, weddings, the New Year, and infant name-giving ceremonies; they are the most important religious practitioners for the Namzi. In 2008, when this tale was collected, only older Namzi women wore the traditional long pieces of black cloth wrapped around the head and long dresses and aprons made from handwoven hemp fabric. Linguists have generally classified the Namzi language within the Qiangic branch of the Tibeto-Burman language family, but much more study is needed to further clarify the linguistic situation.

Li Caifu, of Dashui village, near Xichang city, told "Brother Moon, Sister Sun" to his children (including Libu Lakhi) when they were young, sitting around the hearth after supper. The story leaves a strong impression that siblings should care for one another. Such stories inculcate family values and lull children to sleep.

BROTHER MOON, SISTER SUN

Told by Li Caifu (Namzi)

Look at the moon! See the tree in the moon? This story explains that tree.

Long ago, Brother and Sister's parents died, leaving them to care for themselves. Brother hunted in the wild mountains and forests with his hounds, while Sister did housework at home.

Time passed and, when she reached the age of eighteen, Sister married the son of a rich family who lived far from Brother and Sister's home. Meanwhile, Brother continued his life of hunting with his hounds in the wild. Every day while hunting, he sang to his hounds when he missed his beloved sister:

> I miss you three times if you don't come for a day,
> I miss you nine times if you don't come for three days;
> I wish you could become a cuckoo and hover in the sky,
> I long to become the tree branch you perch on when you tire of flying.

Brother continued hunting and also began searching for Sister, for he did not know exactly where her new home was. Month after month, year after year passed, and, finally, Brother found where Sister lived.

At the doorway of her home, Brother's hounds wagged their tails and happily jumped up on Sister as soon as they saw her. Unfortunately, Sister did not recognize Brother, for he had grown older, and he did not tell her who he was. When it was time to have supper, in spite of Brother's loyal love for Sister, she made Brother eat with his hounds and gave them the food. In spite of being extremely disappointed and in despair, Brother controlled himself throughout the night and decided to leave just as though he were a stranger, without saying anything the next morning.

When the cocks crowed early the next morning, Brother quietly got up, called his hounds, and prepared to leave. Sister's family's hounds and his hounds seemed reluctant to separate—they whimpered and trotted around one another, their tails wagging all the while. When Brother noticed this, he could no longer control himself and sang:

> Though relatives may not recognize each other,
> Hounds recognize that we are brother and sister.

When Sister heard this, she suddenly realized that this man was Brother! She immediately ordered her family members to kill, butcher, and cook cattle and goats to entertain Brother with fresh meat. But she could not stop Brother from leaving. When she caught his hem, Brother cut away his clothes hem, and he cut away the gun butt when she held it.

Finally Sister could only watch as Brother slowly walked farther and farther into the distance with his hounds. She was full of regret and despair that she had not recognized Brother. When Brother was the size of a crow's neck in the distance, she hanged herself from a sandalwood tree. After they both had died, Brother became the sun and Sister became the moon. Their spirits talked to each other:

"I am very ashamed to come out now," Sister said.

"You can come out at night," Brother replied.

"But I'm afraid to come out at night," Sister said.

"Then you can come out during the day," Brother replied.

"But I feel shy during the day," Sister said.

Later, in order to prevent people's looking at Sister, Brother made a bundle of needles and gave them to her. Even today, when we look at the sun, those needles hurt our eyes. Brother became the moon and appears at night with the sandalwood tree. On the night of every fifteenth day of every lunar month, when the moon is round, we can clearly see the sandalwood tree.

NAMZI RIDDLES

Collected by Libu Lakhi (Li Jianfu) (Namzi) and translated and introduced by Libu Lhaki and Kevin Stuart

Namzi riddles are told in the same context as the folktales and powerfully reflect local conditions.[27] For example, the Namzi traditionally used hand- and water-powered millstones to grind barley and corn and to press oil from walnuts (riddle 6), and the goatskin vest is still worn by a few men and women in villages, especially when carrying baskets and wood on the back (riddle 1).

Before a riddle is told, it is common to ask, "If you can't answer my riddle, how many buckets of toilet liquid will you drink?" The person being asked then replies with a certain number. For example, if the listener is confident, he might say, "Ten!" But if the listener is unsure that she can guess the answer, she might say, "One." If the person cannot answer, those in attendance laugh and shout, "Oh, look! He's now drinking it!" which makes the person who could not answer feel shy and embarrassed.

Stories and riddles were heard much less often in 2008, when these were collected, than in the past. More children attend school than ever before and tend to be more interested in watching television and video offerings than listening to local folklore. Television series were particularly popular in 2008; for example, *Journey to the West* continued to be popular with older people, and Korean soap operas were eagerly watched by young people.

Told by Li Caifu (Namzi)

1. One cliff has a grassy side, and the other side is bare. What is it?
2. Two sisters have never seen each other because a mountain range separates them. Who are they?
3. A sow swims across a river, and every time she reaches the other side, she gives birth to a bunch of piglets. What is it?
4. It runs three times around the house and then returns to stand behind the door every morning. What is it?
5. A thousand soldiers are wearing one belt. What is it?
6. It eats from the top and shits in the middle. What is it?

---

27. For a description of the culture, see "Brother Moon, Sister Sun."

Answers: (1) a goatskin vest; (2) a pair of eyes separated by the nose; (3) a ferry; (4) a broom; (5) a fence; (6) a millstone.

TIBETAN FLIRTING WORDS AND TONGUE TWISTERS

Translated and introduced by Lotan Dorje (Tibetan) and Kevin Stuart

Unlike love songs (*layi*), flirting words (*zadem*) are spoken, not sung, between men and women, loudly and rhythmically. Typically, a man begins and addresses a woman on the other side of the valley, across a considerable piece of grassland, or working in a field. He might ask her if she is married, if she has a boyfriend, and if she is interested in him. If they are interested in each other, they come closer and closer until they meet. Lovers and spouses are found in this way. It is taboo to say flirting words in the family, inside the village, and within earshot of relatives. They are most commonly said in the mountains when people are herding. Although popular in the past, they are rarely heard at the beginning of the twenty-first century.

Lotan Dorje (b. 1980), the performer of these flirting words, spent much of his childhood in the Suzi Mountains, in Jiajia township, Jinzha county, Huangnan Tibetan Autonomous Prefecture, Qinghai province, living with Pomo-Zhoma (b. 1927), his paternal grandmother. Lotan Dorje was taught *zadem* by older herders and repeated what he had heard from other herders. These *zadem* were recited from memory.

Few Tibetan tongue twisters (*nhksom*) have been recorded. Jamyang (ca. 1904–1989) taught his paternal grandson, Lotan Dorje, these tongue twisters in Jiajia village. He would say a tongue twister and then praise Lotan Dorje when he repeated it accurately.

Tongue twisters are rarely heard today because of the presence of television, radio, and VCRs in the Tibetan countryside. Tongue twisters developed facility in the Tibetan language and instructed children in human nature, counting, livestock, farming, plants, snow, rain, water, the sun, the moon, and the stars.

FLIRTING WORDS

Performed by Lotan Dorje (Tibetan)

1. Hey, maiden, maiden!

When weeding the fields,
You're the one with no companion.

When strolling down the road,
I'm the one with no companion.

Maybe you can be my companion,
Or I'll be yours.

2. Hey, maiden, maiden!

Your complexion is clear,
Clearer than white paper.

Looking up in the sky,
In the open atmosphere,
I can feel the sun's heat.

Glancing down the road,
Atop a fine horse's back,
I'm the one who goes alone.

On the mirror-flat grassland,
You're the one who stays alone.

Can you come with me?
Or I'll come live with you.

3. Hey, maiden, maiden!

You're like a white silk scarf,
I will be the one to knot the silk.

You're like a white conch,
I'll be the one to polish it.

If you share some special words with me,
It's fine, though we can't be mates.

4. Hey, maiden, maiden!

Seeing the highest mountain,
Makes me think of grass.

Seeing luscious grass,
Makes me think of sheep.

Seeing excellent sheep,
Makes me think of wool.

Seeing white, soft wool,
Makes me think of felt.

Seeing white smooth felt,
Makes me think of you, my lover.

5. Hey, maiden, maiden!

There's no grass on the mountain,
There's no water in the arid gully.
What will the deer eat and drink?

You, girl, have nothing to say,
So what's the point of my waiting for you?

6. Hey, maiden, maiden!

The mountain over there is a golden mountain,
The mountain over here is a silver mountain,
The mountain in between is a conch mountain.

Right on the conch mountain,
There is a turning mill.

When it goes clockwise,
It produces golden flour.

When it turns counterclockwise,
It produces silver flour.

When turning both ways,
It produces conch flour.

When we share conch flour,
May our love be like pure-white conch flour.

7. Hey, maiden, maiden!

The emerging mountain has grown high,
Blocking the world's sun's rays.

The ridge of the dark holy mountain is huge,
Blocking the Yellow River's flow.

We two lovers love playing,
Will your husband disturb us?

8. Hey, maiden, maiden!

In the red mountain cave,
We slept together,
Do you remember that?
If you do,
How do you feel now?

9. Hey, maiden, maiden!

On the narrow bottom,
Of the little valley,
You, cute girl, are as timid as a rabbit.

When I say a word to you,
Your only response is "What?"

When I say a second word,
The response is only "Yes?"

Forget it if you don't want to talk,
Just stay there bouncing your round hips against the ground.

TONGUE TWISTERS

Performed by Lotan Dorje (Tibetan)

1. White horses with black tails,
Black-tailed white horses.
Black horses with white tails,
White-tailed black horses.

2. The red hooves of white bulls are small,
White bulls with red hooves are huge.
The white hooves of red bulls are small,
Red bulls with white hooves are huge.

3. A: What have you got inside your chin?
B: I've got gold in my chin.
A: Can I see the gold?
B: It's in a box.
A: Where is the box?
B: It's under a pile of hay.

A: Where is the hay?
B: It's been eaten by the yak.
A: Where is the yak?
B: It went to the mountain.
A: Where is the mountain?
B: It's been covered by snow.
A: Where is the snow?
B: The sun melted it.
A: Where is the sun?
B: It's everywhere.

4. On the roof of my uncle's home,
Grains of barley and wheat are everywhere.
Look at the way the bird picks grain.
Don't just say "bird, bird,"
The bird has been killed by a hawk.
Don't just say "hawk, hawk,"
The hawk has flown to a cliff.
Don't just say "cliff, cliff,"
The cliff has been covered with weeds,
Don't just say "weeds, weeds,"
The weeds have been eaten by a goat.
Don't just say "goat, goat,"
The goat has been eaten by a wolf.
Don't just say "wolf, wolf,"
The wolf has run to the forest.
Don't just say "forest, forest,"
The forest has been cut by an ax.
Don't just say "ax, ax,"
The ax has been taken by a blacksmith,
Don't just say "blacksmith, blacksmith,"
The blacksmith is stuck in the mud.
Don't just say "mud, mud,"
The mud has dried in the sun.
Don't just say "sun, sun,"
The sun has dropped into a net.
Don't just say "net, net,"
The net has been burned up.

5. Inside the far eastern mountain cave,
People say there are twenty-five golden bowls,
They say nobody can count them in a single breath.
If they are counted with one breath,
It brings the virtue of having chanted one billion prayers.

Golden bowl one, golden bowl two,
Golden bowl three, golden bowl four,
Golden bowl five, golden bowl six,
Golden bowl seven, golden bowl eight,
Golden bowl nine, golden bowl ten,
Golden bowl eleven, golden bowl twelve,
Golden bowl thirteen, golden bowl fourteen,
Golden bowl fifteen, golden bowl sixteen,
Golden bowl seventeen, golden bowl eighteen,
Golden bowl nineteen, golden bowl twenty,
Golden bowl twenty-one, golden bowl twenty-two,
Golden bowl twenty-three, golden bowl twenty-four,
Golden bowl twenty-five.

Chapter 2

FOLK SONG TRADITIONS

Singing has been an integral part of most folk cultures in China since before recorded history. The earliest records of Chinese literature, dating from the era of Confucius (fifth century B.C.E.), are collections of songs from throughout the realm made by government officials. Although polished by their erudite collectors, many of the images of nature and human society in the *Book of Odes* (*Shi jing*), especially the section devoted to folk songs, resonate with those found in the Ming dynasty (1368–1644) collections *Mountain Songs* (*Shan'ge*) and *The Hanging Branch* (*Guazhi'er*) made by the author Feng Menglong (1574–1645) and even with very recent ones. Folk song collecting in modern times began in earnest in the 1920s and 1930s in the wake of the stimulating May Fourth Movement of 1919, in which Chinese intellectuals, following the model set by Japan and Russia in the latter nineteenth century, reappraised and placed new value on folk and popular literature. Scholars such as Gu Jiegang collected thousands of folk songs from every corner of China, influenced in part by developments in Europe and the United States. In the early 1950s, and again in the 1980s and 1990s, massive folk song collection movements took place in China. The use of folk songs and accompanying music to invest dynasties, support rebellions, and promote revolutionary causes has a long history in China, and the revolutionary and political movements of the twentieth century were no exception.

The form, content, vocal techniques, and singing styles of the folk songs vary regionally, as do the tunes to which they are sung. Chinese folklorists use several terms based on folk usage to categorize songs. They include *shan'ge* (mountain songs), *xiao diao* (minor tunes or little ditties), and *haozi* (work songs). Songs in these categories differ in lyrical and musical structure, though they may share many similarities. There are also many other local terms, including *jiuge* (toasting songs), *kujia ge* (bridal laments), *qing'ge* (love songs), and *duige* (antiphonal songs). Besides songs sung in the Han Chinese languages and topolects, most of the minority ethnic groups have rich folk song traditions. Depending on local tradition, songs may be sung by one or more singers on a wide variety of occasions, especially those marking special moments or events in daily life and the life cycle. Folk songs may also be sung as entertainment or as a release of emotions ranging from joy to melancholy. All over China, folk songs have had especially important roles in the courtship and marriage process, whether they are antiphonal love songs sung as a means to meet and get to know lovers or spouses, or bridal laments sung to or by young women about to leave home for an arranged marriage.

The antiphonal style, in which two or more singers "talk" back and forth in song, is ancient and was once popular throughout Asia. Although terminology, line length, tunes, imagery, singing styles, and language differ among these and other folk song traditions, the basic call-and-response dynamic is consistent, as shown by several examples in this chapter. The basic style of the love songs sung in the interethnic singing meets in Guangxi; those of the She people in the mountains of Fujian province, to the east; and the "flower songs" of the northwest is similar.

In northwestern China and parts of the south and southwest, some folk song traditions are still viable, despite a broad decline in interest among younger generations. As is the case with many other oral traditions in China, maintaining a suitable complement of singers is difficult in many places. Many rural youth are drawn to urban areas in search of employment, thus removing them physically and culturally from the local song traditions and experienced singers. Some folk song traditions are in danger of becoming silent or of being voiced only in nontraditional situations, such as staged performances, that rely on electronic or print media (including online postings and locally published song collections) to help perpetuate them, often to nontraditional audiences. In many areas, these new contexts for folk song performance are being created by the rise of ethnic tourism. In places in Guangxi and Yunnan, for instance, traditional folk songs are being learned by otherwise uninterested young people who now perform them for audiences of tourists, most of whom have little or no knowledge of the local traditions. Although some of these new contexts inaccurately represent former or prevailing folk song traditions, they may serve as important stimuli for the continuation of some local singing styles.

A variety of songs from several areas of China are included in this chapter. One song common among the Dong (Gaem) people, who live on the border between Guizhou and Guangxi provinces, is called "Song of the Cicadas," and it is often sung chorally in a unique vocal tradition that mimics the sounds of cicadas. Another song, a kind of bridal lament from the northern steppes, is called a *syngsyma* (weeping song), and it is sung by a Kazakh bride in Xinjiang about to leave her natal place to join her groom. Another song from the northwest, of the Tu ethnic group in Qinghai, is a love song about a "sister from the plain" and a "brother from the valley"; it is rich in images of local customs of herding, plant lore, ritual, and female adornment. Among the several examples of local antiphonal love songs are the "saltwater" songs from the boat people of Hong Kong and Guangdong province, who spend most of their lives on the water. There are also songs attributed to the ancient song goddess Third Sister Liu from Guangxi and those of the mountain-dwelling She people of Fujian province, in the southeast. Mountain songs from Jiangsu province in the Yangtze delta, dating from the Qing dynasty, can be compared with a variety of contemporary songs collected from singers in the same region. These are but a few examples of the many regional traditions of Chinese folk songs.

FLOWER SONGS FROM NORTHWESTERN CHINA

Collected by Ke Yang (Han), Ye Jinyuan (Hui), and Kathryn Lowry and translated and introduced by Kathryn Lowry

Flower songs (*hua'er*), a type of folk song common in northwestern China, are sometimes classified by Chinese researchers as *shan'ge* (mountain songs). Flower songs are sung at local festivals held in rural areas of Gansu and Qinghai provinces and in the Ningxia Hui Autonomous Region, an area of over sixty thousand square miles. The Linxia Hui Autonomous Prefecture, located in southwestern Gansu province, is an area where flower songs and so-called flower song festivals (*hua'er hui*) are especially prevalent. The area is home to approximately sixteen ethnic groups, including Han Chinese, Hui (Chinese Muslims), and Dongxiang. There are also a number of Bao'an, Salar, Tu, Tibetans, and others. As song traditions that involve people of many ethnicities in the region, flower songs employ local Han Chinese dialects (though most participants are not Han), intermingling vocabulary and grammar of the Tu, Salar, and Tibetan languages.

Dozens of flower song festivals take place in northwestern China each year, most of them held in the first and sixth months of the lunar calendar. The festivals in the Hui region in southwestern Gansu, for example, last for three to six days. In this period, festival-goers follow a designated pilgrimage route to visit sites, often on mountains, that may extend to a radius of more than ten miles.

Flower songs sung in Gansu and Qinghai provinces are distinct from one another in regard to language, theme, musical form, poetic structure, and singing style. In Qinghai, they are often referred to as *shaonian* (youth songs). Flower songs are sung to regional melodies, which are unmeasured and melismatic, so that each syllable of text is sounded out as a melodic sequence; the less-skilled singers, however, may strip the melody down so that each syllable matches one musical pitch. The characteristic singing style is high-pitched, in a sharp and nasal "false voice" (*jiayin*). Because there are clear regional and local distinctions between melodic styles, the tunes of each locality have their own melodies and styles of versification. For example, the flower songs of southwestern Gansu consist of two broad types: songs in four lines sung by an individual singer, in which the first line determines the end rhyme; and songs sung by a chorus. The first type of song is most often performed during flower song festivals where two or more sing in an antiphonal format, trading verses back and forth. The second type of song, such as that to the tune "Two Lotuses," may be sung by groups of three or four singers with one person playing the part of conductor and improvisator (or "joiner" [*chuanba shi*]), who dictates the lyrics to the singers while they perform, shouting the lyrics line by line.

Since the 1950s, however, professional or semiprofessional renditions of flower songs for commercial or staged performances have often been enhanced by using a bel canto singing style or adaptations of that style. In recent years, some flower songs have appeared in nontraditional contexts. For example, street buskers in the New York City subways often perform flower songs with *erhu* accompaniment. The Chinese composer Bright Sheng has published transcriptions of flower songs from Qinghai, analyzing some of the characteristic melodic contours and refrains, and has used elements of the flower songs in his compositions.

The antiphonal style is common at flower song festivals and other nonprofessional singing events and takes the form of a contest (*duige*) involving either individuals or small groups of singers. The singers compose or recompose lyrics on the spot, responding to the theme of the previous song. The contest reflects the singers' skills in composing or recomposing lyrics. Singers may elaborate on the topic of the preceding song or answer a question that the other singer has posed. For this reason, the process of exchanging songs is sometimes referred to as "question and answer" (*wenda*). The contest concludes when either one singer or the other can no longer compose or re-create a verse to answer his opponent. While the local singers learn and transmit the songs orally, cassette tapes and digital recorders are now widely available in rural areas and offer new dimensions to transmission and performance.

In southwestern Gansu, in particular, singing flower songs is but one aspect of a more complex event. At festival times, a community stages local opera performances to entertain their local god. The figure of the god is invited to watch the festivities from his palanquin, is shown the boundaries of the community, and is fed and entertained in a temporary shrine. At the same time, some people trade horses and durable goods of all kinds, while others gather in groups of two to eight or more to sing flower songs, often encircled by listeners, who may, at some point, step into the circle to sing. Folklore investigations in the 1930s found that such local festivals were once called temple festivals (*miao hui*) or incense (pilgrimage) festivals (*xiang hui*), suggesting that the mountain pilgrimages and ways of worshipping mountain spirits traditionally associated with the events may have links to indigenous Tibetan religious practice. The festival traditions have subsequently been identified with several disparate belief systems.

After the 1950s, the festivals came to be regarded as secular, with a focus on love songs and singing contests. Since the mid-1980s, festivals have again come to be regarded as popular religious events, commemorating either the local god's birthday or temple founding. They involve ceremonies that may combine Daoist and Buddhist ritual procedures with local traditions of mountain worship. Folklorist Ke Yang, a professor of Chinese and folk literature at Lanzhou University, has suggested that flower song events also provide an occasion for courtship outside the strictures of arranged marriage. Some new flower song festivals have been created since the 1950s to mark political events, such as the founding of Guide Autonomous County, in Hainan Tibetan Autonomous Prefecture, Qinghai province.

Although the majority of flower songs are love songs, some evoke characters and themes from traditional fiction or narrate events from local history. For instance, several vernacular romances are mentioned in the second song—including *Outlaws of the Marsh* (*Water Margin* [*Shuihu zhuan*]), *Legend of the White Snake* (*Baishe zhuan*), *Journey to the West* (*Xiyou ji*), and *Romance of the Generals of the Yang Family* (*Yang jia jiang*)—as well as a reference to "Exiting the Five Passes," a famous passage from the novel *The Vernacular Romance of the Three Kingdoms* (*Sanguo tongsu yanyi*).[1] There are also songs featuring more recent social themes, such as family planning or the success of economic reforms. An example of this type is the fourth song, recorded in 1983 by Ke Yang at the Lianhuashan flower song festival and circulated in a textbook for his classes on folk literature.

As noted, the singers and contexts of flower song performances vary. Some singers are participants in local festivals who generally know a small number of tunes that circulate in locales as small as ten or twenty miles in area; others are professionals who have researched and refined the regional melodies for performance in commercial venues or for sound recording and broadcast. Other singers are semiprofessionals, such as Ye Jinyuan, a forty-three-year-old Hui maintenance worker who assisted in editing a volume of flower song texts published in 1979.

During his active years, Ye was sought out to sing at weddings and festivals in Xining, the capital of Qinghai province, and often lent cassette recordings of his songs to men in the community to help them master his repertoire. Some of his songs were recorded in a district cultural center where he worked. In the wake of the economic reforms of the mid-1980s, Ye abandoned his work as a handyman and editor and opened a restaurant. The singer's career raises interesting questions about the impact of not only access to recording technology but also economic change on the regional flower song traditions.

When barley begins to sprout, its head dips down;
When standing grain starts to sprout, it bends over.
In the midst of a crowd, do not say a word.
Little Sister, why do you hold back your laughter?

Ke Yang, ed., "Flower Songs: Selected Works"

Pole—one length, two long poles.
If you fasten the buttons, I will [find] openings.
The heroes of Mount Liang, or *Legend of the White Snake*,
Journey to the West, or [the episode on] "Exiting the Five Passes"?[2]

---

1. This is an early version of the famous historical novel *Romance of the Three Kingdoms* (*Sanguo yanyi*), referred to elsewhere in this volume.

2. The episode "Exiting the Five Passes" (Chu wu guan) centers on General Guan Yu, in *The Vernacular Romance of the Three Kingdoms*, chap. 7.

Take your pick.[3] Come take a look!
Which thread [of the story] do you like best?

Recorded by Ke Yang at the 1983 Lianhuashan flower song festival

Needle—a fine point, one fine needle.
I shall never forget your kindness.
If I were to forget your kindness,
The act of forgetting would make lightning strike and burn my body.

Recorded by Ke Yang at the 1983 Lianhuashan flower song festival

Steel—one measure, one measure of steel.
As the days stretch on, we grow more and more strong.
I have bought three—no, five bicycles:
A Flying Dove, and a Phoenix to ride.[4]
One is for my wife, and one for my son.
Today I bring along a tape recorder,
To record all of the flower songs that I fancy.

Recorded by Ke Yang at the 1983 Lianhuashan flower song festival

SINGER 1: Oh, an old man is walking along, and takes up his sickle to cut millet.
SINGER 2: Oh, my love, the one I long for, has not come past.
SINGER 3: Oh, the lamp shines through the night, my soul aches with longing, my heart is broken.
IN UNISON: Oh, a flower has two leaves, ah!

Three women, anonymous, ages twenty to twenty-six,
to the tune "Two Lotuses"

Kathryn Lowry interviewed Ye Jinyuan about his work as editor and as maintenance man at the West District Cultural Center, Dongcheng Qu Wenhuazhan, in Xining, on July 11, 1983. He sang the first two verses that follow and explained that they are in the antiphonal style, which he calls question and answer.

---

3. *Tiao,* in the phrase *you ni tiao,* meaning here "pick," is a homophone of *tiao,* meaning "carry," and a play on words, centering on the image of the carrying poles with braided strings hung at the two ends to bear weight. In the following line, "passage" (*tiao* [also "thread or strand" or "section of a story"]) plays with the same image.

4. The Flying Dove and Phoenix are bicycles manufactured in China. They were luxury items in the 1980s when the song was recorded.

At the base of a large rock, the springwater
Has bubbled up for thousands of years;
In the past, I did not recognize who you were,
Or we would have become involved long ago.

From the well, fetch some water, in the garden, now;
Beside the well, rinsing sesame seeds, then.
We ran into good fortune, we met each other by chance.
In our former lives, it was predestined.

The moon is an inkstone; the moonlight is paper.
The painter's brush draws dear sister's likeness.
Dear sister is a fairy maiden in the palace on the moon.
You descended among mortals, now, so fine looking you beat all under heaven.

Ye Jinyuan, to the tune "Major Melody of Xunhua"

The moon shines, this bright lamp, how is it so brilliant?
Who hung it high up over the Southern Heaven's Gate?
Dear sister is the peony, ruler of the flowers.
Compared with a bird in flight,
She outdoes the phoenix up in the clouds.

Ye Jinyuan, to the tune "Major Melody of Xunhua"

Lowry recorded a group of five men as they sang back and forth, exchanging flower songs in Victory Park (Shengli gongyuan), in downtown Xining, in July 1983. They questioned one another, in song, about the deeds of characters in the *Romance of the Generals of the Yang Family* and its storytelling traditions, which have evolved in teahouses and in popular religion. The first man who began to sing, later referred to as "the drunkard" (*jiugui*), addressed his song to Ye Jinyuan. A thirty-year-old factory worker from Xining then joined in the exchange. The drunkard began:

Oh—men who don't value love break nature's laws.
Fine flower, listen.
If he [acts without] reason, demons will catch sight of him.
Oh—the *Yang Generals' Family* and *Three Kingdoms*—sing about them.
If you are defeated by another singer, you know, then demons will catch sight of you.

The semiprofessional singer Ye Jinyuan responded:

Oh—the wind is high, the sky clear, but half cloudy,
Half cloudy, it half casts a rosy glow on my love's face.

Oh—you know that the Yang [Generals'] family is well established.
I'll ask you about Mu Guiying: Whom did she defend, do you know?

The drunkard continued:

Oh . . . —[*first words garbled*] the four, the four directions
I shall explain it all to you, now.
Beyond the high snow-topped mountains the slant of a rooftop shows.
The *Romance of the Yang Generals' Family, Three Kingdoms*—you know them all.
Mu Guiying, the one she sought out was the young master Yang.[5]

Ye Jinyuan responded to him:

Oh—half the sky is clear, and half is cloudy.
Half it's cloudy, half's got the sun coming out.
Oh—this Young Man,[6] listen clearly.
I shall instruct you:
Mu Guiying, she originally defended King Song [of Liao].

Following a series of songs set to a tune known as "The Big Eyes Melody" or "Magpies and Orioles," the factory worker sang:

Oh—on the thirtieth [New Year's] eve, we hang up a golden horse
Hang up a golden horse, and we finally know it is the lunar new year.
Oh—the time to take stock of this year is coming down on our heads.
Coming down on our heads
And we finally admit we are in a difficult situation.

The drunkard responded to him:

Oh—if you can't climb on a mule, ride a horse.
Those who know, listen.
I am going to ride on this darling mix of mule and horse.
Oh—if I cannot find a match, I cannot have a family
Those who know, listen!
I have made up my mind, Little Sister, to become a monk.

---

5. Mu Guiying was secretly married to Yang Zongbao, teenage son of General Yang Yanzhao (the Sixth Son), in the *Romance of the Generals of the Yang Family*, set in the Northern Song (960–1175). Mu Guiying subsequently took charge of the army in a decisive battle against the Liao, a favorite episode in the Beijing opera repertoire.

6. "Young Man" (Shaonian) is capitalized because it refers to the song type, not to a person. As noted, in Qinghai the terms *shaonian* and *hua'er* are used interchangeably for "flower songs."

The drunkard continued:

> Oh—now that you mention Yang the Fifth Son of the Yang Generals' Family[7]
> I will tell you.
> On Mount Tai he has become, oh, a monk, hey.
> Oh—a three-year-old baby no longer suckles milk.
> I will tell you.
> Right after that, then, he wants a wife.

The factory worker responded to his song:

> Oh—the saddle on a camel's back is a saddle made of flesh
> Even a true sword cannot pierce it.
> My heart and liver—take and tear them out to hollow my breast
> In the hollow of my breast, then, hide Little Sister away, now.

7. Yang the Fifth Son, named Yang Yande, is known for being unsuccessful in love. He was the son of General Yang Qiye (called Yang Ye) and became a monk after numerous visits to Mount Tai as protector of the Northern Song emperor Taizong (Zhao Kuangqi [r. 976–997]). Thus he is a historical figure as well as a character in the *Romance of the Generals of the Yang Family* and a protective deity in popular religion.

KAZAKH MARRIAGE SONGS OF LAMENT AND SORROW

Translated and introduced by Awelkhan Hali (Kazakh), Zengxiang Li (Han), and Karl W. Luckert

The Kazakh ethnic group lives mostly in the Xinjiang Uyghur Autonomous Region, in northwestern China, especially in areas bordering the country of Kazakhstan. The traditional economy was based on nomadic herding of sheep and horses, though now many Kazakhs in China follow more sedentary pursuits. Marriages today among the Kazakhs of China are typically arranged by the respective families in accordance with time-honored social rules and Islamic beliefs. In the past, some wealthy men had several wives, though in recent decades monogamous marriages have become the rule.

An important step in the marriage process is determining that the prospective mates are not of the same clan. Other criteria are similar social and economic status and character. The saying goes "The mother is a shadow of her daughter," and representatives of the prospective groom's family will observe the behavior of both the prospective bride and her mother. In determining the sort of dowry demanded, considerations about the economic relations of each family, as well as any other marriages between the families (between other siblings, for example), are taken into consideration.

The wedding rites involve four events at the bride's home: matchmaking, engagement, presentation of the betrothal gifts, and the actual wedding ceremony. Once the bridal party has arrived at the groom's home, there is more gift giving and a welcoming ceremony. Singing, dancing, feasting, and socializing are part of many of these steps. Although such customs are still in play, some young couples establish their own unions.

The series of songs that follows is part of a long and complex series of laments sung by a bride when she is about to leave her home and be escorted to that of her soon-to-be husband. The first passages are laments that the daughter sings to her parents, siblings, and closest kin.

SONGS OF LAMENT

At a certain point in the process of departing her home, the bride removes the cap that is typically worn by girls. An old lady of good reputation and character then covers her head with a veil. This signifies that the bride is now going to leave her home. She begins to weep, and with a soft and mournful voice she sings *syngsyma* songs. It is by way of such songs that the bride pours out her heart and reveals her innermost feelings of anguish. With the words of these songs, a bride bids farewell to her native homestead and to her loved ones.

If only my yurt were set up on the flat grassland,
If only there were a mirror for me to look at my face,
People say, the mother of another is like your own.
How can she be as close as my own mother?
Oh you, my native place!
Good-bye to you, place of my birth!

Farewell, dear Mom, be well!
Let me awaken you and arouse your love for me
Oh my God! Why was I made a girl?
Was it your aim to make me cry?
Oh you, my native place!
Good-bye to you, place of my birth!

Oh, dear Mother, crying with tears,
Where can I find a mother like you?
Not even sixteen years old, you married me off,
Do you not have the strength to stop my father?
Oh you, my native place!
Good-bye to you, place of my birth!

Oh, dear Father, though I am a girl I am like your son,
I am a piece of velvet that you bought at the market,
You forced me to be married,
I am just like a foal, orphaned and helpless,
Oh you, my native place!
Good-bye to you, place of my birth!

If I were a boy, would I not support you, dear Father?
Would I not attend races riding on a dying horse?
As does our native place when blossoms are out,
Would I not make you happy and joyful?
Oh you, my native place!
Good-bye to you, place of my birth!

You forest, swaying before our door,
While I long for you my agony is hard to describe,
The father of another is not the same as one's own,
Who can be compared with you, dear Dad!
Oh you, my native place!
Good-bye to you, place of my birth!

Good-bye, dear Dad. Let me say good-bye,
It is for you that my tears are bathing my face,

O my place of birth! O my kindred! You remain behind,
Today I am saying good-bye to you all,
Oh you, my native place!
Good-bye to you, place of my birth!

Oh dear Brother, I am going far away,
Be fair. Or do I have no longings?
When I step off the threshold of our home,
Come and visit me often,
Oh you, my native place!
Good-bye to you, place of my birth!

We grew up together like foals, dear Brother,
Leisurely carefree times are hard to return to,
I am going to a strange place and am leaving our home,
How can I adapt in a home of others?
Oh you, my native place!
Good-bye to you, place of my birth!

We grew up like lambs and kids, dear younger sisters,
Oh my native *awyl*,[8] you will feel deserted,
Please do not tell why you produce so many tears,
It is difficult to describe the depth of my sorrow,
Oh you, my native place!
Good-bye to you, place of my birth!

I will remember you, my native place,
With me you will lose an ardent lover
From early youth I played and laughed on your grounds,
If I have faults, please forgive, forgive this pitiful girl.
Oh you, my native place!
Good-bye to you, place of my birth!

I have not drunk enough the clear waters of your springs,
I regret not belonging to you anymore,
O God! You take me away from my home,
Why not take away my soul with me as well,
Oh you, my native place!
Good-bye to you, place of my birth!

---

8. The *awyl* is the communal grouping of yurts to which an individual belongs.

Do you hate me, my dear native place?
If you do, please move elsewhere too,
One leaves his home if one is dead,
I leave my home, though I am still alive,
Oh you, my native place!
Good-bye to you, place of my birth!

SONGS OF SORROW

After the bride has sung *syngsma* songs, she steps before her parents, brothers, sisters, and other relatives to begin a song of departure, known as a *köris* song. She is accompanied by two young women. To all her relatives, she sings:

Outside the door is a broad and level place—ah!
Groups of animals are playing on the broad grassland—ah!
Dear relatives, my native place,
I will never forget your great kindness—ah!

While I was young you (my Mother) pampered me,
While I was young I never felt wronged.
How can I be a woman,
If I depart from your side?

How happy it is to climb to the top of a mountain!
Wild sheep are playing halfway up that mountain.
But I was a girl when I was born,
And I became a bag that belongs to others.

Snowflakes are falling thick and fast,
It is you, my Mother, who brought me up.
Dear Mother, I remember you with longing.
Oh, I will spend my time with tears.

I do not want to leave you, my dear Mother,
I cannot stop the tears that flow from my eyes.
In your heart I am your child,
Why can I not stay with you always?

Along the stream stand white birch trees,
I want to treasure and protect them,
As long as I live
I will repay you for your kindness,
Is it a pine or a willow?

Are there trees harder than birches?
Although I say "Don't cry" to myself,
Is there anything as pitiful as girls?

The tea table brought from the market,
How can I take care and not ruin it?
Oh! My Mother, you gave me your milk,
What must I do so as not to disappoint you?

To her father, she sings:

A yellow sturdy horse stands in the horse herd,
A yellow horsewhip lies heavy in your hand
Had I been a boy,
I would stay with you in the *awyl*. Would I not?

Oh! Outside the door are thornbushes,
Oh! Do you know how sorrowful I am?
Father! Please do not send me away.
Let me stay with you for another year!

There is a gray racing stallion in the herd,
Nobody can catch him with bare hands.
You are going to send me faraway,
How pitiful I am, and what can I do?

Today I wear a white skirt,
I comb my hair and wear it in braids,
Oh Father, you said you would not marry me off.
Why do you become so cruel-hearted?

To her brother, she sings:

Dear Brother, please listen to me,
The seat you are sitting on is a throne.
Although we were born into the same family,
We cannot always remain together.

My dear Brother,
I have put the horses out to pasture.
Customs of strange lands I do not know.
How could I know their tempers?

I wish I were a white swan;
I wish I could dwell at the lakeside.
Do not cry, Brother, do not cry.
I hope to join in your song ever after.

There is a brownish mare in the herd,
You ride on her back as you drive our cattle.
Come to me regularly; tarry not too long,
People will say, "Her brother is here."

Birds will flap their wings before flying,
Birds will drop into nets carelessly.
Oh my Brother, you said you will not marry me off.
Why have you, too, been deceived?

To her sister-in-law, she sings:

Bismilla is the beginning of our words.
Tears dropping from my eyes do never cease.
I do not want to leave you, oh Sister-in-law!
Are we going to leave each other like this?

I wear on me a white skirt,
Beautiful flowers are embroidered on it.
O dear Sister-in-law, I love you.
You also liked me in a special way.

The Altai range has high mountains.
Ribbons of our fur hats are made of silk.
Although I say to myself "Do not cry,"
God made us women, inferior to others.

To her younger brother, she sings:

Dear Younger Brother, let me kiss you,
Let me kiss your hair.
How can you remain behind?
We followed each other so closely.

There are corduroys in the market,
You are a good son of our father.
Be a good helper to our father,
These are my words to you, my dear Younger Brother.

Dear Younger Brother, you are like the sun,
My dear one, you never went and left me alone.
But now the time is approaching,
My breath trembles deeply.

The fierce wind is howling,
A well-known mountain is our Sawyr.
I am going away and you are left,
Peace be with you, my dear Younger Brother!

To the threshold, she sings:

Before the door grow burdock plants.
Do not let me go away, my Threshold.
How can I stop the tears that roll from my eyes?
I am so full of sorrow, half-dead.

Larks are flying in the sky,
May the feathers of larks be pure and white.
I cannot avoid having to leave you,
Good-bye now, my dear Threshold.

As she proceeds along her way, she sings another *köris* song.

On me I wear a white skirt,
My folks are sending me away.
The place I go to is far, far away,
Oh, I will remember you with longing.

I am riding on a winged steed.
Flowers are embroidered on my riding boots.
My younger brother is left behind me.
When will he grow up and be a young man?

There is a white horse in the horse herd,
Children cannot catch him.
My father is old, my brother is young,
Dear folks, please look after them.

There are twins in the sheep herd,
The ends of rivers are in the ocean.
My *awyl*, you will no longer call me "Girl,"
From now on you will say, "The young wife is coming."

Köris songs are intoned with deep emotion and sorrow; sometimes they run to a great length. Here is another example.

Oh, my native place and sandy bank,
My Brother, Sister, and Sister-in-law.
When I think about my native place,
My heart feels like stalling.

A willow stands before my door,
What trees are taller than it?
Born at my place, I will grow old on the steppe,
Is there anyone as unfortunate as girls?

Like the marrow in the spine,
My Father, you looked after me as if I were a son.
When you were in debt to someone,
You caught me like a foal to send me away.

I tied a horse to the stable,
I boiled honey in a pot.
O my dear Mom,
I have not yet grown up, and here you marry me off.

O dear Allah! Creator!
The wild horse runs away and is difficult to catch.
Until we meet again, next time,
I say good-bye and wish that you all shall be safe.

There is a horse in the herd,
With a yellow neck and lowered head.
My brothers and sisters remain left behind,
I will never again enjoy happiness with them.

Instead of the *börık*[9] on my head,
My face is covered with a pink veil.
O dear Mother! O my dear!
Your yurt will seem hollow and empty.

When I was born I was not a boy,
I have not driven horses down the mountains.
O dear Dad! O my dear!
[Because a girl] I have not saddled a horse for you.

---

9. The *börik* is a round girl's cap.

Springwater runs down from the mountain,
The fine hair of a small camel is soft.
While I think about my native place,
All my bones and muscles ache.

I ride on a horse, with a whip in my hands.
Tears run down from my eyes.
Like a hired herdsman,
You drive me off from my native place.

A brownish foal plays in the herd,
People will return from summer pasture soon.
Call on me and visit me often,
Or else they will say, "She has none who loves her."

Come call on me and visit me,
Come and give me help.
Before I grow up as a full adult,
Come to me and watch over me.

There is a black foal in the herd,
Pat its back gently.
To part from my native place is not my will,
It will be a long time until we meet again.

Under our luggage is my tea table,
How can I keep from damaging it?
Dear Mother, you brought me up with care,
What can I do not to be unworthy?

I am a lamb in the sheep herd,
I am a foal in the horse herd.
Alongside my parents, Dad and Mom,
I was circling like a swan.

I am a swan and henceforth no longer,
But I will never forget my home and my kin.
I will never forget you like the cloud that floats away.
How can I forget you—Brother, Sister-in-law, Relatives!

I have tied my luggage onto the camel,
I have tied it firm with silk rope.
Good-bye, my native people and kin,
I am crying and telling you.

A shed stands outside our door,
My horse is frightened by the shed.
Although Mother said, "I will not marry you off!"
Now she drapes the veil over my face.

A black rock stands on the mountaintop,
An eagle alights on that rock.
I do not want to leave my home,
Must I leave my home like this, just now?

A pine tree stands on the mountaintop,
Let the larks perch on that pine.
We are age mates, we grew up together,
I regret we cannot be so close anymore.

A black rock stands on the mountaintop,
An eagle alights on that rock,
O my Brother, you said, "I will not marry you off!"
Oh, I cannot remain at your side.

Stones are piled up in the front of the door,
Girls are useless, just as these stones.
If girls are useful, the same as boys,
Then why am I so useless and not like others?

We ate apples and apricots together,
Sister-in-law, you were my companion.
Now I am going far away, my dear,
Your doomed sister, not yet dead.

Large burdock plants are growing by the door.
Wild horses are difficult to catch.
Until I return to this place again,
You all remain safe and sound!

A bluish saddle was bought at the market,
I sit on it and I feel proud.
While I put my feet into the stirrups,
My feelings are difficult to describe.

Licorice plants grow by the door,
Horses stand around the licorice plants.
You who have helped me ride the horse,
How hard-hearted all of you are!

Why did you, oh God, make us girls?
Why, like sheep, for paying family debts?
Girls are made for all the others,
We must act according to the whims of others.

Yesterday the wind was blowing hard,
My *awyl* looks like whipped-up water on the lake.
Now I am leaving, must part from you,
Be safe and sound, all you my brothers.

People are praying in the morning.
Oh, my home looks as lively as a market.
Now I am leaving to part from you.
Oh, where is that place to which I am going?

Many kinds of grasses are growing by our door,
Oh, I drove away three horses.
My older brothers, you said, "I will not marry you off!"
And you handed the reins to me today.

I was so happy-go-lucky at home,
I was pampered and spoiled with tea brought to me.
But all my years of pampering have passed,
I feel sorrowful and upset, Mom!

You are not willing to send me away,
Tears from your eyes do not stop.
The pitiful fetus remains in your womb,
Why am I not at your side now, dear Mom?

There are embroideries now on my sleeves,
Do not cry for me anymore.
While I think about you, my dear Mom,
My heart feels constricted.

I was a girl when I was born,
When God sent me to this earth.
Had I been born a boy,
Would I not remain at your side, dear Brother?

My clothes are sewed with silver buttons,
I have never been beaten by the weather.
I have been so spoiled by my parents,
But what will my future be?

Oh, my hair is soft and long,
I have been so spoiled by my parents.
When I am in a strange place,
Will I be at my wit's end?

I made a chest and covered it with lead,
Patterns I carved upon it.
I entrust my father and my mother
To the one almighty God.

There are carvings on my horsewhip,
When silk is dyed the color does not fade.
No matter how many good people there are,
Nobody is better than one's own mother.

People spend winters near the springs of rivers,
There are velvet decorations on my sleeves.
No matter how many good people there are,
Nobody looks after you like your own mother.

There is a white horse in the horse herd.
"The girl is to be married," spread the word.
"I will not give you to anyone, my dear," said my father.
Why do changes happen so fast?

A foal of last year has become a *tai*[10] by now.
The new moon rises in the sky.
My brothers also said, "We do not give you to anyone."
But words about giving me away they now speak.

A stream is murmuring by my door,
I bow down to wash my face.
Being a girl, I am going to get married,
Do not be anxious, my dear Mom.

I drove the horse to the market,
People are moving onto summer pastures.
To get married I did not agree at first,
You compelled me with force, to agree.

I bought a melon at the market,
I am not willing to leave my *awyl*.

---

10. A *tai* is a two-year-old colt.

My brothers remain behind,
All of them are my own flesh and blood.

Along the river grow trees,
Could I cross the river by holding on to them?
If I had been a boy when I was born,
Would I now sob as I go to another place?

Ears rise up from the barley patch,
The falcon eaglet seeks them out.
When I was born and came to this earth,
God decreed that I leave my native land.

By my door flows a river,
The wind blows hard and raises its waves.
People of the *awyl* said, "We will not marry you off!"
Who is the one that convinced you all?

There is a white-striped horse in the herd,
A boy standing there could not catch him.
People, be considerate toward my dad,
Who pampered me from my childhood.

The yellow buttons bought at the market,
Why has the sewing thread snapped?
"I will not marry you off," my dad said.
But why have you changed your mind?

Swallows are flying to the woods,
Their flapping wings touch tips of grass.
O my dear Mom, who pampered me,
You are the one who pushes me, into living hell.

There are willow bushes by my door,
My sheep are left in the woods.
O *awyl*, you who spoiled me,
The people left behind are weeping.

Low apple trees are thriving,
Narrow-leaved oleasters are growing densely.
Had I been born a boy,
I would remain with you, and rightly so.

Black clouds have blotted out the sky,
My horses are tended on the grasslands.
Do not think that I am still alive,
I am the same as a corpse.

I drove my sheep to the village,
And from the village to the market.
Do not say, "She did not say good-bye."
I said good-bye to all of you.

Bowls, kettles, and teapots,
Are all bought at the market.
Do not say, "She did not say good-bye."
Ladies, I said farewell to you.

Golden horseshoes are made at the market,
Thousands of gold coins are their price.
Do not say, "She did not say good-bye."
Brothers, I said farewell to you.

Floodwaters rush from the mountain side.
The girl's eight braids are of the same length.
Do not say, "She did not say good-bye,"
Sisters-in-law, I said it to you.

I tied the dowry onto a white camel,
The loads at both sides are balanced the same.
Do not say, "She did not say good-bye."
I said farewell and cried bitterly.

I bought a lock at the market,
My desire was not to get married.
To get married is to be doomed.
I wish you salaam, my people back home!

My brownish horse stands in the herd,
I think of you with nostalgic longing.
Oh, my *awyl* is left behind,
I wish good luck to all of you.

How can I endure all the bright days?
How can I endure all the nights?

While I am at such a strange place,
Deep sorrows accompany me from daybreak till dusk.

The ends of rivers run into the sea,
There are animals stout and strong.
Dear Mother said, "I do not marry you off."
Now you let others say, "The bride is coming."

Buttons are stitched and worn at my breast.
O dear Mother, you pampered me,
You who fed me with your breast,
Of your kindness I am unworthy.

Now I wear the unlucky black clothes,
How kindhearted you are, dear Mom!
Peace be with you all your life.
May your life be long, and longer!

With songs such as these, the wedding rites in the bride's *awyl* come to an end. The bride sings *köris* songs and thereby bids good-bye to her relatives. With the help of her brothers, she mounts a horse that has been given to her by her father. Her dowries are loaded onto camels, and—accompanied by her mother, sister-in-law, younger brothers, and younger sisters—she journeys to the bridegroom's *awyl*. Usually the bride dresses in red. A bride from a wealthier family wears an embroidered red dress and a *sawkele*, a Kazakh bridal coronet inlaid with precious stones and fitted with a piece of red velvet to cover her face.

QING DYNASTY MOUNTAIN SONGS

Translated and introduced by John McCoy

Scholars consider folk songs, often associated with professional performances, as an important form of poetry from Qing dynasty (1644–1911) China. While the collection of folk and popular music had antecedents in the Ming dynasty (1368–1644) (notably Feng Menglong's two anthologies, *Mountain Songs* [*Shan'ge*] and *The Hanging Branch* [*Guazhi'er*]), the Qing saw a more meticulous and faithful collection of songs derived from various sources, including the "streets and alleys," the arias of *chuanqi* drama, and the adaptations and recensions for the performance of poems written by famous literati.

The following oral-connected mountain songs are from a number of popular anthologies, with rather varied textual histories, published in the Qing period. Among these collections is *Bequeathed Songs from the White Snows* (*Baixue yiyin*), published in 1828 by Hua Guangsheng, who spent more than a year collecting and sorting the poems. He was aided by friends and others who were interested in collecting and preserving folk music. Another collection, *Supplementary Formulary of the Rainbow Skirts* (*Nishang xupu*), was actually a body of music that had been handed down orally among musicians for generations and was compiled by Yan Zide in 1795. *Little Songs for Strings* (*Sixian siaoqu*) is an anonymous compilation printed in Suzhou in 1736. The book contains 103 songs without any sort of preface or postface. *Myriad Flowers, Little Songs* (*Wan hua xiaoqu*), published in Beijing in 1744, is also anonymous and without preface or postface. *Season's Pleasures* (*Shixing yayayou*) is an anonymous compilation from the Jiaqing reign (1796–1820) that contains 140 songs that were popular at that time. *Beijing Children's Songs* (*Beijing erge*) is a collection of children's songs and poems popular from the reign of Qianlong (1736–1796) into the reign of the Guangxu emperor (1875–1908). *The Heavenly Flute Collection* (*Tianlai ji*) was compiled by Zheng Shudan and published in 1869; it is composed of 48 songs from the Zhejiang area.

A striking feature of these oral poems is the frequent presence of women's voices. Although there were famous women poets in the classical tradition, they seldom described women's lives with the feeling and detail that these folk songs display. One can see the themes of the abandoned sweetheart and unrequited love in such works as the "Midnight Song" (Ziye ge) from as early as the late fourth century C.E. However, it takes folk poetry to bring out such themes as the bitterness of the bride's lot with her in-laws and the desperate frustration of an unhappy nun.

The enormous popularity of these songs is attested to by the fact that the great modern scholar Zheng Zhenduo collected some twelve thousand copies of individually published songs, all of which were destroyed by Japanese bombs in Shanghai in 1932. This is twice the number of songs published in Liu Fu and Li Jiarui's *Draft of a Comprehensive List of Chinese Popular Songs* (*Zhongguo suqu zongmu gao*), and, by Zheng's estimate, this was only 20 percent of the known total.

As a corpus, the poems show a great deal of similarity and frequent instances of outright copying. Although some songs may be quite similar, there is also a great deal of variation, as might be expected in a body of oral-connected lore, where the re-creation of a poem as a song for a performance necessarily leads to differences, just as do separate re-creations of the same song. The need to innovate, to meet the challenge of audience demands, leads inevitably to alteration, rejection, revival, changes in tempo, addition of filler words, and myriad other tricks of the artist.

Thus in most instances, there is no identifiable "original text," except where the song has been adapted from a popular written poem or from a particularly brilliant passage in a stage aria.

A SMILE

A breeze comes blowing from the southeast,
Fresh blossoms open up among the leaves;
Don't smile like that, young miss,
Who knows how many little private thoughts are behind those
smiles?

A STARE

I am always wondering how to be alone with you,
Without needing a matchmaker and a dowry;
When you catch a fish in a silk net it comes up right before your eyes,
And a thousand feet of gauze comes from a single shuttle.

LOOKING

A girl is sitting by the window embroidering a pair of mandarin ducks,
A young rake is just rowing away from shore;
As the girl looks at the boy she pricks herself with the needle,
As the boy looks at the pretty girl his boat is caught crosswise
in the current.

ON FIRE (1)

Really on fire, getting him all worked up,
We meet at the tower of the main gate two or three times a day for
a feel;

I am like the begging monk in the temple who gets a little bit
from everybody,
My lovers are like oarsmen—everyone has an oar and everyone
can row.

ON FIRE (2)

Really on fire, leading him on,
Coolly sitting at the main gate inviting men's stares;
I am like a pair of Hangzhou clogs that anyone can wear,
My lovers are like those old and well-known eating shops that don't need
to advertise.

ON FIRE (3)

When her heart itches she always invites any man's glances,
But when my man goes to her he is not completely satisfied;
Like a fire starting in the ship's bow and raging through the hold,
Fortunately my man was able to save the stern for me.

STUDYING STYLES

The young lady living across from us is having a love affair,
How can I keep from getting excited too?
Around me I see all kinds of this "peach blossom" activity,
How can I bathe in this indigo vat and myself not get blue.

NOT FLIRTING

The famous Tiger Hill is really not too high,
First-class fast boats are not sculled;
A boxing artist worth his salt barely moves his hands,
A young woman who can get an outside lover certainly need not be
too obvious.

EXPRESSING ONE'S FEELINGS

When you pass twenty, twenty-one comes right behind,
If you haven't been in love by then you are really slow;
When thirty has passed the blossoms all wither away,
And if you signal a man with both hands he still won't come.

WITHOUT A LOVER (1)

When the wind rises my heart is sad,
On winter nights without a man I really feel lost;
East, west, north, south—somewhere in this village there must be some twenty-year-old fellow with nothing to do but come and be with me,
Just a temporary companion to pass the cold winter night, and then I'll give him back.

WITHOUT A LOVER (2)

I open the window and watch the snowflakes fly,
When nights are cold and days are freezing I cling to him;
Three layers of cotton quilts still cannot cover my chill,
The only thing that works is the warm skin of my lover's belly.

LOOKING FOR MY LOVER

After you get to know a lover well you are bound to suffer because of him,
Right when you need him most he is nowhere to be seen;
If I could get some officer on his rounds in the village to ferret out my lover and return him to me,
I would gladly present the man with three goblets of wine.

MAKING EXCUSES

Today it's one thing, tomorrow another.
Whenever I want you to come there are always so many excuses;
The girl says, my lover, it is like bamboo shoots that get cut off as soon as they come out,
And arrows made with flowery bamboo are all kinds of colors.

WAITING (1)

I stand by the north window curtains,
I send out my maid to ask for my lover;
The mason has run out of mortar so the bricks are waiting,
My neighbor may take advantage of this situation and have his way with me.

MAKE-BELIEVE

When I haven't seen my lover my heart is painful,
In my imagination I create meetings with him;
I close my eyes and dream and kiss emptiness,
Then I breathe words to my handsome sweetheart.

SECONDHAND

In my heart there has always been a number one,
But while waiting for him so long I became someone else's
for a while;
Since I couldn't have the wonton, the noodles had to do,
When I went with him, at least for the time being it was exciting
and fun.

WAITING (2)

The gardenia opens into six petals,
My lover said he would meet me this evening;
The day is long and drags on endlessly,
I throw open the shutters with both hands to check the sun's
progress.

TEMPTATION (1)

He sees a girl and comes over to make a pass,
But a copper ladle without a handle is hard to fill if it's hot;
The girl says, "Sweetheart, a mortar with nothing in it is a waste of time
to turn.
You might as well sprinkle water on hot coals just to make a hissing
sound."

TEMPTATION (2)

They told me to go out and sit in the cool evening air.
I saw my sweetheart coming over to make a pass.
I quickly sang the little ditty "Firefly, Father and Mother Are Here."
But then I was afraid he would remember the second line
and go look for some "Old Lady Wind sitting in the grass."

DECEIVING MOTHER

Mother watches over me like a tiger,
But I fool her as if she were locked up in a barrel;
It's really like losing the thief right in front of the patrol,
Or assigning an archer to night guard.

HOODWINKING MOTHER

Last night my sweetheart and I slept on the same pillow;
Mother was asleep at the foot of the bed;
I said, "When you're in the middle of the Yangtze,
you should scoop rice with a gentle motion,
And if the iron cable is thick you ought to pull it slowly."

THE TORN SKIRT

We were walking in the alley,
When my sweetheart tore my skirt at the waist;
Back home in front of Mother I said my stomach ached.
I pressed it with both hands and wouldn't straighten up.

WATCHING THE STARS

I opened the window to look at the stars,
Mother knew I was meeting my lover again;
I'm like a bleached white cloth dropped in an oil jar,
Soak it all night in lye and it still won't come clean.

HOODWINKING PEOPLE (1)

Having an affair requires some cleverness,
Let's not make eyes all the time, people will guess;
If we meet face-to-face we can bow politely,
If we bump into each other in a narrow street we should jump apart quickly.

HOODWINKING PEOPLE (2)

Everybody says you and I are lovers.
We will have to stage a fight and get rid of those accusations.

You double up your fist and say you will hit me,
I'll shake my finger at you and scold you soundly.

HOODWINKING PEOPLE (3)

Sweetheart, when you want to come, come by yourself,
Don't pick up some loafer and bring him along;
An extra person is like a crow sitting on the roof,
He always starts cawing before it is even dawn.

HOODWINKING PEOPLE (4)

I have a lover who comes when it is snowing,
If there are footprints outside the house people will guess;
For three coppers he bought a pair of straw sandals and put them on
backward,
They could see only that someone left, but never guess he came.

PREGNANT (1)

He visited once and touched me once,
Already you can see how the waist of my skirt is getting tighter;
The character for "pregnant" doesn't look good when you write it out;
It's written with "son" big inside and "breasts" high outside.

PREGNANT (2)

When I go walking in the streets I go with careful steps,
There are some strange sensations in my stomach;
During the Great Rains at transplanting time there was some extra
propagation done,
And now in the June wedding period my belly is full of wild rice.

PREGNANT (3)

When the pains started she drank the ginger soup,
At midnight in the privacy of her room she gave birth to a little boy;
Holding him in her slender jade fingers and looking at him by
lamplight,
He seemed half to resemble her and half to resemble him.

PREGNANT (4)

My love has left in my belly a little memento of our affair,
Here alone, behind the bed-curtains without my lover, how will I manage?
Wrap it in a reed mat and simply drop it in the lotus pond?
How often such thoughts cross my mind.

PREGNANT (5)

The young lady gave some instructions to the souvenir he left inside her,
"While I am behind the bed-curtains without my lover I can't take care
of you;
Listen until you hear him set a wedding day for me,
Then you can get into my belly."

NOT PREGNANT

We had this love affair and outdid heaven,
Still we don't have a child to burn incense for us;
It's like the gangplank on a powdered lime boat,
You can go back and forth on it for two or three years in vain,
it will still be white.

UNTITLED

The girl says, "My sweetheart,
If you should come at midnight, don't give a rap at the back door,
It would be better to grab a chicken in our yard and pull out some
feathers;
Pretend you are a weasel stealing chickens and make them let out
a cackle,
This will be enough to get me running out in my slip to chase away the
wild cat."

UNTITLED

The woman and her daughter were walking along side by side,
Two fresh flowers, which one is nicer?
The daughter says, "Of the lotus roots in the pond, the tender ones
are better."
The woman says, "Of the lily bulbs from the sand spit, the older ones are
sweeter."

UNTITLED

I agreed with my sweetheart to meet when the moon came up.
Why is it that the moon is on the mountaintops, but I still don't see him?
I wonder if it could be because in my place the hills are low, so the moon
  rises earlier,
Or is it that at his place the hills are high, and the moon rises late?

FOLK SONGS FROM JIANGSU PROVINCE

Collected and introduced by Antoinet Schimmelpenninck and Frank Kouwenhoven

These folk song texts were collected during fieldwork conducted mainly in the southern part of Jiangsu province between 1986 and 1994. A few essential facts about folk songs in this region may be helpful. From all accounts, folk singing was common in many parts of the area in the first half of the twentieth century, before industrialization and political changes put an end to the tradition. Singing used to be particularly popular during the communal work in the fields and in the evening, when people enjoyed leisure after a day of hard work. In the lower central parts of the Yangtze River delta, rice cultivation resulted in rice planting and wedding songs in a variety of forms (solo or with lead singers and chorus). Folk singing was less rich in the outer parts of the delta, the higher ground where cotton (a dry crop) was grown. Today, mainly older people in southern Jiangsu still show an interest in folk songs. The number of active singers is rapidly decreasing, and folk songs are no longer sung outdoors. They are sung mainly in organized recording sessions. Most of the singers we met during our fieldwork were older than sixty at the time of the performance.

As elsewhere in China, love songs are the favorite genre. Songs for ritual occasions include bridal songs, funeral laments, and various chants for worshipping. Poetry dominates over music in the folk songs of southern Jiangsu. Singers know only a handful of tunes to which they sing hundreds of texts. The size of singers' text repertoires ranges from a few lines to ten thousand lines or more.

Outdoor singing used to be loud and vigorous, as everywhere in China. There could be competitive dialogues between soloists or groups. In summer, the air was filled with the sounds of *shan'ge* (mountain songs),[11] which were as familiar to villagers' ears as the twittering of birds or the grunting of pigs. Singers in southern Jiangsu use the term *shan'ge* for at least 90 percent of their song repertoire. The vast majority of these songs are based on a very limited number of local tunes, to which hundreds of different texts are sung. The remaining body of texts is sung to a more varied repertoire of (usually supraregional) tunes that are denoted, by the singers themselves, as *xiaodiao* (little ditties or minor tunes), which are less popular than the *shan'ge*. As far as texts are concerned, there is, in principle, little difference between the two categories, though certain types of padding syllables and the use of refrain verses are typical of *xiaodiao*. The music of the *xiaodiao* is often more regular in rhythm, presumably because it was often sung to instrumental accompaniment. It would seem that the major distinction between the two genres lies in their origin, not in their form or structure. Some Chinese scholars have suggested that *xiaodiao* are of urban origin, while *shan'ge* are primarily a rural genre. We must emphasize that

---

11. See "Qing Dynasty Mountain Songs."

what we describe is the situation in one particular region in China. The meanings of terms like *shan'ge* and *xiaodiao* may be different in other areas, and they may have been different in the Wu area in the past.

Our fieldwork concentrated primarily on the region bordering Lake Tai on the eastern and southeastern side, with the town of Suzhou (ca. 750,000 inhabitants) at the center. This region was once the heart of the semibarbaric Kingdom of Wu (fifth century B.C.E.). Various kingdoms or vassal states of later periods as well as a number of towns and districts in the area eventually adopted the name Wu. Hence they are also called *Wu ge* (Wu songs), a term used in literary and historical writings to refer to the folk songs of this region. The songs are sung in the Wu topolect—actually a group of related dialects found in an area extending far beyond Lake Tai. The exact boundaries are open to discussion. The Nanjing district, in southern Jiangsu, does not belong to this wider Wu dialect area, but the Shanghai district does. Some areas on the northern bank of the Yangtze River are included, as is most of Zhejiang province. All the singers are Han Chinese.

MAIDEN WU (VERSE 1)

Sung by Zhao Yongming

Local people praised Zhao Yongming (b. 1919), a farmer in Luxu, Wujiangxian, for his qualities as a singer by calling him the "mountain song cicada." "Maiden Wu," performed to a local mountain song tune, was recorded on December 13, 1988. It is the beginning of a long narrative love song about Maiden Wu (Wu Guniang), a girl from a rich landowner's family who has an unhappy affair with one of the hired laborers, Xu Atian. Actually this beginning verse (*getou* [literally, "head of the song"]) does not refer to the story and could be used as the beginning of any long narrative song, to "warm up" the singer.

The phrase "my belly," in line 2, is a common way for mountain song singers to refer to the songs that they remember—they keep them "in their bellies." People's existence in the Yangtze River delta depends largely on water, and this fact is reflected in the numerous songs that refer, directly or metaphorically, to the water landscape. In this text, the water of Lake Tai becomes a measure of a singer's memory.

Not singing mountain songs, one forgets them—*eihei wu a heihei!*—easily;
So I go and look for them. My belly still hides 108,900 basketfuls!
Hey ho! To Wujiang's Suspended Rainbow Bridge at Eastern Gate I carry them—and sing them all;
The bridge collapses under their weight. Eastern Lake Tai is flooded with songs!

YEARNING FOR A BELOVED (UNTIL DEATH FOLLOWS)

Sung by Jin Wenyin

Jin Wenyin (b. 1927), a teacher and folk song collector in Shengpu, Wuxian, was recorded on October 17, 1988. Sung to a rhythmically regular *xiaodiao* tune, the text of "Yearning for a Beloved (Until Death Follows)" is Jin's own compilation of three versions that he collected from other singers in the neighborhood.

Virtually every possible aspect of human love is covered in folk songs of Jiangsu, but the most prominent theme is the one found in this song: love longing. It is usually longing on the side of the girl, who is waiting for her beloved or for a future lover. Variants of this text were found in various parts of the Wu dialect area, sometimes with slightly different titles like "Si ao lang" (Yearning for a Beloved Until Death), "Da ao lang" (The Big [Song About] Yearning for a Beloved), or, simply, "Ao lang." To enable comparison, we give one alternative ending of the song as we came across it in northern Zhejiang. The term *shi* (ten) in the title is untranslatable: it is a formulaic device used in many local song titles to indicate that the song has more than just a few stanzas ("ten" meaning "much"). In this particular case, it may also be a misinterpretation of the word *si* ([until] death [follows]).

In the first month, at the arrival of spring, I yearn for a beloved.
I put on my blouse and smooth its front.
In wintertime I wear damask, in summer, thin, white silk;
This matches perfectly with the stockings with mandarin ducks[12]
That women wear in Huzhou streets.
With rough silk, red and white, I embroider my wedding dress.[13]

In the second month, when apricot trees blossom, I yearn for a beloved.
I smarten up a bit. . . . Don't I look pretty?
My hair shines like black silk, my brows are shaped like the character eight,[14]
My eyes are deep as mountain lakes, my face resembles dew on a peach blossom.
My teeth flash between red lips.

In the third month, when the peach blossoms are marvelously red, I yearn
for a beloved.
The incense boat[15] leaves the harbor—what a hustle, what a stir!
In the first vigil of the night I feel numb, in the second vigil I feel drowsy,

12. Mandarin ducks are a symbol of a happy marriage.

13. It is not unusual for a Chinese girl to work on a wedding dress even if no candidates for marriage yet exist.

14. "Character eight" refers to the shape of the Chinese character that corresponds to the word for "eight."

15. The incense boat (*shaoxiangchuan*) takes Buddhist pilgrims to Hangzhou, where they burn incense in temples.

In the third my eyelids are heavy with sleep, in the fourth vigil a golden
pheasant calls.
Then the fifth vigil arrives. Will I manage to get up in the clear early
morning?
Will I stay in bed in the clear early morning? In front I open a gauze window
to the south,
At the back I open a gauze window to the north.
The oil seed flowers are bright yellow, the corn leaves lush green.
Even the ants have now formed pairs.
But I—young as I am—stay home alone.

In the fourth month, with silkworm breeding in full swing, I yearn
for a beloved.
The girls pick mulberry leaves to feed the worms.
I apply some fragrant oil, pencil my brows lightly, powder and paint
my face. . . .
Must I stay at home with my mother forever?
Mulberry leaves fall down. My heart shivers.

In the fifth month, when summer rains pour down, I yearn for a beloved.
I make my up face and do my hair.
In one hand I take an ivory comb, in the other my long, shining black
silken tresses.
I make a knot and coil it once, twice, three times, nine times,
in three braids, like a hollow, curling dragon.
On one side I attach a golden pin, on the other a silver one.
A golden pin and a silver pin have now been stuck into my hair.
Yet such attire does not bring me a beloved.

In the sixth month I yearn for a beloved till I cannot endure it much
longer.
I go out and look at the cocks in the farmyard.
My eyes stray toward the sky—they catch a pair of golden pheasants—
And turn toward the earth—they catch a pair of silver pheasants.
The worms, the ants, and all the other insects, male and female, have
now formed pairs.
But I—beautiful as I am—stay alone.

In the seventh month, when autumn arrives, I yearn for a beloved.
My room is cold and desolate.
In other people's homes women are addressed as mothers,
men as fathers,
But there is no one to address *me* in my own home.
I embrace the flowery cushion in my fragrant room.

In the eighth month, when the osmanthus tree inspires the eye, I yearn
for a beloved.
I hang a red lantern[16] in my room.
I attach it to the highest wall in front of the highest window on the
highest floor.
Passersby believe it spreads its light for anyone to see—actually it should
illuminate my beloved's path.

In the ninth month, when white frost covers the rice fields, I yearn
for a beloved.
I begin to see the truth about my dismal fate.
People in the streets may grow to be one hundred years old.
Which is exactly thirty-six thousand days to count. . . .

In the tenth month, when the days are getting shorter, the nights longer,
I yearn for a beloved.
In my room I prepare my bed.
In the first vigil of the night I feel numb, in the second vigil I feel drowsy,
In the third my eyelids are heavy with sleep, in the fourth vigil a golden
pheasant calls.
The fifth vigil arrives. Will I manage to get up in the clear early morning?
Will I stay in bed in the clear early morning?
In front I open a gauze window to the south, at the back I open a gauze
window to the north.
My eyes are drawn toward the young lads and suitors at the shores of
the Western Lake.
They outnumber the stars.
They are busy pulling carts, and sleep and work in turns.

In the eleventh month, when snowflakes bloom, white frost all around,
I yearn for a beloved.
I take off my embroidered shoes, drop them on the floor and go to bed.
In the first vigil I feel drowsy, in the third my eyelids are heavy with sleep,
In the fourth vigil a golden pheasant calls.
Then the fifth vigil arrives. Will I manage to get up in the clear early
morning?
In front I open a gauze window to the south, at the back I open a gauze
window to the north.
My eyes are drawn toward thick layers of white frost between the roof tiles.
Not even snow is piled so high.
Even in such weather I must live without a beloved!

---

16. "Red lantern" is not a connotation of prostitution; it may serve as a beacon for unexpected visitors.

In the twelfth month, when winter sweet is blossoming, I yearn
for a beloved.
Dear sister-in-law, listen to me, I have to tell you something.
Oh, dear, dear, sister-in-law,
The last three nights I covered myself with three thick blankets with a
stuffing of nine pounds at least.
But all night through I felt weak and chilled to the bone.

[THE SISTER-IN-LAW:]
The last three nights I covered myself with only a single lightly
stuffed blanket.
Yet I felt strong all night and even bathed in sweat.
Your brother is so hot—one could light a coal fire on his body!
How warm and comfortable to share cushion and blanket with him!

[THE GIRL:]
Mama, O Mama! Sooner or later everyone must die.
For me, life is no longer bearable.

[HER MOTHER:]
If you die today you'll have a golden coffin.
If you die tomorrow you'll have a silver coffin.
If you die the day after tomorrow you'll have a pinewood coffin with a
cypress lid,
Two golden trestles to support the coffin, four golden nails to close it off,
And seven Buddhist monks and eight Daoist masters who pray for
forty-nine days
From the *Book of Great Sorrow and Repentance*.[17]
For five miles around people will place red lanterns in the fields.[18]

[THE GIRL:]
If I die today I don't want your golden coffin.
If I die tomorrow I don't want your silver coffin.
I don't need your pinewood coffin with a cypress lid.
I don't need two golden trestles to support my coffin.
I don't need four golden nails to close it off.
I don't need seven Buddhist monks and eight Daoist masters who
pray for forty-nine days from the *Book of Great Sorrow and*
Repentance.

---

17. *Book of Great Sorrow and Repentance* (*Da bei chan*) is a tenth-century Buddhist ritual manual.

18. According to the singer, the placing of red lanterns in the fields to honor a deceased person was a traditional custom in the Yangtze River delta.

I only want a light coffin with a flimsy lid.
Young men—aged around twenty—from the wide surroundings should carry my coffin.
Let them take it to the crossroads.
Let them stop for a while on the Character Eight Bridge.
The coffin must be adorned with flowers on each side, a book on top, and at one end a bowl of water.
Let young men come to pick a flower and smell it.
Let scholars take up the book and read it. Let old people scoop some water and drink it.
Let everyone know that the daughter of Shen Wanshan[19] yearned for a lover from when she was thirteen
Until she died of longing at the age of eighteen.
O please let people send off invitations to arrange a marriage for their daughters in good time!
If that happens, no one will ever again be struck by such a terrible fate!

YEARNING FOR A BELOVED UNTIL DEATH FOLLOWS (FRAGMENT)

Sung by Yuan Xiaomei

This is the final stanza of the alternative version of "Yearning for a Beloved (Until Death Follows)," as sung by Yuan Xiaomei (b. 1922), a singer and farmer's wife in Taozhuang, in northern Zhejiang. This song was recorded on May 29, 1990. From the second line onward, the text is sung in the form of an improvised *jikou* (rapid mouth), with extra words inserted at high speed in the basic line structure. Melodically, the insertion of extra words and formulaic phrases is solved by repeating one or two key intervals in the melody ad lib until the end of the text is reached. The effect is close to (fast) recitation. The *jikou* technique is applied in mountain songs everywhere in the Wu area, particularly in the third line of a stanza.

In the twelfth moon, when no flowers bloom, I yearn for my beloved.
There is now only the white of my eyes, the black pupils are nearly lifeless.
It seems as if I cannot form a pair of happy mandarin ducks with Third Brother anymore.
I say all the time that I'll give up, but how can I give up?
I would so much like to say four, five, or six words to Third Brother to beg him for forgiveness.
If I die today, buy a golden coffin. If I die tomorrow, buy a silver coffin.

19. Shen Wanshan was a wealthy official who lived in the fourteenth century. He donated huge sums of money to the town of Nanjing for the construction of its city wall. His wealth stirred the popular imagination, and Shen's name turns up in numerous folk songs.

If I die the day after tomorrow, buy an ebony coffin with a single lid to close it off.
Attach the lid with twenty-four golden nails.
Mama says, "Girl, O girl, if you die you'll have a red-lacquered coffin with a black-lacquered lid,
Thirty-six large boats will carry it, twenty-four transport workers will bear the coffin on their shoulders.
Large steamed buns will be carried on people's shoulders in osier baskets.
Small steamed buns will be carried on people's shoulders in round baskets."
I don't want seventy-two white birds who come flying.
I only want the third son of Third Uncle's wife[20] to buy—in the east or in the west—a skin-thin coffin for three thousand copper coins.
I want to be laid in it from the upper side, I want it to split on the underside.
Four young men from our neighborhood should wear white kerchiefs
And walk in procession around the shores of the West Lake,
So that everyone knows that I, the girl who yearned for a beloved,
Was buried in a paltry coffin![21]

AT SUNSET, THE WESTERN MOUNTAINS GRADUALLY TURN YELLOW

Sung by Jin Wenyin

"At Sunset, the Western Mountains Gradually Turn Yellow" is another "waiting for the beloved" song, sung by Jin Wenyin, in Shengpu, Wuxian, and recorded on May 19, 1987. It was sung to a local mountain song tune, with *jikou* passages in the second and third verses.

At sunset the western mountains gradually turn yellow.
The girl carries water to heat a bath.
One scoop, two scoops, the bathing water turns warm and bubbles up.
She firmly presses the lid on the tub and waits for her beloved.

I am waiting for my beloved; I look out for my beloved.
I wait until it makes me restless.
With one hand I open the gauze window to the south on the front side, with the other I open the gauze window to the north on the back side.
In the street I see many boys and girls clad in red and green.
The only one I cannot detect is my dear beloved.

---

20. If a Wu song makes a reference to an old woman who is a silent onlooker, a "walk-on part" so to speak, she is often called Sanbo Popo (Third Uncle's wife), a formulaic device.

21. It may seem odd that the "paltry coffin" costs as much as three thousand copper coins, but no importance should be given to the actual figures used in the songs; figures are chosen for their sound, not for their value.

My beloved does not come. I remain on the lookout.
I carry the tub into my fragrant room.
O sweet love, if you come early enough I can share this bath with you.
If you come a little while later, I must throw the water away.

After bathing I decide to enjoy the cool evening air.
I take a small wooden bench outside to the southern yard.
People will think that I am just longing for the cool southern breeze.
Will anyone understand that—at this three-forked road—I'm waiting for my beloved?

IF YOU SING MOUNTAIN SONGS, YOU'LL FIND IT EASY TO COURT

Sung by Qian Afu

Qian Afu (b. 1909), formerly a baker and a shopkeeper, subsequently a pensioner in Dongting, Wuxian, was locally known as the Great King of Mountain Songs. "If You Sing Mountain Songs, You'll Find It Easy to Court" was recorded on April 17, 1990.

Qian Afu loved singing to the point of obsession. He could easily keep going for several hours. During interviews he sometimes shifted from speaking to singing in the middle of a sentence, digging up from his memory a text suitable for the situation. Qian was particularly fond of erotic songs, which he performed "to make people laugh." He referred to them as *cu* (rough) or *buhaoting* (not good for listening to), but he did not mind singing them. Indeed, young people in the audience sometimes encouraged him to sing such off-color songs.

If you sing mountain songs you'll find it easy to court.
If you want to buy meat, buy lean buttock's meat.
If you want to stroke breasts,
Stroke those of an eighteen-year-old maiden, young as a daylily.
If you want to kiss a girl, turn to red lips with shining teeth in a delicate white face.

UNTITLED

Sung by Qian Afu

This performance by Qian Afu was recorded on April 8, 1990. Rough language and obscene words are not necessarily avoided in the songs. But—not surprisingly, in view of severe censorship and violent retribution in the recent past—few people are inclined to sing them in front of a microphone. During intervals in recording sessions while people relaxed and there was no sense of a "performance" going on, singers might suddenly start singing improvised bawdy texts, which would often provoke laughter. Without hiding it, we kept one tape recorder running all the time and recorded a few such songs.

Here's a lad has an eight-hundred-pound prick,
His lassie—a cunt like a city gate.
Twenty-four generals hold a basket under her cunt, oh!
Out comes her son, a great commander he'll be!

RIPPLING WATER, CLEAR AND BRIGHT

Sung by Wu Alin

Wu Alin (b. 1932), a farmer in Huangdai, was recorded on May 7, 1990. Boats with two oars can be found in the Wu area, but they are not common.

Rippling water, clear and bright,
Rippling water, lovely sight.
Boats are admired if they have two oars.
Girls are admired if they have two lovers!

THE PEDDLER

Sung by Jiang Chunshan

"The Peddler" is a love song, sung to a *xiaodiao* tune by Jiang Chunshan (b. 1933), a farmer in Shuangdu, Rudongxian, in northern Jiangsu, and recorded on January 28, 1987.

[THE PEDDLER:]
It is now five, six years since I have left hearth and home.
All alone I traveled the seas,
I sailed the oceans, crossed the seas to sell my merchandise.
I traded everywhere.
Yiya, ye, yederyo a—traded everywhere—*oholei!*

When I came down to this place to sell my goods,
My eye fell on Second Daughter,[22]
Once again I've found a very special and attractive girl!
But it's not easy to bait this little fish . . .
Yiya, ye, yederyo a—not easy to bait this little fish—*ohoholei!*

I drink several bushels of wine on an empty stomach;
The wine goes to my head.

---

22. Children and other kin are sometimes numbered according to their age or order of birth and may be addressed in this way, also by strangers—for example, Second Daughter, Sixth Uncle Liu, and so on.

With a golden ear spoon[23] I pick my ears.
I am in love again—
Yiya, ye, yederyo a—in love again—*oholei!*

[THE GIRL:]
I put some fresh and fragrant powder on my face,
I pencil my eyebrows, cleanse my eyes,
I take some rouge to paint my lips,
My eyebrows are shaped like the character "eight"—
Yiya, ye, yederyo a—shaped like the character "eight"—*ohoholei!*

I put on short trousers and a red-collared jacket;
A sleeveless smock and a skirt complete the outfit.
My white complexion contrasts charmingly with the pleated fine
gauze skirt.
I arrange my hair, put some more powder on my face—
Yiya, ye, yederyo a—put more powder on my face—*ohoholei!*

My left hand holds a fan from Hangzhou and a multicolored shawl,
My right hand holds a graceful thin pipe,
I smoke a wad of love yearning's[24] tobacco—
Yiya, ye, yederyo a—love yearning's tobacco— *ohoholei!*

The little golden lotus feet, three inches high, are very small,
So small and lovely shaped!
With dark-red flowery shoes to cover them,
A silken ribbon on both sides—
Yiya, ye, yederyo a—my little socks are whiter than the clouds!—
ohoholei!

[THE PEDDLER:]
Where other people need two steps I need only one!
I walk up to her door and call three times, in a loud voice:
"It's the peddler here, the peddler! With gold and copper, all for sale!—
Yiya, ye, yederyo a—gold and copper, all for sale!—*ohoholei!*"

[THE GIRL:]
Where other people need two steps I need only one!
I run toward the courtyard,

---

23. Ear spoons (see also the sixth stanza) are tiny sticks with a spoon-shaped end used to clean one's ears. They are still used in China.

24. "Love yearning's" (*xiangsi*) tobacco is a dialect term for local tobacco sold in Ruyi, the area where this song was sung.

Open the door with shaky hands
To find out who is calling—
Yiya, ye, yederyo a—to find out who is calling!—*ohoholei!*

No sooner has the peddler spotted me than he begins to smile:
"Good day, dear girl, good day to you,
Would you buy my knickknacks? Trading suits me well!
Yiya, ye, yederyo a—trading suits me well!—*ohoholei!*"

I offer him a wooden stool and pray him to sit down.
I call the handmaid right away and ask her to bring tea.
Then, while drinking fragrant tea, we discuss his tricks of trade!
Yiya, ye, yederyo a—discuss his tricks of trade—*ohoholei!*

I ask the noble visitor his precious name,
And where he lives and thrives.
He says, "I live and thrive in Nanchangfu, in Jiangxi,
My name, forsooth, is Huang Yucheng—
Yiya, ye, yederyo a—my name is Huang Yucheng—*ohoholei!*

"Dear girl, please buy whatever you wish to buy,
There is no need to bargain—not with me!
Buy whatever pleases you, I have so much variety,
Pick out what you need.
Yiya, ye, yederyo a—pick out what you need—*ohoholei!*"

[THE GIRL:]
I purchase some red satin, one foot, six inches long,
A multicolored shawl, three inches of silk gauze with golden rim.
How many copper coins will you ask me for this?
Yiya, ye, yederyo a—how many copper coins?—*ohoholei!*

[THE PEDDLER:]
You purchase some red satin, one foot, six inches long,
A multicolored shawl, three inches of silk gauze with golden rim.
But I am so fond of you that I don't need your coins.
Yiya, ye, yederyo a—I don't need your coins—*ohoholei!*

[THE GIRL:]
Well, now, why did you come here with your peddler's pack?
One would have thought: to bargain and to trade!
But you try to court me in broad daylight—under the brightest sky!
What's this supposed to mean?
Yiya, ye, yederyo a—you deserve a beating!—*ohoholei!*

No sooner has the peddler heard this than he begins to feel regret.
On both his knees he kneels, down on the dusty floor,
And offers his apologies:
"Next time I will behave myself!
Yiya, ye, yederyo a—I will behave myself—*ohoholei!*"

THE LITTLE CAT

Sung by Li Yunlong

"The Little Cat" is a love song from the male perspective. Sung by Li Yunlong (b. 1929), a farmer and cultural worker in Dasheng, Liuhexian, in northern Jiangsu, it was recorded on May 26, 1987. The song was sung to a *xiaodiao* tune with percussion accompaniment of chopsticks and saucer.

Ah, if only I could be a pair of chopsticks
—In your cherry mouth, dear girl.
If only I could be a silken belt
—Round your slender waist, dear lass.

If only I could be a pair of red-embroidered shoes
—On your lovely feet, dear little girl.
If only I could be a *pipa*. No, a moon lute![25] No, a *pipa*!
—In your caring arms, my little lass.
Ah, if only I could be a snow-white, snow-bright little cat.
—Turning round and round your feet, round your lovely little feet,
dear girl!
Miaow, miaow!
I'd like to jump on you! Ah, dear lassie, ah, here comes your little fellow!

HE GOES EAST, SHE GOES WEST

Sung by Zhao Yongming and Jiang Liansheng

A love song from Wujiang county, "He Goes East, She Goes West" was sung by Zhao Yongming (stanzas 1–5), of Luxu, and recorded on February 23, 1989, and by Jiang Liansheng (stanza 6), of Xinzhuang, Shenta, Wujiangxian, and recorded on December 18, 1988. This song shows that young women in Jiangsu are not always as "subservient" and "shy" as they are portrayed in traditional views. The underdog position of women in traditional China is amply documented, but it does not mean that women are or were always shy and unobtrusive in their behavior. This is also clear from the

25. The *pipa* and moon lute are plucked string instruments.

erotic songs that we collected from female singers. Admittedly, this particular text was sung by men. Zhao Yongming sang it to his favorite mountain song tune, and Jiang Liangsheng sang it to a *xiaodiao* tune that he referred to as "Loumengdiao."

He goes east, she goes west.
This complete stranger smiles at me. *Giggle, giggle!*
This girl says, "Dear boy, why laugh at me—do we know each other?"
He says, "Hidden in your crimson pants you've got a lovely little thing, that's why!"

"Dear boy, don't babble, don't talk gibberish," she says.
"Underneath these crimson pants I wear a pair of knickers.
And on top a pleated silken skirt.[26]
What makes you think that hidden in my crimson pants I've got a lovely little thing?"

"Beg your pardon! I don't babble, I don't talk gibberish!
I happened to pass your southern gauze window—I passed it two, three times.
I saw you take off your pleated silken skirt, fold it neatly, put it on a hanger.
With my own eyes I saw you pull down these crimson pants, and change knickers!"

"A foolish fellow, that's what you are, a really foolish bum!
Why didn't you push open that window and leap into my room?
How foolish not to sail with a favorable wind.
How foolish not to pick a lovely flower when you see one."

"*Aiya*, you say I'm foolish, but I'm not.
I'd have loved to push that window open and leap into your room,
But I was afraid to cause a fire in One Man's Village; nobody there to save me!
What if people had barred the door? What if you had screamed?"

The girl says, "Love, sweet love, a stupid fellow, that's what you are, a really stupid bum!
Why didn't you push open that window and get in?
If there's a fire in One Man's Village, very well then, put it out!
If people bar the door, there is always me to open it for you again!"

26. "Pleated silken skirt" is a free translation of *bafutou luoqun*, an eight-part silk-gauze skirt, presumably of eight strips of cloth sewn together.

A LITTLE STREAM SEPARATES ME FROM MY LASS

Sung by Jiang Liansheng

This performance of "A Little Stream Separates Me from My Lass" by Jiang Liansheng was recorded in Xinzhuang, Shenta, Wujiangxian, on December 18, 1988.

A little stream separates me from my lass.
Groping in the dark I run along the stream, in the second vigil
or the third.
I reach the home of my beloved; that dog will bark.
I drop into my lassie's room; that cock will crow.
"That's how it is—the dog will bark, the cock will crow," she says.
"Tomorrow at dawn, little cock, let me slaughter you!
I'll tear your tendons out and flay your skin!
And may your skin serve as a drumhead ready for beating!
May your tendons serve as horse reins!"

The little cock answers the pretty girl:
"It was not my aim to harm you, intimate pair, close like mandarin
ducks!
But this is how it is: in heaven the golden pheasant cries before the fifth
vigil ends.
Down here the little cock crows before the sixth vigil starts."

The girl says, "Dear little cock,
In the morning I'll bring you sweet brown sugar and mix it with rice.
Let me warm and wash it for you in a golden bowl, then rinse it
in a silver bowl.
At dawn when I open the southern gauze window
You'll be sitting on your lark's throne, tucking into
Sweet rice, preening your feathers!"

The little cock answers the pretty girl:
"Listen, I'm just barndoor fowl. How can I tuck into sweet
brown sugar?
But if you go to yonder courtyard—I mean Third Uncle's wife's
third daughter's place—and get hold
Of their ripe little hen to court with me, sweet little cock,
I'll promise not to crow in the fifth vigil—I'll keep it up
until the sixth."[27]

---

27. The night is divided into five vigils. The "sixth" vigil may be a joke, suggesting that the cock will not crow at all.

THE GIRL LIU (FRAGMENT)

Sung by Han Deru

"The Girl Liu" is an erotic song, sung by Han Deru (b. 1939), a farmer in Shuangdu, Rudongxian, in northern Jiangsu, and recorded on January 29, 1987. It was performed in a half-whispering voice and was broken off by the singer ("I won't sing the rest of it") when he arrived at a metaphorical description of sexual intercourse.

Hey, dear girl Liu. Don't hide behind your fan!
You ask me to come early, you ask me to come late!
I don't know where you live.
Hey, laddie, hey!

Hey, dear girl Liu. I live near Erdajie.
Near the high village bridge.
Hey, laddie, hey!

The black lacquered gate of my home faces the south.
In front of it you'll find three roads.
Run along the curved road in the middle.
Run to me quickly!
Hey, laddie, hey!

Hey, dear girl Liu! There's a garden wall in front of the gate.
There's a tree near the garden wall.
I climb into the branches and across the wall.
Hey, laddie, hey!

If there's someone at home,
Go to the main room and sit down for a while.
If there's no one at home,
Please come to my bedroom.
Hey, laddie, hey!

There's a washing bowl on my footstool,
To wash my feet.
Hey, dear girl Liu!
There are men's boots on my footstool.
Hey, laddie, hey!

You'll find a foot towel hanging near my bed.
Hey, dear girl Liu!
Small feet—rub, rub!

I put them on the bed.
Hey, laddie, hey!

Hey, dear girl Liu,
Don't point your little feet toward me, come over here!
Hey, laddie, hey!
I eat of the forbidden rice. Laddie, hey!

The pied eagle catches a rabbit, hey, laddie, hey!
And jumps down on it. Hey, laddie, hey!

A wooden bench is toppled, legs pointing upward. Hey, laddie, hey!
Entwined like willow branches, hands interlaced. Laddie, hey!

A hen drinks water, turns its little head toward the sky,
Hey, laddie, hey!

PLAYING CARDS AT NIGHT (FRAGMENT)

Sung by Han Deru

A song referring to prostitution, "Playing Cards at Night" was sung by Han Deru, of Shuangdu, Rudongxian, in northern Jiangsu, and recorded on January 29, 1987. The text is unfinished.

Old papa of eighty years is out for pleasure.
He offers two hundred taels[28] in cash.
Well, not for me, I can't agree! *Ai ye hei zi yo,* he's an old bum!
A callow youth of fifteen years is out for pleasure.
He offers two hundred taels in cash.
Well, not for me, I won't agree!
Ai ya hei zi yo, he's just a babe!
A lover of seventeen, eighteen years is out for pleasure.
He offers one copper coin only! Well, not for me, I can't agree!
Ai ya hei zi yo, he can come with me for free!

28. The tael was an ancient Chinese silver coin and, during the Taiping period, a golden coin. Its value fluctuated with the price of the metal.

THE GIRL'S BREASTS ARE WHITE AND FRESH LIKE MILK (FRAGMENT)

Sung by Jin Wenyin

"The Girl's Breasts Are White and Fresh Like Milk," another song about prostitution, was sung by Jin Wenyin, in Shengpu, Wuxian, and recorded on January 9, 1990. The text is unfinished.

The girl's breasts are white and fresh like milk.
A newly opened wineshop attracts no customers.
Old papa of eighty flings money on the counter, but I won't open the
  wine jar for him.
I often give young men a drink on credit.
Aiya, old papa's rage flares up skyhigh!
He smashes his jug to pieces against the wine jar.
"As a young man I was often allowed to drink excellent wine without
  paying for it.
Oh, how true: an old man is like a discolored pearl—no longer
  worth a penny!"

BREAKING UP

Sung by Zhu Hairong

The song "Breaking Up" was sung by Zhu Hairong (b. 1930), a cultural worker in Wuxi, and recorded on May 17, 1987. Songs that appeal to virtue and fidelity are less popular than songs about such themes as adultery and forbidden relationships, but some examples exist. Obviously a call for fidelity may also refer to a forbidden love relationship—that is, a liaison not accepted by the lovers' parents.

If people tie me with a hemp rope, with a metal chain.
Then ask me: Will I break up my bond of love?
I will tell them: You can block the road, break the bridge, block the river.
Break my arms, break my legs. I'll never break up my bond of love!

IF YOU DON'T WALK THE PATH OF TRUE LOVE, YOU WILL LOSE YOUR BELOVED

Sung by Zhao Yongming

This was sung by Zhao Yongming, of Luxu, and recorded on February 22, 1989.

If you don't sing mountain songs, you'll forget a lot.
If you don't walk on that main road, the withered grass will coil everywhere.
If you don't use that sharp steel knife, it will rust.
If you don't walk the path of true love, you will lose your beloved.

CURSING SONG (FRAGMENT)

Sung by Wu Alin

This performance by Wu Alin was recorded on May 7, 1990. Cursing songs were a favorite genre among young boys herding cattle. Basically they could be sung by anyone who needed to air his mind or who sought to provoke his environment. The contents are free but are usually dominated by references to excrement, saliva, pus, blood, dirt, or sex organs. Traditionally, these songs were often heard in the context of quarrels—playful or half serious—between mountain singers, as in the following fragment.

If I'm singing mountain songs, don't interfere!
If you're going to squeeze in your own songs, may your entrails rot.
Yes, let them rot, rot, your guts, your heart, and lungs and all!
Till nothing's left—except your two rotten persimmon legs!
If you sing a mountain song—if you can get it out of your throat, that is—
I will sing one to pit against yours!
Go on then, sing dialogues until blood and pus seep between your teeth.
Ha, with tousled hair and bare feet in your coffin you'll go!

ON A WORN-OUT GREASY CARRYING POLE

Sung by Ren Mei

"On a Worn-Out Greasy Carrying Pole" was sung by Ren Mei (b. 1928) in Wuxi and recorded on January 31, 1989. Not all "vulgar songs" that circulate in southern Jiangsu are necessarily rude or distasteful. Metaphors may be chosen carefully and with humor, as in this fishermen's song. It was one of many fishermen's songs that Ren Mei, a cultural worker, collected in the Lake Tai area from the 1950s onward.

On a worn-out greasy carrying pole,
I take my load of tortoises to Hangzhou.
Tortoises, big and small—I sell them all but one.
No way to get rid of this shoddy beast of mine![29]
Ah well, let me sing a few songs with it.

LET US PLAYFULLY SING MOUNTAIN SONGS TO ASK A QUESTION

Sung by Zhao Yongming

The riddle song "Let Us Playfully Sing Mountain Songs to Ask a Question" was sung by Zhao Yongming to a local mountain song tune, recorded in Luxu on May 17, 1990. Traditionally, riddle songs were often sung in dialogue form, with two singers or two groups of singers competing with each other. The dialogue form is normally referred to as *duige*. The singer's comment to this particular text was "Haha, one has to be clever to think of such a funny reply! How can any person possibly know what a tree weighs? Or how many leaves or roots it has?"

Let me sing a mountain song and ask you a question. How many pounds does the poplar in Third Uncle's wife's courtyard weigh? How many branches does it have? How many leaves? How many stems? How many roots?

Let me sing a mountain song and give you an answer. The poplar in Third Uncle's wife's courtyard weighs three hundred pounds. Except for branches, it's all leaves. Except for stems, it's all roots.

FOURTH BROTHER AND FIFTH SISTER

Sung by Zhu Hairong

"Fourth Brother and Fifth Sister" was performed by Zhu Hairong, who learned it from Qian Afu, a singer in Dongting village, east of Wuxi. It was recorded in Wuxi on May 17, 1987.

The limited number of syllables in the Chinese language offers many opportunities for puns and for semantic ambiguity. Folk songs are full of puns, and Wu songs are no exception. Homonyms have a particularly prominent role in love songs, where there is a constant need for veiled expressions and hidden messages, but they can also feature as wordplay for its own sake, as in this example.

---

29. A tortoise is often used in China as a metaphor for penis, which is what the "shoddy beast" refers to.

If you want to sing mountain songs, I can sing poems in return.
If you sing mountain songs, a smile will appear on Fourth Brother's face.
If I sing Wu songs in turn, the heart of my love will be moved.

An alternative reading of the same text is

If you want to sing three songs, I can sing four songs in return.
Your three songs will evoke a smile on Fourth Brother's face.
My five songs will move the heart of Fifth Sister.

Or, in place of the last two lines:

If you, Third Brother, sing, a smile will appear on Fourth Brother's face.
If I, Fifth Brother, sing, the heart of Fifth Sister will be moved.

SALTWATER SONGS OF HONG KONG

Translated and introduced by E. N. Anderson

In much of eastern Asia, groups of people dwell on boats and make their living from the sea and rivers. They usually share the culture and language of their shore-resident neighbors, but they frequently have their own cultural peculiarities. In Hong Kong and throughout Guangdong province, thousands of Cantonese-speaking boat people maintain a distinctive variant of Cantonese culture. Their lifestyle may date back more than two thousand years, before the Han dynasty (206 B.C.E.–220 C.E.), and some consider them descendants of non-Han peoples. However, if their origin is non-Han, they have forgotten it by now, and most families can trace their descent to ordinary land-dwelling Cantonese who took to the water for reasons of safety or economic opportunity. One of the most unusual features of this waterfront world is the folk song tradition. "Saltwater songs" (Cantonese, *haam seui ko*) are perhaps the best known of the songs peculiar to those who call themselves "the people on the water" (*seui seung yan*).

"Salty" has the same double meaning in Cantonese as in English, and many of the saltwater songs are indeed salacious. Others, especially wedding songs, are more presentable in polite society. Almost all the songs involve double meanings, graphic puns, obscure local references, or other unusual rhetorical devices. Many involve extended references to fish, shellfish, flowers, fruits, birds, and other aspects of the natural environment. Some are known to be centuries old, and certain singers, including some who are illiterate, can chant classical Chinese poems as well as their own folk songs.

Today, saltwater songs are a thing of the past in modern ports such as Hong Kong. Radio and television have had much to do with their decline, but even more important have been social and economic changes. No longer isolated, impoverished, and subjected to prejudice and oppression, the boat people have merged into mainstream Cantonese society, and the contexts for their traditional singing are few.

Saltwater songs were, above all, courting songs. Often, a boy and a girl would exchange lines, in the antiphonal manner so typical of southern China and Southeast Asia. One of the couple would sing two to four lines, or a whole song, and the other would respond. In the floating "flower boats," professional singing girls would sing to entertain clients, who might or might not sing responses. These songs were of the more "salty" sort. At the other end of the social scale were the highly stylized and "proper" songs sung at weddings. Saltwater songs were also sung at feasts or even at ordinary dinners. Individuals alone on the water might sing them in solitary, meditative moods. Often, late at night, when lights were out and other sounds stilled, the song of a lone fisherman or boat girl would float over the harbor under the stars.

Both of the courting songs that follow were sung by accomplished singers and recorded in late 1965.[30] Both were young fishermen and boatmen of Castle Peak Bay and Tai O, in the western New Territories of Hong Kong.

Sung by Cheung Fuk-luk

In this song, the man apologizes for his poverty. The young woman might sing in reply that she does not mind poverty—or she might sing a refusal.

Because I have no money I'll float away:
The penniless man must be always wandering.
Having no money, I work through the watches of the night;
Yes, through the watches of the night, because I am poor.
Corn has so many strands of silk—hard to see its face.

The Buddha statue has a mouth—hard for it to speak.
It's an ancient way: the poor man bears the wind and sun.
I'm too poor to allow us to come together.
My hat full of holes—I take it and put it on;
My clothes, dirt and rags—I must make do with them.
With a cross and a hook, a stroke on the left side, you can write out
"money."
If many men helped me, I'd get wealth and property.
Yesterday I found a friend, we talked together—
A thousand gold pieces can hardly buy a companion in the boat.

Sung by Fung Sam-tsau

This courtship exchange has numerous sexual and other double entendres. Pinching an abacus is a sign of money-grubbing. The great waves are the waves of passion. The dragon boats of the penultimate line are symbolic of the many suitors vying for the girl's attention

HE:
Once more I ask, tender lady, will you go with me?
When you're ready to go, row the boat here.
A new abacus, yet you pinch the wood.
You're a sweet girl, but that's no way to reckon.

---

30. E. N. Anderson offers his thanks to the singers; to Chau Hung-Fai, Choi Kwok-Tai, and Marja L. Anderson for field help; and to the National Institute of Mental Health for funding.

SHE:

Go up the bay, buy a carp, come back down and steam it—
Even with bean paste and soy sauce,
Even with money, I won't love you.

HE:

The dried-up oyster opens, wide as Tai O channel;
If you want to "fire the gun," row your boat here.

SHE:

Yes, step up and "cut flowers," the boy on the left,
But if you're broke, you'll lie alone.

HE:

I start out to fish, but great waves strike the boat.
It's nearly sinking! People grab the rail.
I buy a bowl of chicken soup, give it to her with rice,
As long as I live I will never forget, constant as the North Star.
The moon darkens, sounds fall still, night covers all.
The Sky God says, "Open": through the dark clouds we see the sky.
Row with the sweep, pull the hand lines.
No good working too hard.
The dragon boats are all fast;
We will soon know who loses and who wins.

SONGS OF THE MINDONG SHE PEOPLE

Collected and translated by Charles Ettner

Mindong, a highly mountainous area in northeastern Fujian province, is home to a people officially known in China as the She ethnic group. The She people are skilled at farming the mountainsides, hunting the forests, and fishing the streams, rivers, and coastal areas. However, the She are most renowned for their unique singing skills.

She singing practices engage a multitude of situations, occasions, and purposes. Singing is always performed in the She native language, and both men and women sing in a very high falsetto voice. Songs can be of fixed words ranging from a single four-line verse to more than a hundred verses, or they can be impromptu compositions of any length. Most She songs are sung between a man and a woman of approximately the same age. Others are sung purely solo. Add to this a plethora of song types and singing rules, and it becomes easy to understand why mastering She singing takes years to accomplish.

The following selections survey but a glimpse of the variation, character, and rich content common to She singing culture.

The first two songs typify the work song category. These are songs about typical She labor and provide either methodological information or moral guidance related to the task.

CARRYING FISH GOODS ON A SHOULDER POLE

MAN:
One basket of fish, one of eel.
Carrying fish, often a young girl will tag along.
She asks me how I sell the fish.
I ask a high price and expect a counteroffer.

WOMAN:
I was thinking of buying several fish.
You ask a high price to overcharge me.
Hearing that I turn and walk away.
I don't even want to look at your fish.

MAN:
Seeing you walk away in distrust.
I hasten to ask you not to be angry.
If you want to buy, don't speak of the money.
I will sell to you at any price.

WOMAN:
Carrying fish, often a young girl will tag along.
I urge you don't be a slippery eel.
People like an honest businessman.
To be well liked is more valued than money.

FIELD SONG

WOMAN:
The dike held no water so I came to fix it.
Banks and gates repaired, water flows to the terrace top.
The terrace filled with water makes the rice plants strong.
Next year the harvest will be good.

MAN:
I worked the fields and shared your dam.
Water flows from the dikes you repaired.
When the top terrace has water, the lowest one will too.
Winter harvest will come thanks to you.

WOMAN:
I plant the field with plenty of water.
This field will not need much work.
Your field once again floods full of water.
You'll have two crop harvests this year.

MAN:
Midsummer sun releases the energy.
But it's hard to plow the whole field level.
I plant a field and the water is hot.
You plant a mountain terrace and the water is cool again.

WOMAN:
Planting in cold water is not good.
Cold water is not good for young plants.
A ten-bunch harvest won't equal one handful.
A whole field's harvest won't fill one shoulder basket.

MAN:
Abandon the barren field and go plant the hillsides.
Growing sweet potatoes beats farming barren land.
A ten-bunch harvest won't equal one handful.
But just one sweet potato weighs two and a half pounds.

MATCHMAKING THROUGH SINGING

When celebrating the construction of a new house, an elder's sixtieth birthday, or other family events, relatives or friends coming from afar are treated to a good meal and drink prior to an evening of competitive singing. Most of the songs are impromptu compositions, save for the beginning and possibly the closing songs. A singer from the host family, opposite in sex from that of the guest, begins with a "special event guest song," as in the song that follows. Note that such songs are somewhat teasing in nature and connote a spirit of challenge or competition. Many She songs also draw on historical facts, persons, philosophies, and beliefs in imparting their message. As to the singing and drinking, however, that does continue to alternate throughout the course of the evening.

MAN:
A large camphor tree stands in the front.
I'm so happy to be at the table drinking.
Haven't considered if the wine is good or not.
Haven't worried about if you sing well or not.

WOMAN:
Drink, but no more than the famed Lü Dongbin.
Sing, but not better than a professional singer.
Be an official, but not better than Bao Aizhong.
By day, he judged on earth; by night, in hell.

MAN:
Talking and talking until I am drunk.
If I get too drunk, it will be unfortunate.
If I get too drunk, I cannot think straight.
Still I will sing, and you must answer.

WOMAN:
The words "wine and sex" together enchant you.
Thus aroused you become but a whore hound.
I will offer to you three pieces of advice.
Be not a whore hound, a drunkard, or promiscuous.

MAN:
Such worldly things surely someone will do.
No need for you to labor over such worries.
There are those your age who are beggars.
And others your age who are rich men's wives.

WOMAN:
We will be friends just as buds will be flowers.
In spring the whole mountain will bloom.
Taro can be harvested three times in one year.
Without passing three lives you can't find your mate.

MAN:
The long-tailed oriole comes to sing.
To the base of the tree it descends to cool down.
Money and food can save people's lives.
Our friendship will return, but it may not redeem me.

WOMAN:
Sitting at the table you love to chug wine.
I look at you, an inexperienced man losing face.
You've not considered if the wine is good or not.
How could you even tell if I sing well or not?

MAN:
Now I will sing and you should reply to me.
To and fro we will sing to each other.
You sing many songs and I will sing many songs.
Mounting them up to a mountainous pile.

WOMAN:
Go ahead and start singing and I will reply.
To and fro I will sing as you sing.
You stitch and I will sew.
Together the two will complement each other.

SONG WHEN MEETING SOMEONE ON THE ROAD

When two or more young people of the opposite sex meet on the road or on a mountain path, they are left to their own devices to facilitate introductions. At such times, they may resort to what they call "blocking the road songs" or "blocking the path songs." The man initiates the singing exchange, and the woman is, by custom, required to reply. There are no introductory songs, but the process involves, first, exchanging greetings; second, praising the opportunity to get to know each other; third, testing each other's singing ability; and, finally, singing whatever other songs and kinds of songs they may choose. The woman may choose to politely sing a few songs and then be on her way, or to fully engage the singing event––particularly if neither individual is married. If, however, they choose to sing but one of them has not the time, he or she will sing the reason why and arrange with the other to meet and sing again at another time. At any point, the singers may invite each other to come to their village to sing.

MAN:
Off in the distance I saw someone.
A bamboo hat obscured the person's face.
As we grew nearer, we glanced at each other.
She was a beautiful young girl.
Total strangers and hesitant to speak.
I dare not stare too closely.
A bird won't enter an unfamiliar cage.
Only when familiar will the bird then enter.

WOMAN:
Your white face is so handsome.
I'd like to ask you which village you are from.
I know not where you live.
Total strangers, I am hesitant to ask such questions.

MAN:
You want to ask which village I am from.
You wouldn't even know the place.
Which area is it then that I come from?
Every place that I go is my village.
So, you ask to know the name of my village.
I will tell you the answer truly.
From Yinan, walk on eight *li* up the road.
The name of the village is Bai-lu-keng.

AN APRON AND A RED FLOWER PRESENT

Each special aspect of ceremonious events, such as marriage, has complementing songs that describe, inform, and often serve to aid the participants in negotiating the circumstances. Equally so, the form of the singing sometimes varies according to the situation, such as the crying or wailing form of singing that is used in "An Apron and a Red Flower Present."

Chagang is a hillside She village in the Shuimen district of northern Xiapu county. According to local custom, on the day before a wedding, the bride's parents present her with certain gifts: the father gives his daughter a new apron; the mother gives her a red flower. As the parents send their daughter off to the home of her future husband to be married, the three of them exchange words of farewell in song.

FATHER:
A new apron, that and my daughter will be to another, dear Daughter!

DAUGHTER:
You raised me, but I did nothing for you.
I received so much, but returned nothing, dear Father!

MOTHER:
The flower will wilt in time.
Now is your time for blooming, dear Daughter!

DAUGHTER:
A son would have brought you fame;
his marriage would have benefited you both, dear Mother!

AUNTIE CHATS WITH THE SEDAN CHAIR PORTERS

"Auntie Chats with the Sedan Chair Porters" depicts a verbal joust between the maternal aunt accompanying the bride on her trip to the groom's house to be married and the carriage porters, hired by the groom's family. The song's interplay illustrates the aunt's taking charge of representing the bride and her family and then challenging the character and worthiness of the groom and his family—who are, in turn, represented by the porters (and who are likely to be the groom's family's friends and relatives).

AUNTIE:
You porters aren't doing a very good job.
Four men carry the red sedan chair.
The front man complains every step.
The back man keeps asking to slow down.

PORTER:
Four of us shoulder the carriage.
The red sedan chair is moving along the road.
We must communicate as we go up and down.
Tell the maiden to sit securely.

AUNTIE:
The groom's family is not poor.
Yet they offered a chicken of less than a pound.
That chicken was but half a pound.
Feathers and all, it could not feed you well.

PORTER:
The groom's family is not poor.
The chicken they fed us was over four pounds.
Many thanks for the meal we ate.
You're upset because you got to eat nothing.

FOREVER BY YOUR SIDE

She songs about love are many in both number and kind. They speak to a wide range of emotions and circumstances. The following two songs provide but a partial display of the spectrum encompassing She love songs. The mutual love of two people is the theme of "Forever by Your Side."

MAN:
The knife pulled from the scabbard shines brightly.
To the Fuzhou execution arena I would dare to go.
They could cut off my head, but they can't cut away my heart.
Even after you die I will miss you.

WOMAN:
You pull out your knife and the sun darkens.
But you dare not roll onto the officials' impaling board.
Dearest, you do not fear death.
But if you die, who will give account for your sorrow?

MAN:
Burn a willow tree in a pit alongside the dike.
Burn it this year and next year it will grow again.
As long as water continues to flow to that pit,
In spring the flowers will be as full again as before.
Burn a willow tree in a pit aside the creek.
The wind will sway the black and yellow leaves to and fro.
Dearest, today you are gone with the wind.
I do not know on what day you will return.

WOMAN:
Willow trees sway in the wind aside the creek.
The wind blows its leaves across the water's surface.
I am just like the water that is flowing.
Forever and ever by your side.
A handkerchief with two sides of affection.

I give to you to keep by your side.
Up the mountain and down it will accompany you.
Day and night never leaving you.
A handkerchief with two sides of affection.
At the center of the handkerchief is my heart.
When you wash, our two faces will meet.
When you hold it close, our hearts will touch.
All the mountain toads will bellow.
In the afternoon they will creep up to see you.
Unfortunately, I meet up with your father.
Right away I said I'd come to lend you a waterwheel.

MAN:
Water sprung up from under the rocks is cold.
While on the tree, the flower is fragrant.
You were born a mountain beauty.
Dearest, you sing like a phoenix.
I sit and listen to you sing.
Then I feel like I could fly.

WOMAN:
Water sprung up from under the rocks is cold.
The wild tiger's roar is loud.
You were born truly handsome.
Your words are like honey.
I stop and listen to you speak.
Even listening for one hundred years is not enough.

MAN:
The crescent moon is in the heavens.
My heart is like a bow.
A good archer is needed to pull a good bow.
The greater the strength, the greater it will be drawn.

WOMAN:
The crescent moon is in the heavens.
My heart is like an arrow.
Only a full-drawn bow matches a true and balanced arrow.
No one uses an arrow to pull the string.

HARD TO MARRY A PLAIN-LOOKING GIRL

The She people's songs express quite openly the realities of life, both good and bad. Even in love songs, it becomes clear that not all marriage arrangements are necessarily made in heaven. The notion of a person's fate and, once again, certain beliefs and philosophies that the She people embrace are together manifest in "Hard to Marry a Plain-Looking Girl."

MAN:
It's hard to grow chives in a clay soil garden.
Hard to harvest crops without a sharp sickle.
It's hard to grow rice in an unfertile field.
Hard for me to marry a plain-looking girl.

WOMAN:
Inside your fence no pretty flowers will grow.
Like pouring water onto seeds you plant under rocks.
You're perplexed about marrying a plain-looking girl.
It was all prearranged in your previous life.

A GRANDCHILD WILL BE BORN IN THE FUTURE SOON ENOUGH

The song "A Grandchild Will Be Born in the Future Soon Enough" is one of many that address life in general and the life concerns that the She people attend to, worry about, or feel are important to consider. The singing interplay is among family members displaying a father-in-law's hopes of having grandchildren early, the daughter-in-law's straightforward reasoning for why she has not had children, and the mother-in-law's practical and mediating insights into the whole dilemma.

FATHER-IN-LAW:
A palm-fiber cradle in front of my son's house.
Month after month, year after year it is empty.
Others my age hold grandchildren in their arms.
But there is still no grandchild for me to see.

DAUGHTER-IN-LAW:
A plot of land in front of my house.
Month after month, year after year no cow tills the field.
The field plow can extend only less than three inches deep.
How then can I give birth to a child?

MOTHER-IN-LAW:
This is not the cause; don't speak of this matter.
Don't listen to the old man's muttering either.
My son is still but a very young man.
A grandchild will be born in the future soon enough.

MOUNTAIN SONGS FROM LIUZHOU, GUANGXI (INTERETHNIC)

Collected, translated, and introduced by Mark Bender

The gentle waters of the Liu River half encircle the small city of Liuzhou, an ancient urban center located in the Guangxi Zhuang Autonomous Region, in south-central China. At the annual Midautumn Festival, held in late August or early September, families from the city and nearby rural areas visit Carp Peak (Yu Feng Shan), one of the many fantastically shaped limestone hills that tower on every horizon.

Carp Peak, located in a public park on the banks of the Liu River, is associated with Third Sister Liu (Liu Sanjie), a legendary song goddess said to have lived at the time of the Tang dynasty (618–907). The earliest records concerning her date to the Southern Song dynasty (1127–1279). Numerous written and oral accounts from all over southern China credit Third Sister Liu with introducing the custom of the song festival (*gexu*). Versions from the Liuzhou area relate the way in which she cleverly defeated the representatives of an evil local landlord in a protracted song duel and was soon after murdered. In her memory, the local people placed an offering of two carp beside her grave near the banks of the Liu River. That night, Third Sister Liu suddenly arose from the dead. Mounting one of the carp, she rode it up to the sky. The other fish flipped up on its tail and became Carp Peak.

The general style of singing attributed to Third Sister Liu is common to ethnic groups in many parts of China. In this form of antiphonal singing, two or more singers (often pairs singing against pairs) "talk" to each other in songs, usually in the form of a contest to see which singer or singers can outsing the other side. The Mandarin term for this style of performance is *duige* (antiphonal songs). The most popular songs sung in this fashion in Guangxi are known as *shan'ge* (mountain songs) or *Liu Sanjie ge* (Third Sister Liu songs). Sometimes they are also known as *Guangxi qing'ge* (Guangxi love songs).[31]

In the Liuzhou area, some people who sing mountain songs are of the Han ethnic group, and many are Zhuang. The Zhuang are China's largest ethnic minority group and number around 18 million. The Zhuang language is in the Tai branch of the Sino-Tibetan language family. Due to centuries of interaction, the Zhuang and Han of the Liuzhou area share many cultural traits, including similar styles of clothing and architecture, foodways, and agricultural practices (centering on wet rice cultivation). Most of the songs performed at Carp Hill are sung in local dialects of southwestern Mandarin, though Zhuang is used by some singers.[32]

---

31. Zhong Jingwen, "Liu Sanjie chuanshuo shilun" [Discussion of the Third Sister Liu Legend], in *Zhong Jingwen minjian wenxue lunwen ji* [*Zhong Jingwen's Collected Works on Folk Literature*] (Shanghai: Shanghai wenyi chubanshe, 1982), 93–120.

32. I was accompanied to Liuzhou by Tang Xiaojie and Sun Jingyao, of Guangxi University,

Most mountain songs deal with courtship and love. In some places, though customs vary widely, young Zhuang people still find their spouses by singing. In the evenings, teenage girls gather beside a stream or beneath a large tree near their village to spend hours singing antiphonal love songs with groups of teenage boys from neighboring villages. Among the Zhuang, Miao, Dong (Gaem), Molao, and some other minority groups in Guangxi and nearby provinces, large song festivals may be held several times throughout the year, attracting hundreds or thousands of people, many of whom are young and in search of potential spouses. At Carp Peak, however, most of the singers are middle-aged or older and are already married. For them, singing is a recreational activity. In general, fewer young people are involved in the singing of love songs than in the past due to the forces of modernization and popular culture.

Singers often perform at Carp Peak in pairs. Sitting on the rocks, they may whisper for a few moments about what they wish to say and then sing together in duet (though one singer may be the lead). Very soon, they are joined by a pair of singers of the opposite sex who sing back an answer. The two pairs of singers sit or squat several feet apart and begin to trade songs back and forth in earnest. What results is a sort of lyrical jazz composition that may last for an hour or longer.

Singers draw on a huge stock of traditional lines and motifs that they have heard since childhood or possibly learned from printed song collections. No two song exchanges are ever the same, though in general the pattern is similar to the exchanges of love songs by young people in the villages and includes expressions of initial interest, declarations of love, promises of future meetings, or the decision to never meet again. The tone is lighthearted, and the songs are full of wit, humor, and occasional satire. In some instances, singers may quiz each other with *pan'ge* (riddle songs), such as "What sort of fruit has a comb inside?" to which the answer is "The pomelo has combs inside." (The crescent-shaped fruit segments look like the traditional wooden combs.)

Familiarity with the lyrical tradition and the ability to improvise within it, as well as quality of voice, are all clues to a singer's competence. The singers at Carp Peak often evaluate their opponents' performances through praise or satire, and just as often may offer disclaimers about their own abilities, such as the common beginning phrase "I can't sing." While performing, the singers are often obscured by the audience members, who crowd closely around them. As the singing proceeds, listeners laugh in appreciation or groan in disapproval in response to the quality of the songs. It is not unusual for audience members (many of whom can also sing) to participate by whispering clues in the ears of their favorite singers.

Nanning, where I worked from 1981 to 1987. Liuzhou natives Peng Jialin and Wei Guang aided in the translation. Ke Chi, editor of *Guangxi qing'ge* [*Guangxi Love Songs*] (Nanning: Guangxi renmin chubanshe, 1981), provided me with valuable insights into singing practices and context. Several of his song collections became best sellers in the rural areas of Guangxi in the 1980s.

The most popular form of lyric in the Liuzhou area has four lines, with the verbal equivalent of seven written characters in each line. A less-common form, which is often mixed in with the standard form, has three syllables in the first line, followed by three lines of seven syllables each. Generally, in the standard form, the first two lines introduce and expand on an idea and the last two lines complete the concept, often adding a humorous twist or punch line or suddenly shifting the topic in another direction. In the standard version, it is common for the first, second, and, sometimes, fourth lines to rhyme, though there is much variation. In the second form, it is usual for the second, third, and fourth lines to rhyme. One tune is used throughout a performance, though tunes for a given song vary throughout the Guangxi region.

Numerous conventions are employed in the lyrics. For example, the terms "brother" and "sister" usually mean either "I" or "you." They are terms of endearment between lovers and do not refer to actual siblings. Maidenhood is symbolized by the color red, and certain animals and plants whose characteristics suggest undying love are common motifs. One example is the lotus root, which, when broken, nonetheless hangs together by silky threads of fiber. References to gods, mentions of historical and legendary figures, and quotations from classical literature are frequent. Place-names in Guangxi and the bordering provinces of Guangdong, Guizhou, and Hunan, such as Guilin (in Guangxi) and Guangzhou (in Guangdong), are common. Another feature is the use of words that have one meaning but suggest another because of a similarity in pronunciation. For instance, in the Liuzhou area the words for "star" (*xing*) and "heart" (*xin*) are pronounced similarly. Also, the word for "lotus" is pronounced the same as that meaning "to join" (*lian*). Some lines are stock phrases that have little meaning. However, they are important to the singers as handy fillers when a more original line does not come to mind. Sexual innuendos are also common in the lyrics.

During performances, singers do not normally employ conventionalized gestures or facial expressions, though objects in the immediate vicinity may be incorporated into a song. For example, the arrival of a woman with an umbrella may stimulate a line such as "Sister carries an umbrella from Guangdong" and provoke audience laughter when the singers glance toward the object as they sing.

The following song exchanges were recorded at the Midautumn Festival in 1981 at Carp Peak, Liuzhou. Seven groups of singers were performing on and off around the western base of the hill from early afternoon until late evening. In the afternoon, one woman, seated by herself among the large boulders, was singing out lines in the hope of a response. Plainly dressed in a white blouse and blue slacks, she was evidently well known, since twenty or so people of different ages and sexes had gathered around her. In reply to one of her songs, a male voice answered from the crowd. After they had exchanged a song or two, the man (who was younger than the woman and had a close-cropped head) moved in closer to sit down . . .

WOMAN:
. . . Flowers bloom in Guilin county,
Bearing fruit in Liuzhou city.

MAN:
I can sing—
If one can sing, a crowd will gather.

WOMAN:
If someone's clever, then they often sing,
So ask me to sing some mountain songs.
Everyone says you're a nimble singer—
How shall we go about making a date?

MAN:
Strange, strange that you have talent;
But if not, if not, then no one would come.
Who can compare with Third Sister Liu?
Who has a bellyful of talent like her?

WOMAN:
You're so-o-o nice, so-o-o nice,
Like you just got home from school;
He! I can't even read a book,
So how can I have talent like you?

MAN:
You'll get smarter if you sing,
But I'm just a simple bumpkin;
I've just arrived in the city,
And that's the honest truth.

WOMAN:
So if I'm dishonest, you'd never know it;
Well, here's something to keep in your heart:
Realize there are lots of singers around—
And Brother, do you know any good ones?

[The audience laughs loudly for some time at this suggestion that, although the man is right there, she does not consider him a good singer.]

MAN:
I can't sing, I can't even listen,
There are words in my heart that I can't express;

I have bitterness, but can't share it here,
I dare not tell Sister around so many others.

WOMAN:
When an old man sings
I'm lazy to respond,
Like an old vine wrapping an old tree,
But you, you're just a ginger sprout.

MAN:
How can I reply to that?
I can hardly answer—
Let the audience judge what's best.

WOMAN:
It's like this:
You will sing,
Then I will laugh—
That's how we'll sing together!

[Speaking, she mutters, "I won't sing," and the younger man disappears into the crowd, hiding his head under his bamboo hat in embarrassment. The crowd laughs goodnaturedly at his heroic attempt. After a few moments, the woman again sings out in search of a more skillful challenger.]

As the crowds gathered in the evening, the singing really got under way. In one group, three pairs of singers were performing. Seated on rocks to one side were two women. One was around fifty and rather plump; the other appeared to be in her mid-twenties and had red string tied on the ends of her braids. In duet, these women were performing the role of a young girl singing with a suitor. About ten feet away squatted two men in their forties. They were performing the role of the girl's suitor. Both men wore baggy shorts and loose cotton undershirts. One held a large palm-leaf fan that he kept in constant motion. The only time it paused was when the men hid behind it to whisper about what to sing. In between these pairs of men and women squatted two men in their early twenties who were taking the role of go-between or matchmaker.

This unusual arrangement drew a crowd several layers deep, some people standing so close that their knees sometimes touched the backs of the older men. The following series of songs was taken from this exchange, which lasted for more than forty minutes. In reading the following exchanges, it is important to remember that the singers are pretending to be a teenage girl and boy courting with the help of a go-between. (Although young people in rural areas tend to find their own marriage partners, the match is often finalized when a go-between is sent by the boy's family to the girl's home.)

MEN:
Place a stool at the front door—
Which Huguang fellow has come to court?[33]
Sister has rice stored in the granary
To feed hungry Brother when he works the land.

WOMEN:
Sister, like rice in May,[34]
Is very precious,
So lots of hungry suitors chase her.

GO-BETWEENS:
Sister, you're like a big sheet of paper;
If you're not sold, how long can you wait?
The rice along the big road isn't ripe yet,
The price is low, with little profit.

WOMEN:
When a girl is twenty, she becomes a prize,
When a boy is twenty-two, he heads a household.[35]
If Sister doesn't display herself with pride,
Then what a waste that flower will be.

. . . [*Men's lines unclear.*]

WOMEN:
A camphor tree is tall
But not as fragrant as osmanthus;
Another can care for Sister a long while,
But an apple shines for just a short time.

MEN:
Brother proposes to Sister, but she won't accept.
So hurry home to stay with your mother;
Stay with your mother until you're an old maid—
Then your family will have an old red flower.

---

33. During the Yuan and Ming dynasties, a province known as Huguang included present-day Hunan (which borders Guangxi) and Hubei provinces.

34. Rice is scarce and thus expensive in spring while people await the first harvest in midsummer.

35. According to this song, the ideal marriage age for women is twenty and that for men, twenty-two.

GO-BETWEENS:
Don't marry him, he's not the best;
Lots of suitors will come to your door;
Since you have good luck, a bright moon,
You needn't worry about finding a golden hook.[36]

WOMEN:
From Guangdong comes a potted pine.[37]
Since mother raised Sister as a single dragon,[38]
Since mother raised Sister as an only girl,
She's been kept home to hold up the bamboo roof.

MEN:
Sister's mother raised her as a single mountain,
Hoping to find a son-in-law to help the family;
So if you're looking for a man, then look to me—
I'll provide the cooking oil, salt, and rice.

GO-BETWEENS:
She asks you to join her family,[39] but you'd better refuse.
She just wants to exploit your labor;
Her abacus is very sharp—
Your father-in-law will eat off of you.

WOMEN:
From Guangzhou comes a plate of ginger.
Sister's mother raised her at Tianyang,[40]
Sister's mother raised her
To help support the family.

MEN:
Sister's mother treats her like a dragon's daughter,
Just like a pearl in her palm;
If she's searching for someone to "tie the knot"—
I know the best way to handle that!

---

36. The "golden hook" metonymically refers to a young man.

37. The first line is a stock phrase, whose meaning is obscure. Typically, pine trees symbolize long life, but here the image refers to the girl.

38. Dragons symbolize good fortune.

39. In rural areas, the bride usually goes to live in her husband's home. In some cases, however, a family without sons may arrange to have the groom (usually a man from a poor family) live with the bride's family. The groom may even take his wife's family name in such a case. This form of marriage occurs among both Han and Zhuang villagers in Guangxi.

40. Tianyang is a place-name.

WOMEN:
Look back and forth,
One foot is higher, the other lower.
Who would look for one as unlucky as you?
There'd be no rice if you climbed Sister's stairs.

MEN:
If Sister wears glasses to the market,
Brother will follow on horseback;
Others will praise our comely match
Your single eye and my gimp leg.[41]

GO-BETWEENS:
You've looked each other over several times,
So you can't come blame me later;
Tonight, I'll tell you both the truth:
A one-eyed girl and a lame boy match.

WOMEN:
Dry wood cuts without a knife,
Use hands and feet to break it;
If we love each other, no need for a go-between,
The words we need are few—a wink will do.

MEN:
Loving each other,
If we want to join, we need no go-between;
The go-between is so long-tongued,
He'll only spread gossip far and wide.

GO-BETWEENS:
Now that they are a pair, they kick me away;
So, I say let lightning strike you!
You two are so black-hearted,
A quilt laid crosswise won't cover your heads![42]

[There is long audience laughter.]

---

41. She wears glasses, as becomes apparent in succeeding lines, to hide the fact that she has only one eye. The reference may be to sunglasses.

42. Here the word "head" (*tou*) can also mean "end," implying that the couple will not last long together. (The song exchange is still far from over at this point.)

A SANI BALLAD

Collected by Zeng Guopin (Yi), translated by Zeng Guopin and Mark Bender, and introduced by Mark Bender

The Sani, a subgroup of the Yi ethnic group, are native to Shilin county, which is south of Kunming, the capital of Yunnan province. Numbering about one hundred thousand, the Sani raise goats and other livestock and grow crops such as buckwheat, maize, potatoes, and tobacco in this hilly, rural area. Many Sani women make embroidered handbags and other handicraft items for the tourist trade. Folk songs and folk dances are an important part of Sani life, and impromptu line dances involving dozens of men and women are often held during the evening in the villages and small towns of the area. Some participants play a variety of stringed instruments as they dance, while others simply clap to the lively beat of the tunes led by a small band that includes a flutist. Many types of folk songs are sung on various occasions, and some people are especially noted for their singing ability. Traditional priests known as *bimo* enact rituals on a variety of occasions, including weddings, funerals, and holidays. These specialists sometimes consult chants written in Sani versions of an ancient Yi script that was once also used to record narrative poems and local history. The Stone Forest is the major tourist attraction in the Sani area, and hundreds of thousands of visitors flock to see the oddly shaped limestone formations each year. Among the peaks is a stone formation said to be Ashima, the heroine of a well-known narrative poem about her capture by an evil landlord. In recent years, musicals, holograms, and reenactments of Sani rituals, led by actors dressed as *bimo*, have come to be staged on a regular basis. Although many local Sani people are involved in these productions, some still enjoy the older songs.

The lyric "Four Songs of the Seasons" is a sad song about one's bitter fate. Feelings are evoked by the skillful use of nature metaphors and the sense of prolonged sadness as the various "doors" to the seasons open throughout the year. The number "nine" (or, in some songs, "ninety-nine") simply means "many," though the number sometimes can also have ritual significance. The birds and animals in the song are commonly mentioned in Yi oral literature, often as messengers or harbingers of change

FOUR SONGS OF THE SEASONS

SPRING, THE SWEET TIME

Spring is on its way,
And what opens the door to spring?
Winter winds recede,
The gentle spring wind blows.
The spring winds caress our faces,

The bird of spring, the cuckoo, calls,
Calling, calling, in its fine voice—
The cuckoo, opening the door of spring.

SUMMERTIME

Summer's on its way,
And what opens the door to summer?
As rain clouds roll above,
Summer fields are sown in grain.
Among the stones, maidens look about as
Water cascades down the hillsides,
And mountain pools overflow with water,
Setting the mountain frogs to croaking,
The frogs that open the door to summer.

AUTUMN

Autumn's on its way,
And what opens the door to autumn?
The sky is abuzz with hornets,
Bees buzz all about the earth.
Hornets buzzing,
Bumblebees buzzing,
Autumn is coming,
And it's the bees that open autumn's door.

WINTER, THE WASHING TIME

Winter is on its way,
And what opens the door to winter?
It's the wild goose that opens winter's door,
The flying wild geese with no tails,
Their feet stretching behind them.
Flying, the geese, flying,
Wild geese flying to a sweeter place,
As does the eagle, too,
Flying to a sweet, warm place.
Snow whitens the mountaintops,
Frost falls to the ponds.
The warm days pass, not fit to live.
Nine layers of cloth are needed.
The winds blow through the nine heavens,
And I am poor and brokenhearted;

Even the winds won't blow around me.
Where have the warm places gone?
A burning stump is my warmest place;
Burning, a stump vents its grief with me,
As I gather wild herbs for brunch and dinner,
Finding ginger, but no lard to fry it.
Before life was hard, and now I live
In misery, the story of my life.

TWO FOLK SONGS OF THE DONG (GAEM) PEOPLE

Translated and introduced by Yang Haixia (Dong)

The homeland of the Dong ethnic group (numbering over 360,000) is in south-central China, centered in the region where the provinces of Guizhou and Hunan meet the borders of the Guangxi Zhuang Autonomous Region. Wet-rice farmers, the Dong (who call themselves the Gaem or Kam) share many customs with the neighboring Han, Zhuang, and Miao peoples. Traditional Dong folk-ways include dyed indigo tunics, hammered silver jewelry, sticky rice and pickled fish dishes, and multistoried wooden drum towers and the so-called wind and rain covered bridges made without nails. The Dong speak a language related to Zhuang in a branch of the Tai-language family.

Dong folk songs are rich in content and varied in form. The songs are performed with or without instrumental accompaniment. One popular form is called *pipa* songs (Dong, *gal bic bac*; Chinese, *pipa ge*). The Dong *pipa* is a plucked stringed instrument more like a version of the three-stringed *sanxian* (banjolike instrument) used by the Han people than the Han *pipa* (balloon-shaped guitarlike instrument). Depending on locale and personal preference, the Dong *pipa* may have three or four strings, vary in size and timbre, and be made of various woods, including fir. The larger *pipa* from Liping county, Guizhou, which produces a soft and grave timbre, is more suitable for long narrative poems performed in the drum towers, while the smaller, "brisk and sweet," ones from the Rongshui region, in northern Guangxi, are better for shorter love ballads. In the Sanjiang region of Guangxi, a sort of middle-timbre *pipa* with a deep, rich sound is used for both love ballads and longer narrative poems. According to legend, E Mei, a girl from Zhandong, Guizhou, invented the Dong *pipa*, while historical records suggest their adoption, with no inventor attributed, by at least the Ming dynasty (1368–1644).

Styles of *pipa* songs vary by region, though all are characterized by dainty rhythms and flexible line structures. Rhyme patterns can be complex, including the use of various forms of internal rhyme. Chinese characters sometimes are used for their sound value (rather than their lexical meaning) to write down the *pipa* song lyrics in the sounds of the Dong language, making such songbooks nearly unintelligible to those outside the tradition.

Another Dong folk song tradition is called old songs (Dong, *gal laox*), popularly known by their Chinese name *dage* (great songs). These complex choral songs are usually performed on important occasions, such as festivals or when meeting guests from other villages. Singing groups, of at least two voice parts, are organized from the community. One lead singer sings alto (*seit al*), while other members (which may number in the dozens) sing an undertone (*meix al*) role. The alto is the spirit of the team and has high status among local singers. Content may include love songs, folk wisdom, folk stories and legends, and other subjects, depending on the style.

One type of great song is a short style known as sound songs (*gal soh* or *al soh*, depending on the local Dong dialect), usually performed by women. These short songs are typically inserted into longer performances of great songs in order to change the pace and liven up the atmosphere when the audience gets bored with the performance. The lyrics are minimal, often employing a melody that imitates the sounds of nature, such as birds chirping, a river rippling, and so forth. The short "sound songs" are often named after insects, birds, beasts, or a season. The most famous is "Song of the Cicadas."

YOU WERE LIKE A TENDER SEEDLING, MY SWEETHEART

Collected by Wu Yongxun (Dong)

A love song, "You Were Like a Tender Seedling, My Sweetheart," has appeared in a number of anthologies of *pipa* song lyrics, with versions in both standard and nonstandard character formats. It originally circulated in the Sanjiang area of the Guangxi Zhuang Autonomous Region and was collected by the folksinger Wu Yongxun. The imagery of the local natural world is a common feature in the oral lore of many ethnic groups in the Guizhou and Guangxi regions.

My pretty young girl in the flower of your youth,
I miss you madly day and night.
You were like a tender white-melon seedling
That was just beginning to climb
Uncle's melon shed.
When the millet was already starting to burgeon,
Others took it just as seedlings,
And before it ripened for harvest,
They cut it down and threw it away.
Darling, you were like a flourishing forest tree.
I wanted to plant and water you,
But you were cut down by others, then sent off for use as roofing;
It was I who planted the bamboo while others dug the shoots.
I sit here and sing for you,
But now you belong to someone else.
I still remember the day you gave me a token of our love;
You told me to hide it in the bottom of a chest,
And we swore that we would never leave each other.
You could not live without me,
As a boat cannot sail without a rudder.
Your sweet voice is always on my mind.
I'm deeply hurt because your parents went back on their word;
Their betrayal was because I have no fields.
I would never complain about anything, my sweetheart.

Have you deserted me or is it because
You cannot fight against your parents?
I am so anxious since I have no fields.
We can never feel the warmth of a stove together;
I climb to the top of a high mountain, missing you so much,
I sigh without hope.
I know it is only an empty dream like the moon shimmering in water.
I'm like a mulberry tree growing in the forest;
No one will take care of me.
I groan in my loneliness,
I'm destined not to have you in this life.
You were so soft and tender, my darling,
I loved you so much.
But your mother said:
"It is only a dream for you to love my daughter;
Only sixty years later can you be with her
Like a fish in the river and a dragon in the sea."
Hearing this I realized you were in great trouble;
A hollow candlenut tree is no harder than cold metal.
Uncle is famous in the village for his great fortune,
I have nothing, so how can I match you?
You know it is so hard for me to forget you,
The feeling in my heart grieves me.
I have been waiting for you for three long springs,
But you hide yourself like a fish in a pool.
I have been waiting for you for three lonely winters,
But you are like a bamboo shoot hiding yourself in the earth.
Darling, you are still so young,
But you have married somebody else.
You married into Uncle's family,
Leaving me alone.
Tears are running down my cheeks, how can I forget you?
With no possessions,
Is it possible for me to match you?
A butterfly flies around a flower it loves;
I need you but I only hurt myself;
I want you but can do nothing.
I wish to snatch you back,
But I have no field to mortgage.
It is no use whistling if a thrush does not fly into the cage;
It is no use holding the pole if a fish does not take the bait;
I miss you crazily and tears wet my clothes.
In May, Uncle's wife takes you to the fields;
I am like an arid field without water.

In June, Uncle needs you to weed;
When can you come back to see your mother?
It has been stormy all these days;
When can it be sunny and bright?
You know how pained I was when I left you,
As cows, sheep, and pigs that have left their pen;
It's hard to put a barrel back together
When it is about to fall apart.
Birds fly back to the forest at sunset,
I've come to your home and am waiting for you;
I am barefooted while you are in your fine shoes.
It's silly for a poor fellow like me to miss someone like you,
I am like a hungry fish searching for food in a shallow pond.
Your mother said:
"Don't use dog meat to lure a white swan!"
A little Buddha stands lonely guard over the bronze censer in the temple,
But the earthen bowl in my hands doesn't have your fragrance,
  my darling.
I felt crushed when I heard your mother's words,
As if the sky had burst and the earth were sinking.
I am so lucky that I can hold your hands tonight,
What are you thinking, my sweetheart?
I am desperately lonely without you.
Even if someday you have a child,
I will still be here, with all my heart and soul
Waiting for you.

SONG OF THE CICADAS

Sung by Wu Cuiliang and translated into Chinese by Deng Minwen (Dong)

"Song of the Cicadas" stimulates deep emotions, in part because of its "natural" musical effects that imitate the sound of cicadas in several verses. The cicada sound is reflected in the song's Dong-language title, "Gal laems leengh." This version of the song was sung by Wu Cuiliang, recorded by Wu Hao, and further textualized by Deng Minwen. This song is popular in the counties of Liping, Rongjiang, and Congjiang, in Guizhou province, and in Sanjiang Dong Autonomous County, in the Guangxi Zhuang Autonomous Region. The song is often sung as a choral piece at local, national, and international cultural events by groups of young women representing the Dong ethnic group.

Be quiet, everybody!

I want to sing a song.
Cicadas in April

Fly into forests
Leengh leengh leengh leengh . . .
Leengh leengh leengh leengh . . .

Where are these little cicadas?
Are they lost?
Oh, listen! Their dulcet songs are wafting in the deep,
deep mountains and forests.
Song of the cicadas . . .

Cicadas talk
In songs;
Endless feelings
Are hiding in the deep, deep songs.
Love will never be lost,
And so too the songs
Cicada lovers
Sing in pairs
Leengh leengh leengh leengh . . .
Leengh leengh leengh leengh . . .

Love in this world
Is like the cicadas' song,
Lasting infinitely,
And songs of cicadas will last infinitely.
Leengh leengh leengh leengh . . .
Leengh leengh leengh leengh . . .

SONGS OF THE TU
MOUNTAIN SONGS

Collected by Dong Siyuan (Tu), translated by Limusishiden (Tu) and Kevin Stuart, and introduced by Kevin Stuart

A type of folk song called *ghadani dog* (mountain songs) is still sung among the Mongghul, a subgroup of the Tu ethnic group in northwestern China.[43] Although the songs are now sung mostly in Chinese, they were commonly performed in the Mongghul dialect of Tu before 1950.

Because of their romantic content, the songs are not allowed to be sung in the home. One traditional singing site was a high slope in front of the Number One Middle School in Weiyuan town, the seat of Huzhu county, Qinghai. The slope was called Turen tai (Mongghul Platform). Every year, on the second day of the second lunar month, male and female participants, mostly Mongghul, gathered to sing, and most of the songs were mountain songs like those that follow. It was not only an opportunity for participants to sing songs generally taboo in ordinary life, but also, for a short time, a culturally sanctioned time to find a lover. Today, rural residents still gather on the second day of the second lunar month, but most attendees are Han Chinese.

The following songs were collected in the spring of 1981 in Shgeayili village, Donggou township, Huzhu Tu Autonomous County. The singers were Hao Siyuan (b. 1934), Ma Zhanshan (b. 1935), and Tangja Aadee (b. ca. 1924); no record was kept of who sang which song. Like the three singers, Dong Siyuan (b. 1939), the collector, is a Mongghul from Shgeayili village. After serving as governor of Huzhu county, he moved to Xining city, where he worked on the Qinghai Nationalities Committee. He has actively collected and studied many aspects of local Mongghul culture.

LARINBU AND JIMINSU

Jiminsu, the sister from the plain, and Larinbu, the brother from the valley,
Drive hundreds of horses to mix with hundreds of colts,
Drive hundreds of oxen to mix with hundreds of calves,
Drive hundreds of sheep to mix with hundreds of lambs.

We climb up to the shady side of the mountain and gather lily bulbs,
Climb up on the sunny side of the mountain and break off green cypress limbs,
Climb farther up the mountain and burn incense offerings,

43. See the introduction to "The Qeo Family Girl" (chap. 1).

Prostrate to the sky after sprinkling water on the fire incense,
Pray to the mountain gods after beseeching the great sky.

We two together speak heartfelt words,
Jiminsu, the sister from the plain, and Larinbu, the brother from the valley.
Jiminsu, the sister from the plain, and Larinbu, the brother from the valley.

We come down to the verdant plain and pitch our white tent,
Set up a rough-pottery pot with three stones supporting it underneath,
Pour red tea into the rough-pottery pot after well water is poured inside,
Sprinkle it to the great sky when the white milk is poured into the
rough-pottery pot;
We two meet when the white milk is sprinkled to the mountain gods.

Jiminsu, the sister from the plain, and Larinbu, the brother from the valley.
Jiminsu, the sister from the plain, and Larinbu, the brother from the valley.

I cannot leave you, what should I do?
I offer my golden pins to you.

I cannot leave you, what should I do?
I offer my silver *xangdi*[44] to you.

I cannot leave you, what should I do?
I offer my silver earrings to you.

I cannot leave you, what should I do?
I offer my silver bracelets to you.

I cannot leave you, what should I do?
I offer my golden rings to you.

I cannot leave you, what should I do?
I offer my horse-mounting robe[45] to you.

I cannot leave you, what should I do?
I offer my long-sewn embroidered sash to you.

I cannot leave you, what should I do?
I offer my pink skirts to you.

---

44. The *xangdi* is a pin used in the traditional headdress.

45. The horse-mounting robe is a woman's robe worn only on the day she leaves her parents' home to take up residence in her husband's.

I cannot leave you, what should I do?
I offer my *saliu*[46] shoes to you.

I cannot leave you, what should I do?
I offer my five *chi*[47] body to you.

Jiminsu, the sister from the plain, and Larinbu, the brother from the valley,
Jiminsu, the sister from the plain, and Larinbu, the brother from the valley,

Awulii, Arilolog, Xnjalolog, and Qarilolog (written in a Mongghul romanization) refer to the names of specific melodies. Lyrics sung to these melodies may vary greatly.

AWULII

Li Yanfei[48] strolled on the street selling water,
He watered the withered courtyard peony.
Elder Brother is like a circling bird in the mid sky,
Younger Sister is like a peony in the courtyard garden plot.

The pigeon flew away but the eagle did not,
The bell would tinkle if the eagle flew away.
Her body returned but her heart did not,
How much I would think of her if her heart returned to me.

ARILOLOG

Climb up to the high slope's top,
Look down on the verdant plain;
A gray dragon is turning,
The gray dragon is not true.
Gray water flows,
Clan members are harmonious.
To have a horse but no saddle,
To have a lover but no love,
To have a bit but no rein,

---

46. *Saliu* are Mongghul women's shoes with a raised point at the tip that is sewn with colored threads.

47. One *chi* is about a foot.

48. According to one informant, Li Yanfei was a poor Han Chinese who spent his life carrying and selling water.

To have a heart but no time,
To think that my lover glimmers under my eyes.

XNJALOLOG

Nenbii[49] Plain's crab apple,
A lover's nostrils as nice as a mountain pass,
A lover's eyes as bright as Venus.

QARILOLOG

A lover's eyes as bright as Amdo region's Venus,
A lover's face as red as a Nenbii crab apple,
A lover's flesh as soft as Shaanxi cotton.

FOLK SONG

Collected and translated by Hu Jun (Tu) and Kevin Stuart

This is a song that was sung by He Zhongxiao, of the Xian Feng Brigade, in the winter of 1988, in south Minhe county, Qinghai province. Older people usually sing "Six Persuasions for People's Hearts" to educate youth, since it specifically sets forth the duties and responsibilities for the young people within a home. A Minhe Tu wedding is an enormously complicated affair that lasts for a full three days and features innumerable songs.

SIX PERSUASIONS FOR PEOPLE'S HEARTS

Sung by He Zhongxiao (Tu)

The first persuasion of the heart is for parents to hear.
Parents are old and live a hundred years.
Parents' hearts are turned to the children,
But children's hearts are turned to stone;
The more children reared, the more trouble,
No children reared is a great grief.

The second persuasion of the heart is for brothers to hear.
Brothers should be unified and discuss together.

49. Nianbo in Mandarin, the plain is in Ledu county, in east-central Qinghai province, in the Haidong region adjoining Huzhu county.

All things inside the family are Eldest Brother's duty;
People coming and guests leaving are Second Brother's duty;
Turning grain over and paying taxes are Third Brother's duty;
Watering fields and making dikes are to be done in turn.

The third persuasion of the heart is for sisters-in-law to hear.
Sisters-in-law should be unified and discuss together.
All things inside the family are Eldest Sister-in-law's duty;
All needlework is Second Sister-in-law's duty;
People coming and guests leaving are Third Sister-in-law's duty;
Carrying ashes and water are to be done in turn.

The fourth persuasion of the heart is for girls to hear.
Girls should embroider in the embroidery room,
Pomegranate flowers embroidered on pillows,
Peonies embroidered on shoes;
Someday go to Mother-in-law's home;
In Mother-in-law's home you are to be staunch and strong.

The fifth persuasion of the heart is for students to hear.
Students are to study in school.
Big characters are to be written well in square form;
Small characters are to be written in bright beauty;
Someday enter the university,
Serve the people well.

The sixth persuasion of the heart is for the clan to hear.
The clan should be unified and discuss together;
Both sides deserve blame when children quarrel,
Otherwise elders' hearts will break.

Chapter 3

FOLK RITUAL

Rituals are integral to the wide range of belief systems making up China's complex religious heritage. The most popular of the formal ritual traditions are the Three Teachings, based on the doctrines of Daoism, Confucianism, and Buddhism. Localized belief systems, some rooted in the very ancient past, include animism, shamanism, and ancestor reverence. These beliefs find local expression in a multitude of forms that are often a synthesis of elements of several belief systems. Moreover, it is not uncommon for gods and spirits from many traditions to be worshipped in the context of a particular ritual. Other major traditions originated in the Middle East. Judaism and Christianity have historically had limited followings in some areas. Islam, however, has followers in many parts of the country, especially in the western border regions. A number of folk rituals are presented in this chapter, while other ritual-linked traditions appear elsewhere in the volume.

Efficacy is an underlying concern in ritual behavior throughout China. Rituals may be conducted by individuals or ritual specialists to implore supernatural beings to provide water for crops, to protect a household from fire and sickness, and in hopes of success and safety in other aspects of life, including the accumulation of wealth, travels, harmonious marriages, the bearing of healthy and abundant progeny, and long life. Those conducting the ritual may call on beings from a number of belief traditions to share in a ritual feast, sometimes with entertainment in the form of folk music, singing, drama, or storytelling. These entertainments, presented to please the beneficent spirits, are also of great interest to the living audience members. A good example is the Jingjiang "telling scriptures" selection from the lower Yangtze delta region, in which a storytelling genre is performed in conjunction with child-protection rituals and other life-cycle rites. Although they are now mainly secular, the rice-planting song (*yang'ge*) dance dramas of northern China are linked to ancient planting and harvest rituals. In this chapter is an example of clan-protection rituals conducted by Manchu shamans in northeastern China. These complex rituals often include battles with malevolent forces while on journeys to the spirit world. The efficacy of the rituals is linked in part to these strong dramatic elements by which shamans demonstrate their power over supernatural opponents.

Traditionally, a huge variety of local ritual activities took place at family gatherings, festivals, and temple fairs throughout the year all over the country. Such ritual activity, however, was suppressed during the Cultural Revolution (1966–1976) and at other moments in recent history. Beginning in the early 1980s, there has been a great revival (and sometimes reinvention) of local ritual traditions, which has continued unabated. Elaborate wedding ceremonies and funerals, made possible by the enhanced economic environment, are now common in many areas. Rituals such as shaman rites in northeastern China and the rituals of native priests among the Yi and Naxi ethnic groups in the southwest, once banned from public performance, are now celebrated in museums and interpretive parks. In various parts of the country, many rituals have been radically simplified or changed in new performance contexts created by the boom in ethnic and local culture tourism. This blossoming has resulted in a great deal of fieldwork by scholars to document folk rituals in many parts of the country and among many ethnic groups. The recruitment of ritual specialists is now difficult in some areas, however, and searching for persons to conduct traditional rituals forces some rural communities to import specialists from other areas or forgo the rituals altogether. Among the contributing factors to this lack of tradition bearers are the availability of modern medicine and education and the lure of secular urban lifestyles that draw younger generations to new rhythms of life and new expressions of ritual behavior.

The following selections are drawn from some of the lesser-known but very rich traditions of the minority ethnic cultures, particularly those of the diverse southwest. All were chosen as much for their artistic appeal as performances as for their illustration of the beliefs they exemplify. Most concern very immediate needs of a family or small community: a song to placate the spirit of a tree that is to be felled, words integral to the consecration of a marriage, or a story associated with dispelling harmful forces from the home. The examples include a now obscure ritual from ethnic Koreans (Chaoxianzu) in northeastern China held to propitiate the many gods overseeing the welfare and harmony of the house and to cleanse the home of malevolent forces at the New Year. It was collected from an elder in 2001 and illustrates the precarious nature of some ritual traditions in China. There is a chant from the Wa ethnic group in southern Yunnan province recited in a ritual to call back the wandering soul of an older woman, and one from the Yi ethnic group in northern Yunnan to entice the lost soul of a child. Similar rituals are still conducted among a number of ethnic groups in southwestern China and seem to be part of an ancient tradition of soul-calling rites, as evidenced by chants in the *Elegies of Chu* (*Chu ci*) dating from the third century C.E. The marriage prayer of the Lahu people of Yunnan province illustrates a ritual related to a major life-cycle event and emphasizes the important cultural values of cooperation and harmony in married life. The dramatic Nuosu chant from Sichuan, "The Origin of Ghosts," is recited by priests as a necessary assurance of efficacy in a ritual for casting away malevolent forces.

A CHAOXIAN LUNAR NEW YEAR EXORCISM RITUAL

Collected, translated, and introduced by Peace Lee

Approximately 1.9 million ethnic Koreans (known as Chaoxianzu, or Chaoxian ethnic group) live in China, most concentrated in the northeastern part of China called the Yanbian Chaoxian Nationality Autonomous Prefecture, in Jilin province.

The following text is only one example of ethnic Korean ritual tradition. It is a chant performed to propitiate the house gods that traditionally were thought to inhabit each home. This version of a house god chant (*seongjupuri*) was performed by Li Jiaoyong, of Antu county, Jilin province, in February 2001. According to Li, the house god chant was performed by a local farmers' band as a part of a ritual held to exorcise negative forces known as *jisinbalpgi*. The *jisinbalpgi* cleansing rite was one of many rituals performed during the lunar New Year. The process of the *jisinbalpgi* ritual began with the band's visit to the oldest tree in the village, asking its blessing for the success of the exorcisms that were to take place. Then the performers visited all the important places in the village, such as freshwater springs or wells, in order to ask the supernatural beings for a good year. Once the propitiations were made, the band paid a visit to every house in the village in order to perform the *jisinbalpgi* exorcism. The clang of a brass percussion instrument known as a *kkwaengguari* signaled the arrival of the band at each door. After the group entered each home, the *jisinbalpgi* took place. Every part of a house was exorcised of unclean and unlucky forces. The last part of the ritual was the performance of the *seongjupuri*, the house god chant, which was accompanied by offerings of rice while the performers wished for prosperity for the homeowners.

This tradition, described as a form of "superstition" by Li, is no longer practiced. When Li presented this version of the house god chant, each line was followed by a brass gong performance. Shamans have different versions of house god chants in their repertoires.

HOUSE GOD CHANT

Performed by Li Jiaoyong (ethnic Korean)

Where is the origin of *Seongju*?
Gyeongsang province, in the land of Andong.
Swallows return, it must be spring;
Take pine seedlings from the spring swallow,
Toss them here and there.
Nights, covered with cold dew,
Days, shining with sunshine,

Became young pine saplings;
Young pines grew and grew,
Became tall thick pines.
You, carpenter Gim! across the street—
You, carpenter Yu! in the house above—
Let's go logging.
Grab your tool bags,
Walk over this hill, that hill,
Take a look at one branch, at
The branch leaning south.
Storks, red birds, fly in,
Fouling things with their droppings.
Walk over one more hill,
Grab a branch and look at
The branch leaning north.
Crows and magpies built nests in
This tree, also fouled.
Walk over one, two hills,
Go over three hills.
Tall, exuberant pine trees—
Pull saws, *seo-reong, seo-reong.*
Upright trees, chop their fronts;
Curved trees, cut their backs;
Prepare timber for a house.
Invite the priest Muhak;[1]
Smooth the site according to feng shui;
Build a small cottage.
Beginning that night, dreams come:
Look at Lady Gachwa;
Night and day without a rest
Carrying in pure well water
To offer at the temple of Samsin.
When signs of pregnancy appeared,
Ten months had passed by,
A precious baby boy was born:
Seongju is his very name.

---

1. Muhak was a famous Buddhist monk who had a close relationship with the founder of the Joseon (Chosŏn) dynasty (1392–1910).

MANCHU SHAMAN SONGS FROM NORTHEASTERN CHINA

Collected by Shi Guangwei (Manzu) and Luo Lin (Han) and translated and introduced by Juwen Zhang (Han)

The Manchu (Manzu) are one of China's largest ethnic groups. Once rulers of the great Qing dynasty (1644–1911), which collapsed in Sun Yat-sen's Republican Revolution, many Manchus are today regaining a sense of ethnic pride. The Manchus originated during the Ming dynasty (1368–1644) as an entity formed of the Nüzhen and other ethnic groups in northeastern China (the present-day provinces of Heilongjiang, Jilin, and Liaoning). At the time of their rise to power, they formed military units known as banners, which sometimes included people from other ethnic groups. The word "shaman" is a Tungus-Manchu word (*saman*) variously rendered as "one who knows" or "ecstatic" dancer or ritualist. The earliest Chinese record of the term is in reference to shape-shifting female ritualists who had the ability to communicate with gods and spirits. Written by Xu Mengshen (1126–1207), of the Southern Song dynasty (1127–1279), the text is called *A Compilation of the Northern Alliances of the Three Reigns* (*Sanchao beimeng huibian*).

Shamanism was an integral part of the religious activities of Manchus at all levels of society. Shamans performed sacrificial rituals for the imperial court at the Divine Peace Pavilion (Shenning) and at the Peaceful Longevity Pavilion (Ningshou), in the Beijing Imperial Palace, and at the Tranquil Peace Pavilion (Qingning) in the Shenyang Imperial Palace. Shamans were invited to dance and sing at court and folk events ranging from routine household and clan protection rituals to rites for the ancestors and special sacrifices to heaven. Today, shamanistic rituals are held for the benefit of family and clan, as well as for harvests, prosperity and offspring, avoidance of disease, happiness and longevity, ensuring a safe journey to a relative's village, and redeeming a vow to a supernatural benefactor.

Songs and chants are key ingredients in shamanic rituals. Scholars began collecting and classifying written shaman texts as early as the reign of Emperor Qianlong (1736–1796). Many of them were translated into Chinese for broader circulation. *The Imperial Ceremonies in the Manchu State for Offering Sacrifices to Gods and Heaven* (*Qinding Manzhou jishen jitian dianli*) was such a book. Completed in 1747 and comprising six volumes, it included dozens of songs modified and polished by Emperor Qianlong himself. Although use of the Manchu language was in decline by the end of the Qing dynasty, a number of songs were recorded in the Manchu script. In recent decades, folklorists have conducted fieldwork to rescue many songs in the oral tradition, as exemplified by the following two pieces. Such records are precious texts in the study of Manchu folk culture, which has undergone many changes in the past two hundred years. Today, shaman performances are one of the very few situations in which the Manchu language is used.

When conducting their rituals, shamans use a number of different musical instruments and props. These are usually a large drum (*taigu*), a row of elongated waist bells (*yaoling*), a hand drum (*shougu*), a brass mirror (*tongjing*), brass bells (*hongwu*), and clapping boards (*zhaban*). Two shamans may interact during some rituals. The so-called family shaman (Mandarin, *jia saman*; Manchu, *zaili*) represents the human realm and begins the event by singing songs for the gods or spirits. The chief shaman (*da saman*), representing the gods, acts as a medium, singing out lyrics, after the spirits enter his body, that express their will. Sometimes one shaman takes both roles. In the course of a ritual, the shamans dance, make music, and sometimes shout or talk as they sing. As the shaman conducts the ritual, the audience participates at some points by answering the shaman's questions or by singing along.

Since shamanism is not a formally organized religion, its continued existence depends solely on its deep roots in folk life. Thus shamanic songs are not only an important component of shamanic rituals, but also the basis of Manchu oral literature and the primary medium for the expression of the shamanistic worldview.

SACRIFICE TO THE PYTHON GOD

Performed by Shi Qingming (Manchu)

"Sacrifice to the Python God" is part of a ritual sacrifice to the Python God and was performed in the Shi family in Little Han village, Hujia commune, Jiutai city, Jilin province, in May 1979. The Python God is one of the many animal gods worshipped by the Manchu. This performance was held to pray for the peace, health, and happiness of the clan.

At the beginning, the shaman lies down in front of a high table serving as an altar, facing up to the sky, with a stick of burning incense laid horizontally across his nose. With his hands across his chest, he creeps across the ground by moving his shoulders back and forth and twisting his body, imitating a python. In this way, he moves from the altar to the hallway, and then returns. At this point, it is believed that the Python God has entered the shaman's body, and the sacred song in the voice of the Python God can then be performed. In some cases, a chief shaman performs the ritual with the assistance of a family shaman. Shi Qingming is the family shaman of the Shi family and a descendant of the Pure Yellow Banner of the Manchu army. The lyrics were sung in the Manchu language. The collector, Shi Guangwei, is a government-trained local folklorist.

For what reason and
Who is offering?
Live among the supreme peaks,
In the White Mountains,
Through the white clouds and silver valley,

Arrive now at the ridge,
By riding the cloud and descending
On the bank of River Nishiha.

Eight *tuo* huge Python God[2]
Nine *tuo* huge Snake Immortal.
No difference from day to night,
Enter the sacred caverns as gods.
The family Shi is here praying,
Raising heads for fortune and happiness.
Offer sacrifices to the Great Bear,
Ask what animal is associated.
I am the Manchu *erzhen*,[3]
Inviting all the gods to the feast.
Request in loud voices,
Reply in gentle sounds.
Hand drums in flurries,
Sitting drums are booming.
The spirit has entered the body,
The shaman is washed clean,
Became a master after apprenticeship,
Walked back into the family door.
Now inviting gods at the front gate,
With offerings on the high table,
Followed by all the family clans,
Repeating the words eight times.
Learning to sing the words,
To contribute to all the gods.

We invite gods in the grand temple,
Offering sacrifices at the family shrine,
Praying for health and peace,
Happiness and fortune all on the way.
Spring and summer have passed,
Golden autumn is ready to come.
We bid good-bye to the old month,
And welcome the new month.
Choose a lucky day,
Pick an auspicious hour.

---

2. One *tuo* is the distance from one hand to the other hand when the arms are stretched out horizontally.

3. *Erzhen* is a transliteration of the Manchu word for "chief" or "master."

Grind the yellow glutinous rice,
Humbly make delicacies for gods.
First light the rue incense,
Then burn the Han incense.
Offer with proper rites,
Tell the reasons and wishes.

For peace and joy for the offspring,
For harmony with the seasons,
For health and safety,
We pray for blessings and protection from the gods.
As the shaman in the family,
I sing the words tonight.
Drums are booming,
Three times incense is burned.
Ready to bid to all the gods,
And accompany the return,
To the mountain peaks.
All set off on their journeys,
But what is left for the shaman?
Live your life the best you can,
As the shaman in the family,
Pray for utmost happiness.
Safety and tranquillity, health and peace,
Pray for these all the time.

A SONG FOR THE GOD OF SACRIFICES

Performed by Guan Zhiyuan (Manchu)

"A Song for the God of Sacrifices" was performed in the Guan family clan in Hantun village, Wulajie township, Yongji county, Jilin province, in July 1981. The god of sacrifices is believed to be in charge of all the sacrificial foods offered to the various gods and spirits (which might number in the hundreds). The dance for the god of sacrifices is also called shaking the grain. The lyrics are sung before the incense is burned and the shaman performs his dance. Glutinous rice cakes are the main offering in this ritual. "Shaking the grain" refers to the shaman's movements as he imitates the manner of sifting grain to make glutinous rice cakes. As he dances, the sound of drums and bells alerts the gods and spirits to the delicious offering.

At the start of a ritual, a table, used as the family altar, is placed in the middle of the yard. On it is positioned a wooden grain measure (*dou*) full of sorghum and covered with red paper. In front of the measure is an incense burner. An offering table with a red tablecloth is set in front of the family altar table. A pair of incense burners, a pair of candles, three cups of rice wine, three dishes of glutinous rice cakes, and some fruits are placed as offerings on the table. A drum is suspended from a roof beam. Carved wooden incense burners are placed before the shrine to the family gods and ancestral spirits on the southern heated earth-brick bed (*kang*), before the Foduo Mother on the northern brick bed, before the Aoduo Mother in the outer room, and an old willow branch is placed on the wall in the southeastern corner of the outer room.[4] A young man known as the incense-lighting boy lights all the incense burners after kowtowing in front of them. "Han incense" and "rue incense" are separately placed in the two incense burners on the offering table.[5] After these steps, the family shaman kowtows in front of the family altar. At this high point in the rite, he starts to dance. Singing while dancing, he symbolically enacts the entire process of washing, drying, steaming, and grinding the glutinous rice, and finally offering the cakes on the table. Guan Zhiyuan is a professional shaman and a descendant of the Rimmed Yellow Flag Banner. Luo Lin, the collector, is a folk-culture worker conducting fieldwork in the area.

Suhalihala,[6]
Here is the family with the name of Guan.
I, your servant, make vows
With all my family members standing by.
Bid the old month good-bye,
Welcome the new month,
Choose the lucky days,
And make offerings to all gods.

Cook delicacies,
Prepare yellow wine,
And light the rue for sacred spirits.
Respectfully invite Tangzi and Tuoli,[7]
And Zusebeizi,[8]
With favors from all the gods.

---

4. Foduo Mother is a transcription for "goddess of reproduction." The Chinese meaning is "mother of loving kindness." According to a Manchu folktale, the first emperor of the Manchu, Nurhaci, was once saved by a Han Chinese woman. The Manchu feel obliged to her for their later success and make offerings to her as their goddess of family peace and offspring. Aoduo Mother is held to be the original ancestress of the Manchu. She is also known as the goddess of war.

5. Han incense (or joss incense, also called thread incense from its shape) is so called because it is used mainly by the Han Chinese, while rue incense, made from the medicinal herb common rue (*Ruta graveolens*), is used mainly by the Manchu people.

6. The Manchu word Suhalihala, transcribed here from the Mandarin, signifies the god of family names, regarded as the basis of the group.

7. The Manchu word Tangzi signifies the sacred hall, and Tuoli indicates the brass mirror or the god of the sun. Both are transcribed from the Mandarin.

8. The Manchu word Zusebeizi, or Zushebeile, transcribed from the Mandarin, refers to the god of agriculture.

I, your servant, and the family members,
All kowtow while waiting here.
The old are replaced by the young,
Praying for your blessings and protection.

While the shaman in chief is getting old,
The young constantly practice,
With the words of the gods borne in their hearts,
Pray for blessings from the gods,
For I, your servant, who is growing old.
May there be no disasters for a hundred years,
May there be no disease for six decades.
We burn the incense high,
Make a feast with filled tables.
Pray for blessings from the gods forever,
For peace and fortune in the family,
For countless animals and full barns.
Pray for protection from the gods forever,
Please accept, Dafu and Yuhuang,[9]
Respectfully and humbly,
We, your servants, pray to all the gods,
With burning incense,
For your constant blessing and protection.

---

9. The Manchu word Dafu signifies the gods in heaven. Yuhuang is the Jade Emperor of Daoism, where he reigns over all, but he is not the supreme god in shamanism.

A WA SOUL-CALLING CHANT

Collected by Ni Ga (Wei Deming; Wa) and translated and introduced by Kun Shi (Han)

The Wa (Va) are one of the smaller ethnic groups in China, and one of the few groups in the country who speak Mon-Khmer languages. In China, the Wa number around four hundred thousand and live in the southwestern part of Yunnan province. Hundreds of thousands of Wa also reside in Burma and other parts of Southeast Asia. Dialects of their language spoken by various subgroups include Wa, Ahwa, and Ba'rek (Parauk), all meaning "mountain folk." Once hunters and gatherers, Wa who live in rural areas are now mostly mountain farmers and traders. Mountain villages with wooden stockades, huge ceremonial drums carved from giant trees, hunting crossbows, and women's garb of silver crowns and bracelets, long unbound hair, and tube skirts woven on backstrap looms are representative of some aspects of the traditional folk culture.

Most Wa today follow Theravada Buddhism or Christianity, though polytheistic and shamanistic beliefs are common. Beliefs concerning souls loom large in traditional belief systems. As among many peoples in southwestern China, persons are believed to have multiple souls, of which one is the vital soul. When a person dies, this soul must be sent to the other world, lest it prove troublesome to the living. It is also widely believed that when a person is sick, his or her soul is wandering. A shaman is often summoned to call the soul back to the stricken person's body with a special chant in which the soul is promised protection, succor, and a variety of comforts such as fine food and clothing, all to induce it to return. After the ceremony, thread is often tied around the patient's hands. Roosters with colored feathers or colored eggs are commonly used in the ceremonies, while white chickens are reserved for ceremonies to exorcise evil spirits.

"Daxga Calls Back the Soul of Amrong" was recorded by Ni Ga in the spring of 1982 in a Wa area near Shanyun and Wendong, Yunnan. Daxga, the performer, is a follower of Theravada Buddhism. Amrong, Daxga's wife, was in her sixties and suffering from malaria when this healing song was chanted. Auspicious days are the best for chanting, especially the day of the tiger (dragon days are best for rainmaking). Depending on the circumstances, such ceremonies can be performed in the home or on a hilltop.

DAXGA CALLS BACK THE SOUL OF AMRONG

Performed by Daxga (Wa)

Oh! Amrong, Amrong!
Amrong is frightened, startled!
She is frightened by insects,
She is startled by buffalo;
She is frightened by snakes,

She is startled by leeches.
Thus I am calling back her soul,
Thus I am calling back her life.
The calling should be made on a useful day,
It should be made on a lucky day.
(Wandering souls) do not stand on the ground,
Do not separate at the crossroads.
We offer complete bundles of thread,
Complete skeins of silk thread,
A full bottle of wine,
And a whole piece of sugarcane.
We use a sickle to cut the sugarcane,
We use a hook to get the bananas.
We do not let you stay in low, wet places,
Nor let you stay in deep grass,
Nor let the flood carry you away,
Nor let the flood drown you.
So we gladly call you,
So we call in loud voices.
We call you back by offering one *jin* of gold,
We call you back by offering a silver bracelet.
Threads are in bundles,
Silk threads are in skeins.
Do not stand at the crossroad,
Do not stop on flat ground.
Please stay in a smoke house,
Please stay in a dry warehouse.
Please break and eat the egg,
Please warm yourself by the fire.
We treat you with a rooster,
We entertain you with the first egg.
So you must come back,
So you must return home.
You can live in the main roof beam,
You can sit in the central room.
You can hide in the long trunk,
You can hide under the red rock cave.
Come back from the place you were frightened,
Come back from the place you were startled.
After you were frightened away by insects,
After you were startled away by buffalo,
After you were caught in a landslide,
After you were hitched by a rope,
We now treat you attentively.

You, ancestral spirits, Luan![10]
You are the lords of the souls.
So we invite you here,
So we beg you to return.
Come back at an auspicious time,
Come back on a lucky day.
We'll treat you to rooster meat,
We'll feast you on the best eggs.

---

10. Luan is a reference to the local ancestors of the Wa.

A LAHU MARRIAGE PRAYER

Collected, translated, and introduced by Anthony R. Walker

Speakers of a Tibeto-Burman language, the Lahu of southwestern Yunnan spill over into the four neighboring states of Burma, Thailand, Laos, and Vietnam. In the People's Republic of China there are over 450,000 Lahu. Perhaps 150,000 Lahu live in Burma (there are no accurate figures), possibly as many as 100,000 in Thailand, over 5,000 in Vietnam, and 10,000 in Laos. In addition, a few hundred live in the United States, principally in California.

Living mostly in the mountains on both sides of the Lancang (Mekong) River in Simao and Lincang prefectures, the Lahu of Simao prefecture occupy relatively small village communities, which are scattered among settlements of other ethnic minority peoples, principally Wa (or Va) and Hani (Akha). (In the north of Lincang prefecture, Lahu settlements tend to be much larger.) In their population centers, the Lahu's immediate neighbors in the lowlands are the Dai. Although, in historical terms (as is evident from the language they speak), the Lahu are to be counted among the Yi peoples, over the centuries their social, religious, political, and economic institutions have been greatly influenced by the cultural ideology of their Theravada Buddhist Dai neighbors. The Lahu are essentially an ethnic minority people living on the peripheries, both geographic and cultural, of Dai civilization. Only in the past two centuries has it been necessary for some of the Lahu to make significant adaptations to Han civilization.

In 1953, in pursuance of the Communist Party's policy of regional autonomy for ethnic minority peoples, the Chinese authorities set up the Lancang Lahu Autonomous County; in the following year, the Menglian Dai-Lahu-Wa Autonomous County was established. More recently, in 1985 and 1990, respectively, Shuangjiang Lahu-Wa-Bulang-Dai Autonomous County and Zhenyuan Yi-Hani-Lahu Autonomous County have been created. All but Shuangjiang county (part of Lincang prefecture) are in Simao prefecture. Over half of all Lahu in the People's Republic of China live in Lancang county, where, constituting about 48 percent of the county's population, they make up the largest ethnic group.

The traditional Lahu economy is based on shifting, or swidden, agriculture, the farmers cultivating rice as a subsistence crop and various other crops—such as cotton, corn, and opium poppy—both for domestic use and for sale or barter outside the community. Lahu in the more northerly areas of southwestern Yunnan learned plow agriculture from Han immigrants, while those in the southern areas picked up similar skills from their Dai neighbors. But not all Lahu live in areas where irrigated rice agriculture is a viable alternative to their traditional swidden farming technology.

Lahu villages are controlled by headmen, known as masters of the village, who are assisted, informally, by the elders of the community. Individual households enjoy much autonomy under the joint leadership of the "master" and "mistress" of the house. While some Chinese scholars infer a former matrilineal, even matriarchal, social system for the Lahu, bilateral kinship coupled with an uxorilocal postmarital residence rule seems to be the present norm among the great majority of Lahu communities. But sociocultural generalizations are always difficult concerning this essentially language-based ethnic group, which is divided into several important subgroups, Lahu Na and Lahu Shi (Black and Yellow Lahu) being the two principal ones.

Lahu marriage is traditionally monogamous and comes about usually after a brief period of courtship initiated by the young people themselves. Village festivals, especially the festival of the new lunar year, are favorite occasions for initiating courtships, for it is at these times that young people are free from farmwork and able to congregate. Youthful visitors come from other Lahu villages, and they sing and dance far into, or throughout, the night. Antiphonal group singing around a large bonfire some distance from the village is a favorite festival activity. Couples may break off from these parties in order to make their own fires in more secluded spots and there enjoy more intimate association than is possible in the larger group. In some Lahu communities, it is customary for a boy to ascertain his girlfriend's intentions toward him by "stealing" her turban. If she demands its return or makes any serious attempt to get it back, the boy is to understand that she rejects his advances. But if she protests little or not at all, he knows that he may proceed with his courtship.

Once a couple has decided on marriage, it is the young man's duty to approach his parents, who, in turn, will obtain the services of a village elder, not closely related to them, to act as mediator between the two families. It is customary for this go-between to take tea, wine, and possibly some other gifts to the girl's parents, who will accept them if they accept the marriage proposal; otherwise, they reject everything that is offered to them. Since much freedom is granted to the young people themselves, rejections seem uncommon, provided that the boy and girl are not descended from a common great-grandfather: "[Those related within] three generations may not marry," Lahu are frequently heard to say.

The nuptial rites vary from one Lahu community to another, and Christian Lahu have, of course, digressed in the direction of Protestant or Roman Catholic nuptial liturgies. But common traditional elements seem to be the lighting of candles, the binding of the couple's wrists with cotton strings (a rite supposed to preserve a person's spiritual essence, or "soul," within his or her body), and the chanting of the marriage prayer. This ceremony usually takes place in the bride's parental house, the master of ceremonies sometimes being the village headman, sometimes just a respected elder. After the ceremony, chickens are killed and leg-bone omens read. All partake in a ritual meal.

The marriage prayer chanted by the officiating elder is frequently rather short, but invariably poetic. In essence, it announces that an unpaired couple is now being paired by the community's elders and that this paired condition is the "natural" one for humankind, as it is for many other entities: sun and moon, mountain and valley, big cooking spoon and little cooking spoon, and so on. (The Lahu follow the same duodenary cycle as the Han Chinese. Each day has a guardian animal [in order: rat, ox, tiger, rabbit, dragon, snake, horse, sheep, monkey, fowl, dog, and pig], and children are frequently named after the presiding animal of their birthday. Thus in the marriage prayer, Ca Va[11] [Mr. Pig] and Ca Fa [Mr. Rat] are named after their respective calendar animals. One alternative to the animal-day system is to name a child according to birth order. Thus Na Ui [Miss Big] indicates that she is the firstborn child.)

THE MARRIAGE PRAYER

Oh, Ca Va and Na Ui, this evening you two are not one pair; so we white-haired people and black-haired people,[12] we take you and make you into one pair.

Within the four corners of the village, all the white-haired people and the yellow-haired people[13] take you and make you one pair.

Today and hereafter, you two will work for Ca Fa.[14]

Guardian spirit of the village, carefully look upon and take care of this pair; guardian spirit of the house, carefully look upon and take care of this pair; guardian spirit of the temple,[15] carefully look upon and take care of this pair.

The sun and moon are one pair; these two are not one pair; so here, this evening, we of this community, all of us together, take Ca Va and Na Ui and we make them one pair.

---

11. The male prefix "Ca" is pronounced "cha."

12. The poetic couplet "white-haired people and black-haired people" means "old people and young people" and, so, "the whole community."

13. "White-haired . . . yellow-haired" make a couplet with "white-haired . . . black-haired" and have the same meaning; Lahu youngsters do not, of course, have yellow hair.

14. The couple will reside uxorilocally and work for the bride's father, Ca Fa. After the completion of the duties of the bride service and a somewhat shorter period of service for the boy's father, the couple is free to set up a household of its own, usually in the wife's village.

15. Some, but by no means all, Lahu villages have temple buildings dedicated to the worship of their highest divinity, the creator divinity G'ui sha. But here the elder calls on the protective spirit of the temple, not on G'ui sha himself.

Let them enjoy health and prosperity;[16] let their children be as plentiful as the fruit of the *tao ma* tree, as plentiful as the fruit of the *hk'a ca* tree.[17]

Open this blessing upon Ca Va and Na Ui; enwrap them both with this blessing alone.

The grasshoppers, they say, are in pairs; the caterpillars, they say, are in pairs; these two are not one pair, so we take them and we make them one pair.

Oh, when these two work in the fields, may they obtain good yields; wheresoever they prepare their fields, may they obtain food; wherever they wish to work, may they obtain everything they need.

The small bamboo spoon and the big bamboo spoon are one pair;[18] these two are not one pair; so we take them and we make them one pair.

Oh, today, we take these two and make them one pair; may they both live to the same age.
May the headman and the priest help these two, may the white-haired people and the black-haired people, all together, help them.

May they not die, may they enjoy long lives; may they suffer no sickness, may this blessing alone always be upon them.

As the hills and streams do not separate, so may these two not separate.

May the solar scribe and the lunar scribe,[19] like the sun that can look in ninety thousand directions, watch over and be mindful of them.

Today and hereafter, when these two climb the hills, may the spirits of the hills protect them;
When they go down to the valleys, may the spirits of the valleys protect them.

Oh, these two people will live with and work for Ca Fa; like heaven and earth, may they not separate.

---

16. Literally "to stay easily and to have easily."

17. Both trees are said to be notable for the quantity of fruit they yield; *tao ma* is Indian gooseberry (*Phyllanthus emblica*), but I am unable to identify *hk'a ca*.

18. The small spoon and the big spoon are used, respectively, for stirring and ladling food.

19. Some Lahu talk of the solar and lunar scribes, who record every action of mankind, through day and night.

May they both enjoy health and prosperity; today and hereafter, may they suffer neither death nor sickness.

When they have children, may the children not die; let there be many animals underneath the house[20] and let there be many people inside the house.

Let this blessing be opened upon them, let them be enwrapped by this blessing.

Oh, good fortune, good fortune to Ca Va and Na Ui!

20. Lahu houses frequently are raised on piles. Domestic animals like pigs, fowl, and dogs sleep underneath the house, and horses and mules are frequently tethered there at night as well.

YI CHANTS FROM CHUXIONG PREFECTURE, YUNNAN

Introduced by Mark Bender

The following chants were collected in the Chuxiong Yi Autonomous Prefecture, in north-central Yunnan province. The Yi are one of the largest ethnic minority groups in China, numbering over 7 million, with dozens of subgroups living throughout the mountains of southwestern China. The largest Yi subgroups in Chuxiong prefecture are the Lipo and Lolopo. Most Yi in the prefecture are farmers who raise rice, buckwheat, and other grains; hemp; and goats, chickens, and other livestock. Traditional-styled houses are made of adobe brick, rammed earth, and sometimes logs.

Language and custom vary widely among the Yi, especially in Yunnan. While certain commonalties exist with the Nuosu of southern Sichuan and northwestern Yunnan, there are many differences between them and the Chuxiong Yi in terms of folk literature, costume, housing styles, burial practices, and other customs. Many Yi in north-central Yunnan have lived in proximity to Han Chinese for generations and have been influenced more strongly by Han culture than have Yi in other places. In recent years, as native language use has decreased in parts of Chuxiong prefecture, folk songs have come to be sung in Chinese to Yi tunes (a phenomenon also seen in other ethnic minority areas). The following chants were taken from a collection of songs and chants (many sung in Chinese) collected in the 1980s by researchers in Chuxiong prefecture.

CALLING BACK A CHILD'S SPIRIT

Performed by Yang Shi (Yi), collected by Yu Weiliang (Yi), and translated by Mark Bender and Fu Wei

"Calling Back a Child's Spirit" is an example of a soul-calling chant from the Lufeng area of Chuxiong prefecture. Like other ethnic groups in southwestern China, the Yi have many traditional beliefs about wandering souls. If someone dreams about a living person, it is thought that the person's soul has actually entered the dream. If, instead, a deceased person is seen in a dream, the next morning prayers and sacrifices are made to appease the wandering soul. In cases of chronic illness, it is thought that the soul has wandered from the body. Therefore, certain rituals are performed by the Yi priests (*bimo*), who read the sacred scriptures calling back the soul from the mountains, rivers, valleys, and woodlands. In some areas, bowls of rice, water, and wine are placed in front of the doorway to refresh the returning soul.

"Calling Back a Child's Spirit," shorter and less complicated than many sung by the *bimo*, may be sung by a sick child's mother. She will sing the lyrics at daybreak, her hands on her child's head. Many Yi women still know such songs.

Little one!
The sky is brightening.
Come home!
The sky is brightening, it's nearly dawn.
Hurry on home!
If you're frightened, don't fear,
Get up and hurry home;
Don't keep wandering about there.

In a dream,
Uncle Zhou told me
That you are in the piney rocks.
I'll go a thousand miles to meet you;
When my calls echo through the mountains,
You should answer;
When my calls echo along the rivers,
You should answer;
When my calls echo through the mountains,
You should walk on home;
When my calls echo along the rivers,
You should ride a boat on home.

Don't go to the places the crows are calling,
Don't go to the places with crags and crevices;
Don't stand beside the rivers and waters,
Don't stay by the foot or top of the village.
When it's cold, come back, get better dressed;
When you are hungry, come back for your supper.

The sky brightens,
It's time for you to come home.
Hurry back to put on clothes,
Hurry back for supper.

Come back, come back!

CLOSING THE COFFIN

Performed by Zhou Cong (Yi), collected by Zhe Houpei (Yi) and Yu Lihang (Yi), and translated by Mark Bender and Fu Wei

"Closing the Coffin" is part of a series of funeral chants sung by a Yi priest, known as a *bimo*, during lengthy and complex funeral rites. An important role of the *bimo* is conducting the soul of the dead to the land of the ancestors. As such chants unfold, the soul is guided through the landscape in which actual (or sometimes forgotten) towns and places are named. This chant follows a similar pattern, in that in stressing the filial piety of the deceased's children in the search for the objects needed for the funeral, many familiar places in the landscape are noted. It is believed that when the deceased hears the song, he or she will rest in peace, on the soft cotton supplied by the descendants. All the towns and cities named in the chant are in northern Yunnan, while the Awa (a local name for the Wa) live farther south near the border with Burma. The numbers nine and seven (in reference to the children) may be related to the nine young men and seven young women who, in the ancient creation myths, were told to make the heavens and earth, respectively. The chant is only one part in a long series covering every step of the burial process. Unlike the cremation practices of the Nuosu of southern Sichuan, earth burials are the norm in most of Yunnan.

Elder of this clan,
Today you have passed away;
No longer can we let you
Sleep upon a bed.
Your children will carry you,
Place you
Inside the wooden casket.

You have raised nine sons,
As well as seven daughters;
Your children will carry you.

Your sons' hands do hard work each day,
Using the hoe and plow on the earth.
Digging dirt and cutting wood
Has calloused those hands.
Of those nine sons,
Each one's hands are hard.
They cannot softly carry you.

Your daughters' hands spin hemp,
Your daughters' hands sew clothing.
Thus your daughters were asked to
Carry you—
Yet, though your daughters' hands are soft,
A mattress still had to be found.
But where could one be found?

In the town of Zhennan,
Only banjos were for sale;
And in Gongtong,

Not one mattress was seen;
And in Lufeng town,
There were only bamboo mats.

In Liangxiangguan,
Only scissors were for sale,
Not one mattress was seen;
In Kunming,
Goods were heaped in mountains,
But not one mattress was seen.

Returning to Dingyuan,
There were only metal wares.
Going to Yaoan,
A son went out,
Went to the region of the Awa,
To bring back some Awa cotton.
A cotton worker was called to fluff it,
Then to make the mattress.
The mattress was placed in the coffin;
And how soft the cotton is!

Lightly, softly they carry you,
Carry you to the coffin,
For a comfortable sleep.

CUTTING THE NEW YEAR'S FIREWOOD

Performed by Qumulashi (Yi); collected by Jimoreko (Yi), Jihuowangjia (Yi), and Wang Jiaxing; edited by Yang Jizhong; and translated by Mark Bender

There are many chants connected with the various festivals marking the yearly calendar, as is true for many of the ethnic groups in China, and those associated with the festivals greeting the New Year are particularly numerous. "Cutting the New Year's Firewood" recognizes the life of a tree used in the New Year celebrations of certain Yi communities in Yongren county, Chuxiong prefecture. The Yi believe that trees have spirits and that there is a firewood spirit. A simple ceremony is held when wood—old beliefs say that it must be pine—is cut for the New Year's ceremony. Before making his first cut, an axman places a bit of food and drink before the tree, and then recites songs similar to the following one. Later, while chopping the wood and carrying it home, he chants a succession of other lyrics.

Straight, straight grows this pine tree. You stand before me—
Today I want to cut you, cut you for the New Year's firewood.

When the sky created mankind he also created the myriad beings:
The sons of snow were in twelve divisions,[21]
And you are among the bloodless ones.
Yet the bloodless divisions were also divided:
First was the Muwugezi group,[22]
Second, the Geziechu group,
Third, the Echuxuezi group,
Fourth, the Xuezierbo group,
Fifth, the Erbonisa group.
These five generations were further divided into tens,
With grandchildren covering the earth.
You are the eldest of the trees, you are that one, the progenitor.
Of all the spirit trees on earth, you are the greatest;
Of the tree and grass spirits,

You are the most powerful.

Today I come to cut you,
Cut you for the New Year's firewood.

It's not that I fear you that I cut you, and not that I hate you that I cut you, and neither is it that I can find no other tree for firewood.
It is because of the tenets of the ancestors; it has been said for certain that it is only you that can be cut.

21. This line and the next reflect the local Yi belief that humans and other living beings were transformed from snow. According to legend, the snow had twelve sons; five became "bloodless flora," and seven became fauna with blood.

22. Muwugezi refers to the first god of firewood; the other names are his successors in later generations.

A NUOSU MYTH FROM SICHUAN

Collected, translated, and introduced by Bamo Qubumo (Yi)

The Nuosu, numbering more than 2 million, are the largest subgroup of the Yi ethnic group of southwestern China. Most Nuosu live in the Liangshan Mountains in Sichuan and Yunnan provinces, raising sheep, goats, cows, pigs, chickens, and a variety of upland crops including potatoes and buckwheat. Hunting (and a keen interest in hunting dogs) is still a part of traditional life, though this is more restricted than in the past. Muntjac (*Muntiacus*) and river deer (also called water deer [*Hydropotes inermis*]) are favorite prey. Clan ties and ties of blood and marriage are a central aspect of the Nuosu worldview and identity; references to all sorts of relationships are common in Nuosu oral and oral-connected narratives. Among the most elaborate of Nuosu narratives are the *bbopa* (origin narratives). Such stories are usually sung by priests, called *bimo*, in a variety of ritual settings, though shamans (*sunyi*) are often called on to perform many ghost-ridding rituals.

"The Origin of Ghosts" is usually sung as part of a ritual to exorcise ghosts from a home.[23] If, for instance, lightning strikes a house, a *bimo* will be called on to chant an origin narrative dealing with ghosts in order to rid the home of harmful forces that may cause horrible diseases such as leprosy. In order for the exorcism to succeed, an account of the origin of ghosts must first be told. Before the telling, a fire is started in the home to assemble the supernaturals and aid the *bimo* in his work. The family "ghost boards" (boards painted with ritual drawings used in creating spells targeted at ghosts) are also brought out. The most common text for such events is "The Origin of Ghosts" (Nyicy bbopa), also known as "The Beautiful Zyzy" (Zyzy hninra), and "Scripture of Ghost Spells" (Nyicyssy teyy). The content concerns the activities of a ghostly femme fatale. The word *zyzy* refers to a type of bird, while *hninra* means "beautiful"—such a name implies that the young woman has no clan ties (and thus no real origin) and is thus a different sort of being. Although written versions of the story exist, *bimo* priests normally recite the texts, composed in five- or seven-syllable line units, from memory.

The following text is based on a performance in Nuosu dialect by the *bimo* Qubi Dage, recorded and translated by Yi epic scholar and poet Bamo Qubumo in 1992. Among the stylistic features of the text are the predominance of five-syllable lines, repetition, formulaic beginnings and endings of some passages, and the insertion of short accounts on the early life of the hero Hxoyi Ddiggur (as in episode 4). Before actually performing the Zyzy Hninra story, the *bimo* will recite several other origin narratives, beginning with the origin of the *bimo* priests. As the ritual proceeds, the *bimo* inserts the *bbopa* where appropriate, often when particular ritual objects are being employed.

---

23. A version of the translation first appeared in Bamo Qubumo, "Traditional Nuosu Origin Narratives: A Case of Ritualized Epos in *Bimo* Incantation Scriptures," *Oral Tradition* 16, no. 2 (2001): 453–79.

Certain verbal effects, often enhanced by gestures and bodily movement, are part of the narration. For instance, in some passages the lines are strung together "like pearls" and spoken in rapid sequence or enhanced in other ways; one example is the deer's speech in episode 3. The description of the lovely Zyzy Hninra (episode 6) freshly changed from a deer is the sort of passage subject to elaboration in the act of performance. Another example is the ghost-cursing speech of the *bimo* priests in episode 10. Such passages—or "verbal riffs" (*kemgo kaxie bi*)—are often not found in the written versions. As an oral feature, their use allows performers to demonstrate their ability as singers, display their knowledge of traditional lore, and make the tales more exciting for their audiences. The final line of the text is delivered in a thundering voice, as if the curse were fiercely cast toward the ghost: "*Yy a kekemu!*" (Torrents of curses upon you!)

It should be noted that ghosts are an important part of the Yi supernatural world, with a variety of manifestations, characteristics, and powers. Many are derived from persons who suffered violent or early deaths and are sometimes associated with natural phenomena such as lightning, and living people may transform themselves into ghosts.[24] Ghosts are often associated with pestilence and disease, and some are especially known for being duplicitous. Besides ghosts, the story also presents an array of wildlife native to the Liangshan region.

THE ORIGIN OF GHOSTS

Performed by Qubi Dage (Yi)

EPISODE 1

Chanting loud and long—
Once upon a time,
When that time of heaven and earth in chaos had passed;
Once upon a time, when time had already flown,
Past the age of the six suns and seven moons . . .
At that time, when the cock crowed at dawn,
And the swallows soared in the clouds,
And dawn was brightening—
Toward the direction called *zyzy puvu*,
In the land of the Aji clan of Nuosu nobles:
The old man got up and made the fire,
The old woman got up and set the pot;
The maiden got up and prepared the dog food,
The child got up and tied the leash to the dog.
In the land of the Nuosu noble clans,

24. See "Cannibal Grandmother" (chap. 1).

The Ajis had for three years raised hunting dogs,
The Ajis for three months had woven dog cages.
The three lads arose,
Whistling to their hunting dogs for a chase in the mountains.
The white hunting dogs arose like sheep;
The black hunting dogs arose like bears;
The piebald hunting dogs arose like magpies;
The red hunting dogs arose like badgers;
The yellow hunting dogs arose like tigers;
The gray hunting dogs arose like wolves. . . .
The three lads whistled up their hunting dogs and left,
Left, they, for the forest.

EPISODE 2

At this time, responding to a dog's bark,
A white river deer was driven from a bamboo grove.
As the deer was fleeing, it came round three hilltops
While running through nine stands of forest;
It jumped three times over gullies while nine times wading through rivers;
Finally reaching the bank of the Anning River, from the mountain Sypy Ggehxo.
At this time, responding to a dog's bark,
The deer ran across the headman Nzy Miajy.
Drawing his silver bow,
Fixed with a golden arrow,
He released it toward the white river deer.
The arrow point flew toward the clouds,
Yet, no one saw where it fell.

At this time, responding to a dog's bark, the deer ran into Moke Ddizzi,[25] the wise;
Drawing his copper bow,
Fixed with an iron arrow,
He released it toward the white river deer,
The arrow point flew toward the mists
Yet no one saw where it fell.

25. Moke Ddizzi assists the rule of the Aji.

EPISODE 3

At this time, responding to a dog's bark,
The deer ran near the famous warrior, the hero Hxoyi Ddiggur,[26]
Who drew his huge wooden bow, with a fixed bamboo arrow;
As he settled on his target,
The white river deer, just at that moment, suddenly spoke out:
"Hxoyi Ddiggur, don't shoot at me.
Ddiggur, don't shoot at me.
You were born as a human in Momupugu,
I was born as a beast in the same spot.
So we share the same birthplace,
Ddiggur, don't shoot me."
And she explained it again and again,
"The divine beast with a single horn am I.
Even though a beast at which to aim,
I am not supposed to be hit.
Even if hit, I am not supposed to drop to the ground;
Even if dropped, I am not to be butchered;
Even if butchered, I am not to be cooked;
Even if cooked, I am not to be eaten;
Even if eaten, I am not to be digested.
Were they me to shoot, a white river deer such as I would
Either break nine strong bows or injure nine archers;
If butchered I would either break nine long knives or injure
nine butchers;
If cooked I would either damage nine iron pots or hurt nine eaters;
If eaten I would either nip nine white teeth or hurt nine gluttonous
tongues. . . ."[27]
"Hxoyi Ddiggur, don't shoot at me;
Ddiggur, don't shoot at me.
You were born as a human being in Momupugu,
I was born as a beast in the same spot.
So we share the same birthplace,
Ddiggur, don't shoot at me."
And she explained again and again,
"I have been looking for you so long,
Since your parents asked me to send you their words.

---

26. Hxoyi Ddiggur serves the Aji.

27. The verses are joined like a string, and the voice is sounded in rapid succession like a chain of pearls, such as a series of statements or words poured in an ascending order of rhetorical force or intensity, especially from the mouth of the river deer in the first person's speech.

Your father was melancholy as he missed you so much.
Your mother was not herself as she was always thinking of you.
When your father missed you,
In the daytime he would wander at the entrance of the valley
And take seven wrong roads,
While at night he was so sad his tears wet the pillow and bedclothes;
When your mother thought of you,
In the daytime her mind was uneasy and her eyes were so dizzy,
She would go to ten different places outside the village;
While at night she cried so hard that tears flowed from the hands
With which she covered her eyes, and the tears would wet three layers
of soil."
Hxoyi Ddiggur
Drew his huge wooden bow,
The bamboo arrow fixed.
When settling on his target, the white river deer,
Just at that moment, he suddenly cast a spell:
"The sun rises in the east—and my arrow flies like a dragon!
The water in the rivers flows to the south—my arrow is ever victorious!
The sun goes down in the west—my arrow can sweep away all obstacles!
The source of water is in the north—my arrow will miss no targets!"[28]

No matter how the deer begged and cajoled,
It could not stop the flight of Ddiggur's lethal arrow.
As the deer was shot,
The arrowhead point broke from the shaft,
Driving straight through to its tail.

EPISODE 4

Hxoyi Ddiggur,
When five years old,
Went to play on the dam with the swineherd.
He caught big snakes,
Playing with them as if they were fish.
He caught toads,
Playing with them as if pieces of stone.
When six years old, he hung around the hills with shepherds,
Catching gray leopards and riding them as if steeds.
He caught red tigers,

---

28. This is an example of *kemgo kaxie bi*, an oral text riff not found in the incantation scripture.

Making them plow like cows.
He caught wild boars, riding them as if steeds.
He caught old bears, too, making them plow like cows.
He led jackals and wolves as if leading dogs;
He caught muntjac and river deer,
Yelling to them as if stock.
When seven years old, he wove mats,
Wearing them as armor.
When learning martial arts,
He crouched agilely to dodge the flying stones.
On the battlefield,
He would meet an enemy head-on,
Facing the spear thrust toward him.
He walked like a fish leaping,
Moving freely along the cliffs, amid
Spears like bamboo groves and
Arrows like falling stars.

EPISODE 5

When the hunters ran to the place where the deer had fallen,
They could not see a trace of the deer;
Hearing the sound of a hunting dog barking ahead,
They followed the sound to investigate.
The whole pack was barking at a stand of red blooming trees.
Ddiggur thought there must be something hidden in those trees,
So he anxiously drew an arrow and shot toward the trees.
When he shot off a branch, it fell to the ground and disappeared;
Standing in front of him was a maiden,
The incomparably beautiful Zyzy Hninra.

EPISODE 6

Look at Zyzy Hninra:
Her plait is black and glossy with smooth, soft hair;
Her forehead's wide and flat, a nose in exactly the right place,
Neck slender and upright;
Lips thin and delicate,
Cheeks soft and tender,
Eyes bright and shining, eyelashes upturned.
Look at Zyzy Hninra:
Her fingers delicate and arms slender,
Soft and dainty legs, plump and round;

Her dress, long and graceful.
Oh, Zyzy Hninra,
Her appearance is as beautiful as a charming moon on a fall night;
Her carriage as elegant and smart as the river in the sloping fields;
Her voice as melodious as a skylark in a vast field.
A lovely maiden she is indeed![29]

EPISODE 7

One day,
The head of another Nuosu tribe, Nzy Awo Nyiku,
Took his hunting hounds to the forest to look for game,
And soon was face-to-face with Zyzy.
He was stricken at first sight,
And Zyzy Hninra followed Awo Nyiku to his clan's village,
Where the two lived happily together.

EPISODE 8

The first year,
Hninra was a beautiful wife,
With a face like flowers and a bearing like the moon,
And the second year she was a wise and capable spouse.
But in the third year,
Zyzy Hninra began to change,
To become nasty, evil, and cold,
And in the village people started dying,
One after another, for no apparent reason.

She was born with two pairs of eyes that were separately
Set in the front and at the back of her head,
With the front ones to watch the roads,
And the back ones to see human beings.
She was born with two mouths that, too,
Were set front and back of her head,
With the front one to eat food,
And the back one to devour human beings.
She was born with two pairs of hands,
Set both in front and back of her body,
The front ones for collecting firewood,

29. This is another example of *kemgo kaxie bi*.

And the back ones for ripping out human hearts.
She would eat the corpse when someone died in the village;
She would devour the remaining bones
When a corpse was burned on the mountain.

In the fourth year,
Awo Nyiku took ill.
One day he asked about Zyzy Hninra's family tree
And where she was from,
And she told him a plausible story.

EPISODE 9

Awo Nyiku was very afraid,
And began to plot to control Hninra,
And pretended that his illness was worsening.
Hninra tried to cure him,
And one day she turned into a red-winged kite,
And flew in an instant to an island
In the middle of the sea
To bring back a swan egg;
Another day, she turned into a banded jackal,
And in the wink of an eye ascended a tall mountain,
Boring into a black bear's chest to steal the bear's gallbladder;
Another day, she changed into an otter,
And instantly dove to the bottom of a river to bring back a fish's heart. . . .
But none of this had any effect.

One day Awo Nyiku said that, with the exception of snow
From the peak of the great mountain Minyak Konkar,
Nothing could cure him.
Zyzy Hninra was determined to save her husband,
And decided that no matter what, she would go
To that thousand-tricent[30] distant snowy mountain to fetch the snow.
Before she left, Zyzy asked Awo Nyiku to promise her:
"After I go, don't burn the stone used to exorcise evil spirits at home,
Or you will get a headache.
Don't burn wood,
Or you will get asthma.
Don't burn the fire made to exorcise evil spirits in front of the house,
Or you will feel dizzy.

---

30. One tricent (*li*) is three hundred steps, or about one-third of a mile.

Don't sweep the rubbish in the house,
Or you will feel nervous.
Don't let a *bimo* speak in the village,
Or you will become deaf.
Don't pick up the exorcising branch,
Or you will get lumbago."[31]

EPISODE 10

After Zyzy had left,
Awo Nyiku quickly summoned ninety *bimo*
From the upper end of the village,
And seventy *sunyi*
From the lower end of the village
To his house to read texts and perform rituals.

"Let me chant out a loud and long howling.
Zyzy Hninra, you used flattering words and a pretty appearance
To baffle human beings,
And you used your witchcraft to mislead common people.
You'd better submit to the magic arts immediately! . . .
Zyzy Hninra, you are the spirit of the trees on the wild mountains
And the licentious birds in the sky.
Now your witchcraft has lost its effect,
And you'd better submit to the magic arts immediately! . . .
I will dispatch the flood dragon to the sea,
So that you will not be able to hide yourself in the water.
I will dispatch the divine snake to the earth,
So that you will not be able to hide yourself in the earth!
Curses cast toward the ghost like rapids rolling fiercely away!"[32]

EPISODE 11

At that time, as Zyzy Hninra had completed a thousand travails
And was on her way back from the snowy peak,
Because of the spells and curses of the *bimo* and *sunyi*,
She slowly changed into a light-gray mountain goat with a red tail;
The snow that she had fetched for Awo Nyiku still stuck on her hoofs,
Caught in her wool, stuck in her ears,

---

31. All these things are taboo in the world of ghosts; consequently, all Zyzy's cautions to Awo Nyiku ironically constitute a manual for performing rituals against ghosts, but in reverse!

32. This is another example of *kemgo kaxie bi*.

And adhered to her horns.
She knew her life was nearing its end,
And wanted to ride the wind back home from the snowy mountain.
She wanted to bring back the snow, to express her undying love
for Awo Nyiku.

EPISODE 12

But Awo Nyiku summoned ninety young men,
And shot with an arrow a tired old goat,
Which they bound and took into a cave in the mountainside.
Before long, the goat that Zyzy Hninra had turned into
Washed out of the cliffside cave into a river,
And fell into a cloth fishing basket
Used by three herders from the household of Vusa Jjujjo,
And was skinned and eaten by people who knew nothing of it.
As a result, the people who died from eating the goat that Zyzy Hninra
Turned into, became ghosts who injure people everywhere.

The goat was taken out from the water.
On a slate cutting board, the herdsman skinned the goat
And then the skin was stretched on the ground.
The young girls dealt with the goat intestines,
Placed the meat on a bamboo sifter,
Cut up the goat intestines with a sickle.
But many people died of poisoning after eating the meat.[33]

EPISODE 13

Many tribes and clans were completely destroyed by the ghosts of
Zyzy Hninra,
So the *bimo* and *sunyi* of every tribe and every clan all curse Zyzy
Hninra
With a thousand curses, and all say that Zyzy Hninra was the origin of
ghosts.
Yy a kekemu! Torrents of curses upon you![34]

33. These are taboos in everyday Nuosu life.
34. The final line of the narrative is an ending formula.

Chapter 4

THE EPIC TRADITIONS

What is an epic? In recent decades, this is a question that has come to concern scholars of oral literature around the world. As researchers in Africa, Asia, the Americas, Australia, and Europe have systematically examined the performed narratives of many cultures in these regions, the standard definition of "epic" as a long poem of history focused on a hero—based on the model of the Greek epics of Homer—has widened to include material that makes neat definitions of the term difficult. In addition to the increased awareness of the wealth of epics around the globe, scholars have come to realize that living epics are dynamic and multifaceted traditions of performance. Thus the tag "epic" has been given to an increasingly wide variety of orally performed narratives, many of which have a more pronounced dramatic element than usually has been ascribed to ancient Greek epics (of which, unfortunately, there are no taped live performances!).

In the spirit of this more encompassing approach to epics, Finnish scholar Lauri Honko described the epic as a long poem about exemplary characters.[1] His definition was based in part on his research on written and live performance versions of the Siri epic, of the Tulu people of southern India, which was part of a large project intended to document endangered epic traditions on the Silk Road and to increase familiarity with a host of epic traditions elsewhere.

1. Lauri Honko, *Textualising the Siri Epic*, Folklore Fellows Communications, no. 264 (Helsinki: Suomalainen Tiedeakatemia, Academia Scientiarum Fennica, 1998).

Honko found that not only are heroines more prominent in some traditions than heroes, but the requirements of a historical component and the association with the martial values of valor and military prowess are not necessarily aspects of the many long poetic narratives that have been documented. As for performance, through the work of many scholars it has become obvious that, in the oral tradition, epics are seldom, if ever, performed in whole: it is more the norm for them to be recited or enacted in parts. A single singer or group of singers may know only one portion of a larger story that exists as a whole only when the various parts are recorded, transcribed, edited, translated (if necessary), and published. Uniformity has frequently been the goal of epic collectors and editors as they seek to "textualize" their findings, but in the oral realm, variation and versions are the norm, as with other folk activity. Thus epics are more often than not performed in segments, and these segments, even if performed by the same singers, vary in accordance with the particulars of the performance situation and the state of mind of the singers and even the audience. While singers may have a mental version of a full episode, or even a whole narrative cycle, each time the singers perform, they draw on and recombine parts of the mental version to voice a re-created version of the story suited to a particular audience.

This new scholarly orientation toward the epic has allowed many researchers to recognize that China, which some Western literary scholars once claimed did not have epics, is actually a place where many different epic traditions have flourished in the past and where some survive as living traditions. This awareness has grown over the past fifty years in China because of the efforts of many folklore collectors of various ethnic groups involved in both large- and small-scale collecting and translation projects, which have often received government funding and logistical support.

The epic traditions of China tend to be divided into two broad categories: the heroic epics of the northern and western borderlands and the creation-oriented epics of the south and southwest. For the most part, these traditions are the cultural products of a number of ethnic minority groups. In recent years, however, examples of creation epics and long narrative poems have been found among some Han groups in rural southern China. Although there is some rationale for considering the long prosimetric performance traditions (and related written ones) of some Han local cultures as epics, these traditions (such as Suzhou chantefable and precious scrolls) are usually classified in China as forms of *quyi* (art of melodies), and they are presented in the sections on northern and southern prosimetric forms in chapter 6.

Examples of the heroic epics from the northern borderlands are a Mongol version of the famous epic of the legendary Tibetan king Gesar. As adapted by Mongol epic singers hundreds of years ago, the story of the hero—named Geser Khan—has taken on new content and meaning. Of especial prominence are the passages concerning the multiheaded ogre who seduces one of Geser Khan's wives and is later killed by the hero. Such tales of multiheaded human-eating ogres are common among the various Mongol groups and other cultures all across the northern steppes and among the forest-dwelling peoples of northeastern China. Also included is a passage from the native Mongol epic from western Inner Mongolia about the hero Jangar. The epic relates the exploits of heroes who exist in an imaginary world of lavish banquets, manly sport, kidnappings and rescues, battles with ogres, and courting of beautiful women. Among the many epics and narrative poems of the Yi people in southwestern China is *The Palace Lamp of the Nanzhao Kingdom* (Chinese, *Nanzhao gongdeng*), which was discovered in Yunnan province in the 1970s. Written in a form of Yi script, the text relates the rise of a young king in an ancient kingdom that once ruled a large part of southwestern China and northern Southeast Asia around the eighth century C.E. The southern creation epics are represented by *Miluotuo*, a tradition-oriented version of a Yao creation epic written by an ethnic poet based on traditional materials. The story relates the creation of the sky and earth and the actions of the female creator as she makes the forests, plants, animals, and humans. Many of the motifs in the epic are common to creation epics all over southern and southwestern China. Among certain Miao groups in southeastern Guizhou province, short lyrics known as song flowers are intertwined with passages of the epics, which are called ancient songs. Two such flower songs (completely different from the songs of a similar name from northwestern China) are also included in this chapter.

AN EXCERPT FROM THE EPIC *GESER KHAN*

Translated from Mongolian into Chinese and edited by Ankeqinfu (Mongol) and Qimudedao'erji (Mongol), translated from Chinese into English by Mark Bender and Chao Gejin (Chogjin; Mongol), and introduced by Chao Gejin

The epic tale of King Geser (Tibetan, Gesar), of Tibetan origin, is among the longest epic poems ever created.[2] The narrative, consisting of three major parts, concerns the life and deeds of a great supernatural king who brings peace and harmony to the three realms of the heavens, earth, and underworld. Each of the three parts is composed of many episodes. The first part deals with the supernatural birth and early life of Geser, who is the son of the god Hurmusta and is reincarnated on earth as a weak and deformed young man. Later, Geser distinguishes himself in a series of manly contests at a festival, winning the hand of a lovely wife and transforming into a handsome superhero, eventually becoming a king. The second portion of the epic relates various military campaigns and battles. The last section involves his pacification of the various realms and rescue of his mother and wife from the land of the dead in the underworld. In the end, he returns to the heavens. Since telling the entire tale might take years, the story is never told as a whole, and bards tend to choose those portions with which they are most familiar.

This Tibetan tale has been adapted by a number of other ethnic groups in Central Asia and the northern steppes. Of these adaptations, the Mongol versions—in which the hero is called Geser Khan—are the best documented. The following selection is taken from a Mongol version of *Geser Khan* sung by the singer Pajie (1902–1962) in China in the early 1960s, just before such folklore-collecting activities were ended by the onset of the Cultural Revolution in 1966. Pajie (also known as Pajai) is said to have had an incredible memory even as a child and could memorize performances of famous epic singers upon one hearing. After spending years in training as a lama, at age eighteen Pajie began a career as an epic singer, performing epics about heroes battling the multiheaded monster ogres known as *manggus*. He also performed Chinese-derived tales, called *bensen uliger*, such as "Wu Song Fights the Tiger" and other parts of the classic fictional work *Outlaws of the Marsh* (*Water Margin* [*Shuihu zhuan*]).

The action surrounding the canto "The Twelve-Headed Monster" is as follows: While Geser is away on a campaign, his evil uncle attempts to seduce Geser's wife Aralu Gowa, taking a current plague as evidence that Geser will not return. In order to escape the uncle's advances, Aralu Gowa runs off in search of Geser. Her travels lead her to the realm of a monster—a human-eating ogre. She eventually allows herself to be seduced by the monster-king. Returning

2. The basic features of Mongol epic poetry (which are in ways similar to Turkic and Tibetan epics) are discussed in the introduction to *Jangar*.

from his journey, Geser sets out to find Aralu Gowa. Eventually finding her in the monster's realm, he, too, comes under the monster's spell but eventually frees himself with the aid of his flying wonder horse, who tells Geser of the monster's weakness. Once free, Geser banishes Aralu Gowa to wander in the wastelands. Geser then returns home to his second wife but soon sets off on another adventure. The following passage opens with the image of Aralu Gowa's wandering alone into the realm of the monster-king.

THE TWELVE-HEADED MONSTER

Sung by Pajie (Mongol)

Lady Aralu Gowa left home alone in sorrow
Obstinately traveling between the horizons and to the edges of the seas,
Floating along year after year, month after month through wind and rain.

Finally one day
She came to the white-earth place,
The domain of the white-animal tribe,
Who sent out heavenly steeds to greet her.

Such an honorable welcome,
Such a warm reception.
They presented her with white clothes and a white horse,
Inviting her to pass through their lands.

After another day
She came to the domain of the striped-antelope place,
The domain of the spotted animals,
Who sent out cakes with which to welcome her.

Such a grand welcome
With slow, graceful dances,
They entertained her as though an honored guest,
Escorting her on her passage.

After another day,
She came to the yellow-earth place,
The domain of the yellow-colored animals;
A laughing fox came to welcome her.

Such a grand welcome,
Such a moving reception.

Gladly, with pomp and ceremony,
She was safely escorted through the territory.

After yet another day
She came to the blue-colored place,
The domain of the blue-colored animals.
The hedgehogs came out to greet her,
Making a rude tea
Offered as if a rare and excellent food,
They screeched and squeaked,
Making sounds of welcome.

Her horse's hooves never stopped moving
Until the lady arrived at the dark monster's valley.
All she could see from sky to earth
Was nothing but dense, churning mist.

Beneath the mountain was a black sea
With fiercely crashing waves
And a dry, parching wind
That caused her body to tremble.

The mountaintop held a single peak,
A jagged spire piercing the sky,
The frigid wind whipped all about,
Causing her whole body to ache.

Beholding the horrid vista
Aralu Gowa's spirits sank;
With an uncontrollable start,
So frightened, her eyes saw stars.

Just as the path seemed to end
And the mists betrayed no opening,
She beheld a black monster
Lurching toward her.

As the monster stared at the beautiful lady
He suddenly let forth a crazed laugh
That shook the earth
And echoed through the mountains.

When the lady heard it, her hair stood on end
And she warily stole a glance.

She saw a body the size of a mountain
And a head the size of a cart wheel.

The ferocious teeth gleamed brightly,
With canines flashing,
Lightning bolted from its roving eyes,
And twelve horrible heads waved about.

One head was for gnashing teeth,
One head was for keeping a lookout,
One head was for cursing,
One head was for seducing,
One head was for arrogant blather,
One head was for causing disasters,
One head was for causing plagues,
One head was for being ferocious,
One head was for committing crimes,
One head was for releasing horrid smells,
One head was for killing horses,
One head was for poisoning babies.

It was none other than the horrendous monster-king!
Peerless in strength;
Poor Aralu Gowa,
She nervously asked him:

"Are you the emperor of the sky,
Or the ruler of the underworld?
Are you the master of the four seas,
Or the king of the monsters?

"Are you a king beneath the sky god,
Or the overseer of the mountains?
Are you the warden of the seas,
Or an officer of the monster?"

The gigantic monster
Widened his eyes and replied:
"Beautiful Lady Aralu Gowa,
Please, listen attentively to my reply.
In the golden world I am also called great,
In heaven and earth I am called ruler,
If you have heard of the twelve-headed monster,
Then that is my name, known throughout the world.

"Knowing of your arrival,
I have especially come to welcome you,
Since you are in such straits,
I wish to express my deep sympathy toward you.

"That Geser of yours,
Gave up his life sometime ago,
And your three tribes
Have already met with disaster.

"Most honorable lady,
You needn't have the slightest worry,
Follow this powerful monster-king,
To live a happy, carefree youth."

Beautiful Aralu Gowa was captured by the horrible monster-king,
And before she could open her eyes,
She had already flown across the crystal wall of the moat.

The snow-white walls
Seemed to reach the heavens,
The stench of little monsters
Wafted between heaven and earth.

Weird monsters
Hobbled all about
Fluttering their bloodshot eyes,
With ugly, hooked noses.

Gnashing their gnarled teeth,
They wildly called to eat and drink,
They stretched forth hairy arms,
Begging for a share of food.

Upon seeing this, Aralu Gowa
Was filled with disgust,
Thinking of her beloved Geser,
She could not control her warm tears.

There were three fresh young maidens,
Who knelt beside the door to greet the monster-king,
In his wicked manner, the monster-king
Roughly kicked them aside.
With his iron-clawed hand the monster-king

One by one picked them up by their throats,
Ripped off their clothes and
With a mighty gulp swallowed them into his stomach.

Upon seeing this, Aralu Gowa
Began to shiver with fright,
Yet this human-eating monster-king,
Didn't even bat an eye.

The monster-king laughed savagely,
And said to Aralu Gowa:
"Don't be afraid, precious lady;
Follow me and you will have endless happiness."

INTRODUCTORY CANTOS FROM THE MONGOL EPIC *JANGAR*

Translated by Mark Bender and Chao Gejin (Chogjin; Mongol) and introduced by Chao Gejin

The Mongol word for "epic" is *tuuli*. The two major epic stories of the Mongols in China are the story of Geser Khan (Tibetan, Gesar), a supernatural hero of Tibetan origin, and an epic of Mongol origin about a hero named Jangar. Researchers have identified three major centers of epic performance, all connected with local cultures. The Bargu and Horchin centers are located in the northeastern end of Inner Mongolia, while the Oirat center is associated with groups of Oirat and Chahar Mongols in Xinjiang. At least seventy written versions of various other epics (excluding *Geser Khan* and *Jangar*) from these centers have been published in China. Many print editions of the two great epics have also appeared over the past few decades, in Mongolian, Chinese, or bilingual editions.

The Oirat center is most closely associated with the *Jangar* epic traditions. Like other Oirat epics, versions of *Jangar* tend to exceed two thousand lines in length and have many characters. Although the hero Jangar was not a historical figure, some singers feel that they are telling a historical story. Records from the seventeenth century indicate that one singer, Tar Bayar, from the Oirat region, could sing seventy cantos of the *Jangar* epic. The epic is thought to have been formed between the fifteenth and seventeenth centuries.

The epic singers are known as *tuulchi* or *Jangarchi*, and they perform with the accompaniment of stringed instruments. The main theme of *Jangar* is the deeds of the khan Jangar, his twelve able men, and his thousands of soldiers. The epic cycle consists of a series of similarly structured cantos. The cycle begins with a preface describing Jangar's kingdom, his deeds, the twelve heroes, and his lady. In some cases, this material is repeated in some form in succeeding cantos. A typical canto begins with a feast of the heroes that is interrupted by news that a ravaging *manggus* (multiheaded ogre) has invaded the realm. One of the heroes then sets off to subdue the monster, and his difficulties and successes in the process are recounted.

As recently as the 1980s, there were 106 active singers (among them, 3 were women) of the *Jangar* epic, though only 2 knew more than twenty cantos, and many knew only one. Estimates vary as to the total number of cantos, and seventy-two is the highest number reported. It was considered taboo, however, to know all the cantos and unlucky if a singer did not finish a canto once started. The epic was frequently performed in winter around a fireplace, by itinerant singers, at camps inhabited by a few families. At one time, princes sponsored epic-singing pageants—a context that has been revived in recent decades by government sponsorship.

Certain rituals were performed before the epic singing began. Stringed instruments used in performances included the two-stringed plucked lute (*tobshur*), the horse-head fiddle (*morin huur*), and the four-stringed lutelike *pipa*. Traditionally, the epics were sung in a special and conservative language register used only in the epics. In recent years, the singing tradition has declined, and fewer singers are able to sing in the old way; most singers now speak the epic in language quite close to everyday speech.

The *Jangar* epic exhibits all the major traits of the Mongol epic traditions. These include a story pattern focusing on fighting, courtship, and marriage; a sequence beginning with the hero's birth and ending, after a series of adventures, with his return home; the use of head rhyme (rhymes at the beginning of a line) and parallelism; performance in a special language register more or less different from everyday speech; the use of formulas (often in descriptions of characters); and the appearance of numbers (often multiples of seven or nine) indicating large numbers of people, objects, or years. The hero has a supernatural horse that thinks, talks, and sometimes flies; the hero's archrival tends to be a multiheaded ogre that savors human flesh, or the enemy may occasionally be a rival khan. The return of the hero is marked by a great feast. The influence of Buddhism and other cultures, such as Tibetan or Turkic (sometimes in the realm of language), on Mongolian epic is also felt.

The following cantos were translated into English from a Chinese-language version based on performances in Mongolian. Canto 1 is the sort of preface that normally begins epic performances. The action is set in a long-ago time, and Jangar's palace is located at an auspicious place called Bomba—though the origin of the name and its location have not been established. The passages tell of the humble origin (he was born an orphan) but worthy lineage and early feats of the hero, his marriage to the incomparably lovely and talented Agai Xabtala, the building of his palace by six thousand craftsmen, and the introduction of his horse, Aranjal, and of his most capable and loyal men—each of whom is introduced (along with his horse) and described in accordance with his rank and traits. The themes presented in the following passages are similar in many ways to those of other Mongol epics, though in some cases the khan may simply be a capable hunter (*mergen*) on a quest to save a bride or parent captured by a hulking ogre.

The cantos include many references to humans and monsters inhabiting the epic world that are part of the "history" of the epic. While many of these references are obscure, they serve to ground the narrative in a kind of epic existentiality that is closer to the world of fairy tales than to mundane reality.

CANTO 1

In that ancient golden age,
The time of carrying forth the power of Buddha,
Was born the orphan Jangar,
At the place called Bomba.

Jangar, a descendant of Tahijolai Khan,
The grandson of Tangsug Bomba Khan,
And son of Ujung Aldar Khan.

When Jangar was just two years old,
An ogre invaded his motherland,
And Jangar was orphaned,
Experiencing the bitterness of life.

When Jangar was just three years old,
The horse Aranjal was only four years old;
The little warrior perched atop the wonder steed
Broke apart three great battle formations,
Conquering the most evil ogre, Goljin.

When Jangar was just four,
He broke apart four great battle formations,
Causing that yellow monster, Duleidung,
To give up evil ways for good.

When Jangar was just five years old,
He captured the five monsters of the Tahai region,
Ensuring that they would never again do evil.

And when he was just five years old,
He was captured by the wrestler Mongon Sigsirge,
The orphan becoming a captive of the strongman.

When Jangar was just six years old,
He destroyed six great battle formations,
Breaking to bits countless swords and spears,
Facing down the eminent Altan Qegeji.

Altan Qegeji's palace
Was pretty as a picture;
Under Jangar's command,
He took a seat at Jangar's right hand.

When the orphan Jangar was just seven,
He conquered seven countries in the east;
The hero's name spread in the four directions,
Known to everyone under the heavens.

When Jangar's steed, Aranjal,
Speedily galloped along,
When Jangar's long golden lance
Was sharp beyond compare,
Jangar displayed his heroism.

In the springtime of his youth,
He refused the daughters of the forty-nine surrounding khans
in the region;
From the southeast,
He chose the daughter of Nomintegus Khan as wife.

The horses raised by Jangar
Were fast beyond compare;
Jangar's conscripts
Were all warriors beyond compare;
The lands of the forty-two surrounding khans,
Were each enfeoffed to the glorious Jangar.

Jangar's place, Bomba,
Was a paradise on earth;
The people there were always young;
Always looking as if they were youths of twenty-five,
They never looked old, and never died.

In Jangar's happy land,
It is always springtime,
There are no parching droughts,
There are no bone-chilling cold spells;
Fresh breezes softly sing,
Precious mist descends on the hills;
Flowers blossom everywhere,
And the grasses flourish.

Jangar's happy land
Is vast beyond compare;
Fast steeds can run for five months,
Yet still not reach the borders;
Here the five million blessed subjects
Can live rich and fulfilling lives.

Elegant peaks, white-capped and lofty, touch the skies,
Shimmering under the golden sun.

From the great, green lake Sirato Dalai,
Rivers issue both north and south,
Rippling day and night like laughter,
Enlivening the rich verdure.

Jangar drinks the waters of the Huiten River,
So clear and sweet, bubbling on its way,
Never stopping, no matter the season.

The master of Bomba,
Once the orphan Jangar,
Has supreme power,
Bringing fortune to his people;
The hero's deeds shine among the people,
The hero's beautiful name is known everywhere.

CANTO 2

In that pure white *ger*,[3]
Six thousand and twelve warriors cried out:
"We want to build a palace;
The palace will be splendid and strong,
Beyond compare with anything on earth."

The forty-two surrounding khans discussed things:
On what precious, auspicious land
Will the palace be built?
It must face the light, must face the sun,
In the verdant southern reaches of the grasslands,
To the south of the tablelands,
At the confluence of the twelve flowing rivers,
On the western flanks of the white-capped mountains,
On the shores of Bomba Lake,
In the bosom of sandalwood and poplars,
Building a fantastic palace in that most auspicious place.

On the best day,
At the best time,
The forty-two khans
Assembled six thousand and twelve skilled craftsmen
To break ground and begin the work.

---

3. The *ger* (yurt) is the round felt tent of the Mongol nomads.

Coral and agate were laid in the foundation,
And walls inlaid with pearls and gems;
The tops of the north wall were set with lion's teeth;
On the north wall, sika[4] antlers were set in place.

Old Altan Qegeji
Foretold the coming ninety-nine years of fortune and evil,
Fixing in memory events of the ninety-nine years past.
In a clear voice he declared:
"This palace must be strong and protective,
Just short of heaven by three spans;
If it were built all the way to the ninth layer of the sky,
It would be unlucky for Jangar."

The six thousand and twelve skilled craftsmen
First built the central palace
Then built five great corner halls.

The entrance to the palace
Is mounted with glimmering slabs of crystal;
The egress of the palace
Is decorated with flame-red glass.

The lucky people to the north have plentiful milk and food,
The north walls are covered with spotted deer hides;
The blessed people of the south have plenty of meat and food,
And the south walls are covered with sika hides.

The four directions around the palace
Are set with blazing mirrors;
In the four corners inside the palace
Stand warrior attendants of the Buddha.

This palace of Jangar's
Is ten levels tall,
Grand in every way, the five colors blazing,
Standing tall and upright on the green grasslands,
Majestic, grand, symmetrical, and refulgent.

The forty-nine monster-kings surrounding the region
Were terrified by the sight, fearing to invade and plunder.

---

4. The sika (a northern variety of *Cervus nippon*) is one of several species of deer commonly hunted by the Mongols.

In front of the palace
Hangs a shimmering golden banner,
While inside the flag sheath
It sends out a red glow;
Taken from the flag sheath,
It releases the rays of seven suns.

CANTO 3

Greatest of the great
Was the orphan Jangar;
He sat upon a throne of forty-four legs,
Shining and glowing like a full moon.

Jangar wore a greatcoat of black satin;
This coat was tailored with great care by his wife, Agai,
And fervently sewn by the wives of his men.
Jangar sat on his precious throne,
Stroking his mustache, shaped like swallow wings,
Expounding to his men about running across the land.

If someone asked
When Jangar's steed, Aranjal,
Ran most speedily,
And when Jangar's long lance
Was sharp beyond compare.
Jangar's heroic demeanor
Gained in the spring of youth.

He refused the beautiful daughters of the surrounding forty-nine
khans
And wed a wife from the southeast,
Nomintegus Khan's daughter,
Who seemed forever a sixteen-year-old maiden,

What was this Agai Xabtala like?
When Agai looks to the left, her left cheek shines brightly,
On her left hand, the waves of the lake waters shimmer,
As the small fish in the great lake jump for joy;
When Agai looks to the right, her right cheek shines brightly,
On her right hand, the wavelets of the great lake shimmer,
As the small fish jump for joy.

Agai's face, a complexion white as snow,
Agai's two cheeks, red as fresh blood,
Agai's hat, a lovely pure white,
Tailored by her nimble-fingered mother,
Embroidered by the great officers' wives' loving hands.

Agai's long hair
Is raven black, thick, and shining;
It is covered with a black satin headdress,
Caressing her face,
Waving left and right.
Agai's earrings
Are big as camel dung,
Shining beneath her ears.

Agai's silver lute
Has ninety-one strings
And can play twelve tunes;
The lute sound is sweet to the ear,
Like the joyful cries of a swan in the reeds,
Having just laid its eggs;
Like the joyful songs of a banded duck at lakeside,
Having just laid its eggs.
When Agai plays the lute
Who in this world can match her strains?

Only Jangar's master of ceremonies,
A handsome man, Mingyan,
Accompanied by the silver lute, sings the moving lyrics.

Jangar's right-hand man
Is called Altan Qegeji;
With his far-reaching eyes, Altan Qegeji sits upon his black satin cushion,
Holding sway over Bomba's seventy fiefs;
No matter what sort of trying circumstance arises,
He is able to resolve it smoothly and without flaw.

Jangar's left-hand man
Is pure and honest Honggor.
He is descended from the great strongman Tebxin,
The only son of the wrestler Sigsirge,
And the beloved son of his virtuous mother, Lady Zandan Gerel,
Who bore him in her twenty-second year.

Honggor is Jangar's helper,
Pride of the seven-hundred-thousand-man army;
Honggor is Bomba's sacred sky pillar,
A model for a million warriors.

In battle, Honggor
Never knows the meaning of retreat, like a tiger or wolf;
Honggor put forth his precious life,
And by himself, with his horse, single-handedly defeated
Seventy monster-kings.

Below Honggor in rank
Sat a giant mountain of a warrior;
He was Gujegen Gombo Noyan.
When he sits with his legs apart, he occupies fifty-two seats;
When he sits with legs folded,
He occupies twenty-five seats.
His great power startles people,
And his martial skills are replete.
The iron fork in his hand
Is a monster-stabbing tool.
His high-headed black charger
Is big and strong,
With four great hooves,
Like four great bowls.
Gombo's mouth is like a river,
Spilling forth endless advice on statecraft.

Below Altan Qegeji in rank
Was the "Eagle among the masses" Sabar,
Nicknamed "Iron-Arm Strongman."
As an infant, Sabar
Used ten thousand slaves
To exchange for a chestnut horse,
A chestnut horse, speedy and beautiful.
He wields a battle-ax eighty-one spans long,
A blade that never leaves his shoulder.
Sabar has superhuman strength;
No matter how strong a match he meets,
In one toss all are thrown from horseback.

The third right-hand hero
Is Hara Sanal;
He has a beautiful crimson horse.

He left his felicitous and virtuous father,
Letting his father lose his felicity.
He left behind his kind and loving mother,
Letting his mother be without a son;
He abandoned a million slaves,
Letting them be without a master.
He left behind his pretty young wife,
Letting her be without a husband;
Bolingar's son,
The divine warrior Sanal,
Took his crimson horse
And followed Jangar to Bomba.

These peerless warriors sit together in seven circles,
And at banquets also sit a circle of silver-haired old men;
Wise and compassionate old women with bright red faces,
Pretty and lovely wives, gentle and obedient,
Beautiful and cultivated maidens with pink cheeks,
All sit in circles respectively,
And in one circle sit the innocent, lovely children;
At the banquets is endless yogurt and koumiss,
And an unlimited amount of fragrant venison.

The warriors drink until sotted,
Hot blood pulsing through their veins,
Their joyful, ringing laughter filling the hall.
The warriors grab each other's shoulders
Singing in high voices:
"Of all the lands on earth,
Which is like this Bomba, so rich and powerful?
Of all the warriors on earth,
Which among them are like those of Bomba?
So strong?
When have we encountered comparable opponents?
When have we encountered such hunt-worthy mountain goats?"

A DAUR BALLAD

Translated and introduced by Mark Bender

The ballad "The *Mergen* and the Fox-Fairies" is attributed to the Daur people of northeastern China. It is based on an oral singing style known as *uqun*, and it shares features with the longer heroic epics of northern Asia. Like other Daur folk stories, such ballads were often performed on the family *kang* (brick platform bed) as after-dinner entertainment during the long winter nights. The *mergen* is the hunter-hero par excellence of the Daur, Hezhen, Mongol, and other regional ethnic groups. Shape-shifting fox-fairies or fox-demons are part of the folklore of many peoples in northeastern Asia. This particular ballad, translated from a Chinese version, includes references to a number of items of clothing, tools, and architecture from the traditional Daur lifestyle.

THE *MERGEN* AND THE FOX-FAIRIES

In the town of Dedu once lived a *mergen*,
Whose family, for three generations,
Was famed far and wide as hunters.
With a bow and arrows he was fantastic;
His swordplay was like magic;
River and roe deer fled at his footstep;
Roving beasts dared not pass near his village;
Birds of the air warily gave him wide berth.

Three thousand *li* from Beijing is Dedu;
A towering golden peak stands nearby;
Within the peak three fox pups lived,
Their fur growing white as they grew up into fox-fairies.
Their skill in deceiving men's eyes and ears was great,
Since they had the power to transform at will.

Third Brother Fox declared one day:
"There is a famous *mergen* in Dedu;
How surely must men praise and flatter him in every way.
Why don't I pay him a visit, and we'll see who's most powerful!"
As he yelped these words, the wind suddenly blew full of whirling
snowflakes.

By midnight, snow thickly blanketed the ground.
Third Brother Fox flew on the wind to Dedu; pricking up his ears,
He listened quietly in the *mergen*'s courtyard.

Softly, he crept before the doorway and left his spore.
He then circled the courtyard three times, but all remained still.
He lay for a while before a window,
Then for a moment on the threshing ground.
Finally, in triumph, he left the village and made straight for the cave.

Next morning, as the east brightened,
The *mergen* came out to view the falling snow.
The snow-filled sky made his spirits rise,
But the sight of the fox tracks startled him.
He thought to himself, "My two hunting dogs didn't discover these prints,
They must have been left by a fox-fairy!"

Turning back inside he cooked up a batch of trail food,
Called to his dogs, and made ready his bow and arrows.
He slipped his white wool sheepskin coat atop
His roe skin leggings, to cut the cold,
Pulled a fox skin hat onto his head,
And slid *qakamin*[5] boots onto his feet.

When he was on horseback, his eyes traced out the fox prints;
As he hastened toward the peak,
The two dogs raced ahead, sniffing along on the track.
Laying back his ears,
Third Brother Fox flew like the wind.

In a twinkling, noon saw the fox hard-pressed for his life.
Two bounds more and a tumbling roll brought out his magic—
He arose as a gray-headed old man.
The *mergen* saw not a fox but a human form,
And a man's footprints where a fox's had been.
He was hard-pressed to figure out the change.

The *mergen* was quick to ask the old man:
"Did you see a fox pass this way?"
The old man replied, "You're just a young man;
Why hunt the white foxes?
If you'd worship them instead
Your herds would surely multiply,
A full and happy life you'd lead."

---

5. *Qakamin* is a kind of leather and fur winter boot.

As these two talked, the dogs were furiously barking,
Making mad circles around the old man;
The *mergen*'s eyes burned like bright stars:
"Nonsense, you old beast,
A good fox skin can keep out the cold;
Any hunter worth his salt knows that much."

As he spoke he mounted an arrow and let it fly,
"What the . . . ?!" the old man exclaimed as he dodged.
Tumbling down and rolling on the ground,
He resumed his real shape and sped off frantically.
The dogs ran hot on his tail;
The *mergen* soared up behind on his horse.

In what seemed like moments, dusk was coming on;
Surely, the fox had little chance to escape with his life.
Rolling to the ground once more, he changed into an old fisherman,
Walking along, carrying his ice-fishing gear.
The *mergen* approached and made to speak,
But the fisherman spoke first, saying:
"You're just a young man,
Why be out hunting the white foxes?"

As he spoke, the dogs sprang toward him,
Circling, covering the fisherman's every move,
"It's just another trick to hold me up."
The *mergen*'s mind was now as clear as his sight.
Tumbling down and rolling on the ground, the fisherman
Appeared again as a fox running for his life.

The *mergen* lashed his horse to keep up,
The fox, at wit's end, dived into the cave,
The *mergen* and his dogs rushed right in behind,
Where he found three houses with bright tile roofs.
Entering one, he saw atop the heated *kang* an old-style
Four-sided "eight fairy" table
And three old men chatting leisurely over cups of tea.

The old fellow sitting in the seat of honor queried in a low voice:
"Might you be the *mergen* in pursuit of the fox-demon?"
As he spoke he shoved the old fellow nearest him down off the *kang*,
Adding: "You're asking for whatever trouble comes your way."
The *mergen* replied: "Hunting is what hunters do;
If someone invites trouble, I oblige."

Grabbing Third Brother by the scruff of the neck,
The *mergen* dragged him from the cave;
Third Brother bumped along, shaking in fright,
Then changed from an old man into a freshly killed fox.
The *mergen* stripped off the pelt,
The hide thick and the fur silky.
There are no immortals in the eyes of a hunter,
Proof enough the Daur will worship no fox-fairies!

SELECTIONS FROM A YI EPIC

Collected and edited by Nienu Baxi (Yi) and translated and introduced by Mark Bender

The Yi ethnic group, numbering more than 7 million, is among the largest of China's minority ethnic groups. There are over seventy subgroups of the Yi, who refer to themselves by names such as Nuosu, Nisu, Nasu, Lolo, Lolopo, Lipo, Axi, Azhe, Misa, Gepo, Sani, and Luo. In the past, many of the groups today classified as Yi were called Lolo, which in many contexts was the equivalent of "savage." A number of these subgroups are represented in this volume.

Most of the Yi live in the provinces of Yunnan, Sichuan, and Guizhou. To varying degrees, many Yi in Yunnan and Guizhou, though culturally distinct, have been influenced by Han Chinese culture since the sixteenth century, when a large number of Han began immigrating into southwestern China. In many areas, the Han took control of the scarce bottomlands, the displaced natives seeking refuge in mountainous areas. Until the 1950s, however, there existed in the Liangshan Mountains of southern Sichuan an independent stronghold of Nuosu aristocrats who ruled a hierarchy of lower-class serfs. Since the 1950s, the more remote Yi areas have gradually opened to the outside, and, like other ethnic groups in southwestern China, the Yi are engaged with the forces of modernization and change.

The Yi languages belong to the Tibeto-Burman family. In Yunnan, many Yi languages have a large number of borrowings from southwestern Chinese dialects: in certain areas, some styles of Yi folk songs are now sung in Chinese. Although it varies by region, traditional economic pursuits include the farming of buckwheat and other grains and potatoes and the raising of goats and horses. Some scholars credit the forebears of the Yi with initially establishing the Nanzhao kingdom (737–902), the forerunner of the Dali kingdom (937–1253), which ruled most of what is now southwestern China and a sizable portion of Southeast Asia for several centuries, until it fell to the Mongols. The ancient city of Dali, now associated with the Bai ethnic group, still stands on the southern shore of scenic Lake Erhai and is a popular tourist destination.

The Nanzhao kingdom is the setting for a recently discovered epic of heroism and loyalty recorded in Yi writing by ritual specialists called *bimo* (in some areas, *baima*, *bema*, or *bipo*) at least as early as the Ming dynasty (1368–1644). *The Palace Lamp of the Nanzhao Kingdom* was collected by Nienu Baxi in the early 1970s from a *bimo* in the Honghe Hani-Yi Autonomous Prefecture, in southern Yunnan, a homeland of the Nisu subgroup of the Yi. Baxi, who is a Yi folklorist, translator, and author, comes from a family of five generations of *bimo*. Baxi supplied the title to the previously unnamed, anonymous text, which was written in a local version of Yi script. Baxi is one of only a few dozen researchers in the world who can read any of the traditional Yi scripts, which consist of several thousand written graphs and which vary by region. Although the shape and style of many of the characters are similar, in many cases the local traditions of Yi writing are only partially mutually intelligible. (A standard syllabary of 819 graphs based on a selected number of traditional graphs from traditional texts in Sichuan has been developed; however, it has only limited local usage.) Yi writing was used primarily by the *bimo* to record lore such as funeral chants, divination rites, genealogies, stories, history, and narrative poems. The narrative poems are performed at a variety of ritual events, particularly at wedding parties and after funeral services. In some places, *bimo* gather to compete over knowledge of the ancient books, each contestant chanting from memory the ancient songs as he rings a brass handbell. The prize for such a contest, which in parts of Yunnan may last for three days and nights, might be a flower made of silver leaf. When conducting the lengthy Yi funeral rites, *bimo* in some areas wear feltcovered bamboo hats dressed with iron eagle claws and recite the written scriptures either sitting or standing with a pine staff and a bell (though such accoutrements vary).

The plot of *The Palace Lamp of the Nanzhao Kingdom* concerns the rule of a legendary young prince, Luoshengyan. After receiving the throne upon his father's death (as described in the two following cantos), Luoshengyan carries on his father's just and peaceful rule under the guidance of a general who had been his father's most trusted adviser. All is well until Luoshengyan marries a bride from a rival kingdom. Falling under the influence of her emissary, the young king ignores the advice of the trusted general, eventually exiling him and diverting the Nanzhao army to the task of building a large pleasure ground. Ultimately, the rival kingdom attacks Nanzhao but is defeated in a great battle thanks to the efforts of the loyal general, who has raised a force in a remote corner of the kingdom. The young king restores the loyal general's position, calling him Palace Lamp of the Nanzhao Kingdom.

The content is similar to that of numerous stories of wronged loyal advisers in the Chinese histories. Although the exact time of the narrative has yet to be determined, the Nanzhao did have relations with the Chinese court throughout much of the Tang dynasty (618–907). In 736, the Tang emperor recognized Piloge (P'iloko) as "king of Yunnan." Things were not always peaceful, and Nanzhao became involved in shifting alliances in wars between the Chinese and the Tibetans. In 829, Nanzhao invaded Sichuan province, enslaving over ten thousand artisans, craftsmen, and officials who contributed significantly to the sinification of Nanzhao court culture.

In the following selections of the twenty-two-canto work, a notable aspect is that of "performances within performances." In canto 8, the assembled *bimo* chant scriptures at the king's cremation that are similar to those still used at Yi funerals, while in canto 9 we hear official oratory and the folk songs of the people. These descriptions of performances are framed within an epic narrative tradition performed orally by real-life *bimo*. Although *The Palace Lamp* was probably intended for oral performance, as was most Yi narrative poetry, the original text was written in five-syllable lines. Another feature, also typical of Yi epic literature, is the shifting narrative focus on phenomena in the heavens, to an earthly scene, to a specific human event, as in the first stanza of canto 8. Moreover, when different classes of people are mentioned in the text, the usual order of appearance is a descending hierarchy of nobles, officials, ritual specialists, and common people, reflecting ancient Yi social divisions. The translation is based on a portion of a handwritten bilingual Yi and Chinese text compiled and edited by Nienu Baxi in the early 1980s. A similar version was published in that decade in the "for scholars only" press in Yunnan.

THE PALACE LAMP OF THE NANZHAO KINGDOM

CANTO 8. THE ROYAL CREMATION

From the sky a bright star fell,
On earth a sky-supporting tree collapsed;
The news of the royal death spread throughout Nanzhao,
Heralding to subjects high and low the demise of the ruler.

The high mountains drooped their heads,
Tears falling like waterfalls;
The wailing of the rivers filled the mountain valleys.
One by one the leaves wept silently;
One by one the stars wept silently.

In the palace, the prince sobbed, brokenhearted,
His tears drenching the breast of his robe;
With bowed heads the officials stood at vigil by the coffin,
Grieved as if ten thousand needles had stabbed their hearts.

The rulers and the people formed a great line,
Every face was streaked with tears;
One by one they kowtowed before the head of the bier,
Consoling the king's righteous soul.

Reed trumpets blew in the capital from dawn to dusk;
Outside the palace walls, cannons shook the heavens.
Seventy-two groups of lion dancers seemed like butterflies dancing;
Gongs resounded endlessly in the four directions.

The funeral rites were carried out in accord with tradition,
As was proper to the prestige of a king;
The funerary goods were of every sort and kind,
Filling to capacity the width of the palace.

Golden boys made of paper carried wine pots;
Jade girls made of paper held food trays;

Magic cranes made of paper rested atop the casket;
Riding horses made of paper were mounted with golden saddles.

Soldiers made of paper waved precious swords,
Attendants made of paper held aloft parasols;
All were to protect and serve the king,
All were to accompany the king in his cremation.

White sandalwood was used to make the coffin,
The black lacquer cover was rimmed with gold;
On the right of the coffin gold tigers roared,
On the left of the coffin dragons writhed in the clouds.

Seventy-two wise *bimo* were called to recite incantations,
To drive away all evil spirits;
Wagging brass bells, they danced around the coffin,
Releasing the great king's soul from this world.

The seventy-two *bimo* turned the pages of the sacred books,
Singing the funeral lyrics in accord with Yi tradition;
The sound of the singing was like a great bull's bellowing,
The lyrics were like an endless, flowing river:

"King who is dead, you should not be resentful,
The first to sicken, the first to die, is not you;
The winged ones in the air all die,
The legged ones on the earth all expire.

"All the officials and commoners wished you long life,
Wished you to live a hundred years;
The old ones who don't die are the sun and moon—
When people grow old, they must decline.

"Others may blow air into your mouth,
But you shall never again raise your arms;
Others may trade you their legs,
But never again shall you mount a steed.

"Fallen leaves won't grow again,
When the aged die, they never revive;
Had the world a life-reviving herb,
The officials and commoners would rip out their hearts and lose
their skulls for it.

"King who has died, ah,
Your body is worth a thousand pieces of gold;
But gold mountains and silver rivers, ah,
Will not buy back your beating heart.

"Go slowly, O king who lives in the hearts of the officials and common folk,
A circling phoenix shall accompany you on the road to the ancestors;
In peace, leave behind your great name for the ages,
Your spirit body shall reside in the realm of year-round birdcalls and fragrant flowers.

"Ducks don't make friends with eagles,
You, follow the ancestors to assemble in one hall;
Your spirit should not follow the path of demons,
You must live in peace and tranquillity with the ancestors.

"Go, follow the kings already with the ancestors,
Do not dwell on leaving your golden walled, splendid palace;
Leave, O king who is summoned by the ancestors,
Do not dwell on thoughts of your silks and gold fan.

"Everyone has done their best to satisfy your every need,
Now you must protect the good folk and officials,
Keeping all disasters from Nanzhao,
Allowing the succession of kings, sons to grandsons, to continue on and on."

The day of the cremation arrived,
The court officials carried the casket out of the palace;
The funeral procession like a river of humanity;
The casket was escorted by the human river straight to the burial ground in the mountains.

Piece by piece, the wood was piled into a high mountain,
The casket placed high on the pyre, touching the sky;
The fierce flames raged,
Sending up spirals of blue smoke.

The sound of wailing arose,
Some people, breaking through the wall of mourners, threw themselves into the fire.
Tears of hurt and grief, *ya*,
Splattered the flames, dousing the great immolation again and again.

The great blaze burned for three days and three nights,
The people cried their eyes dry of bloody tears;
The royal remains were entombed in the grounds of the Precious Dragons and Tigers,
Only then did each and all disperse.

CANTO 9. THE ENTHRONEMENT

The proclamation of Luoshengyan's succession
Spread like a turbulent wind swirling throughout Nanzhao;
Wherever the happy news spread,
People became as excited as a nest of sparrows.

Nanzhao seethed like a cauldron of boiling water,
People worked madly for the new king's ceremony of enthronement;
In all directions, colorful door banners were raised,
Every village and hamlet unfurled streamers and flags.

The palace doors were plated with silver wash,
To the throne was added a brilliant golden sheen;
The dragons on the palace pillars churned in the waves,
The phoenixes on the palace walls danced about lightly.

From dawn to dusk the palace lamps shone,
Like blossom after blossom of rhododendron blooms;
The palace gates were hung with silk door banners—
When the wind caught them they were like rosy clouds.

The auspicious day arrived,
The ritual volleys marking the ascension shook the mountains and valleys;
Joyous people arrived from each and every direction,
Like a great tide surging into the palace.

Luoshengyan, with the semblance of a martial hero, donned the royal vestments.
The crowds that came to worship the lord
Were like ants climbing a tree;
The celebrants in the courtyard couldn't be more numerous.

Every one of the gift horses was strong and robust,
Each of the gift antlers, in velvet, was like a newly sprouted bamboo shoot;
The tributes of precious stones were heaped on tray after tray;
Gold given in tribute to the king was piled in a huge golden mountain.

Rhododendron blossoms, like balls of fire,
Gave all Nanzhao a russet glow;
The royal succession ritual
Was full of pomp and ceremony.

The officials wore beautiful vestments,
Bowing in deep reverence before the king;
Holding large sticks of red incense,
They uttered their heartfelt congratulations:

"Best wishes for the young king's ascension,
Best hopes for an auspicious rule;
Let the throne be firm as the rocky cliffs;
Let the king rule with monumental achievements.

"Let the Nanzhao kingdom thrive and prosper,
Let the king's power be without compare;
May officials and common folk hold unwavering allegiance,
That, by the grace of the king, all shall live and work in peace
and happiness."

The leaders and people all dressed festively,
The brass drums' beats were like waves of sound;
Dancing in unabashed revelry,
Each song came from each heart:

"Higher than high, O King,
You are more radiant than a bright moon;
You have fortune greater than the sky,
You have the courage of a fanged tiger.

"We wish that your fortune may light the four directions,
We hope your prestige lasts longer than the sun and moon;
The throne is like a boulder of jade from afar,
And your name glimmers radiantly.

"We beg that the king, protected by the sky spirit,
Let ruin and disaster blow afar like clouds;
We hope that your every day is happy,
We hope that your every year is healthy.

"With your intelligence and courage,
Common folk and officials shall certainly live in health and safety;

With your wisdom and martial skills,
Nanzhao shall be as fragrant as osmanthus.

"You are the king bee of Nanzhao,
The folk are like bees, every day busy among the flowers,
So that you may smoothly lead a life of leisurely luxury,
So that you may pass your days in a sea of wealth and riches."

The young king strode out from the golden palace,
Strode out to the crowd that was the size of the sea;
Like a red sun rising from above the water,
He went forth to accept the lustration of the officials and folk.

The crowds turned into mountains of color,
The crowds turned into a sea of song;
The mountains were happy and the waters smiled,
The sound of rich laughter rose up to the sky.

During the great enthronement ritual,
There was celebration for three days and three nights in the palace;
Mount Weibo bent itself in laughter;
In the happy waters of the Yanggua River, fish leaped merrily.

The officials had no thought of returning home,
The common folk had no thought to leave;
Everyone was like a golden deer attracted to a spring,
Everyone was like butterflies intoxicated by the flowers.

A TRADITION-ORIENTED YAO CREATION EPIC

Edited and translated into Chinese by Sha Hong (Zhuang) and translated into English and introduced by Mark Bender

Miluotuo (Miloto)[6] is a female creator figure in the mythology of certain groups of the Yao nationality living in the mountain areas of the Guangxi Zhuang Autonomous Region, in southwestern China. The Yao (also known as Mien and by numerous local designations) number over 2 million and live in communities in the mountains of Guangxi and other areas of southwestern China and Southeast Asia. Most Yao are wet-rice farmers and engage in timber and forest products industries. Yao women are known for their weaving and garment crafts. Many traditional beliefs have elements of animism and shamanism, folk Daoism being an influence in some areas.

Scholars in the Bama, Donglan, Tiandong, Nandan, Dayao, Du'an, and other areas of northern Guangxi have collected versions of the Miluotuo myth that detail the figure's role in the creation of the creatures of the earth. In the Bama and Du'an autonomous counties, Miluotuo's story was performed at Yao New Year's (fifth lunar month) and at various life-cycle events, including wedding celebrations and funerals, by male and female singers. According to Sha Hong, during the festival the story was performed by male and female singers accompanied by bronze drums.

As with many minority epics published in China during the late 1950s and then (after the Cultural Revolution) in the 1980s and afterward, collectors, researchers, and editors often worked together to create "ideal" versions from a number of texts based on oral performances of a core story. Until recently, before tape recorders and video cameras had become common, collection methods required laborious hand transcription—often through layers of interpreters. As can be imagined, these limitations often influenced the storytelling situation. Moreover, oral epics everywhere tend to vary from performance to performance (even by the same singers) in terms of length, content, and elaboration; also, it is rare that an entire epic cycle is sung at a single setting. In striving to reach their goal of an aesthetically pleasing whole that did not stray too far from politically sensitive norms, the editors often pieced together a number of versions to create a final, printed text that would be available to an educated reading audience. In some cases, writers and poets were involved in these projects, which sometimes resulted in artistically enhanced works that took rather wide liberties with traditional material. Sometimes, the opposite occurred. Translators attempted (within the limits posed by editorial

6. Miluotuo is the Chinese pinyin rendering of the Bunu Yao romanization of the name Miloto. Since the pinyin version is much more widely used in printed versions and online sites in China, it is utilized here. Other names and terms are also in pinyin.

guidelines on "politically correct" content) to follow the original style and content, at times attempting to "purify" the final texts of obvious influences from other cultures so as to reveal the true beauty and national essence of the texts.

In both instances, an important motive was to contribute to raising the status of ethnic minority culture in the eyes of the Han Chinese and provide the individual groups with evidence of their own proud traditions. Such creations can be described by Lauri Honko's term "tradition-oriented epics" in the sense that, although they are based on traditional material, the resulting texts have gone through a process of editing that yields more a literary work than an ethnographic recording of a specific performance event. An early example of this type of production is the Sani narrative poem from Yunnan province called *Ashima*, which features a young heroine kidnapped by an evil landlord.

The Chinese translation of *Miluotuo* is thus a tradition-oriented epic. It was collected from various Yao singers in the Bama region by researchers from the Guangxi Folk Literature Research Organization (Guangxi Minjian Wenxue Yanjiuhui). In the collection process, a singer would first sing a portion of the epic in Yao. As the local Yao communities are interspersed among both Han and Zhuang peoples, many people are bi- or trilingual. Thus, after singing, the singer was then asked to translate the song word for word into Mandarin, with the researchers writing everything down each step of the way.

Sha Hong (1925–1985), a Zhuang nationality poet and researcher, organized and selected among the sections of the resulting texts and made certain alterations for style and content. He attempted to follow the original style of the verses where possible, while avoiding the tendency to interpret things in terms of Han or Zhuang culture. The Bama versions were utilized because of their relative completeness. In the editing process, Sha Hong organized the sections of the mythic narrative into chapters, forming a sequential story line. Certain stylistic elements of performance, such as recurring refrains of sonorous syllables, which add to the effect of the singing, were not represented in the translation. A more intrusive change was the deletion of a portion of the tale involving the creation of humankind. In the interests of "ethnic harmony" (*minzu tuanjie*), sections that would have proved offensive to various groups were deleted or modified (much in the same spirit that some fairy tales in the West were either bowdlerized for sexual content or, in more recent times, rewritten to accord to prevailing notions of political correctness). Such changes have been made in other creation epics from southwestern China as well, usually in scenes describing the origins and social status of particular ethnic groups. Despite certain modifications, the overall themes in these epics—especially those relating to the creation stories—are similar across southern China.

The story of Miluotuo is one such account of the creation of the heavens and earth. Events include the dismembering and transformation of parts of a creator entity (in this epic, the Master Craftsman), propping up the sky, stitching together the edges of the heavens and earth, and creating geological features and celestial bodies; the walking, flying, and swimming creatures; the five basic grain plants; wet-rice fields; and the Thunder God. Like the cosmic wind that created her, Miluotuo is impregnated by the wind, giving birth to nine sons, who aid in creating the forests on the hillsides. Various cultural items associated with humans are described, such as houses, which are built from the newly grown trees with stone tools. In some cases, simile and metaphor are used. For example, the newly made mountains and valleys look like the pleats in the traditional skirts of Yao women, and axes are sharpened as sharp as a tiger's tongue. Etiological tales, such as why monkeys' faces are red, are part of the epic as well.

Later in the epic, the twelve suns in the sky are melting everything on earth. With their mother's encouragement, Miluotuo's nine sons shoot down the excess ones (in versions of this event from other mythologies, such as the Han and Miao, one heroic figure shoots down the extra suns). This is followed by the story of a battle against a marauding tiger. Even though the creature was created by Miluotuo, it begins to cause trouble and eat goats around the brothers' settlement. One of her sons eventually devises a plan by which the tiger is tricked into neutering itself, thus ending the threat of nature's most fearsome beast.

Finally, Miluotuo decides to find a place to create humans, a task that requires the help of a number of different birds and animals, including an eagle—a bird that figures frequently in myths from southwestern China. After numerous tribulations, everything is ready, and Miluotuo forms her creations out of beeswax; they become humans after they are placed in an earthen crock for nine months. In the end, the babies are suckled; they learn to speak Han, Zhuang, or Yao by listening to the sounds of rustling bamboo (another common motif); and later they are divided into various clans. Thus ends the mythic epic of Miluotuo, one of several female creator figures from southern China. A parallel in Han Chinese mythology is the goddess Nü Wa, who created humans out of earth, and the anthropomorphic Butterfly Mother (Mai Bang) of Miao groups in southeastern Guizhou province, from whose eggs the ancestors of humans hatched.

A number of tree, animal, and place-names in the text are obscure.

MILUOTUO

PART 1. CREATING HEAVEN AND EARTH

A long, long time ago,
What created Miluotuo?
A great wind came blowing,
Creating Miluotuo.

Long, long before,
What had created the great wind?
A great dragon blowing,
Had created the great wind.

Long, long before that,
What had created the great dragon?
The All-Knowing Master Craftsman,
Had created the great dragon.

When the Master Craftsman died,
What did his rain hat become?
The Master Craftsman's rain hat
Was used by Miluotuo to create the skies.

When the Master Craftsman died,
What did his hands and feet become?
His two hands and two feet became four pillars.
Miluotuo took the four pillars
And propped one in each of the four corners of the sky.

When the Master Craftsman died,
What did his body become?
His body became a great column;
Miluotuo took that great column
And propped it up in the middle of the sky.

Miluotuo created the skies.
What else did she create?
Miluotuo created the skies,
And she also created the earth.

She created the sky narrower than the earth;
She created the earth wider than the sky.
Miluotuo took up a thread to sew,
She sewed the edges of the sky and earth together.

Miluotuo drew the thread tight,
The edges of the sky and earth were joined snugly;
The sky sat crooked like a pot lid,
The earth was wrinkled like a pleated skirt.

Pleats were folded one after another;
The tips became high mountaintops.

The pleats were made line after line;
The dips became riverbeds.

Miluotuo created the sky.
What else did she create within the sky?
Miluotuo created the sun and moon in the sky,
Miluotuo created the stars in the sky,
Miluotuo created the Thunder God in the sky.

Miluotuo created the earth.
What else did she create upon the earth?
Miluotuo created the water channels and field banks,
Miluotuo created the five grain crops,
Miluotuo created the flying birds and walking beasts,
Miluotuo created the fish and shrimp in the rivers for netting.

PART 2. CREATING THE FORESTS

Miluotuo created the heavens,
Miluotuo created the earth;
But she created a bare earth,
She created an earth without trees.

Miluotuo went atop a mountain,
A great wind blew against her side;
Miluotuo became pregnant,
And bore nine sons:
The first was called Abo,
The second was called Bunong,
The third was called Buluo,
The fourth was called Ha'ang,
The fifth was called Suoliang,
The sixth was called Kunwen,
The seventh was called Liuban,
The eighth was called Guyayu,
The ninth was called Taoyaye.

Miluotuo gave birth to nine sons,
Then called the nine sons together for a meeting:
"I created this place,
But it seems scorched bare.
I created this place,
But who can provide the dark shade?"

The nine brothers were silent,
Miluotuo thought of her neighbor Youli,
Youli's home had tree seedlings they could plant.

When the cocks crowed the next morning,
Miluotuo rose from bed,
Rose from bed and went at once to find Abo:
"Abo, Abo!
Go to Youli's house,
To Youli's house for trees to plant."

Abo quickly answered:
"Today I must go work in the mountains;
I can't go."

Miluotuo asked Bunong:
"Bunong, Bunong!
Go to Youli's house
To get some trees to plant."

Bunong quickly replied:
"Today I must make roads;
I couldn't go if I wanted to."

Miluotuo asked Buluo:
"Buluo, Buluo,
Go to Youli's home
To get some trees to plant."

Buluo agreed.

Just as the sun was setting,
Buluo carried back the seedlings
And placed them outside the door.
He entered the house and tricked Miluotuo, saying:
"Miluotuo, Miluotuo,
I was halfway back
When all the seedlings fell into the river."

Miluotuo was hurt,
And complained to Buluo:
"Why weren't you more careful,
Since seedlings are so hard to come by?"

Miluotuo couldn't sleep;
At midnight she heard a big dog bark.
So Miluotuo went out the door.
When she saw the seedlings, she chuckled to herself.
The wonderful seedlings,
Bouncing about in a big basket;
It seemed they wished to leap right out,
And climb up onto the hillsides by themselves.

The east slowly brightened.
Miluotuo called to Buluo:
"The seedlings are outside the door,
Why did you trick me?
Quick, go call your brothers,
Today we all go to the hills. . . ."

The nine brothers climbed up the hillsides;
The seedlings couldn't be scattered by the handfuls,
It was one by one that the seedlings
Were planted.

Suddenly, a great wind blew across the hills,
The great wind blew bringing happiness;
Miluotuo let the seedlings in her hands
Be blown by the wind high and low.

Nine months passed,
The spring winds blew on the hillsides;
Suoliang went to the hills to hunt.
The seedlings had sprouted thickly;
Suoliang was joyful,
And told Miluotuo.

Miluotuo was joyful,
Miluotuo laughed to herself;
The hills were covered with forests,
The hills now had green shade.

Nine more months passed;
Suoliang went hunting in the hills;
Each of the saplings had grown into trees,
The thick trees reached clear up to the sky.

All the hillsides were deep green,
All the hillsides were richly verdant;
Golden fruit hung on the trees,
And the trees bore red blossoms.

Suoliang ran back home,
And told Miluotuo:
"Grass and trees are everywhere on the hillsides,
Flowers and fruits are everywhere, too."

Miluotuo went up into the hills,
From top to bottom the hills had changed;
Such wonderful trees!
The thick trees had grown as high as the sky!

The hillsides had grass and trees,
The hillsides had flowers and fruit,
But there was nothing to pick the flowers,
And nothing to eat the golden fruits,
And nothing to eat the green grass,
And nothing to come build nests,
And nothing to hide themselves in the forests.

Miluotuo created bees and butterflies,
Which tended the flowers.
Miluotuo created monkeys and civets,
Which ate the golden fruits.
Miluotuo created cows and horses and sheep,
Which ate the green grasses.
Miluotuo created eagles and long-tailed birds,
Which came to make nests.
Miluotuo created bears and wild boars,
Which hid in the forests.

The hillsides had big trees,
The hillsides had living creatures;
Miluotuo still wanted to make people,
But the people had no houses to live in;
Miluotuo wanted to create houses.

PART 3. CREATING HOUSES

Miluotuo wanted to create houses,
But she had no axes,

Nor saws,
Nor brush knives.

Miluotuo opened a chest,
Took out some stone and gave it to Buluo.
Buluo took the stone and gave it to a stonemason,
Gave it to the mason to make axheads.
Buluo took the stone to the mason to make a saw,
Buluo took the stone to the mason to make brush knives.

The mason made many axheads,
The mason made many saws,
The mason made many knives.
Buluo went to sharpen the axheads,
He sharpened them as sharp as a tiger's tongue;
Buluo went to sharpen the saws,
He sharpened them as sharp as knife-grass leaves;
Buluo went to sharpen the knives,
He sharpened them as bright as springwater.

Buluo took the axes home,
And gave them to Miluotuo to see;
Buluo took the saws home,
And gave them to Miluotuo to see;
Buluo carried the brush knives home,
And gave them to Miluotuo to see.
When Miluotuo saw the axheads,
When Miluotuo saw the saws,
When Miluotuo saw the brush knives,
Miluotuo was joyous,
Miluotuo liked them very much.

Miluotuo called the nine brothers,
The nine brothers went to Liulipo,
And used the axes to chop down the trees,
And used the saws to saw up the trees,
And used the knives to split the trees.
Cut down and sawed,
Sawed up and split.
Split the big trees for mortises,
Split the big trees for tenons,
Cut the small trees for rafters,
Cut cogon grass to thatch the roof,
Cut bamboo to weave a fence.

As the sun set,
The nine brothers carried back the wood,
The nine brothers carried back the grass,
The boards and grass were all there.

Now Miluotuo wanted to build a house,
But what sort of house would she make?
She wanted to create a great house,
One that would last for ten thousand generations!

Miluotuo called Buluo,
Called Buluo to go to Changshu.
To Changshu to choose a good day.
The necromancer chose the ninth day of the month;
The ninth day belongs to the tiger,
So the ninth day is a lucky day.

Buluo returned;
When the ninth day arrived,
The nine brothers went to Liulipo,
To Liulipo to build a house.

The big logs were used as posts,
And the posts were put in first.
The boards were used to make the walls,
And in the walls were made window frames.
The grass was used to cover the house,
To cover it very smoothly.
The bamboo was used to weave a fence,
Which was woven around all four sides.

When the tables and chairs were arranged inside,
When the beds were placed inside,
The nine brothers walked out of the house,
The nine brothers looked over the house;
The big house was dark,
The big house wasn't bright at all.

The nine brothers returned home and said:
"Miluotuo, Miluotuo,
We made a great big house,
But the big house is so dark;
The big house isn't bright at all!"

Miluotuo opened a chest,
And took out some glittering silver water.
The nine brothers took the silver water and
Washed the house posts till they sparkled;
The nine brothers took the silver water and
Washed the doorframe till it glistened.
How the house shone!
It looked like the rising sun!

When the big house was all cleaned,
They invited Miluotuo to come and live in it;
The nine brothers went out and cut some bamboo
And wove a sedan chair.
The nine brothers called two young girls to carry
Miluotuo to Liulipo.
The nine brothers picked up her clothes,
The nine brothers picked up her pigs and chickens,
And escorted Miluotuo to Liulipo.

Miluotuo got out of the chair,
Miluotuo looked over the big house;
The wide house was big and tall,
The big house was bright and shiny,
It would surely last forever!

Outside the house were rows of mountains,
And water flowed beneath the mountains,
Beside the water were fields,
With fragrant flowers all year-round.

Miluotuo, leading the nine brothers,
Walked into the big house;
Miluotuo leading the nine brothers,
Moved into the big house.

Miluotuo moved into the big house,
Miluotuo opened up the wastelands,
In the low spots rice was planted,
In the highlands millet was sown.

In the ninth month when the rice was yellow,
Miluotuo called the monkeys to come,
Called the monkeys to come see the rice.

In the ninth month when the millet was like torches,
Miluotuo called the grasshoppers to see the millet.

When the monkeys came,
They stole the rice and ate it;
When the grasshoppers came,
They ate the grain's leaves.

A monkey scolded a grasshopper:
"Why did you eat the leaves of grain?
I'm going to tell Miluotuo."

The grasshopper scolded the monkey:
"You were first to eat the rice,
Go ahead and tell on me, I'm not afraid."

The monkey was undaunted,
The monkey challenged the grasshopper to a fight;
The grasshopper didn't fear the monkey,
The monkey, likewise, didn't fear him.

The monkey wanted to fight;
He picked up a stick and came
Out from the gully.
Then he struck at the grasshopper,
But the grasshopper flew onto the monkey's face.

The monkey could not see the grasshopper,
But he used the stick to hit the grasshopper.
So he hit himself in the face—
Right on the bridge of his nose!
From that time on the monkey's face was red,
From that time on the monkey's nose was flattened.
The monkey failed to hit the grasshopper,
So he ran atop the white cliffs.

PART 4. SHOOTING THE SUNS

When Miluotuo created the skies,
She gave birth to twelve suns.
The twelve suns in the skies
Looked just like twelve firepots.
They scorched the big trees till they

Were a withered yellow.
They scorched the big rivers till they were dry.
The corn in the fields was dry as kindling,
The grain in the paddies drooped to the ground.

The nine brothers cried and cried,
With long faces they said:
"Miluotuo, Miluotuo,
There are twelve suns in the sky;
They are all very evil.
Everything has been burned to death,
We'll all be baked, too!"

The suns burned brightly,
The suns were very evil-hearted.
Later, when she created humans,
They would certainly be scorched to death.
Miluotuo called the nine brothers together:
Upon the twelfth day
They must shoot down the twelve suns.

When the twelfth day arrived,
The nine brothers held long spears,
The nine brothers wore stone hats,
The nine brothers wore stone shoes,
And walked to three forks in the road;
There at the forks of the road they waited.

The twelve suns showed their faces,
Flames raging in the sky,
Flames raging down on earth.
The nine brothers raised their spears,
But the spears were burned to a crisp,
The nine brothers wore hats of stone,
But the hats of stone melted,
The nine brothers wore stone shoes,
But the stone shoes became soft.
The nine brothers failed to strike down the suns,
The nine brothers were instead burned by the suns.

The nine brothers turned back home,
Crestfallen, the nine brothers said:
"Miluotuo, Miluotuo,

We failed to strike down the suns."
Miluotuo was upset,
Miluotuo didn't know what to do.

"The trees and grass on the mountains are all withered;
Only the wild hemp hasn't yellowed;
You all go and strip off some wild hemp fibers,
And bring them back to make a bowstring.

"The trees and grass on the mountains have all withered,
Only the steel-star tree is still green;
Cut down the steel-star tree
And bring it here to make a large bow.

"The trees and grass on the mountains have all withered,
Only the bamboo leaves are still green;
Cut down some big bamboos,
And bring them here to make arrows."

The nine brothers stripped off some hemp fibers,
The nine brothers chopped down the steel-star tree,
The nine brothers cut down some big bamboos,
And made a great bow and arrows.

Miluotuo again ordered them:
"You must climb up the hills to get medicinal herbs;
Pluck twelve kinds of herbs
And grind them into a paste;
Then coat the arrows with it."

The nine brothers went up into the hills,
And brought back the medicinal herbs;
They ground the herbs into a paste,
Then coated the arrows with it.

Miluotuo was still not confident.
She told the nine brothers to take the bow and arrows
And shoot a chicken.
A chicken is stronger than the suns,
Therefore if the bow and arrows killed the chicken,
They could shoot down the suns.
The nine brothers put an arrow on the bowstring
And with a "plunk,"
The chicken was struck dead.

Miluotuo was still not confident.
She told the brothers to take the bow and arrows
And shoot a pig;
A pig is stronger than the suns,
Therefore if the bow and arrows killed the pig,
They could shoot down the suns.
The nine brothers put an arrow on the bowstring
And with a "plunk,"
The pig was struck dead.

Miluotuo was still not confident.
She told the brothers to take the bow and arrows
And shoot a cow;
A cow is stronger than the suns,
Therefore if the bow and arrows killed the cow,
They could shoot down the suns.
The nine brothers put an arrow on the bowstring
And with a "plunk,"
The cow was struck dead.

Miluotuo was still not confident.
She told the nine brothers to take the bow and arrows
And shoot a horse;
A horse is stronger than the suns;
Therefore if the bow and arrows could kill a horse,
They could be used to shoot down the suns.
The nine brothers put an arrow on the bowstring
And with a "plunk,"
The horse was struck dead.

After another twelve days,
The nine brothers carried the bow and arrows on their shoulders,
The nine brothers held their lunches in their hands,
The nine brothers came to three forks in the road,
And at the three forks, they waited.

The twelve suns in the sky
Rode upon twelve white horses;
The twelve big white horses came charging toward earth,
The nine brothers' hearts were burning with anger,
The nine brothers' faces were red,
Abo drew back the bow,
Buluo pulled back the string

And shot two arrows,
Which whizzed through the heavens.

Two of the suns were struck by the sharp arrows,
Two of the suns spun round and round
As twelve head of horses galloped toward them,
The nine brothers drew back the bow
And used the sharp arrows to shoot ten of the suns;
Then there were only two left to hide behind the mountains.

The skies still had two suns,
But the two suns weren't shining;
The sky was very dark,
The earth was very dark, too.

The nine brothers became worried,
The nine brothers returned home,
"Miluotuo, Miluotuo,
The suns in the sky are no longer shining,
Day and night are both dark;
We can't see where we are,
We can't even see our doorsteps!"

Miluotuo became angry,
Miluotuo scolded the suns:
"Why don't you shine?
If you don't start shining again,
I will destroy you completely!"

The two suns were very frightened,
The two suns became very nervous;
The two suns appeared again,
The two suns began to shine.

Ten of the suns had died,
The two remaining suns were lonely,
The two remaining suns had an idea:
They secretly wished to be married.

Miluotuo thought it over—
If the two suns get married,
Then they'll have children,
All life on each couldn't continue.

Miluotuo picked up a bowl,
Miluotuo said to the suns:
"If you two were meant to be married,
Then this bowl cannot be broken.
If the bowl breaks,
Then you must part."

Miluotuo hit the bowl,
The bowl broke.
The two suns didn't get married.
The two suns parted forever.

From then on, one shone in the day,
From then on, one shone at night.
The one that shines in the daytime is called the sun;
The one that shines at night is called the moon.

The sun and the moon
Still meet once a month.
They can still see each other.

The nine brothers returned,
Their lunches were covered in the suns' blood;
So they fed their lunches to the pigs,
But the pigs just snorted at the food and left.

The nine brothers returned,
Their lunches were covered with the suns' blood;
So they fed their lunches to the dogs,
But the dogs only sniffed at the food and left.

The nine brothers returned home,
Their lunches were covered with the suns' blood;
So they fed their lunches to the roosters;
The roosters gobbled it down and
From then on roosters' combs have been red,
Just like the suns' blood.
So, each day, when the sun rises,
The roosters will crow to greet it.

PART 5. KILLING THE TIGER

Miluotuo wanted to create people;
Miluotuo picked up some stones,

And put them in an earthen crock.
After nine months,
The stones turned into tiger cubs.
The tigers ran up on the white cliffs,
The tigers hid in the forest.

Miluotuo then created people.
Miluotuo took up a piece of stone,
And put it in an earthen jar.
After several months,
The stone had made baby stones.

Miluotuo went out to the fields,
And left the baby stones at home.
When Miluotuo returned home,
She couldn't find the baby stones anywhere.

Behind the house was a winding path,
Miluotuo followed the winding path,
And walked up to the white cliff tops,
Where the tigers were eating people.

Who was being eaten?
The baby stones were being eaten.
Miluotuo was brokenhearted;
Miluotuo was furious.

Miluotuo returned to Liulipo,
She called to the nine brothers:
"The tigers are eating the people!
The tigers are harming the people!"

Abo heard her call,
And told Miluotuo not to grieve.
Abo wanted to climb the mountain to get rid of the tigers,
So he immediately rushed to the mountain forest.

As Abo walked along,
He formed a plan.
When Abo arrived at the cliff,
He called out to the white cliffs in a great voice,
"Old Friend, Old Friend!
Are you up there on the white cliffs?

Follow me to go hunting,
Follow me somewhere for a good time."

The tiger heard Abo call,
The tiger was very happy.
He followed Abo to go hunting,
He followed Abo up the mountains.

Abo went to Liulipo,
Abo said to the tiger:
"You wait up on the mountain,
I'll drive at the foot."

The tiger climbed up the slope;
Abo started a fire at the foot of the mountain;
The fire burned its way up the slope,
The tiger lunged into the roaring flames.

The fire burned the tiger's whiskers,
The fire burned the tiger's fur;
From then on the tiger's body
Was striped.

The fire burned across the slope,
Abo cried to the tiger:
"Old Friend, Old Friend,
I've been driving down here at the foot.
Has any game run up the hill?"

The tiger slapped at his burning body,
"I haven't seen any game;
My body's been burned,
My whiskers were all singed off!"

Abo pretended to scold the tiger:
"Why didn't you run away?"
The tiger didn't make a sound;
The tiger then went home.

Abo still didn't feel avenged,
Abo's hatred was hard to dissolve;
After three or four days passed,
He again called the tiger to go hunting.

Abo went to the white cliffs,
And again cried loudly to the cliffs:
"Old Friend, Old Friend,
Are you up there on the white cliffs?
Follow me to go hunting!
Follow me along somewhere for a good time!"

When the tiger heard Abo's cry,
The tiger was very happy,
And again he followed Abo to go hunting,
And again he followed Abo to the mountains.

Abo went up to the mountain,
Abo said to the tiger:
"This time you wait at the bottom of the mountain,
I'll go drive game down from the top!
When the animals run down,
Use your jaws to bite them!"

Abo climbed up the mountain,
Abo pried out a hunk of stone;
The rock went rolling down,
The tiger couldn't see it clearly,
The tiger opened his mouth—
In a great bite he snapped off several of his teeth,
And blood dripped out of his mouth.

Meeting a goat running down the hill,
The tiger caught the goat in his jaws.
The goat bleated,
And Abo ran down the slope:
"Brother, oh Brother,
Did you catch the goat?"

With a bloody mouth
The tiger raised his head and looked at Abo;
Abo didn't make a sound,
But grabbed up the goat and skinned it.
Abo called to the tiger as he
Lit a fire and roasted the goat meat.

While the tiger was still far away,
Abo picked up the big stone

And rubbed the goat blood on it;
The stone was dyed red all over,
And looked just like a great piece of meat.

The tiger returned;
Abo laughed to himself as he said:
"Old Friend, Old Friend,
You bit the goat to death;
Thank you for your work.
You take the goat meat,
I'll take the goat guts."

The tiger nodded his head,
The tiger gave a wide grin,
Picked up the great stone,
And happily went on home.

The tiger returned home
And started a fire;
He put the stone on to cook,
It boiled and boiled, but still it wasn't done,
So he ran to find Abo.

Abo had sliced up the goat,
And given a piece of it to the tiger to eat.
The flavor of the goat meat was delicious.
The tiger asked Abo:
"How do you roast goat meat?
How do you boil goat meat?"

Abo had an excellent plan:
"You go on home,
Set up a great big kettle,
And fill the kettle with water.
Call your children to the side of the fire pit,
Call your wife to hold the kettle handles.
You take the goat meat upstairs,
Then with all your might, throw it into the kettle;
This way the goat will boil deliciously,
This way the goat will boil till it's done!"

The tiger listened,
The tiger then ran home.

He called to his children,
He called to his wife.

The children gathered around the fire pit,
His wife picked up the great kettle;
The fire below it was burning hot,
The water in the pot was at a rolling boil.

The tiger picked up the great stone,
And climbed up to the top of the stairwell.
The tiger faced the great kettle,
And dropped in the great stone.
Splash! The kettle water splattered everywhere,
Scalding to death the tiger cubs,
Scalding to death the tiger's wife.

The tiger cried for three days,
The tiger cried for three nights.
He cried as he walked along,
As he walked to Abo's home:
"Brother, O Brother,
Why did you deceive me?
My wife and children were all scalded to death,
And my great kettle was broken."

Abo pointed at the tiger's nose:
"I'm so kind and goodwilled,
How could I deceive you?
It's you who messed everything up!

"You boiled the water,
Then put in the goat meat.
How could you not help but scald them to death?
How could you not help breaking your kettle?"

The tiger felt very hurt,
And tucked his head and cried.
The tiger bowed his head,
And went off toward his home.

After a few days,
Abo again called the tiger to go hunting.
He cooked some animal liver

And tied it to his thigh.
Then he went into the shady forest,
Into the cool shade.
In front of the tiger, he cut off a piece of his thigh,
Cut off a piece of himself to taste.

The tiger found the meat so fragrant
That spittle ran out of his jaws:
"Old Friend, Old Friend,
What are you eating?
What can smell as good as that?"

Abo replied:
"I am eating *niejilin*.
Here, I'll give you a little to try."

The tiger ate the liver;
The liver was sweet and fragrant.
Abo ate a little and gave him a little to try.
Abo asked the tiger:
"Cut off a piece of yourself for a taste."

The tiger asked him how to cut it.
Abo told the tiger to go home
And put an edge on his cooking knife;
Sharpen it until it glistened.
Then he was to hold the knife in his right hand,
Spread his rear legs apart,
Look up to the sky,
And cut "it" off with a knife.

The tiger memorized the instructions,
Then returned home.
He locked his door,
And sharpened his cooking knife till it glistened,
Then he cut off his *niejilin*.
And from then on there were no tigers on the mountains.

PART 6. FINDING A PLACE

After Abo killed the tiger,
Abo returned to Liulipo Place:
"Miluotuo, Miluotuo,

The mountain tigers have all been killed.
If you want to make people now, you can go ahead."
Miluotuo was very happy,
Miluotuo was very glad.

If Miluotuo wanted to create people,
She first had to find a proper place.
Who could she ask to find such a place?
First she asked a deaf pig.
After the deaf pig ate breakfast,
It went to find a suitable place.
When the deaf pig was halfway there,
It found an earthworm nest,
And dug all the worms out to eat.
When the deaf pig had eaten its fill,
It went back home.

Miluotuo stood by the door and asked:
"Were you able to find a place?"
Stuttering, the deaf pig said:
"I went halfway
And dug up some worms to eat;
I didn't see any good places."

Miluotuo was very upset,
Miluotuo was very angry.
She picked up a stick and beat the deaf pig.
She beat its ears hard,
And from then on the deaf pig was deaf,
And it had to hide in the mountains.

Miluotuo called a long-tailed bird,
And told it to find a suitable place.
When the long-tailed bird flew to the mountainside,
It saw the slopes had red fruit.
After the bird had eaten its fill,
It went back home.

Miluotuo stood by the door and asked:
"Were you able to find a good place?"
The long-tailed bird replied:
"I flew to the hillsides
And picked red fruit to eat;
I didn't see any good places."

Miluotuo was very upset,
Miluotuo was very angry.
She took up a bow and arrow,
And shot the long-tailed bird;
She shot it in the rump,
And the long-tailed bird grew a very long tail,
Then flew up into the mountains.

Miluotuo called a crow.
After the crow ate breakfast,
It went to look for a suitable place.
The crow flew into the mountains,
And saw the slopes were on fire.
It flew into the dense smoke,
And flapped its wings playfully in the fire.
As the sun was setting,
The crow flew home.

Miluotuo stood before the door and asked,
"Were you able to find a good place?"
The crow replied,
"I flew to the mountains,
And saw a forest fire.
I flew there to play in the fire;
I didn't see any good places."

Miluotuo was very upset.
Miluotuo was very angry.
She took up some indigo ink,
And splashed it on the crow's body.
From then on the crow was black,
And it flew into the mountains.

Miluotuo called an eagle.
After the eagle ate breakfast,
The eagle packed its lunch,
And went to find a suitable place.
The eagle flew nearly half the day
Till it lit for a rest in a kapok tree.
On the white cliffs was a puff of smoke,
The eagle picked up a spark,
Then made a fire and began cooking its lunch.

On the white cliffs was an old man, who said:
"Why have you come here?"
The eagle said to him,
"Miluotuo wants to create people.
She asked me to find a suitable place."

The old man immediately grew serious, saying:
"I created this place;
No one else can look at it.
No one else can live here."
The old man took a rope
And snared the eagle's feet.
He put it in a cave,
And locked it there for three years.

The old man bought some wine;
The old man wanted to kill the eagle;
But the eagle knew what he was planning
And begged the old man:
"I am going to die soon,
Please open my cage,
Let me gaze at the sky,
Let me look at the earth."

The old man opened two of the bars,
And the eagle gazed about at the sky.
But it could not even see half of it.
The eagle looked at the land,
But it could not even see half of it.

The eagle again begged the old man,
So the old man opened four of the bars.
The eagle spread its wings
And flew out of the cave,
All the way back to Liulipo Place.

When the eagle flew home,
It saw Miluotuo.
It asked her for something to eat,
It asked her for water to drink,
But Miluotuo scolded the eagle:
"You were gone for three years,

And now you've come home.
I have food, but I'll give you none.
I have water, but I'll give you none!"

The eagle's body and feet were weak,
So the eagle tremblingly said:
"Miluotuo, Miluotuo,
After I've eaten my fill,
After I've had enough to drink,
I have something to tell you."

Miluotuo gave some food to the eagle,
The eagle ate the food;
Miluotuo gave some water to the eagle,
The eagle drank its fill.
Then it said,
"On the white cliffs
There is a devious old man.
He said he created that place;
He wouldn't let me see it,
And shut me up in a cave.
He shut me in there for three years."

Miluotuo thought to herself:
"Who could be living on the white cliff tops?
Who could be so devious?"
Miluotuo thought to herself
That the fellow living on the white cliff tops
Was certainly Ha'ang.
Ha'ang was double-hearted,
Ha'ang was two-faced.

Miluotuo opened a chest,
Seeking stone to give the eagle a beak;
Miluotuo opened a chest,
Seeking stone to make the eagle claws.

The eagle's beak was like a spike,
The eagle's claws were sharp;
Miluotuo bade it
Bring Ha'ang back.

The eagle flew off,
Flew atop a mountain;

It opened its stony beak
And snatched up a white pheasant.

The eagle flew to the white cliff top:
"Old Friend, Old Friend,
I want to set things right with you again,
So I'm giving you this white pheasant
For you to eat with your wine."

When Ha'ang heard the eagle's cry,
He became very happy and said,
"You have brought a white pheasant,
I'll get up a fire and cook it."

Ha'ang was excited,
Ha'ang blew into the fire,
But it only became smokier.
So the eagle said to him,
"You don't know how to blow a fire,
You're only making it smokier.
Please close your eyes,
I'll help you to blow."

As Ha'ang closed his eyes,
The eagle opened its talons
And grabbed Ha'ang by the nape of his neck;
Holding on to Ha'ang, it flew into the sky.

Ha'ang cried from the sky,
But the eagle flew higher and higher;
Ha'ang looked down at the earth—
The rivers looked like pieces of string.
The eagle said to Ha'ang:
"Master, Master,
I'll let you fall to earth!"

Ha'ang was terrified,
Ha'ang cried for the eagle not to drop him;
The eagle flew on and on,
Right to Miluotuo's home.

When Miluotuo saw it was Ha'ang,
Miluotuo became angry:
"I want to create mankind;

I told the eagle to go find a good place.
Why did you lock him up?
You are bad-hearted,
I'll put you in the earthen dungeon!"

After Ha'ang was put in the dungeon,
Miluotuo called to two girls
To take food to Ha'ang.
Ha'ang again grew devious.
Ha'ang made tongs of bamboo in the dungeon,
And with them broke the girls' hands,
Causing the two girls to die.

Miluotuo was brokenhearted,
Miluotuo was furious;
She took the two good girls
And buried them in the Moon Temple.
Then she created human beings,
And she bade the girls to watch,
And she bade the girls to be happy.

Ha'ang was very worried,
Ha'ang was very sad.
A rat burrowed inside
And saw Ha'ang at the end of its hole.
"Old Friend, Old Friend,
Why are you living here?"

Ha'ang said to the rat:
"Miluotuo wanted to create humankind,
Miluotuo shut me up in here.
Do you have any relatives?
If so, bring them here to help me."

Thinking of its old friends,
The rat called a pangolin to come.
The pangolin made a hole;
It dug a hole right up to a tree root;
But the big root couldn't be dug through.
Ha'ang asked the pangolin,
"Do you have any relatives?
If so, please bring them to help."

Thinking of his old friend,
The pangolin called a sharp-toothed rat.[7]
The sharp-toothed rat's teeth were so sharp
They seemed like knives.
It gnawed right through the big root
And dug a big hole.
Ha'ang could then escape,
And he ran out of the dungeon.

PART 7. CREATING HUMANKIND

Miluotuo then created humankind;
Bunong went to the mountains to play.
Beneath a kapok tree
Was a bee's nest.
Bunong dug out the larvae,
And put them in his mouth.
The larvae were very sweet,
And tasted like honeyed wine.

Bunong took home the larvae,
And gave them to Miluotuo to see.
Every larva was white and fat,
Just like a baby's face.

Miluotuo called the nine brothers;
The nine brothers took axes to the hillsides
And cut down the kapok trees.
They pulled out the roots,
Dug out the larvae,
And rooted out the beeswax.

Miluotuo was joyful.
She took the larvae to create humankind,
And used the beeswax to shape the heads,
And beeswax to shape the hands,
And beeswax to shape the feet.
This way she shaped humankind;
Shaped them one by one,
And put them in an earthen crock.

---

7. This may be a bamboo rat (Rhizomyinae), a burrowing mammal that eats rhizomes.

Miluotuo stood beside the crock and said,
"If they are baby chicks,
They will take twenty days to hatch;
If they are puppies,
They will take two months to be born;
If they are colts,
They will take twelve months to be born;
If they are calves,
They will take nineteen months to be born;
If they are children,
In nine months they'll be born!"

When the ninth month arrived,
Miluotuo went to the crop fields;
The nine brothers were all at home.
Suddenly, they heard sounds of crying
Coming from within the earthen crock.

The nine brothers opened the crock.
The larvae had changed into human beings!
Some were male and some were female;
And each one was white and fat.

Miluotuo returned home;
The nine brothers said to her,
"The larvae have turned into humans!"
Miluotuo opened the big crock,
The babies moved their hands and feet.
Miluotuo was joyous,
Miluotuo was so glad.

Miluotuo took rice to feed the babies,
But the babies wouldn't eat it;
Miluotuo brought wine for them to drink,
But the babies wouldn't drink it.
Miluotuo called Miling to come;
Upon Miling's chest were two outcroppings,
Inside them was milk.
Miling used them to suckle the babies.
The babies drank the milk,
And each day they grew bigger.

The wind blew through the southern bamboo grove.
The bamboo rustled and creaked;

By listening to the sounds of the bamboo,
The babies learned to speak,
But their speech wasn't all the same:
Some spoke Han Chinese,
Some spoke Zhuang,
And some spoke Yao.

As Miluotuo saw them off,
Miluotuo told them to marry:
Those named Lan and those named Luo should pair up,
Those named Wei and those named Meng should pair up,
Those named Lan were to go to Niehuoniedong,
Those named Luo were to go to Poshanpo,
Those named Wei were to go to Poxipomeng,
And those named Meng were to go to Kechangkesuo.

TWO MIAO (HMONG) SONG FLOWERS

Translated and introduced by Mark Bender

The Miao ethnic group (officially known as Miaozu in China) is a large and diverse people living in China, in parts of Southeast Asia, and in diaspora communities around the world. Outside China, Hmong is often the preferred name, though there are many local designations. More than 7 million Miao people live in the mountainous regions of southwestern China, particularly in Guizhou, Hunan, and Guangxi. The two songs presented here were collected in the Southeast Guizhou Miao-Dong Nationalities Autonomous Prefecture, a nexus of Miao culture. Locals tend to live in upland villages and raise rice, vegetables, fish, and pigs. The area is known for folk festivals such as the Sister Festival, held in Taijiang county each spring. Clad in elaborately embroidered tunics and skirts and enormous amounts of fantastic silver jewelry, young women hold large circle dances on the riverbanks. Later in the summer, the rivers are filled with lively crews racing long wooden boats in the Dragon Boat Festival.

Such festivals, as well as weddings, house raisings, and certain ritual events, are times when antiphonal folk songs are performed. Although the Miao have a rich tradition of antiphonally sung love songs and drinking songs, a few singers still participate in an antiphonal style of epic singing. The subject matter of the epics (or "ancient songs") is typically the creation of the world by mythic beings, including the making of the suns and moons from gold and silver, the shooting down of excess suns when the earth began to melt, the planting of the landscape with trees, and the birth of a creator figure, known as Butterfly Mother (Mai Bang). Butterfly Mother lays her eggs in a sweet-gum tree. After being hatched by a mythical bird, the culture hero Jang Vang emerges from his shell. Industrious, but something of a trickster, Jang eventually gets into a tiff with the Thunder God over an ox, resulting in rains that flood the earth. Jang Vang and his sister survive the flood inside a giant calabash. Following the pattern found in many traditional myths collected in central and southern China, the brother and sister reluctantly marry and the world is again repopulated. Other epics tell of legendary migrations.

The epics are usually sung by two pairs of singers, often two men and two women, who sit opposite each other at a table. Each pair sings together in one voice; partners or the opposing singers are referred to as brother or sister. The singers, who are surrounded by audience members and supplied with food and drink, can exchange portions of the epics for hours or even for days and nights on end. Structurally, the epics unfold as narratives punctuated by questions. One group sings a certain portion of a section and then asks a question. The other side repeats some of what has just been sung and answers the question, thus providing new content and moving the narration along. Occasionally, the "bone" of the narration is enhanced by the insertion of what are called song flowers (*bang hxa*). The "flowers" are short, lyrical poems that often have nothing to do with the content of the epic but provide variety, humor (especially when the singers poke fun at themselves or the opposing singers), and a further chance for the singers to exhibit their singing skills and knowledge of tradition. Once a song flower has been sung, the singers revert to narrating the epic. Both "How Much Do You Really Know?" and "Don't Weave Cloth Without a Loom" were collected in Taijiang county, southeastern Guizhou, in the 1990s and edited in a bilingual volume by the epic scholar and singer Jin Dan.[8]

HOW MUCH DO YOU TWO REALLY KNOW?

Sung by Gang Yenf Eb Ghob (Miao) and collected by Xenx Jenb Eb Ghob (Miao)

How much do you two really know?
I'm afraid I'm old, my body's weak.
As my teeth fall out, my cheeks grow hollow.
As my cheeks cave in, my lips stick out,
And the notes of my songs are not so round.
Were I as young as you,
My Mandarin would flow like yours,
And one by one would my Miao songs ring.
This one singer could outsing ten,
Making them cry for their pa and ma,
Causing their tears by the hundreds to stream,
Stream like rivers to float a boat
Clear to Shanghai, that far-off port,
Clear to a big official's door:
That's what I call singing.

DON'T WEAVE CLOTH WITHOUT A LOOM

Sung by Fuf Nix Khat Gad (Miao) and collected by Qenf Dangk Khat Ged (Miao)

Don't weave cloth without a loom,
Don't sing songs without the rules,
Follow the song path when you sing,
Sing them all from head to toe,
Without missing anything in between;
If anything in between is missed,
Then we'll not sing in harmony.
If you want to sing a new song,
That we two haven't learned,

8. For a version of the Miao epics, see Mark Bender, *Butterfly Mother: Miao (Hmong) Creation Epics from Guizhou, China* (Indianapolis: Hackett, 2006).

We'll have a hard time following Sister.
We'll have to owe Sister a little favor,
But don't feel bad over a favor owed,
Don't be sad on account of Brother.
As teachers, companions, walking a familiar road,
Since we're so close, let's be friends,
Become dearest kin for life.

Chapter 5

FOLK DRAMA

In China, traditional drama has had a complicated and fertile relationship with other expressive arts, including the storytelling arts called *quyi* (art of melodies), various musical traditions, and popular literature. All told, Chinese scholars have documented more than 360 different local styles of drama within the borders of the country. Those offered by professional troupes, in particular Beijing (Peking) opera (*jingju*), constitute the best known of the forms, though there are vast numbers of lesser-known local styles, with varying levels of organization. The styles are differentiated by ethnic group, local tradition, language, music, and emphasis on certain dramatic conventions. Despite such a wide variety, a large percentage of the dramatic styles share basic features, including a mix of stylized conventions of song, speech, and movement, and characters that fall into conventional role types.

Although the early history of drama in China is still filled with numerous question marks, the antecedents of drama likely include shamanistic ritual that featured dancing and singing. References to rituals known as *nuo* date to at least the Spring and Autumn (770–476 B.C.E.) and Warring States (475–221 B.C.E.) periods of the Zhou dynasty (1045–221 B.C.E.). Such dramas seem to have been performed as much for the gods and spirits as for human audiences. This feature of performance and reception is still part of some local dramatic forms, such as the *nuotang* opera (*nuotangxi*) traditions of Guizhou and other provinces in the southwest in which performers wear ritually consecrated wooden masks representing a host of characters. Other early performance traditions include court entertainers such as dancers, jesters, and musicians, as well as puppetry and comic games, such as combat between men and animals.

Influences from Indian and Central Asian narrative, dramatic, dance, and musical traditions entered western China on the Silk Road, especially as vehicles for spreading Buddhism. Records and artistic images from the Tang dynasty (618–907) indicate that plays were widespread by that time and were performed in contexts ranging from government-sponsored performances in the imperial palace to those given on mat-shed stages at festivals, markets, and feasts for various levels of elites and common folk. By the Song dynasty (960–1279), styles of drama known as *zaju* and *yuanben* had developed, which featured role types still familiar in many traditions. With the invasion of the northern Jurchen (Jin) people, which pushed the Chinese capital southward to Hangzhou, there was a mixing of northern and southern dramatic traditions. One influence from southwestern China was Cuan drama, which featured elaborate dances.

The greatest influence on the development of drama in China, however, was the Mongol conquest. During the ensuing Yuan dynasty (1271–1368), Mongol leaders like Kublai Khan facilitated the spread of drama throughout the realm. Some disenfranchised Han Chinese scholars contributed to this development by writing lyrics or plays, sometimes in direct cooperation with actors. Over the course of the Ming (1368–1644) and Qing (1644–1911) dynasties, traditional drama achieved its fullest elaboration, and regional forms developed.

These included the influential and elegant *kunqu* opera of Jiangsu province, which flowered in the late Ming and had declined by the early nineteenth century in the Qing. By the mid-nineteenth century, a robust form of opera had developed in the northern capital that combined musical and dramatic styles from Anhui province in the south with the acrobatic theatrical elements of northern opera. Over a period of decades, this marriage formed the style now known as Beijing opera, the best known and most widespread of the traditional styles of regional drama that have expanded across the country since the Ming dynasty.

Among the major regional opera styles are Cantonese opera, the operas of Fujian and Taiwan, Shaoxing (Yueju) opera (with some all-female troupes) in the Yangtze delta, the Qinqiang traditions of Xi'an and parts of northwestern China, Hunan opera in south-central China, and the amazing Sichuan opera in the southwest, in which actors change thin masks in the blink of an eye. Along with basic conventions and many overlapping play plots, these "major" styles feature large troupes of professional actors (primarily, since 1949, with government support) and informally associated groups of avocational performers and fan clubs. As parallel forms to human-actor drama, various types of puppet drama also have long histories in China.

Traditionally, Confucian values of filial piety and Buddhist tenets of selflessness were frequently embodied onstage. During the twentieth century, revolutionary movements used folk dramas to promote their causes, and new ideas displaced the more traditional ethos, especially in the decades leading up to and immediately following 1949. Since the late 1970s, many styles of traditional drama have reappeared following years of suppression imposed by the Cultural Revolution (1966–1976), a period dominated by a limited number of highly politicized dramas that were widely performed throughout the entire society.

Troupes of itinerant actors once performed all over China. Some dramatic traditions were community based, offering involvement to locals as organizers, actors, and audience members. In recent years, state-run opera troupes in various parts of China have had to deal with declining audiences and limited funding, but at the same time there has been a revival, expansion, and reinvention of dramatic traditions among groups of middle-aged people all over the country. Other local dramatic forms have been co-opted or even created by the needs of the tourist industry. These less formally organized, highly localized traditions combine in various ways and to varying degrees singing, speaking, dancing, stylized movements, and musical accompaniment. Among the most widespread of these local styles are revived versions of various types of "rice-sprout" (*yang'ge*) performances of the north and so-called lantern operas (*huadeng xi*) of the southwest that are based on earlier traditions associated with the agricultural cycle of planting and harvest.

The major forms of Chinese opera have been treated in many other volumes. Our selections, by contrast, are examples of more local styles that suggest the importance of drama in the fabric of folk and popular arts of China. *Records on Rescuing Mother*, from Shaoxing, in the eastern province of Zhejiang, is a dramatic version of a popular Buddhist tale about the filial son Mulian that dates to the Tang dynasty. *A Worthy Sister-in-Law* is an example of a *yang'ge* used to promote socialist ideals in the decades after the founding of the People's Republic. A comical shadow-puppet playlet from northern China, *All Three Fear Their Wives*, features a cast of colorful characters who like to gamble, are "stubborn and mouthy," and spitefully engage in domestic violence. The chapter also includes a modernized hand-puppet performance from Taiwan featuring dramatic effects like smoke caused by aerosol sprays and flashing electric lights.

HAND-PUPPET THEATER

Collected, translated, and introduced by Sue-mei Wu

Hand-puppet theater (*budaixi*), a kind of puppet show featuring figures made of tiny sacks topped with painted heads and manipulated by hand, developed in the Ming dynasty (1368–1644) and was introduced to Taiwan by immigrants from Fujian province. During its over two hundred years of development in Taiwan, *budaixi* became intertwined with Taiwanese local customs and practices, emerging as a valued component of Taiwanese culture.

A traditional *budaixi* troupe usually includes two groups: the puppeteers and the musicians. In general, a performance requires two puppeteers. The chief puppeteer, who generally is the director of the troupe, stands behind the stage, manipulating the main puppets, performing the difficult scenes, and singing and narrating. A supporting puppeteer manipulates the other puppets in coordination with those of the chief puppeteer, takes care of the stage setup, changes the puppets' costumes, changes the music (if on tape), and produces the special effects. The relationship between the two puppeteers is usually one of master and apprentice. Frequently, the master trains his sons to succeed him as puppet master. The musical group consists of usually four or five musicians who sit behind the stage. The main instruments include the Chinese two-stringed violin (*erhu*), gong (*luo*), cymbals (*ba*), drum (*gu*), castanets (*paiban*), and a trumpetlike wind instrument (*suona*). The drummer is in charge of directing the musicians during the performance.

Budaixi troupes are usually organized and sponsored by folk organizations. The troupes are invited to perform when there are temple festivals, occasions honoring deities, and other auspicious or happy events such as weddings, births, and promotions. The main stated purpose of *budaixi* is to thank and entertain the deities. The limited entertainment options in Taiwan in the 1950s and 1960s, however, meant that it also served as a popular means of folk entertainment at the time.

The stories to be performed are usually selected from popular folktales, such as *Journey to the West* (*Xiyou ji*); historical serial novels, such as *Romance of the Three Kingdoms* (*Sanguo yanyi*); and the martial arts world, such as *Outlaws of the Marsh* (*Water Margin* [*Shuihu zhuan*]). The stories can also be newly created stories set in ancient China, for which the martial arts world is the most popular.

The main language of traditional *budaixi* performance is Taiwanese with a literary flavor, including some poems and literary idioms. In order to entertain the audience, however, words and expressions from other languages—such as Mandarin, English, and Japanese—are sometimes added for humorous effect.

Since *budaixi* is a folk entertainment form enjoyed by ordinary people, it is easily influenced by new or popular things. In the past two decades, *budaixi* has had to struggle to compete in a world of ever-increasing entertainment sources.

Troupes have begun to use new technologies to entertain audiences—for example, dry ice, laser lights, and taped songs. In addition to its adaptation to competing forms of entertainment, *budaixi* is being preserved and promoted as one of the most representative aspects of Taiwanese culture. As a result of these multiple influences, four distinctive types of *budaixi* performance have evolved in Taiwan: open-air performances for temple festivals, television performances for entertainment, exhibition performances for preservation and education, and a new experimental form designed to promote and educate people about Taiwan's local history and geography. Of these four, television *budaixi* has become the most popular, because the medium allows a high degree of technological advancement and audiovisual special effects, and the shows can reach more people than can live performances.

The following selection presents an open-air hand-puppet theater performance by the Zhang Shuangxi Hand-Puppet Troupe. It was staged during a temple festival in Sanchong city, in the suburbs of Taipei, Taiwan. On March 21, 1996, an open-air hand-puppet theater performance was scheduled in honor of the alleged millennial anniversary of the local temple, Shuntian Gong (Shuntian temple), located in an alley of Sanchong city.

The performance utilized a truck bed as the base for a highly portable stage. This stage was positioned to face the local deities, so they could conveniently watch the show. There were two puppeteers: the director of the troupe, Zhang Shuangxi, and his wife, who served as the assistant puppeteer. A tape of music and dialogue was used, enabling the performers to concentrate on manipulating the puppets. Special effects, including multicolored flashing lights and smoke produced from aerosol cans, made the scenes more eye-catching.

Before the show, background music was played, consisting of renditions of Taiwanese popular songs without their lyrics. Then the puppeteer used the microphone to announce that the day was the celebration of the Shuntian temple and that his troupe was going to perform a "Judge Bao" story. The selected scenes that follow constitute about fifteen minutes of the ninety-minute show.

EXCERPTS FROM A TEMPLE FESTIVAL PERFORMANCE

Performed by the Zhang Shuangxi Hand-Puppet Troupe, Taipei, Taiwan

Scene 1

(*Up in the Cuifeng Mountain stockade, a* LADY BANDIT LEADER *and one of her followers are talking.*)

BANDIT (BIG HEAD): I'm coming! I am the Big Head, Chen Chaoqing. Does my lady leader have any orders for me?

LADY BANDIT LEADER: Now the food stocks of our stockade are almost used up. We need to go down the mountain to block the passersby and ask them to pay a toll. If the passersby plead with you, then grab half the money and leave half to them.

BANDIT (BIG HEAD): All right! Now I am going down the mountain to rob!

LADY BANDIT LEADER: You all go down the mountain to rob. I shall guard our Cuifeng Mountain.

Scene 2

(*Down the mountain, the* BANDIT [BIG HEAD] *is talking to a poor scholar,* YAN ZHICHANG.)

YAN ZHICHANG: If I gave all my money to you, Big Brother, how could I go to the capital to seek scholarly honor and official rank?

BANDIT (BIG HEAD): Stop it! Stop it! I have heard this kind of excuse a lot. Give me your money!

YAN ZHICHANG: Big Brother, may I ask how much you want?

BANDIT (BIG HEAD): The more the better!

YAN ZHICHANG: I have only six *liang*.

BANDIT (BIG HEAD): Then give me all six *liang*. I may leave you some change.

YAN ZHICHANG: Please, Big Brother, I beg you: let me owe you this six *liang*. Please let me go!

BANDIT (BIG HEAD): Ah! What do you mean! What are you talking about! I'm robbing you of your money and you want me to let you pass with an IOU!

YAN ZHICHANG: I am going to the capital to seek honor and official rank. Please let me owe you this six *liang*. I will write down your name and address; then let me go through. When I succeed, I will definitely bring the money to you.

BANDIT (BIG HEAD): Nonsense! You think I'm a kindhearted donor! I am robbing you!

(*A fighting scene follows. The* BANDIT [BIG HEAD] *chases* YAN ZHICHANG. YAN ZHICHANG *is driven into the wilderness. He is defeated and flees. The tempo of the music speeds up and is accompanied by the sounds of yelling and screaming, further enhancing the fighting scene. [Behind the stage, the puppeteer, Zhang Shuangxi, is controlling both puppets, one in each hand. The assistant puppeteer, Zhang's wife, is busy controlling the overhead lights. She makes smoke to indicate a change to another scene.] Another puppet comes onstage.*)

Scene 3

(*A knight-hero,* WU DAZU, *enters.*)

WU DAZU: I am Wu Dazu, a wandering knight. I have a strong sense of justice and I help the weak. Now I am in a wild field and see a group of people attacking a scholar. Let me go and see what is going on.

(*The fighting music continues.* YAN ZHICHANG *runs and runs and then bumps into* WU DAZU. WU *helps him along.*)

YAN ZHICHANG: Thank you for upholding justice. I hope that you will rescue me!

WU DAZU: How did you, a weak scholar, come to be fighting with this group of people? What is the reason?

YAN ZHICHANG: It is hard to explain in a few words. Please allow me to tell the story.

(*The background music switches to a rhythmic accompaniment.* YAN ZHICHANG *mimes telling the story.*)

WU DAZU: That's wrong! That's unfair! You step aside. Let me, Wu Dazu, deal with it!

YAN ZHICHANG: Thank you, Hero!

WU DAZU: Step aside!

Scene 4

(WU DAZU *intercepts the* BANDIT [BIG HEAD].)

WU DAZU: Hold it! Stop!

BANDIT (BIG HEAD): Ah! I was just about to get the money from the young man, and now suddenly someone gets in my way. To be frank, you can ask for anything, but you shouldn't ask for death. You can eat your own food, but don't mess in other people's business. I'm warning you now. You should be more realistic!

WU DAZU: You, mountain bandit, you've gone too far!

(WU DAZU *fights with the* BANDIT [BIG HEAD]. *The background music quickens. [The assistant puppeteer sprays smoke.] The* BANDIT *is badly defeated.*)

BANDIT (BIG HEAD) (*running and panting, then in an out-of-breath monologue*): I, the Big Head, Chen Chaoqing, am shamed. I am very good at kung-fu techniques such as Tiger Fist and Bear Fist. But now I encounter this youngster, and I cannot match him in a fight. I am going to ask help from our lady leader, Jin Cuilian. She can fight at your level. We will see if you will be arrogant then. I am running back to the mountain. Hurry up!

Scene 5

(*The* LADY BANDIT LEADER, JIN CUILIAN, *enters.*)

JIN CUILIAN: Big Head reported to me that this guy is very good at kung fu. I will stay in this mountain and remember the words of my Lady Master. Now I am going to use the technique of Divided Body and Spirit. One is the spirit, and the other is the original physical form.

(*The background music becomes fast paced. A roll of grass, representing* JIN CUILIAN'S *spirit form, goes out and fights with* WU. WU *fights and runs and eventually gets caught.*)

BANDIT (BIG HEAD): I am the Big Head, Chen Chaoqing. My Lady Master is great. She employed her technique of Divided Body and Spirit, and then it was too late for the youngster to escape!

Scene 6

(JIN CUILIAN *and* WU DAZU *are onstage.*)

JIN CUILIAN: You, young man, have been caught by me. Now what do you have to say?

WU DAZU: Once caught by you, whether I live or not is up to you!

JIN CUILIAN: You were caught by me and yet you don't beg, but on the contrary are arrogant and show your pride in front of me. Do you want me to send you to the West Mountain?[1]

WU DAZU: I usually help good people and remove bad elements. Today I am at Cuifeng Mountain and encounter this evil lady bandit leader, who has captured me. I, Wu Dazu, am a disciple of the master Huang Shigong. Is this the place I will be buried?

JIN CUILIAN: Ah! You are a disciple of the master Huang Shigong? Let me untie you.

WU DAZU: You, evil lady bandit, heard my name, Wu Dazu, and quickly untied me. What is the reason for this?

JIN CUILIAN: Wu Dazu, if you had reported your name at first, then there wouldn't have been this unfortunate misunderstanding. Now that the mistake is already made, let's let bygones be bygones. I will untie you and explain the reason to you. I have a golden letter written with gold ink that was given to me by my Lady Master. Now take a look at it, and then you will understand.

WU DAZU: Who is your Lady Master?

JIN CUILIAN: The golden letter is here. After you read it, you will know the story. It will explain everything.

WU DAZU: I see. Let me open and read it. What is this golden letter about?

(WU DAZU *opens the golden letter and reads through it.*)

I opened and read the golden letter. As pointed out by the Lady Master, you and I are destined to be together.

JIN CUILIAN: You are destined to be my husband! I have been waiting here for you for a very long time! Welcome, my husband, on your arrival to Cuifeng Mountain. We can get married here.

WU DAZU: Since we are destined to be a couple, we shall get married. However, I have one condition. You must open the path on Cuifeng Mountain for all the passersby.

JIN CUILIAN: Yes, I accept my husband's instruction.

WU DAZU: Let's bring my friend, Yan Zhichang, up Cuifeng Mountain together with us.

---

1. The West Mountain implies the land of the dead, and thus the words are a death threat.

Scene 7

(YAN ZHICHANG *and* WU DAZU *are onstage.*)

YAN ZHICHANG: I am Yan Zhichang.

WU DAZU: I am Wu Dazu. I came to Cuifeng Mountain and married my wife.

JIN CUILIAN: We have been married for three days. Now I would like to become sworn brothers with you. You are the big brother.

YAN ZHICHANG: My little brother, you saved my life! But I have been on Cuifeng Mountain for three days. I need to move on and go to the capital.

WU DAZU: My brother is going to the capital to seek honor and official rank. As you are a weak scholar, I should ride a fast horse to escort you there. However, my wife and I have been married only three days; it would be inconvenient for me to leave. I have one hundred *liang* here for your expenses. Please accept it.

YAN ZHICHANG: No! I cannot take it. You saved my life and now you want to give me your money!

WU DAZU: You think it is too little, right?

YAN ZHICHANG: No! I don't mean that!

WU DAZU: If you don't mean that, please accept it.

YAN ZHICHANG: I see. Thank you, my little brother, for your righteous and generous help. In the future, if I, Yan Zhichang, have success, I will never forget you.

WU DAZU: My older brother, don't thank me. It is nothing. Inside the four seas we are all brothers. You must be very careful on your way to the capital.

YAN ZHICHANG: Okay. I am leaving now. Good-bye!

WU DAZU (*to himself*): My older brother, Yan Zhichang, has left Cuifeng Mountain. I will stay at Cuifeng Mountain to wait for his success. His name will be written on the golden board. Now let me return to Cuifeng Mountain.

A POSTMIDNIGHT SHADOW PLAY FROM SHAANXI

Collected, translated, and introduced by Fan Pen Chen

Also known as extra or additional plays (*shaoxi*) and ribald plays (*saoxi*), postmidnight plays (*houbanyexi*) are basically comical, skitlike playlets performed very early in the morning, after all the women, children, and elderly audience members have left following the nighttime performance. They exist in both shadow-type and human actors' theater. In the shadow-theater troupes of Shaanxi province, these highly entertaining but unseemly skits used to be performed by secondary performers, the musicians of the troupe, rather than by the main singer and master puppeteer. While they provided lighthearted entertainment for the audience and helped lift its spirits during the early hours of the morning before the continuation of the serious, main plays, their performance by an alternate cast also afforded a rest for the main performers.

Unlike the main plays, these skits are very short and last only about fifteen minutes. They are usually orally transmitted and hence performed without playscripts. The audiences of these postmidnight plays are mostly young and middle-aged men who obviously enjoy sarcasm, exaggeration, and scatological and sexual jokes, as well as laughing at people worse off than themselves. They reflect the taste, concerns, and mentality of these peasant audiences. Only in such skits would the clown role (*chou*) and the flirtatious young female role (*huadan*) be allowed to become protagonists. The characters are exaggerated, and none command respect, but they must have been plausible to their audiences. While the wives being ridiculed tend to be a sorry lot, the husbands are, as a rule, no better. In the following playlet, the husband is a lazy good-for-nothing whose "ingenious" plan to buy things to please his wife depends on his confident assumption that he will win at the next local gambling session.

The traditional daughter-in-law was apparently not as helpless as one might believe. In this play, her room seems to be a sacred space protecting her from the nagging of her mother-in-law. In fact, the mother-in-law is afraid of being caught by her son near her daughter-in-law's room; even the husband of its occupant cannot enter if she refuses to open the door. Much as she yells at and abuses the younger woman, the mother-in-law is not able to beat her and seems to exert practically no influence over her. The daughter-in-law defies her authority and leads a life of leisure and gossip with the neighbors.

Both women manipulate their husbands through a most powerful threat: they get their way by threatening to commit suicide. Power through sexuality on the part of the young woman is also hinted at. The mother exerts no influence over her son and must rely on her husband to discipline him. Hence it becomes apparent that the play expresses a popular fear that a son might actually side with his wife against his parents. Filial piety is totally absent in this dysfunctional family.

All Three Fear Their Wives is a popular shadow play of northwestern China, found in Gansu, Shaanxi, and Henan provinces. The version translated here was transcribed by a Daoist shadow-theater troupe in Lingbao, Henan. Headed by Suo Xinyou, members of this Daoist troupe considered themselves proselytizers of Daoist tales and thought and performers of some Daoist rituals. Postmidnight plays are not part of their traditional repertoire, but they adopted them from shadow performers in Shaanxi to "lighten up the audience's spirit before sending them home."

The henpecked husband or husband who fears his wife is a popular theme in postmidnight shadow plays. The fact that men enjoy watching henpecked husbands suggests that this is a subject close to their hearts and that women have not been totally powerless.[2]

ALL THREE FEAR THEIR WIVES

Performed by a Daoist shadow-theater troupe in Lingbao, Henan

CHARACTERS

SON: Wang Qi, a young clown
DAUGHTER-IN-LAW: Woman Ying, a flirtatious young female
MOTHER: An old female clown
FATHER: Wang Gongjing, an old male clown

SON (*enters and recites*):

So muddleheaded I am,
Can't tell the first from the middle of the month.
Beating up and scolding my parents,
I am filial to my wife instead.

(*Speaks*): I am none other than the kid Wang Qi. I live at Duyu Village, of Shaanzhou. I love to do nothing more than gamble every day. It's early morning; I think I'll take a stroll down the main street.

(*Sings*):

A new emperor has just ascended the throne,
I have here a story I would like to tell.
At the area of Wentang, in the county of Shaanzhou,
Within Wentang, there is a village called Duyu.
I have a father by the name of Wang Gongjing,
He gave birth to me, his son—my name is Wang Qi.
Each day instead of tending to chores on the farm,
I smoke, borrow money, and spend my time gambling.

(*Speaks*): I'm going to go and try to borrow some money. (*He exits.*)

2. Judging from details in the postmidnight shadow plays collected by the translator from Shaanxi, the majority were created during the Qing dynasty.

DAUGHTER-IN-LAW (*enters and sings*):

I, Woman Ying, will now tell you about myself.
Wang Qi married a daughter of the Ying family,
By nature I am stubborn and mouthy,
Unwilling to tend to chores of the house;
I spend my time creating havoc among the neighbors.
Everyone blames me for our neighborhood problems,
But what do I care—I just stare right back at them.

MOTHER (*enters and sings*):

The minute this Old Lady sees her, I'm mad as hell,
I scold her: Woman Ying, you good-for-nothing!
Instead of doing household chores, you gossip among the neighbors.
Everyone blames you for all the problems;
Totally embarrassed, where can I put this old face of mine?
The more I speak, the angrier I feel,
I'll give the slut a sound beating—what am I afraid of?

DAUGHTER-IN-LAW (*sings*):

When I, Woman Ying, see a beating forthcoming,
I run quickly to my own small bedroom.
Hurriedly I turn around and close my door,
And pressing my hands to my eyes, I begin to weep.
In the small bedroom, I, Woman Ying, lament my fate.

MOTHER (*sings*):

Standing outside her door, I, Old Lady, am unsatisfied,
Most unhappy that I, Old Lady, am unable to beat her.
I scold: Listen to me carefully, you lowborn slut,
I won't say anything else about you,
I'll only say that you were born by a pig and raised by a bitch.
Just as I, Old Lady, am in the midst of my scolding—

SON (*enters and sings*):

In comes through the door little old me, her son, Wang Qi.

MOTHER (*sings*):

Discovering the arrival of my son,
I, Old Lady, rush away in shock.
Hiding under the window of the small bedroom,
I hold my breath and listen quietly,
Waiting to see what goes on between the couple.

SON (*sings*):

I, Wang Qi, arrive at the door of the small bedroom;
Why is it that I hear my wife crying and weeping?
I walk forward and bang on the door,
I call out: Dear wife, open the door!

DAUGHTER-IN-LAW (*sings*):

I, Woman Ying, am weeping in the small bedroom;

Suddenly, I hear someone calling outside my door.
I walk forward and open the door,

SON (*sings*):
In from the outside arrives the kid, Wang Qi.

DAUGHTER-IN-LAW (*sings*):
Seeing the arrival of my husband,
I, Woman Ying, can't help but weep even harder.

SON (*sings*):
I move forward and bow to her,
I ask: Dear wife, what is the matter?
Did you quarrel with my parents?
Did the neighbors next to us mistreat you?
Tell me, Wang Qi, nothing but the truth,
Dear wife, I'll go to the city of Shaanzhou and sue them.

DAUGHTER-IN-LAW (*sings*):
Ah, my dear husband!
I did not quarrel with your parents,
Nor did the neighbors mistreat me.
I have nothing to say about your *da*,[3]
But your ma is quite something else!
She yells at me from morning till afternoon,
Then from afternoon she scolds again till sunset.
I can't say much about the other things she called me,
But she said that I was born by a pig and raised by a bitch.
You and your da and ma can take your time living out your lives,
I'm going to pull up my hair and hang myself instead.
If I, your wife, leave this world,
Your ma can find you a better substitute.
I, Woman Ying, announce: I want to die!

SON (*sings*):
Listening to her, I, Wang Qi, got ever so worried,
I walk forward and tug on her clothes.
I kneel down before her in the middle of the room,
I plead: My dear wife, please don't kill yourself,
I have something to tell you, pray listen to me.
There'll be a market gathering tomorrow east of the village,
I'll go to the market and do some gambling.
I'll win lots of money at the gambling table,
And buy lots of things to make you happy.
I'll first buy you a nice gauze handkerchief,
Then I'll deck you out with silver jewelry.

---

3. People in Shaanxi and its vicinity call their fathers *da*.

You'll have a *qilin*-patterned[4] hairpin for your hair,
And a pair of earrings with bamboo leaf and plum flower motifs.
You'll have a sterling-silver bracelet imprinted with orchid flowers,
And three strings of agate beads hanging down from it.
I'll first buy you a padded jacket of bright red silk,
And then I'll get you the best woolen skirt, nice and soft.
A red padded jacket to match the skirt;
On top, you'll also wear a necklace with a *qilin* pendant.
But let's not talk about these lovely things for you to wear,
Let's talk about the delicious foods I will also bring.
I will first buy eight sweet baked cakes,
I will then buy four solid and juicy pears.
We'll eat the cakes in the middle of the night,
And after finishing the cakes, we'll eat the pears.
You can have the flesh, I will eat the peel.
The pear seeds we'll throw under our brick bed,
Lest the two old ones find out about it.
If they find out about it, they'll denounce me, Wang Qi, as unrighteous.

DAUGHTER-IN-LAW (*sings*):

Hearing this, I, Woman Ying, smile with content,
Walking forward, I approach my husband and help him up.
I was only teasing you, my dear husband,
Why would someone as young as I want to die?
You and I shouldn't stand around here all day,
Let's take advantage of the darkness of our small bedroom.

NARRATOR (*speaks*): Let's speak no more of Wang Qi and his wife.

MOTHER (*sings*):

Let us now talk about me, Old Lady, who has been listening.
The more I listened to them, the angrier I got;
Let me go to the master bedroom to find the old dog.
One foot inside the door, one foot still outside,
I yell to my husband: Old Dog, listen to me carefully.
You really did a good job of teaching that son of yours,
Now he won't do anything but please his wife.
When the market is on tomorrow east of the village,
You son plans to go gambling at the market.
He plans to win at the gambling tables
And has promised to buy her all sorts of gifts.
He will first buy her a bright red padded jacket,
He will then get her a woolen skirt, nice and soft.
A red jacket, a woolen skirt,

---

4. The *qilin* is a propitious lion-like mythical animal with antlers.

On top, she'll have a *qilin* pendant.
Let's not say any more of these lovely things to wear,
He also promised to buy her delicious foods to eat.
He will first buy eight sweet baked cakes,
He will then get her four smooth, solid pears.
His wife will eat the pears, he will eat the peel.
The pear seeds they'll throw under their brick bed,
Lest you and I would find out about it
And denounce them as unrighteous.

FATHER (*sings*):
I, the old man, walk forward and gag her mouth;
I tell her: Old Lady, listen carefully.
Don't blame the son and the daughter-in-law,
Remember how many things I got you in the past?

MOTHER (*sings*):
Ah, Old Dog, ah!
As I, Old Lady, speak, tears fill my eyes,
I tell you, Old Dog, listen to me carefully.
You and your son and daughter-in-law can take your time living out your lives;
I'll go to the dike by the Yellow River and plop myself in.
If I, Old Lady, leave this world,
Your son can find you a young partner instead.
Saying this, I announce: I want to die!

FATHER (*sings*):
Hearing this, I, the old man, got ever so worried.
Old Lady, please go back to the master bedroom,
I will go find the little kid, Wang Qi.
Hearing her, I, the old man, got ready for action.
In one step, I jump smack into the middle of the courtyard,
Opening my mouth, I yell at Wang Qi to box his ears.
I scold: Wang Qi, you good-for-nothing,
In the past, your grandpa was henpecked by your grandma;
Your ma also had me so scared that I used to tremble.
I thought that the trend would change with you,
Wonderful son of mine, why, you turned out to be as henpecked as we were!
I don't know whether it's the location of our ancestral graves or that of our gate?
I'll have to hire a geomancy specialist tomorrow,
And consult him as to the locations of our buildings.
I'll have our ancestral graves moved backward,
And the gate of our house moved forward.

SON (*sings*):

Listening to him, I, Wang Qi, am all smiles,
You don't need to do all that, my dear old man.
There's no need to hire a geomancer tomorrow,
Find my uncle instead and we'll split the household.
We'll divide the family properties one by one,
You can serve your wife and I will serve mine.
You can serve my mother in the master bedroom,
I will serve my wife in the small side bedroom.
Although I'm quite civilized now,
I can also give you a beating—who's afraid of that?

FATHER (*sings*):

Wang Qi, don't you be bad now,
The Five Dragons in heaven will come after you.

SON (*sings*):

The little dragons in heaven aren't strong enough to capture me,
But I can't afford to be caught by the old ones.
Since I'm too scared to give you a beating,
Let me smear your face with shit and piss.

FATHER (*sings*):

Seeing this, I am so consumed with fury,
The kid, Wang Qi, has really gone too far.
Yelling and beating me are bad enough,
But he really shouldn't have smeared me with shit.
If you wish to know the name and title of this play,
This play is none other than *All Three Fear Their Wives*.
I'm not going to stand around here any longer,
I'm heading for the city of Shaanzhou to sue my son.

A RICE-PLANTING DRAMA

Translated and introduced by Ellen R. Judd

Yang'ge (rice-planting songs) is a term used to denote a set of popular performing genres widespread in Han areas of northern China and linked to similar forms in the south. It can be traced at least as far back as the Song dynasty (960–1279), and the famous Song poet Su Dongpo (1037–1101) has been credited with creating some of the earliest *yang'ge* known in the Ding county area of Hebei province, though there is no firm evidence to support this claim. The name itself suggests that it originated as a type of work song, and this, too, has been posited. Whatever its history, by the twentieth century *yang'ge* were being performed in rural northern China in a variety of genres, ranging from simple but distinctive street dances to small-scale local dramas.

Yang'ge's roots in the northern countryside, where the Communist forces had their main bases during the Yan'an period (1937–1947), formed the basis of its adoption as the centerpiece of the era's reform of popular literature and art. In 1949, the *yang'ge* dance was performed in urban streets as a celebration of liberation, but new *yang'ge* drama was by then already well established as a genre in the recent popular literature and art.

A Worthy Sister-in-Law exemplifies the new *yang'ge* dramas that were created and promoted during this era, and especially from 1943. These new *yang'ge* dramatized and advocated some aspect of official policy in the Communist Party's border regions, such as increasing production, maintaining good relations between the army and civilians, and instituting various moderate social reforms. *A Worthy Sister-in-Law* is an adaptation of an already existing item in the local dramatic repertoire. The new *yang'ge* text presented here shows the continuing attention of *yang'ge* to the important matters of everyday rural life, such as family relations, and to its role in advocating policy and promoting change—in this case, literacy for women. The resolution of this short drama illustrates the idea of success on the road to change, while established values of familial harmony are retained and even enhanced.

A WORTHY SISTER-IN-LAW

Performed by the Qiaozhen Township Yang'ge Troupe

CHARACTERS

OLD MOTHER LI
ZHOU SHI: Old Mother Li's daughter-in-law, twenty-six years old
GUI JIE: Old Mother Li's daughter, eighteen years old
LI RONG: Old Mother Li's son, thirty years old
ZHANG: Head of the Women's Federation, twenty-six years old

MOTHER (*sings*):

Say that I'm bad, well then I'm bad,
I won't let my daughter-in-law learn to read.
Say I am odd, well then I'm odd,
But I can't stand my daughter-in-law's learning to read!

(*Speaks*): I'm Old Mother Li, and I have one son and one daughter. The son is called Li Rong and the daughter is called Gui Jie. The boy has been able to read since he was young and is now working in the fields—he's not only able to write and reckon, but he's a good worker, too. The girl spins cotton. The family's really not doing badly and my heart would be content, except that just now things are strange. Here there's a night school being organized, and there's a reading class, bringing a lot of young men and women together. These young people! What good is there in young wives' learning to read! My Gui Jie is grown up now and wants to join a reading class. I can't control her and can't bring myself to beat her. But that daughter-in-law of mine also wants to join a reading class! I don't want to let her, but I'm afraid of the others.

Today, while my son's at the harvest, what's to prevent me from calling my daughter-in-law and giving her a good talking to? Cursed daughter-in-law—why aren't you out here!

DAUGHTER-IN-LAW (*enters singing*): *Ai!*

In early morn learning to read while spinning,
I hear my mother-in-law calling to me.
I quickly hide my reading book,
And rush off to her room.

(*Speaks*): Mother, what are you calling me to do?

MOTHER: Did you wash up after eating?

DAUGHTER-IN-LAW: It's all washed up.

MOTHER: Have you fed the pigs?

DAUGHTER-IN-LAW: I fed them.

MOTHER: Have you fed the chickens?

DAUGHTER-IN-LAW: I fed them.

MOTHER: Have you carried the water in?

DAUGHTER-IN-LAW: It's carried in.

MOTHER: Then why haven't you spun any cotton thread?

DAUGHTER-IN-LAW: I've already spun two ounces.

MOTHER: Ah! You've washed up, fed the pigs, fed the chickens, carried the water in, and also done some spinning, eh? What are you dressed up like an empress for—are you going to visit relatives or going to watch opera?

(*The* DAUGHTER-IN-LAW *is startled and drops the book.*)

Ah—what's that?

DAUGHTER-IN-LAW: Nothing.

MOTHER: Hand it here and let me see. Oh! It's that devilish book again. How is it that the reading class leader comes around every day? What are you doing, running around day and night, putting on airs, collecting books like an old monk? Didn't I tell you long ago that I'm not letting you join the reading class—but you went and joined it on the quiet, eh!

DAUGHTER-IN-LAW: Mother! The reading class is a good thing. Look, Gui Jie has joined the reading class, too.

MOTHER: You cursed daughter-in-law, you dare compare yourself with my Gui Jie?!

DAUGHTER-IN-LAW: Mother! Gui Jie is a person, and I am also a person. If she can join the reading class, why can't I?

MOTHER: Heh!

(*Sings*):

Cursed daughter-in-law,
You're too brave with words.
Talking right back to your mother-in-law.
Gui Jie is my own born and raised;
How can a daughter-in-law match her?
With this stick in my hand I'll beat you.

(*She's just about to strike when the head of the Women's Federation knocks on the door.*)

(*Speaks*): Who is it?

ZHANG: It's me.

MOTHER: And who are you?

ZHANG: I'm Zhang.

MOTHER (*opens the door*): Ah, the head of the Women's Federation has come. Let's sit down. What's brought you here?

ZHANG: Ah, the township has sent us a reading teacher today, so I've come to call your daughter-in-law and Gui Jie to come to class.

MOTHER: Ah, but we haven't had supper yet.

ZHANG: All right, when you've had supper, send them along. You two should hurry. Now I'll be going.

MOTHER: Won't you eat before you go!

ZHANG: No, I'll go now. (*Exits.*)

MOTHER (*shuts the door angrily*): Heh, you think that because the head of the Women's Federation came, you can have your own way! Well, you can't!

(*Sings*):

This old mother will never change.
No matter what, no matter what,
This old mother can't stand the sight of you. (*Beats her* DAUGHTER-IN-LAW.)

GUI (*enters singing*):

I hear my sister-in-law calling out,
And rush up to ask her why. (*Sound of clapper*)
Hai! I'll go up to mother and ask her why,
What cause to beat my sister-in-law?

(*Speaks*): I'll ask my mother to tell me plainly. Mother! Why are you beating my sister-in-law?

MOTHER: Cursed daughter-in-law, do you still dare to talk back? (*About to hit her*) Oh, it's my Gui Jie!

GUI: Why do you want to hit my sister-in-law?

MOTHER: Gui Jie, you don't know—

(*Sings*):

Oh, Gui Jie, just you listen as your mother tells you plainly:
How I hate that cursed, awful daughter-in-law!
Up in the morning eating food, but doing not a speck of work,
In her hands a reading book, going on "ni ni nan nan."[5]

GUI: Mother! Reading is a good thing!

MOTHER (*sings*):

Chickens not fed, pigs not fed, water not brought,
And all day running all around the village.

GUI: My sister-in-law never goes visiting!

MOTHER (*sings*):

Because I called her to give good advice,
She even argued back to this old mother.

GUI: Mother! Nonsense, my sister-in-law never talks back.

(*Sings*):

My sister-in-law is able and pure,
Spins thread, weaves cloth, and never talks back.

MOTHER (*sings*):

Little one, you are trying to deceive.
Not beating her just won't do.

(MOTHER *and* DAUGHTER *struggle for the stick.*)

GUI: Mother! Don't beat my sister-in-law. If you want to beat someone, beat me! (*Kneels.*)

MOTHER: With my cursed daughter-in-law on the ground, my heart is like oil poured on stone—cold, cold. With my Gui Jie on the ground, my heart feels as if needles were stuck in it—layer upon layer of pain. Gui Jie, get up.

GUI: When you let my sister-in-law get up, then I'll get up.

If you don't let her get up, then I won't get up!

MOTHER: You're kneeling, you're kneeling. . . . Oh, this daughter-in-law of mine is a good daughter-in-law: her hair is black, her face pale, her eyes large, her eyebrows long, and her feet small. She's a really good daughter-in-law. Eh, will you still not get up?

GUI: Is Sister-in-law getting up?

MOTHER: Gui Jie, get up! Oh, you really must get up for me.

---

5. The sound of reading aloud, which is how most Chinese students traditionally learned to read.

SON (*enters singing*):

September's come and hills are yellow with millet,
Each and every household busy with the harvest.
In a twinkling, the sun sets behind the hills,
And sickle in hand, I make my way home.
But then I hear voices raised at home. (*Sound of clapper; he enters.*)
So it's my old mother being angry.
I'll go up and ask her why.

(*Speaks*): Mother!

MOTHER: My son! You're back. While you were on the mountain cutting millet, that wife of yours was at home—not working but holding a reader in her hand: "ni ni nan nan." Your mother tried to give her a few words of advice, and she hit me with one hand and pulled my hair with the other. She shook me, and my body is swollen all over.

(*Sings*):

Rong, my son, hear your mother's words,
Daughters-in-law have now rebelled.
They rise up early,
They rise up early and eat a meal,
But then they don't do a speck of work,
Reader in hand, "ni ni nan nan," they run around town.
I advise her, and she ignores me, opposes me.

SON: Mother! Don't cry.

MOTHER: Rong! Do you want your mother, or do you want your wife?

SON: Mother! Why do you say that?

MOTHER: If you want your wife, your mother can't go on living.

(*The* SON *is speechless.*)

If you want your mother, you must cast off your wife and send her home.

SON: Mother! Nowadays people don't cast off wives, and anyway reading is a good thing. If others know about this they won't support it.

MOTHER: If reading is a good thing, then how about running around on the street all day visiting, is that a good thing? If you don't send her away, your old mother won't go on living—won't go on living.

SON: Mother! I'll send her away, ah! How does one write this?

MOTHER: Ah! You can't even write a statement renouncing your wife. Come here, I'll tell you what to write:

(*Sings*):

First, cast off the Zhou woman, who is not filial to Mother.
Second, cast off the Zhou woman, who dares to curse her husband.
Third, cast off the Zhou woman, who's not of proper appearance.
Fourth, cast off the Zhou woman, who has a roving heart.
Fifth, cast off the Zhou woman, whose hands and feet are clumsy.

Sixth, cast off the Zhou woman, who is not filial to Mother.
Seventh, cast off the Zhou woman, who is not filial to Mother.
Eighth, cast off . . . oh, just write it that way.

SON (*writing while singing*):

First, cast off the Zhou woman, who is not filial to Mother.
Second, cast off the Zhou woman, who dares to curse her husband.
Third, cast off the Zhou woman, who's not of proper appearance.
Fourth, cast off the Zhou woman . . .

MOTHER (*sings*):

Fourth, cast off the Zhou woman, who has a roving heart.

SON (*sings*):

Fourth cast off the Zhou woman, who has a roving heart.

MOTHER (*sings*):

Fifth, cast off the Zhou woman, whose hands and feet are clumsy.

SON (*sings*):

Fifth, cast off the Zhou woman, whose hands and feet are clumsy.

MOTHER (*sings*):

Sixth, cast off the Zhou woman, who is not filial to Mother.

SON (*sings*):

Sixth, cast off—

GUI (*comes forward and grabs the statement from her brother, sings*):

Elder Brother, you aren't a real man, a real man doesn't think like this.
She not only reads but also works,
To send her off is just not right;
Brother's statement I'll tear into bits,
And see what Mother can do to me.
Sit still, Mother, and listen to me,
Hear this comparison from your child:
Aunt Zhang is fifty and more
And gets on well with her daughter-in-law,
The two of them spin thread together,
And together in the evening learn to read.
My sister-in-law is a virtuous woman, in working and reading a model in both.

(*Speaks*): Brother! You see my sister-in-law does fine sewing and spinning while up on the *kang*, and when she comes down, cooks tasty and tender food. A daughter-in-law like this you'll not find anywhere, even with a lighted lantern. As I see it, you shouldn't send her away!

MOTHER: Sending her away is already decided.

GUI: Mother! How old am I now?

MOTHER: Two years ago you were sixteen; when the year turned you were fifteen; and now you are fourteen.

GUI: Mother! You're mixed up. How can a person grow younger!

MOTHER: Ha! You made me so angry, I got mixed up. Two years ago you were sixteen; when the year turned you were seventeen; now you are eighteen. That's right, isn't it?

GUI: Right. I'm already twice nine, or eighteen. A good father-in-law and good mother-in-law must be found. What if I find a mother-in-law like you, beating me one day and cursing me the next, then after a few days casting me off and sending me home? Mother, how will you keep face then?

MOTHER: Eh, the cursed daughter-in-law is the cursed daughter-in-law, and Gui Jie is Gui Jie. How can she compare with you! Casting her off is set.

GUI: Is it set?

MOTHER: It's set.

GUI: Then I'm going to call the head of the Women's Federation. (*Exits and calls from offstage*) Head of the Women's Federation!

MOTHER: She doesn't dare go.

ZHANG (*enters*): What are you up to?

MOTHER: Heh! Head of the Women's Federation, you've come to our place. Listen and I'll tell you—

ZHANG: Slowly. What are you sending her away for?

MOTHER: You see, this daughter-in-law of mine doesn't work hard, doesn't look after anything, and when I tell her to join a reading class—reading is a good thing—she won't go. I give a few words of advice and she hits me.

GUI: Head, don't listen to my mother. She's got it all backward.

MOTHER: Cursed daughter. You're speaking out of place.

ZHANG: Gui Jie, speak up.

GUI: To begin with, my sister-in-law is a good worker. The day before yesterday when you came, she and I both joined the reading class. My mother told her not to join and said that it's useless for wives to learn to read and called my sister-in-law to come and get a beating. Today she is forcing my brother to cast her off.

ZHANG: Li Rong, are you willing to divorce your wife?

SON: I'm not willing! But if I don't send her away, my mother will kill herself!

ZHANG: Woman of the Zhou family, are you willing to divorce your husband?

DAUGHTER-IN-LAW: I'm really not willing, but I'm not wanted!

ZHANG: Old Mother Li, see—your son and daughter-in-law don't want to get divorced.

GUI: Let's call the masses to judge this.

ZHANG: Right. Everybody, Old Mother Li wants to cast off her daughter-in-law today because she wants to learn to read. Do you support this or not?

MASSES (*first person*): Don't support it!

(*second person*): Send away such a good daughter-in-law?!

(*third person*): Struggle against her!

(*fourth person*): Put this on the blackboard for announcements!

GUI: Mother! See, they want to struggle against you and put you on the announcements blackboard. What's to be done? Not send her away!

(*The* MOTHER *is silent.*)

ZHANG: Learning to read is a good thing! Your daughter-in-law is a good worker to begin with and now joining the reading class is a good thing! You are a sensible person. Problems can be resolved best by understanding. Look, your son likes her and so does your daughter. How good it is to have a happy family—you mustn't quarrel and beat her as you do.

GUI: Mother, see, the head of the Women's Federation has spoken with you. You should understand!

MOTHER: Eh, my good head of the Women's Federation! Your words have made me fully understand. Before, this old head just couldn't turn itself around. My dear daughter-in-law, just now I was at fault. In the future we can learn to read together. But don't make a fuss about what just happened. Everybody, if I hit my daughter-in-law again, I'll accept your judgment.

DAUGHTER-IN-LAW: I won't make a fuss!

ZHANG: That's good!

MOTHER: Dear head of the Women's Federation! This owes much to you. Woman of the Zhou family, cook a meal, and let's keep the head of the Women's Federation to eat with us.

ZHANG: No, I must go. There is so much to do at home! (MOTHER, DAUGHTER-IN-LAW, *and* GUI JIE *see* ZHANG *out.*)

(*All sing*):

The wind blows and scatters the clouds.
An old mind can be turned around.
Men and women, old and young, join reading classes,
Learning to read and working as well,
Abundant clothing and ample food are happiness, indeed.
We sufferers of old have made a new start;
Masters of the new society are we.
Chairman Mao leads us all forward.

A LOCAL DRAMA FROM SHAOXING

Translated and introduced by Rostislav Berezkin

Dramas on the theme of the monk Mulian's rescuing his mother from hell are well known in many areas of China. The following excerpt is a translation from the voluminous text (more than a hundred acts) of the drama *Records on Rescuing Mother* (*Jiu mu ji*), from Shaoxing county, Zhejiang province. The Mulian drama enjoyed popularity in this area and was mentioned with praise by the great writer Lu Xun (Zhou Shuren [1881–1936]), a native of Shaoxing. The modern edition of the text is based on an undated manuscript that came to light in the 1950s.

The story of Mulian's (a disciple of Buddha, in Sanskrit he is known as Mahāmaudgalyāyana) rescuing his sinful mother from her punishment in the afterlife comes from *The Ullambana Sūtra Expounded by Buddha*. The monk Dharmarakṣa (Zhu Fahu), in the fourth century, called it a translation into Chinese, but it may be an apocryphal work. The story in a more elaborate form has been found in the manuscripts of Chinese popular literature discovered in Dunhuang—"transformation texts" (*bianwen*) and "tales of conditional origin" (*yuanqi*) (eighth–tenth centuries). In the twelfth century, a drama dealing with this story was performed in Kaifeng, the capital. The Mulian dramas are among the earliest to have been performed in Chinese theater, but early Mulian drama texts have not survived and are known only by name or in passing references. The oldest extant edition was compiled by the literatus Zhen Zhizhen (1518–1595). Most Mulian dramas performed in various parts of China use texts that derive almost entirely from Zhen Zhizhen's version. The Shaoxing version also follows the main story line presented in Zhen Zhizhen's text, but it also has many episodes not found there.

The play depicts the life of the family of the merchant Fu Xiang, a virtuous Buddhist layman. As a reward for Fu Xiang's piety, the Jade Emperor orders an astral deity to be incarnated as his son, Fu Luobu (Turnip). Luobu is the secular name of Mulian. Later, the Jade Emperor summons Fu Xiang to heaven. Then Fu Xiang's wife, Liu Qingti, attending to the advice of her brother Liu Jia, stops fasting (that is, maintaining a vegetarian diet) and starts to kill living beings (that is, eating meat). In order to avoid the remonstrances of her son Luobu, Qingti sends him out on a business trip. Then the Jade Emperor punishes Liu Qingti for her evil deeds: her soul is taken away by divine messengers and imprisoned in hell.

Luobu decides to rescue his mother's soul, so he becomes a monk and goes to the Western Heaven (India), where he meets the Buddha and asks for his help. Then Luobu travels through the ten divisions of hell in search of his mother, and the play describes all the kinds of suffering that sinners endure in the afterlife. After searching through many parts of hell, Luobu at last finds his mother, who then receives rebirth as a dog. Luobu later helps Liu Qingti attain a better rebirth, and finally the whole family is reunited in heaven.

The selection translated here, act 47, from volume 5, depicts the conversation of Liu Qingti and Liu Jia. It is important inasmuch as it reveals the conflict between the two systems of ideology in the play. The first, cultivated in the Fu family, incorporates Buddhist regulations (fasting and religious precepts) into the Confucian outlook. The second, adopted by Liu Jia, refutes Buddhist rules on the basis of the more ancient Chinese virtues of filial piety and sincerity. The act is also noteworthy for its depiction of scenes from everyday life in the household.

The text of this Shaoxing drama is written mainly in simple classical Chinese, especially in the prose dialogues. However, it also includes many elements of colloquial language typical of traditional drama and novels. Many expressions are formal, and the translator has tried to convey this. Furthermore, the text contains elements of the local Shaoxing topolect. This influence is revealed mainly in the character substitution made on the basis of local pronunciation in the original manuscript. One also finds several local expressions and even nonstandard characters that have been invented for recording topolectal words.

RECORDS ON RESCUING MOTHER

Act 47. "Exhortation to Refrain from Vegetarian Fasting"

CHARACTERS

Lead female: LIU QINGTI (Mulian's mother)
Second male: LIU JIA (Liu Qingti's brother)
Young female: JINNU (Golden Servant)

JINNU (*enters and sings*):

Every day at the clear dawn, I splash water
And sweep the space in front of the hall and inner chambers.
First I splash water on the floor to settle the dust,
And then I sweep the ground with a broom very neatly.
Ah! The hall of Buddha should be clean, should be clean;
Buddha's image is the golden body.
How silent are the inner gates;
The wind raises the pearl curtains;
Incense smoke swirls;
Everything is blurred as in the realm of the immortals.

(*Speaks*): Old mistress! Oh, old mistress!

(*Sings*):

How nice it is to enjoy prosperity and thus spend your lifetime!

LIU JIA (*enters and sings*):

I deserve pity:
Our parents gave birth to the two of us.
In previous days I went on business to other districts,
And my elder sister often asked for news of me, ah!
Yesterday I returned to the gates of my home,
And upon returning home I received some news.
I learned that my elder sister's husband had passed away.
How pitiful they are: the mother and the son, all of a sudden they were all alone.
Now I shall go to their house to ask how they are.

(*Speaks*): I have arrived. Might there be somebody inside? Jinnu, how is your mistress?

JINNU (*answers*): By the grace of your blessing, she is doing fine. I, Jinnu, have a matter to bother you with, Uncle.

LIU JIA (*speaks*): I already understand! I see that you have already grown up, and you want me to be a matchmaker for you?

JINNU (*speaks*): It's not that.

(*Sings*):

It is only about my mistress observing fasts, eating vegetarian food,
And reading sutras.
My master ate vegetarian food and succumbed to illness,
And mistress in vain discusses sutras.
Ah! Uncle, may I trouble you to urge the mistress
To stop her observation of vegetarian fasting as soon as possible?
A common saying holds:
Three cups of perfect wine and one cheerful heart,
This is good enough to express one's feelings freely,
And for the rest of one's days to enjoy heaven's destiny!

(*Speaks*): My old mistress! Oh, my old mistress!

(*Sings*):

What is the use of observing fasts and reading sutras?

LIU JIA (*speaks*): There is no need to speak more. Ask your mistress to come out. I, Uncle, have my own idea.

JINNU (*speaks*): I see. Mistress, please come out!

LIU QINGTI: What is the matter?

JINNU: Uncle is here.

LIU QINGTI (*enters and sings*):

I hear that my younger brother has entered the gate.
It is really that the so-called Emperor of Heaven[6] has drawn his merciless sword

---

6. The Emperor of Heaven (or Celestial Emperor) is the supreme deity in Chinese popular belief.

And cut the feelings of husband and wife in the human world.
I hear that my younger brother has entered the gate,
And cannot prevent my tears from flowing in streams.

LIU JIA (*interrupts*): My sister!

LIU QINGTI (*sings*):

Oh, my brother, oh!
Previously, when your sister's husband was alive,
When he heard that you, my brother, would come,
He definitely would go far to meet you,
And after you went he would see you off!
But now he has left his wife without care,
And abandoned his son without concern.
In the vague distance, where did his soul go?
Oh, my brother! Now I do not see even the shade of my husband,
How can your sister dispel her sorrow? Ah!

LIU JIA (*speaks*): Greetings to my sister!

LIU QINGTI (*speaks*): Greetings to my brother!

LIU JIA: Sister, please sit down!

LIU QINGTI: Brother, please sit down!

LIU JIA: Sister, I came a while ago [but I have not seen my nephew]; where is he?

LIU QINGTI: Yesterday, there was a fasting feast at a neighbor's house,[7] and today he went to thank them for the feast.

LIU JIA: In your home everything is about fasting; you cannot speak without mentioning the word "fast"! My sister, it would be better to stop fasting!

LIU QINGTI: My brother, it is better to observe fasts!

LIU JIA: It would be better to stop fasting!

LIU QINGTI: My brother, what are you talking about? I exhort you to perfect yourself and to do so as quickly as possible. As to the reason for observing fasts and eating vegetarian food: if when alive, we eat food of all kinds of tastes, after we die, how would we be able to add even a few drops of oil to this? It is still better to observe fasts.

LIU JIA: My sister, I have an example to tell you, so please listen. All these Buddhist and Daoist monks who wander around strictly observe fasts and engage in repenting. Their faces are yellow, and their bodies are skinny as sticks. Once they die in the middle of the road, there are no coffins to bury them in the mountains. After all, it would be better to stop fasting!

LIU QINGTI: It is better to observe fasts.

LIU JIA: Listen now to what I shall say:

(*Sings*):

I argue that man is the supreme spirit among the myriad things.
I argue that man is the head of the myriad things.

---

7. To pay monks for conducting rituals, pious families often gave vegetarian feasts in which both monks and laymen participated.

The fact that taste enters through the mouth and tongue is worth paying attention to.
Why should people not eat that for which there is a natural basis?
Cattle and sheep originally were borne by heaven to nourish our bodies.
Chickens and ducks are things that constitute the nourishment of the people of the world,
Fish and meat are products that nourish human life;
Turtles and tortoises are cooked with soy sauce.
Though it is hard to equal Zeng Yuan and Zeng Shen,[8]
Wine and meat, the fat and the sweet, nourished both my parents!

LIU QINGTI (*sings*):
I argue that fasting and precepts can nourish your mind:
One can compare fasting and precepts with holy enlightenment.
Fasting and precepts cause the joy of the Celestial Emperor.
To feed your mouth and stomach—people despise it.
To feed your mind and will—people respect it.
If one does not know hunger and thirst—it will turn into a defect of the mind.
Why should I be troubled that my life span will not reach that of other people?

LIU JIA (*sings*):
I argue that fasting and precepts for people of
The past and the present are different;
The past and the present had two modes of thinking.
People of the past observed fasting and precepts in a sincere way;
In recent times people observe long fasts just to delude the spirits.
Having made a show, their hearts turn calm;
But, before fortune comes, disaster has already arrived.
I encourage you, my sister, to drink wine and eat meat,[9]
Please do not observe long fasts and deceive others!

LIU QINGTI (*sings*):
When I heard these words, I suddenly awoke;
I regret now that I have not awakened all these years.
Now I have overcome the obstacle that deluded my soul;
From now on I shall leave off thoughts of praying to Buddha.
I cannot bear to betray my husband's words,

---

8. Zeng Shen (or Can, courtesy name Ziyu, also known as Zeng Zi [Master Zeng, 505–436 B.C.E.]), a disciple of Confucius and himself a philosopher, was known for his great filial piety. Zeng Yuan was the son of Zeng Shen and took care of his father during his last years. Once Zeng Yuan refused to change a mat that Zeng Shen found too bright and not consistent with ritual, so Zeng Shen changed it himself, but then died because of his anxiety. Accordingly, Zeng Yuan is regarded as an unfilial son in comparison with his father.

9. Buddhist fasting requires eating vegetarian food. Spices and wine are forbidden because they stimulate earthly feelings.

But I fear most that my son will not approve.
Today I shall tell my son about this,
Then I shall feed my body with wine, meat, unctuousness, and sweetness!

(*Speaks*): From now on, I shall follow your words, my brother.

LIU JIA (*speaks*): If so, then I shall bid you farewell. I urge you, Sister, to drink wine and eat meat.

LIU QINGTI: I still cannot get rid of one thought.

LIU JIA: Your brother is going.

LIU QINGTI: My brother, do not hurry; my brother, please come back.

LIU JIA: What do you still have to say, my sister?

LIU QINGTI: When your nephew returns, what is best for me to do if he does not approve?

LIU JIA: My sister, please calm yourself. When my nephew returns, if he approves, let him stay at home, and you will enjoy prosperity together. If he does not approve, it's not difficult either: give him a thousand in capital funds and send him away on business together with the servant Yili. Is not this good?[10]

LIU QINGTI: My brother, this is really a good plan. Take care!

LIU JIA: My sister, please come back.

LIU QINGTI: What do you still have to say, my brother?

LIU JIA: My sister, when my nephew returns, you definitely should not say that I was here.

LIU QINGTI: I understand. You do not need to remind me again.

LIU JIA: I am just a neutral person. Good-bye!

LIU QINGTI: Take care! (*Leaves.*)

10. Yili's name means "surplus profit."

Chapter 6

PROFESSIONAL STORYTELLING TRADITIONS OF THE NORTH AND SOUTH

Over three hundred local storytelling traditions, performed by both professional and part-time or avocational storytellers, were active in China in the late imperial era at the beginning of the twentieth century. Most of these traditions, collectively called *quyi* (art of melodies) since the 1950s, involve a combination of speaking and singing (that is, they are prosimetric in form) and are often performed by one or more storytellers with some sort of musical accompaniment. Traditional venues for these professional performance genres ranged from districts in urban areas that featured all sorts of acrobatics, magic acts, and other entertainments to marketplaces, private homes, teahouses, pleasure boats, and special houses for storytelling and music. By the 1930s, some forms of *quyi* and drama were being broadcast on radio. With the advent of the social changes brought about by Westernization and, in recent times, by globalization, many of the traditions have died out, though a number still survive, sometimes in newly emerging contexts, including tourism. Written correlates or imitations of some of these traditions make up a large part of traditional popular (or vernacular) literature.

Many professional storytellers learned their art in apprenticeships to master storytellers. Some performers were organized in guilds. After 1949, most *quyi* performers were absorbed into government troupes, and part of or all their storytelling repertoires were revised or replaced with content that accorded with the political needs of the day. In some cases, experiments were made in the number of performers, instruments, and especially music, which in some styles became considerably enhanced. Many professional storytellers were forced to stop during the Cultural Revolution (1966–1976). In the early 1980s, many styles were revived, though by the late 1990s many storytelling troupes were struggling economically and there was widespread fear that some styles would not be viable. Today some professional storytellers in Beijing and Shanghai engage in profitable cameo performances at special events in restaurants, clubs, and companies, but less-fortunate performers must make do with a share of ticket sales in the remaining story houses, where audiences are rapidly aging.

Many of these storytelling styles involve the use of various musical instruments to accompany the singing or speaking. Those using drums are particularly common in northern China. Some styles, such as the "big drum" (*dagu*), feature flat drums supported on stands. They are struck by hand or drumstick in complex patterns on the heads and sides and are sometimes used in concert with other instruments. Some northern storytelling styles use only clappers, made of wood, metal, or bamboo. Two well-known ones are clapper tales (*kuaibanshu*) and fast tales (*kuaishu*). Held in one hand, the clappers add a rhythmic, paralinguistic dimension to performances and thus serve to attract, hold, and sometimes refocus audience attention. Stringed instruments are especially common in storytelling traditions in regions farther south and to some extent in the northwest. For instance, the four-stringed lutelike *pipa*, the three-stringed *sanxian* (banjolike instrument), and the two-stringed *erhu* (fiddle) are among the instruments used in these traditions, some of which go by names such as *tanci* (literally, "plucking verses" or "plucking lyrics"), *tanchang* (plucking and singing), *xianci* (*sanxian* verses), and *pingci* (narrative verses); they are sometimes translated as "chantefable," "story singing," and other terms.

Several traditions, though, typically involve lively speaking on the part of a single storyteller, who uses conventional gestures, body movements, and facial expressions in the performance. There is typically no musical accompaniment, but stories may contain the occasional short song or rhyming passage. Acoustic effects are sometimes made with a small rapper made of wood or stone, a folded fan, or, in some Sichuan traditions, a stick with metal jangles. These styles of narrative are often known as *pinghua* or *pingshu*, which can be roughly translated as "plain talk," "straight talk," or "straight stories." Regional traditions of these styles are found in northern, southern, and southwestern China. Like many other *quyi* performers today, these storytellers often wear long robes (or gowns, if women) while performing, though formal Western dress is also seen. Stories were often very long, and some performers could tell elaborated versions of traditional novels such as *Romance of the Three Kingdoms* (*Sanguo yanyi*) in daily sessions that might last a year. Since the 1930s and 1940s, many styles of storytelling have increasingly borrowed from one another, some new forms have emerged, and stories tend to be shorter (an average of two hours a day for two weeks in many Yangtze delta story houses). A popular form of comic dialogue called *xiangsheng* (cross talk) shares some features with these storytelling traditions and is often heard on radio. Current audiences for all sorts of professional storytelling seem interested in increasingly lively and fast-paced performances, in contrast to the often slow pace of delivery and relatively reserved performance styles typical of a former era with fewer alternative forms of entertainment and no input from the buzzing world of electronic media.

Southern China is a mosaic of local customs, architecture, food traditions, languages, and topolects. Local performance styles also mark and differentiate the diverse local and ethnic cultures. The styles of *quyi* and oral-connected written traditions we are calling southern prosimetric are in many ways similar in form and content to performed and written forms from other parts of China that combine singing and speaking. However, the southern styles have always been regarded by locals as different. In contrast to many northern styles of storytelling—especially those in which excitement is increased by clappers and drums—southern styles and their stories are often seen as more gentle, refined, and intricate. These differences are also paralleled in the traditional operas, which share many stories and some conventions with certain oral-storytelling forms. While Beijing opera has a robust gymnastic and martial component, the "softer" schools of southern drama, such as Kunqu and Yueju opera from the Yangtze delta (and Cantonese opera from even farther south), rely more on refined singing and have comparatively subtle movements. Suzhou chantefable (*Suzhou tanci*), for example, has been especially influenced by the Kunqu tradition in terms of character roles, voice registers, and hand movements. While raucous and rambling stories of gallants such as Wu Song are popular in northern repertoires, complex love stories that stimulate subtle emotions and center on relations between gifted scholars and upper-class beauties are more typical of storytelling south of the Yangtze River. Even when stories of heroes are told in regions "south of the river," the depictions and presentations tend to be less flamboyant. Located at a cultural crossroads, between northern and southern China, the city of Yangzhou is the home of professional storytelling styles that reflect both northern and southern sensibilities.

As mentioned, oral-connected written correlates exist for some of these *quyi* performance styles, and some forms of popular written literature mimicked oral conventions. These texts were often cheaply printed editions of popular stories represented in a writing style that was either relatively near or distant from actual styles of performance. The texts could be read wholly independently of the performances, though in some cases they were read aloud to small groups of listeners. This seems to have been a fairly common activity among women in the Yangtze delta and farther south. Both the oral performances and the written correlates used a language style that tended to mix vernacular speech (sometimes local topolects) with quasi-literary Chinese, similar in some ways to language styles in Chinese drama and popular fiction. In the north, these oral-connected texts included *zidishu* (bannermen's tales, once used by Manchu bannermen in Beijing and northeastern China) and various prosimetric forms known by names such as *guci* (drum songs). Among the written southern prosimetric traditions are various forms of *tanci* chantefables of the lower Yangtze delta, Cantonese wooden-fish songs (Cantonese, *muk'yu*; Mandarin, *muyu*), and other forms from the coastal cultures of Fujian and Guangdong provinces. Many such texts also circulated deeper in the Chinese heartland thanks to merchants and officials (or their wives) and were sometimes produced locally in printed or handwritten form.

In this volume, examples of these traditions of *quyi* and written correlates include recent texts based on living performance traditions and oral-connected texts dating from the Qing dynasty (1644–1911). Two works, "A Bannermen's Story of Hua Mulan" and the drum song "The New Edition of the Manchu–Han Struggle," are from a Qing dynasty compendium of oral-performance-connected texts known as the *Tune Book of the Manor House of Lord Che* (*Che Wang fu qu ben*). The collection has been acclaimed as one of the most valuable assemblages of late imperial Chinese popular and entertainment literature ever discovered, owing as much to the nature of its contents as to the vast amount of material it contains. The title indicates its provenance in the manor house of Lord Chedengbazaner, an important Mongolian official of the Qing dynasty imperial government who had close ties to the ruling Manchu elite. *Tune Book of the Manor House of Lord Che* consists of nearly five thousand manuscript volumes comprising nearly two thousand works that fall roughly into the three categories of operatic, prosimetric, and popular song texts.

Another selection, associated with Mount Hua, in Shaanxi province, is "The Precious Scroll of Chenxiang." Precious scrolls (*baojuan*) were once a common form of oral singing and telling performance found in many parts of China. They were often connected to local ritual traditions. Examples of living northern traditions include fast tales, clapper tales, a Peking (Beijing) drum tale, and a form known as a medley tale. Also included are two versions of the story "Wu Song Fights the Tiger" told by different storytellers in the Yangzhou *pinghua* style of storytelling.

Selections from southern China include "Suitable Attire," an excerpt from an oral-connected "women's chantefable" taken from a million-word work written by a young eighteenth-century woman from the Yangtze delta. Two longer selections also represent the living Suzhou chantefable tradition. One, a famous episode from the classic story *Pearl Pagoda* (*Zhenzhu ta*), describes a young woman hesitantly walking downstairs to meet her lover. An exciting feature of this text is the use of the convention of "inner voices" to reveal her thoughts as she takes each step. The other, "The Thrice-Draped Cape," is an example of a story composed in the early socialist era and based on a traditional opera plot. Here also are two versions of the classic tale of the ill-fated lovers Liang Shanbo and Zhu Yingtai: one from an eighteenth-century prosimetric text from Suzhou and the other from a Cantonese wooden-fish story. Comparing the styles between generations of storytellers and local traditions allows insight into how similar stories play out in local traditions.

From Yunnan province, in southwestern China, there are two examples of a *quyi* tradition from the Bai ethnic group. Living on the shore of Lake Erhai, these people share many elements of culture with the Han Chinese. The "great volumes" tradition has persisted into recent times as a live performance tradition in which written script books are consulted by singers before, or even during, performances. One selection about an ancient virtuous official named Wang Shipeng, "Wang Shipeng Sacrifices to the River," was recorded live in the 1990s. The other, a portion of "Singlet of Blood and Sweat," is based on versions of a story also set in ancient times that was created in the post-1949 era and explicitly concerns women's issues. This chapter also includes examples of storytelling traditions in Hangzhou and the "telling scriptures" (*jiangjing*) tradition of Jingjiang county, in Jiangsu province, which is regarded as a "living fossil" of a once widespread style of prosimetric storytelling.

Northern Prosimetric

A MEDLEY SONG FROM NORTHERN CHINA

Translated and introduced by Rulan Chao Pian

Traditional Chinese narrative art is rich in musical resources and variety of delivery style. Some forms alternate between purely spoken narration and singing, such as the "West River Drum Song" (Xihe dagu), and others are delivered in various degrees of a half-sung and half-spoken manner practically throughout, like the "Peking Drum Song" (Jingyun dagu). Of course, there are also those that are completely spoken. The medley song (*danxian paizi qu*, or either just *danxian* or *paizi qu*), especially in this particular version, consists largely of melodious singing, using one tune after another. In putting a story such as "The Courtesan's Jewel Box" into the medley-song form, the plot has been made much more compact, while some of the potentially lyrical moments in the story have been expanded.

The medley song, a northern Chinese narrative genre known as far back as the eighteenth century, was still performed in public places, as a kind of popular entertainment, well into the middle of the twentieth century. Today, only a small number of artists can still perform a few pieces in this genre. Originally the singer accompanied him- or herself on the *sanxian* (three-stringed banjolike instrument). (The term *danxian* means "[singing] alone [while accompanying oneself on a] string[ed instrument].") Toward the beginning of the twenty-first century, the stringed accompaniment was delegated to another performer. Subsequently, the singer would often play the so-called eight-cornered (octagonal-shaped) tambourine during the instrumental interludes in the performance. Even though the tambourine is not really as important as the *sanxian* in the performance, this type of narrative art is sometimes also referred to as an eight-cornered tambourine song (*bajiaogu*), as are some other narrative genres using this percussive instrument.

A complete medley song may use as many as a dozen or more different tunes, or as few as three or five tunes. One of the shorter names of this genre, *paizi qu*, simply means "a song of traditional tunes." Another term for this genre, *zapaizi*, meaning "assorted tunes," is also used. Many texts of medley songs are still preserved in writing, in which, though no music is written down with the texts, the titles of the tunes are regularly indicated at the beginning of each section.

The tunes used in the medley song are from various sources, including well-known folk songs, ballads, and arias from older forms of classical contemporary narrative arts. The adaptation of existing tunes (which may be called tune types) to fit the style of a particular genre and the needs of various new texts has a long tradition in China and is widely practiced in both sophisticated art songs and popular entertainment. Texts are typically in couplet form. Each tune, usually rather short, is repeated several times in succession according to the needs of the story. Each tune is chosen for a given scene of the story, as one can see in "The Courtesan's Jewel Box."

The *sanxian*, which is active throughout, plays sometimes in unison with the voice and other times independently. At such times, the voice seems almost unaccompanied, with only a few quick strummings on the strings that merely serve to punctuate the voice lines. At other times, the voice and the instrument simply alternate, overlapping each other by a few notes.

The story told in "The Courtesan's Jewel Box" is a familiar one in China. In the written short story form, which is still commonly read, it is known as "Decima Angrily Throws Overboard Her Treasure Box" (Du Shiniang nu chen baibao xiang), published in 1624 among other stories in the collection *Comprehensive Words to Admonish the World* (*Jing shi tongyan*), edited, and possibly rewritten, by the late Ming dynasty writer Feng Menglong (1574–1646). A slightly earlier version of this story, written in the form of the classical tale by Song Maocheng (1569–1622?), is called "The Faithless Lover" (Fu Qing nong juan) and dates to not long before this version.

In the original story, Du Shiniang (which means "tenth daughter," or, as translated into Italian here, Decima) is a girl sold into a "green building" (*qinglou*), or bordello. After working for several years as a popular companion to merchants and other upper-class men, she begins a relationship with a rich young playboy named Li Jia. Eventually, Du Shiniang falls in love with Li Jia and decides to marry him. She concocts a clever plan by which Li Jia can convince his father to accept her. But one night, while his boat is anchored not far from present-day Yangzhou, in Jiangsu province, Li begins drinking and gambling with a salt merchant in another boat. As the night progresses, the merchant convinces Li Jia that his father will never accept a woman from the pleasure quarters as his daughter-in-law. Li Jia ends up selling Du Shiniang to the salt merchant, who has heard Du Shiniang singing in her quarters. The next morning, after learning of her fate, Du Shiniang proceeds to the prow of the boat carrying a large wooden box. Opening the box, she then drops handfuls of gold, silver, and jewels into the river. As her aghast lover Li and the salt merchant look on, Du Shiniang casts herself into the churning water, leaving her coldhearted lover behind. The story has been adapted into many local styles of opera and storytelling, including a famous "opening ballad" (*kaipan*) version in the Suzhou chantefable tradition.

In the *Comprehensive Words* version, as well as in the literary Chinese source, Shiniang first throws her jewels into the river, meanwhile denouncing her lover and, particularly, her would-be purchaser, and then shows some marvelous pearls, evidently an even greater treasure, before jumping in herself, clutching the box with the pearls. The process has to be drawn out in this way so that she can denounce the two men while the spectators admire the beautiful treasures. In the source, at least, the denunciation is the high point of the story.

Versions of this story can also be found among several present-day regional operas.

THE COURTESAN'S JEWEL BOX

THE PROLOGUE

Decima, by sad fate,
Lived the life of a courtesan.
She staked her future on Li Jia
And swore her love to him, *ai!*

Alas, the single-minded, love-blind
Girl, she met a faithless young man,
That Li Jia; before they reached home,
He had already changed his heart.

Poor Decima,
She cast her jewels into the river
And threw herself in,
Taking with her endless regrets, *ai!*

THE RECITING TUNE

Decima, following Li Jia,
Begins a new life;
The couple start sailing for home
Down south.

There is a tiny little
Suitcase
Decima keeps constantly
By her side.

One day, as they approach
Gua Zhou,
A storm approaches, so they anchor the boat.

The next morning she rises and
Finishes her toilet;

As she empties the washbasin, she
Meets Sun Fu face-to-face.

Seeing Decima, a most rare beauty,
At once an evil thought
Comes to his mind.

As Li Jia steps ashore
　　To take a brief stroll;
That Sun Fu following close,
　　Calls out, "Honored Brother!"

Approaching Li, he greets him
　　With salutations;
Inviting him to go for a drink,
　　To have a friendly chat.

With money he bribes
　　Li Jia;
Through a cunning trick he separates
　　The pair of lovers.

That Li Jia will sell Decima
　　To Sun Fu;
The price, white silver—
　　A thousand taels.

They are to meet in the morning,
　　When money and goods will be exchanged;
The two men thus in agreement,
　　Each goes back to his boat.

THE *NAN CHENG* TUNE

Decima comes forth to greet him,
　　All smiles;
"In such a storm, where have you been to amuse yourself?

"For you, my love, I have warmed the
　　Teapot and washed the cups clean;
For you, my love, I have prepared
　　Good wine and succulent food.

"For you, my love, I have prepared the
　　Bedding, filled the cabin with incense;
If you are still chilly, I have a
　　Fur coat to cover you."

Reaching out for his hands,
　　She asks him what he wishes;

The wretched lover, tongue-tied,
Knits his brows together.

"Is it that, my dear one,
You have had a fight?
We're far from home, there is no
Choice but to be a little patient.

"Is it that you miss your parents
And are anxious to move on?
It is only a matter of days before
We shall all be reunited.

"Is it that, I myself have
Offended you?
Dearest love, please be tolerant,
Give me time to learn."

The gentle Mistress Decima
Solicits with tender words.
The faithless lover, sighing, regretting,
Lies in his bed.

Decima says, "What puzzlement!
How can I solve it?
Can it be so unspeakable that you
Hide it from me?"

Li Jia says, "Unspeakable it is, but
I have to say it."
He tells her the agreement in the
Wineshop; not a word does he spare.

Decima listens and she
Shivers a little.
"Why, is that all? That's not worth
Worrying your handsome head about!

"Fine, so you've sold me!
Then I'll just go with him;
Get it settled tomorrow,
We must not delay.

Your dinner and wine are still warm there,
Go help yourself;
Excuse me for not waiting on you,
I must get ready for bed."

THE *SI BAN* TUNE

Decima, in anger,
Feels her body go limp;
Slowly she staggers
Back to her bed.

"My lover cares for money more than
He cares for me;
He has forgotten our escape together,
And our promises together.

"He has forgotten that, with heart and soul,
I've given myself to him;
He has forgotten that, risking life and death,
I struggled to leave the brothel.

"I had thought I had met a kind man
And found a new home.
Who would guess that on our way, already
He has changed his heart?

"So be it, for me
There is nothing left;
My only wish now is to die;
I shall not linger anymore."

Decima sits before the lamp,
Her heart utterly broken.
One hears the drum beat in the watch
Tower announcing the small hours
Of the night.

THE *HU GUANG* TUNE

At the first watch, one o'clock,
The snow blows across the boat;
Li Jia—*ai!*—he is fast asleep,
Mumbling loudly in his dream.

His words are clear, again and again,
"The right price for the right girl";
Decima, her hot tears—
Bu-yo-ai-yo!
Falling on her breast.

At the second watch, two o'clock, you
Hear the owl hooting in the co-old;
Decima, listening, her heart—ah!—
Is as though seared in oil.

"Such is my lot; from childhood, when
I was sold to the brothel;
I hate you, Father and Mother—
Bu-yo-ai-yo!
I hate you, heaven above!"

At the third watch, three o'clock,
Moonlight pierces the window;
Decima looks at the jewel box;
An idea comes to her mind.

"Perhaps my treasures will
Persuade this heartless man;
But then—a bought love—
Bu-yo-ai-yo!
Will it last?"

At the fourth watch, four o'clock,
The waves splash louder and louder;
The wick in the candle is flickering,
Burned down to the dish.

"It is a pity, that my life
Will not outlast this candle;
That this river, of all places—
Bu-yo-ai-yo!
Should be my last home."

At the fifth watch, five o'clock,
Decima weeps no more;
On the shore the cock crows;
It is dawning in the east.

Decima, facing the mirror,
Determined, makes up her face once more.
She combs her hair, puts on her earrings. *Ai!*
Bu-yo-ai-yo!
And her best new clothes.

THE *YUN SU* TUNE

Suddenly she hears some one calling,
"Brother Li!"
It is that evil Sun Fu
Stepping onto their boat.

Li Jia quickly
Goes out to greet him.
The two men standing at the box
Chat cordially.

"I say, about our contract yesterday,
Have you attended to it?"
"Why, yes, of course! With us gentlemen,
A promise is a promise."

Hearing this, Decima's face
Flushes with anger;
With her jewel box in her arms
She approaches them.

Saying, "Now, both of you,
Wait a moment;
I still have a little business
To attend to."

Slowly, with her lily-white hand,
She opens the box;
She says, "Mind you,
Look very carefully."

Precious stones and rare jades;
Nothing in the world would compare
With them;
Sparkling and shining,
One's eyes are blinded by the brilliance.

She asks, "Heartless Li Jia,
See for yourself;
Is this worth the thousand taels of
Silver that you will get from him?"

Li Jia, shocked, says,
"I know I was wrong;
Please, my dearest,
Will you forgive me?"

With a bitter smile she says,
"Ah—but it is too late;
Don't you know that once water is spilled
On the ground it cannot be collected
Again?"

She lifts the box high
Over her head;
Aiming at the heart of the river,
She casts it down.

THE *LIU SHUI* TUNE

Decima turns to Li Jia
And addresses him;
In plaintive voice
She begins to speak.

"Remember when you went to the capital
To take the examination;
You failed and were feeling
Despondent.

"Quite by chance you came to
My quarters;
We fell in love and gave our hearts
To each other.

"You swore by heaven and earth
You would never change;
We'd live happily,
Happily ever after.

"Then the money that you had brought
Was all exhausted;

In desperation you even
Pawned your clothes.

"The merciless bawd would have you
Turned out;
But I risked everything to keep you
By my side.

"With my secret savings I
Paid your debt;
I paid my own ransom
To follow you home.

"I looked forward to a life
Of lasting love;
I did not foresee that, on our way,
You would already change your
Heart.

"What a man you are:
Six full feet tall,
You studied to no purpose,
You moralized for nothing.

"Money is your goal,
Cheating is your skill.

"What virtues you have:
Full of cowardice,
Full of greed.

"You keep no promise,
You show no faith.

"You've no sense of shame,
You've no sign of humanity.

"I wish you:
A peaceful journey,
A safe arrival.

"I wish you for the rest of your life:
High appointments,
Stylish living,

"Noble in-laws,
Filial children.

"May you bring glory to your
Ancestors,
Be the sage at the court."

Turning to Sun Fu she continues;
"Pay good attention to my words.

"It's a shame that you
Bribe men with your wealth and power;
Hurt innocent people with your devious ways.

"Now you have come between
A loving couple, like
The wild wind that blows apart
Two mandarin ducks,
The waves that scatter two fish
Swimming together.
The rain that shatters two flowers
Grown on the same branch.
You've ruined two people's noble
Friendship;
You've broken two people's
Marriage vows.

"What a shame that you won't be
Punished for this.

"Surely it is
The neglect of heaven,
The impotence of the gods,
The indifference of the emperor,
The unfairness of the judges.

"That let you get away with it all,
That let you live at peace."

Decima looks up to the sky and
Weeps bitterly.

She cries:
"My ancestors who created me,
My old mother who bore me,

My sisters and brothers who cared
For me, where are you now?
Good-bye to you all; in this life
We shall not meet again.

"How I have been wronged! Yet my wrath
Will sink with me,
For this ill-fated maid will
Die today."

She weeps and weeps, with her face
In her hands;

And now she
Twists her eyebrows,
Closes her eyes,
Clenches her teeth,
Braces her heart; with a
Stamp of her foot, she
Jumps off the boat.

The frightened,
Guilty Sun Fu, he is
Out of his wits;

And that
Mercenary
Cruel, brutal,
Callous Li Jia
Shakes with his knees
Buckling under him.

And so this is my story of Decima, who
Had met the wrong man;
She cast her treasures in the river
And then threw herself in.
It is a legend that everyone sings
About, sighs about.
Such is Decima,
She was strong and heroic,
But she met a hard fate.

AN ANONYMOUS WORK FROM THE *TUNE BOOK OF THE MANOR HOUSE OF LORD CHE*

Translated by Max L. Bohnenkamp and Na Xin and introduced by Max L. Bohnenkamp

"A Bannermen's Story of Hua Mulan" (Hua Mulan zidishu) is a remarkable adaptation of one of China's best-known legends of all time, that of Mulan, the girl warrior. The earliest and canonical version of the tale is "The Ballad of Mulan," an anonymous lyric that entered into the written literature through its inclusion in the sixth-century *Record of Ancient and Modern Music* (*Gu jin yue lu*). It has been hypothesized that the original ballad of Mulan came to China from the oral tradition of the non-Sinitic Xianbei (Särbi) people when the Xianbei Tuoba (Tabgatch) clan established the Northern Wei dynasty (386–535) and unified northern China. The Tuoba, whom the Han Chinese regarded as "barbarian" nomads, gradually adopted the Han Chinese language and customs after assuming power over what was then a far-flung, multiethnic empire. However, it has been thought that some of the anonymous ballads written down in the Chinese language during the Northern Wei dynasty reflect something of the contribution the nomads made to Chinese culture. Mulan's courage and military prowess, her uncharacteristic flouting of gender roles, even her name—all have been cited as indications of the northern steppe people's cultural influence as seen through the legend of the girl warrior.

In sixty economical lines, "The Ballad of Mulan" narrates the story of the teenage girl's decision, inspired by her profound filial devotion to her ailing father, to masquerade as a man and take his place in battle, thereby satisfying the khan's military conscription. Mulan succeeds in tricking her comrades-in-arms over a military campaign of twelve years, distinguishes herself in battle, and returns home victorious, only to resume her life as a maiden. The original poem ends provocatively as Mulan appears to the astonished men who served alongside her and regard her in her feminine finery for the first time. She challenges them with the query: "Though the male hare has a thumping foot, and the female a misty eye, when the two scamper side by side, could you tell which one is which?" Along with the lyrical artistry of "The Ballad of Mulan," its extraordinary combination of fanatical filial devotion, titillating gender-bending, and suggestion of equality between the sexes has secured it a special place in the literary tradition and cultural imagination for over a millennium and a half.

"A Bannermen's Story of Hua Mulan" is an oral-performance-related literary text from the late Qing dynasty compendium *Tune Book of the Manor House of Lord Che* (*Che Wang fu qu ben*). The version manages to amplify the original story as well as make a special contribution to its telling. Although classical literary tastes may always prefer the succinctness and elegance of the original "Ballad of Mulan," the unique qualities of the bannermen's story genre (*zidishu*) and the anonymous Qing author's clever embellishment of Mulan's tale result in a much more detailed and dramatic rendition of the story. With its longer format, the genre has given ample room for the development of an animated narrative, deep characterization, colorful dialogue, and evocative description.

The "bannermen's story" is a narrative oral-performance genre that arose in northeastern China; as the name suggests, its origins are thought to lie in the shamanic and heroic narrative songs of the Manchu Eight Banners military elite. In the Qing dynasty, under the urban conditions of Manchu–Han cohabitation in northern cities such as Beijing and Tianjin, the bannermen's story assumed a genuinely popular status, becoming familiar to Manchu and Han, elite and commoner alike. Descriptions of bannermen's song performances from Qing dynasty writings indicate it was usually performed by one singer with drum accompaniment, though other performance configurations may also have existed.

The genre's basic metrical unit is the paired seven-syllable line with intermittent embellishments that result in the occasional longer line. The last syllables of each second line display a consistent, though not strict, rhyme scheme. As a narrative genre, the plots are propelled primarily by action, dialogue, and characterization. However, there is also a rather free shifting from the dominant mode of narrative development, on the one hand, and a more expressionistic, lyrical descriptive mode, on the other. If at times the tone of "A Bannermen's Story of Hua Mulan" veers from elegant lyrical metaphor to straightforward vernacular statement, it is surely evidence of its success in recasting the original tale into an engaging and entertaining popular style that harnesses a wide spectrum of language registers for narrative effect.

The extant copy of "A Bannermen's Story of Hua Mulan" from the *Tune Book of the Manor House of Lord Che* does not tell the entire Mulan legend as it is known from its original version, but deals with only the narrative from Master Hua's order for military conscription up to the disguised Mulan's arrival in the army camp. Along the way, each of the piece's six chapters manages to intensify the dramatic tension and expand on the themes of the original. Of course, this version's most fundamental contribution to the legend is its detailed and beguiling portrait of Mulan herself, presenting the willful and heroic girl determined to flout gender distinctions in order to make a higher sacrifice for the safety of her family and nation. The portrait of her offered here has psychological dimensions not present in the original ballad: this Mulan is a realistic and sympathetic character who vacillates between her determination to do battle, her sadness at leaving home, and her fear of having her gender discovered.

Also significant in this version of the tale is its development of the domestic dynamic that Mulan confronts with her unconventional proposition, presented here in the second chapter's absorbing dispute between the parents and their daughter over her plan to impersonate a man in the military and in the third chapter's touching depiction of their late-night farewell after she convinces them to let her go. "A Bannermen's Story of Hua Mulan" also richly develops the basic theme of the girl's cross-dressing, spectacularly describing her transformation into a masculine warrior in the second chapter but also humorously depicting the challenge of maintaining the ruse when she lands in the midst of a great many male soldiers in the camp. Among the narrative elements of the piece that do not appear in the earliest version of the legend of Mulan, perhaps the most tantalizing is the hint of romantic tension between the handsome General Liu Qing and the girl he mistakes for a man. Although revelation of the full implications of their meeting and special friendship is precluded by the incompleteness of this version of the text, it is more than merely hinted that the fates of Mulan and the dashing general are intertwined and that their relationship may present further risks for the maintenance of her male persona.

As a final observation, it is compelling to consider the relevance of such tales as "A Bannermen's Story of Hua Mulan" to our knowledge of the themes and sentiments that shaped the popular consciousness of the creators and audiences of such works. There is evidence of a complex interplay among late Qing elites, professional performers, and masses in the shaping of such popular literary traditions as the bannermen's stories. Consequently, in the case of such an anonymous text as "A Bannermen's Story of Hua Mulan," it is hard to verify its place in the social context of authorship, performance, or reception. Furthermore, coming as it does from the *Tune Book of the Manor House of Lord Che,* a collection associated with the elite connoisseurship of popular and entertainment literature, it remains difficult to attribute any definite social intention to the thematic concerns of this tale of a girl warrior. Still, there is a strong current of popular consciousness in Mulan's assault on the gender chauvinism of Confucian propriety and in another pervading theme of the piece: its deep sympathy with the hardships faced by the common folk under the rule of imperial militarism and the devastating effects of war. In this regard, it is not only Mulan's heroic decision to save her family by taking her father's place in battle that makes the tale so poignant, but also her doing so with the knowledge that war is never a glorious business, that it is nonetheless absolutely unavoidable for the protection of one's own family and nation. Perhaps this is what makes the various lyrical interludes describing the terror and desolation of war and its destructive effect on society among the most vivid and stirring passages in these six chapters of "A Bannermen's Story of Hua Mulan."

A BANNERMEN'S STORY OF HUA MULAN

1. THE ALARM

Martial skill, cultured refinement—how hard to achieve both equally!
How many men of great accomplishment have there truly been?

If the brushes that write history will not record one's fame,
Then only by taking up the sword may one transmit their name!

Don't place last in the official examinations!
Head-to-head in close competition, fight to be first!

Sigh for those bearded ones whose lifelong hustle and bustle only buries them in emptiness,
And who are still no better than the Hua Mulan who marched to war in her father's place!

This beautiful maiden, just sixteen years old, awaited a husband in her chamber,
And was naturally endowed with a lotuslike face and a jade complexion.

How pleasing that her brows were not knit with romantic longing!
She shut her eyes firmly to the temptations of springtime.

Clever like Ban Zhao,[1] she was capable of writing histories,
Brave like Xun Guan,[2] she could wear the armor of a knight.

And gracefully poised like a young flower,
So that even stony-hearted and iron-willed men would adore her at one glance.

What's more, her brows were verdant without any painting,
And her lips were scarlet without any rouge.

Sometimes when peering into the mirror she even fancied herself,
Staying hidden away and letting no outsiders look.

Her fingers had grown tired of stitching mandarin duck embroidery,
Her mouth too used to reciting the *Biographies of Exemplary Women*.[3]

---

1. Ban Zhao (45–120?) is considered to be the first female historian of China because she completed the official *History of the Former Han* (*Han shu*), which had been left unfinished by her father, Ban Biao (3–54), and brother, Ban Gu (32–92). She also wrote the seven-chapter *Admonishment to Woman* (*Nujie*).

2. According to the *History of the Jin* (*Jin shu*), the thirteen-year-old girl Xun Guan saved her father, Xun Song, the prefect of the city of Xiang, from siege at the hands of an enemy army. The girl took up arms and led a troop of warriors through the enemy's blockade and came back with reinforcement troops. Her heroism succeeded in driving away the enemies and saving the city.

3. The *Lienü zhuan* is attributed to Liu Xiang (79–8 B.C.E.), of the Han dynasty. Each of its seven chapters tells the story of a different remarkably chaste and virtuous woman from Chinese history; it was considered the canonical moral text for women's education.

When idle, she studied sword fighting with her old father,
And, just like Lady Gongsun,[4] with a miraculous dance she brought heavenly flowers down before everyone's eyes.

She said, "How could I ever master the martial arts of the immortals, who fight miraculously with only their hands,
I'd have to attain the skills of a swordsman if ever I hoped to vanquish villains and traitors."

Her father, Master Hua, declared, "It's useless for girls to practice fighting.
Besides, it's impossible to attain the peak of perfection in every pursuit.

"Just look at the women of the world, who of them have ever been like the Scarlet Thread Maiden?[5]
Most of such tales found in books are merely the fabrications of writers.

"I'm just the feeble old man that I am, pitifully bored, and whiling away my idleness,
By teaching you sword fighting to keep you from playing on the swing.

"Who could have known you would become serious about learning the martial arts?
If you were to master them, doubtless you would still try to run off to the borderlands!"

Mulan retorted, "Are the stories of women warriors all untrue?
Is the Mirror Grinder Couple also just a fiction?[6]

"On the contrary, I have good intentions for pursuing this study,
And never meant that Father was at fault.

---

4. Lady Gongsun was a dancer of the Imperial Theater of the Tang dynasty (618–907), immortalized in the poem "A Song of Dagger Dancing to a Girl Pupil of Lady Gongsun" (Guan Gongsun da niang dizi wu jian qixing), by Du Fu (712–770). She excelled at the dagger dance and was a source of inspiration for some of the era's master calligraphers.

5. The Scarlet Thread Maiden, Hongxian Nü, was famous in legend from the Tang dynasty on for her bravery and martial arts excellence. The adopted daughter of the military commissioner Xue Song, she preempted an attack from her father's enemy by dressing in black and using her amazing skills of stealth to break into the home of the villain and steal his official seal.

6. The Mirror Grinder Couple is the legendary female swashbuckler of the Tang dynasty, Nie Yingniang, and her humble husband, who made his living by grinding mirrors.

"You deny the ancients and say they're all lies,
So in the future if your own child were to shake the earth and astonish the heavens, who would dare believe it?"

Master Hua answered, with a hearty guffaw, "Now your thinking is getting more foolish.
You're just a little girl, what could you do to shake the earth and astonish the heavens?

"In the future just be filial to your in-laws and don't rebel against your husband or sons,
The Three Points of Obedience and the Four Virtues are to be taken for granted."[7]

Mulan replied, "Nothing can be predicted before it takes place,
Changes in the human world are not just of one order."

In the midst of their debate, Mother exclaimed to the girl, "Stop raising a ruckus!
Listen, there's someone knocking on the door outside."

Master Hua, dragging his cane, opened the door for a look,
He saw that it was a county clerk and a sergeant standing out front.

They folded their own hands together in greeting and said, "Good news!
Grandfather will be sent to help rid the lands of the southern barbarians."

Master Hua laughed out loud and said, "What's the matter?
You two are just toying with me."

They explained, "Here we have an official imperial order from the court,
You better respect it and follow the orders. Do not regard them as trivial."

They took out a military order and showed it to Master Hua,
Saying, "Elder, please don't get upset."

Master Hua spoke, "I'm an old man who will soon reach seventy,
And I'm the only adult male member of this family.

---

7. The Three Points of Obedience and the Four Virtues were the basic Confucian code of behavior for women in traditional China. They are obedience to the father before marriage, to the husband during marriage, and to the son after the husband's death, and the virtues of morality, proper speech, modesty, and diligence.

"Furthermore, I'm crippled and unable to walk;
My feet have been racked by disease for as long as ten years.

"I am begging you two to show some compassion;
Find a good excuse for me and plead my case in front of the officials."

They answered, "Each home must send one male of age in order to be impartial and fair.
If you don't go, who will take your place and be sent to the borderlands?

"If you can hire a servant to go in your stead and evade the conscription,
Then of course we can handle everything."

Master Hua still wanted to express his distress,
But the two men said good-bye and left, disappearing like smoke.

Master Hua exclaimed with a long sigh, "What can be done?"
He entered the room and, the women having heard the news, his wife and daughter's tears were gushing like a spring.

2. THE PLAN

For ages the people have suffered like those of Stone Moat Village,
Under duress there are always those who jump the courtyard walls to escape.[8]

It would be sweeter to be clutched in the jaws of a tiger than to live under such a sad and cruel reign;
"The earth is vast and heaven is high," grieve the common folk.

Who considers the weak and feeble when men are freely conscripted into service?
How unbearably heartbreaking it is that the old and sick be forced into the army.

How regretful that the fisherman wouldn't reveal the true paradise of the immortals,

---

8. This is a reference to Du Fu's heartrending poem "The Shihao Officer" (Shi hao), in which an old man escapes over the village wall to evade the clutches of an officer who is conscripting the last men left to go to war.

And kept the Peach Blossom Fountain as his own hiding place
from Qin.[9]

Husband and wife, father and daughter, they all let out a long, deep sigh.
His wife cursed the ministers at court through clenched teeth.

"To think that they've deceived the emperor and lured invaders to our
borders for combat.
They're displaying their weapons, parading their armies, and upsetting our
powerful neighbors.

"They're using this to draw praise from the emperor in order to be
promoted in rank,
And don't care what damage it does to the populace.

"I'm afraid that you'll be killed before you could ever receive a title or
lands for military distinction;
All that would be left behind would be tens of thousands of years of
curses on those crooked ministers."

Mulan waved her hands and said, "Mother is mistaken.
I doubt that the officials really dare raise armies just to taunt our
powerful neighbors!

"What they are is corrupt, and their extortion forces the people to rebel;
First they profit off of folks for their own gain, and then they push them
away.

"Like a sore growing into a fatal disease, this can no longer be hidden,
But, pressing on the borders, the enemy troops already pose a grave threat.

"How lamentable that the homes on the enemy's path are being trampled;
Families are scattering apart and people are fleeing, not one out of a
hundred remains behind.

---

9. This is a reference to the poetic tradition of celebrating the paradise of the Peach Blossom Fountain. Perhaps the closest textual referent to this instance is the short verse from scene 28 of the Qing dynasty play *The Peach Blossom Fan* (*Taohua shan*), by Kong Shangren (1648–1715), in which the scholar Hou Fangyu extemporizes on the theme of having been expelled from paradise: "I dwelt in the hidden cave by Peach Blossom Fountain, / But on my way back I could not find the road. / For the fisherman had misled me over the mountain, / To keep this sanctuary for his own abode." All such accounts go back to the famous *Record of the Peach Blossom Spring* (*Taohua yuan ji*), by Tao Yuanming (365–427).

"Now misfortune has reached the fish in the pond, the ripples of this disaster have spread to us, too,
And the royal court is sending out brave villagers."

Her mother exclaimed, "Why can't we all just flee in escape?"
Master Hua spoke up, "How could one betray the emperor's benevolence and still call himself a man?

"We use his fields and streams and must now show our gratitude.
What's more, to abandon the battlefield on the eve of war is a grave offense.

"It would be worse to end up as a dungeon ghost
Than to die on the battlefield fighting the enemy.

"I should just risk this old life and go off to fight!
Isn't that better than dying of some illness in one's own bed, buried with no recognition by the world?

"I only regret that my energies are all used up and my body is sickly;
Even lifting my feet to walk has become so hard that I'm already a cripple.

"I think that before I could even reach the barracks,
I would become a hapless soul that had passed away out in the open.

"Women, if you want to retrieve my body, you'll have to search in the middle of the road.
Don't let the wild dogs and foxes scatter my bones.

"If you can, bury me alongside our ancestors,
That way you can fulfill your moral obligations as filial daughter and virtuous wife."

His wife said with great sorrow, "It's destroying me,
Heavens! Why must we have been born to this place!

"Though heaven and earth are vast, I have nowhere to hide.
Before my very eyes, father and daughter, husband and wife are being torn like bones from flesh.

"I hate the enemy—why do they kill people and set fires at will?
How miserable that the court can't just disavow war and concentrate on cultivating civility.

"Now, from door to door, every household must sacrifice a man to war.
Where could I beg for someone to take my husband's place?"

Hua Mulan, indignation swelling in her chest, raised her eyebrows,
And said, "Father, Mother, please put your hearts at ease.

"Having a girl or having a boy, it's all the same.
Your daughter has the perfect plan for repaying your parental kindness.

"Think of that time when Xun Guan broke through the enemy lines and saved her father;
Ti Ying risked her life to repay her father's benevolence.[10]

"Although I am just a girl, I do have some resolve;
I'm determined to step up to the example of these ancient heroines.

"Your daughter is going to dress like a man for expediency;
By going under Father's name, I will take his place in the army."

Master Hua gave a long sigh and exclaimed, "Do not speak such nonsense!
The girl is completely out of her mind.

"You have never had a taste of the world outside,
You have heard nothing about the life in the barracks.

"Just wait and let me tell you everything in detail from the start;
If I make it known to you then your zeal will surely diminish.

"On the battlefield, the mountains and rivers, grasses and forests all lose their beauty;
The rain pours, the wind blows, and the mist is heavy.

"In daylight, the whistle of the fife can be heard lilting and soldiers are in misery;
At night, ghosts can be heard murmuring desolately as fireflies light up anew.

---

10. Ti Ying was a remarkably filial woman who lived during the reign of Emperor Wen (180–157 B.C.E.), of the Han dynasty. According to *The Records of the Grand Historian* (*Shiji*), by Sima Qian (ca. 145–90 B.C.E.), and *The History of the Former Han*, she was determined to sell herself to save her father from severe punishment by the court. The emperor was touched by her filial piety and reduced her father's sentence.

"You'll look in the four directions endlessly, but which way is home?
It is like living with ghosts as constant companions.

"And the most bitter and painful part of it is, warriors' lives are nothing more than weeds;
If you can't conform to army life, you'll end up put to death by your own commanders.

"If you really do go to battle against a strong enemy, then it quickly becomes a real struggle of life and death,
And this will surely scare your soul right out of you.

"You will hear the sound of drums shake the earth as the plundering enemy arrives,
Filling the horizon and covering the fields, their army billows like the clouds.

"Arrows fly like a sudden rainstorm, a swarm of locusts,
Men are like leaves falling from the trees of late autumn.

"Flashing blades strike one another, they shine like ice;
The painted drums repeatedly pound, the troops are as thick as a forest.

"Weapons fly through the air, bones rattle, but you have not died in the fight;
Their arrows all gone and bows broken, the enemy has stopped advancing.

"Even brave knights and heroes all will lose their nerve when faced with such a scene,
Not to mention a woman like you standing in her chamber door."

3. A CHANGE OF APPAREL

A hundred objections could not reverse the conviction of this remarkable girl;
She was of one mind to help her father and serve in his place.

Her name survived in the histories, making the bearded ashamed of their inadequacy;
Her filial devotion moved heaven's heart, and astonished the spirits and ghosts.

How admirable that this girl might strive to exceed people's expectations,
But how difficult it is for a woman to really change her looks and shift her shape.

From the bedchamber came a deed to inspire awe for eons,
Shining brightly in the eyes of budding young men.

Master Hua announced, "I will persuade the child not to think such thoughts;
Sitting quietly in the boudoir is the only proper thing for a girl.

"You are a fresh flower, just newly blossomed;
How could you assume my aged, withered willow appearance?

"Rather than let my dear daughter become a ghost on some battlefield,
It would be better that I, this old bag of bones, march to my destiny.

"Besides, you have never left your parents' side in your whole childhood,
How could your mother ever be willing to let her child go off to join the army?"

Her mother said, "If my dear daughter left, this old soul would surely die soon,
I would be waiting on the path to the Yellow Springs for your spirit.[11]

"What your father has just said,
Every sentence of his description of marching off to war is true."

Mulan retorted, " 'The Memorial of the Ancient Battlefield' tells of it thoroughly,[12]
Your humble daughter has also read 'Marching with the Army.'[13]

"Such stories are nothing more than the work of fabulists hoping to frighten people with the thought of death,
As long as I have the will to give up my life, how could I ever fear the enemy's iron chariots, though they be thousands strong?

"Besides, my skill is well known to Father,
With such excellent mastery of the martial arts, your daughter is a veritable heroine.

---

11. Yellow Springs is the dwelling place of the souls of the deceased.

12. "The Memorial of the Ancient Battlefield" (Diao gu zhanchang wen) was written by the Tang dynasty literatus Li Hua (d. 766) and tells of the desolation and destruction of battle.

13. "Marching with the Army" (Cun jun xing) is the title of an old Music Bureau ballad included in *Explanation of the Old Titles of Music Bureau Ballads* (*Yuefu guti yaojie*), by Wu Jing (670–749), which evocatively depicts the lives of the soldiers on the borders and the hardships of military life.

"If I were to go, I would raise a heavenly imperial regiment to scare off any thieving army,
Report victory to the emperor, and return with the soldiers amid laughter and chatter.

"If you keep me trapped in my bedroom, I can only go on with my head buried waiting for death;
It would be better to end my life with hanging.

"Besides, how can Father and Mother stay on constant watch?
Given the chance, I will steal away in the middle of the night and run straight to the army's barracks."

Her mother spoke, "You can't really mean to abandon me?
It's hard to believe that your heart could be so hard as iron and stone that you could cut off all filial emotion.

"How pitiful that I raised this child as tenderly as one would a fledgling phoenix!
I regret I cannot hold you protectively in my own mouth, in the center of my palm.

"How pitiful that I went to such pains to nurse you for three years;
I regret that I couldn't bring you to adulthood with just one blow of my breath.

"How pitiful that I have endured dampness to keep you dry, suffering many hardships,
I regret that I couldn't find the right way to truly cherish you.

"Now you are all grown up and want to leave your father and mother,
And don't care that your old dad and mom are like candles flickering out in the wind.

"Just look at your delicate beauty, like a flower or a jade!
How would you stand going on remote long marches, bathed by rain, hair blown by the wind?

"Besides, there is no end to the bitterness of life in the army;
How could it not break my heart?

"Heaven should strike down the old man who taught this girl the martial arts for no reason at all,

Feeding her ambition and raising her expectations so high that she wants to go take up arms."

Master Hua protested, "Mother, don't blame Father,
This is our daughter's goodwill, a result of her deepest sincerity."

Mulan, sobbing, spoke, "Don't blame Father!
Your daughter will do this because there's absolutely no other solution.

"Let Daddy stay here to care for the family, and raise my young brother,
So that in the future he'll not let the incense of the ancestral shrine burn out and may pass on the family name.

"If we let Father join the army,
Then our family will only perish from cold and hunger and will not be able to live on."

Master Hua said, "Even though this is true, we still need to talk;
In every problem, only after three considerations may one act.

"Anybody can speak of war on paper,
But if you were actually facing a scene of battle then you'd really repent your inadequacy.

"Anyway, it is not easy for a girl to masquerade as a man,
And you know nothing about life under military regulations.

"If, for instance, your trickery was not well hidden and discovered by someone,
You would drown Daddy's noble reputation of half a century."

Mulan declared, "Pretending and imitating are something anyone can do,
Laying it on thick and overacting are lowly affairs.

"I have seen the fellows in the 'Pear Garden'[14] climb up on the stage to put on a drama,
And nowadays it is customary for men to impersonate women there.

---

14. "Pear Garden fellows" was a euphemism for actors dating back to a Tang dynasty coinage by Emperor Xuanzong (r. 712–756) in reference to the imperial dancers, singers, and actors whom he had employed in his Pear Garden.

"The world's ways have been turned upside down, people's hearts are no longer like the ancients',
Men being women, women being men, no one can tell them apart.

"Daddy, if you don't believe me, then let's just have a try;
Just wait while your daughter goes to dress up; in a moment I'll be transformed."

Leaving the boudoir, she went to the eastern room and went about dressing in soldier's garb;
Carrying a painted halberd she stepped into the central hall with a totally different countenance.

Mother and Father examined their daughter, Mulan, with great care,
From head to toe she was done up quite impressively.

Red tassels streamed from on high, her head was swathed in a double headband,
Her military gown was the bright scarlet of a newly dyed cloth.

A bow on her left, arrows on her right, she carried a *kunwu* saber at her side[15]
And wore a belt of braided silken ribbons.

Her eyebrows had become swords, her eyes stars, and her face as white as powder,
Her arms were long like a monkey's, her waist thin as a wasp's, and her fingers long and white as onions.

It was also noticeable that her spirit was up, her wrath blazed, and her eyes would be unmoved by any enemy invaders;
Her will was strong, her muster was up—she looked around in a heroic stance.

Her old mother was both saddened and delighted by this and began to cry.
She said, "My child looks just like Master Bingling."[16]

---

15. A *kunwu* saber is an unbreakable sword smelted from the superior iron mined from the mythic Kunwu Mountains in western China.

16. Master Bingling is the legendary third son of the god of Mount Tai and had a temple devoted to him at the foot of the mountain in the Song dynasty (960–1279). To Master Bingling was attributed many of the qualities of a courageous and upright general.

Master Hua added, "Even though you do look like a man, how can we
bear to let you go?"
Mulan answered, "What's the matter? Just let me go to the battlefield
and prove myself."

Mother exclaimed, "This is such a dilemma, I have no idea what to do."
Mulan replied, "There is no need to discuss it anymore, I am determined
and must follow my will.

"Your daughter will set off now and no matter if I should fail or succeed,
I will leave my name in the histories,
I will be loyal and fulfill my filial obligations to bring glory on our
household."

4. A FAREWELL FEAST IN THE NIGHT

Cold dew, transparent frost, the night is dark gray,
The plaintive call of a goose pierces one's heart.

Ravaged leaves are blown by the sorrowful whistling of the wind;
The stars shine dismally and the moon is bitterly cold.

Along the Yi River, a loud song bids the brave hero farewell,[17]
At the foot of Yan Mountain, a willow branch is broken at the departure
of the painted beauty.[18]

From the four distant directions, the faint sound of crying can be heard;
It is the sound of the young men, having abandoned their work and
families, going off to war.

Hua Mulan gathered up her horse and weapons, getting them all ready;
She didn't dare to distress her friends or relatives, and was cautious to
conceal her tracks.

---

17. This is a reference to the "Song of the River Yi" tradition, covered by the *Intrigues of the Warring States* (*Zhanguo ce*) and the poets Song Yu (290?–222 B.C.E.) and Tao Yuanming (365–427), which celebrated the departure of the famous swashbuckler Jing Ke from the kingdom of Yan to assassinate the emperor of Qin at the behest of the prince of Yan. A farewell feast was held on the banks of the Yi River for Jing Ke, and as the gathered officials saw him off, a performer sang a mournful song of farewell to the hero, who was not expected to return.

18. This line invokes the early Han custom of seeing off a departing traveler with the gift of a willow branch, immortalized in Music Bureau balladry.

To set off during the daytime, she would have to fear folks' noticing;
At night she secretly crept away, hiding from the neighbors' eyes.

Her father and mother clandestinely saw her off to the desolate outskirts of the village;
In this lonely place, they poured a departing libation.

The old couple took their places, and right after they sat down,
Mulan knelt down in respect to her father and mother.

She declared, "Today your unworthy daughter leaves her parents,
Not even knowing in what year she can reunite with them and pay her proper respects.

"In vain you have spent over ten years raising this child;
Your endless and deep generosity is impossible to repay.

"There is absolutely nothing good about the person you see before you;
Always whining, I excelled only at angering Father and Mother.

"Today, fortunately, I can do a little something to compensate for past misdeeds,
And this can count as the benefit of having raised a daughter.

"I only hope that you, my parents, will be strong and healthy,
And can spend your time free from disaster or sickness.

"In your declining years, as the sun sets, drink more tea and eat more rice,
When the frontier wind blows hard, wear a few more layers of clothing.

"Help and encourage Younger Brother to study the classics and histories,
Don't let him play around wildly and neglect the smell of ink on paper.

"If he can raise his name and assume a position on the golden roster of officials,
Then he will avoid serving in the army and entering the battlefield."

Father and Mother exclaimed, crying, "What you have said is right;
How will we repay your deep sympathy for the rest of our lives?

"We only hope that you quickly defeat the thieving enemy,
Lead your army back to the court, and return to your hometown soon.

"You must be careful with yourself, protect your precious body, worth thousands in gold to us;
Wherever you are, watch out and be on close guard.

"Be prudent in front of officials;
Don't behave arrogantly among your fellow soldiers.

"We will wait for your messages and letters to arrive often;
Don't make unnecessary tears flow from our eyes or tie our stomachs in knots.

"But now that you are placing your life in front of blades and arrowheads, your fortune is hard to guarantee;
From ancient times, only a few ever return home from serving in the army.

"If our dearest daughter were to become a ghost on the battlefield,
It would make this helpless couple die at home in pain."

Mulan replied, "Don't worry too much,
Father and Mother have no need to feel knots in their stomachs.

"For this bit of sincerity, your daughter will be blessed by the heavens;
I expect that, in the future, my deed will result in a positive end.

"But there is a matter in my heart that I find difficult to speak of;
If I mention it I fear you may be annoyed.

"Daddy, if you do worry about your daughter,
Please don't hurt Mother with your words.

"Mommy, if you truly worry about your daughter,
Please don't fight with my father over little things.

"You are an old couple and should take care of each other,
So the household will be harmonious and good luck will come to you.

"This will indicate that you two old folks really love and think of me;
Though I will be far away and we will be separated by the Guan Mountains, I will still be able to put my heart at ease."

After Mulan finished speaking, she left her seat, bowed,
And said, "Please, Father and Mother, go back home.

"Look to the east, it will be morning soon and the sky will brighten,
Take advantage of the hour, hurry home as quickly as you can and avoid leaving your tracks in sight."

The old woman tightly embraced the beautiful girl and announced, "It's killing me!
Oh my daughter, you are tearing my guts out."

Master Hua cried aloud and said, "Daughter, you must remember,
Leaving now, your fate will be unforeseeable.

"You must know that showing duty to country and sacrificing your life is really no great matter,
Protecting the body as if it were jade is the most important thing.

"If you run into savage winds and torrential rains, be very careful,
If the butterflies flutter wildly or the bees go mad, you must hold your own.

"Your daddy's half-century-old, noble reputation depends entirely on you;
If your true appearance is revealed you will bring shame upon yourself at once."

Mulan replied, "Don't worry so much,
If one's heart is resolute, the heavens will be moved.

"Your daughter is going to be slaying the enemy, rousing her heroic spirit,
How could she 'steal jade and rob incense,' and do such demeaning things.

"I hope Father and Mother can act according to the situation by protecting themselves like a thousand weight in gold,
And wait for the sounds of the victory song and our reunion in the family hall."

Holding back her tears, the young beauty announced, "Your daughter departs."
The draft horse whinnied and neighed, and the night became gray.

In an instant the heavens and earth grew dark and gloomy, and a sad wind blew up from the four corners,
The old couple cried themselves half to death and sobbed their hearts out.

5. AN UNEXPECTED MEETING

The moon hangs low in the sky, crows caw, and the steed whinnies;
Frost blankets the ground like flowers, a chilly evening wind blows desolately.

Wisps of smoke rise up from cooking fires, villages are hidden in the distance,
An endless stream of snow falls as thick as reeds, the field becomes a blur.

The eyes are met with nothing but desolation, and there are no companions in this place,
A person so lonely and miserable has no one to depend upon.

In the midst of her journey, Hua Mulan suddenly had her first taste of the sadness of autumn;
How many tears of grief poured out of her eyes!

The beautiful maiden slowly whipped her dappled steed along,
And turned her head around to gaze at the mountains of her home, but the road back was already hazy.

Who would blame these woods?
It's just that the morning light is so dim.

How could she stand the frost coming up her sleeves, the army uniform was so cold?
Leaves danced in the air, and the shadows of trees were sparsely scattered.

She said, "Who knows how long Old Father and Mother stayed up crying?
I just had to harden my heart and make my departure.

"I grieve for this humble homebody who has suddenly become a traveler on such a long journey;
My eyes look to the rugged road twisting on the distant horizon.

"All I can hear is the babbling of the flowing Yellow River,
And the cawing of crows perched on ancient trees.

"Fortunately I have iron guts like Jiang Boyue,[19]
And my courage is as triumphant as a Lady Yanzhi's.[20]

---

19. Jiang Boyue was the historical figure General Jiang Wei (202–264), of Shu-Han, whose courage was depicted in *Romance of the Three Kingdoms*.

20. A reference that remains rather vague, this appears to evoke the title *yanzhi*, used for the

"If I were to be afraid of 'wolves in front and tigers in back,'
Then it would be hard for me to take even one step in this journey of a thousand miles."

The girl traveled until it was almost noon,
When suddenly she saw a chattering magpie fly up alongside her horse.

Mulan sighed, "I have nothing to be happy about;
You clever bird, there is no use for you to report any good tidings to me."

Seeing her horse lift his head and let out a long whinny as he darted toward a spring,
The girl also felt that her stomach was empty.

She said, "Why don't I find a place to sit and have a little fried rice to eat,
And find a gushing spring to water my horse."

The girl sat beneath a stone wall,
And for no reason, her thoughts began to be stirred by poetic inspiration.

She sighed deeply and announced, "Today, I'm 'Watering My Horse at a Long Wall Hole,'[21]
Why don't I chant a few short lines of poetry and write them here on this stone fence?"

She concentrated her attention for a short while and began to write on the stones,
Nimbly producing four lines of verse.

The poem read:
Alone, I am going ten thousand tricents[22] to the battle;
The horses and foxes gallop so fast that they have taken flight.
The moon's cold shine sparkles on my bronze armor;
The wild fire burns heavily and contrasts with my iron garb.

---

royal wives of the Xiongnu khan dating from the Han dynasty. The suggestion seems to be tied to the theme of the political betrothal of Chinese brides to the northern barbarian rulers known widely from the *Records of the Grand Historian* and the Han histories.

21. "Watering My Horse at a Long Wall Hole" (Yin ma chang cheng ku xing) is the title of a famous Music Bureau ballad invoking thoughts of a traveler led far from his loved one by military duty in the northern borderlands.

22. One tricent (*li*) is three hundred steps, or about one-third of a mile.

After writing the poem, Mulan began thinking about how to sign her name to it;
Suddenly she saw the shadow of a person pop out from beside her,
exclaiming, "Magnificent versification!"

Mulan, surprised, turned her head around for a look;
She saw a young general who was extraordinarily handsome.

His general's scarf had a red spot on the front, dyed a deep scarlet;
There were thousands of brocade flowers embroidered on his military gown.

From between his brows projected the air of a hero;
His face was smooth and shiny like a beautiful piece of jade.

Whatever talk you may have heard of brocade horses and supermen in
praise of gods and emperors,
It matches our handsome general perfectly, so hard to faithfully portray.

Mulan put her hands together in greeting and spoke up, "The poem
displays my foolishness;
Even though it is laughable, please offer me some enlightening guidance
and forgive me for my ignorance.

"May I ask, what is my respected brother's honorable name?"
The man said, "My name is Liu Qing, and I am the seventh oldest in
my family.

"I suppose that Respected Brother comes from the same village as I."
Mulan replied, "I am Hua Qing, and my ancestors are from Wei county."

Liu Qing said, "Brother Hua is more brilliant than one could expect."
Mulan replied, "I would that you might use your 'tree trunk' of a brush to
produce a poem in reply to mine to the same tune."

Liu Qing said, "Your little brother has no talent, but I'm willing to make
a fool of myself,
I hope that Brother Hua can help 'chop it down to size.'"

After saying this, he wielded his brush and began writing a poem,
Inscribing it under Mulan's and following her rhyme scheme exactly.

It read:

Leisurely expressing refined admiration for literary creation,
Eagerly grabbing the wine cup, I take flight.

To the dragon's abyss, to the fish's seaweed abode, I calmly go,
I take off this soldier's garb and change into embroidered silks.

After reciting this poem he bowed slightly, and said, "It needs your critique."
Mulan said, "I enjoyed your poem, it is precious without a doubt."

Liu Qing said, "Respected Brother's learning is so excellent,
Why are you riding this horse, dressed in a military uniform, going off to battle?"

Mulan replied, "I had no other choice,
Each home must send one man—who would dare disobey?

"Respected Brother, are you too on your way to the barracks?"
Liu Qing said, "Your little brother is a minor official; it is merely an inherited position."

Mulan asked him, "Please do me a favor by taking me there as your companion."
Liu Qing answered, "I'm willing to follow your whip and stirrup, and cherish this valuable friendship."

The two finished speaking and both climbed on their horses;
The whole way they were bathed in rain and their hair blown by the wind—their suffering can be imagined.

But it was good that they were able to appreciate each other;
It was likely an ancient, long-standing destiny that made it so.

After a few months their journey brought them to the barracks;
Seventh Son Liu held an inherited post and was of unusually good character.

Hua Mulan was given some assignments in the army camp;
It was all thanks to Liu Qing's support and help.

6. IN THE ARMY

The great banner flaps in the wind as the setting sun's rays scatter;
The flat sands stretch on endlessly and the road is long and boundless.

The fife of the steppe lands sounds like sobbing, it breaks one's heart;
There is the clanging of a bronze brazier: the night is getting late.

Somewhere blue-green fireflies chirp, sounding like the murmuring of ghosts;
Thousand-year-old white bones are washed up on the river's sandy banks.

Please, kind audience, do not envy those who have received official rank;
The success of one general is the demise of tens of thousands of lives.

After the beautiful maiden moved into the army barracks,
It was like treading on thin ice and facing a deep abyss.

Her entire person and everything she did was completely different from before;
There were hundreds of things to conform to, and restraint was quite hard to achieve.

She was not afraid of sleeping alone, or of hearing the sound of the water clock;
The only time she worried was while in the midst of the raucous, laughing soldiers.

For a young girl to be out and visible is intimidating enough,
Even more so to be shoulder to shoulder with such men—how could she not feel embarrassed?

"I must harden my heart, and pretend to be older and tougher,
Show off my nerve, and thicken my skin.

"I've got to put on a more mature appearance, and lose my childish air,
Make myself like all the rest of the bunch, not at all different.

"Taking brocade, I bind my breasts tightly in the dark,
I stuff cotton into my socks, to make the tips of my boots look rounder.

"It's so ridiculous, every time I bow and salute I have to sneak a look at others;
I seem just like a young southern barbarian just arrived in the capital.

"Before I walk toward people, I make sure to take very steady steps;
When speaking, I must tense up my throat and thicken my voice on purpose.

"All the day long, who would dare comb her hair and wash her face?
The whole time, the thing I feared most was suffering torture, and now my life is no different than torture.

"I hate that this pretty face of mine cannot be changed into a common, coarse countenance,
That this beautiful appearance can't be moved onto someone else's body.

"It's a pity that the wind and sand can't stain this pearl-like face;
Looking at the reflection on the water's surface, I can still tell that my old looks haven't changed.

"Whenever possible, I pick the lice off of myself so quickly, I should be called 'Fast Hands,'
Whenever I get a chance, I change my undergarments to feel more comfortable.

"Whenever we're eating, I act like a feasting wolf and a devouring tiger;
Before we enter battle, I rub my hands together and punch my fists into my palms on purpose.

"In the middle of dreams, I suddenly wake up in fright, scaring myself and feeling bewildered;
Sometimes, in the middle of the army tent, I lift my head and can't tell where we are or what day it is.

"How pitiful that all day long I don't dare once to drink even a little water or tea:
It would be awful if I had to go to the latrine and I couldn't wait until it was very late and everyone was sleeping quietly under the half-moon.

"I'm sick to death of this, being as young as a boy who has just barely reached manhood and having to study well the ways of these much older men;
There's nothing to be done—here I am wishing I could chat about books and learning while serving in the army.

"During sword and spear corps training, I always volunteer to go first;
Whenever the others are playacting and joking around, I never say a word.

"When meeting people I act haughty and proud, but who wants to be this way?
Confronting all these men, so strong and fearsome, I feel uneasy.

"In my heart I've had tens of thousands of different thoughts and ideas,
Of how to find new ways to make people loathe me.

"I've provoked some of my comrades into complaining about me often;
Behind my back, they talk about me in groups of twos and threes.

"They say, 'This Elder Hua who has just arrived—
His page-boy appearance is warm and friendly, but his personality is rough and bad-tempered.

'For no reason at all, he'll make a long face,
And if he finds other people's talk disagreeable, then he opens his eyes wide with a glare.

'What a pity that such a face would belong to his body;
He's so cunning and loathsome that it's impossible to deal with him.

'He takes advantage of Captain Liu's power to bully us around;
This little twerp incurs hatred wherever he goes.

'In the future he will definitely end up a ghost of the battlefield,
Let's not mess with him, just wait until he meets his end, then he'll have a hard time feeling sorry.'

"Who could know that they're doing exactly as I wish;
Quite the contrary, now that they see me like this, I can begin to put my heart at ease."

Let's not talk about Miss Mulan's experience in the army for now;
Who knew that someone had secretly spoken to Liu Qing?

One day, Liu Qing had nothing to do and at leisure paid a visit;
Mulan welcomed him in and they bantered idly.

Liu Qing asked, "Why hasn't my worthy brother come to see me these last few days?"
Mulan replied, "I didn't want to bother your mess cooks and waste their time."

Liu Qing said, "Worthy Brother is showing too much consideration for me,
Taking such pains to show so much care, but I've no complaints to make.

"Your brother has a word to say in persuasion:
Being a man means forming ties of friendship wherever one goes.

"I have once heard: A true sage does not become attached to things,
But is still able to collaborate with others.

"Not to mention that life and death are not guaranteed in the army:
We are all together in fear and peril, in suffering and hardship.

"Oh, Worthy Brother! Why can't you open yourself up to accepting other people?
The great blue sea has always accepted the hundreds of rivers."

These few sentences stirred something deep in Mulan's heart;
Uncontrollably, she felt a sour pang in her heart and her tears flowed like a gushing spring.

Liu Qing was aghast and asked, "What has made you react this way?
Your foolish brother has spoken only loyal words.

"Is it not that someone has bullied you?
My power is surely enough to put him in his place."

Mulan spoke up, "Under your protection, my brother, who would dare bully me?
It's just that everything your younger brother has encountered has been difficult indeed.

"Who would be willing to invite the hatred and complaints of others for no reason?
Who would be willing to pretend to be all alone and high above all others, provoking their slander?

"Who would be willing to turn his own comrades into enemies before even facing the true enemy?
Who would refuse to tackle his own faults and attribute them to the others around him instead?"

Liu Qing inquired, "If what you say is so, then what does Brother truly mean?"
Mulan explained, "It is indeed hard to explain what your brother has residing in his heart.

"Either I will die in conflict on the battlefield and turn into a spirit,
Or I will be lucky enough to succeed and return to my home.

"By that time, only if the clouds have opened will the moon be seen on the horizon,
And only by the sight of falling water will we know there is a spring beneath the mountain."

AN ORAL-CONNECTED DRUM SONG FROM THE *TUNE BOOK OF THE MANOR HOUSE OF LORD CHE*

Translated and introduced by Ok Joo Lee and Delia Noble Zhang

"The New Edition of the Manchu–Han Struggle" is a drum song (*guci*) drawn from the Qing dynasty compendium of oral-connected literature known as the *Tune Book of the Manor House of Lord Che* (*Che Wang fu qu ben*). Written drum songs are associated with northern China; they are regional forms of oral-connected literature that are in some ways similar to the written *tanci* chantefables and wooden-fish songs (Cantonese, *muk'yu*; Mandarin, *muyu*) of southern China. Drum songs are a type of prosimetric literature characterized by alternations of spoken and sung parts. When performed, drums and clappers as well as stringed instruments and even flutes are used as accompaniment.

This work is written in a style reflecting oral performance. Although little is known about how this drum song was actually performed, it is written in a manner that retains some aspects of a live performance. In this work, prose and verse alternate in the telling of the story. The verse consists of a regular rhyme pattern of seven syllables. While some lines are actually more than seven characters in length, it is speculated that in these lines the first few characters would have been sung twice as fast as the remaining characters in the line, maintaining an even seven-beat rhythm throughout the songs. Unfortunately, the tunes of the songs are not recorded and cannot be reconstructed.

In addition to speaking and singing, this work also includes recitation of classical poems. The poems use a strikingly different style of language than the sung verses, and they are more serious in nature, teaching morality and Daoist philosophy. These poems tend to lend a moralistic view to the work, excusing the outrageous stories contained in it as merely didactic rhetorical tools.

In the story, the narrator frequently speaks directly to the audience, just as one might in an oral performance. The narrator often switches to new characters in order to maintain the audience's interest and advance the plot, just as in many modern "soap operas." In an oral performance, the performer must use various methods to attract and hold the audience's attention, a need met in this work through the interpolation of short stories. Such "teasers" tend to have few characters, and the plots are sometimes not even wrapped up before the performer moves on to the main story.

Two such short stories are inserted into the main text of "The New Edition of the Manchu–Han Struggle." Both may seem offensive in the modern "politically correct" world, because they poke fun at characters who have physical limitations. The intrigue of these short stories is generated by the difficult situations in which these characters find themselves. Although the stories are rather crude, they are left in the text in order to preserve the original flavor.

The plot itself also contains some rather vulgar story lines, intended to tantalize the audience and make its members want to stay for the outcome. The story is divided into six chapters; the chapter divisions represent pauses in performance. Each chapter breaks at a new peak of anticipation, making the audience want to read on to find out how the story is resolved. The first volume of this work is the only section translated, and it also ends at the height of anticipation. Perhaps the reader will also crave more after finishing this selection.

The story takes place in the Qing dynasty during the reign of Qianlong (1736–1795). Liu Tongxun receives the commendation of the emperor, permitting him to travel incognito to Shandong. Gentleman Liu's true reason for going to Shandong is that he has suffered the loss of two of his three sons because of treachery in Shandong.

The story also tells of Jin Haoshan; his wife, Lady Wang; and his two teenage daughters, Jinjie and Fengying. Because of a severe drought in Shandong, the family has lost its means of supporting itself and sets out for Beijing, the capital, to seek help from relatives. On the way, the family encounters two villains, brothers named Li Tang and Li Hong. The Li brothers lure Jin Haoshan and his family to their compound in order that they might take as wives the beautiful daughters Jinjie and Fengying. A maid named Chunhong devises a plan in which the girls agree to marry the Li brothers but get away before their conjugal union. Following Chunhong's instructions, the girls narrowly manage to escape from the compound. The first volume ends when Gentleman Liu meets Jinjie and Fengying and inquires about their injustices.

THE NEW EDITION OF THE MANCHU–HAN STRUGGLE

CHAPTER 1. LIU TONGXUN RECEIVES AN IMPERIAL DECREE

Scholars have myriad elegant verses.
Of these, we can select but a few good and satisfactory works.
They are tranquil, having the proper Way, without selfishness.
In them the Way and the three powers[23] *are unified.*
Taken altogether the gods of fortune, prosperity, and longevity
Shine within like spring.
They possess sincerity, propriety, fortune, and wealth.
From Pangu[24] *till now it has been said:*
Such things arise from the natural order, not the self.

Now I have finished reciting this guiding lyric poem, "The Moon on the West River," and I will present a drum song. Gentle audience, if you do not take offense at listening to a long tale, please let me tell you the following nonsensical story. Oh! The first chapter begins:

---

23. The three powers are heaven, earth, and humanity.

24. In Chinese mythology, Pangu is the creator of the universe. The phrase "from Pangu till now" means "for all time."

There once was a fellow three *cun* three[25] tall.
The brim of his huge one-*cun* hat fell to his shoulders,
His two-*cun*-five robe dragged along the ground,
His one-and-a-half-*cun* boots looked like pants.
North of his house was a half-*mu*[26] field;
Although the land was flat it took half a year to till.
At the crack of dawn he carried a hoe out to the field;
He swung at a bunch of beanstalks with his hoe.
His beautiful wife carried some food to him with a shoulder pole;
She could not find her husband anywhere.
She separated the beanstalks looking for her husband,
But she saw only beanstalks swinging back and forth.
As soon as his wife saw this, she became quite annoyed:
"I'm going to send you to hell!"
Impulsively she threw the baskets of food onto the ground
She took up the pole and smashed the ground mercilessly,
Hitting the ground with great fierceness.
[Her flailing dislodged] a greenish insect, which sprang away with the fellow on its jagged back;
He flew off the insect and fell into a ditch.
He urgently cried out,
He could only shout, "My virtuous wife!"
And he continued, "Listen to me, good wife.
Come quickly to save me! Come quickly to save me!
Your husband is drowning, and it's not a joke!"

Gentle audience, you must be wondering what he fell into—
Bull in a china shop.
That was a story about a short man;
The following will be the main story.
In what follows I will tell you no story other than
A story about the Qing dynasty.
The title of this story is "The Manchu–Han Struggle";
First I will tell you just the background.

The story takes place at the Brocade River Mountain of the unified Qing dynasty,
When the emperor was righteous, the officials were good, and all the people were at peace.

---

25. One *cun* is the equivalent of just over an inch; the man's height was thus a little over four inches.

26. One *mu* is 667.5 square meters, about one-sixth of an acre; the field was thus considerably less than one-tenth of an acre.

They developed the wastelands, pulling up the weeds and planting seedlings;
There was a bumper crop of the five cereals[27] throughout the peaceful, tranquil year.
It was the inauguration of the reign of the Qianlong emperor;
All the civil and military officials came to the royal court.
Grand preceptors were lined up on the left, grand inspectors on the right;
Eight great officials were lined up in two groups.
Forty-eight sons of imperial concubines were present.
The civil officials stood to the east and the military officials stood to the west.
The Qianlong emperor ascended the imperial dais;
He declared, "Ministers, deliver my message to those below."
Even before the emperor's words were completed,
The eunuchs knelt before the imperial table.

The Qianlong emperor ascended the imperial dais, with the civil officials to the east and the military officials to the west, standing in two lines. The emperor began his imperial proclamation, "Ministers, deliver my message: If someone has any matter to present, step forward immediately to speak. If no one has any matter to present, let us roll up the screen and disperse." The ministers responded and shouted the proclamation to those below: "All civil and military officials below, please listen carefully! The emperor has a message. If you have any matter to present, step forward immediately to speak. If no one has any matter to present, we will roll up the screen and disperse." One minister stepped out from the group on the left. The following exchange ensued: "Please do not disperse yet." "Who has a matter to present?" "Liu Tongxun has a matter to present." "Obey the emperor and state your matter." "Long live the emperor! Long live the emperor!"

Even before the ministers' words were completed,
A sudden response from the group was heard.
Who made the first response?
It was the honorable Liu of Shandong.
He adjusted the official's hat on his head;
He arranged his great red robe.
He pulled his Manchu–Han jade belt tight;
He stamped his feet in his boots once or twice.
In dynasties of old, officials held their tablets upright before their chests;
The Qing dynasty officials held their jade bottles in front of their chests.
He ascended the steps and approached the imperial dais;

27. The five cereals are rice, wheat, beans, and two varieties of millet.

He said, "Long live my lord and emperor!"
He bowed seven times to the front, nine times to the rear, and eight times to the center.
In all he bowed twenty-four times, saying each time,
"My lord and emperor."
The Qianlong emperor's eyes became bright with expectancy.
He glimpsed the chief minister coming forward:
"Chief Minister, whatever matter you have,
State everything clearly from the beginning.
Whether you present a civil matter or a military matter,
Whether you present a matter of treason or a matter of loyalty,
Every official is asking you to present it.
I manage everything with the fairest mind."
Gentleman Liu kept nodding his head as he listened to the emperor.
He said in a loud voice, "My lord, please listen to me.
I am presenting neither a civil nor a military matter,
Nor am I presenting a matter of loyalty or treason.
I have a personal matter that I must present.
I humbly beg my lord to listen to me.
I have heard that there has been a famine in Shandong for three consecutive years;
For several years there has not been any harvest there.
I have a mind to visit Shandong incognito.
The purpose of the visit is to see if the common people are at peace."
The Qianlong emperor was greatly pleased:
"I truly must make you into a minister.
Visit Shandong incognito as planned.
Listen and I will give you an official title.
I will give you three bronze daggers and two swords;
You must follow my decree to go with an envoy to Shandong."

Gentleman Liu kept nodding his head as he listened to the emperor:
"I greatly appreciate my lord's giving me an official title."
Why did Gentleman Liu plan to go to Shandong incognito?
It was because of his grief over his son's death.
He had three sons, and two had already passed away.
He wanted to visit Ye Lihong the Elder.
"I have to discover the real situation
So that I and my son will be rewarded for our bitter sorrows.
If I cannot discover the real situation,
I will never be able to get revenge."
Gentleman Liu walked down from the imperial dais;
All the officials accompanied him to the Cow Gate Garden.

Who was busy at this moment?
It was two brothers, Wang Liang and Wang Yi, who were in such a hurry.
As soon as the emperor gave the word, they quickly brought a palanquin,
Following his decree without stopping even once.
All the servants carried the palanquin;
Gentleman Liu ascended it.
In front there were twenty-four horses in two lines to pull a carriage at a fast clip;
In the back there was a group of young men;
Their quivers were full of arrows with birds carved on them.
They carried carved bows across their backs.
There was a battalion of soldiers on each side of the palanquin.
A flag was flapping in the wind, a sight that would shock even the spirits of the dead!
There were also foot soldiers encircling the group;
There were five battalions encircling the entire envoy.

A pair of wooden clappers and a pair of sticks,
A pair of iron locks and a pair of ropes,
Metal "melon" spears, axes, and pickaxes faced the sky.
There was row upon row of padded wheels.
"Absolute *silence* and absolute *avoidance*" was written on standards everywhere;
Spectacular flags were flying high in the sky.
People wearing black and red hats were shouting;
Every word sounded like the roar of a tiger.
Above the palanquin a red silk umbrella was opened;
The palanquin was carried on the shoulders of eight men.
Gentleman Liu gave the command, "Go forward";
All the men moved forward without stopping.
They traveled three tricents and passed Peach Blossom Inn;
After ten tricents they passed Apricot Blossom Camp.
In great dignity and power they progressed forward;
There was row upon row of soldiers in the envoy.
From dawn to dusk they traveled for many days,
Until one day they saw Liangxiang far off in the distance.
As soon as Gentleman Liu saw this, he immediately ordered:
"Enter the prefecture, which is ten tricents from the city."
Gentleman Liu entered the prefecture and sat down;
Many soldiers relaxed in comfort.

At this point I will cease to speak of Gentleman Liu.
I will shift to another topic.
What will I speak of next?
Let me talk now of Shandong.

Bird Landing Prefecture in Shandong
Administrates a small county called the Jin Family Camp.
In the Jin Family Camp there was a man named Jin Haoshan;
He passed the civil service exam and became a candidate.
There was a continuous drought,
And for several years there had been no crops harvested.
Jin Haoshan had no food and sold his land,
As well as all his mules, horses, cows, and sheep.
As a result there remained only he and his wife
And their two daughters.
The older daughter was named Jinjie;
The younger daughter was named Fengying.
The older daughter was sixteen years old;
The younger daughter was barely fourteen.
They grew up without anyone to rely on,
So they wanted to go to Beijing to get help from their relatives.
Haoshan decided upon his plan.
He walked toward the back of the compound.
When he entered the women's quarters[28]
He began to speak about his plan.

When Jin Haoshan entered the women's quarters, he met his wife, Lady Wang, and said, "I have a matter to discuss. I don't know what my good wife will think about it." Being virtuous, Lady Wang said, "I don't know what my husband would like to discuss." Jin Haoshan said, "I have a mind to go to Beijing to get help from my relatives, and I will bring you and our daughters together with me. I don't know what my good wife thinks of this." *The next chapter explains this.*

CHAPTER 2. JIN HAOSHAN GOES TO VISIT RELATIVES IN BEIJING

In the previous chapter I spoke of Jin Haoshan's discussing with his wife, Lady Wang, about going to Beijing to visit his relatives. "I don't know what my good wife will think about it." Lady Wang said, "I will do whatever you say." Lady Wang said, "When does my husband plan to leave here?" Jin Haoshan said, "I will leave today." They packed their belongings, and they wrapped their valuables in their clothing. When they finished packing, Jin Haoshan lifted his bedroll to his shoulders. His wife and daughters followed him, leaving their house and going outside, then locking the door. Then they passed through the gate and locked it. They came to a road crossing and their relatives came out to send

28. The women lived in an apartment behind the main building.

them off, saying to them, "Have a safe trip!" Lady Wang said, "No one is at our house. You must all look after it." They said, "Of course." They left weeping. Jin Haoshan . . .

Carried his bedroll on his shoulders, leading the way;
His wife and two daughters followed him.
They traveled on an uneven road,
And passed over some winding paths.
The two sisters had difficulty walking because of their small, bound feet;
While walking their feet tingled in pain.
They would walk a tricent, rest a tricent,
Walk for a while, then rest for a while.
They traveled ten tricents and passed Peach Blossom Inn,
Then traveled five more tricents and passed Apricot Blossom Camp.
A beautiful woman came out from Peach Blossom Inn;
The food was good at Apricot Blossom Camp.
For many days they began at dawn and ended at dusk;
One day they saw Liangxiang far off in the distance.
It was very difficult for the sisters to walk;
They sat down on a patch of even ground with a "thump."
Jin Haoshan looked up at the sky and let out a deep sigh,
Calling out to the heavens a few times.

At this point I will not speak of this family.
I will shift the story to some other people.
Who will I speak of next?
Let me talk now of Li Tang and Li Hong.

Two fellows, Li Tang and Li Hong, lived in the Li Family compound. They robbed men, mistreated woman, did all kinds of bad things, and certainly did no good things at all. On this day they were sitting in their reading room, when suddenly they remembered that there was something happening in Liangxiang county. They ordered their servants to bring their palanquins. When their servants heard this, they carried over two large palanquins. The brothers left their house and got into their palanquins. They ordered more than ten thugs to accompany them. They ran to the main road in Liangxiang county.

That is to say . . .
They gave the order and it was not neglected;
The servants followed their orders without stopping.
In great dignity and power they progressed forward,
But they noticed several people on the roadside.
Two ladies were sitting on the roadside;
They were at most teenagers.

They looked like celestial beings,
As though immortals descended from heaven.
As soon as Li Tang saw them he ordered:
"Quickly rob those beauties!"

Li Tang gave the order, "Rob them!" Li Hong said, "Stop!" Li Tang said, "Why this 'Stop'?" Li Hong said, "I heard that a certain Gentleman Liu has come from Beijing. He has been granted the emperor's decree and is accompanied by an envoy. He carries three bronze daggers and two swords and has the right to first kill, only afterward making a report to the emperor. If Gentleman Liu knows what we have done, then we will be terribly punished, and even my cousin Ye Lihong will be terribly punished. I have an idea that is not as good as kidnapping them to our house, but that makes sense."

The two brothers discussed it and made up their minds. They gave the order to lower their palanquins and went over to Haoshan, then clasped their hands in front of their chests and made a bow saying, "Cousin, how are you?" Jin Haoshan did not recognize them at all and felt a bit panicked. Li Tang said, "We have not met each other for about ten years. Don't you recognize your cousins? This is not a good place to stand around talking. Let's go home and get reacquainted. We brought three horses, so the three of us can ride them. Your wife and daughters can ride in the palanquins." They said, "Return home."

That is,
They gave the order and it was not neglected;
Their servants followed the order and turned back.
This will be cut short and finished quickly:
If I talk on and on, you won't bear to listen.

In a moment's time they arrived at their house, got off the horses, and lowered the palanquins. Li Hong ordered the maids to lead the wife and daughters to the women's quarters. The three men went to the main building and ordered the servants to quickly prepare some tea. They poured tea into the teacups.

That is to say . . .
Li Hong immediately gave the order;
The servants followed the order without stopping.
Even though they were not high officials,
The mountains of meat and oceans of wine served were the same as
for such.
The wine exceeded three rounds and the dishes exceeded the five flavors.[29]
Li Hong spoke with a smile on his face.

---

29. The five flavors are sweet, sour, bitter, hot, and salty.

Li Hong said, "How strange it is that you, my cousin, don't recognize me. But I also forgot your name." Jin Haoshan said, "My name is Jin Haoshan." Li Hong said, "Oh! Right! Cousin, where do you plan to go?" Jin Haoshan said, "I plan to go to Beijing. I am going there to get help from relatives, and if I can get some work it will be really good!" Li Hong said, "Why go to get help from others? My uncle is in Beijing and is one of its highest officials. I will write a letter for you to take, so that when you go to Beijing, there will be no reason why you can't find work!" Jin Haoshan said, "Thank you for taking care of me, good cousin." Li Hong ordered his servants to bring his writing utensils. He ground his ink stick, he formed the tip of his writing brush into a point, and with a few strokes and dots, he finished the writing at once. Jin Haoshan stood by his side watching, and found no errors at all. Li Tang said, "Cousin, rest at our home for a few days." Jin Haoshan said, "I have to leave today." Li Tang gave the order to prepare a white horse, and someone brought a well-fed horse. Why would they bring out such a well-fed white horse? Li Tang had a mind to get rid of Haoshan by sending Flying Legs Wang Biao to follow and catch up with him in order to kill him. *This part of the story comes later, and I won't talk about it now.*

Li Tang also ordered his servants to bring ten *liang*[30] of silver coins for traveling and two strings of copper coins.[31] After he had finished giving his orders, the three men left the house and went as far as the main gate to send off Jin Haoshan. Jin Haoshan said, "Cousins, please take care of your relatives, my wife and daughters. They are totally dependent on you." Li Tang and Li Hong said, "Of course." Jin Haoshan got on the horse, bid them farewell, and left quickly. *For the time being I will not talk about him.*

Li Tang and Li Hong returned to their reading room and ordered their servants: "Quickly call Flying Legs Wang Biao to come here!" The servants called Wang Biao to come, and he said, "Who is ordering me to come?" Li Tang said, "Just now I sent Jin Haoshan to Beijing to get help from relatives. Go quickly to catch up with him and kill him. I will reward you with ten *liang* of silver coins." Wang Biao said, "I will follow your order!" When Wang Biao went to his own house, how did he disguise himself? He wrapped a patterned handkerchief around his head and wore a tight-fitting jacket and small pants that were tight in the crotch. He stepped into his boots like a tiger pouncing on the ground. In his hand he carried a steel jackknife. He left the compound and quickly ran to the main road in Beijing.

That is to say . . .
Jin Haoshan's horse proceeded forward;
He thought to himself:

---

30. One *liang* is 1.75 ounces.

31. Copper coins were round with square holes in the middle and were carried on strings.

"How good it is[32] that on my way to Beijing to get help from relatives,
I met up with good relatives!
If I can get work in Beijing,
I will never forget the kindness of these two."
As Jin Haoshan traveled along the road of human reality,
He never realized that he was entering the city of the bitterly
sorrowful dead.
Haoshan kept traveling onward.
Suddenly he heard someone's voice behind him;
Wang Biao shouted, "Wherever you are going,
You will never be able to run away!"
As soon as Haoshan heard this, he was frightened;
He got off the horse to give it up.

He could not say anything else,
But could only call out to that "brave man":
"You can take my belongings and my horse,
But by all means please let me live."
When Wang Biao heard this,
He called out to that "good man":[33]
"Who are your cousins?
You haven't even asked their names.
My masters really go by the name of Li.
One is Li Tang and the other is Li Hong.
They saw how beautiful your daughters are
And want to get married to them.
They intentionally planned to trap you
And deceived you into coming to their house.
They want to kill you.
You will never be able to get away!"
Wang Biao immediately raised the knife
And venomously stabbed him and finished the matter.

I don't know if he was killed or not;
The next part of the story will speak of this.
I will stop right here,
And if you want to listen, it will be in the next section.

---

32. The phrase "how good it is" consists of the same words as in Haoshan's name; another play on his name happens again in this passage.

33. The term "good man" is written the same way as Haoshan's name. The juxtaposition of Jin Haoshan as a "good man" and Flying Legs Wang Biao as a "brave man" is made clear in the original since the two phrases rhyme.

CHAPTER 3. LI TANG AND LI HONG FORCE A MARRIAGE

The vanities of the world are not worth desiring;
Fame, wealth, power, and arms always increase.
I encouraged the emperor not to entrust himself to the insignificant opinions of men.
If it is not about what to eat, it is about what to wear.

These four verses open our story. Now I will present a drum song. If you don't mind listening to a long story, please let me tell you the following popular vernacular story. Gentle audience, please sit down and cross your legs and let me tell you a story. It goes like this . . .

Having nothing to do, I went to the south to spend some time,
And saw two blind men rolling on the ground fighting.
Blind Man Zhang was holding Blind Man Wang;
Wang was grabbing Zhang's clothes at the waist.
Wang forced Zhang to fall on the ground.
When Zhang fell down he grabbed hold of dog feces;
As soon as he smelled it he thought it smelled very strong.
He didn't know what it was
And said, "Wang, listen up!
I just touched something very sticky;
It seems like a slice of jujube cake."
Wang had always had a strange temperament compared to Zhang,
So he didn't want Zhang to take advantage of this delicious opportunity.

He stealthily grabbed some and bit into it, oh! "This good stuff smells terrible." Zhang said, "That is really a bit of stinky dog feces. This time it turns out that you lost." Wang's eyes rolled back in contempt, showing only the whites. Zhang got up and left. *This story of the blind man who ate dog feces is finished. Gentle audience, please listen to the following story.*

The last chapter was about:
Jin Haoshan was in the middle of the road.
On his knees he knelt with his head close to the ground.
He said only one thing,
And he continuously called out "good fellow":
"I want neither my luggage nor my horse,
But please spare my life."
Haoshan broke his tongue begging for mercy,
But it was only like wind passing by Wang Biao's ears.
Haoshan said, "Even if you have no regard for me,
At least you can show your reverence of Buddha.

If you cannot respect a humble fish,
Show your regard for the ocean [in which it swims].
If you have no regard for water or fish,
Then have sympathy for me,
As I am far from home and all alone."
Haoshan spoke and cried loudly,
Realizing his mistake:
"From the beginning I was wrong;
I should have asked them their names."
At the moment Haoshan realized his mistake,
Flying Legs Wang Biao killed him.
There was only the sound of the "chop,"
And his head fell to the ground.
Flying Legs Wang Biao returned home;
He quickly arrived at the courtyard.

Wang Biao returned to the compound and entered the reading room. He told about how he had killed Jin Haoshan. When Li Tang and Li Hong heard this, they were very happy. They walked back to the women's quarters and met Lady Wang, saying: "Mother-in-law, how is everything?" Lady Wang said, "How is that you address me like that?" Li Tang and Li Hong said, "We saw that your two daughters are very beautiful, so we tricked you into coming to our house. We murdered your husband on his way, and we plan to marry your daughters." When Lady Wang heard this, it was as if her heart was pierced with a sword. She cried loudly and said, "You wicked men, aren't you afraid of disturbing the natural order?" She pointed her finger at them and accused them: "You wicked men, aren't you afraid of divine retribution?"

Lady Wang cried loudly,
And accused them: "You wicked men, you are truly horrible.
Your family has sisters, too,
So why don't you marry your aunts!
Today, you think that I will give in to you,
But even if you make me blind through torture, you will still be wasting your time!"
When Li Tang heard this he was annoyed,
And he had her taken to the South Prison Chamber.
He immediately ordered her to be taken to the South Prison Chamber.
The two sisters shouted loudly
And pointed at them, accusing them:
"Sons of bitches, you beasts!
Let us suppose that you dare to meet us again:
Even if you arrange the ceremonial paintings everywhere,
Have our images memorialized in paintings,

Put our paintings on the North Wall,
Burn incense and offer sacrifices for us,
We still will not give in to you even in death!"
Li Tang and Li Hong were annoyed by their reproof.
With indescribable fury,
They ordered: "Servants, tie them up.
Suspend them from the roof of the East Stable.
Dip the whip into water for lashing them.
Give them a lashing, then see if they agree.
Give them another lashing and ask them again.
See if they are willing to marry or not."
The servants followed the order, and it was not neglected;
With a "whoosh" they came together like a swarm of bees.
They tied up the young women from head to foot;
If any ropes were loose, they tightened them, pressing with their feet.
When Li Tang saw this, he hurriedly ordered:
"Suspend them from the roof of the East Stable."
The servants followed the order, and it was not neglected;
They suspended them from the roof of the East Stable.
They suspended them from the second support beam;
They were like coils of ropes hanging in the air.
They were about to lash them with the water-dipped whip.
One of the servants, Chunhong, was startled.
She spoke to them and no one else:
"Masters, please listen . . ."

Chunhong said, "If you listen to the opinion of a servant, then you, my masters, don't have to lash them." Li Tang and Li Hong said, "Why not lash them?" Chunhong said, "If you beat them black and blue, how can they marry you? If you listen to the opinion of a servant, bring them to a 'cold' attic, giving them no food but only drinking water. Let your servants watch over them so that they cannot commit suicide. Don't worry about whether they will agree to marry." Li Tang and Li Hong were greatly pleased and said, "Let's follow your plan." Chunhong quickly untied the ropes and said, "You two sisters follow me to the attic."

What a clever girl Chunhong was!
She lowered the sisters to the ground.
The servants went as a group,
Pushing and shoving one another as they went.
In a moment's time they arrived at the women's quarters;
All the servants went to the courtyard.
Chunhong saw this and began to speak,
And she called out a few times, "Maidens!"

Chunhong said, "You sisters had better agree to this marriage. How splendid it will be with all those carriages and palanquins going to and fro!" The two sisters said, "Why do you use your mouth so much! We would prefer to die. We won't agree to a marriage!" Chunhong said, "Are you telling the truth?" The two sisters said, "How could we lie?" Chunhong said, "If you are serious, I can help you run away. Today, act as though you are willing to marry, then go through the marriage ceremonies. After the late watch, I will secretly let you escape." The two sisters said, "You are really foolish. If we marry them, and you give us the cold shoulder, then we could never purify our bodies, even with water."[34] Chunhong said, "If you don't believe me, I will swear by heaven." She hurriedly opened the door and looked about to see if there was anyone nearby. Chunhong knelt down on the floor and swore by heaven.

That is . . .
The servant knelt on the floor.
She prayed to the host of gods in heaven:
"Great and small gods in heaven,
Reveal your powers, I beg of you.
If I plan to deceive these two sisters,
Then by all means let me be punished by five loud peals of thunder!"
The servant straightened up and took a serious oath;
This made Jinjie and Fengying exceedingly happy.
They came to her and quickly helped her up;
They called her "Sister Chunhong" several times:
"Stand up, stand up;
If you keep kneeling it will break our hearts."
The servant heard this and said respectfully,
"Maidens!"

Chunhong said, "I want to tell you something that you must bear in mind. If you agree to this plan, at night you must make these two men drink until they sweat wine and they agree to three requests. First: Today is the wedding day. The maids must help cut the grass and feed the horses. Give each maid a bottle of wine and a piece of meat so that everyone can retire early to drink wine. Do not let them be in attendance. Second: Tonight do not make the servants draw water from the well. The well is in the flower garden, so I'm afraid that you might meet up with them by chance. Third: Do not make them keep the watch. Make them all drunk. When the watch is over, I will send you to the gate of the flower garden to run away." The sisters said, "We will keep these things in mind."

---

34. That is, even if they drowned themselves.

CHAPTER 4. CHUNHONG LETS THE TWO LADIES ESCAPE

Chunhong did not neglect these things;
She did them quickly without stopping.
There was a mirror stand, washbasins, and a wardrobe;
The highest quality clothing was already prepared.
The servants hurriedly carried in water for face washing;
The two sisters worked without stopping.
Holding ivory combs,
They put on makeup.
Their left hands combed, and their right hands made chignons;
Their left hands combed, and their right hands fluffed their forelocks.
Fragrance on the chignons;
Scents on the fluffed forelocks.
They powdered their reddened faces,
And put Jiangnan rouge on their red lips.
They wore eight-treasure earrings weighted with gold;
They wore jingling bracelets on their arms.
The older sister liked wearing a parrot-green dress;
The younger sister liked wearing a pomegranate-red dress.
They wore green pants and snake-leather belts;
They carefully tied their red silk slippers embroidered with flowers.
The sisters finished making themselves up.

Chunhong was kept busy too—
She hurriedly went downstairs,
And in a minute she arrived at the parlor.
Chunhong entered the room and called, "Two Masters":
"Those two decided to agree."
The two men heard this and were very happy;
They hurriedly gave orders.

Li Tang and Li Hong ordered: "Quickly look to the incense altar!" The servants tended to the incense and the horse paintings and arranged them properly. They ordered the servants: "Quickly go to the women's quarters and bring the two ladies out to get married."

The servants listened and did not neglect the orders;
In a short time four people came.
They hurriedly went upstairs
And ascended thirteen rungs of the ladder.

They put three-*chi*[35] black silk cloths over their faces
And were led down to the courtyard.
They looked like willows waving in the wind as they walked
And looked like immortals descended from heaven.
They passed through several side gates
And walked down several paths.

You may want to know the main story.
Gentle audience, you must have become sleepy hearing me talk on and on.
Let me make it short and sweet:
They immediately arrived at the front building.
Who is busy now?
Li Tang and Li Hong.
They went to the front and bowed to heaven and to earth.
Hurriedly they gave orders again.

Li Hong ordered: "Prepare a table of good food and wine. Today I want to drink the wedding wine." While he was speaking, the four people entered the bridal chamber. The two sisters were so embarrassed that their faces were completely red, all the way to their ears, even though they were powdered. The wedding feast was prepared immediately. The two sisters said, "Husbands, today is the happiest day of our lives. We must drink many cups of wine." After they said this, each one filled a cup to the brim and gave it to Li Tang and Li Hong, saying, "Husband, please drink much wine."

As for the two sisters . . .
Unable to drink wine, they learned how,
And they drank until their tongues hurt.
Drink a cup, pour a cup,
Drink a glass, pour a glass.
One sister called out, "Husband,"
And the other sister called out, "Husband."
As for the two brothers, a cup for you, a glass for me;
A glass for you, a cup for me;
In a short while they were dead drunk.
The two sisters said,
"Today is the happiest day of our lives;
Please grant us several requests."

---

35. One *chi*, usually translated as a "foot," equals 1.09 feet; thus the length of the sides of the square cloth was 3.3 feet. The cloth was draped over the head of a bride when she was presented to her husband for the first time.

Li Tang and Li Hong said, "What are your requests?" The two sisters said, "You must grant us three important requests." Li Tang and Li Hong said, "Don't say two or three! Even if you have eight or even ten requests we must grant them." Li Tang and Li Hong said, "But we don't know which three you have." The two sisters said, "Today is the happiest day of our lives. All the people in the compound, the young and old maids, those who tend the grass and feed the horses—please give each of them a bottle of wine and a piece of meat and make them retire early so they can drink their wine. Do not make them stay in attendance." Li Tang and Li Hong immediately had the order carried out. Li Tang and Li Hong asked again: "What is the second request?" The sisters said, "Tonight do not make the servants draw water from the well. Today is a day of great happiness. We are afraid that they will fall into the well by mistake. This would not be good." Li Tang and Li Hong agreed to this request. Li Tang and Li Hong asked about the third request, and the sisters said, "Do not make the night guard keep watch." The two brothers said, "That cannot be! Our compound is very large. What if someone steals our gold and silver treasures? We absolutely cannot agree to that!" When the sisters heard this, they came up with a plan: "Today is our wedding night. This first night we will not come together as husbands and wives. Even though this is not good, it is better than two sisters' dying at once!" When the sisters finished speaking, they stood up and ran directly at the wall.

The two sisters immediately stood up;
They ran into the walls in an attempt to kill themselves.
Who was busy at that time?
The servant Chunhong;
She came forward and grabbed hold of them quickly;
Li Tang and Li Hong were shocked.

Li Tang and Li Hong said, "You sisters do not have to die. We two brothers will drink less wine and that is that." They ordered the night guard not to keep the watch.

The two sisters were very happy.
They called Chunhong
And ordered: "Quickly switch to the big cups.
We four people will play a drinking game."
When the servants heard this, they did not neglect it;
They quickly switched to large cups.
The two sisters were busy pouring wine,
Giving it to Li Tang and Li Hong.
A cup for you, a cup for me;
A glass for you, a glass for me.
They drank one and became dead drunk;

They drank another and became helplessly drunk.
They lay down on the bed and fell into a deep sleep.
The two beauties were busy.
They went forward and spoke loudly,
Calling out, "Husband" several times:
"Quickly get up, quickly get up;
We four are playing a drinking game."
They called out several times but there was no answer.
Chunhong was busy;
She came forward and grabbed hold of them:
"Maidens, follow me."
In a minute they arrived in the flower garden;
Looking to all sides it was dark everywhere.
They had not thought that the wall would be so high, making it difficult
for them to run away;
They wanted to go over the wall but were not able.
The two sisters sat on the ground;
In a flood of tears they rolled on the ground and sobbed pitifully.
Looking toward Shandong, they cried loudly
All the while crying out about their parents' lack of sons:
"Other people raise sons and thus acquire land;
You raised daughters, having nothing in return.
Today we will die in the flower garden;
We will never be able to get revenge."
The sisters cried like sotted fools;
Chunhong was madly busy.
Hurriedly she made a plan;
Suddenly a plan came to her mind.

When the young servant had thought it through, she made a plan: "You two sisters do not have to cry. At the top of the flower pavilion there is a ladder for picking flowers. If we move it to the wall, you two can jump over the wall and run away." Chunhong quickly brought the ladder and leaned it against the wall: "You sisters quickly climb the wall and run for your lives!" Jinjie and Fengying quickly stepped up to the top of the ladder. Using their hands to feel around, they found that—"Uh-oh!"—on top of the wall were thorns preventing them from crossing. At the top of the ladder they cried loudly again: "We sisters' lives must end now."

Jinjie was on the top of the ladder;
She shouted to heaven:
"I will certainly go to Hades;
I can never run away.
People live to be one hundred but eventually die;
I'd rather die early and not go to Hades!"

The two sisters cried loudly;
Chunhong was kept busy.

Chunhong said, "You two sisters don't have to cry so pitifully." She felt around her and found a wooden handle and she gave it to Jinjie, saying, "Take this scythe and swing at those thorns as though you were cutting down grass with one swift chop." Jinjie took up the scythe and took a swipe at the thorns, knocking down a whole batch. After that, she used her sleeves to wipe them off the top of the wall. Then she shouted, "Sister, come quickly and climb over!" Fengying climbed over the wall and looked down. She did not know how far it was to the ground because it was terribly dark, so the two sisters sat on top of the wall. They started crying again.

The two sisters shouted several times toward the ground:
"My mother!
You are suffering in the Southern Prison Chamber;
We don't even know if you are dead or alive.
Your daughters are unable to run away as we look over the wall;
We've tried over and over again but cannot succeed."
The two sisters cried loudly.

Let me tell of the spirits of those who have died unjustly.
I don't know where these spirits of those who died unjustly came from;
I will explain in the next chapter.

CHAPTER 5. CHUNHONG DROWNS HERSELF IN THE FLOWER GARDEN WELL

On the far bank of a river lies a bar of gold.
The sight brings happiness to my eyes and joy to my heart.
I desire to cross the river and obtain the treasure,
But there is no one to row me to the opposite shore.
It seems that all things arrive through destiny;
Not one thing comes from human effort.
I stamp my feet in great fury!
All the world's treasures cannot change a poor man's destiny.

I have finished reciting "The Moon over the West River." Now I will continue the story of the previous chapter.

The two sisters Jinjie and Fengying were trying to escape from the wall of the rear flower garden. The wall was more than several *zhang*[36] tall, and the

36. One *zhang*, usually translated as "ten feet," equals 3.6 yards.

ground on the opposite side was like a dark hole. The sisters were worried that they could not jump down from the wall, so they kept crying. Their crying alarmed the spirits of those who had died unjustly. *You may ask, where did these spirits come from? Gentle audience, there is something you don't remember.* Li Tang and Li Hong robbed men and mistreated women. They did all sorts of bad things, killing those men and women, the elderly and the young, throwing them into the well in the flower garden. The spirits of the dead were countless, calling out to one another, "Older Sister"; or another calls, "Younger Sister"; one calls, "Older Brother" or "Younger Brother"—"Today we are gathered in this place. If we do not help save their lives, who can get revenge for us?" All the spirits immediately said, "Aye!" This frightened the sisters so that they fell to the ground. *One would ask, how could they fall and not die? Gentle audience, under that wall was a big fluffy pile of hay, so they did not die.* Those two sisters climbed out of the haystack. They could not get their bearings. They wanted to run away quickly and so they just went forward. It was very dark, and they didn't know what direction to go.

Those sisters stood up and went forward,
But they did not even know which direction was which.
Trembling with fear, they went forward.
Weeping, they cried to heaven:
"Heaven help us to reach the capital
And arrive at the government office to report our grievance."

Now I will not tell of these sisters;
Let me tell of Chunhong:
"The two maidens crossed over the wall;
I am left behind, and it would be difficult to leave.
I want to return to the main building,
But I am afraid that they will ask about my clever trick.
If my two masters find out,
It will be even more difficult to run away!
People live to be one hundred but eventually die;
I would rather die early and enter the world of ghosts forever!"
When the servant finished her thoughts, she walked forward.
The well was in front of her, not far away.
In desperation she decided to jump into the well.
The cries of the spirits reached heaven:
How pitiful that Chunhong died!

Now we will talk of Li Tang and Li Hong again.
After several hours, they woke up and opened their eyes,
But they could not find their servant Chunhong.
Where were the two beauties?

They hurriedly called all the servants.
When the maids heard this, they all came;
Li Tang and Li Hong began to speak.

Li Tang and Li Hong said, "Did you see where Chunhong and the two ladies went?" None of the servants knew. After Li Tang and Li Hong thought for a long time, they realized that the three must have run away. They ordered the servants: "Bring lanterns and torches and search everywhere." When they heard this, the servants lit the lanterns and torches. They found that the front gate had not been opened, so that they must have run away through the rear flower garden. Li Tang and Li Hong said, "The wall of the flower garden is too high to cross over." All the servants came to the flower garden. Using the lanterns they looked around and found a ladder leaning against the wall. After finding it they reported it to Li Tang and Li Hong. The two brothers heard this and supposed that the two sisters could not have gone far. They opened the gate of the compound and went out to pursue them.

That is,
When they heard the command, they did not neglect it;
They went through the gate of the compound and proceeded forward.
All the servants were like tigers and wolves;
Behind the two sisters, the sound of shouting did not stop.
While the sisters were walking forward,
Suddenly they heard the sound of people behind them.
The two sisters were frozen in fear;
With a "thud" they fell over on their sides.
There was no one to help the two sisters.

Let me skip this part and talk of another story.
What will the story be about now?
Let me speak of two Venus stars, Li and Jin.
The star Jin was in his seat;
His infirmity prevented him from hearing well and seeing straight.
Why was his right eye straight but his left eye crooked?
Why was his right ear a good ear but his left ear deaf?
Where is the sky high but without rain?
Where is harvest lacking because of floods and droughts?
Where do virtuous and filial women come from?
Where do parents and beauties suffer?
Heaven and earth know [the answers to these questions];
All the spirits gathered in that place know [them, too].
"If I don't help them, who will help them?
If I don't take care of their suffering, who will take care of it?"
The star Jin quickly left his seat.

Riding a cloud in the sky, he spurred it on.
The star Jin hurried the cloud forward.
He saw the two beauties.
Pointing his finger, he changed heaven and earth,
Hu la, hu la, a loud wind rushed by.
The wind blew so hard that heaven and earth were darkened,
And all kinds of cattle were blown everywhere.
When the servants saw this they couldn't open their eyes.
They tried to go forward but were not able to move.
Their lanterns and torches were all blown out
And everything was dark before them.
Li Tang immediately ordered:
"Let's go back to the compound—don't stop."
I will not speak of Li Tang's returning to the compound;
I will present someone else.
Who will the story talk of now?
Let me talk of Gentleman Liu once more.

Gentleman Liu woke up at dawn, ate breakfast, and said, "Shao Qing and Shao Hong, go to the gate and give explicit instructions to those soldiers: if any great or small official comes to pay his respects, tell him he doesn't have to see me and that I am sick and do not feel well." Shao Qing heard this, went to the gate, and told this to the soldiers. The soldiers answered in agreement. He went back to Gentleman Liu, and Gentleman Liu ordered again: "Shao Qing, go to the main road and buy a beggar's clothing. I have a plan to visit Liangxiang county incognito. Quickly measure out five *liang* of silver coins." Shao Qing heard this and immediately measured out five *liang* of silver coins and went to the main road. He went along the main road. A beggar came from the west. *What do you think this beggar looked like?* He wore a flower hat, a patched jacket, a rice-grass belt, and lantern pants. He wore a "left" boot on his right foot and a shoe with a broken sole on his left foot. Shao Qing came forward and bent over, saying, "Dear beggar, if you please." The beggar answered, "Yes?" Shao Qing said, "Dear beggar, are you willing to sell your clothing?" The beggar heard this, lowered his head, and thought: "His voice sounds like that of a southerner. He might be a southern savage and a treasure hunter. I've always heard that southerners have keen insight, so he must see that there is some kind of treasure in my body. If there is a treasure, then I don't know about it, but if there is no treasure, then I will not lose anything. It's difficult for treasure sellers like me to meet up with treasure buyers. I am a frank person. I will sell my clothes to him as a deposit, then it can be a done deal." The beggar casually said, "I'll sell." Shao Qing said, "If you want to sell to us, I must explain that you cannot sell your clothes individually. If you want to sell, I need the whole set." The beggar said, "Why don't you buy me?" Shao Qing said, "I do not need anything that breathes, I just want your clothing." The beggar said, "If you want to buy my clothing, I will sell, but you must pay the full price." Shao Qing said, "If you want to sell, I want to buy. Name your price." The beggar thought for a long time. This is a good saying: "Don't let a golden opportunity slip through your fingers." Then the beggar said [to Shao Qing], "I want five *liang* of silver coins." Shao Qing said, "If you want more, I don't have it. I have exactly five *liang* of coins." *I don't know how this turns out. The story will continue in the next chapter.*

CHAPTER 6. GENTLEMAN LIU VISITS LIANGXIANG COUNTY INCOGNITO

In the last chapter I talked of how Shao Qing bought clothing and paid five liang *of silver coins.* Shao Qing said, "If you will sell, please go behind the temple with me." The beggar said, "I can't go there." Shao Qing said, "Dear beggar, don't be mistaken. This is a very busy road, so if you take off all your clothes, it is not convenient." After the beggar thought about this, he said, "That's right!" The two went behind the temple, and the beggar took off his flower hat, his rice-grass belt, his patched jacket, and his lantern pants, and he removed his mismatched boot. "I don't want this shoe with its broken sole, so I will give it to you." He grabbed the silver coins and ran away quickly.

Now I will not speak of the beggar;
Let me speak of Shao Qing again.
Hurriedly he turned back;
The prefecture was just ahead, not far way.
Shao Qing entered the prefecture
And explained to Gentleman Liu what had transpired.

Shao Qing approached Gentleman Liu and reported: "The beggar's clothing has arrived." Gentleman Liu ordered: "Put it in a steamer and steam it." *One might say, forget about it. These clothes are neither stuffed buns nor steamed bread for eating. These are only torn clothes, so what is the use of steaming them? Gentle audience, Gentleman Liu is afraid that he will be bitten by fleas, so that's why he wants them steamed and roasted.* Shao Qing gave the order to steam and roast the clothes. Then Gentleman Liu got dressed and put on the patched jacket, the rice-grass belt, the lantern pants, the mismatched boot, and the broken shoe. He finished putting on his disguise and said, "Shao Qing, do I look like a beggar?" Shao Qing answered, "No beggar has a white official's face like yours, two gold earrings like the ones you have, and such distinguished eyebrows." *Audience, Gentleman Liu's eyebrows are very distinguished indeed.* He is the Qianlong emperor's favorite official, so the emperor gave him two gold earrings, and that is why he has them. Gentleman Liu said, "Shao Qing, I changed everything else, but I cannot change my face." Shao Qing said, "If you permit me to do something, I can change your face too." Gentleman Liu said, "I permit you. Go ahead." Shao Qing immediately felt around in a pile of cooking-stove ashes and found some mud. He said, "Master, please close your eyes." Gentleman Liu heard this and closed his eyes. Shao Qing used his hands to pat the mud on Gentleman Liu's face and then took a sip of tea and sprayed it all over his face so that his face was streaked and muddy. Shao Qing said, "Master, please look at your clothing in the mirror and see whether you look like a beggar." As soon as Gentleman Liu looked at himself, he laughed loudly and said, "This flower hat cannot cover the two gold earrings." Gentleman Liu found an earwax pot and put it over his head to cover his gold earrings. Gentleman Liu finished getting dressed and ordered Wang Liang and Wang Yi: "Today I have a plan to visit Liangxiang county incognito. I will return in the afternoon. If I don't return, wait for me at the office in Liangxiang county." Gentleman Liu gave orders to those guarding the gate, explaining clearly: "When I arrive at the gate, make the soldiers shout at me to prevent a rumor from being spread and to prevent others from knowing my secret." All the people agreed and immediately they arranged everything correctly and followed his orders. Gentleman Liu took a yellow clay pot and a stick to beat off dogs, as well as writing tools. He left the gate of the prefecture quietly. The soldiers shouted, "Hey! Where did this stupid beggar come from? This is the prefecture. Is this a place for a beggar like you to be hanging around?" Gentleman Liu did not respond but just left.

Gentleman Liu left the prefecture;
He walked forward just like a tiger.
Gentleman Liu got lost as he walked
And followed the main road to the west;
He did not know how to get to Liangxiang county.
Gentleman Liu got lost that day;
He could not get his bearings.
Altogether he walked more than ten tricents;
His legs became numb, making it difficult to walk.
In front of him there were several willow trees;
He was able to rest there.
Gentleman Liu sat down on some level ground;
He looked east and west.
Gentleman Liu found
Two beauties coming from the southeast.
Gentle audience, you may want to ask who they are:
They are Jinjie and Fengying.
The two sisters were cursing as they walked.
They were cursing Li Tang and Li Hong:
"How can we get revenge and show our hatred?
They killed our family, causing us all to suffer bitterly.
We sisters are going to Beijing;
We can report our grievances at the office there."
The two sisters walked forward;

They looked east and west.
The sisters continually looked behind them;
They were afraid of Li Tang and Li Hong.
The sisters did not say that they were afraid,
But Gentleman Liu, looking on, could discern it clearly.

Gentleman Liu was sitting at the side of the road. From the southeast came two ladies who continually looked behind them. They looked different, unlike the daughters of a poor family. Why were they walking as if they had an important reason to be walking? Gentleman Liu liked to poke his nose in others' business. He called out, "You two ladies, come here." As Jinjie and Fengying were walking, they heard someone calling them, and it frightened them so much that they trembled. They thought that Li Tang and Li Hong had followed them. When they looked around, they found that no was following them, but it was a beggar sitting there who had called.

Fengying said, "That beggar most likely plans to rob us." Jinjie said, "Look, that beggar is more than eighty years old. His beard is full of silver hairs. He will probably not rob us. Let's rest for a while and ask him what he wants to talk with us about." The two sisters came close to him and said, "Beggar, do you have something to tell us?" Gentleman Liu said, "You two do not look like the type of people who try to avoid others. Why are you so busy looking behind you? You must have some reason. Tell me what it is." The sisters said, "We have a reason, but you cannot help us." Gentleman Liu said, "Don't think that I'm just a beggar. I am especially able to resolve people's injustices. If you have some kind of trouble and if you have been treated unjustly, I am able to write a lawsuit for you." The sisters said, "We have been treated unjustly, but we are afraid that you cannot help us. We sisters have a complaint, so we want to go to Beijing to report it." Gentleman Liu said, "Who do you want to ask to write your lawsuit?" The sisters said, "We heard that there is a man named Gentleman Liu in Beijing, and we want to ask him to write it." Gentleman Liu said, "If you spoke of anyone else, I would not know of him, but I do know of Gentleman Liu." The sisters said, "If you know which district and which county Gentleman Liu lives in, please tell us." Gentleman Liu said:

"Listen . . .
I know the Gentleman Liu that you speak of;
His family lives in Old Shandong,
Qingzhou prefecture in Shandong, and
Administrates a small county named Zhucheng.
There is an eight-tricent area of land in Zhucheng;
In Pangu village there is a courtyard.
The two of us are good friends;
From childhood we diligently studied together.
One day the emperor hosted civil service examinations;

The two of us entered Beijing to take the exam.
He passed the exam,
But I failed, so I am now poor.
The two of us are the best of friends;
It is as if we were one and the same man."
Gentleman Liu talked as if telling the truth.
He again asked Jinjie and Fengying about their problem.

"I have told a long story. What unjust treatment has been done to you?" The sisters said, "Even though we have been treated unjustly, you can't write a lawsuit for us. You don't have a brush and ink. You also have no paper." Gentleman Liu said, "I am able to write a lawsuit for you. I just picked up a set of writing implements and paper from a shop. Where do you two live? What are your names? Who do you want to report? Tell me everything in detail." The sisters said, "Beggar, listen." *Let me explain this in the next chapter.*

THE PRECIOUS SCROLL OF CHENXIANG

Translated and introduced by Wilt L. Idema

Mount Hua, in modern-day Shaanxi province, has been venerated as a holy mountain since time immemorial. Located just to the southwest of the place where the River Wei joins the Yellow River as it sharply turns east, its many steeply rising peaks offer an imposing sight. Ancient legend holds that the mountain had acquired its characteristic features when the god Giant Spirit (Julingshen) severed Mount Hua, with one blow of his axe, from the mountains to the other side of the Yellow River, in order to give the Yellow River a passageway to the sea. Since the Han dynasty (206 B.C.E.–220 C.E.), Mount Hua has received offerings as the Western Marchmount, one of China's five holiest mountains. A huge temple complex has been built to the north of Mount Hua, close to the county capital of Huayin.

The cult of Mount Hua flourished especially during the Tang dynasty (618–907), when Mount Hua marked the midway point of the road linking Chang'an and Luoyang, the two capitals of the dynasty. By this time, the god of the mountain had acquired a large family, whose members also enjoyed veneration. But both he and his womenfolk, according to legend, quite often behaved in ways not befitting their divine status. While the god preyed on (the souls of) mortal women, his wives maintained amorous relations with mortal men. The god's third daughter bewitched male visitors to her shrine with her beauty, and often such affairs resulted in sons.

In later centuries, the stories of the amorous adventures of Third Daughter of Mount Hua were transformed into the legend of Chenxiang (Aloeswood). Chenxiang is the son of Third Daughter and her mortal lover, the student Liu Xiang. His name is derived from an aloeswood fan pendant, a family heirloom that Liu Xiang is given by his mother when he leaves home to travel to the capital to sit for the examinations, which he in turn leaves with his divine paramour when the preordained time of their life together has come to an end, and which she in turn attaches to the baby boy born from their union, whom she brings to Liu Xiang to raise. Third Daughter now has an elder brother in the figure of the god Second Son (Erlangshen). This god originally had no connection to Mount Hua, since his cult would appear to have originated in the area of Chengdu. However, in due time, as his cult spread to larger areas, Second Son was identified with many local deities. Modern Chinese readers probably are best acquainted with his great magical might and transformational abilities from the pages of popular sixteenth-century novels such as *Journey to the West* (*Xiyou ji*), in which he battles Sun Wukong, the Great Sage Equal to Heaven. Once Second Son's name had made him a suitable candidate for the role of elder brother to Third Daughter, legends developed linking him to Mount Hua. Eager to suspect other female deities of amorous adventures, Second Son flies into a rage as soon as he hears that his own little sister is pregnant by a mere mortal, and he punishes her by imprisoning her under Mount Hua. It will be left to Chenxiang to eventually save his mother and, by doing so, to exemplify the foundational virtue of filial piety.

Other divine characters in the story include the Jade Emperor, Great White, the bodhisattva Guanyin, the Queen Mother of the West, and the Eight Immortals. Highest authority in heaven is embodied in the Jade Emperor, but his role is largely reactive. When he is persuaded to take action, it is often Great White, the Star of Metal (the planet Venus), who is dispatched to solve the problem. Great White manifests himself to mortal eyes in many guises—one moment as an old man, the next as a young buffalo boy. The bodhisattva Guanyin takes a more active role in human affairs as she "listens to the sounds of the world" and is eager to display her mercy. The Queen Mother of the West rules all female immortals; she resides atop Mount Kunlun in the far west, where she celebrates her birthday each year on the fifteenth day of the (lunar) eighth month, at the time of the Midautumn Festival, with the Banquet of the Peaches of Immortality. This banquet is attended by all divinities, and so we find among the attendants the Eight Immortals. Three of the Eight Immortals are mentioned by name in "The Precious Scroll of Chenxiang": Zhongli Quan, Lü Dongbin, and Immortal Matron He (He Xiangu). Zhongli Quan had been a general during his mortal lifetime, and Lü Dongbin is usually depicted carrying a sword. It is therefore no wonder that they, like practically all other gods (both male and female), are redoubtable warriors whenever the occasion calls for a display of their might. Immortal Matron He is the only female member of the group of the Eight Immortals, and it is therefore perhaps not surprising that other divinities at times suspect her of having improper liaisons with one or more of her constant companions. Each of these gods, of course, has his or her own entourage of divine servants, from golden boys and jade maidens to infernal judges, ghosts, and ugly demons known as *yakshas*. In the final violent confrontation between Chenxiang and his uncle, Second Son, many other divinities join the fray, but since they are brought in only as extras, there is no need to detail the background, nature, and appearance of each of them.

While we have references proving the existence of the legend of Chenxiang at least as early as the fourteenth century, we have to wait for the nineteenth century to have full narrative accounts of the tale. The anonymous "Precious Scroll of Chenxiang" (Chenxiang baojuan; also known as the "Precious Scroll of the Amulet King") is the shortest and the simplest of the many versions of the legend. This text must have been in existence by the middle of the nineteenth century, and it is known through numerous manuscripts. The precious scrolls genre certainly existed by the middle of the fourteenth century and may even go back to the early twelfth century. Originally the genre was devoted to Buddhist legends, and from the sixteenth century it was also utilized by a number of newly emerging religious teachings to spread their messages by oral and written means. By the nineteenth century, the genre had come to include a wide variety of stories from a non-Buddhist background, but the performance of precious scrolls still had, as a rule, a strongly ritualistic character. With the rise of a modern printing industry in Shanghai in the early twentieth century, texts in this genre were also widely distributed as entertainment reading. Of its original religious nature, little remained beyond a few introductory and concluding verses. One trait of many nineteenth-century narrative *baojuan* is that they often provide complete versions of tales in relatively short texts, where the same narrative might appear in much greater length in other genres. Actually, we have at least two more adaptations of the legend as a "precious scroll," of which each is at least twice the length of the version translated here. These other versions often carry in their name a reference to a "precious lotus lantern" as the magic weapon of Third Daughter, but this version does not mention that gadget.

The story of the "Precious Scroll of Chenxiang" happened to a descendant of Prince Jing of the Han dynasty, during the reign of the Son of Heaven Emperor Jing. There was a rich man with the name of Liu Guangrui who owned millions but lacked an heir.

> He lived in Qingzhou prefecture of Shandong province
> In the county of Anqiu he had lived for many years.
> He had amassed a fortune of many millions,
> And the wife to whom he was married was Lady Li.
>
> The high hall and great rooms were all in good order,
> Towers, terraces, halls, and pavilions reached to the clouds.
> No need to describe the wealth and status of the family—
> But because he was without a son he was not happy.
>
> Light and shade, so swift and quick, easily pass by,
> It came to pass that his wedded wife was pregnant.
> And on the first night of the new spring,
> Exactly on the fifteenth day, she gave birth at midnight.
>
> To their great joy she gave birth to a male child,
> And for his name they chose Liu Xiang.
> The first and the second year easily passed by,
> And in his third and fourth years he easily grew up.
>
> When he was five and six he reached understanding,
> At seven he started to study, read the books of the Sage.
> Light and shade, so swift and quick, easily passed by,
> And he became a student at the prefectural school.

At that time he was just sixteen years of age;
His sole ambition was to jump across the Dragon Gate.[37]
He spoke to his rich father in the following words:
"Your son wants to leave home to pursue a career and fame."

The lady, his mother, immediately replied:
"My son, now just listen to what I have to say.
Your old parents have no one else on whom to rely,
We rely solely on you, our son, to take care of affairs.

"To become an official far away, to scheme for fame and profit—
Much better you stayed at home and took care of your parents!"
When Liu Xiang had heard her words, he replied as follows:
"My dear mother, please listen to what I have to say—

"Ten years of study by the window—no one knows your name,
A single success in the exams—the whole world knows your fame!
Even though our family may have a treasure of a thousand gold,
In the end we are only common citizens of no status at all.

"As soon as I obtain a single office or only half a job,
It will change our status and turn us into people of rank!"
The lady, his mother, was unable to keep him at home this time,
And as soon as he had packed, her son started on his journey.

So she gave his two servants the following order:
"Be careful in whatever you do while on this trip!"
She took a rare treasure of aloeswood from her chest,
Which she gave to her son to carry on his person:

"Above there are the sun and moon to light your way as yin and yang;
Below there are the mountains and streams in the eight directions.
As long as you carry this invaluable treasure on your person,
You are bound to pass the examinations as top of the list!"

Once Liu Xiang had received this treasure of aloeswood,
He took leave of his parents and left for the capital:
"Today just so happens to be a Yellow Way day,[38]
The wind is fine, the weather warm, so I'll be on my way!"

---

37. To jump across the Dragon Gate was to pass the civil service examinations and become an official.

38. Traditional Chinese were conscious of whether a day was astronomically auspicious or inauspicious and would avoid setting out on a trip when it was not a good day. In contrast to Black Way days, Yellow Way days were considered auspicious.

All the way he made rapid progress,
Till before him appeared a large temple.
He descended from his horse and entered the temple,
Burned incense, bowed down, and implored their help.

When Liu Xiang arrived at the temple, he burned incense and threw the oracle blocks.[39] But it just so happened that Her Majesty, Third Daughter of Mount Hua, was not present in her temple. It was the Midautumn Festival of the eighth month, and on this fine day, the birthday of the Queen Mother of the West, all the gods and immortals in each of the three ranks had gone to Jasper Pond in order to celebrate her birthday and wish her long life at the Banquet of the Peaches of Immortality. So the infernal judges and ghostly underlings were in no position to settle this oracle and left the oracle blocks suspended in mid-air. Shouting with fury, Liu Xiang pulled away the screen and beheld the image of the goddess.

As soon as Liu Xiang had seen the image of the goddess,
He inscribed a four-line poem on the wall for all to see:

"How bright the hues of red and green: the image of the goddess!
'Tis sculpted of clay, carved from wood, decorated with gold.
If you have only one breath of life in your beautiful body,
I'll wed you as the wife who shares my couch and blanket."

No sooner had he finished the poem than he made himself scarce,
As he hurried on and pursued his journey.
He had gone only three or four miles, when
Third Daughter of Mount Hua returned from the feast.

She put her cloud on the ground, entered the temple,
And immediately was startled out of her senses:
"The ink is not yet dry on this four-line poem
That clearly inappropriately makes fun of me!"

The infernal judges and ghostly underlings, dumbstruck,
Hurriedly informed her of all that had happened:
"There was this student by the name of Liu Xiang,
He hailed from Qingzhou prefecture in Shandong province.

"On his way to the capital to search for fame and glory,
He arrived at Mount Hua and wanted to consult you.

39. Oracle blocks were cast on the ground for purposes of divination.

As you had gone to the Banquet of the Peaches of Immortality,
We kept his oracle blocks suspended in midair,

"Whereupon the student in his furious rage
Inscribed the poem on the wall, cursing Your Majesty."
When the goddess heard this story, she was filled with fury,
And her flowery face turned into the shape of a *yaksha*.[40]

She stepped on her cloud and left with great speed,
In order to catch Liu Xiang, the author of the poem.
But as soon as she caught sight of Liu Xiang's face:
"His brilliance rises straight up—a handsome fellow!

"He looks like an immortal lad reborn on earth,
And resembles a Song Yu[41] who has returned to life!
Any god would be pleased as soon he saw him,
Even immortals would feel the urge of desire!

"I wanted to cut off his head and kill him,
But alas, he is such an adorable person.
This man really is the man of my dreams:
While alive we'll share a pillow, after death a grave!"

She turned around and asked the Old Man in the Moon:
"Inspect for me without mistake the register of marriages."
The Old Man in the Moon hurriedly took a look:
"Your Majesty, you will marry this man surnamed Liu, under

"The rites of the duke of Zhou: you'll give birth to a boy
Who will continue the line of the house of Liu."
Hearing his words, the goddess was filled with joy;
She took her leave of the Old Man in the Moon and departed.

"'This very night the marriage will be consummated,
I'll display a miracle to show my miraculous power."
In the endless expanse of wilderness before her,
She conjured up a fairy mansion, in all respects complete.

In the front she constructed a high hall, in the back a tower,
In the flower garden she constructed a flower-gazing pavilion.

---

40. The Sanskrit word *yaksha* means "demon."

41. Song Yu was a famous lover of antiquity.

It is impossible to describe all the beautiful features,
Pearl curtains were hung up high for all to see.

She also transformed her serving women
And turned them into four pretty young maids.
Her Majesty's magic was wonderful in all respects;
It allowed this heavenly immortal to descend to earth.

Immediately she recited spells and incantations:
The thunderstorm and raging winds were terrible!
Liu Xiang was scared out of his wits
And repeatedly called out to his servants.

When suddenly the thunder rumbled and lightning flashed, while deafening thunderclaps filled the sky, our student Liu Xiang was at his wit's end, without a road to ascend to heaven or a gate to enter earth. But when he lifted his head and had a look, he dimly discerned a village manor, so all he could do was go up to the gate and say to the gatekeeper: "Sir, while on our journey we have run into this downpour, so we would like to rest here. Please report us to your master." The gatekeeper immediately went inside to report his arrival. He opened the main gate and said, "Please come inside and take a seat!" When the young maids had served him fragrant tea, Her Majesty came forward and greeted the student. As soon as she had taken a seat, she asked him: "What is your name? Where do you live? How old are you? Please let me know!"

Liu Xiang immediately told her the full truth:
"Mademoiselle, please listen to my words.

"I live in Qingzhou prefecture of Shandong province,
And I was born in the county of Anqiu.
My father is known as a rich man because of his millions,
And my mother, Lady Li, is his main wife.

"My own name is Liu Xiang, and I am a student,
Eighteen years old, in the prime of my spring.
Mademoiselle, may I ask how old you are,
And why you are dressed in mourning's white?"

The immortal maiden replied in the following words:
"Young man, please listen to my words.

"My father has passed away and my mother is deceased,
I am eighteen years old and not yet married.

If you, student, do not despise me for my ugliness,
I'd like to tie the knot with you as man and wife!"

Liu Xiang answered her in the following words:
"Mademoiselle, please listen to my words.
I am currently on my way to the capital,
Once I've achieved fame and glory, I will respond.

"I am deeply grateful for the favor you show me,
But you'd better find someone else as your husband.
Moreover, my father and mother are both still alive,
To marry without their permission would be a major crime!"

Upon hearing his words the immortal maiden was filled with
 fury,
And she cursed him: "Young man, you insult me!"
She ordered her maids, all four of them:
"Throw the three of them out of the house!"

When Liu Xiang had been told this, he left in a hurry,
He pressed on, whether the road was high or low.
We will not say how Liu Xiang made his escape,
Let us describe how the goddess displayed her powers.

She took a single golden hairpin from her head,
And transformed the pin into a striped old tiger.
Then she took a handkerchief on which she blew,
And it was transformed into a huge long snake.

She threw an incense burner high into the air:
It turned into a high mountain jutting into the sky.
She also took off an embroidered shoe, threw it up into the air,
And turned it into a Yellow River, ten thousand fathoms deep.

As the master and his two servants were pursuing their journey,
A sudden whirlwind filled them with fear:
A striped tiger jumped into the road,
Baring its fangs, stretching its claws, ready to devour them.

At first sight of the creature, Liu Xiang was scared,
But then an evil serpent blocked his way:
Its maw like a bowl of blood, its fangs like swords,
It stretched its neck as if to swallow him whole!

While in haste and hurry they fled over small byways,
A high mountain blocked their road, so they could not proceed.
And as they searched for a road to go around the mountain,
The Yellow River with its myriad fathoms was as deep as the sea.

When the student saw this, his mind was scattered,
And the two servants were so scared they lost their minds:
"East, south, north, and west: nowhere a road,
We can only go back and make amends!"

When Liu Xiang had entered the hall once again and greeted the young lady, he made a very deep bow, and said, "Demoiselle, I have offended you, please forgive me!" The immortal maiden asked, "Why did you come back after you had left?" Liu Xiang told her: "In front of me there was a fierce tiger, and behind me was an evil snake. To the left was a high mountain, and to the right the Yellow River. I was so scared that I didn't know where to run. I was really frightened! I could only come back to your mansion and implore you to show me your kindness. If you agree, I will be happy to marry you."

Upon these words the immortal maiden was filled with joy,
And she ordered her servants to make everything ready.

On a stand the wine of union was displayed,
And hastily she was dressed as a bride.
With black thread her coiling-dragon chignon was tied up,
But no sight of rouge or powder as she made her entrance!

She was dressed in a bright-red jacket with massed flowers,
And under that she wore a five-colored green-tide skirt.
She looked just like Chang'e[42] as she leaves the moon,
She resembled a fairy maiden descending to earth.

In the hall the flowery candles had been arranged.
Flower and candle in the bridal chamber: husband and wife!
Filled with joy and happiness: like fish and water—
One quarter of a spring night equals a thousand in gold!

Her Majesty Third Daughter of Mount Hua said, "Young man, I have a riddle here in the form of a poem that you have to solve. And the poem goes:

42. Chang'e is the goddess of the moon.

From afar I gaze on the high mountain, oh green so green:
A man who is lost on the mountain roads sits by the side of the path.
A farmer all by himself is passing through the fields,
Taking off his straw cape he rests by the bank."

When Liu Xiang had heard the poem, he thought to himself: "A 'man' 人 by the side of a 'mountain' 山 has to be the character for 'immortal' 仙. And if you add 'clothes' 衣 to the character *shen* 申 you have the character 'divine' 神. So you are a divine immortal!" The immortal maiden told him: "I live in the palace of the Dipper and the Ox, and I have been enfeoffed as a divinity in the temple of Mount Hua. Because you asked for an oracle and inscribed a poem, I inquired of the Old Man in the Moon, and it turned out I was destined to be your wife for three nights. That's why I kept you here and slept with you. But the three nights of married life are over now, and today we have to go our separate ways!"

Upon these words Liu Xiang was startled out of his wits,
He knelt down on both his knees in the dust and the dirt.
"I am only a mere mortal person,
So how could I marry an immortal maiden?"

The immortal maiden helped her husband to his feet,
Calling him "My husband!" a number of times.
"I have nothing special to give you as a parting gift,
So I will give you three magical treasures:

"One night-shining pearl to accompany you,
One girdle of pearls to express my love,
And then there is this glazed bowl of green jade—
These I give to you to cheer you up."

Upon these words Liu Xiang dissolved in tears,
And he took his aloeswood to express his love:

"If later you give birth to a son of the house of Liu,
Give him the name of Chenxiang [aloeswood].
And then later, when he will have grown up,
Let him take this aloeswood to his father as a sign."

Liu Xiang took his leave and went on his way,
And Her Majesty returned and went to her temple.

I will not speak of the maiden who returned to her temple;
Let me speak of Liu Xiang, who will meet with disaster.

There was the evil minister, Chancellor Hu,
Who, after drinking with colleagues, returned to his office.

Liu Xiang and his two servants pursued their journey. Evening was falling, and as he looked up, he saw a wineshop and inn, so he decided to get down from his horse and stay there for the night in order to leave early in the morning.

I will not tell how Liu Xiang went into the inn,
I will tell how that most evil man in court
Just happened to pass by in front of the inn
Where a hundred shafts of brilliance lighted up heaven,

So he thought: "Some treasure must be hidden at the inn,
Could it be that some small demon or monster is staying here?"
He ordered his bodyguards, all four of them:
"Break open the gate of the inn, without delay!"

Liu Xiang was fast asleep in his bed when the four bodyguards broke into the inn. They saw a red light, a purple haze, shimmering in one of the guest rooms where a man lay asleep on his bed. The bodyguards said, "Get up! Who are you? Where did you steal those treasures? His Excellency is here, so confess without delay!" Liu Xiang was scared out of his wits: "Could these be robbers?" He could only get up. When he was brought before the high official, he could only kneel down and report:

"Your honor, my name is Liu Xiang
And I hail from Qingzhou prefecture.
Because of my trip to the capital for fame and glory
I met with an immortal maiden at the foot of Mount Hua.

"The immortal maiden gave me this gold and treasure,
I intended, once in the capital, to present these to our lord."
Upon these words this evil villain was filled with fury,
And the first words he spoke were: "Arrest this cheat!"

So immediately Liu Xiang was put in shackles,
Straightaway he was pushed to the execution ground:
"I'll first have you beheaded, and only then report to the throne,
Best is that I grab your treasure and pearls."

Liu Xiang at this time was overcome by grief,
He wailed and screamed as he wept and tears coursed down.
The injustice he suffered rose straight to heaven,
And so the immortal maiden of Mount Hua was informed.

Swiftly she dispatched heavenly troops and generals
To save the man surnamed Liu on the execution ground:
Just as the executioner raised his sword to cut off his head,
Blue-faced, large-fanged demons protected Liu Xiang!

As a tornado touched down with its whirling winds,
Sand and stones flew about and rain poured down.
The dragon towers and phoenix pavilions all were shaken
And in his golden palace hall [the emperor was frightened].

Our lord and king was frightened out of his wits,
Civil and military officials all were scared.
A member of the Hanlin Academy, Secretary Wang,
Stepped forward and submitted the following request:

"I beg Your Majesty to display his kind grace
And pardon from death that student Liu Xiang."
Upon these words the emperor issued an order:
"The man surnamed Liu is spared from execution."

Liu Xiang and his servants were all pardoned,
With twenty-four bows they expressed their gratitude,
At this sight His Imperial Majesty was very pleased:
"What is the reason that brought you hither?"

Liu Xiang knelt down in the golden palace hall:
"Your Majesty, please listen to my words.
The only reason for me to come to the capital
Was my wish to present treasure to Your Majesty."

When the emperor saw the treasure he was overjoyed,
And he appointed him to office, and not the least!
Liu Xiang was selected to serve as prefect of Yangzhou,
There to be in charge of both military and civil affairs.

Liu Xiang immediately expressed his gratitude
With twenty-four bows, calling himself "your slave."

A good hour was selected, a Yellow Way day:
The order given, he ascended his horse, started on his
  journey.
Very soon after he had left Chang'an,
Mount Hua already appeared before him.

After Liu Xiang had left the capital, he passed by Mount Hua. He quickly ordered two secretaries to prepare incense and candles, and he entered the temple to burn incense and bow before the altar. Liu Xiang said, "That day when I was shackled on the execution ground, it was only through your help that I was saved. Now I have arrived here today, immortal maiden, I hasten to express my gratitude. And I also want to take my leave of you before I pursue my journey."

At this time Liu Xiang took his leave of the immortal maiden,
As filled with love and longing his tears coursed down:
"Before this I consummated my marriage with you,
But now we are separated and apart as yin and yang."

Let's not tell of Liu Xiang's love and longing—
His trip went as easy as if the wind were speeding a cloud.
Earlier than expected he arrived in Qingzhou prefecture,
And the county capital of Anqiu appeared before him.

All the officials of the prefecture came out to greet him,
To welcome His Honor, Prefect Liu!

His parents were filled with joy when they saw their son,
And spread a banquet in the hall, offering drinks.
All his relatives and relations showed up for that feast,
Even those who never had been relatives now were relatives!

Let's not speak of the pride and joy of his parents,
Let's tell how Liu Xiang traveled to his post.
After he had selected a lucky hour, a Yellow Way day,
He took leave of his father and mother.

Let's not waste time on telling of the road he traveled:
Soon Yangzhou appeared before him.
As soon as His Honor had entered his office,
His predecessor transferred all the files.

Let's not speak about the prefect of Yangzhou,
But let's tell instead what happened at Mount Hua.

The fifteenth of the eighth month each year is the birthday of Her Majesty the Queen—Mother of the Western Pond. And all immortals go to Jasper Pond to celebrate her birthday.

Let me tell about the Queen Mother of the West,
Among all immortals of this world she is foremost.

She celebrates her birthday on the fifteenth of the eighth,
The Banquet of the Peaches of Immortality is her feast.

As soon as Jingyang struck the bell three times,
The divine immortals of all directions arrived.
They all arrived at Jasper Pond for the celebration,
Crowding the Garden of the Peaches of Immortality.

Among the immortals who attended the celebration there was a great immortal by the name of True Lord of Mysterious Miracle, who liked to make jokes, so he said teasingly: "Immortal Matron He, Immortal Matron He, everybody claims you have a husband!" Immortal Matron He replied, "I don't have any husband at all, but your own younger sister has one. I'll be happy to tell you all the details!

"No one believes what you tell about me,
But what I'll tell you is not so pretty.
Your own younger sister, Mount Hua's Third Daughter,
Married a mortal man called Liu Xiang.

"Ten months pregnant, she is heavy with child,
That's why she did not show up to meet the immortals."
The immortals who heard this collapsed with laughter:
"Is this juicy scandal really true?"

When the True Lord had heard this, he thought to himself:
"Could it really be true she had an affair?"
His cheeks flushed with red, and he turned around,
Leaving without a good-bye to the other immortals.

Borne on his cloud he traveled fast,
And soon Mount Hua appeared before him.
These are the first words the True Lord spoke:
"Why did you not show up at Jasper Pond?"

Her Majesty Third Daughter of Mount Hua replied, "Brother, I am right now suffering from a serious illness, that's why I did not go to Jasper Pond." The True Lord said, "That's a good one! By day you did not practice meditation, and by night you did not seek enlightenment. And why? Because you wanted to act the slut! At the Banquet of the Peaches of Immortality I have learned all about your sordid little affair. Do you, bereft of all shame, still want to deceive me? Confess!"

When confronted with these questions Her Majesty turned face,
And within a moment she got on her golden-lily feet.

Immediately heaven and earth were darkened and black,
As innumerable divine soldiers rushed out to join battle.

The True Lord recited his miraculous incantations,
And rose into the air, borne aloft on a cloud under his feet.
You with your saber and I with my sword:
The battle of all against all gave rise to clouds of sorrow.

Because Her Majesty was heavy with child,
She eventually had to concede defeat on the battlefield.
When the True Lord saw that his sister started to flee,
He changed into the Long River to block her way.

Her Majesty's miraculous powers were extensive and her magic was without limit, but because she was heavy with child she had to wrap up her cloud and flee over land. When she went on, she saw herself blocked by the Long River and could not pursue her flight. She thought to herself: "As I cannot flee my brother, I will have to fight him once more!"

But the True Lord bound his younger sister with the Lasso That Ensnares Immortals and imprisoned her under Mount Hua, as he shouted, "You may be spared the penalty of death, but you cannot escape your punishment as long as you are alive!" He took up his brush and wrote out three powerful amulets, and so sealed the gate of her grotto. Immediately he dispatched the god of the mountain and the god of the soil to guard Mount Hua and never let her out again!

Let's not describe how the True Lord wrote his amulets,
Let's tell how Her Majesty met with disaster:

Now she was imprisoned under Mount Hua,
Just as the child in her belly was about to be born!
Light and shade, so swift and quick, easily pass by:
On the twenty-sixth of the ninth he was born at midnight.

"My husband gave me a fan pendant of aloeswood,
So I will call him Chenxiang as a sign for his father."
Hastily she plucked a stalk of lucky grass
And wrote a letter as her tears coursed down.

She also took the aloeswood treasure she bore,
And wrapped it all up in the same package.
She then dispatched a single *yaksha* ghost
To take the child to the prefect's office in Yangzhou.

I will not tell how the ghostly judge delivered the child,
Let me tell instead about the prefect of Yangzhou.
Just as he was sitting and pondering in his study,
He suddenly saw right before him a *yaksha* soul!

At that sight the prefect was dumbfounded with fear:
"What injustice have you suffered that brings you here?"
The *yaksha* did not speak the language of the living
And limited himself to placing the letter before him.

Outside the door he heard a little baby crying,
And when he opened it, he was flabbergasted:
The prefect saw the aloeswood fan pendant
And the letter in blood that provided an explanation.

So long as he had not seen the letter, things were fine,
As soon as he had read the letter, tears coursed down.
"It is not that I, Liu Xiang, was without decent feelings,
But I am a mortal man and you are an immortal maid."

He picked his son up from the ground, held him in his arms,
And when he looked at him carefully, he was overcome by
grief.
A flat neck, a broad forehead, heaven's storehouse full;
With tiger back and dragon waist it was a fine young man!

Light and shade are like an arrow and easily pass by:
Chenxiang at seven years of age read the books of the Sage.
And when he had reached the age of twelve, he asked:
"What is the reason that I never see my mother?"

Chenxiang called, "Father,
Where is my mother to be found?"
At this question Liu Xiang's tears coursed down:
"My son, listen to what I will have to say.

"Your mother is not a woman of this mortal world,
She was a goddess in the temple on Mount Hua.
Since she was married to me,
Your uncle is the god Second Son.

"Your mother is imprisoned under Mount Hua,
And no one is able to save her, so what's to be done?"

Upon these words Chenxiang wept and screamed,
And he collapsed right then and there on the ground.

At that sight Liu Xiang started to weep and wail,
With both his hands he helped his son to his feet.
The first words the boy spoke were: "Father,
Tomorrow I will go and save my mother!

"Your son is willing to go and cultivate himself,
And become a wandering Daoist priest.
I will find an enlightened master to be my teacher,
And learn the magic techniques to save my mother."

He did not choose a good hour or a lucky day—
Rare to find is such a filial person as Chenxiang!
On his head he wore a Daoist priest's cap,
His body was wrapped in ocean-blue silk.
A yellow cord of silk was tied around his middle,
And both his feet were shod in red shoes.

Their loud weeping was truly heart-piercing:
Father and son said good-bye—such terrible grief!
The little child left to look for his mother:
There was no end to the weeping of the whole family.

I will not tell of Liu Xiang's weeping and wailing,
I will tell how Chenxiang moved as fast as a cloud!
When he had been on the road for a full six months,
Mount Hua appeared before him.

When Chenxiang had been walking for half a year, he arrived at an old temple on Mount Hua. He went inside to burn incense and to make his bows. He saw the image of a goddess and cried out, "Mother!" Following this, his heart was overcome by sadness. Weeping, he walked out of the temple gate and went straight to the foot of the mountain. He cried, "Mother! Mother!" But, no matter how often he did so, there was no reply. A bystander who saw him said, "This man must be a simpleton!" Upon these words, Chenxiang wept only louder: "My mother, this suffering is unbearable!"

As the red sun's disk sank down in the west,
He rented a room in the inn near the bridge.
Thereupon he suffered a terrible sickness,
It left him no ease by day, no rest at night.

Because Chenxiang was spitting blood,
The innkeeper, who looked after him, was at his wit's end.
After he had been ill in the inn for half a month,
It was clear that this illness would carry him to the grave.

Great White, the Star of Metal, descended to earth,
And manifested himself as a mortal medicine peddler.
As he was passing by the gates of the houses,
He cried again and again, "Miraculous medicine!"

As soon as the innkeeper saw the doctor, he said, "I have here a young traveler from Yangzhou who is beset by an illness. Doctor, do you have some miraculous medicine to save him?" Great White, the Star of Metal, said, "Where is he now? Let me feel his pulse so I can diagnose his illness."[43]

Great White, the Star of Metal, determined the causes:
"One dosage of cool medicine will remove the root of the illness.
He has been exposed to wind and frost in a terrible manner,
So now his body suffers form a severe blood disease."

From his gourd he poured a magic cinnabar pill.
As soon as it was taken, the illness diminished.
Chenxiang immediately got on his feet again,
And with a bow thanked the doctor for saving his life.

As soon as he was done bowing, a whirlwind arose,
And suddenly the doctor was nowhere to be seen!
All the guests in the inn called it a miracle,
And Chenxiang was extremely happy.

His sole desire was to save his mother,
So he took his leave of the innkeeper and traveled on.
Let's not waste any words on the road he traveled—
Before him appeared a pavilion for taking a rest.

Wherever he looked all around him, he saw no man,
Then suddenly a heavy snow started to fall in profusion.
The hunger in his belly was truly unbearable,
But in front of him there was no inn, behind him no village.

---

43. Pulse taking is the chief diagnostic method of Traditional Chinese Medicine.

The sad desperation in his heart was indescribable,
It again alerted Great White, who descended to earth.
In the expansive wilderness on one side,
He conjured up a three-bay[44] straw-thatched cottage.

As Chenxiang was pained by hunger,
He was overjoyed at the sight of the cottage.

The cottage Chenxiang had seen turned out to belong to a soothsayer, who said, "Please come in!" After he had greeted him with a bow, [Chenxiang said:] "I would like to stay here for the night, so I can go on tomorrow."

Furtively Chenxiang silently prayed:
"May this soothsayer tell me my future!"
To this the Star of Metal replied,
"Young man, please listen to what I have to say.

"Your mother endures a thousand kinds of misery,
It is her fate to suffer disaster at Mount Hua.
If you want to meet your mother face-to-face,
You'll have to study with an immortal on Mount Zhongnan."

Upon these words Chenxiang was overjoyed,
Only to be scared by a sudden whirlwind.
In an instant, the soothsayer had disappeared,
No trace was left of the straw-thatched cottage.

Chenxiang said, "Isn't that strange! He must have been a divine immortal! Or could he have been an old mountain sprite?"

Chenxiang bowed to the air to thank the divinity,
And all alone he went ahead on his journey.
Up mountains, across ridges—such toil and suffering,
And soon a high mountain appeared before him.

Chenxiang came to a fork in the road:
"I don't know which road leads to Mount Zhongnan!"

As Chenxiang lifted his head and looked around him,
He saw in front of him a woodcutter.
Immediately he asked the woodcutter:
"Which is the road to Mount Zhongnan?"

---

44. The bay, the space between two columns, is the basic Chinese architectural unit.

When the woodcutter heard this question, he replied, "I wouldn't know whether Mount Zhongnan exists or not. I spend my days cutting wood, so what do I know about the roads? Young man, please go ahead and ask someone else."

Upon these words Chenxiang hastily went on ahead,
And all of sudden he started to wonder:

"The sun sets behind the western hills, it's getting dark,
Where will I be able to rest for the night?
No one's in sight on these towering mountains,
And the sound of the wind in the trees is terrifying.

"In the wild mountains all around I'm bound to die,
A broken thread, a finished road—too painful to bear!
I'm starving with hunger and freezing with cold:
Tonight is going to be the end of my life!"

His loud weeping and great sadness were truly miserable,
It startled the Great White Star in highest heaven.
Great White, the Star of Metal, transformed himself,
He transformed himself into a little buffalo boy.

Astride his buffalo he appeared in the distance on the mountain,
Blowing his short transverse flute without ever stopping.
Just as Chenxiang was about to commit suicide,
The buffalo boy repeatedly called out to him.

After the buffalo boy had saved his life, Chenxiang saw that his savior was a buffalo boy, and he said, "Brother, many thanks for saving my life!" The Star of Metal spoke: "Hurry on!" Chenxiang came forward, grasped the tail of the buffalo, and followed behind him.

At first sight the buffalo boy smiled from ear to ear,
Repeatedly, a number of times, he called out, "Chenxiang!
If you still want to go to Mount Zhongnan,
Follow me and we'll go there together!"

Before he had said these few sentences,
They came to a frightening stone bridge:
"This stone bridge is only three inches wide,
How do you expect me to cross this bridge?"

As soon as Chenxiang saw this bridge, he was frightened out of his wits, and he called out to the buffalo boy: "Brother, this bridge is only three inches wide,

I am bound to slip and fall into the river and die!" The buffalo boy replied as follows: "Young Master, don't be frightened! Hold on to the tail of the buffalo and follow me across the bridge. You will be safe, I assure you!" Chenxiang thought to himself: "I have no choice but to cross this bridge. I can ponder a thousand possibilities, but I can die only once."

As he heard the wind swirl by his ears,
He held on to the tail and crossed the bridge.
But when he looked up to see the boy's face,
He had turned into thin air and disappeared.

When he looked and gazed all around him,
A high mountain appeared before him.
On it was written: "Number One, Mount Zhongnan."
At this sight Chenxiang was filled with joy.

Hurriedly he walked up to Mount Zhongnan,
And as he looked up he saw two men.
Chenxiang immediately knelt down
And repeatedly addressed them as "Master!"

When Zhongli Quan saw him, he laughed out loud,
When Lü Dongbin saw him, he smiled from ear to ear.
Their first words to Chenxiang were the question:
"For what reason have you come to this mountain?"

Chenxiang gave them the following answer:
"Immortals, please listen to my words.
I, your disciple, hail from Yangzhou,
And the two syllables Chenxiang are my name.

"I was born thirteen years ago,
I have suffered this much to save my mother,
All because my uncle hurts my mother—
Imprisoned under Mount Hua she suffers."

Upon these words, Zhongli Quan replied as follows:
"Chenxiang, please listen to my words.
If you want to save your mother, this is the mountain!"
Chenxiang was overjoyed when he heard those words.

White cranes were dancing in pairs in the air,
Magic mushrooms and immortality flowers shone
brightly.

White and fragrant jade trees swayed in the breeze,
The water in the brook by the grotto was blue and clear.

Following the two immortals, Chenxiang arrived at the door of their grotto. All he saw were dark pines and green cypresses; the stairway of white jade was embellished with all kinds of gems, and rustling and verdant bamboos were on all sides surrounded by a balustrade. While many of the immortals there were playing Go, others were humming poems or writing rhapsodies, yet others were playing the flute or other instruments, and some were singing ballads of ancient sages.

The immortals asked him the following question:
"For what reason have you come to Mount Zhongnan?"
Chenxiang answered immediately:
"Immortals, please listen to my words.

"I, your disciple, hail from Yangzhou.
Chenxiang is my name, I am surnamed Liu.
It's because my uncle harms my mother,
I beg you, immortals, to save my mother!"

When the immortals heard the words of Chenxiang, they realized he was a filial son. Light and shade, so swift and quick, pass by easily, and the Midautumn Festival of the eighth month had arrived. When the immortals left for the Banquet of the Peaches of Immortality, [they said:] "We entrust you with the care of everything in this grotto!"

After these orders the immortals left on their clouds,
And Chenxiang could not contain his joy,
As he looked up he saw an immortal peach:
As soon as he swallowed it, his strength doubled!

In the grotto he also found a gourd,
Its long rays of light lit up the universe!
It was filled completely with cinnabar pills,
So he swallowed them all, to the very last one.

Thereupon Chenxiang walked farther inside,
And, lifting his head carefully, looked around.
On a little table stood a bowl of immortal wine,
He promptly drank it to the very last drop.

When he lifted his head again and looked intently,
A precious sword manifested its precious clouds;

A book on the arts of war was lying there,
And at that sight Chenxiang was overjoyed.

When he had then gathered all these treasures,
His strength had immediately multiplied.
In his body he combined all magical powers,
He was capable of thousands of transformations.

"Now I have to hasten quickly to Mount Hua!"
And with his stolen treasures he left on a cloud.

After Chenxiang had stolen all these treasures, he arrived at Mount Hua, riding a cloud. He loudly called out, "Mother!" but no one replied. But to the left of him in the clouds he heard someone hollering, "Chenxiang, you daredevil, shouting and screaming like this!" The god Second Son had arrived!

At the sight of his uncle Chenxiang was startled,
And on both knees he knelt down on the earth.
He called himself a "nephew of a different surname,"
And repeatedly, two or three times, said, "Uncle!"

Upon these words the True Lord was filled with fury,
And cursed him: "Chenxiang, you are no human being!
If you want to meet your mother face-to-face,
You will have to display your might before this mountain!"

To these words Chenxiang replied as follows:
"Uncle, listen to what I have to say:
Don't mess with me if you have no magic!"
Immediately the two of them rose on their clouds!

The True Lord thereupon displayed his might,
And Chenxiang's powers fell somewhat short.
But let's not tell the tale of the battle of these two,
Let me speak about the immortals of the eight grottoes.

When the White Crane acolyte was passing by Mount Hua, he saw two people waging a fierce battle in the clouds, so he could not but stop and watch. The one in front who was fleeing was Chenxiang, while behind him the god Second Son was in close pursuit. As soon as White Crane saw this, he turned his cloud around and hastened to report this to the immortals.

The divine immortals of the eight grottoes were on their way back,
And met with White Crane, who informed them of the situation.

Upon his words the Eight Immortals were filled with fury,
And the Dark Maiden of the Ninth Heaven followed along.

All the immortals of Penglai Island came, to a man;
Fourth Sister of the Hundred Flowers descended from heaven.
When they arrived at Mount Hua, they displayed their might,
And at their sight the True Lord truly was startled!

The True Lord thereupon recited his magic spells,
And heavenly troops and officers joined in the fray—
The four heavenly marshals, Ma, Zhao, Wen, and Yue,
The lord of thunder, the mother of lightning, the six *jia* gods!

The thunder rumbled, lightning flashed, mountains were shaking,
Flying sand and moving stones disturbed the cosmos.
In the front line mountain-shattering cannons were fired,
Heaven was darkened, earth lost its luster because of the fighting!

At the sight of this, the immortals were all dumbfounded,
It startled the bodhisattva Guanyin of the Southern Sea.
From her clouds in the ninth heaven, she observed the fighting:
"The filial son Chenxiang wants to save his mother!"

Riding her cloud she arrived at the Hall of Numinous Heaven,
Where she reported the situation to the Jade Emperor:
"I beseech Your Majesty to swiftly give out the order
That both sides have to lay down their weapons without delay!"

The Jade Emperor agreed to Guanyin's proposal,
And dispatched the Great White Star of highest heaven:
When Great White, the Star of Metal, came down to earth,
Each and every immortal laid down his weapons.

Chenxiang was thereupon filled with joy,
He hastened to Mount Hua and shouted, "Mother!"
He searched east, he searched west, but found her nowhere,
Before the mountain, behind the mountain—not a ghost!

Chenxiang wept till his liver and innards burst to pieces,
He cried, "Mother" some several thousand times,
Until the god of the mountain and god of soil told him:
"Your mother is imprisoned under Mount Hua!"

Upon these words, Chenxiang was filled with grief.
He gripped the mountain-splitting battle-ax in his hand,
Heaved it high, and brought it down with a crashing sound,
And the hundred miles of Mount Hua had been cleft in two!

In the grotto he clasped his own mother in his arms,
Wailing and weeping without restraint he shouted, "Mother!"
This meeting of mother and son was truly bitter—
Heaven was darkened; earth lost its luster because of his weeping.

"Lacking in filiality your child has committed a crime,
Being so late in saving my mother—a major crime!"
His mother may originally have been an immortal maiden,
But now her face was yellow with hunger—she looked like a corpse!

With her unkempt hair and bare feet she was an ugly sight,
She looked exactly like a king of ghosts in her frailty.
Her eyes both lacked sight, she could not see a thing,
She was incapable of walking for even a minute!

When Chenxiang saw his mother, he knelt before heaven:
"Protect my mother and give her back her former beauty!"
In this way Chenxiang practiced his superior filiality—
Her Majesty the Dark Maiden said, "Younger Sister,

"I have here a numinous cinnabar pill;
This is a pill that you should swallow."
As soon as she had swallowed the cinnabar pill,
Her sight was restored, her beauty regained!

Her Majesty expressed her thanks to everyone,
She bowed before the persons who kindly had saved her life:

"You accepted my son as your disciple,
You taught him magic so he could save his mother.
When long ago I had him delivered to Yangzhou,
I did not expect that today we would meet."

After mother and son had thanked all of them,
They arrived before the southern gate of heaven.
Her Majesty arrived at the Hall of Numinous Heaven,
She implored the Jade Emperor to pardon her crime.

The Jade Emperor, the Great Thearch, very happy,
Repeatedly said, two or three times: "Excellent, excellent!
Rare to find is this great filiality of Chenxiang,
We appoint him as Lord of the Amulets of the middle realm."

On receiving this order, mother and son were filled with joy,
And after thanking the Jade Thearch, they descended to earth.
After mother and son had taken their leave,
He returned to Yangzhou to see his father.

Liu Xiang was just sitting and pondering—
How could he know his child was able to ride a cloud?
Five years of separation—his heart was filled with longing,
Day and night he longed for him as his tears coursed down.

"Is your mother alive? Where is she now?
Did you manage to save her or not?"
Chenxiang replied by telling him everything,
And upon his words Liu Xiang was filled with joy.

As father and son wanted to travel to Mount Hua,
They rode on his cloud and set out on their way.
Her Majesty Third Daughter came out to welcome them:
Husband and wife were reunited, a family of three.

We've narrated the "Precious Scroll of the Amulet King":
May immortals and bodhisattvas be filled with joy!

A PEKING DRUM SONG

Collected, translated, and introduced by Kate Stevens

Drum song (*dagu*) is a genre of prosimetric narrative, once common in northern China, performed by one storyteller using a drum. Peking drum singing (*jingyun dagu*, or Peking-accent drum singing) is especially well known for its refined and sensitive portrayal of characters. In Peking drum-singing performances, the drum singer plays the drum and wooden clappers (three pieces of wood); additional musical accompaniment may include the three-stringed *sanxian* (banjolike instrument), a four-stringed spiked fiddle (*sihu*), and, sometimes, even a four-stringed lutelike *pipa*. The pace is set by the singer; the accompanying instruments follow. Line lengths vary and are end-stopped both linguistically and musically, though performers sometimes add variation by transgressing this convention. The overall pace and percussive beats differ in diverse styles of drum singing.

The most famous drum singer of the early twentieth century was Liu Baoquan (1869–1942), "King of the Drum Singers." Liu drew on the drum-singing traditions of Hebei province, which were extended prosimetric narratives, with self-accompaniment. However, after moving to Tianjin to seek a better living, he found that the city audience demanded short pieces. In order to succeed with the city audiences, he adapted short "warm-up" pieces, mostly martial in content, that he had previously used to introduce long narratives. Among the stories he adapted were "City of Baidi" (Baidi cheng), "Visiting Qingwen" (Tan Qingwen), and "Returning by Boat in Wind and Rain" (Fengyu guizhou). His "On the Slopes of Changban" (Changbanpo), an adaptation of an earlier Manchu bannermen's narrative text (*zidishu*), appealed to the generations of women drum singers who followed Liu, the result largely of its depiction of the resolute, wise, and tender Lady Mi. Among them was Zhang Cuifeng, a drum singer who performed the piece in the 1950s in Taipei, Taiwan. The version presented here is based on a 1950s performance by Zhang and a very similar 1982 performance by the accomplished Peking drum singer Sun Shujun.

"On the Slopes of Changban" is based on an episode in the classic novel *Romance of the Three Kingdoms* (*Sanguo yanyi*), set in the third century, following the collapse of the Han dynasty. Versions of the story have also been performed in the northeastern drum-song (*dongbei dagu*) style and in the Suzhou storytelling tradition.

ON THE SLOPES OF CHANGBAN

1

On old roads and ancient hills, bitterly they contend;
The black-haired people in extremis, blood flies red.
Lamps shine on yellow sands, heaven and earth dim;

Dust obscures the constellations, a sound of ghosts crying.
"Loyal and Just" his name resounds, weighty through the ages;
Valiant, indeed, whose death to him is trifling as a feather.
There on the Changban slopes, shedding sweet blood,
Tested to the utmost, is that general, Zhao Zilong.

2

Liu Bei sought refuge in Jiangling, to put up arms and build morale;
All unawares, on Dangyang Road, he met pursuing soldiers.
Breach the circles:
Amid the thicket of sword and spear, lord and vassal torn apart;
Tread the wastes:
Amid the shouts and cries of "Kill!" the princeling drifts abandoned.
The Lady Mi Shi, A Dou at her breast,
Blindly follows moon's light, tears cast on the autumn wind.
Arrows wound her:
As night comes, she swoons away upon the grassy ground;
There is naught but panting breath,
A tiny thread as yet unbroken until the morning dawn.
Mi Shi has swooned away; ah! She once again awakes,
Willowy graceful body just as cold as ice.
Suddenly was heard close by autumn cicada's call;
All I can feel is—
In my thigh—the arrow's wound throb on throb.
Soft eyes slowly open, flitting fireflies in wild dance;
Lift snowy bosom only to find—A Dou lies at my breast.
Fallen leaves heap up in mantle, my self all icy dew;
And vaguely seen—
Fading stars not yet dispersed, a darkling moon.

3

Frail body quivering, Mi Shi sits erect;
See chill mist press the ground, sere grass stretch to horizon.
Dust entombs the lady's sleeves, her fragrant skirt chill.
Blood bestains her lily feet, soaks her stockings red.
Reach forth a hand into my breast, stroke the little prince;
Ah? How can it be . . . ?
He stirs not by a hair, his mouth is closed in silence.
The lady in alarm goes pale, and looks more carefully:
Of course! What's happened is the infant A Dou has cried himself weary
    and fallen fast asleep.
Head bent toward my dear son, "Come now, wake up"—

See the princeling's tiny hands stretch out, eyes open slowly.
He looks at her. As eyebrows knot up, the mouth cracks wide;
The little face nudges at her bosom, knocks against her breast.
The lady, so painfully: "Dear heart, you've woken up.
My son, you will be wanting milk, your little tummy's empty.
How I lament, beloved with a harsh fate, the hunger you endure.
Who can say where your own mother, Gan Shi, is drifting now?"
The lady held the princeling tight, her heart wracked with pain;
Little A Dou, alert and understanding, didn't make a sound.
By this time—
Through lifting fog and thinning mists, dawn about to break;
On treetops and hilly peaks a sun already red.
Shows bloody water in the ditch, stray arrows, bows snapped in two—
Tattered are the tents of war, drums and banners strew the ground;
A few warhorses without saddles do wildly leap and neigh.

4

The lady gazed upon the field of war, her heart broke with pain;
In this dire state who can say if my lord's alive or dead?
I expect that Lady Gan has forfeited her life;
And no sign of Mi Chu, Mi Fang, or Jian Yong.
Of Third Brother Zhang Fei there is no word;
More dreadful yet—
In the melee of battle has he died, the general from Changshan,
  Zhao Zilong?
If lord and liegemen all have fallen at Cao Cao's hand,
I'm left alone, a single woman,
Shorn of land and fief; how could I raise this orphan child?
The lady thought to this conclusion: naught remains but death;
Turned once more to A Dou at her breast as tears welled up.
"*Ai!* Alas for his father—
He wandered for half his life, no other child than this;
A little speck of flesh and blood, not yet fully grown.
If I preserve my honor, then you, son, must surely die;
And at the Yellow Springs,
How shall I face the House of Liu and all its ancestors?"
The lady, full of her predicament, dropped her head and wept;
Ya! From afar I see that
Suddenly the enemy approaches o'er the plain.
Too desperate to take thought of the ache of my wounds,
Clench silvery teeth, set hand to gravestone and pull myself erect.
By the road I espy a peasant hut—Cao's soldiers burned it down,
Leaving there just half an earthen wall where one might hide.

Child in my arms, each step a swoon, I force myself on;
Alas for the lady—
Resolute to raise the orphan, I must endure the pain.
She reached the wall of yellow earth, just beside a well;
Where she stepped
Blood stained the weedy growth, all the ground was red.
How the wound wracked her—pierced her heart, infused her bones;
With panting sighs she drew short breaths. Weak from hunger.
Her cries tremble;
Sweat streaks her powdered face, lustrous orbs close;
Her neck droops; hairpins fall among the weeds, ravaged her visage.
All of a daze, my eyes perceive a vision of army pennons;
All in a blur, my ears hear the sound of army drums.
Body weakened, strength spent, she faces the final test;
Suddenly one voice cries out:
"*Ya!* Right here, after all, is where she lies concealed."
What I see
Is the quick sword and sure lance, all blood bespattered;
White armor, silvery robes covered up with mud.
His all-seeing eyes encompass the whole world;
One man's pure heart revealed to heaven and earth.
Mi Shi lay concealed beside the dried-up well;
A turn of her head showed Zhao Yun's horse come right up to the wall.

5

See the lady, A Dou at her breast, sit with drooping head;
Tragic how disheveled hair and streaked face take away her beauty.
Zhao Yun hurried to dismount, spear in ground, tied up his horse;
Hastened forward to kneel with a flourish and perform obeisance.
He kowtowed and said,
"Milady has been affrighted! Is the young prince safe and sound?
The blame must rest on me, Zhao Yun, your general has failed you."
The Lady Mi,
Joy and sadness intertwined, asked, "Does my lord still live?"
Zhao Yun kowtowed:
"He broke through the enemy ranks, headed straight east."
The lady said,
"This is our nation's fortune, good fortune for the world."
Then she asked, "Who is with him?"
Zhao Yun kowtowed: "Zhang Fei attends him."
The lady nodded, "Zhao Yun, please take your ease."
Zhao Yun stood up erect and bowed deep once more.
"Milady, pray demean your honored self and get upon my horse;

When breaking through,
Above all, hold the princeling tight, don't become alarmed."
The lady said, "You, General, will fight on foot?"
The hero said, "Just so.
Count only on my full hot blood, my scrap of foolish loyalty.
Quickly let Milady make haste to mount my horse;
Your servant will forfeit life itself to see you back to camp."
Lady Mi heaved a sigh, the tears spilled down:
"Only now do I realize what my lord saw so clearly.
Precious are those fine sharp eyes that knew ability,
General Zhao, to the prince's father you are a strong right arm."
Weakly, so weakly, with limbs enfeebled, Lady Mi knelt down:
"General Zhao,
This salute of mine is not made to your person;
I salute your loyal heart."

6

Zhao Zilong knelt down in agitation, and made a kowtow;
See the lady
Speak in mournful tone, tears of blood blown in the wind.
Sadly, so sadly.
Her hand points to her breast, her eyes on the tiger-hearted:
"Take pity on one unaware, unknowing, a little tiny child.
Alas for his father, life half spent, no other son than this;
Now I give up this heavy burden, turn it over to you, Zhao Yun.
This tiny life
Will live or die, survive or perish—it all depends on you;
I pray you act
Half for loyalty and justice, half to store up good deeds.
Could the debtor to your kindness be just Liu Bei and him alone?
Our whole Liu clan's progenitors in the Yellow Springs will bless your generous deed."

7

That good brave man,
Hero's heart wracked with pain, could only bow his head;
See how the lady stands back up, loosening her gown.
From her breast she lifts out A Dou, lays him on her palm;
Her gentle mien bent close to her son's face, a heart full sore.
Saying "Son of mine—
Our joined life as son and mother today has run its course;
Dear little heartache—

Don't yearn for your mother, don't shy away from strangers;
You must not cry, son, and if you meet your august sire,
Just say that as your mother, I . . .
Oh! Let it go! As yet you have no speech."
To Zhao Yun: "Today I turn A Dou over to you—
I don't expect you need me to tell you what to do.
Except that when
Horses surge and men press in, sword blades have no eyes;
You must take care to guard the princeling's life, and protect your person.
My son's hold on life is tenuous, his very bones are soft;
Don't draw your breastplate armor tight, nor leave it too loose."
Zhao Yun said, "Pray Milady, mount my horse with A Dou at your breast;
So that your servant,
Single spear in hand, can break through the enemy camp."

8

The lady, most soberly, said, "General, you err,
A woman, severely wounded, how can I go along?
I cannot ride your mount, and you must use your steed;
It can't be that
'Mid these myriad foes you'd run on foot and fight?
One A Dou in safety is worth a thousand of Lady Mi;
This child is, after all,
The one clan member who can carry on the line.
Just think—
Though one may live a hundred years, yet death comes at the end;
And so today I rejoice in death, and die in a good cause.
On my behalf, over and again salute our ruler's throne;
May his heaven-bound heart ever and always be with the common people.
With great sword sweep clean the dust of war, defeat the nation's traitors;
Hold on high the red sun, reestablish glorious Han.
General Zhao, keep this in your heart; now take the child and go."
Zhao Zilong would not take the princeling, just urged Mi Shi to mount.
The Lady Mi said, "Look over there, enemy forces come."
General Zhao turned back, to get a clear look.
That wise determined woman
Took the weeping infant, resolutely set him down;
She spun about and cast herself into the well, her spirit sent to the shades.
Gladly she chose the right, found eternal rest;
Bury the moth eyebrows in the rush of the Lo River, the chill of the west
wind.
Her praise shall be
Pure as gold or jade, word and deed equally fine;

His heroism
A red sun in clear sky, "loyal and just" made plain.
Zhao Zilong's spear
Pushed over the earthen wall, covered the well mouth over;
As he girded for
A break through the enemy line to save A Dou and go to meet Liu Bei.

A PEKING DRUM SONG

Collected, translated, and introduced by Rulan Chao Pian

The following selection is a translation of part of a recording of "Zi Qi Listening to the *Qin*," a Peking (Beijing) drum song based on the ancient Chinese story of two people who became loyal friends through their shared interest in *qin* (lute) music. The Peking drum song is one of the best-known forms of traditional narrative songs of northern China in recent centuries. It is outstanding in its tuneful melody, strong rhythmic drive, and the highly dramatic quality of its delivery. The virtuosity of its most famous master, Liu Baoquan (1869–1942), also contributed much to the popularity of this art.

In recent years, interest in various kinds of Chinese narrative songs has increased among modern scholars. The songs reflect the interests and tastes of a large cross section of Chinese society; they draw on various traditional musical materials, ranging from folk tunes to sophisticated operatic arias. Many pieces are the product of the skillful polishing and refining of professional performers.

In present-day practice, the Peking drum singer beats, with the right hand, a small, flat drum (about twelve inches in diameter) placed horizontally on a stand and plays, with the left hand, a pair of wooden clappers. The singer is also accompanied by a *sanxian* (three-stringed banjolike instrument), a *sihu* (four-stringed fiddle), and occasionally a *pipa* (four-stringed lutelike instrument). The drum is used today mainly during the preludes and interludes rather than during the singing.

The singer uses, on the whole, a fairly natural voice production. Often the singer adds a broad vibrato on a long-held or an important note. The melody is characterized by a wide range and angular lines with frequent wide skips. Because of this feature, the imitation of speech tones is especially effective. For emphasis, there is frequent use of the two-against-three rhythm both in the voice and in the instruments. At other times, for the sake of emphasis and clarity, words or sentences may be spoken at highly dramatic moments.

This entire piece lasts about twenty-five minutes, approximately the average length of Peking drum songs. There is a fairly long passage sung in the *erhuang* melody style borrowed from Beijing opera. This is a common practice in Peking drum songs, and in "Zi Qi Listening to the *Qin*" the passage appears about one-third of the way from the beginning. Another structural feature, which appears even more regularly in full-length performances, is a section of much faster tempo, with a more clearly defined meter (very often triple time). This usually occurs in the latter portion of the song.

The content of this essentially popular song deals with *qin* music and its ideology, which, even to most Chinese, is an esoteric subject. Near the end, in the climactic section, the rapid questions and answers about the cosmological symbolism of the *qin* remind one of the question-and-answer technique typically found in ballad singing.

ZI QI LISTENING TO THE *QIN*

The lords of the Warring States were in bitter strife;
It was a time to show who was able, who was good.

There was a man called Boya, also known as Yourui;
He was a minister from the state of Qin.

One day the duke of Qin sent him on an errand;
On a trip to pay homage to the king of Chu.

The mission done, the minister got ready to leave;
He boarded the boat; it was the middle of autumn.

They arrived at Han'ang and moored for the night;
Dark clouds were gathering and the rain came fast.

Soon the rain is over, the sun sets in a clearing sky;
You Boya pushes open the cabin door.

Thousands of ripples sparkle like silvery snakes;
Whiffs of sweet-olive fragrance come from the shore.

The autumn breeze again and again is refreshingly cool;
The wind brushes the water, and the water rises against the wind.

In our ears we can hear the rustling, crackling sound of the wind in the autumn leaves,
Falling and scattering all through the autumn forest.

The autumn stars are bright, quiet autumn cicadas hiding in the autumn grass on the autumn hills;
You can hear the poor insects shivering, their chattering, pitiful tone.

The autumn grass is turning brown, the autumn scene fills your eyes, Ah!
Behold, on the eastern horizon rises a brilliant autumn moon.

[*In the* erhuang *melody*]
"Such a beautiful autumn scene brings inspiration;
Come, my servants, bring out the *qin* and light the incense.

"I'll play a piece to amuse myself."
Just then a woodcutter comes walking along the shore.

"Zhong Zi Qi is my name, that's what people call me.
I live at the foot of Saddleback Mountain, the sages' village eight miles away.

"There was a time when I studied hard, but I refused to take an official post;
That is because my parents are old, and there is no one else to assume their care.

"Every day I go into the hills cutting wood to earn my living;
I walk the woods, climb the cliffs, in this way passing my days.

"Today, with my load, I was wending my way home;
When the thick clouds gathered and a shower came.

"In such a storm I could not return;
I hid myself in an old abandoned temple.

"The rain is now over, it is getting dark.
The wind is clear, the moon is bright; with bright moon and clear wind I start my way back.

"In hurried steps I run along the path on the riverbank;
Suddenly I hear someone playing the *qin* near the shore."

At the sound of the *qin*, the woodcutter stops and stands still,
Setting his bundle down on the dusty ground.

It is the tune about Confucius's lamenting the talented Yan Hui, whose life was short;
Then suddenly a string snaps, frightening You Boya out of his wits.

[*In the Peking drum song melody*]
With a string broken, Boya is stunned;
"What? Can there be prowlers on the shore?"

He asks his servants, "Where are we moored?"
The oarsmen reply, "At the foot of a hill."

There are trees and bushes along the banks;
But there are no houses or villages around.

Boya thinks, "So this is a deserted region;
Surely there can be no one listening to me play!

"Men, come in and hear my orders;
Go ashore and search carefully around.

"Look in the reeds, search the shadows under the willow trees";
Then suddenly a voice from the shore speaks: "Please, Your Honor—

"There is no need to search—there are no thieves or robbers here;
It is I, a humble woodcutter, listening to you play.

"I am a woodcutter living in these hills;
I was returning home, when I heard the sound of music.

"Seeing that it was you playing on the *qin*, I stopped in the middle of my way."
You Boya bursts out laughing, "So it is a woodcutter, eh?"

[*Speaks:*]

"So after all this talk, he is nothing but an ignorant woodcutter in these hills. In such a deserted, uncivilized countryside, what learned conversation would you expect from him? He actually claims to be enjoying my *qin* playing! What audacity! Ha, ha, ha!"

[*Sings:*]

Zi Qi says, "If no one in this deserted, uncivilized countryside can appreciate your playing,
Surely you must know that, since there are the *qin* Rules of the Six Taboos, the Eight
Restraints, and the Seven Refusals, you should not be playing when there is not a proper listener around!"

Hearing this, Boya thinks, "His words are well said;
I should not despise this humble country region.

"Servants, go ask him in.
Fetch that woodcutter. I want to talk to him."

A servant, answering, steps off the boat.
He approaches Zi Qi and gives him the message.

Says he to the woodcutter, "When you see His Lordship, kneel and kowtow with respect;
Whatever His Lordship asks you, be sure to answer with care."

Ignoring him, Zi Qi steps on the boat with his head held high;
He salutes Boya simply and says, "I pay my respects."

Boya, maintaining his dignity, does not return the salute;
"Sit down there, I wish to have a chat with you."

Zi Qi calmly accepts and sits himself down.
Boya is dismayed, a frown appears on his face.

With no tea offered, the two sit opposite each other.
"Well! So it was you on the shore listening to my *qin*?"

Zi Qi replies, "My knowledge is very little, it is quite superficial;
Please do not overestimate me."

Boya says, "You claim that you know something about the *qin*;
I have several questions to which I know that few people can
answer.

"Let me ask you, who first handed down this instrument?
Where did he leave it, and why is it called a Yao *qin*?

"What is the proper wood for making the instrument?
Who was it who constructed this particular *qin*?

"If every word you say is accurate,
I shall grant you, Woodcutter, that you are a cultivated man."

Zi Qi answers, "This instrument was handed down by Fuxi;
He left it in Yao Lake, hence it was called a Yao *qin*.

"A *qin* should be made from a paulownia tree;
The upper part of the tree is too light, the lower part too dense; if you cut
out the central portion, the wood is just right.

"There was a famous Zi Qi;
He was the one who made this *qin*."

Boya asks, "In former days, who was the most expert player?
It is said that while he played, certain unusual people often appeared.
At what point did this happen, and who were these men?

"Who lost his life as a result of playing this instrument?
Who laid a charge against another while playing his *qin*?

"If every word you say is accurate,
I shall grant you, Woodcutter, that you are a cultivated man."

Zi Qi answers, "King Wen was the most expert player;
At the climax of his piece, supernatural beings often appeared.

"The son of King Wen, Bo Yikao,
Had once laid charge, while playing the *qin*, against the evil King Zhou,

"Whose consort, Da Ji, plotted a wicked scheme:
She had King Wen eat his own son's flesh, and that was how the young man lost his life."

Boya asks, "How many inches does this *qin* measure across the front?
How many inches at the tail?

[*In fast rhythm*]
"What does the top surface of the instrument stand for?
What, in terms of feet, inches, and fractions is its total length?

"Who was the virtuous Sage, who the man of courage?
How many strings altogether stretched over the top of the *qin*?

"If every word you say is accurate,
I shall grant you, Woodcutter, that you are a cultivated man."

Zi Qi replies, "The *qin* measures eight inches across the front;
The tail end four inches, which stand for the four seasons.

"The rounded top of the fingerboard represents the rounded sky;
Three feet, six inches plus one-tenth of an inch is its total length.

"King Wen was the virtuous sage-king, Wu the man of courage;[45]
Thus there are seven strings stretched over the top of the *qin*.

"The music can reach beyond the clouds and affect the phoenix;
The sound can touch the mountains and the sea, pacifying the tigers and the dragons."

Boya says, "If indeed every word you say is accurate,
Can you tell me what was the theme of the piece that I have just played?"

---

45. The implication is that five of the seven strings use the sol-fa names of the pentatonic scale, while the other two are called *wen* (literally, "civil") and *wu* (military).

Zi Qi replies, "It was about Confucius's lamenting Yan Hui, whose talents were high but whose life was short;
It was the moonlight and the autumn river that moved you to play."

Hearing this, Boya nods his head with amazement;
Wondering how in this country place there is such a learned man.

Boya exclaims, "Marvelous, marvelous, you are really marvelous!"
Zi Qi smiles quietly with calm self-assurance.

Thus the two men, through the *qin*, swore eternal friendship;
Which led to the day when You Boya came once again to Saddleback Mountain to offer sacrifice to his dead friend, smashed his *qin*, never to play again.

AN EXCERPT FROM *JOURNEY TO THE WEST* IN FAST BAMBOO CLAPPER–TALE STYLE

Collected, translated, and introduced by Kate Stevens

"Triple Theft of a Magic Fan" is a scene from the famous Ming dynasty prosimetric novel *Journey to the West* (*Xiyou ji*), written by Wu Cheng'en (1504–1582) and told by Wang Xueyi in the fast clapper-tale (*kuaibanshu*) style of storytelling. In this style, a single performer recites the tale to the rhythm of two handheld clappers: the left clapper is made of five short pieces of bamboo; the right, of two longer pieces.

Wang's performance was videotaped by Kate Stevens and Susan Blader in 1982, during a series of special performance engagements held at Peking University. A number of well-known storytellers, representing diverse storytelling styles in China, participated. Kate Stevens has a long career as an avocational performer of clapper tales in both Chinese and English translation. She constructed the following translation with a beat reminiscent of the original rhythms. As this translation was rendered specifically for oral performance, readers are encouraged to "voice" the text in performance by reciting it out loud.

"Triple Theft of a Magic Fan" is but one of a series of fascinating episodes in *Journey to the West* that have been adapted to an oral medium. The scenes adapted for performance differ greatly from Wu Cheng'en's written text (if that is indeed the source) in terms of language and content, while still following the general plotline of the written text. Wang's version is a synthesis of two of the eighty-one episodes in *Journey*, in which the monk Tripitaka sets off on a long and dangerous journey to India to bring the Buddhist scriptures to China. Set in the Tang dynasty (618–907), the tale unfolds across the exotic lands of western China and Central Asia. On the way, the monk rides a white horse and is accompanied by an anthropomorphic pig named Pigsy, a simple but strong monk named Sandy, and the ultimate trickster figure, the Monkey King, capable of innumerable transformations. On their epic journey, the group is confronted by formidable terrain and endless antagonists, who also have magical powers and use them to try to block their eventually successful quest. In Wang's performed version of this episode, Lady Raksha is one such antagonist whom they meet on their journey.

TRIPLE THEFT OF A MAGIC FAN

Told by Wang Xueyi (Han)

The road to the west is perilous and long,
Where Tripitaka, in search of Buddhist sutras, hurried on.
He rode upon White Dragon, his mount,
Pigsy toted his muckrake and a case of documents,

Sandy had the baggage, monk's staff on shoulder sitting;
Up front scouting out the path was the Heavenly Rioter,
Great Sage Equal to Heaven, Dear Monkey!
As teacher and disciples continued on their way,
The farther they went, the hotter it became.
Pigsy, from behind, kept up his complaint—
"I say, Brother Monkey, let's rest for a bit ere you press on again.
This place is so terribly hot
Old Pigsy may be finished off.
From top to toe I'm oven-broiled,
My heart's a bubbling pot of oil.
My mouth is dry, my tongue's on fire;
Each breath my last ere I expire.
If we go on without a rest,
Old Pigsy will have breathed his last."
Tripitaka called out, "Monkey, disciple, let's stop here—
I too am drenched in sweat; the heat's hard to bear.
The height of late autumn should be coolest of all;
Why is this place just like a cauldron?"
Monkey said, "Teacher, for now, wait by the roadside.
Once I've found out the cause, a plan we'll devise."
As he spoke, quick as a flash he was off ahead—
Saw a white-haired elder by road's edge.
Monkey came over and bowed low—
"Dear sir, may I bother you?
Why does this place heat up so?
Why do earth, sky, hill, and stream give off a red glow?"
The elder turned and gazed his way—
Ai! He couldn't help how his heart did quake.
Saw Monkey's pointy mouth, puffy cheeks—what a sight;
From both eyes there streams out golden light.
The elder looked, then went on to say—
"You . . . you . . . you must be some kind of demon come this way."
When Monkey heard this he laughed out loud—
"Dear elder, no need to fear, no need to cower.
My teacher is Tripitaka—
I'm from Fruit and Flower Mountain,
    Great Sage Equal to Heaven, the Monkey King!"
When the elder heard this, he nodded his head;
Hand stroking his beard, these words he said:
"This place has been hot for quite some time;
Throughout the four seasons it's always the same.
It's all because, off to the west sixty miles away,
The ridge of Fiery Mountains blocks the way.

The mountain flames shoot up ten miles high,
Reach to the clouds, block sun from sky.
For miles about, in a circular course,
No blade of grass, the earth all scorched.
Stones cook until they just dissolve,
Lumps of iron melt, like a bowl of broth.
To make our meals, no fire is lit;
It cooks so fast, you can't believe it.
On the walls is where our hearth cakes cook.
Set a pot of water in the yard, it boils in a trice, makes noodle soup!
You can tell it's really hot!"
Monkey said, "In such heat, how can crops be made to grow?"
The elder said, "Just heed my tale, don't press me so.
On Jade Cloud Mountain, there's Palm Cave.
Over three hundred miles from here—southwest it lies.
In Palm Cave lives Lady Raksha, a female demon;
Her husband is known as the Ox-King Demon.
In that cave, minor demons, one after another—
They all call Lady Raksha Queen Mother.
She has one treasure, a palm-leaf fan,
It's an object with powers grand.
If you use it to fan at those mountains just once,
On the spot, the fire's put out, light is smothered.
If you fan the mountain a second time,
Sand and stone fly about, the winds are wild.
If you fan the mountain three times in all,
The heavens open, kind rains fall.
Each decade we ask her to visit one time,
So we can put out the flames, plant our grain.
It's no easy matter to ask her here,
We must bring peaches and wine, duck, chicken, fish, and flesh of ass,
  horse, ox, and sheep."
When Monkey heard this, he said his thanks,
Took leave of the elder, returned to road's edge.
He told Tripitaka what had been said;
It left Tripitaka worried and sad.
"Oh? Monkey, with such fierce flames, how can we pass?"
Monkey said, "Teacher, don't worry, don't get upset.
Let me go to Palm-Leaf Cave and borrow that fan;
We'll fan out the flames, then make up the time."
He turned to his brothers with these words—
"You must take care of Teacher, stay on guard."
Pigsy and Sandy replied, "We know;
Brother, you needn't worry so."

Monkey nodded and said, "Here I go!"
In a flash of golden light, he headed off to the southwest.
Monkey, with one somersault, could span one hundred eight
thousand leagues,
So for a mere thousand—he gave a little wiggle—he's there.
At the door of the cave, he looked with care—
It happened the maidservant was standing there.
Monkey said, "Maid, please go inside and pass the word on—
Just say I have urgent business and need your mistress for a consultation."
The maidservant asked, "What's it about?
Who are you to come to our spot?"
Monkey said, "My name is Pilgrim Sun,[46]
My teacher is the monk, Tang Sanzang.
We four go to the Western Land to get the sutras true,
But find the Fiery Mountains block our way through.
So we came to borrow the palm-leaf fan,
To fan out the flames and cross the mountain pass."
When the maid heard this, so diligent,
She hurried inside to see her mistress.

Monkey's every word to her mistress she relayed;
When Lady Raksha heard it, on the spot her face went yellow with rage.
"Damned ape! I remember how you wrongly killed my own dear son;
Son and mother torn apart—what desolation!
I was going to find you to settle the score;
How convenient you brought yourself right to my door."
With a clang she drew her sword as she rushed outside:
"You impudent monkey, don't think you can hide!"
Monkey hurried over to bow in greeting—
"Dear sister, tell me, how are you keeping?"
Lady Raksha pointed right at him: "Hold your tongue!
You call me 'sister'—what's the reason?"
Monkey said, "Brother Ox and I have sworn brotherhood.
If I call you 'sister,' why so I should."
"Since you admit the sacred pledge you made,
Then why—then why did you cause the ruin of my young lad?"
Monkey said, "Red Boy thought to eat my teacher Tripitaka's flesh,
That is why he was suppressed.
The Goddess of Mercy has taken him in—
He's become her Boy of Goodly Wealth, that's better than being a demon."
Lady Raksha said, "Oh, if my son's not met his death,

46. His surname, Sun, also means "monkey."

When can he return to his mother's hearth?"
Monkey said, "First, you'd better lend me the fan;
The rest can wait for a later plan."
When Lady Raksha heard he would borrow her fan,
With a cold laugh she spoke her mind:
"Heh, heh, heh! You can borrow it, no trouble there—
Just let me first take three sword swipes at you—then I'll concur."
Monkey said, "Okay, you're on.
Eight or ten strokes will do no harm."
As he spoke, he doffed his cap, neck out straight.
Lady Raksha took sword in hand, on high 'twas raised.
Shua, shua, shua, with never a pause she sliced down with verve.
How she yearned to turn Monkey into meat conserve!
Who'd have thought, as she sliced away ten times and more,
Solid as Mount Tai he stood at her side—
Giggling with laughter, face upraised?
When Lady Raksha saw things weren't going well,
With hurried steps she turned and fled.
When Monkey saw this, he moved fast,
Came right up and caught her dress.
"Sister, if that fan to me you'll lend,
It'll save getting into an argument."
    Lady Raksha said, "I won't agree,
Let's see the worst you can do to me."
Monkey said, "If that's your decision, let's have no regrets—
First, I'll give you a taste of my rod—how does it set?"
As he spoke, into his ear he reached his hand;
Took out Sea Queller, his Gold-Tipped Staff.
And then he called out one word, "Expand!"
It grew thick as a bowl, with a six-foot span.
With a rush, he laid it on—
Tried Lady Raksha with "Ridgepole Pressed on Mount Tai."
Lady Raksha saw trouble ahead—
Used her twin swords for self-defense.
There in the cave the two joined battle:
  One to, one fro,
  One up, one down,
  One left, one right,
  Over and under,
  Every place.
Shadow of a staff, gleam of a blade.
You couldn't have drunk a cup of tea down
Ere Lady Raksha was so weary, sweat soaked her gown.
She just parried his blows, couldn't attack,

Eyeballs aspin, she thought of a trick.
Stretched out her hand for the magic fan—
Reached out to meet him, like a great arched span.
Aiming right at Monkey,
    She gave the fan a great swing—my goodness me!
On the spot she
    Fanned away Great Sage Equal to Heaven, Dear Monkey King!
Monkey felt the wind go past his ears in a whistling blast,
Floating and whirling, he headed southwest.
Lady Raksha put the fan away, went on in,
Got washed up, put fresh clothes on.
With a gesture, she summoned the serving maid, "Maid!
Brew me up some tea, what a thirst I have."
The maidservant poured out a cup of tea,
Brought it in, and set it down quite deftly.
Lady Raksha took up the bowl and looked it over;
The tea had a strangely yellow color.
She blew off the leaves, and drank the brew:
Gulp after gulp, it tasted good too.
In a trice, that ape's been fanned off myriad leagues;
When he tries to return—it'll be some time before he reappears.
Lady Raksha felt quite pleased with herself;
When suddenly a voice was raised in a yell:
"Fierce, fierce, very fierce!
Hard, hard, hard to handle!
Far, far, so very far!
Fast, fast, so very fast!
With one stroke, I was fanned off fifty thousand leagues;
Yet, at my return, you've only just made the tea!"
When Lady Raksha heard this, she got a scare—
"Maid, who is it yelling wildly here?"
The maidservant came forward to respond:
"Well, my guess is, that monkey bonze."

"Why can't I spot that damned ape anywhere?"
When Monkey heard this, he laughed aloud
And from her belly he spoke up and said:
"Sister, don't look further, don't ask about,
I'm hidden right inside your gut!"
"What?!" Lady Raksha heard this and felt afraid;
Screwed up her courage before she said:
"Damned ape, with one stroke I fanned you some thousands of leagues,
How come you got back with such great speed?"
Monkey said, "One somersault can take me myriad leagues;

This little trifle is nothing to me.
Let me tell you—I've got a pill to hold the wind in thrall;
Your palm-leaf fan can do me no harm at all."
Lady Raksha said, "Humph! My vitals are fierce-burning fire;
Get out or, in a bit, I'll scorch off all your monkey fur."
Monkey said, "Laozi's furnace was hotter still;[47]
While in it, I complained of a chill.
Just look! Here's your heart, liver, and lungs;
This your kidney, that your gut."
As he spoke, he did monkey *taijiquan*,
Used her liver and lights as his exercise camp.

Lady Raksha with a thump falls to the ground—
Rolls in agony as her cries resound:
"*Aiya! Aiya! Aiya! Ma!* How it hurts!
    Aiya! Uncle! Uncle! Please spare me, do!"
Monkey said, "How does the flavor appeal to you?
Maybe your teacher should practice with his Gold-Tipped Staff?"
"Dear uncle! Dear uncle! No more drills, no more drills—
    We can make an arrangement about the fan."
Monkey said, "Decide! Will you lend it or not?"
"I will! I will! It's already waiting on the tabletop."
Monkey said, "Open your mouth wide while I look outside."
Lady Raksha hurried to spread her mouth wide.
Monkey crept right up her throat—
The fan really lay on the tabletop.
With a whirr, out he flew,
Seized the fan, his shape resumed.
Taking great strides, he headed outside,
"Thank you, Sister, for your aid. Good-bye!"
In a flash, he somersaulted from the scene;
Lady Raksha ground her teeth, swore at Monkey King,
"You damned ape! You say you have the better art;
This time we'll see who wins, who loses out.
My fan will bring about your demise—
Fan away! The more you fan, the fiercer the fire.
Laozi's furnace didn't do you much damage—
Fiery Mount will turn your monkey fur to ash."
Lady Raksha was all riled up, scolding Monkey King,
Of a sudden from the doorway, *pa pa pa!* rang sounds unceasing.

---

47. This refers to a famous episode from the early part of *Journey to the West* in which Monkey is imprisoned in a fiery alchemist's furnace.

"Hey! Open up!" The maid came forward to report:
"Mistress, my goodness, there's someone at the door."
"Yes, I heard them. I'll open up, no need to fret."
Lady Raksha opened the cave door, attentively looking—
Oh! It was her own husband, the Ox-King Demon.
See how he held the reins of his Beast with Golden Eye;
On its beast neck hung small bell chimes.
Lady Raksha came forward, a greeting she gave;
The maidservant came up to take the reins.
The Ox-King bowed in return and went on in.
Lady Raksha's eyes were tear-filled and red-rimmed.
Ox-King came to the banquet, took his seat;
"Wife, you're sobbing and weeping, why is that?"
Lady Raksha told what had happened from the beginning,
Ox-King gave a strange cry, swore at Monkey King.
"Damned ape! You are really too unmannerly and wild!
You're in my hands now—
I'll have your noggin move house, leave your neck behind!
I'll eat your monkey flesh for food,
And make your monkey blood into soup!
What remains of monkey bones,
Gnash and gnaw—they'll feed the wolves."
As Ox-King spoke, his anger soared,
Lady Raksha, at his side, kept saying, "My lord!
My lord! Over such a trifle, why let your temper flare so high?
Should rage make you ill, it's not worthwhile!"
Ox-King said, "Now you've gone and lent our fan!
You've got to expect me to get mad."
When Lady Raksha heard this her smile grew broad;
Face wreathed in smiles, addressed my lord:
"My lord, just now I lent him a fan that was fake—
So if he isn't dead yet at least his monkey fur is burned to ash."
"Oh, if that's so, where is the real fan to be found?"
Lady Raksha said, "Hidden right here in my mouth."
As she spoke her mouth opened wide;
Spat out a tiny fan bathed in golden light.
No bigger than a peach leaf, furled;
With marvelous dangles set with pearls.
As she spoke she handed it over.
Ox-King took fan in hand, over it did pore.
"Wife, why is this fan so very small?
Not like it used to be at all?"
"Dear Ox-King, you've been away two years, no more;
Yet our family treasure—you've forgotten its lore.

Don't worry about its seeming small;
Stroke the dangles—on the spot it's twelve feet long."
"Oh, that ape got me so angry my head could burst—
So I'm all topsy-turvy, my head's in a whirl."
Whereupon he took a sip of wine,
Into his mouth was the fan consigned.
"Dear wife, just now you spoke of the Monkey Pilgrim—
I, too, am a bit afraid of him."
"Ah? Ox-King! You're scared too?" "Just so.
Remember how, at Fruit and Flower Mountain, he was the chief—
Everyone praised him, within the Four Seas?
In heaven, he defeated spirit-led brigades;
In hell he altered the Book of Life and Death.
He can summon wind and rain, on thunderbolts ride;
He can make hill and sea move aside.
He wields an iron staff, tipped with gold;
Comes and goes like a demon, martial and bold.
His seventy-two transformations, wondrous to see;
Make gods and spirits tremble, demons shake with fear.
Of course, Wife, you would hesitate;
But even I, the old Ox-King, should I face Monkey, might meet my fate."
"Dear Ox-King, can it be . . . can it be you've had too much wine?
You praise that ape so, tell me why?"
When Ox-King heard this he laughed in derision—
"Wa ha, ha ha, Sister! How could you have thought Monkey was the Ox-King Demon?"
As he spoke, hand o'er face passing,
Revealed Sage Equal to Heaven, Dear Monkey King.
Lady Raksha gave a weird cry and drew her sword—
Monkey flew out the cave door, giggling still more.
Of a sudden from on high there came a cry "Hey!
Upstart ape, don't think you can hide!"
Monkey looked up, gazed around—
It was Lady Raksha's husband, the real Ox-King.
You can tell Jade Cloud Mount will be a battle scene—
Next time, Monkey will contend against the Demon Ox-King!

TWO SHANDONG FAST TALES

Collected, translated, and introduced by Eric Shepherd

Shandong fast tales *(kuaishu)*, as they are performed today, represent a relatively new oral-performance genre, having evolved in the 1930s out of a similar genre known as telling Wu song. A form of rhythmic storytelling, Shandong fast tales involve a single performer chant-singing to a rhythm set by rapping together two half-moon-shaped brass plates. Performers wear traditional storyteller's robes and use no other props. Most stories are characterized by end rhyme and a single rhyme that is maintained throughout the whole story (in all voices other than plain speech). Shandong fast-tale performances are delivered in a generic Shandong dialect that originated in the southwestern area of the province but has incorporated characteristics from other areas of Shandong, so that it is an artistic language that does not match the speech patterns of any one locality. Performances are marked by the extensive use of bold body movements, abundant facial expressions, and other paralinguistic devices.

"Second Brother Ma" and "Learning to Write" are Shandong fast-tale performances given by Wu Yanguo, a professional storyteller from Qingdao who was fifty-five years old when his stories were videotaped in 2004. No written form affords the opportunity to experience Wu Yanguo's unparalleled comical expressions, to hear the beat of the brass plates or the different voices of the various characters, or to see how Wu's demanding physical movements enhance the verbal portion of the performance. In an attempt to convey a sense of the acted delivery, some movements, expressions, and voice shifts are indicated in brackets.

SECOND BROTHER MA

Performed by Wu Yanguo (Han)

[*Narrator's voice*] There once was a comrade called Second Brother Ma.
[*Turning to the side to address an audience member*] This comrade asked, "Who is Second Brother Ma?" Big Brother Ma's little brother! [*Small pass on the brass plates to set the rhythm*]
There once was a comrade called Second Brother Ma,
One day, he was holding a straight razor, shaving his beard raw [*leans forward to shave*].
There was this fly that began to really piss him off,
It landed on the tip of his nose, and to and fro it began to crawl [*crosses eyes*].
Second Brother Ma itched so bad he couldn't stand it at all.
He wiggled and squiggled his face into a ball [*contorts face as if annoyed by fly*].
[*Addressing the audience*] He went after him with this kind of vigor . . . [*looking cross-eyed at the fly on the tip of his nose and concentrating with all his might*].

That fly just couldn't keep his balance and was about to fall;
He could only spread his wings and fly toward the wall [*pointing in the direction of the insect's flight*].
Second Brother Ma again picked up the straight razor to shave his beard [*picks up razor*].
When back came that fly to flirt with him and all [*appears to see fly coming and landing on his nose*].
He thought to himself [*shifts to young male voice*]: "You little rascal [*looking at fly*]—
If I don't make minced meat of you today,
There's no way this beard of mine is going to get shaved at all."
[*Shift to narrator's voice*] You can just see him holding that straight razor [*as if holding razor in left hand*].
Like this, inching it forward little by little [*moving razor closer and closer to nose*],
His mind set only on killing that fly.
The only sound was the "swoosh" as he let the razor fall [*making chopping motion*].
The tip of his nose was chopped into a little ball.
He hurt so bad he grabbed at his nose [*dropping razor*],
As the razor in his hand dropped to the floor.
How could it be such a coincidence?
His toes were covered by only a sandal.
There was only the sound "kerplunk,"
Ouch! His toe was chopped clean off [*jumping and cringing in pain as razor hits toe*].
He picked it up and pushed it on his nose [*reaching down*],
Stitching it up without a wrinkle [*covering nose and stitching it up*].
He rubbed on every oil and balm [*reaching for balms and rubbing on nose*],
Grabbing a bandage he wrapped it in a ball [*wrapping nose again*].
In merely two days it began to grow,
Second Brother Ma wasn't ashamed to be a regenerative surgeon at all.
There was just one little problem,
It's on the tip of his nose that he has to trim his toenail [*making cutting motion with two fingers in front of nose*].

LEARNING TO WRITE

Performed by Wu Yanguo (Han)

[*Facing audience in narrator's voice*]
Comrade Zhang was learning to write;
His teacher patiently taught him just right.
When learning to write, start with the easy;

In the beginning, it can't be too difficult.
The character "one," is one line [*holding up one finger*];
For the character "two," draw two strokes [*holding up two fingers*].
When Comrade Zhang heard this, he thought to himself:
"No need to ask. The character 'three' is definitely three strokes" [*arrogantly shaking his head and holding up three fingers, in young man's voice*].
[*Narrator's voice*] Oh so clever! Oh so ingenious!
His guess was a perfect match to what the teacher said.
So he didn't ask how to write the character "four" [*holding up four fingers*],
Just gathered up his things and headed out the door [*gathering imaginary things*].
No matter whom he bumped into, he opened his mouth,
He bragged to everyone how easy it was [*bragging in young man's voice*]:
"It's not that I'm tooting my own horn,
But I can draw up any kind of essay you can think of!"
[*Plain speech, aside to audience as performer*] Other people write but he draws!
One day, Old Man Ten Thousand from the PLA paid him a call.
[*Narrator's voice*] Old Man Ten Thousand in his left hand carried a letter [*carrying imaginary letter*];
With his right he led his granddaughter, Xiaohua [*leading imaginary Xiaohua*].
They entered the gate and called out to Comrade Zhang:
[*Plain speech; knocks on imaginary door while making knocking sound followed by the sound of door opening; facing left, speaking in old man's voice*] "Is Comrade Zhang at home?"
[*Turning to face right, speaking in young man's voice*] "Oh, please come in, please come in. Make yourself at home."
[*Turning to face left as old man*] "Oh, I
Want to ask you to write a letter for me,
Asking my son to make a trip back home."
[*Plain speech; turning to face right as Zhang*] "Goodness, Grandpa, a matter as small as this is no problem at all! No problem at all! Old Man Ten Thousand, what is your son's last name?"
[*Plain speech; turning to left as old man*] "Comrade Zhang, my last name is Ten Thousand. My son's last name is *also* Ten Thousand!"
[*Plain speech; turning to right as Zhang*] "Oops, Grandpa, how silly of me. How silly of me. What is your son's first name?"
[*Turning to left as old man*] "Comrade Zhang, the characters in my son's first name are 'one hundred' and 'one thousand.'"
[*Shift to narrator's voice*] Comrade Zhang thought: that's a problem.
[*Shift to young man's voice*] "Ten Thousand, Hundred, Thousand. Ten Thousand, Hundred, Thousand. That means I have to write eleven

thousand one hundred strokes!" [*Shift to narrator's voice*] Comrade Zhang was at a loss for words,
So he pulled out his ballpoint and just began to write [*pulling out imaginary brush*].
He drew a line on top [*as if holding writing brush, moves it in each direction he speaks*],
On the bottom he drew,
To the left he drew,
To the right he drew,
He drew a horizontal line,
And drew a vertical mark,
Half here, half there,
Another over there.
In all he drew for two straight hours [*holding up two fingers*],
Until his two arms were completely numb [*holding arms as if numb*].
To the side, Xiaohua couldn't keep quiet anymore [*looking up to the left, in girl's voice*]:
"Uncle, Uncle, write faster. I want to go home for dinner" [*pointing toward home*].
[*Shift to narrator's voice*] Hearing this, Comrade Zhang got really fired up,
Put down his ballpoint, and had his say [*puts down brush, looking down to the right, in an angry man's voice scolds Xiaohua*]:
[*Plain speech*] "Little girl, little girl. You think your uncle writes too slowly, do you?
You didn't stop to think your dad's [*pointing and accusing*]
Name is really quite complex.
For the character 'one' you have to draw one stroke,
The character for 'two' takes two lines,
This 'Ten Thousand, Hundred, and Thousand'—
Altogether I have to draw eleven thousand one hundred strokes."
"Oh, Uncle, Uncle, don't get mad [*looking up to the left, in girl's voice, dancing and holding skirt as if excited*].
If writing a letter is just making some marks,
There's a really good way to quickly make marks.
At our house we have a big broom [*pointing in direction of home*].
One swipe with that, and you've got several hundred strokes [*using both arms, making a sweeping motion*]!
[*Plain speech*] Uncle, I'll go get it for you."
[*Looking down to the right, in old man's voice, motions for Xiaohua to come back, then points in direction of home*] "Xiaohua! Wait a second, your grandpa also has a big mop. I think you better bring that back, too,
So the two of us can help him write." [*Both arms make sweeping motion*]

TWO VERSIONS OF "WU SONG FIGHTS THE TIGER" FROM THE YANGZHOU *PINGHUA* TRADITION

Collected, translated, and introduced by Vibeke Børdahl

Yangzhou storytelling (Yangzhou *pinghua*) has more than four hundred years of documented history and is still a living tradition. Situated at the junction of the Grand Canal and the Yangtze River, Yangzhou was formerly a city of great cultural and commercial importance. Dependent for its wealth largely on the salt trade and river transport, it was famous for its exquisite garden culture, its arts and handicrafts, its rich intellectual milieu, and its proud tradition of storytelling.

Around the turn of the twentieth century, Yangzhou had more than twenty sites for daily storytelling, either in teahouses or in so-called storytellers' houses (*shuchang*). The storytellers would alternate among the venues, usually working for a period of three months at one place. Often they would take to the roads and accept work in towns and villages all over the area where the dialect is spoken, including Nanjing and Shanghai.

In Yangzhou, the most respected storytellers' houses were situated in the middle of the old town, in the area called Jiaochang, where the present-day storytellers' house is still to be found: the Great Enlightenment Storytellers' House (Da Guangming Shuchang). Usually an engagement is for a couple of months, during which time the artist performs a cycle of tales in daily installments of two hours' duration. Each day's performance adds a new episode to the story, and the audience, mostly elderly men, is therefore of a rather constant character.

The Yangzhou dialect as spoken by the storytellers carries on a long historical tradition of speech with special characteristics, different from the language of ordinary townsfolk. The local dialect is modified according to the special demands of the acting and telling technique, comprising a number of different speaking styles (*shuokou*), or registers. The storytellers have developed a correspondingly rich vocabulary of technical terms for their art. For example, the speaking styles of "square mouth" (*fangkou*) and "round mouth" (*yuankou*) have a major role in dialogue as well as in narrative passages. "Square mouth" is spoken with a distinguished slow pace and manifests a number of phonetic and grammatical features reminiscent of old-fashioned "Yangzhou officials' language" (*Yangzhou guanhua*) or "northern dialect" (*beifanghua*). This style is used for impersonating the dialogue of high-status characters, for reciting poems, for narrating more serious portions of the plot, and for presenting some storyteller's comments—for example, those in which the moral is pointed to in the form of a saying.

"Round mouth" is very close to the way the dialect is spoken by ordinary citizens of Yangzhou, but there are certain special pronunciation habits among the storytellers that characterize even this register as a particular artistic medium. "Round mouth" is used for impersonating the dialogue of low-status characters and ordinary persons, for narrating less serious and humorous portions of the story, and for presenting most of the storyteller's comments.

Yangzhou storytelling, like other local traditions of storytelling in China, is divided into a number of specific schools of storytelling (*jia* [house], *men* [door], *pai* [branch]), classified according to their repertoires and founding masters. The oldest and major schools of Yangzhou storytelling have grown up around the themes of *Romance of the Three Kingdoms* (*Sanguo yanyi*) and *Outlaws of the Marsh* (*Water Margin* [*Shuihu zhuan*]). Apart from these great tales, Yangzhou storytelling comprises about sixty other themes or cycles of tales, called books (*shu*), but fewer than half of them are still in living memory.

Ultimately, themes from *Water Margin* go back to China's "father of storytelling," Liu Jingting (1587–ca. 1670), who came from Yangzhou prefecture and was most famous for his performance of "Wu Song Fights the Tiger," which was described in a lively fashion by a contemporary witness:

> Pockmarked Liu from Nanjing had a dark complexion, and on his face there were lots of scars and pimples. He was careless and indifferent about his looks, as if he were made from clay or wood. He was a master of storytelling. He told one session of storytelling a day; the price was a tael of silver. Even if you came ten days ahead to make an appointment and pay the fee, you could not be sure he would be free. . . . I once heard him perform, in the plain style of telling [without musical accompaniment], the tale of "Wu Song Fights the Tiger on Jingyang Mountain," and it was very different from the version transmitted in books. His descriptions and illustrations went into the finest details, but he also knew where to cut the thread and make a pause, and he never became talkative. His voice rang out like a big bell. Whenever he came to an exciting point, he bellowed and raged so that the noise seemed to make the house fall down. At the point where Wu Song arrives in the inn and orders wine, there is nobody in the inn. At the sudden outcry of Wu Song, the empty jars and pots send out a ringing sound. Thus he would add color to every interval, and he did his utmost in his care for detail. Only when his hosts were sitting quite attentively and cocking their heads to listen would he begin to tell the story. But if he noticed some among the servants whispering to one another, or if the listeners were yawning or showing other signs of sleepiness, he would stop immediately, and nobody could force him to start again. Every evening when the tables had been wiped and the lamps snuffed, and the simple tea bowls were passed around in all calmness, he would slowly begin to speak.[48]

Historical sources do not allow us to establish a direct lineage from Liu's time to present-day storytellers. The cycle of *Water Margin*, transmitted in an unbroken

---

48. Zhang Dai (1597–1684?), *Tao'an meng yi* [*Recollections of Tao'an's Past Dreams*] (Shanghai: Shanghai guji chubanshe, 1982), 68.

chain from master to disciple, goes back in direct lineage seven generations to the founding father, Deng Guangdou (fl. 1821–1862), and the so-called Deng school of *Water Margin*, but it also has a parallel lineage going back five generations to Xu Dianzhang (fl. 1821–1862) and his disciple Song Chengzhang (fl. 1862–1908), after whom the Song school of *Water Margin* was named.

The Wang school of *Water Margin* (Wangpai Shuihu) takes its name from the most famous storyteller in China in the twentieth century, Wang Shaotang (1889–1968), and his descendants. The history of the Wang school goes back four generations as a family tradition, and its repertoire consists mainly of four ten-chapter cycles telling the adventures of four famous heroes among the outlaws in Shandong during the twelfth century: Wu Song, Song Jiang, Shi Xiu, and Lu Junyi. The sagas are called, respectively, "Ten Chapters on Wu Song" (Wu shi hui), "Ten Chapters on Song Jiang" (Song shi hui), "Ten Chapters on Shi Xiu" (Shi shi hui), and "Ten Chapters on Lu Junyi" (Lu shi hui).

Wang Shaotang's father and uncle, in their youth, changed profession from small moneylenders to storytellers. The two brothers studied with masters from the two lines of *Water Margin;* one belonging to the Deng school, the other to the Song school. Wang Shaotang's father, Wang Yutang, combined elements from both schools in his repertoire, and Wang Shaotang further developed this trend and also learned much from other contemporary great masters. He was a highly creative artist, and through study as well as personal life experience, he managed to elaborate and swell his performances of the "Ten Chapters on Wu Song" to seventy-five days of daily sessions in the storytellers' house, about double the length of his elders'. His performances of the other ten-chapter cycles of the full repertoire underwent similar growth and expansion.

Wang Shaotang was extremely careful and strict in the education of his heirs. Since he had no son of his own, he accepted and adopted his brother's son, Wang Xiaotang (1918–2000), as his son and disciple. Later, Wang Xiaotang's daughter, Wang Litang (b. 1942), was also educated in the family tradition, by both her father and her grandfather. There were also storytellers from other schools who wanted to learn from Wang Shaotang and who took a personal initiative in this direction, such as his colleague Ma Fengzhang (1899–1965) and the storyteller Li Xintang (b. 1935), who also studied with Wang Xiaotang. In 1960 and 1961, the government arranged for a group of young aspiring storytellers to have classes with the old master: Ren Jitang (b. 1942), Hui Zhaolong (b. 1945; also a student of Ma Fengzhang), and his last student (*guanmen dizi*), Chen Yintang (b. 1951). They studied irregularly under his guidance for a couple of years, and some continued as students under Wang Xiaotang and Wang Litang. Thus as late as the 1990s, there was still an active group of middle-aged storytellers who saw themselves as the heirs of the Wang school tradition. In recent years, the young storyteller Ma Xiaolong (b. 1980) has studied with Ren Jitang and Hui Zhaolong and has both the "Ten Chapters on Wu Song" and the "Ten Chapters on Lu Junyi" in his repertoire.

The following two versions of "Wu Song Fights the Tiger" are based directly on oral performances, recorded on audiotape. The first text was translated from a copy of a radio broadcast by Wang Shaotang in Nanjing in 1961. The second text was translated from a tape recording of a performance by Wang Xiaotang in his home in Zhenjiang in 1992. The texts are rendered in authentic, nonrevised form, and passages that are the same in both versions are translated in the same way, so as to reveal more clearly to the reader both the similarities and the differences between two storytellers in a close hereditary relationship. Thirty years divide the performances by the two masters of the Wang school, father and son. (Some readers may wish to read only one of the versions, since they are quite similar, despite differences in details. It is, however, instructive to see the differences and similarities selected by the members of different generations of storytellers.)

The recording by Wang Shaotang includes the first session of thirty minutes of the series he performed for the radio: the beginning of the episode of "Wu Song Fights the Tiger" in which Wu Song arrives at the inn of Jingyang town, drinks the strong wine "Three bowls and you cannot cross the ridge" (San wan bu guo gang), and leaves the inn, whereupon the young innkeeper and the waiter Xiao'er (Little Second) start quarreling about the silver piece that Wu Song left as payment and tip.

Wang Xiaotang's performance has the length of a normal session in the storyteller's house, about two hours, including a break in the middle. This version includes the episodes that would usually be told on the first day of the saga "Ten Chapters on Wu Song," continuing after the quarrel over Wu Song's tip with the story of Wu Song's climb up Jingyang Ridge, where he discovers the official proclamation about the dangerous tiger, his falling asleep on a flat rock, the tiger's appearance (with a digression about the tiger's love story), the tiger's prey, the wind that follows the tiger and awakens Wu Song, the climactic fighting scene, the killing of the tiger, and the appearance of two more tigers! Here the story ends on the first day. It is typical of the traditional performance at the storytellers' house that it ends this way: this is the technique of the so-called selling a crisis (*mai guanzi*)—that is, stopping at a point of suspense in order to encourage the audience to return the following day.

WU SONG FIGHTS THE TIGER

Told by Wang Shaotang (Han)

Chai Jin accommodates guests in Henghai county.
Wu Song fights a tiger on Jingyang Ridge.

Second Master from Guankou, Wu Song, was in Henghai county at the estate of Lord Chai when he received news from his elder brother. He bade farewell to Chai Jin and went off to Yanggu district in Shandong to find his brother. He was not just one day on the road—he marched for more than twenty days—and on this day he had reached the boundary of Yanggu district in Shandong, more than twenty tricents from the city. It was in the middle of the tenth month, and now the sun was slanting steeply toward the west.

Our hero felt hungry in his stomach and wanted to take a rest. The moment he looked up, he saw in the distance a pitch-black town. Our hero shouldered his bundle and, holding a staff in his right hand, he marched forward in big strides, making his way to the gate of the town. When he raised his head again and looked up, he saw the wall piled up with flat bricks all the way to the roof and the round city gate. Above it there was a whitewashed stone with three red characters: Jingyang town.

As he entered the gate, he saw a broad alley, neatly lined with shops on both sides, most of them thatched cottages. There were also quite a few people around. Walking along, he noticed an inn to his right, a brand-new thatched cottage with three wings. Under the eaves a brand-new green bamboo pole was stuck in, and, hanging on the green bamboo pole, there was a brand-new blue wine banner. On the blue wine banner a piece of brand-new pink paper was glued. On the pink paper were written five big brand-new characters: "Three bowls and you cannot cross the ridge!"

The moment he glanced inside the inn, he saw brand-new tables and stools, a brand-new kitchen stove, a brand-new chopping board, a brand-new counter, and also two brand-new people. You must be joking! Other things can be "new," but how can people be "new"? Why never ever?

Behind the counter sat a young innkeeper, just in his twenties. In front of the counter stood a young waiter, eighteen or nineteen. Probably young people could be called "new" people. And then it follows that old people might be called "worn" people. The proverb is right: "Wave upon wave, the Yangtze River flows; new people overtake the elder generation."

So people can also be counted as "new."

From the other side of the counter he saw the butler standing in the main room. That's what he is called in storytelling—but actually, it's just the waiter. He was handsome, with a clear brow and bright eyes, white teeth, and red lips, and a delicate mouth with thin lips: he certainly looked like he had a glib tongue. On his head he wore a soft cap, around his waist he had tied an apron as clean as can be, and below his feet showed in cotton socks and cotton shoes. With both hands on his hips, he glanced out from the door of the inn. Why did he stand there and look? He was on the lookout for business. Suddenly he caught sight of a customer, bundle on shoulder and staff in hand, who was approaching and had made a halt. Sure enough, this must be someone who wants to drink some wine.[49] A businessman who sees business coming his way will always give it a warm welcome! So the young fellow, all smiles, hurriedly took a

49. The alcoholic drink in question is technically "brew" or "ale," not "wine." But it functions socially in the same way as wine in Western literature, so in translations from Chinese it is given that name by convention.

few steps forward, greeting the customer with both hands clasped and a mouthful of phrases in a so-so Beijing accent:

"Sir! Does Your Honor want to take a rest in our humble inn? Millet gruel, sorghum, chicken, pancakes, steamed rolls—the food is fine and the prices are reasonable. Please, come in and have a seat, sir!"

"Xiao'er [Little Second]!"

"Yes, sir!"

"Do you have good wine in this inn?"

Why would Wu Song pose as such a connoisseur? Even before he had entered the door of the inn, he began to ask if they had good wine. Well, he had this kind of lofty and unyielding character, not like just anybody. People of former times had four words they couldn't do without: wine, sex, wealth, and vigor. These four words are actually not for the good. So people nowadays don't care too much about those four words. But at that time, they didn't have any good education, so they couldn't do without those four words. But Wu Song cared for only two things: he was fond of drinking good wine, and he was fond of using his strength on behalf of innocent people, he was so full of vigor. These were at the same time his weak points, impeding him his whole life. He saw that the town was small and the inn was small, too, so he was afraid that they did not have good wine. He didn't care for wine that was diluted with water; if it were, he would rather refrain from taking this rest. Therefore even before Second Master Wu had entered the door, he first asked whether they had good wine.

"Oh! Sure, sir! In our humble inn, we wouldn't boast about other things, but the quality of the wine is amazingly good. People from afar have given our humble inn eight verse lines in praise."

"What eight lines?"

> "It is like jade nectar and rosy clouds,
> Its sweet bouquet and wonderful taste are worth boasting about.
> When a wine jug is opened, the flavor will make people tipsy three houses away.
> Guests passing by will pull up their carts and rein in their horses.
> Lü Dongbin once paid with his famous sword,
> Li Bai, he pawned his black gauze hat,[50]
> The immortal loved the wine so much he never went home . . ."

"Where did he go then?"

> "Drunken, he tumbled into the West River, embracing the moon!"

---

50. Lü Dongbin was one of the Eight Daoist Transcendants. Li Bai (701–762), a famous Tang poet, was extremely fond of drinking; the legend recounted in the following line is one of the many tall tales that are told about him.

When Second Master Wu heard this, [he said]: "Good!"

Why did he say "Good!" in this way? There was a reason for it. The wine of this inn was not only good, it was extraordinarily good. When they opened a gallon of wine, the neighbors three houses away would become tipsy; just by smelling it you would get tipsy. What else was it that was so good about that wine? Lü Chunyang [Lü Dongbin] loved the wine of this house so much that he drank up all the money he carried in his belt and even pawned his famous sword to pay for more. Li Taibo [Li Bai] also loved the wine so much that he drank up every penny he had, whereupon he tore off his black gauze hat and pawned it to pay for more wine. How could it be true that Li Taibo pledged his black gauze hat or that Lü Chunyang pawned his famous sword? No such thing ever happened. This was only flattery from the guests. But since the customers had thought out these phrases in order to flatter the wine of the inn, one can imagine that their wine was indeed good.

Highly pleased, Second Master Wu followed Xiao'er to the door and stepped into the hallway of the inn. They passed through a half door and came to the next wing, with a small courtyard and a thatched hall just opposite. The thatched hall was clean and nice, with seven or eight tables. But there was not a single customer. What was the reason? It was already long past the lunchtime rush. The sun was slanting steeply toward the west.

As Second Master Wu walked inside, he took down his bundle and staff, placed his bundle on the corner of a table to the right, and leaned his staff against it. He brushed the dust off his clothes and sat down at the main seat of the table right in the middle. Xiao'er wrung out a hot napkin and served him a cup of tea:

"Master, what do you want to eat with the wine?"

"Good wine and good food, and be sure there is enough, too!"

"Ow! Yes!"

Eh? How come the waiter, Xiao'er, had changed his accent? A moment ago at the doorway he was saying everything in so-so Beijing accent. Why did he afterward begin to talk in the dialect from the district north of the Yangtze River? What was the reason? There was some sense in it. This young man, Xiao'er, was from the district north of the Yangtze River, so he was our fellow townsman. How come he was able to speak Beijing dialect? Because he used to stand at the doorway of the inn looking out for business. The travelers from south and north were not acquainted with the dialect from north of the Yangtze River. Therefore he had made a special effort to study a few sentences of Mandarin in order to be able to deal with the customers. But he had learned only a few phrases, uncivilized whelp as he was, and he wasn't able to keep going much longer. At this moment he wasn't able to turn out any more phrases in Beijing accent. He had better be honest and stick to his own dialect. Therefore his pronunciation was different.

Xiao'er went to the front and took a big piece of beef, more than two pounds, and cut it into thin slices, a big plate of chopped fragrant red meat, just the right size. Apart from that, he peeled a dozen eggs; he peeled the shell off the boiled eggs. He sprinkled [the meat] with gravy. [The eggs] were snow-white and tender. He put a handful of white salt on a small plate; the salt was for the eggs. Then he filled two other plates, one with steamed rolls and another with pancakes. When he had filled a mug with wine, he arranged cup and chopsticks on the tray and carried everything over to the thatched hall in the rear wing. He placed the tray on the table where Second Master Wu had left his bundle, and then he arranged the snacks, wine and food, beef, cup, and chopsticks in front of his guest. Xiao'er removed the tray, took up a position to the left of our hero, and looked, smiling at Wu the Second. Second Master Wu pushed his teacup away and reached for the wine mug:

"Get me a big cup instead of this one!"

"You are welcome!"

His wine cup was exchanged with another, much bigger one. This wine cup was almost as big as a rice bowl: *Sh-sh-sh* . . . he poured himself a cup: "Uh! This wine is not good. Its color is not right, and it doesn't have any flavor. Such wine probably doesn't have the least spirit. Let me try and have a sip! Let me see how it tastes in the mouth!" Second Master Wu took two sips of the wine: "My goodness! This wine is really bad! It is watery wine and it has no body to it. Strange, it is not in line with what the waiter told me a moment ago at the doorway. I had better ask him!"

"Xiao'er!"

"Yes, Master!"

"Is this the good house wine?"

"Oh, no! This is only a medium good wine of our inn!"

"Ah, why do you not bring the good wine?"

"If you want the good wine, it's surely not bad. If it's the good wine that Your Honor wants, it's 'Three bowls and you cannot cross the ridge.'"

"Fine!"

Oh, my, how glad Second Master Wu was! Sure enough, before he entered, he had noticed a piece of pink paper glued to the wine banner of the inn with the inscription "Three bowls and you cannot cross the ridge." "I do not understand; I have no idea what it means. Why not ask him?"

"Xiao'er, what does it mean: 'Three bowls and you cannot cross the ridge'?"

"Well, Master, our small town, this town of ours is called Jingyang town, and west of the town, seven tricents along the highway, there is a mountain ridge, called Jingyang Ridge. The highway runs east to west and the mountain ridge runs north to south, so all the travelers going west must cross the ridge at this point. But you should not drink the wine of our humble inn, or else only the medium good wine, because if you really do drink the best wine, then after only three bowls—when you have drunk three bowlfuls—you cannot cross that Jingyang Ridge ahead. That's why people have given the wine of our humble inn this name: 'Three bowls and you cannot cross the ridge.'"

"Fine! Bring me a mug to taste!"

"Oh, don't be in a hurry to do that! Ordinary people cannot drink this wine, or else they get drunk!"

"No harm in that!"

"Well, Master, if you insist on having that wine, that's up to you, but I should like to ask a question: after you have dined and wined, do you plan to stay overnight in our humble inn? We can find a room for you, and in that case I shall serve you promptly. But if you want to travel onward after your meal, that won't do!"

"I'll travel on!"

"You cannot travel on!"

"Why not?"

"In case you want to travel on, and in case you are going west, as I can see you are, I'm afraid you cannot cross our Jingyang Ridge, and what will you do then?"

"What nonsense are you talking? Are you poking fun at an outsider for having no drinking capacity? I can drink thirty bowlfuls and still go straight across the ridge! Bring the wine!"

"Oh!"

Xiao'er was frightened. The voice of his guest resounded like a bronze bell and the whole place trembled at his shouting—it was deafening. Glancing at his guest's face, he saw him rolling his eyes and blinking, *wa-da-wa-da,* his fists each as heavy as a five-bushel willow basket! A businessman is not very brave. As soon as he is scared, he has no guts to refuse; acting by his order, the wine was brought to the table. The mug of bad wine was removed and changed for a mug of wine from the front, and be sure it was "Three bowls and you cannot cross the ridge."

"Please, Master!"

"Fine!"

Wu Song gripped the handle of the wine mug and filled himself another bowlful. Ah, interesting, no need to sample this wine—just a glance would tell how good it was: the green and clear color, the fragrance attacking the nostrils, and wine "crystals" clinging to the edge of the bowl. What is a wine crystal? Wine crystals are the same as wine "flowers" [bubbles]. What kind of wine was it, this wine? "Three bowls and you cannot cross the ridge." This name "Three bowls and you cannot cross the ridge"—how to explain it? No need to come up with explanations. Such names are simply fabricated by the wine merchants. After serving you a good wine, they may overhear the names you people invent. There are lots of such names, not just one name, all kinds of odd and strange names that they have overheard from wine bibbers who like to outdo each other by voice power. For example: "The fragrance penetrates the bottle," "Clear like seizing the moon," "A gust of wind and you collapse," "You will collapse before paying your bill," and then there is also the name "Three bowlfuls and you cannot cross the ridge." Searching for the root and source of such names leads to nothing but the fact that it is an exquisite wine, an original brew. Anyhow, it is just a good wine, and that's all. What good is there in drinking good wine? I think there isn't necessarily any good in it. But according to those who like to drink, drinking this wine had two advantages. Which advantages? When you drink it there are two flavors! First the flavor you feel when you take a sip of the wine in your mouth and it smells so delicious. After a while, you may have a good burp: *a-a-ah!*—again you feel the delicious smell. Apart from this there are no other advantages.

Second Master Wu had great capacity. After three large cups, the wine mug was finished. It would be unfair to say that there was too little wine in the mug: the reason was that the cup was particularly large. Well, if he had stopped drinking, that would have been the end of it. But after these three cups he looked both greedy and thirsty and stared at Xiao'er like a greedy caterpillar hanging on a straw. Xiao'er was standing silently beside him, biting his tongue: "The drinking capacity of that fellow is frightening. Our large cups are as big as rice bowls, but he empties them in one mouthful. Although he has a capacity like the sea, I'm afraid he is good and drunk by now!"

"Xiao'er!"

"Master!"

"Fill it up!"

"Uh, you must be joking! Just think of the way Your Honor is eating, I've never seen the like, and those three bowlfuls Your Honor downed, that's quite something! You shouldn't drink more! More of this wine and Your Honor will surely get drunk, and then you cannot cross Jingyang Ridge ahead!"

"What nonsense are you talking? Are you poking fun at an outsider for having no drinking capacity? I can drink thirty bowlfuls and still go straight across the ridge! Bring the wine!"

"Sure, sure!" Xiao'er did not dare to refuse him, noticing how his eyes were beginning to roll again. He left to get him another mug, which he filled up: *hua-a-a* . . . .

"Bring the wine!"

"Here you are!"

"Fill up!"

"Please!"

Just like the rich and wealthy who know no limits, Wu Song was drinking deep. How much had he drunk? Five mugs. Each mug held three bowlfuls, and three times five is fifteen. Henceforward he began to shout and cry ever more rudely and roughly, to the alarm of the other, the young innkeeper at the counter in the front. The young innkeeper was astonished. He couldn't figure out what was going on in the rear, and he couldn't relax because of the way they were shouting and quarreling. The young innkeeper lifted up his gown, stepped down from the counter, and went over to the half door, where he glanced inside: "Hm!" All he saw was that single customer sitting and drinking with Xiao'er attending to him. The young innkeeper called in a low voice. What did he call? He called:

"Wang Er!"

The waiter's surname was Wang and he was second among his brothers, so the young innkeeper called him Wang Er [Wang Second]. As soon as Wang Er heard his boss calling, he hurried over to the half door at once:

"Hello, Boss, why do you look for me?"

"Why does the customer over there quarrel with you?"

"For no reason—he wants to drink!"

"If he wants to drink, please, serve him! We innkeepers are not afraid of big-bellied guys!"

"Do you realize what kind of wine he is drinking?"

"Eh?"

"It's 'Three bowls and you cannot cross the ridge'!"

"My goodness! You can't let him drink much of that wine!"

"Exactly my words!"

"How much has he drunk?"

"Five mugfuls!"

"Oh, ay! You stupid fool! Other people cannot take even one mug of that wine, and you have served him more than five mugs!"

"But he ordered me to!"

"Does our guest want to drink more?"

"No idea!"

"Let me give you a hint: if he doesn't order any more, well and good! But in case he orders more . . ."

"Yes?"

"Then you have to fix it a bit on the sly!"

"Sure!"

What does it mean, "to fix it a bit"? It is a secret expression used by people in that trade, something they cannot say openly. If a customer shouts for more wine, you may dilute it with a little water; you cannot give him more of the real stuff. But since you cannot admit openly that the wine is diluted, you just "fix it a bit" on the sly. It is only the insiders who understand it; outsiders have no idea. When the young innkeeper had left, Xiao'er did as he was told. What about Second Master Wu? Second Master Wu still wanted to drink. He was in high spirits. Had he not drunk his fill long ago? He certainly had drunk his fill. Why did he then want to drink more? Because a moment ago he had uttered a certain sentence: "Are you poking fun at an outsider for having no drinking capacity? I can drink thirty bowlfuls and still go straight across the ridge!" As said, so done. Since he had said how much he could drink, then he had to drink that much. Since he had said he could drink thirty bowlfuls, he couldn't stop short of a single bowl. One mug equaled three bowls. He had drunk five mugfuls. Three times five is only fifteen bowlfuls. He was only halfway through and that's why Second Master Wu wanted to drink more.

"Xiao'er!"

"Yes, Master!"

"Bring more wine!"

"Please!"

"Fill it up!"

"There you are!"

Thereupon another five mugfuls went down the hatch. The last five mugfuls were, however, far less potent than the first five. The first five mugfuls were from the original brew, but the next five were diluted with water, three parts wine to seven parts water. At that moment Second Master Wu couldn't tell the difference anymore. Why? The more he drank, the less he was able to cope. He sure had an enormous drinking capacity, but now he had downed almost ten mugfuls and his face had turned the color of crimson silk, he looked blank, and his tongue was glued to his gums so that he could hardly speak:

"Xiao'er!"

"Yes, Master!"

"Bring more wine!"

"Does Your Honor want still more? It's no joking matter! Hasn't Your Honor had enough?!"

"What nonsense are you talking? Are you poking fun at an outsider for having no drinking capacity? I can drink thirty bowlfuls and still go straight across the ridge!"

"You have already had thirty bowlfuls!"

"Have I?"

"Yes! Please have a look, Your Honor, and count the mugs! On the table there are altogether . . . five . . . ten . . . about eight or ten wine mugs. One mug holds three bowlfuls, ten mugs of wine for sure equals thirty bowlfuls!"

"Ha, ha!"

"Why do you laugh?"

"I laugh at [your poking fun at] an outsider for having no drinking capacity. Now I have drunk thirty bowlfuls, and what has it done to me, pray?"

"Sure, Your Honor has a considerable capacity, were it not that your eyes look blank and your tongue is glued to your gums, stiff as a plank!"

"What nonsense are you talking?"

Second Master Wu had stopped drinking, and now he was busy eating the steamed rolls, pancakes, and beef. Otherwise, he cared only about drinking, not about eating. But at this moment he was eating, not drinking. Even the eggs were eaten up by him, to the very last: "Burp!" He was full. Since he was full, he stopped eating. Xiao'er wrung out a napkin for our hero to wipe his hands and face.

"My bill!"

"Sure! Will Your Honor please come over to the counter?"

"Okay!"

Second Master Wu rose to his feet, gripped his bundle and staff, and stumbled and staggered forward . . .

"Oh, no need to hurry, be careful not to fall, let me give you an arm!"

"No-no-no need for your arm!"

Second Master Wu had arrived in front, and Xiao'er was right behind him ready to give account:

"Hello! Listen over there at the counter! Our guest wants to pay his bill! Four silver ounces and five coppers all in all!"

This meal didn't cost more than four silver ounces and five! In those days prices were much lower.

Second Master Wu stopped in front of the counter, placed his bundle on top of the counter, and leaned the end of his staff against the counter. The young innkeeper looked at Wu Song and nodded, well aware that he was drunk: that was obvious from the expression on his face and the blank look in his eyes. Second Master Wu opened his bundle and took out his black silken silver-wrapper from the bundle. He had more than thirty taels[51] of silver in his wrapper. Originally, when he set out on this trip from the Chai estate, the Lord of Liang had just presented him with fifty taels to cover his travel expenses. On his way he had used up about ten taels, so he still had a nice sum left. The larger pieces weighed more than two taels and the smaller four or five ounces. Second Master Wu deftly fished out a piece—a piece that, as I, the storyteller, may inform you, weighed more than one tael—and placed it on the counter:

"Please, count it!"

"Oh, sure!"

The young innkeeper hurried inside to fetch his steelyard. When he returned, he climbed the bench again and turned his face toward Wu Song. His full attention was fixed on the face of Second Master Wu. After scrutinizing him for a moment, the young innkeeper put the silver piece on the pan of the steelyard. With two fingers of his right hand he picked up the string of the steelyard and with his left hand he picked up the stick of the steelyard. The sliding weight hanging from the stick was moved to the point of balance, horizontal position. Then he removed his left hand, while his right hand still held the string of the steelyard. He looked at the silver piece, lifted his head, and looked at the face of Second Master Wu, and then he announced the amount:

"Master, this silver piece of Your Honor's, I have just weighed it, it is one tae-e-e . . . e-e-el minus one copper!"

Why did he talk like that? As if he tried to press the counterweight out of balance! What was the reason? Well, this young innkeeper was harboring evil intentions. He had noticed that his guest was fond of drinking and now was good and drunk. He also saw what a large silver piece this was, and he wanted to swallow the whole piece. He meant to let a big piece seem like a smaller piece. How heavy was this silver piece after all? He had just weighed it and found out it was actually one tael, five ounces, and four coppers. How much did he say it weighed a moment ago? He said one tael minus one copper! Do you see how much he wanted to grab for himself? One tael minus one copper, that's

51. "Tael" is a Malay word indicating a unit of weight ten times greater than an ounce.

nine ounces nine. Do you see what he was up to? If it were nine ounces nine, why not say nine ounces nine? Why did he have to draw out the "one tae-e-e . . . e-e-el" and then add "minus one copper"? For what reason did he have to break the sound halfway? Well, he had his means and ways. Even though he saw that his guest was drunk, could he be sure whether his guest kept good account of his silver? If he did keep good account, as he usually would, and if you said that this silver was nine ounces nine, it would be like dressing with your arms stretched out stiffly—you can't turn a corner! If the guest did keep good account of his money, he would be likely to swear at you and make a mess: "What scoundrels you are in this inn! You dare to lie about my silver!" In that case he would have no reply in defense. Therefore he used this alternative way of saying it, making it "one tael minus one copper," which allowed him two ways out. He would draw out the sound of "one tael," and while he was still saying this and drawing it out, he would fix both of his eyes on the face of Wu Song. "If he actually does keep good account of his silver, and he hears me say one tael, he will begin to quarrel and shout: 'How can this silver piece be only one tael?' but then I'll just add: 'and five ounces!' And so I will steer clear." At the moment when the word "one tael" came out of his mouth, he saw that his guest didn't react and so it was clear enough he didn't keep account of his silver. Since his guest didn't care, he promptly took his eyes away, adding: ". . . minus one copper!"

Let's slow down a bit! Did Wu Song actually keep account of his silver? The money was a gift from a friend, how could he be so narrow-minded as to weigh piece after piece? And even if he had weighed his silver, he wouldn't be able to remember. Otherwise, he would have had to stick slips of red paper to each piece and bother somebody to keep them. Second Master Wu simply used his money as need be. No need to blame him for not keeping good account, but even though he used to keep account, he didn't do so right now. Why so? He had drunk too much wine. And Second Master Wu was in no mood to waste words:

"Is this piece of silver too much or too little?"

"This silver piece is a little too much!"

"If there is too much, then give the surplus to Xiao'er!"

Xiao'er was standing at the half door and looking. He saw the young innkeeper weigh the silver. He heard the young innkeeper announce the amount. Xiao'er was smart, he, too, so he hurried out in front to take a good look at that piece of silver. Why did he do that? He guessed what his boss was up to, that he was cheating the other man out of his money. But Xiao'er was not as crafty. When Xiao'er heard the guest say that the surplus was for him, he was quick in his reply:

"Thanks a lot, Master, excuse me for not seeing you off, Master, please come again early tomorrow!"

Second Master Wu put the rest of the silver into his bundle, tied it up, and flung it over his shoulder. He took his staff and walked out the door. As he lifted his head and looked up, oh, my! To the east the moon was already up! The moon was already up! Well, today it was in the middle of the tenth month, and when he had arrived at the town the sun was already slanting steeply toward the west. He had been drinking for quite some time, too, and in the tenth month the days are at their shortest. "In the tenth month there is hardly time to comb one's hair and eat a meal." But now the moon was up. Second Master Wu shouldered his bundle and headed straight to the west.

The young innkeeper and Xiao'er didn't waste another thought on Wu Song. All their interest was concentrated on the silver. The interest of Xiao'er was also concentrated on the silver, since he was well aware that his boss had cheated the other man of his money. The young innkeeper had evil intentions about the money he had cheated; he wanted to pocket it for himself, not give it to Xiao'er. There they were, equally suspicious, when the young innkeeper deftly grabbed the silver piece and put it into his drawer. Xiao'er was on the spot:

"Hey, Boss!"

"Eh?"

"Don't put it into your drawer! A moment ago the guest said that he wanted to give me the surplus!"

"Did he want to give it to you?"

"Sure he did, he gave it to me! Please, give it to me!"

"I shall, but this piece is too much! You don't mean to grab everything including the money for the meal, do you? This piece is nine ounces nine, our guest's meal amounted to four ounces five. Now I first take this piece of silver and then I'll return a piece of five ounces and four coppers to you, all right?"

"What! You can't fool me with your piece! Give me that piece of silver! Give it to me! Later this evening when we do the accounts, I'll of course return your money!"

"Let's solve the question right now, all right?"

"We make up this evening, please give it to me first!"

"Why do you want that piece of silver?"

"Why do *you* want that piece of silver, pray?"

"I have my reason why I want this piece of silver. It's because some days ago your sister-in-law asked me to have a hairpin made for her. But the silversmith of our town doesn't have good-looking silver, and to take the trip to the city seems a bit far. So my plan was to have a hairpin made for your sister-in-law . . ."

"Take it easy! My sister-in-law is a widow. Why would you make a hairpin for her?"

"Please, don't suggest that kind of suspicion! It's not the sister-in-law of the family on your side, it's a female relative on my side!"

"A female relative on your side! How could that be my sister-in-law?"

"We call each other brothers, I'm older than you, so my wife is of course your sister-in-law!"

"Aha! Not bad, not bad, not bad at all!"

Just as the two of them were debating, the old innkeeper stepped into the inn.

WU SONG FIGHTS THE TIGER

Told by Wang Xiaotang (Han)

Chai Jin accommodates guests in Henghai county.
Wu Song fights a tiger on Jingyang Ridge.

Second Master from Guankou, Wu Song, was in Henghai county when he received news from his elder brother. He bade farewell to his lord, and went off to Yanggu district in Shandong to find his brother. He was not just one day on the road: he had marched for more than twenty days, and today he had reached the boundary of Yanggu district in Shandong. There was still a distance of more than twenty tricents to the city along the highway. It was in the middle of the tenth month, and now the sun was slanting steeply toward the west.

Our hero felt hungry in his stomach and wanted to take a rest. The moment he looked up, he saw in front of him a pitch-black town. He shouldered his bundle and went in big strides: *ta-ta-ta-ta* . . . forward to the gate of the town, and there he stopped in his tracks. When he raised his head and looked up, he saw the wall piled up with flat bricks all the way to the roof. Here was the round city gate. Above it was a whitewashed stone. On the whitewashed stone three hollow characters were engraved: "Jingyang town."

As our hero spread his legs and entered the city gate, he saw a broad alley, neatly lined with shops on both sides. He passed by the fronts of more than ten shops, and then to his right there was an inn, a brand-new thatched cottage with three wings. Hooked on to the doorway of the shop there was a brand-new green bamboo pole, and hanging on the green bamboo pole there was a brand-new blue wine banner. On the blue wine banner a piece of brand-new pink paper was glued. On the pink paper were written five big brand-new characters: "Three bowls and you cannot cross the ridge!" When our hero glanced inside the inn, he saw a brand-new kitchen range, a brand-new chopping board, brand-new tables and stools, a brand-new counter, and brand-new people. Why?

In this world *things* can be "new"; can people also be "new"? Yes! Behind the counter sat a young innkeeper, no more than twenty-one or twenty-two this year. In front of the counter stood a young waiter, Xiao'er, not yet twenty years old. The proverb says:

> Wave upon wave, the Yangtze River flows;
> New people overtake the elder generation.

Just as Wu Song prepared to enter the inn, that waiter of the inn, Xiao'er—who would have imagined it?—was so eager to try out the tricks of the trade that he came forward to the door, all smiles, lifted both his hands in salutation, and looked at Wu Song:

"Oh! Yes, sir! Do you want to take a rest in our humble inn? Millet gruel, sorghum, chicken, pancakes, steamed rolls; the food is fine and the prices are reasonable. Please, come in and have a seat, sir!"

"Xiao'er!"

"Yes, sir!"

"Do you also have good wine in this inn?"

Oh, that was strange! Even before Wu Song had entered the inn, he asked for good wine, how come? People of former times in their daily life had four words of importance to them: wine, sex, wealth, and vigor. But Wu Song cared for only two things: he was fond of drinking, and he used his strength on behalf of innocent people. He saw that the town was small and the inn was small, too, so he was afraid that they did not have any good wine in this inn. Therefore even before he had entered the inn, he would first ask whether they had good wine.

"Oh! Sure, sir! In our humble inn, we wouldn't boast about other things, but the quality of the wine is amazingly good. People from afar have given our humble inn eight verse lines in praise."

"What eight lines?"

> "It is like jade nectar and rosy clouds,
> Its sweet bouquet and wonderful taste are worth boasting about.
> When a wine jug is opened, the flavor will make people tipsy three houses away.
> Guests passing by will pull up their carts and rein in their horses.
> Lü Dongbin once paid with his famous sword,
> Li Bai, he pawned his black gauze hat,
> The immortal loved the wine so much he never went home . . ."

"Where did he go then?"

> "Drunken, he tumbled into the West River, embracing the moon!"

"Good wine!"

My goodness, how Wu Song was comforted in his heart! The wine of that inn must be extremely good. When they opened a jug, the flavor of the wine would make people tipsy three houses away. Those people didn't even need to drink the wine, just by smelling the flavor of the wine they would become drunk. Don't you think the wine of that inn was good? The immortals loved the wine so much, one lost his famous sword as a pledge, another pawned away his black gauze hat. Oh, that wine must be good. Wu Song followed Xiao'er into the inn. They went through the front wing, passed the half door, and came to the next wing. Oh, the roof of the hall was thatched. The tables and stools of the hall were neatly arranged, the whole place fresh and cool. But there was not a single customer. Quite right, it was already long past the lunchtime rush. Wu

Song took down his bundle, placed it on a bench beside him, and seated himself at a table right in the middle. Xiao'er wrung out a hot napkin for Wu Song to wipe his hands and face, and brewed a pot of tea for him. Then Xiao'er stepped over beside Wu Song:

"Master, what do you want to eat with the wine?"

"Bring me some good wine and good food, and be sure there is enough, too!"

"Ow! Yes!" Xiao'er turned around and off he ran.

Strange! Didn't that waiter turn out a fine Beijing accent a moment ago at the gate? Why does he afterward begin to speak in local dialect? Oh, that was just because his inn was situated in the area of Shandong. Because there was a lot of traffic in front of the gate, people traveling from south to north, people speaking in all the southern and northern idioms. Suppose you were standing at the gate of the inn; then, if you were speaking the local dialect and wanted to do some business, some people would not be able to understand. Therefore he had studied a few Beijing dialect sentences. But he had learned only these few sentences. If you asked him to continue speaking, he couldn't turn out any more of them. In that moment his foxtail would show[52] and he would betray himself.

Xiao'er went out in front, where he cut some beef, put steamed rolls on a plate, poured wine, and at the same time arranged cup and chopsticks on a tray, and then carried it back to the rear wing. When he stepped into the rear wing, he placed the tray on a table beside Wu Song. Then he arranged the wine and food on the table in front of Wu Song and took away the tray. Then Xiao'er took up a position ready to serve his guest.

When Wu Song saw that the wine and food had arrived, he placed the wine cup in front of him, lifted the wine mug, and, *sh-sh-sh* . . . , poured himself a cup. Then he put down the wine mug while he gave some clicks of dissatisfaction and shook his head. "According to Xiao'er, his house wine should be very good. But I think that when I poured it, the color didn't look right and it didn't have any flavor. Hm, perhaps it is no use looking at it, maybe one absolutely must taste it. Let me try and have a sip." Our hero lifted the wine cup. My! When he had a mouthful, it didn't have any strength at all. "Oh, this must be a joke! I must ask that waiter, Xiao'er, about it."

"Xiao'er!"

"Yes, Master!"

"Is this the good house wine?"

"Oh, no, no, no! This is only a medium good wine of our inn!"

"Why won't you serve me the good wine?"

"Master, if Your Honor actually wants to drink our good wine, then that is the one called 'Three bowls and you cannot cross the ridge.' "

---

52. This Chinese idiom means that he would reveal his true colors. In Chinese folktales, foxes often take on human shape and seduce or otherwise trick people, but they are sometimes revealed by their foxtails.

"Fine!"

Oh, my! Wu Song became glad at heart. No wonder that before he entered the inn, he had seen those five characters on the wine banner of the inn: "Three bowls and you cannot cross the ridge." But he did not understand the meaning.

"What does it mean, 'Three bowls and you cannot cross the ridge'?"

"Oh, Master, that is because the wine of our humble inn is very good! So if you have drunk three cupfuls, then you will not be able to climb that ridge on the other side of our town, that ridge seven tricents from our town along the highway, called Jingyang Ridge. You will not be able to cross Jingyang Ridge, because you will be drunk from the wine. And that's why people have given this name to our inn: 'Three bowls and you cannot cross the ridge.'"

"Fine! Bring me a mug to taste!"

"Oh, don't be in a hurry! After you have dined and wined, do you plan to travel onward, or do you plan to stay overnight in our inn?"

"I'll travel on!"

"Ah! That is no joking matter! If Your Honor wants to continue and you are going from east to west, you've got to cross Jingyang Ridge. But you will not be able to climb it, not after the wine 'Three bowlfuls and you cannot cross the ridge.'"

"Bah! What nonsense are you talking? Hm! I can drink thirty bowlfuls and still go straight across the ridge! Bring the wine!"

"Oh!"

Xiao'er looked at him again: Gosh! That customer was no good talking to: his eyes blinking, *wa-da-wa-da*, his fists almost as heavy as a five-bushel willow basket each! No, a businessman couldn't afford to quarrel with him. He had better just simply bring a mug of wine and ask him to do as he pleases. He snatched away the wine and the wine mug in front of Wu Song and hurried out to change it into a mug of "Three bowls and you cannot cross the ridge." Then he placed it in front of Wu Song and stood as before beside him, ready to wait on him.

When our hero saw that the wine had been exchanged, he put the wine cup in front of him and lifted the wine mug: *sh-sh-sh* . . . Good, ah, good things and bad things can hardly be compared; if you do compare them, the difference between high and low is revealed. Have a look! This color was green and clear, and it had that fat, limpid quality. This wine was good. He put down the wine mug and lifted the wine cup: "gulp!" Ah, that wine, dear me!—coming down your throat, it was almost like a fireball, rolling and rolling all the way down into your stomach. Ah, could it be that such good wine had only this single effect? Oh, no, according to the saying, when you drink good wine there are three flavors! What three flavors? First, the flavor you feel when taking a sip of the wine in your mouth. Then after a while, when you exhale the spirits, the flavor is still there. And besides, when you fart, it also has this flavor! But that was three bowlfuls, already! One mug of wine would pour you three bowlfuls, and then it was empty. When Wu Song began drinking, could he be slow?

"Xiao'er!"

"Yes, Master!"

"Bring more wine!"

"Here you are!"

"Fill it up!"

"Oh, please!"

Xiao'er didn't dare to refuse, and in front of Wu Song were standing one mug to the left and one mug to the right. After a while he had downed five mugfuls.

After sitting and drinking for some time, Wu Song became more rude and rough in shouting his orders. Since his voice resounded like a bronze bell, the moment he said something, the whole place started to tremble, and even the young innkeeper at the counter out in the front was alerted. The young innkeeper lifted up his gown and stepped down from the counter, then went over to the door in the corner and looked inside. Oh, there was only a single customer sitting in the hall and drinking with Xiao'er attending to him!

"Wang Er! Wang Er!"

Whom was he calling? He was just calling the waiter, Xiao'er. Xiao'er and I are from the same family; his surname is Wang, too. He was the second child in his family, and he had not changed his first name; he had not studied, you see, so people just called him: Wang Er [Wang Second]. The moment Wang Er heard the young innkeeper calling, he at once hurried over to the door in the corner.

"Yes, Boss!"

"That customer sitting and drinking in the hall over there—when did he arrive?"

"Oh, he has just arrived!"

"What kind of wine is he drinking?"

"He drinks 'Three bowls and you cannot cross the ridge.'"

"How many mugfuls has he drunk?"

"He has drunk five mugfuls."

"You stupid fool, you! Other people cannot hold even one mugful, and you have served him five mugfuls!"

"But he ordered me to."

"Does he want to drink still more?"

"I do not know."

"In that case, if he does not order any more, that's that. But if he wants you to bring more, then you will have to fix it a bit on the sly."

"Sure, sure."

The young innkeeper disappeared. What does it mean to "fix it a bit"? It is a slang expression used by people in that trade. It means that, if this person wants still more wine, you cannot give him the good wine, so it is best to add some water to the wine. Why didn't he tell him to add water, then? Oh, it is no joking matter! If you were to say it quite plainly and ask him to add water, and if the customer heard that, he might bang on that big table! So in this situation, he tells him to "fix it a bit" on the sly; that is the slang of the trade, secret language.

Xiao'er returned to the hall and immediately took up his position beside Wu Song.

Did Wu Song then want to drink more? According to Wu Song's drinking capacity, those five mugfuls of wine were just right for him. If so, didn't he stop drinking, then? Oh, no, he couldn't. Why? "A moment ago I said to Xiao'er: 'I can drink thirty bowlfuls and still go straight across the ridge.' These words came from my mouth. One word from the noble man is like putting spurs to a flying horse. How can I go back on it? I must go on drinking."

"Xiao'er!"

"Yes, Master!"

"Bring more wine!"

"Oh!"

"Fill it up!"

"Oh, there you are!"

After this, another five mugfuls were consumed. How would he know that these five mugfuls were far less potent than the first five? The first five mugfuls were taken from the exquisite original brew, but the next five mugfuls, I'm sorry to say, had been filled with wine and water three parts to seven. But even so, Wu Song was now sitting there and staring, his face looking like red silk, his eyeballs fixed in a blank look. When he wanted to talk his tongue didn't follow suit.

"Xiao'er!"

"Yes, yes, Master!"

"Bring more wine!"

"Do you want still more? I think Your Honor shouldn't drink any more now. You look almost like a piece of red silk in your face, and you can hardly pronounce clearly."

"What nonsense are you talking? I can drink thirty bowlfuls and still go straight across the ridge!"

"Oh, but you have already drunk thirty bowlfuls!"

"Have I?"

"You have, you have! Look, look, try and count your wine mugs! Over there are nine mugs, and here is one mug, that's ten mugs, and one mug holds three bowlfuls, ten mugs hold thirty bowlfuls, isn't that so?"

"Ah! Ha, ha!"

"Oh, why do you laugh?"

"I have drunk thirty bowlfuls, and what has that done to me?"

"Sure, Your Honor has capacity like the sea, only your tongue tends to get a little twisted."

"What nonsense are you talking?"

"Oh, oh, it has nothing to do with you, nothing to do with you! Will you, please, come to the front to pay your bill?"

Wu Song nodded. Our hero rose to his feet and shouldered his bundle; he felt the ground swaying and swinging under his feet. Xiao'er cleared the table and carried the tray out to the rear, then he followed behind Wu Song in order to give the account.

"Hello! Do you hear me out there at the counter! Our guest owes four ounces in silver and five coppers!"

"Okay!" The young innkeeper answered at once.

When Wu Song came up to the counter, he took down his bundle, placed it on the counter, and opened it. He took out his silver-wrapper from it and opened that. There were still twenty to thirty taels of silver pieces in it. He picked out one piece and placed it on the counter, then looked at the young innkeeper:

"Weigh it and count it!"

"Oh, sure!"

The young innkeeper fetched a steelyard and put the silver on the pan. With one hand he held the string of the steelyard, and with the other hand he balanced the stick of the weight. He lifted his head and looked at the expression on Wu Song's face, then he lowered his head and looked at the silver piece, and after that he said:

"This silver piece of Your Honor's weighs one tae-e-e-e-e-el minus one copper!"

One tael minus one copper! Why not simply say: nine ounces and nine? And why did he draw out the sound and then break it off halfway? Well, no—who would imagine that this silver piece of Wu Song's was not merely one tael and that the young innkeeper was harboring evil intentions and wanted to make the piece appear less than its true worth? If he wanted to let it appear as worth less, why not say it was worth less? Don't be a fool! If at this very moment you were to say it was worth nine ounces and nine, how were you to know if this customer kept account of his money? Since it was his own money, he might very well keep account of it. And if he did keep account of it, he might start shouting: "What? How can it be only nine ounces nine?" That would be a mess. Therefore he made it "one tael" in the first place to see how the land lay: "This silver piece of Your Honor's weighs one tae-e-e . . . " and then he would draw out the sound while looking at Wu Song's face. If Wu Song pulled a long face, he would continue as follows: " . . . el plus five ounces and some." But the moment he saw that Wu Song didn't react, he understood that Wu Song didn't keep account. And since he didn't keep account, the innkeeper had better simply go on like this: " . . . el minus one copper." Did Wu Song actually keep account of his silver? How should he keep account? When he left the Chai estate in Hebei province, the Lord of Liang, Chai Jin, had given him fifty taels to spend on the road. The money was a gift from a friend. How could he weigh piece after piece in his hand? Therefore he didn't keep account.

"Is that piece of silver too much or too little?"

"Oh, oh, Master, if you want to pay your bill, then this piece of silver is a little too much."

"If there is too much, then give the surplus to Xiao'er!"

Who would have thought that Xiao'er was right on the spot:

"Oh, thank you, Master, thanks a lot, Master!"

Wu Song tied his silver-wrapper and put it into his bundle; then he tied his bundle and flung it over his shoulder. Thereupon, he walked out the door, staggering and stumbling. Then he began to march toward the west.

As soon as Wu Song had left, Xiao'er stepped forward to the counter. The young innkeeper was just about to put that piece of silver into his money box.

"Hello, Boss, don't put that piece of silver into your money box, give it to me!"

"Why should I give this silver piece to you?"

"Well, just a moment ago you weighed it, and that silver piece was nine ounces nine. Our guest dined for four ounces five, and he said he would give the surplus to me, which comes to five ounces four, right?"

"Sure!"

"I shall give you the four ounces five of his bill, and then will you, please, give me that silver piece!"

"Come on, this piece of silver is nine ounces nine. Our guest dined for four ounces five. The surplus is five ounces four, so I'll give you five ounces four."

"Oh, no, no, no! Please, give me that silver piece!"

"Why do you want that silver piece?"

"Oh, take it easy, Boss! Why do *you* want that piece of silver?"

"Let me tell you: the day before yesterday your sister-in-law said to me: 'Couldn't you have a silver pin made for me?' I had a look at the silver in the silver shop, but it didn't have a nice color. In our town there are only a few, small silversmiths, but I don't dare to go to the city. I think the silver piece of our guest's today looks very nice, and therefore I plan to have a silver pin made for your sister-in-law from it."

"Hey, Boss, there is something odd about what you are saying! My elder brother has died, so my sister-in-law is a widow, how come she would ask you to have a hairpin made?"

"Oh, no, no, no, don't suggest that kind of suspicion! Even if the two of us are boss and waiter, we do call each other brother, don't we? I am about two years older than you, so I'm a kind of elder brother, agreed? And so my wife is a kind of sister-in-law, agreed?"

"Well, but please express yourself clearly!"

Just as they were standing there and quarreling about the silver, the old innkeeper came home from the neighbor's. The old innkeeper had been on a visit to the neighboring tailor's when he heard a quarrel was going on at home. The old innkeeper stroked his long, full beard:

"Young fellows! All day long business has been fine, so I cannot imagine why you are quarreling!"

"Oh, oh, our old boss has come home. Let me explain to you!"

"Very well!"

"A while ago there was a guest here who dined for four ounces and five coppers, and he paid with a silver piece. This piece of silver was weighed by our young boss, and it is worth nine ounces nine. The guest said he would give the surplus to me. So then I asked our young boss to give me that silver piece, and then I would hand him the four ounces and five coppers of the bill, you see? Do you find anything wrong in that calculation?"

"Nothing wrong with that."

"Well, since nothing is wrong, then that's settled!"

"Young fellow, please, give it to him!"

"Why should I give it to him? My dear father, I have figured this out, too! This silver piece is nine ounces nine, our guest has dined for four ounces five, so there is five ounces four too much. If I give him the surplus—five ounces four—doesn't that come to the same?"

"Yes, not the slightest error!"

"Well, that's agreed, then!"

"No, Old Boss, please tell our young boss to give me that piece of silver!"

"Let's have done with it, young fellow, give it to him!"

"How could I give it to him? Come on, this silver piece is worth much more!"

"Worth much more?"

"Yes, I told him it weighed less than it actually did. You must understand that this piece is not just nine ounces nine."

"How much more is it worth?"

"This silver piece is actually worth one tael, five ounces, and four coppers."

"How much did you tell our guest?"

"I told him nine ounces nine."

"Good gracious! Young fellow, your heart is black through and through! I don't understand what you are up to! How can you play such tricks? That person may return to our inn and make a row . . ."

"No, no, no, no, he is well on his way. He shouldered his burden and off he went!"

"Where did he go?"

"From the east to the west."

"Did he go toward the west?"

"Yes, he went toward the west."

"So he went toward the west. Did you then tell him about Jingyang Ridge to the west? And that there is a tiger on Jingyang Ridge! Did you tell him that?"

"Too bad! Father, I forgot all about it!"

"Young fellow! All day long you put your heart only into making money, and so you don't care about the lives of our guests! A fine young fellow you are!"

Then he turned his face and looked at Xiao'er.

"Yes, sir."

"Come here quickly! Will you hurry up and get hold of our guest and bring him back here! As soon as you have brought him back, I shall give you the whole piece of silver."

"Okay!"

Diddleli-diddleli-diddleli . . . Xiao'er immediately took to his heels and left. Why did the old innkeeper immediately act with such urgency? He was anxious. What was he anxious about? Because the local officials had put up a proclamation: For military and lay folk alike, if they notice a traveler, they absolutely must keep him back, he must not cross Jingyang Ridge. If you do not keep him back, and the traveler is killed by the tiger, then the local officials will treat the case severely. Can you imagine how anxious the innkeeper was?

At that very moment Xiao'er rushed out the door and headed forward: *Diddleli-diddleli-diddleli* . . . He looked into the distance. "Hello!" There he saw Wu Song still stumbling and staggering forward. That was because now Wu Song was tipsy. If he hadn't been tipsy but had strolled along with his usual big strides, could Xiao'er have overtaken him? You wouldn't be able to overtake him in your whole life. But it was because today he was tipsy, his head was heavy, and his feet were light; when he walked it felt as if the ground under his feet were swaying, and therefore he was walking rather slowly just now. Xiao'er closed in on him:

"Hey! Master, don't go any farther!"

There in front, Wu Song heard him: "Why? That sounds like a well-known voice!" Then he turned his head and looked: "Oh, it is Xiao'er from the inn. Wine in your belly, but master of the situation!

"Xiao'er!"

"Yes, yes, my goodness! I have been running for my life to catch up with you, sir! Your Honor, please, stop!"

"Why?"

"Why ask why? You are going west! When you come out of our town to the west and continue along the highway for seven tricents, then you come to Jingyang Ridge. And on Jingyang Ridge there is a tiger! If you go on to that place and get eaten by the tiger, how terrible! Turn around, please! Hurry up and come home with me to pass the night in our inn."

"What? Is there a tiger on the road ahead?"

"Yes, on Jingyang Ridge ahead there is a tiger."

"Why didn't you tell me that before?"

"I forgot all about it at first, and then from the very moment I remembered it, I hurried after you to tell you."

"I understand!"

How should he be able to understand? At this moment Wu Song was getting suspicious, believe it or not. That was because during the Song dynasty the roads were dangerous; every thirty tricents there was a mountain stronghold, every fifty tricents a camp of brigands, every eight or ten tricents there would be a holdup or a blackmailing; in every other inn they would mix sleeping medicine into the wine. In former times there were all too many sinister inns. Wu Song thought to himself: "When I entered the inn, none of you told me there was a tiger on Jingyang Ridge, and when I left the inn, none of you told me there was a tiger on Jingyang Ridge. Only now at this very moment do you hurry after me and tell me there is a tiger on Jingyang Ridge! So I understand! When I was standing at the counter and paying my bill, I opened my silver-wrapper, and you saw that pile of snow-white silver of mine. Seeing these riches, you began to make schemes, and so you would try to cheat me to return and spend the night in your inn. Then when I have slept until the third watch, then the two of you, boss and waiter, will come crawling in and take my life." Wu Song was mistaken, however.

"Ha, ha! Do you know, today the tiger on Jingyang Ridge has invited me for dinner?"

"Oh! Hm, hm! Your Honor is witty, very witty. But I'm afraid it is rather you who will be served as dinner for the tiger! I think you had better return at once."

"What nonsense are you talking? Off with you!"

Then Wu Song hurried ahead. Now, if you were Xiao'er, would you run after him? Well, Xiao'er couldn't give up. Why? The old innkeeper had said he must go on. He must bring this guest home with him, for only then would he get that silver piece. If he couldn't bring his guest back, he wouldn't get that silver piece. Therefore he was getting very anxious in his heart, and he stretched his arms out in order to drag Wu Song back.

"Master, please, don't go!"

Just as Wu Song was about to shoulder his bundle, Xiao'er, too, clutched at Wu Song's bundle. Our hero turned his head once more, and now Wu Song was getting angry: "You! You try to scare me with a tiger, and when I don't go back with you at once, you have the nerve to rob me of my bundle! Since you don't mind robbing me of my bundle, I don't mind beating you!" Our hero turned around and raised his right hand, with two fingers—and these fingers of his sure looked like iron rulers—he hit Xiao'er on the left shoulder.

"You bastard, off with you!"

Swish! He struck him only once.

"Help!"

Hullabaloo! Z-*z-z-z-z-z* . . . ! Bang! Where did all those sounds come from? How would you guess that, when his body was set in motion, in that very moment he was stumbling against somebody else's solid wooden door. And in the very middle of that solid wooden door there was a half door, and the bolt of that half door had not been bolted, so at this very moment the half door opened with a creak: *z-z-z-z* . . . ! And "bang!" he tumbled inside. Inside there was an embroidery shop. The old owner of the embroidery shop was standing at the counter doing the accounts. Junior was standing beside him. As the old owner was doing the accounts he suddenly heard: "*z-z-z-z* . . . ! Bang!"

"Good gracious! Young fellow, go and have a look!"

"Yes!" Junior went out to the main door of the shop and looked around:

"Oh, oh, Father! It is not a stranger—it is Xiao'er from that inn, Wang Er! Wang Er! Have you got epilepsy?"

He saw at once that Xiao'er was holding on to his shoulder and his mouth was covered with saliva and foam.

"He's done for!"

"Who is done for?"

"I'll tell you: just a while ago such and such a thing happened, and then so on and so forth."

"Enough! He wasn't willing to return, so you just have to go home!"

"Go home! I cannot even get to my feet."

"What do you mean you cannot get to your feet?"

The old owner heard them: "Well, well! Go over to the shop and call two men to carry him home."

His son called two men from the shop, and they lifted him up and carried him home. The old innkeeper was kind, indeed. When he understood what Xiao'er had gone through, he gave him the piece of silver. When he was given the silver piece as a gift, wasn't it easy money? Well, he sure got some easy money. My God! How it hurt on that spot! He had a terrible bruise, you see! What to do about it? Ask a doctor to cure it. The doctor treated him for one day and for two days, but did it do him any good? Then the doctor told him: "The pharmacy Eternal Life Hall has a kind of plaster that is especially for curing bruises caused by falling or being beaten. Try to buy one and put it on and see!" But the price of such a plaster was very high. Well, better get hold of one and put it on and see! Oh, who would have imagined that, as soon as the plaster was put on, he felt a little better. And since he felt a little better, he had to change it after a couple of days. And so he put on one to the left and then one to the right, one to the left and one to the right, and as soon as he had used up these few coins of easy money, his wound was healed. That is called: "Ill-gotten wealth will not better the fate of a poor man." That's the moment I'll leave them, in order to follow Wu Song.

After Wu Song had thrashed Xiao'er from the inn, he turned around and said to himself: "Ha, ha! To try to scare me with a tiger!" Then he hurried on out of the town. When he came out of the town, he had a strong west wind dead ahead, blowing right into his face. He was good and drunk. Wonderful! The wind was so pleasant! Wu Song was still staggering and swaying. He walked and walked, but he had covered only three and a half tricents. Our hero hurried ahead, taking advantage of the moonlight. He discovered something beside the road. When he took a closer look, he saw there was a Temple of Earth at the roadside, and on the eastern gable a snow-white thing was hanging. What was it? At this moment our hero was stepping up in front of the Temple of Earth, and, availing himself of the moonlight, he fixed his eyes on it. Oh, it turned out to be a proclamation from the local authorities. How could he know? Because a notice had been put up, and at the bottom it was stamped with a neat square seal of the local authorities. And as for the characters on the proclamation, Wu Song was even able to recognize some of them, too.[53] Although Wu Song had never been to school, he had studied a bit on his own, memorizing and asking meanings. Skimming through this from the beginning to the end, he couldn't fail to notice a sentence like "A tiger obstructs the road." At this moment our hero was standing there and staring, but I had better read it aloud. The first line is nothing but official titles:

> On special order from the main office of Yanggu district, Dongchang prefecture in Shandong, we, Shi Wenhui, holding the honorary office of the tenth rank, ten times promoted, shall hereby make public the following instructions:
>
> Hereby it is notified that, concerning the area east of the city, Jingyang Ridge, which is the main thoroughfare that travelers and merchants have to follow. Unfortunately, this autumn a fierce tiger has appeared. It obstructs the road and kills people, causing extreme suffering and grief. The local headman must at all events prevent the traffic. It is permitted to cross the ridge every day only during the three watches from ten to four o'clock. Travelers should form groups, and the headman should beat a gong; everybody should carry cudgels, so that they can safely be escorted over the ridge. If innkeepers do not keep people back, headmen do not prevent them from crossing, and travelers are thus killed by the tiger, those parties concerned will be severely punished when our district finds out, and it will absolutely not be tolerated. Special warning against violating this edict!
>
> *Xuanhe year [1119 C.E.], X month, X day, issued and pasted up at the Temple of Earth, east of Jingyang Ridge.*

"Oh, my! Good grief!" What? Why was Wu Song so despairing when he saw that proclamation? Why did he stamp his feet? When Wu Song saw that proclamation, oh, woe to him! Poor Wu Song! "It was my fault, my fault! You see, just a while ago Xiao'er came hurrying after me to tell me that there is a tiger on Jingyang Ridge. Not only didn't I believe him, I even thrashed him. You see, so here is the proclamation pasted on the wall, and the proclamation states that there is a tiger on Jingyang Ridge. It must be true! It carries the stamp of the local authorities. Since this is the case, then hadn't I better return? Oh, no, I cannot. A moment ago I boasted and said that the tiger had invited me for dinner. If I go back, Xiao'er will laugh at me." In the next moment Wu Song thought: "Come on!" Our hero thought to himself: "What is

---

53. It would be unusual for a person of Wu Song's background and status in traditional China to be even partially literate. He certainly would not have been able to read the whole of the government proclamation, though he might have been able to pick out a few simple characters such as the one for "tiger."

the point of learning the martial art of boxing and cudgel play? We learn it for self-defense and protection. The tiger—enough about that tiger! How fierce could the tiger be, after all? Moreover, this tiger is obstructing the road and killing people. Shouldn't I do away with this evil for the people who travel here? I simply have to kill this tiger!" Therefore, at that moment, Wu Song thought: "Come on!"

> Clearly knowing there was a tiger on the mountain,
> He obstinately climbed that tiger mountain.

Our hero again hurried ahead, still staggering and stumbling. At that time he was already feeling a little better, because a wind was blowing, so that the wine—his drunkenness—was evaporating a little.

Then he walked another three and a half tricents. Since leaving the town, he had progressed altogether seven tricents along the highway, and just now he had arrived at the foot of Jingyang Ridge. That ridge wasn't so very big, nor was it so very high. Usually Wu Song could have crossed the ridge in a single breath. Hm! Today it didn't work, because today he was drunk. When he walked, the ground under his feet shook. Swaying along, he forced himself ahead up the ridge. When he had come halfway up, oh, God, he wanted to take a little rest! He looked around and spotted a moss-grown stone beside the road, seven feet long, three feet broad, and about two feet thick. On top it was oily smooth, as if coated everywhere with velvet. How could it be oily smooth? How could it be coated in velvet? A rock should be rough and rugged, shouldn't it? Well, no! This was Jingyang Ridge, where the tiger was, but at the time when there was no tiger, this ridge was the main road of traffic. For instance, some people traveled empty-handed, and some shouldered heavy loads, and when one of those with a load on his shoulder pole came to this place, wouldn't he be tired of carrying it? And since he was tired of carrying the load, he would fling it down and sit down on this stone to rest. After he had had a rest, he would again shoulder his burden and go on. In this way—maybe you, maybe he—would come here and sit down, and so—maybe your, maybe his—clothes would rub the surface of the stone. Day by day, year by year, this stone would be rubbed and rubbed, until it was oily smooth. As the occasion would have it, our hero sat down on the stone, took his bundle down, and placed it on the stone. He put his left arm on the bundle, clenched the fingers of his left hand into a fist, and rested his temple on it. He closed both his eyes firmly. Wu Song placed his right hand over his chest. When he fell asleep in this way, he really looked like "the immortal goddess He languishing on an ivory-inlaid bed."[54] At this moment Wu Song felt a wind sweeping by, swooshing over the stone. Oh, how comfortable! As soon as he

---

54. He (pronounced somewhat like "huh") is the name of the goddess of dawn, who is here represented as still fast asleep.

relaxed, he began to snore: . . . *z-z-z-z* . . . He had been on his feet day and night during this trip for so many days and had suffered hardships, so now he fell asleep just like that. He slept all the time until the second watch. At that time the tiger came out to look for food.

Where was the tiger? South of Jingyang Ridge. South of Jingyang Ridge the tiger had its den. The tiger was waiting at the opening of its tiger's den. Propping itself up on its forepaws and squatting on its hind legs, it raised its tiger's head and stared at the bright moon in the sky. This tiger . . . , you see, earlier there had been no tiger there. Why suddenly this autumn had there arrived a fierce tiger? Had that tiger fallen from heaven? Or had it sprung from the earth? Tigers cannot fall from heaven, and neither can they spring from the earth. This tiger had met with misfortune at home, and so it had sneaked away. What kind of misfortune had it met with? Misfortune in tigers' mating. When one day a tiger has grown up and begins to feel lust, and it wants to mate, then it does not hunt for food, it only roars. For example: the male tiger roars to attract a female tiger, and the female tiger roars to attract a male tiger, and then they mate, don't they? No, they do not mate. They stand face-to-face and take turns roaring:

Ma-a-a-a . . .

What for? They talk and have fun! They like to get friendly! And then by and by, they begin to roar louder and louder and are filled with lust, and then they mate. But on this day of mating, our tiger was not very successful, because this male tiger—or man tiger—had a thorn on his male member. So as for the tigress, in her female opening, it felt like a furnace, as if she had caught fire. One of them was aching like being burned, and the other was aching like being stabbed, and they both gave a roar! When finally the lust had passed, one of them ran straight east, and the other ran straight west. After running so far, all his lust had worn off, and our tiger had hollowed out a cave and hidden himself there. So this tiger had been thrown out of his old lair because of tiger mating.

At this moment the tiger stepped, swaying and swinging, out of the tiger's den. The tiger swayed along with steps exactly like an official's. It walked all the way to the road west of the ridge, and then to the fringe of a grove; it hid in the thicket of dry grass. It lay down its two forepaws, and curled up its two hind legs, let its lower jaw drop down on its forepaws, and began to stare at the moon in the sky with those tiger eyes. That beast had a strong desire to swallow up the moon! And so the tiger was lying right there and staring at the moon. Who would have thought that this tiger had actually had nothing to eat for three days? How come? Couldn't it eat people? There were none! It had eaten them up! When travelers came to this place, it used to eat them. But lately a proclamation from the local authorities had been put up: people were allowed to cross the ridge every day only during the three watches from ten to four o'clock. Travelers were to form groups and the local headman was to beat a gong, everybody was supposed to carry cudgels, so that they could safely be escorted over the ridge. They did not come one by one or two by two—no, they formed groups of two to three hundred. So even if this was such a beast—as you could see—an enormous beast, and very intelligent, too—when it saw such a crowd of people, it didn't dare to come forward. In such circumstances it could not eat people. What about winged game and four-footed beasts? Couldn't it eat them? There were none of them, either. The tiger had already eaten them all up. For example, the tiger may sit on top of the ridge, look into the sky, and catch sight of a sparrow. The sparrow comes flying by. A tiger cannot fly! In the first place, if the tiger had a pair of wings, that would be disaster! Even more ferocious! However, it only has to lift its head and give a roar:

Ma-a-a-a . . . !

From its mouth streams a foul smell. It opens its mouth wide and gives a roar, letting out breath that carries the smell up into the air. The sparrow flying in the sky has to rely on its two wings. Pressing them against the wind, it is able to fly along, but when it smells that stench, it suddenly folds up its wings and falls to the ground: "plop!" The tiger steps forward and has it for breakfast. Another example is the rabbit. Can it not run away? Those four legs of the rabbit's sure run fast! The moment it sees a tiger, off it goes, running straight into its hole. The tiger's head is so very big, and how big is a rabbit's hole? When the tiger spots a rabbit, it probably sets out chasing after it? No, it doesn't. The tiger lies prone on the ground and:

Wu-u-u-u . . . *ma-a-a-a* . . . , it roars.

Ma-a-a-a . . .

A gust of wind carries along the stench from its mouth. Over there the rabbit is running at full speed, but when its smells that stench, it begins to shiver. And as soon as it sits there shivering, the tiger—in no haste and no hurry—walks over to it, and—"flop"—has it for lunch. The monkey, however, it can climb very high, isn't that so? As soon as a monkey sees the tiger, it clings to the top of a tall tree. The two hind legs sit on a forking branch, and the two forepaws clutch some twigs. Then it looks down toward the tiger, blinking with those monkey eyes: *wa-da-wa-da*. It says to itself: "Elder Brother, I don't care if you are fierce! Can you climb, perhaps? Can you come up here? What can you do to me?" But the tiger is even more ingenious. The tiger will sit down in front of that old tree and stare at the monkey:

Ma-a-a-a . . . ! it roars.

As soon as the monkey sees it roaring, my goodness, it begins to shiver in its heart. But when you shiver, the tiger goes on roaring:

Ma-a-a-a . . . !

And the more fiercely the tiger roars, the more fiercely the monkey shivers. And thus shivering and shivering, shivering and shivering, its hands loosen their grip. And when the forepaws have lost their grip, the hind legs also slacken and it falls down: "plop!" Then the tiger steps forward and—"flop"—has it for dinner. In the evening the tiger goes down to the river to drink. The water flows in through the left side of the mouth and out through the right side. Not one single fish or shrimp will escape, and that will do for supper. Four meals a day!

Winged game, four-footed beasts, fish and shrimp, everything had been eaten up by now. Oh, it could not get hold of any creature from around there. But what about stray animals? Couldn't it eat some stray animals passing through the area? No! After the tiger had settled there, all the winged game and four-footed beasts of the area had fled and gone to other places. For example, at the moment a crow was leaving the place, it might meet another crow and scream:

Du-u-u-u-u-u . . .

What did it scream?

"A tiger! Don't go to Jingyang Ridge! There is a tiger! There is someone having free meals!"

Everyone had heard the news, and therefore the tiger had nothing to eat. If it had nothing to eat, it must be fated to die from hunger! Three days had gone by! Don't take it too seriously! No problem! Assuming there were people around, then it ate people. If there were winged game and four-footed beasts, then it ate winged game and four-footed beasts. But now it couldn't get hold of any; it just couldn't get hold of any. Day after day it would drink the dew to allay its hunger and pretend to be full.

At this very moment the tiger was lying prone in the dry grass west of the ridge, and once again it emitted a tiger's roar . . .

The west wind was very strong: *wu-u-u-u-u* . . . ! The wind blew from the west toward the east. Wu Song was sleeping on the stone halfway up the eastern slope of the ridge. He was so soundly asleep. The stone was flat and smooth, the wind refreshing, and the wine had already evaporated almost totally. At this moment, Wu Song woke up from his sleep. "Oh, my!" The wind blew so cold that the hairs of his body were standing on end! How cold it was! It was the weather of late autumn.

"Oh, my!"

Our hero opened his eyes, leaned on his elbows, bent over, and sat up. A gust of wind passed by, and on the tail of the wind Wu Song became inadvertently aware of something. He sniffed again. Hm, there was a foul smell. Hm, hm! That was probably the tiger out hunting. Wu Song had "wine in his belly, and something on his mind!" He thought about what had happened earlier in Jingyang town and that someone had told him there was a tiger on Jingyang Ridge. How could he know that at this very moment the tiger was coming out hunting? That was because when he had been at home, he had made friends with some hunters, and those hunters had told him:

"Whenever we go to the deep mountains and the wild moors, and a strong wind blows up, and if the tail of the wind carries along a foul smell, then that means a wild beast is out hunting."

It could only be the tiger's opening its mouth wide resulting in that bad smell. So, when Wu Song inhaled the smell, he must have had tremendous resistance or otherwise he would never have been able to stand it! Yes, the tiger was out hunting! Wu Song didn't bother about his bundle but pushed himself up with his hands and onto his feet. He got to his feet and he leaped and bounced: "pooh-pooh-pooh-pooh . . ." On and on he went, until he reached the top of the ridge. When he was on top of the ridge, he took the position of "the golden pheasant standing on one leg." He stood on his left leg and kept his right leg hanging in the air. His left hand was clenched into a fist, akimbo on his hip. He lifted his right hand to shade his eyes from the moon in the sky, and stared in all four directions.

He was looking for the tiger. He was looking for the tiger and he had not yet found it. But the tiger had caught sight of him! The tiger was at the fringe of the grove nearby. It was lying in ambush in a thicket of dry grass. Since it was late autumn, the grass had turned yellow. The fur on the tiger's body was also yellow, and therefore, for quite some time, Wu Song was unable to recognize it. At this moment the tiger spotted Wu Song: "Oh, goodness me!" That big beast was clever. The tiger felt too happy for words! Oh, my! It was so glad! How did it look when it was so glad? It would stretch out and bury its forepaws in its own fur and flesh and scratch itself on the breast, so glad was it! "Woe! For three days I have eaten no man. But the man who comes there is a big one! Uhm! Today I'll have an ample meal!" Then the tiger conveniently propped itself up on its four paws, stretched its forepaws forward, stepped back onto its hind legs, arched its back like this, put down its tiger's head, and lifted its tail upright—what for? It gave a stretch! A tiger, you see, is almost like a cat. A cat looks like a tiger, a tiger looks like a cat, you see. For instance, if you take a cat, and if it is wintertime and it is sleeping in the firewood basket and it is purring in its sleep, and then you come along and as usual pat it gently, at that moment it jumps down. And when it has jumped down, it stretches its forepaws outward, it puts its head downward, it raises its tail right up in the air, and then it arches its back, and in this way it stretches itself just like us human beings. The tiger in such a moment does the same thing, and it is called tiger's stretch. After the tiger's stretch, it lifted its forepaws and stepped onto its hind legs and:

Wu-u-u-u . . . !

Plop! It leaped onto the road and landed on its four paws. When it had landed, it lifted its tiger head upward and stared at Wu Song. It swayed its head and swung its tail, bared its teeth and flaunted its claws, and then it broke into a tiger's roar.

How could one imagine that just as Wu Song was standing on the very top of the ridge, and exactly when he was about to look around, just preparing to look for the tiger, then suddenly—"plop!"—something nearby leaped out. It leaped onto the road and landed there. In the light of the moon he now saw this tiger:

"Ugh!"

Why did he say "Ugh!"? Hm, Wu Song had another look: "Damn it! Such a tiger!" No wonder it had killed quite a few travelers. My God! This tiger must be one of the largest. It was as big as a bull, and, when it opened its mouth wide, it looked like a pail of blood. Its teeth were as sharp as swords and its tail was like a steel whip. Under the eyes of Wu Song the tiger looked up at him. At this moment Wu Song felt a little—well, he became a little afraid. In fact I have a few verse lines to praise the tiger:

Seen from afar it looked like a bull ox with one horn.
Seen from nearby it was a mottled wild beast.
The left ear was spotted with red color, like the sun,
The right ear was spotted with green color, like the moon,
Between its brows, a "king's" character,
Like a prefect inspecting the mountains.
Its twenty-four straws of whiskers
Were like needles and barbed wire.
Four big teeth, eight small teeth
Were like iron cramps and steel nails.
Its eyes were like bronze bells, their light like lightning.
The tiger's tail was like a bamboo whip.
In front were the paws, behind were the legs.
When it put its paws to the ground, it could climb the mountains
And bounce from hill to hill.
When it lifted its hind legs, it could jump over gullies and cross rivers.
When it lifted its head and roared in the wind,
The winged game in heaven all lost courage.
When it lowered its head and drank of the water,
The fish and shrimp of the stream all lost their wits.
Among the four-footed beasts he alone stands out.
Deep mountains and desolate moors are his home.
When he has not eaten human meat for three days,
He will swing his tail and sway his head and grind his teeth.

It looked at Wu Song, swinging its tail and swaying its head, baring its teeth and flaunting its claws. "Hm!" Wu Song took another look at it: "You beast, you are so terrible! So fierce! So ferocious! You have killed so many travelers! Just by looking at your appearance, one can imagine your ferocity. Today I have come, and I am bound to kill you! My God! Is the tiger so terrible? And if it is so terrible, what to do? And even if it is so terribly dangerous, I am still a man, not a beast! Come on! You come and try to kill me! If you don't come, that's it! But if you do happen to come, I'll first kick blind those two eyes of yours. And then I'll watch how a blind tiger like you is going to eat a man! When you don't know either east or west, north or south, where are you then going to find me?" Therefore the man, Wu Song, as he is found in the cycle called "Opening with the Tiger and Closing with the Dragon," from the "Ten Chapters on Wu Song," throughout these ten chapters of storytelling, the actions of this man should be called not only brave but also resourceful. He is a great hero of both wit and courage. So Wu Song had already made a plan. First he was to attack the tiger's eyes. When our hero had made up his plan there and then, he put his scarf right, tightened his belt, tucked in the loose corners of his clothes, then he stamped his feet into his boots, rolled up his sleeves, and rubbed his hands: "pooh-pooh-pooh-pooh . . . !" He was standing about ten feet from the tiger. Our hero was standing in the posture of "three tips closely together." The "tip" of his nose and the "tips" of his feet were coordinated and ready. Wu Song stared at the tiger without blinking at all. This man, Wu Song, had never been defeated, whatever he had done. He was awfully coolheaded, ready to cope with the situation. "Come on! Come on! I'll handle you as I see fit!" Thus, at this very moment Wu Song was standing there and watching the tiger attentively.

The tiger, certainly, was a beast! When the tiger had caught sight of him, it lifted its forepaws and rose on its hind legs:

Ma-a-a-a . . . ! and—"thump!"—it sprang toward him. With its two forepaws it aimed at Wu Song's left and right shoulders and sprang! Hm, hm! He was not going to get caught! If it caught Wu Song, he would be squeezed flat. As soon as Wu Song saw the tiger springing, its two forepaws aiming at his own left and right shoulders, our hero at the right moment turned his body and leaned to the left side. The tiger made a jump into the air:

"Huh!" and with this jump it landed to his right side. As Wu Song saw it lying prone in front of him, our hero planted his left foot firmly on the ground, lifting his right leg, and then he twisted the tip of his right foot and aimed at the tiger's right eye:

"Got it!"

"Phew!"

When he kicked it this time, he hit it very deftly. The tiger broke out in a roar:

Wu-u-u-u-u . . . !

Why? It truly roared! My goodness! The tiger was hurt to the marrow of its bones! Wu Song had kicked the tiger right in its eyeball so that it exploded. That damned old eyeball looked exactly like a small egg being squeezed out, dripping with blood. Didn't the tiger have to recover from the pain? At first the tiger didn't move. Our hero prepared to catch hold of it. From time to time the tiger raised all the hairs on its body:

Wu . . . *ma* . . . !

Suddenly it leaped forward. Our hero turned his body again. But the tiger had no mind to give in. Sure, it had not had its free meal! But it had had a lot of hardship, and now it had gotten severely wounded. It made a jump upward, turned around in the air, and stood again face-to-face with Wu Song. Because of the moon in the sky, our hero was able to see the tiger:

"Well!"

My goodness! How well he felt! "Ugh! You beast, haven't you had one of your eyes blinded? You try and come! If you come again, I'll kick out the other eye of yours! Then let me see how a blind tiger like you can eat people!" That tiger, sure, was a beast! And now it had suffered badly. As soon as it looked at Wu Song, it lifted its forepaws and rose on its hind legs:

Wu . . . *ma* . . . !

Again it aimed at Wu Song's left and right shoulders. At the same moment Wu Song saw that it was about to spring and:

"Hey!" bent his body and leaned to his right side. Again the tiger had jumped into the air:

"Huh!"

After this jump it landed on his left side. Our hero planted his right foot firmly on the ground and lifted his left leg up in the air. He concentrated all his energy in the tip of his left foot and aimed at the tiger's left eye:

"Got it!"

"Phew!"

When he kicked it this time, the tiger was to be pitied:

Wu . . . ma . . . !

Good gracious! It hurt! How it hurt! Who would have thought that its left eye would be blinded, too? Wu Song had kicked the tiger right in its eyeball so that it exploded. It looked like a small egg, dripping with blood. Now the tiger had been blinded in both eyes. It didn't know east, west, north, and south anymore. Didn't Wu Song let it run then? No, our hero took the opportunity to step forward and prepared to catch hold of it. The tiger wanted to turn around. Yes, now the tiger wanted to turn. You want to turn, and you cannot for your life do it! The tiger's head was just there to the left of Wu Song. Our hero lifted his left hand:

"Hey!" And he took a firm grip on the tiger's neck. He took a firm grip, but the tiger was about to leap forward. Wu Song saw this: "So you are about to jump off and run away! Where do you think you are going?" Wu Song's five fingers were like iron hooks. In this instant our hero was holding it so tight, it couldn't get away. The next moment he twisted his left arm:

"Hey! Hey!"

Wow! Terrific! How on earth could that be an arm? It was more like a thousand-pound iron pillar. When the tiger got that blow: *wu-u-u* . . . ! it couldn't even move anymore.

However, there was the tiger's tail, swinging—"flop, flop"—from side to side. And the four paws were scratching the earth below. Wu Song watched it intently: "Poor you! Poor you! So you are still swinging your tail, you beast? Are you? Well, if that tiger's tail slaps me, that will feel like a steel whip! I don't want to taste that!" Our hero bent forward and placed himself opposite the tiger's left hip. He planted his left foot firmly on the ground and lifted his right foot into the air. With his right foot he made a sweeping movement along the tiger's back, and then he kicked it. That is, he aimed at the root of the tiger's tail with his heel and kicked:

"Got it!"

"Phew!"

It gave a sound:

"Crack!"

That sound—"crack"—came from the bone that was broken. The tiger's tail was drooping to the ground and it could not swing anymore. The bone of the tail had been broken by that kick! Do you think it could still swing? The tail drooped to the ground, and Wu Song took the opportunity to mount the tiger. He didn't treat it like a tiger; rather, he treated it like a head of cattle. The tiger was suffering badly. It had never carried anything so heavy on its back before. Didn't the tiger feel worried?

Wu . . . ma . . . !

It stubbornly tried to raise its head. Wu Song was holding it. He watched it intently: "Do you have the guts to raise your head again?" Then he raised his right fist and concentrated all his energy:

"Got it!"

"Phew!"

This time he beat it on its right eyebrow.

Wu-u-u . . . !

The tiger again put down its head. Our hero concentrated his energy in his right fist and aimed at its right flank:

"Hey! Hey! Hey! Hey! Hey!" swooping down on it a dozen times or so. That can't be right! He killed the tiger with three knocks and two kicks! How could he beat it a dozen times or so? Well, not so! When he beat it a dozen times, he didn't hit it on a lot of different spots, but beat it on only that very spot he had aimed at. Therefore it was counted as only one knock when later on he arrived at the office of Yanggu district and the inspector performed an autopsy. Therefore, even though he had beaten it more than a dozen times, since it was not at different spots, it was taken as only one knock, you see!

Wu Song had beaten it a dozen times.

"Yo-ho!"

My God! Wu Song said to himself: "If I carry on this way, will I ever be able to go to the battleground again and fight? Will I ever be able to raise my hand against an enemy again? Will I? I can't even kill a tiger! How am I to take the life of an enemy? Oh, I have an idea! When you fight a man and want to kill him, you have to wound him on his deadly spot. If you don't wound him on his deadly spot, how on earth is he to die? A tiger, well, a tiger is of course like a man. Man is no different from all the living creatures. Where does one find those deadly spots on a man? The ear is such a deadly spot. Hm, the right ear of the tiger is exactly under my hand. Come on! Let me box him on his ear for once!" Our hero raised his fist and concentrated his energy:

"Got it!"

"Phew!"

This time his force was enormous! How could the tiger guess that it was to get such a blow?

Wu-u-u-u . . . !

The tiger gave a snort, it couldn't even roar anymore. From its left ear something looking like a red silk thread gushed forth more than ten feet: *sh-sh-sh-sh . . . !* What was it? Blood! Blood from where? Blood flowed from its right ear. Blood from its right ear? That ought to drip from its right ear or gush forth from its right ear! Why did it gush forth from its left ear? Oh, that was because the force of Wu Song's fist was so enormous that he had blocked up the main door. When you cannot take the main door, you have to go to the back door, and so it gushed forth from the left ear: *sh-sh-sh-sh!* When this blood gushed forth, the tiger didn't raise its head anymore and it didn't scratch with its paws anymore. Before it had dug out four deep furrows in the ground, but now it did not move anymore. Wu Song said to himself: "It's dead! It's dead, dead, dead! Beware! Such a beast has many a trick! Maybe it pretends to be dead! Come on! Let me ask and see!" With his left hand he pinched it twice. It didn't move. It didn't move, so it was probably dead. Our hero rose to his feet. He swung his right leg over to the other side, put his weight on his left foot, raised his right foot, and gave it another kick—"phew!"—"thump!" The whole body of the tiger fell down to the ground. Did the tiger fall down? Yes, it fell down. It shouldn't do so! Isn't it so that "a dead tiger keeps its posture"? Oh, no, no, no, no! It's true that "a dead tiger keeps its posture," but it depends how it dies. If the reason is that it has caught some illness, and it understands it is going to die, it cannot move anymore, then it always finds a crossroads of three or four roads, where it props itself up, opening its mouth wide and stretching its tongue as long as it can. Then it sits there, and if passersby suddenly catch sight of this tiger:

"Help! My God!"

As soon as they detect the tiger, they scurry off in a hurry. But actually, it is a dead tiger. Even after it is dead it can frighten people. The great generals from former times used to compare themselves to tigers:

"My lord, you are certainly a tiger general!"

However, this tiger had been beaten so viciously by Wu Song that its posture had collapsed totally. How could it stop falling? It fell down, and our hero stepped over it to the other side and watched it intently:

"Ha, ha! You monster! Where is your majestic air?"

> Second Master Wu, his courage was strong,
> Stood up and went straight to Jingyang Ridge;
> With his clever fist he killed the mountain tiger,
> Since then his great fame has swept over all the world.

At this moment Wu Song hurried to the east side of the ridge; he wanted to go back and get some sleep. That place where he had been sitting, wasn't there a moss-grown stone? First he sat down to relax a bit, and then he wanted to return and get some sleep. He had that bundle of his, and now he shouldered his bundle and crossed the ridge:

"Pooh-pooh-pooh-pooh . . . !"

When he had come about two tricents down from Jinyang Ridge, he caught sight of something in front:

"What?"

He suddenly saw a crossroads: "*Aiya!* Two roads, one to the right and one to the left. Which one of these roads leads to Yanggu district? Too bad, at this time there are no travelers, and moreover there are no peasants around to ask. What direction should I take?"

Just as Wu Song was standing there and speculating, he suddenly heard something at the rim of his ear:

"Ding-dong-ding-dong . . . "

To the left of him this sound was ringing, as if it were a bell ringing. He turned his head to the left and looked:

"My!"

Good gracious! Wu Song got really scared! On his left hand he saw a big forest, and at the fringe of the forest two tigers were lying in wait. How could one imagine that the sound of bells came from the tigers' necks?

"Ding-dong-ding-dong . . . ," they sounded.

Wu Song said to himself: "My God! How many tigers are there after all on Jingyang Ridge? Please? I have just killed one tiger on top of the ridge. And now I am completely exhausted. Two tigers more at this moment, well, those two tigers, I do not have more force! What can I say?" At this moment Wu Song was just about to flee, but the tigers came rushing toward him!

Southern Prosimetric

HANGZHOU STORYTELLING AND SONGS

Translated and introduced by Richard VanNess Simmons

Since at least as early as Southern Song times (1127–1279), when the city served as the dynastic capital, Hangzhou was a flourishing center for storytelling and oral performance. Historical records indicate that Hangzhou storytelling artists were loosely organized since at least the beginning of the nineteenth century, when the Storytellers Society (Pinghua She) was founded. The activities of the Storytellers Society culminated yearly in a Storytelling Festival held during the Chinese New Year. In the early Republican period, the name of this organization was changed to the Story Revival Society, and it continued to operate until several years after the Communist revolution in 1949. After the revolution, the storytellers were reorganized into the Hangzhou Storytellers Troupe.

Several types of traditional folk performance have already been lost in Hangzhou, including a form of traditional southern opera known as Hangzhou opera (Xiwen). As late as the early 1980s, however, there were occasional performances of Hangzhou *tanhuang* and *Wulin diao*, the former an elegant form of local opera said to have emphasized poetic diction and a refined musical score, and the latter a form of opera noted for a grander, bolder musical style. Traditional puppet plays, both hand-puppet shows (*muren xi*) and marionette shows (*tixian xi*), were also extremely popular in Hangzhou during the early half of the twentieth century but are not performed today.

In recent times, the Hangzhou storytelling tradition has struggled to survive the onslaught of modern popular culture. Traditionally called straight storytelling (*pinghua*), Hangzhou stories are performed on a small platform about eighteen inches high and fifty-four feet square, equipped with only a narrow table and a chair or stool for the storyteller behind it. The table is the resting place for the artists' few props: a fan, a small towel or handkerchief, and the awakening block (*xingmu*). The last is a small block of wood used to rap the table at highlights in the narrative (some claim that it also serves to wake up dozing members of the audience!) and is the trademark of the local storytellers' profession. In addition, there is usually a cup of tea on the table to moisten the artist's tongue. While a storyteller may occasionally gesture with the teacup, it is not considered a regular prop in the Hangzhou *pinghua* tradition. Storytellers usually wear a simple, loose-cut mandarin gown (*paozi*).

During a performance, the *pinghua* artist sits or stands behind the table and gestures frequently as he spiritedly acts out the roles of the characters in his narrative. He is skilled at manipulating exaggerated expressions on his face to serve the purpose of his tale and makes full use of different voices and turns of accent. His fan may come out of the background as he uses it to represent a sword or knife, a window or door, a maid's platter or shopkeeper's tray, or anything else, as he sees fit. His handkerchief, too, while often used to wipe the sweat from his brow, may be employed to portray an imperial edict, a romantic letter, an embroidered pouch, or even the head of a slain enemy. And the awakening block may spring from its ordinary role as a clapper to become a silver ingot or perhaps a Daoist's spirit tablet. Now and then, the storyteller may insert a rhymed descriptive passage (*fu'er*) into his narrative to more fully describe a particular scene or the appearance of a character.

Most of the Hangzhou storytellers perform stories that have been transmitted orally, traditional tales that the artists breathe fresh vigor into by telling anew. Some storytellers invent their own narratives, presenting them onstage in the traditional *pinghua* format. Their repertoire includes narratives based on legends of the Eastern Han dynasty (25–220) and Three Kingdoms (220–280); tales of martial heroism and chivalry, such as *Outlaws of the Marsh* (*Water Margin* [*Shuihu zhuan*]) and stories based on the Yue Fei legend; so-called *gong'an* stories of officials, legal cases, mystery, and intrigue; and tales of ghosts and the supernatural, such as the adventures of Ji Gong.

The pieces chosen to represent the Hangzhou tradition here are short forms that, all written by their performers, can be appreciated as independent compositions. "Old Hangzhou Bridges" is an example of an opening poem (*jieshi'er*) sung during a chantefable performance locally called *pingci* (narrative verses). As in other regional chantefable traditions, *pingci* are also known as little story (*xiao shu*) because of the focus on themes of amorous intrigue and domestic adventure. The genre is performed with the storyteller's occasionally interspersing his tales with a musical flourish on the *erhu*, the two-stringed fiddle played with a bow that a *pingci* artist always has at hand. The accompaniment of the *erhu* is also a required element of the *jieshi'er* sung at the commencement of a *xiao shu* narrative. *Jieshi'er* is the Hangzhou term for what are more widely known as opening ballads (*kaipian*), songs and poems presented at the opening of many varieties of traditional plays and narratives in the Yangtze delta region. "Old Hangzhou Bridges" served as a *kaipian* sung to *erhu* accompaniment by the venerable sixty-five-year-old Hu Zhenghua during his performance of *Pair of Pearl Phoenixes* (*Shuang zhu feng*). The piece is an amusing, tongue-in-cheek play on the names of bridges in Hangzhou, a city that was crisscrossed by canals and bridges in traditional times.

"The Market Scene" and "The Cooper" are examples of *xiaorehun*. *Xiaorehun* are short, amusing stories or anecdotes tunefully chanted to the accompaniment of a small *luo* (gong); hence they are also called *xiaoluo shu* (small-gong stories). Fast paced and compact, *xiaorehun* provide a succinct illustration of some of the more colloquial elements in Hangzhou oral literature. Both pieces were sung by a celebrated *xiaorehun* performer and Hangzhou native, An Zhongwen, who was sixty-six at the time of the performance. "The Market Scene" is on a modern theme, playfully depicting a squabble between goods at a market; "The Cooper" is a short excerpt from the tune "Cheap Goods" and is on a more traditional theme about a barrel maker. The translations are based on performances recorded in 1990.

Reflecting their different genres, the *kaipian* is in a rather literary style, while the *xiaorehun* are in a more vernacular style. Where the idiom differs (only slightly overall), it reveals a skillful use of language to fit the genres. Hu Zhenghua consistently used regular, traditional Hangzhou readings—which carry greater prestige—in his more literary piece. An Zhongwen's pieces are more unabashed in their use of a clearly dialect vocabulary.

OLD HANGZHOU BRIDGES

Written and performed by Hu Zhenghua (Han)

When the Southern Star and the Northern Dipper hang high,
Master Hongchun fancies a leisurely stroll.
Lonely is his study where he daily sits in quiet solitude,
When he'd like to step out and enjoy himself at Gongchen Bridge,[55]
Secure the double spring lock on his gate,
Keeping the Key Bridge with him as he goes,
A handsome Young Page [Bridge] walking ahead to show the way,
While behind follows a boy named Silver Grotto Bridge.
The boy would like to sink his teeth into Mongol [Cake] Bridge,
When the master steps onto Horse Watering Bridge.
Encountering a peak at Phoenix Peak Bridge,
He doesn't pause to enjoy the view of the hills;
Coming upon a stream, he avoids gazing into Clear Water Bridge,
And he has no desire to look around Six Parts Bridge.
In the brisk cold he wanders by Xiling Bridge.
He has the urge to enter Qiantang Gate;
But in error unwittingly wanders over Jingting Bridge.
Then Master Hongchun lifts his head at Look Toward Bridge,
And catches a glimpse of a maiden,
As her Fragrance [Bridge] wafts by on the breeze.
He notices that her willow leaf brows form the Character for Eight Bridge,
Her eyes are autumn pools—
Gilt Pool Bridge and Clear Pool Bridge.
[She has] a fine jade nose,

---

55. In traditional times, many of the bridges named in "Old Hangzhou Bridges" had specific associations, some of which Hu Zhenghua has alluded to in this composition. Gongchen Bridge was located near a district of brothels. Lock Bridge (Suo Qiao) and Key Bridge (Yaoshi Qiao) once existed near Qingbo Gate; the former was not well known, and the latter, being only twenty inches wide, was not used. "Handsome Young Page" alludes to Golden Grotto Bridge, a place once found in Hangzhou together with the matching Silver Grotto Bridge, though no actual bridge is extant for either name. Xiling (Western Briskness) Bridge was also known as Su Xiaoxiao Bridge. Su Xiaoxiao was a courtesan of the Southern Qi dynasty (479–502) said to have been buried in the vicinity. Mao'er Bridge was a gathering place for fortune-tellers. The jail used to be located at Small Carriage Bridge. Prisoners were led past Vexation Comes Bridge on their way to the execution grounds.

Cherry skin and a touch of Rouge Bridge;
From head to foot she is dressed most fashionably,
Upon her neck she wears Locket Bridge.
"What's your name?" he ventures to ask.
"Ah! Master, I go by the name Beauty Bridge."
Their meeting a fortunate chance of Three Lifetimes Bridge,
The two talked and chatted at Undulant Dragon Bridge.
He inquires of the maiden's marriage plans,
And finds her as speechless as Mute Bridge.
"Ah! Master, if you wish to inquire of my betrothal,
I must ask Grandmother at Old Lady Bridge."
So the young master burns incense at Iron Buddha Temple Bridge,
Supplicates the gods and Buddha at Divine Protection Bridge.
Rushing to kneel beside Six Parts Bridge,
He fervently reveals his wish to Upper Celestial Bridge.
The old lady is delighted when she hears,
And inquires of a blind medium at Mao'er Bridge.
The soothsayer wishes to select an auspicious day,
And comes up with the Lingyin Midday Bridge.
The bridal chamber is built beside New Palace Bridge;
The lamps and streamers hung at the gate are as colorful as Market Bridge.
Scholar Li Bridge serves in the accounting room;
And offerings are presented to the incense burner at Lion and Tiger Bridge.
They invite the Zhang Family Bridge,
As well as the Ling Family Bridge.
Then the groom is seen with an Embroidered Sash Bridge upon his head,
And Wearing a Dragon Robe Bridge,
A Jade Belt Bridge strapped tightly around his waist,
His two feet upon the East and West Cloud Slipper Bridges.
Then the bride appears,
Riding in Small Carriage Bridge,
And the groom is invited to Ascend the Hall Bridge.
Guests and visitors Stream Through Bridge.
A pair of newlyweds form decorative candlesticks,
As they bow to heaven and earth at Harmony Bridge.
Today the whole family is at ease and Peace Bridge.
For the future promises a house full of descendants,
And Overflowing Happiness Bridge.
The crash of drums roars toward the heavens,
Excitement at its peak;
And at the gate they roll out Camel Rug Bridge.
It is simply hoped that man and wife reach old age together.
In time a son is born [named] Long Life Bridge.
But as time passes husband and wife grow to quarreling.

They are fated foes of a former life—Vexation Comes Bridge.
When the rooster's crow issues thrice at Heavenly Water Bridge,
The maiden Beauty Bridge is no longer to be seen.
And if man and wife are to meet again,
It will only be the image of a dream reflected,
In the effervescence at Sea Moon Bridge.
Then, as Master Hongchun blinked,
His spring dream passed,
And road returned to road;
And bridge returned to bridge.

THE MARKET SCENE

Written and performed by An Zhongwen (Han)

At the little market by Longxiang Bridge,
Day and night the goods roll in—
It's truly a lively bustle.
Here they're deliverin' large winter melons;
While there they're bringin' in dried ribbon fish.
On the subject of dried ribbon fish,
Let me sing a tale of a dried ribbon fish.
One such fish saw in the market that the winter melon's cheap.
And so spoke forth with great swaggerin' pride,
Sayin':
"Hey winter melon!
I, the dried ribbon fish,
Have traveled far across the seas to land here at Hangzhou,
Where the seafood company assigned me to this little market.
See how everyone welcomes me,
How long the line is here!
That's 'cause I'm quite nutritious,
Containin' phosphorus, protein, and fat.
Steamed or fried,
With a little vinegar and salt,
I've got a delightful taste,
Fresher than fresh and more fragrant than ever.
You, the winter melon,
Are neither fresh nor fragrant,
But pudgy and tubby,
Remarkably resemblin' a brazier urn.
Six dimes'll buy a whole catty.
Not even ten catties of winter melon,
Can fetch the price of a catty of dried ribbon fish."

Hearin' this,
The winter melon went blue in the face;
His belly swelled with rage.
"Dried ribbon fish," he snapped,
"Your sneerin' slurs are uncalled for!
I, the winter melon,
Have a build more stout than yours.
Soup of winter melon with salted vegetable,
Is thrifty and practical, moreover easy to cook.
Winter melon rind and seeds,
Also make good herbal remedies.
A dried ribbon fish has never been in the herbalist's!
I, old winter melon,
Can be sent to the candyin' plant,
And pressed into winter melon strips,
Sugared through and through,
Then delivered to the store in bright glass jars.
Dried ribbon fish,
If you go on a-braggin',
This sixty-eight catty winter melon,
Will roll on over,
And squish you to death,
You hopeless dried ribbon fish!"

THE COOPER

Written and performed by An Zhongwen (Han)

Strike up the little brass gong,
And sing a fussy old tune.
At Hangzhou's Maojiabu,
A fellow,
His surname Gu,
All on account of his wife,
Stirred up a great ado,
A great, great ado.
At Maojiabu,
There was a cooper,
Gu A-Wu.
When he was just fifty years of age,
His son had already taken a wife,
And his daughter had been married off,
Leaving the old couple alone,
At Maojiabu.

The old lady boiled tea,
Cooked the meals,
And kept house.
A-Wu repaired foot basins,
And hammered out coopering hoops.
After food and expenses,
They had plenty extra.
Life was altogether pretty darn easy.
Who would have known,
That on the fifth of the year's first month,
Just after dinner,
A storm would arise in these quiet parts.
A-Wu had slept till just past midnight,
When his teeth grew clenched,
His fists tight,
His legs stiff and straight,
And, alas,
He died!

JINGJIANG "TELLING SCRIPTURES" FROM THE *SAN MAO PRECIOUS SCROLLS*

Translated by Qu Liquan and Jonathan Noble and introduced by Jonathan Noble

San Mao Precious Scrolls (*San Mao baojuan*) is a transcription of a *jiangjing* (telling scriptures) performance from the late 1980s in Jingjiang county, Jiangsu province. Telling scriptures represents one of the few current storytelling traditions that preserves and expresses certain performative elements of the *baojuan* (precious scrolls, or precious volumes)—orally performed prosimetric narratives and related texts dating back to the Yuan dynasty (1271–1368) and associated with Buddhist teachings. The *baojuan* tradition had entered the Jiangsu region from the north by the Ming dynasty (1368–1644). The flourishing of sectarian religious associations that promoted a syncretic belief system by integrating Confucian values with popular Daoism and Buddhist iconography contributed to the popularization and secularization of the *baojuan* tradition during the late Ming and early Qing (1644–1911) dynasties.

The telling scriptures tradition shares certain storytelling conventions—the use of specialized registers of narration and dialogue and the narrator's enactment of different character roles—with other regional storytelling arts (Yangzhou *pinghua* and Suzhou *pinghua*) and regional forms of chantefable (*Suzhou tanci* and *Yangzhou xianci*). Yet the telling scriptures tradition exhibits a number of important distinctive features, including its framing within a sacred or secular religious context and the audience's role as chorus. A ritual specialist-cum-storyteller, called a *fotou* (Buddha head), who often sits at the storytelling table surrounded by the chorus, leads the performance, which involves the use of various ritual paraphernalia, including paintings of Daoist immortals and Buddhist deities, a censer, food trays, and red candles. The storyteller may use an awakening block (*xingmu*), a brass bell, a wooden striker, and a carved percussion instrument called a wooden fish (*muyu*), typically used in Buddhist ceremonies, during the performance to invoke spirits and accentuate action in the story.

The storytelling follows a general pattern usually involving an invocation to the gods to attend the event, followed by alternation among sung passages (to set tunes, or *dian* [*dan*, *ping*, and *gua*]), spoken narration, the dialogue of various characters, and the responses of the chorus. The chorus is cued to respond by shifts in the storyteller's voice, and these refrains may include Buddhist elements, such as the chanting of "adoration to the Amitabha Buddha." Stories told at night, though involving certain religious activities and items, are of a secular nature, while those told during the day are conducted in association with religious rituals and involve a more prominent invocation of the gods and more elaborate religious paraphernalia and religious offerings.

San Mao Precious Scrolls illustrates a conflict between Confucian familial harmony and the quest for Buddhist salvation. The youngest son in the prime minister's family desists from studying the Five Confucian Classics and turns to meditating and chanting Daoist scriptures—in particular, the *Scripture of the Three Visualizations* (*San guan jing*). The son's actions transgress the important Confucian ethical principle of filial piety (*xiao*) in several ways: the son jeopardizes his family's status and wealth by refusing to prepare for the imperial civil service exam to secure an official title; he abandons the filial obligation of producing progeny by practicing meditation in reclusion from his wife and their bedchamber; and he disobeys his parents' instructions to return to his study and bedchamber.

The prime minister returns home and admonishes his youngest son. Ironically, in order for the prime minister to take leave from the court, he must deceive the emperor into thinking that he is ill. Upon his father's return, the "wayward" son announces his disavowal of all worldly pursuits. Angered by his son's disobedience, the prime minister locks him in a cangue. Abetted by a fellow adept of their patron Daoist deity, the son escapes and ascends into the heavens after proving his devotion to the Daoist deity. The comical and often satirical language colors the story's presentation of the conflict between familial obligations and individual salvation, scholastic merit and spiritual attainment, and worldly and transcendent pursuits.

THE PRIME MINISTER IS SUMMONED HOME

Chanted [*nian*]:
Aboard a skiff of worldly suffering,
Onward bound with no way back.
Despite the raging waves on attack,
One can proceed only along this track.

[Dan *tune*]
Third Young Master Jin meditates upon the skiff of worldly suffering,
Confronting the three perils and six hardships, refusing to turn back.
No notice he takes of the violent and fierce waves that attack;
The sail is raised, and he continues ahead along his chosen track.
Let us return now to where we left off in our story;
Onward we journey to Third Young Master meditating, holed up in a wooden shack.

In the previous chapter, we already told of how the third son of Prime Minister Jin had ordered An Tong, the servant, to move his belongings into the Western Garden's Wood Fragrance Shed. There, every morning and evening, Third Young Master recited the *San guan jing* scripture. He meditated on the Dao all day long, thus reaching a state of eternal peace.

[Ping *tune*]
We will not tell of Jin's meditating on the Dao,
But rather tell of his wife, Madame Wang.

When Madame Wang saw that her husband was leaving their bedchamber in Mellow Fragrance Pavilion, she wept with anger. Her maid, Plum Fragrance, said to her: "Mistress, your husband is as strong willed as you—how can you hope to control him?"

[Ping *tune*]
Despite your urging, he will still meditate each day;
Entreat someone more commanding to compel him to stay.

Madame Wang replied: "Plum Fragrance, who is more commanding? Who can control my husband?" Plum Fragrance spoke: "As husband and wife, you are of the same generation, so you are of the same stature. Your husband's mother, Madame Qian, is a generation older, so she is of a higher stature. Since your husband is not willing to be persuaded, you must enlist the assistance of Madame Qian, and then your husband can be controlled." Upon hearing this advice, Madame Wang had little doubt as to what she must do, and she said: "Plum Fragrance, please lead the way and take me to see my mother-in-law."

[Ping *tune*]
Plum Fragrance grasped Madame Wang's hand,
Shuffling their golden-lotus feet on their way out.

After ambling along a winding path, they arrived at the Pavilion of Warmth, Madame Qian's chamber. When Madame Wang approached Madame Qian, she knelt on both knees and spoke: "Long live Mother!" Madame Qian responded: "My third daughter-in-law, if you have come here just to pay your respects, then why are you crying so?"

"Dear Mother, it is nothing but . . . well, my husband, your beloved son, is meditating and . . ."

Madame Qian said: "Why is his meditation any concern of yours?"

Upon hearing this, Madame Wang wailed, her heart torn by grief.

[Ping *tune*]
Dear Mother,
Even though your third son's meditation is no concern of mine,
It will sever the progeny in our family line.
Dear Mother, by his meditating at such a young age,
You also lose a hand to serve you soup and tea.

Upon hearing this, Madame Qian thought this to be a grave matter indeed. How could the little rascal have turned to meditating on the Dao? Certainly he must be cognizant of the three violations of filial piety. Not having progeny, isn't this the gravest infraction?

Madame Qian continued: "Third daughter-in-law, is this indeed the case?"

"Mother-in-law, I swear it to be true."

"Where is he meditating?"

"Dear Mother, he is in the study."

Plum Fragrance spoke: "Grand Madame and Mistress, third son is no longer in the study. He has now moved into the Wood Fragrance Shed."

Madame Qian said: "How terrible! How terrible! Third daughter-in-law, don't be too upset. Allow me to handle this matter. Let us go together." Madame Qian tied up her hair with a blue silk ribbon, leaning on her walking staff . . .

> [Ping *tune*]
> If the little squirt doesn't come around,
> This cane's dragon handle will beat him to the ground.

Madame Qian and her daughter-in-law bade farewell to Plum Fragrance, and they set off on the path to the Western Garden's Wood Fragrance Shed. Madame Qian emitted a cough outside the shed, startling her son. Lifting his head, he peered outside: "Oh, what misfortune! My mother has come!" He concealed the Daoist scripture with his hands and approached his mother, before whom he knelt and proclaimed: "Mother has come! Her son offers his deepest regards!"

"Little rascal, I don't want your respect. I have something to ask you. If you are not in your study reading the classics, what are you doing holed up in this shed?"

"Oh, Mother. How I long for a mind empty of worldly concerns! Little do I care for physical austerities. Since coming to the shed, my mind has been quite at peace."

"My son, when you were reading the classics in the study, did anything disturb your tranquillity?"

"Well . . ."

"Don't hem and haw. Show me what it is exactly that you are reading."

> [Ping *tune*]
> Just as long as your writing is sincere and heartfelt,
> When sent to the capital, the emperor will receive it with favor.

Jin said: "Mother, I am reading the scriptures, not the classics." His mother replied: "Oh, such as the *Book of Songs*, the *Book of History*, and the *Book of Changes*?"

[Ping *tune*]
Oh, Mother,
I am not reading the *Book of Songs* and the *Book of History*,
I am reading only the Daoist scripture *San guan jing*.

Madame Qian said: "What is the use of reading this Daoist *San guan jing*? Will it assist you in passing the civil service exam, to become an official and govern the empire?"

"Mother, it is read only for meditation. It will not assist in governing the empire."

"Then why are you reading it?"

"Mother, since you don't understand, please allow me to explain. Reciting the *San guan jing* while you and Father are still alive augments your good health, allowing you to live a very long life. After you and Father pass away, I will still recite the *San guan jing*. In this way, your sins will be atoned for in the nether world, and you will quickly be released from the suffering of reincarnation."

[Ping *tune*]
Avoiding the suffering of reincarnation,
Repaying one's parents by praying for mercy.

Upon hearing this, Madame Qian became very distressed. "You nitwit! How can you only recite the scriptures! How can you become an official if you don't study the classics! Don't you care at all about what others may think of you?"

[Ping *tune*]
The prime minister's son is meditating on the Dao,
You will be the laughingstock of the imperial court!

Jin was speechless. Madame Qian asked again: "Little rascal, how many chapters of this scripture do you intend to chant?"

"Mother, time is all that matters, not the number of chapters."

"Then, how long do you plan to chant?"

"Three hundred years."

"You are not making any sense. People do not live to be one hundred. Flowers cannot bloom for a hundred days. Will you live for three hundred years?"

"Mother, why would I not live for three hundred years?"

[Ping *tune*]
The immortal Pengzu[56] lived for eight hundred years,
And Chen Zhuanyi[57] slept for one thousand years.

---

56. Pengzu is the Chinese Methuselah.
57. Chen Zhuanyi is the Chinese Rip Van Winkle.

Madame Qian spoke: "Little rascal, you don't really want to chant for three hundred years. In any case, I will not permit you to chant for even thirty."

"Mother, please let us talk this over. Will you let me chant for at least thirty years?"

"No, even thirty years is too long. I can't allow it."

"Mother, then you'll let me chant for three years!"

"Even just half a month is not acceptable."

Upon hearing this, two teardrops rolled down from Third Young Master's eyes.

> [Gua *tune*]
> O Mother, when reading the Five Classics in the study,
> My mind was overcome by despondency.
> The day I went to delight in the spring scenery at your behest,
> An old Daoist adept in Sanqing Temple did I meet.
> He kindly bestowed upon me this *San guan jing*,
> And consequently, each and every day my afflictions lessened.
> If now I do not recite the *San guan jing*,
> To my grave I will be sent by the return of my former maladies.

Madame Qian pondered for a moment. After all, she had raised the little rascal. Her heart was torn by both adoration and indignation. If she dealt with him too strictly, and it backfired, it could result in the loss of the family's livelihood!

"Son, I'll permit you to chant for half a month. On the sixteenth day, you must quit that shed."

"Mother, I understand."

Madame Qian then turned and said to her daughter-in-law Zizhen: "Daughter-in-law, you have heard, right? Wait half a month, and let him gradually come around. Then, he will go back to your chamber." Upon hearing this, Madame Wang was overcome with joy. Madame Qian returned to the Pavilion of Warmth, and Madame Wang returned to the Mellow Fragrance Pavilion.

Following this incident, from the first day to the fifteenth, Madame Wang pined for her husband's return each morning and counted down the nights. On the sixteenth day, Madame Wang lit a silver lamp, ordered a feast and wine to be prepared, and waited with anticipation until midnight. But her husband never came! "My husband is cunning," she thought, "and perhaps he has decided to wait one more day before coming back." On the evening of the seventeenth night, she once again lit the silver lamp, ordered a feast prepared, and waited until past midnight. But her husband never came. Madame Wang trembled like thunder, and she furiously shook her finger in rage.

> [Ping *tune*]
> When the sun came up, it was already the seventeenth day,
> My husband, why have you not yet come here to stay?

Breaching your appointment with your wife is just a small affair,
But disobeying your promise to your own mother, how can you dare?

Madame Wang was at a loss, so she wept the entire night until sunrise. In the quiet night, her weeping startled Madame Xiong and Madame Gui, her two sisters-in-law, who conferred: "Why is Third Son's wife weeping all night long? Let us go and pay a visit. Plum Fragrance, please come with us to see her."

[Ping *tune*]
Plum Fragrance in front led the way,
The two sisters-in-law followed from behind.

Weaving along the path, they reached the Mellow Fragrance Pavilion. Madame Xiong and Madame Gui asked: "My sister-in-law, it is late, and the night is calm; why are you weeping with such despair?" Ah, Madame Wang was in such a pitiful state. She tried to speak, but the words got stuck in her throat, and she could only weep: "*Aaaaai*, my sisters!!"

[Ping *tune*]
You continue to get happier,
While I just despair more and more each day.

Madame Xiong and Madame Gui said: "Sister, why are you crying? Prithee, tell us!" Fragrant Plum interrupted: "Madame Wang is too angry to speak. Let me tell you." Fragrant Plum then recounted the events that had triggered Madame Wang's utter despair.

Madame Xiong and Madame Gui said: "Sister, please don't cry. We will go confer with him." Madame Wang replied: "He won't listen to your urging." Madame Xiong said: "When I confront him, he will certainly be scared stiff, trembling with fright from head to toe. Where is he?" Madame Wang reported: "He is in the Western Garden's Wood Fragrance Shed."

"Oh, let's go. As we all know, an elder brother is like a father and an elder sister-in-law is like a mother. If he doesn't heed me, then I, becoming incensed, will tie his hands behind his back and beat him."

Madame Gui said: "Don't speak such nonsense. How could you confuse it so? It is not that an elder brother is like a father and an elder sister-in-law is like a mother. Rather, it is said that an elder brother is to be obeyed, and an elder sister is to be learned from. For example, if the parents of a younger brother pass away, then the elder brother must raise him and his elder sister-in-law should goad him in his studies and demand that he do the appropriate chores. How could an elder sister-in-law be so unbridled as to tie his hands behind his back and beat him?"

[Ping *tune*]
Brother-in-law and Sister-in-law are picking a fight,
How many people will laugh over such a sight?

Madame Xiong said: "What should we do?" Madame Gui replied: "The way I see it, when Brother-in-law is meditating, we should go and make a commotion. We will yell and shout until he becomes frantic. He will then be compelled to bring his wife back to their chamber."

Madame Xiong said: "Then we should split up and ambush him from all directions. We will each shout out, urging Third Young Master to come to his senses."

[Ping *tune*]
The three sisters rushed like a strong gale,
Toward the Wood Fragrance Shed without fail.

After devising their plan, the three sisters arrived outside the Wood Fragrance Shed. Two sisters faced west while one faced east. Pretending that they had unwittingly run into one another, Madame Gui said: "Hey, Elder Sister, where are you going?"

"Well, I have heard that there is a living Buddha in the garden, and I want to ask him when my husband will get a promotion. How about you, Second Sister, where are you going?"

"Well, I have also heard that there is a living Buddha in the garden, and I have come to ask when my husband will have the title of duke conferred upon him. And Third Sister, where are you going?"

"Well, I have also heard that there is a living Buddha in the garden, and I have come to ask when my husband will come to his senses and stop reciting the *San guan jing*."

The three sisters then pretended that they had forgotten an important matter, exclaiming, "Oh no . . ."

[Ping *tune*]
Running helter-skelter, bustling all about,
They had forgotten to prepare the incense and candles.
Plum Fragrance, the garden has not yet a candle shop,
So dirt must be scooped up to pay offerings to the gods.

Madame Xiong and Madame Gui said: "Pray to this living Buddha from the south for me." Third Young Master thought: "They have come to pester me. Although I meditate all day long, I have received only a few merits. Now that they kowtow to me, all my merits will be canceled. Oh no, they are kowtowing from the south! I had better turn around and face the north." Plum Fragrance saw him turn around, and she kowtowed from the north. Third Young Master had to turn around again, this time facing the east. Madame Xiong and Madame Gui said: "Plum Fragrance, kowtow toward the west for us, okay?" Jin again turned to face the east. "Plum Fragrance, you have many sisters. Have them surround him from all directions for us. Now we will see how this Buddha will spin about trying to find a way out." Third Young Master panicked, as there was no escape. He stood as if he were brandishing a winch hammer: "Don't kowtow, don't worship me, I'm not a Buddha yet." Madame Xiong and Madame Gui clapped their hands together in merriment and burst out laughing.

> [Ping *tune*]
> From the antiquity of Pangu[58] until now,
> This is the first revolving Buddha to have ever been seen.

Madame Xiong and Madame Gui looked at Third Young Master and feigned a look of astonishment: "Oh my, there is no Buddha! It is only Third Brother-in-law!"

"Oh, it's just my two sisters-in-law!"

> [Ping *tune*]
> You two must know the strict rules of our family:
> Without serious business, you are not permitted to run about.

Madame Xiong and Madame Gui said: "Third Brother-in-law, the rules of the master no longer apply to this house. When he left for the capital to serve the emperor as prime minister, the rules went out of the house with him. Some of us are serving as officials, while others are just monkeying around."

"Sisters-in-law, you don't want to say anything to malign another. Pray, tell me who are serving as officials? And who is monkeying around?"

> [Ping *tune*]
> Your two elder brothers are officials,
> You are up to no good in the thatched monastery.

Third Young Master said: "Sisters-in-law, don't ridicule me."

> [Ping *tune*]
> Although my two elder brothers are high officials,
> It cannot compare to me sitting in the monastery.

"If you don't believe me, watch me impersonate the emperor. Your two elder sisters-in-law will play your two elder brothers, one a civil official and the other a military official. Here, I tap on your wooden fish, which is usually used by

58. In Chinese mythology, Pangu is the first living being and the creator of all.

monks when reciting scriptures. But, now, pretend it is like the sound of bells and drums in the imperial palace, summoning you to come into the palace. Hah! You can't simply run into the palace! When ascending to the palace, you must crawl one hundred steps forward and then crawl one step backward." Madame Xiong and Madame Gui retorted: "Isn't that the way a ghost moves?" Third Prince Jin burst out laughing: "Well, there you go!"

[Ping *tune*]
My two elder brothers serve in the court,
Ghosts they are, till they depart.

Madame Xiong and Madame Gui said: "Younger Brother-in-law, don't talk nonsense. We have come to beg you to come to your senses. We want your wife to be happy, reunited with her husband."

Third Young Master said: "If you want me to quit chanting, it is rather simple. I ask of you only to solve a riddle. If you get it right, I will stop meditating. If you get it wrong, however, I will never change my mind no matter what you do." Third Young Master thought for a while before coming up with a riddle: "What is a little bit red, fits tight, issues orders, and asks for the emperor's conferral."

Upon hearing this, Madame Xiong could not conceal her glee: "I've got it. The answer to this riddle is my husband. If you don't believe me, just listen."

[Ping *tune*]
The black gauze cap atop my husband's head is a bit red,
The ceremonial robe about his body tight.
His hand holds a vermilion brush, for issuing orders;
He enters court with a request, asking for the emperor's conferral.

Third Young Master said: "Elder Sister-in-law, your guess is incorrect." Madame Gui then spoke: "Third Brother, I know the answer. This riddle is about my husband."

[Ping *tune*]
The warrior's cap atop my husband's head is a bit red;
The bright helmet and armor about his body tight.
His hand holds a spear while issuing orders.
After forcing the enemy's retreat, he asks for the emperor's conferral.

Third Young Master said: "Elder Sister-in-law, isn't this what I have already told you? No matter what, you can't help but put on airs for the Jin family. Without rank and status, how can you put on airs for your family? If I did gloat like you, it would be only about myself."

[Ping *tune*]
When the sun rises in the eastern sky, it is a little bit red.
The thatched monastery encloses me tight.
I take my orders from the true scripture of *San guan jing*,
Meditating to acquire merit, asking for conferral from the Jade Emperor.

Madame Xiong and Madame Gui responded: "Younger Brother-in-law, isn't it too soon for you to ask for conferral from the Jade Emperor? Why don't you allow us to confer a title upon you first?"

[Gua *tune*]
Third Brother meditates very diligently on the Dao,
The top of his head lurching forward in a bow.
His underside can shelter one from rain,
While his backside is flat enough to plant onions.
The day you finally become enlightened,
You will ascend to heaven as a Buddha completely famished.

Third Prince Jin said: "It makes no difference. Anyway, I have already become a famished Buddha." Madame Gui replied: "Wait, wait, I want to add to Younger Brother-in-law's conferral."

[Gua *tune*]
Third Brother-in-law meditates, his heart all flustered.
His face becomes colored yellow just like paper.
His eyeballs receding into the sockets of his skull;
His back as haggard as a bed of rice;
His ribs as fragile as a paper-crafted window;
Feet and legs withered like wooden stakes;
Hands and arms scrawny as a wooden pole.
The day you finally become enlightened,
You will be like a skeleton when you see the god of death.

Madame Xiong said: "I will also add a conferral upon Third Brother-in-law."

[Gua *tune*]
Third Brother meditates on the Dao so diligently,
His wife left in a cold room, forsaken pitifully.
Starving, he breathes only the west wind inside the thatched monastery;
His spine like a bow bending,
His feet swollen like a lantern.
The day when you finally become enlightened,
No air will your nose still be inhaling.

Third Young Master said: "Ladies, you are cursing me as if I had tossed your babies down a well. You don't just say that I will become a famished Buddha! You also hex me to die!" Madame Xiong said: "Precisely. Plum Fragrance, to show your respect for Third Brother, please pour him a cup of tea." While Plum Fragrance was pouring him tea, Madame Xiong said:

> [Ping *tune*]
> Brother-in-law, our words have offended you,
> Please forgive us as much as you can.

Third Prince Jin replied: "All right. We should be friends, not enemies. As you have apologized, let's just forget it. I will ask for the family's forgiveness."

> [Ping *tune*]
> Eldest Sister offers a cup of tea,
> Steeped with chrysanthemum petals.
> Elder Brother, an official of high eminence,
> Ensuring sons and grandsons will enjoy much glory.

Upon hearing this, Madame Gui was overcome by happiness. "Brother-in-law's meditation has finally led him to say sensible things. I will also pour a cup of tea to apologize to my younger brother-in-law." Third Young Master said: "If Second Sister-in-law also makes peace with me, I will also ask for the family's forgiveness on her account."

> [Ping *tune*]
> Second Sister-in-law pays her respects with a cup of tea,
> Steeped with osmanthus petals.
> Second Brother, a general at a station along the border:
> You wear silk in the winter and chiffon in the summer.

Madame Wang said: "My two sisters, in pouring tea, have shown their respect, so I will also apologize to my husband." Third Young Master looked at his wife:

> [Ping *tune*]
> Madame Wang offers a cup of tea,
> Steeped with magnolia flowers.
> I meditate in my thatched monastery,
> Now my wife looks shabby like a beggar.

Madame Xiong responded: "Well, my husband is an official, so I have a life full of riches. If Second Brother-in-law is an official, Second Sister will have a life of comfort. If you are reclusive in the thatched monastery, Third Sister's tears will never run dry." Third Young Master responded: "My sister-in-law, please don't get worked up. Listen to what I have to say again. Since now is neither a special occasion nor a holiday, when you wear flashy attire, you are even uglier than a ghost."

[Gua *tune*]
Eldest Sister-in-law wears flashy reds and blues,
So the devil believes her to be a demon.
Second Sister wears bright red, her hair ornamented with many flowers,
So the devil thinks she is but an urchin.
My wife doesn't adorn herself in the least,
Dressed plainly just like a grown, honest woman.
The devil extends her an invitation,
Thinking she is a living Guanyin from the Southern Sea.

Madame Xiong and Madame Gui said: "You are so cruel, comparing us to demons but comparing your wife to Guanyin! We are not ghosts! Rather, by meditating so much, you have turned into a ghost! Your two elder brothers are serving as officials in the emperor's court. They always ride in palanquins, with sentries hailing in front and crowds rushing from behind. The sound of gongs signals for a path to be cleared, and *suonas*[59] and trumpets announce the procession. Eight attendants carry a sedan, as if they were carrying a living Buddha."

"Well, Elder Sister-in-law, you must know that those in high office may be well known, while those who meditate on the Dao have a peaceful life. But, in the end, high officials will not enjoy a good fate. A minister who follows an emperor is like a lamb following a tiger."

[Ping *tune*]
A minister following an emperor will end in tragedy;
A lamb that follows a tiger will always be killed.
A general surely ends up deceased on the battlefield.
Even a ferocious tiger can't easily escape from a pit.

Third Young Master asked Madame Xiong: "Elder Sister-in-law, did you catch the drift?"

"No, I didn't."

"Since you can't understand it, allow me to explain again. When a tiger and lamb are in each other's company, if the tiger is not hungry, they will get along quite well together. However, when the tiger gets hungry, since the lamb's strength cannot compare to the tiger's, it will be eaten by the tiger. My elder brothers serving as officials in the imperial court are just like lambs. When

---

59. The *suona* is a loud, double-reed instrument with a flaring bell opposite the mouthpiece.

everything is going well, then the ruler is content. If something bad happens, however, then the ruler will become very angry."

[Gua *tune*]
The emperor's brow moves up and down;
The emperor's brush dangles from his palm.
Although my two elder brothers are not yet dead,
In the emperor's jail, they are locked up with dread.
If dismissed from office, their official caps stripped away,
Your phoenix coronets and capes can no longer stay.

[Ping *tune*]
When the sisters heard this,
They became infuriated.

Madame Xiong, enraged, said: "What kind of person are you? You just can't listen to reason. Second Sister, let's go. Let him hang himself." Madame Wang said: "Sisters, wait for me!" Madame Xiong and Madame Gui said: "Where do you think you are going? Since your husband is reciting the *San guan jing*, you should recite liturgical blessings to ensure the safety of your two elder brothers."

[Ping *tune*]
Ensure that your elder brothers return home safely;
Guarantee that they will stay healthy.
If something horrible goes astray,
You will certainly have to pay.

Upon hearing this, tears began to pour from Madame Wang's eyes.

[Ping *tune*]
My husband, your wicked words do not distress me,
But to your sisters-in-law, you ought to be more mannerly.
My husband, if you fail to come to your senses,
I will never return to our bedchamber.

Madame Xiong and Madame Gui said: "Third Sister, don't be like that. Since we have come together, let us also leave together. We have failed to make him come to his senses. Perhaps there is someone else who can."

[Ping *tune*]
The three sisters stood up,
And reported to their mother-in-law.

The three sisters arrived at the Pavilion of Warmth and kowtowed to their mother-in-law. When Madame Qian saw that the three wives had arrived, she raised her eyebrows and grinned: "Daughters, has the little rascal come to his senses?"

"O Mother!"

> [Ping *tune*]
> Third Brother has not come to his senses,
> Rather, he just sniggered and laughed at us.

Madame Qian asked: "What did the little rascal say?"

"He said that those in high office gain fame, while those who meditate on the Dao have a peaceful life. But, in the end, high officials will not enjoy a good fate. Moreover, he said that high officials must meet an inauspicious fate. He said that a minister who follows an emperor is like a lamb following a tiger. A minister following a ruler always ends in disaster, just like a lamb that falls into a tiger's lair will always be eaten. He also said that Eldest Brother and Second Eldest Brother—"

> [Ping *tune*]
> In court, if one day the emperor's rules they disobey,
> The emperor will send them to prison.
> Dismissed from office and the official's cap taken away,
> Our phoenix bonnets and capes, no longer can we wear.

Madame Qian said: "Daughters, these are not the words of an oracle. He was just being carefree and talking nonsense." Madame Xiong and Madame Gui then said:

> [Ping *tune*]
> Mother, we can forgive him for profaning our husbands,
> But, Father, as well, follows the emperor's every call.
> As smashing a water vat damages the surrounding wall,
> So Father is also implicated in Third Young Master's scorn.

When Madame Qian heard this, she was angered and shook like thunder: "All right! The rascal is not willing to come to his senses. We will then write a letter to the capital, asking Father to come home and teach him a lesson!"

> [Ping *tune*]
> Despite our urging, the rascal still meditates on the Dao,
> So request that our honorable father return home now.

When Madame Xiong heard this, her entire body regained its previous strength. She grasped some paper and a brush, dipping it in ink: "Mother, I will first write a few lines."

[Ping *tune*]
Kowtowing, kowtowing, three times,
Kowtowing to my most honorable father-in-law.
Of the three sons whom you have raised,
Two are in the imperial court much praised;
The third, however, is at home not studying as he ought.
Avoiding the classics and becoming a Daoist hermit.
We entreat Honorable Father to return home as fit,
And instruct him to correct his ways and study the Five Classics.

Upon finishing, Madame Xiong put down the brush. Madame Gui said: "Let me also write a few lines."

[Ping *tune*]
Kowtowing, kowtowing, three times,
Kowtowing to my most honorable father-in-law.
In court, serving as a high minister,
You are earning great wealth in silver.
With a ladle, it is measured for all in the family,
With a dustpan, it is dispensed generously.
One of your sons, whom Honorable Father has born,
Is reluctant to read the classics, but insists on reciting the scriptures.
Hoping that Honorable Father will quickly return home,
To instruct and admonish Third Brother to quickly grow up.

Upon finishing, Madame Gui put down the brush. Madame Wang said: "Let me also write a few lines."

[Ping *tune*]
Kowtowing, kowtowing, three times,
Kowtowing to my most honorable father-in-law.
Permitting my family to take your son as a son-in-law,
You used your power to marry me into your family.
Your son each day is meditating on the Dao,
Hurting your daughter-in-law Wang Zizhen.

Madame Qian received the letter, looking at it: "Oh no, rather than humbly inviting your father to return home, you blame him. You do not want to blame and curse him! Let me write to him myself." Madame Qian thus picked up the brush and wrote:

[Ping *tune*]
Wishing my honorable husband peaceful days within the imperial court,
Wishing eternal happiness and the emperor's kindness.
We have together raised three sons, no less;
Two of our sons have proudly joined you in the imperial court.
The third son, however, harbors no aspiration at home;
Avoiding reading the classics, he has become a Daoist recluse.
Your wife's old age makes it hard for her to correct him,
So I humbly hope that my honorable husband will quickly return home.

The three sisters looked upon the letter: "Oh, Mother is after all more knowledgeable than us. She has written with great politeness." Madame Xiong and Madame Gui said: "Inviting a general is fine, but it is better yet to rouse a general. What if we each add a few lines." They wrote:

[Gua *tune*]
Kowtowing, kowtowing, three times,
Kowtowing to my honorable father-in-law.
If you return upon reading this letter,
You will pacify this household matter.
If, rather, you do not return upon reading this letter,
The four of us will have to go to the imperial city.
The family letter has now been written,
We will seal it as tightly as we can.

Madame Qian quickly summoned A Long and A Feng,[60] two of the family's strongest servants. After eating breakfast, they put the letter inside a cloth and hurried on their way. The two servants were ordered not to rest during the day and not to stop for lodging in the evening, traveling both night and day. Jin Long and Jin Feng said: "Madame Qian, during the day the road is easy going, but at night we will be interrogated at the patrol stations." Madame Qian replied: "Don't worry. When your master entered the capital, he didn't take his lanterns, so now you can carry the lanterns with you and no one will dare stop you."[61]

[Ping *tune*]
Take the lanterns with gold letters on your trip,
No barriers then can hinder you.
If someone questions you on the road,
Then just say you are delivering a letter from the prime minister's family.

---

60. The "A" (pronounced "ah") of these names is a preposed syllable indicating a colloquial form of address.

61. These are official lanterns indicating imperially bestowed status.

At this, Jin Long and Jin Feng prepared their saddles and fed the horses with ample hay.

> [Ping *tune*]
> Leaping upon the silver-maned horses,
> All the way to the emperor's Wuchao Gate they galloped.
>
> [Gua *tune*]
> The family servants quickly traveled,
> Not even stopping for a short rest.
> Because of the family's letter they carried,
> They were able to enter the capital at night.
>
> After they were past the gate about a mile,
> They passed four or five houses with chimneys.
> They saw six or seven elaborate terraces;
> Eight, nine, or ten fragrant flowers.

When one goes slowly, it is like clouds obscuring the moon. When one goes quickly, it is like a shooting star, which doesn't admire the landscape upon approaching a mountain or inquire as to the depth of water when approaching a lake.

> [Ping *tune*]
> Traveling on the road for several days,
> Finally catching sight of the imperial city's outer wall.

Jin Long said to Jin Feng: "My brother Jin Feng, what everyone says about the imperial city being grand is certainly true."

> [Ping *tune*]
> But they don't have the leisure to admire the imperial city,
> Rushing toward the emperor's court.

Jin Long said: "Brother Jin Feng, this is our first time to enter the capital, and we don't know where Prime Minister Jin's office is located." At this moment, an imperial guard, walking stick in hand, was pacing on the side of the road. Jin Long and Jin Feng dismounted and walked up to the imperial guard and kowtowed: "Sir, please be so kind as to tell us the whereabouts of Prime Minister Jin's office?"

"To get to Prime Minister Jin's office from here, you need to go east, turn right, and then it is on the street that is paved with white jade stones."

[Ping *tune*]
The two family servants went on their way,
The prime minister's waiting room up ahead lay.

Jin Long and Jin Feng swung off their horses and tied them to a flagpole. They knocked on the door, and the doorkeeper An Tong answered: "Who's there?"

"I am Jin Long, from the prime minister's house in Bingzhou. I have come to deliver a letter from his family." An Tong opened the door to look: "Well, if it isn't my two brothers."

[Ping *tune*]
Just wait a moment outside the door,
I will quickly report to the prime minister.

When the prime minister was told that a letter from his family had arrived, he immediately ordered An Tong to open the official door to his office, inviting in the bearers of his wife's letter.

[Ping *tune*]
An Tong hurriedly rushed about,
Inviting the family's letter into the office.

The prime minister received the letter, and he ordered Jin Long and Jin Feng: "You have been on a long journey, enduring much strain and hardship. Please go to the kitchen for a meal."

[Ping *tune*]
To the kitchen for snacks, the family servants went swiftly,
The prime minister read the letter until he understood clearly.

There is a popular saying: "The inside of the prime minister's stomach can hold a boat." This is not to say that his stomach is so large that a boat can fit inside. Rather, it means that his knowledge is very broad, his wisdom acute, and he possesses well-calculated plans. While the prime minister was reading the letter, he entered into conversation with it:

"Thanks, thanks."

"Exactly, exactly."

"Not at all, not at all."

An Tong heard the prime minister and said: "Prime Minister, to whom are you speaking?" The prime minister replied: "My wife's letter says: 'Wishing my honorable husband peaceful days within the imperial court, wishing eternal happiness and the emperor's kindness.' So, I responded with: 'Thanks, thanks.' She wrote: 'We have together raised three sons, no less; two of our sons have proudly joined you in the imperial court.' So I answered: 'Exactly, exactly.' She has written: 'The third son, however, harbors no aspiration at home; avoiding reading the classics, he has become a Daoist recluse.' I thought: 'Not at all, not at all.' As I have not returned home for such a long while, they just use this as a pretext to get me to go back for a visit."

[Ping *tune*]
Jin Long, you can confirm how winding is the long mountain road;
An old fellow like me cannot grow wings and fly.

Jin Long said: "Master, keep reading, there is more." If the prime minister hadn't looked at it, it would not have been so, but since he did . . .

[Ping *tune*]
So angry that his face became pale like none,
The threads on his shoes breaking one by one.

"An Tong, go to the senior official's compound and summon my eldest son for me!"

[Ping *tune*]
An Tong went to carry out his order,
Not daring to delay even one second.

When An Tong arrived at the prime minister's son's compound, he passed on the prime minister's order. My listeners, usually when Elder Brother Jin receives an invitation, he follows the protocol of presenting a calling card to the host, and he travels in a palanquin attended by eight servants. This evening, upon hearing his father's summons, he dared not dillydally, and he immediately jumped into a small palanquin and set off.

[Ping *tune*]
Quickly traversing the streets and alleys,
He sped straight to his father's office.

When he arrived at the office, he kneeled down on both knees and said: "Eternal happiness to my father! Why have you summoned me?" The prime minister said: "It is just because your mother has sent a letter. You will understand when you read it." Official Jin received the letter and read it very carefully from beginning to end.

[Ping *tune*]
When he had finished reading the letter,
He flung it to the ground.

The prime minister's beard quivered, and his eyes flared in rage: "You scoundrel!"

[Ping *tune*]
Tossing the family letter to the ground is no trivial matter,
As you have disobeyed your own mother.
At five in the morning, I will face the emperor and report this letter,
Your betrayal of your mother and father is not a light crime.

When Official Jin saw that his father had misunderstood his feelings, two tears rolled down from his eyes.

[Ping *tune*]
O Father, the only reason I tossed the letter to the ground,
Is because I just hate my brother for meditating on the Dao.

The prime minister said: "Son, if it as you say, don't weep. Let's talk this over. Do you think I should return home?"

"Father, you certainly should go back. If you don't, your wife and three daughters-in-law will rush to the capital. When they are seen by the officials in the imperial court, you will certainly lose face."

[Ping *tune*]
The four women entering the imperial city,
Encouraging the mockery of the court's military and civil officials.

The prime minister said: "Son, my court affairs are multifarious, how could I possibly afford to go home?" Jin Long and Jin Feng said: "Those now serving in office have several ways in which to take leave. Some return home on account of their age, others because of illness, and some even resign. Our master could return home on account of illness."

[Ping *tune*]
Master will say he has an illness,
Returning home for convalescence.

The prime minister said: "What you have suggested, however, is far from the real situation. My face is robust and rosy, my body is plump and healthy. I don't even have a cough. How could I ask for sick leave? You should all know, if my excuse is found to be wanting, my position will not be stable."

Jin Long said: "Master, this is not a problem. Just go to the apothecary and buy a half ounce of gardenia and three capsules of lotus leaf. Use locust-tree flowers to rinse out your ears, and the lotus-leaf water to wash your face. If you do so every day, washing three times, washing nine times in three days, then your face will become yellowish and withered, and you will appear to be sick."

The prime minister then gave An Tong a few spare silver ingots and sent him to the apothecary to buy five ounces of locust-tree flowers, a half ounce of gardenia, and three capsules of lotus leaves. He washed every day three times, nine times in three days, and then the prime minister looked at himself in a bronze mirror and burst out laughing:

[Ping *tune*]
No wonder the Jin family is so wealthy,
I always have crafty people giving me clever ideas.

When his son saw him, he said: "Father, this is perfect. Your face really looks yellow and withered. You truly look like you have become ill."

[Ping *tune*]
O Father, your face is like yellow paper;
Your eyes have recessed a half inch deeper.
It looks as if your illness were truly severe;
It is certain that you can return home on account of illness.

Official Jin wrote a sick-leave request for his father. At five in the morning, he approached the emperor: "Emperor, your humble official's father has a sick-leave request, and I humbly ask that Your Majesty take a look."

The emperor read it and said: "Oh my, my respected minister's health is not normal, please bring him to see me at the palace immediately!" Official Jin thought: "Amitabha Buddha, I hope he feigns illness well, otherwise I fear for our lives!" Official Jin immediately went to his father's chamber: "Congratulations, Father, the emperor has requested to see your illness to verify the request letter. You will need to feign with exaggeration. Speak in a softer voice, as you want to really seem like you are overcome with illness." At this, Prime Minister Jin supported himself on his son's shoulder, who held his father's elbows.

[Dan *tune*]
Official Jin accompanied his wobbly father into the palace.
When his foot stepped up, his hand slipped.
Prime Minister Jin stumbled into the palace.

The emperor asked: "Minister, who is that behind you?"
"Emperor, it is my father."
"Revered Prime Minister, raise your head and look at me!"

[Ping *tune*]
The prime minister raised his head and focused his eyes,
Saying "Long live the emperor," repeatedly, and then:
"Emperor, my head aches as if by a thousand swords it is being chopped;

My stomach hurts as if by ten thousand arrows it is being pierced.
My eyes and ears are unclear;
My four limbs lack strength and vigor.
Emperor, I am burning up like a flaming stove;
Freezing like water about to become ice.
Emperor, my illness has become this severe,
I don't know if my life will be spared."

Prime Minister Jin was a renowned minister, so when the emperor heard that his illness was like this, he was very concerned indeed.

[Ping *tune*]
My revered minister, only three days ago,
Your complexion was exuding red like a peach blossom in March.
Now, how can it be like a chrysanthemum suffering frost in September?
My revered minister, are your heart and lungs not well,
Or is your temperament in disorder?
Please tell your humble majesty your true condition.

Prime Minister Jin said: "Emperor:

[Ping *tune*]
Although I never had problems before,
I have become ill suddenly.
Last night, the cold wind and rain chilled me,
And my body couldn't normally adjust to the temperature."

The emperor said: "My beloved minister, don't worry, this is called 'catching a cold wind.' The countryside has a doctor for the people, while the court has an imperial doctor. I will summon the imperial doctor and have him prescribe medication for your illness and observe your illness carefully, so that your body will quickly recuperate."

When Official Jin heard this, he was scared out of his wits. He thought to himself: "If the imperial doctor discovers that my father is really not sick, how could we bear the great crime of deceiving the emperor?" He kowtowed, kneeling, and pleaded:

[Ping *tune*]
Emperor, forgive me but my father has a family in his hometown,
Please allow him to return home to see my mother.

The emperor responded: "My beloved minister, your humble ruler's country is very important, and your father is important to the country's ruling. If he is absent from court, then who will take care of the country's affairs?"

Official Jin responded:

[Ping *tune*]
Emperor, when my father is not in court,
There will still be my brother and me.
I am adept at maintaining peace throughout the nation with my brush,
My younger brother uses his sword to pacify heaven and earth.[62]

When the emperor heard this, he was very pleased: "My respected minister, your humble ruler has approved your request. Please quickly return to Bingzhou so that you may recover. My minister, you are an accomplished official, so I will spare no expense and will bestow upon you half an imperial entourage, with an eight-servant palanquin, to accompany you to Bingzhou."

When Official Jin heard this, he knelt down and said: "Please, Your Majesty, don't extend your royal kindness. If my father were to return in a royal entourage, then when he arrives, the provincial officials and the local government officials will wish to greet him. This will waste time on the road, making it difficult for him to take his medicine and delaying his recovery. I humbly beg you not to provide him with an entourage!"

[Ping *tune*]
Returning to the province does not require being met by provincial officials;
Returning to the local government does not require being met by local officials.

The emperor consented with his request of doing away with the royal entourage. Official Jin thanked the emperor for his majestic beneficence, and he retreated, returning to his chambers, and said to his father:

[Ping *tune*]
If we had not been able to turn that corner in the palace,
Then we would have had to descend and enter the devil's gate.

"Oh Father, Third Younger Brother is still at a tender age, please be patient when you return to admonish him. You should not use the methods for castigating the lower officials."

[Ping *tune*]
Don't use three bats and five clubs to beat him,
Otherwise you will let my mother down.

62. These references are to the civil and military divisions of government.

AN EIGHTEENTH-CENTURY VERSION OF "LIANG SHANBO AND ZHU YINGTAI" FROM SUZHOU

Translated and introduced by Wilt L. Idema

The origin of the tale of Liang Shanbo and Zhu Yingtai can be traced back to the Song dynasty (960–1279) and perhaps even to the Tang dynasty (618–907). Zhang Jin (ca. 1130–ca. 1180) writes in *Maps and Facts of Siming in the Qiandao Reign* (*Qiandao Siming tujing*) a description of the Ningbo area:

> The Grave of the Loyal Wife is the place where Liang Shanbo and Zhu Yingtai were buried together. It is found ten li to the west of the county capital, behind the Court of Reception. There is also a temple there. Old records tell that the two of them had studied together in their youth, and that for three years Shanbo did not realize Yingtai was a girl—such was his guileless simplicity! When the *Shidao sifan zhi* [*Record of the Ten Circuits and the Four Barbarians*] reads: "This is the common grave of the Loyal Wife Zhu Yingtai and Liang Shanbo," it refers to this location.

Record of the Ten Circuits and the Four Barbarians is credited to a certain Liang Zaiyan of the late seventh century. A more detailed account of the tragic love of Zhu Yingtai and Liang Shanbo is said to derive from the Tang dynasty short story collection *Heated Room Records* (*Xuanshi zhi*), by Zhang Du (second half of the ninth century):

> Yingtai was the daughter of the Zhu family in Shangyu. She disguised herself as a man in order to travel and study, and she devoted herself to her work together with a certain Liang Shanbo from Guiji. Shanbo's style name was Churen. Zhu returned home first, and only when, two years later, Shanbo paid her a visit did he realize that she was a girl. He was greatly disappointed as if he had lost something. He told his father and mother to ask for her hand, but she had already been promised in marriage to a son of the Ma family.
>
> Later Shanbo served as magistrate of Yin county. When he died of an illness, he was buried on the west side of the city of Yin. When Zhu was on her way to marry Ma, her boat passed by his grave. Wind and waves prohibited the boat from going on. When she learned that this was the location of his grave, she left the boat and wept for him. The earth then suddenly split asunder and swallowed her. This was the way she was buried together with him.
>
> The chancellor of the Jin, Xie An (320–385), reported this to the throne, which bestowed upon it the title "Grave of the Loyal Wife."

But since this account is first encountered in an eighteenth-century compilation, its authenticity is doubtful. Be that as it may, by Song dynasty times the legend had been enriched by the detail of the lovers' transformation into butterflies, and from the late sixteenth century onward, most retellings bring the lovers back to life in one way or another and allow them an eventful career. This career would grow longer and more complex as both Liang Shanbo and Zhu Yingtai acquired in subsequent versions more and more magical and military skills. But modern retellings of the story tend to stop at the butterfly transformation.

A few scenes of Ming dynasty dramatic adaptations of the legend have been preserved. The earliest completely preserved prosimetric version of the legend, *The Ballad of Liang Shanbo and Zhu Yingtai's Common Study as Sworn Brothers* (*Liang Shanbo Zhu Yingtai jieyi xiongdi gongshu ci*), probably antedates these dramatic adaptations and may date from the fifteenth century or even earlier. Another early ballad version is the *Song of Liang Shanbo*, which was printed in 1660 and written in stanzas of seven-syllable lines. The version translated here belongs to the genre of *tanci* (literally, "plucking rhymes" or "plucking lyrics"). It survives as a single manuscript copy, made by a professional artist in Suzhou in 1769. In this retelling, the action is set during the lifetime of Confucius, which is identified with the reign of King Ding (r. 606–586 B.C.E.) of the Zhou dynasty (1045–221 B.C.E.). From the nineteenth century and later, we have a great number of adaptations in practically all genres of prosimetric "speaking and telling" literature (*shuochang wenxue*). From the same period and later, we also have access to a large number of versions in various forms of local drama (in many of these local drama genres, it is traditional to have both Zhu Yingtai and Liang Shanbo played by women). In the twentieth century, the tale was also adapted for the screen. The first screen adaptation dates from 1926. Another very successful version was produced in China in 1954, while the Shaw Brothers of Hong Kong had a huge hit with their 1963 version.

In the twentieth century, the story of Liang Shanbo and Zhu Yingtai has often been hailed as an expression of women's desire for literacy and equal educational opportunities, and as a reflection of the evils of the traditional marriage system in the old society. In more recent years, the legend has been claimed as a charter by the Chinese queer movement.

The *tanci* (translated as "chantefable" throughout this volume) was a popular genre of prosimetric literature in the modern provinces of Jiangsu and Zhejiang from the sixteenth century onward. The majority of the texts in this genre are very long and are mostly written in lines of basically seven-syllable verse, interspersed with short passages of prose. The seven-syllable line in the verse sections is sometimes replaced by two short lines of three syllables each, or it may be extended by adding one or more characters at the beginning. The verse sections were sung to the accompaniment of one or more stringed instruments, played by the singer or a musician. The genre had both male and female performers; whereas male performers told their stories in the region's teahouses for a mostly male audience, female performers, until the second half of the nineteenth century, usually performed in private homes for a female audience.

Each major locality in the region developed its own style of *tanci* performance, but the locality best known for its *tanci* is the city of Suzhou, where local performers trace their tradition back to great performers of the eighteenth century. "The Newly Compiled Tale of the Golden Butterflies" dates from that formative period in the development of the *Suzhou tanci* and can be considered an oral-connected text. Although conventions in both the singing and dialogue roles differ from those of *tanci* performances today, the interplay among speaking, singing, and dialogue in the text suggests the performance dynamics of an earlier era. Its relatively short length makes it possible to include a complete translation of the text. The version starts out by having its two protagonists introduce themselves in the first person and in the sequence that was customary on the traditional stage, which may suggest that the anonymous author of the *tanci* was inspired by a play, but for the remainder of the text he (or she?) sticks to the traditional format of third-person omniscient narrative, interlarded with ample dialogue.

THE NEWLY COMPILED TALE OF THE GOLDEN BUTTERFLIES

There is a poem that goes:

> Master Qiu, that wise Sage of the Zhou dynasty, Confucius:
> His teachings have been transmitted throughout the world.
> His three thousand disciples were all distinguished by talent,
> While the seventy-two elders were accomplished in learning.[63]

[*Speaks:*]

"My name is Liang Shanbo. For generations my family has lived in Shaoxing prefecture, and I hail from Zhuji county. My parents are of the same age and approaching sixty. I am their only son, and I have just turned seventeen. Fortunately, my family is quite well off, so I can devote myself fully to my studies. I have been told that Confucius, Master Kong from Shandong, is roaming throughout all the states, widely teaching the study of the Odes.

[*Sings:*]

"This very moment he has established himself as a teacher in Hangzhou,
That's why I took leave of my parents and started out on this journey.

---

63. Kong Qiuni is, in the West, best known as Confucius (551–479 B.C.E.), a Latinization of the expression "Kong fuzi" (Master Kong). The total number of his students during his lifetime is said to have been three thousand. Seventy-two (a magic number throughout Eurasia) of them are venerated with the Master in Confucian temples. During his lifetime, Confucius, who hailed from Qufu, in modern Shandong, visited many of the feudal states of Zhou dynasty China (needless to say, he never visited Hangzhou). Confucius is also credited with editing the Classics, including the *Book of Odes* (*Shi jing*).

The only servant I brought with me goes by the name of Four-Nine;
I've departed from Zhuji and hurry on with all possible speed.
Just look, as I am traveling it happens to be the third month of spring:

"Red peach blossoms and green willow leaves fill mountain and village.
Let me not narrate how Shanbo traveled on his journey,
Our story will have to tell of yet another actor on the stage!"

[*Speaks*:]
"My name is Zhu Yingtai, and I hail from Xinghua village in Yuezhou prefecture.

[*Sings*:]
"My father and mother are both alive and quite well-to-do,
Their only children are my elder brother and little me.
My elder brother has already married a sister-in-law,
He takes care of gardens and fields with great competence.

"Slaves and servants are ready in droves to do his bidding,
Our granaries are filled with rice, while silver fills the vault.
I am conversant with all forms of a woman's needlework:
My embroidered dragon and phoenix have brilliant colors!

"Considering that my pretty face has quite exquisite features,
I want to become a person who is perfect in talent and beauty.
I've been told that Master Kong, roaming through the states,
Now has opened a school and is teaching in Hangzhou.

"He is a famous teacher, who is revered by all and sundry,
So I want to go and travel there so as to study with him.

"If I would be able to achieve an understanding of the Odes,
I would establish an eternal reputation as a famous talented woman.
Now I've pondered this awhile, I've grown quite enthusiastic,
So let me go to their room and discuss this with my parents."

[*Speaks*:]
So she said: "Father and Mother, ever since my birth I love to study, so I regret I have no excellent teacher to instruct me. Recently I've learned that Master Kong is teaching in Hangzhou. That is a unique opportunity I cannot afford to miss!

[*Sings*:]
"My dear parents, I have come here to inform the two of you
That I want to leave home in order to study with that teacher!"

The lady her mother and the squire could not hide a smile
As they addressed their darling daughter in the following words:

"It's only boys who devote themselves to the study of books,
There never have been girls who devote themselves to study!
Look at all the civil officials and military officers at court:
They all, to the very last man, are males, masculine fellows!

"You, moreover, are a girl in a skirt, wearing hairpins,
How could you go off and study together with boys?
Go to your room and devote yourself to your embroidery,
Such womanly work is your proper and classical text!"

After Yingtai had heard these words from her parents,
She addressed them once more in the following words:

"Your daughter may be a girl in a skirt, wearing hairpins,
But when I dress up as a man you can't tell the difference!
My parents, please be so kind as to give me your permission,
Only if I can study *Documents* and *Odes* I'll be happy!"[64]

[*Speaks*:]

The squire said: "If you talk like this, dress up as a man and show yourself to me. Only if I indeed fail to recognize you will I give you my permission to leave home and study."

[*Sings*:]
When Yingtai heard these words, she was filled with joy,
And went back to her own room, to her private apartment.
After she had boiled lotus-leaf water, she washed her face,
She took off her hairpins and rings, removed her scarf.

A square hat of the latest fashion she put on her head,
A blue gown replaced the skirt and shirt she then wore.
Her embroidered shoes were replaced by red-cloud boots,
As she dressed herself up as a traveling fortune-teller.
In her hands she carried an abacus as sign of his trade,
And for accent she adopted the dialect of Lanxi county.

When all her servant girls came out to have a look,
Each of them had to laugh so much her belly hurt!

---

64. The *Book of Documents* (*Shu jing*) and the *Book of Odes* are two of the Five Classics.

"Demoiselle, you indeed are so cunningly clever,
Now you're dressed as a man, none knows the truth!"

Once Zhu Yingtai had left her private apartment,
She hurried through the back garden to the street.
Arriving in front of the gate she called out loudly,
And Mr. Zhu, when he heard this, thought to himself:

"Yingtai wants to leave home, study with a teacher—
I just wanted to invite a specialist and have our fortune told."
So he ordered a servant to invite the gentleman in,
And the fortune-teller immediately entered the house!

Mr. Zhu invited him hastily into his study, and said:
"I'd like to ask you to compute our daughter's fortune.
This year she turned just sixteen years of age,
She was born on the seventh of the seventh, at noon.

"If you compute her future correctly, make no mistake,
I will show you my gratitude in no slight way!"

The fortune-teller promptly started the computations,
And then addressed Mr. Zhu in the following words:
"The Star of a Team of Four Horses moves in this fate:[65]
She has to leave home, and will rise to great glory!
But if she stays home, she will meet with disaster,
From which she can escape only by leaving home."

Upon these words Mr. Zhu was filled with joy,
And he made ready to pay the gentleman his fee.
When the gentleman saw this, she started to smile,
As she shouted: "My daddy, you were deceived!
I am none else than your own darling daughter,
Who dressed up as a fortune-teller to try you out."

Upon these words Mr. Zhu laughed out loudly:
"My child, you truly are quite determined!

"In disguise you could fool even your own father,
So I am sure that others, too, will be deceived.
As it is your desire to devote yourself to studies,
Be careful as you leave and go on your way."

---

65. In ancient times, a team of four horses pulled the carriage of a high official.

When her sister-in-law in her room heard of this,
She came to see her parents-in-law and said:
"When my sister-in-law is going off to Hangzhou,
She is bound to find herself a husband there.

"All the students are boys, and she is a girl—
It is improper, such mingling of boys and girls!
My parents-in-law, your have to make a decision,
You cannot allow your daughter to go to a school!"

Upon these words her parents-in-law had no reply,
But Zhu Yingtai, Ninth Sister, raised her voice:[66]
"If ever I will harbor any villainous desire,
Blue heaven above will be my witness!"

A flower vase stood, she saw, before the Buddha,
So she turned around and went into the back garden.
She plucked there a single peony flower,
And she stuck it in that flower vase:

"I make the following vow in respect to this flower:
This flower will be exactly the same as my body.
If once in Hangzhou I allow my body to be broken,
This flower, too, in its vase will wilt and die!

"But if I in the academy preserve my virginity,
This flower, too, in its vase will continue to bloom!"
Upon these words her parents were overjoyed:
"Of course, my child, you are not the common sort!

"Leave early, come back early, take good care.
Remember this well before you speak your mind."
Little Miss Zhu Yingtai said she had understood,
And with lowered head she bowed before her parents.

First she bowed to her father, next to her mother,
Third she bowed to her brother and sister-in-law.
Fourth she bowed to the neighbors and all relations,
And she informed each of them of what had transpired.

---

66. In some retellings of the tale, Zhu Yingtai has not just one elder brother but eight elder brothers, which makes her ninth in the order of siblings.

Fifth she bowed to the chests and trunks in her room:
"I'll not wear my clothes for a while, store them safely!"
Sixth she bowed to her powder and powder box:
"For a while now I will not look at my face!"

Seventh she bowed to her box of hairpins:
"When I come back I will again put up my chignon!"
Eighth she bowed to the flowering trees in the garden:
"Let me pour out this cup of wine to the clear breeze!"

Ninth she bowed to the golden carp in their pond:
"When I come back I'll ready again my angling gear!"
Tenth she bowed to pavilion and water kiosk:
"For a while my white hands will not open the blinds."

Once she had finished taking her leave with a bow,
She prepared her luggage and was ready to depart.
But first her parents gave her the following advice:
"When on the road and traveling, be very careful!

"When you meet someone, don't tell him the full story,
You cannot immediately bare to him all your secrets.
Stay at most three years away, but better just two,
Come home as soon as you have finished your studies.

"Make sure you strictly observe the precepts for women;
If someone finds out, it would be quite an ugly scandal!
The Zhu family has a well-established reputation,
You should keep that, my child, in mind at all times!"

Yingtai had the following answer to those good words:
"My parents, don't worry, I will be smart enough!"

She took her servant girl Renxin along with her,
And had her dress as a servant boy to serve her.
After she had said good-bye to the crowd of relatives,
She went out through the gate and set out on the road.

Just look how fine the spring scenery is before your eyes:
Red peach and green willow fill mountain and village.
In pairs the powdered butterflies dance through gardens,
In twosomes the yellow birds are singing in the trees.

But she has no desire to watch this boundless scenery,
Her only desire is to hasten on to the city of Hangzhou!
In front of her she sees a pavilion for taking a rest:
"So let's stop for a while and then slowly go on!"

But when master and servant go inside the pavilion,
They find another student is already resting there.
He also has a servant with him, who waits on him,
And he rises to greet them, his face one great smile.

When Yingtai stepped forward and greeted him,
That student asked her the following question.

[*Speaks:*]

He said: "May I ask who you are?"

"I am Zhu Yingtai, and I am on my way to Hangzhou to study with a teacher. May I ask your name?"

"Ah, so you are Brother Zhu! I am Liang Shanbo, and I am also on my way to find a teacher. Why don't we team up and travel together?"

[*Sings:*]
Upon these words Yingtai was filled with joy,
And promptly she asked him the following question:
"May I ask you when you were born, how old you are?"
And Liang Shanbo replied in the following manner:

[*Speaks:*]

"I am seventeen, and I was born on the seventh day of the seventh month, at noon."

"In that case you are one year my senior. But the hour, month, and day of birth are exactly the same. If you are agreeable, I would like to honor you as my elder brother."

[*Sings:*]
Upon these words Shanbo was filled with pleasure,
The two of them teamed up and continued their trip.
In the first village the two of them went into a wineshop,
The two of them swore friendship: elder brother and younger!

From then on the two of them traveled on together,
Teamed up as a pair they headed for Hangzhou.

When in the west the red sun's disk was sinking,
Each and every house and family lit its red lantern.

The two of them hastened on, found an inn for the night,
And after their evening meal they had a discussion.

[*Speaks*:]

Yingtai said: "Brother Liang, I have to confess to you that ever since my earliest childhood I have been very sickly, and that is why I do not undress when I go to sleep."

"Well, if that is the case, then you just sleep with all your clothes on."

[*Sings*:]
There is no need to speak about their quiet night of sleep,
The next day they continued their journey at break of dawn.
The masters and servants, all four of them, left the inn,
And, crossing the Qiantang River, they reached Hangzhou.

Just look at those thirty-six lanes of flowers and willows,
And then those seventy-two drinking establishments!
Each of the three hundred sixty trades and guilds may be found;
People are conversant with all sixty dialects of traveling folk.

The two of them had no desire to take in the sights;
They located the academy, presented themselves to the Sage!
The master promptly asked the two of them as follows:
"Where do you hail from, from which prefecture and county?"

Yingtai and Shanbo immediately replied as follows,
And they said: "Revered Teacher, please listen to us.
We both are students from Shaoxing prefecture,
And hail from the two counties of Guiji and Zhuji.

"The name by which I am called is Liang Shanbo,
And the name by which he is known is Zhu Yingtai.
I am the elder brother, while he is the younger brother,
We swore friendship while traveling, are best friends!

"We have come here together for finding a teacher,
We hope that you will accept us as your disciples."
Upon these words the Master was filled with joy,
And he taught and instructed this twosome with care.
At night they shared a bed, each a separate blanket,
But by day they sat together and walked together.

When the master observed Yingtai's features closely,
It was clear to him that she was a beautiful girl.

But while he knew this, he did not disclose it,
And he taught and instructed the twosome with care.

Yingtai, too, pondered the situation and thought:
"I cannot join them in defecating or urinating.
All the others are boys here while I am a girl,
If they find out I'm a girl, I would be mortified!"

She proposed to the master to hang out a tablet:
People would have to take turns and not go together.
The master considered it a very good proposal,
So he hung up a tablet and told all his students:

"For defecating and urinating you go in turns,
You're not allowed to go in pairs and fool around.
Every person who does not stick to this rule,
Is punished with twenty strokes of my thorny rod!"

All the students obeyed the rule to a man,
So Yingtai was extremely well pleased.

The days and month passed by oh so quickly,
All of a sudden more than half a year had passed.
Shanbo still was somewhat deficient in his studies;
Yingtai performed considerably better than he.

That day the weather was hot, the heat oppressive,
So she went to her room and opened her gown,
Without expecting that Shanbo would enter and see
Her snow-white body and her bared breast.

Shanbo then promptly asked her the question:
"Why do you have such boobs with nipples?"
Yingtai immediately replied to that question
And said to her fellow student, her sworn friend:

"Don't you know that a man with big boobs will attain high office?
Physiognomy provides us a clear explanation!"
This was the way Shanbo was kept in the dark,
And could not figure out Yingtai was a girl.

In the sixth month's hot weather: wet with sweat!
But Yingtai did not dare to take off her clothes,
So Shanbo called out to Yingtai: "Little Brother,
Don't be so prudish; take off your clothes!"

Yingtai answered him in the following words:
"There's something that I have to tell you.

"Because I've been sickly from earliest youth,
Even in hottest weather I do not undress.
Even if my clothes are wet all through with sweat,
I would fall ill as soon as I took off my clothes."

When Shanbo saw he refused to take off his clothes,
He was filled with suspicion and thought to himself:

"Everyone pees standing up when they take a leak,
But Yingtai squats down when he has to pee.
By the looks of it, he does not act like a guy,
Could it be after all that he is a pretty girl?"

So that time he also asked her as follows:
"Why do you have to squat down when you pee?
I am your roommate and your fellow student,
We eat together, sleep together, share a room.

"All the other people say that you are a girl,
And I, too, am puzzled by the way you behave.
So I beseech you, Brother, to tell me the truth,
I definitely will not tell your secret to others!"

Yingtai hastily answered Shanbo as follows:
"How come you cannot come to understand?
I've read *Treatise of Stimulus and Response*:
'Don't spill your piss on the Three Lights.'[67]

"To stand and pee brings down the wrath of heaven,
You'll not live long and die before your time.
How is it possible that you would not know?
But you have to claim that I am some floozy!"

Upon those words Shanbo was flustered and afraid,
He did not dare bring up the question with her again.

---

67. The *Treatise of Stimulus and Response* (*Ganying pian*) was, since the Song dynasty, a widespread moral treatise. The Three Lights refer to the sun, moon, and stars.

Yingtai devoted herself completely to her studies,
Her literary accomplishments were without compare.
She excelled in writing poems, composing couplets,
Greatly pleasing her teacher, a man full of learning.

Without her noticing, light and shade passed swiftly by;
All of a sudden it was the spring of the third year.
At that time of the third month the peach trees blossomed
And everyone wanted to go out and enjoy spring.

So the students informed their teacher
They wanted to enjoy spring and have some fun.
Shanbo and Yingtai went along together
To take in the brilliant, charming new spring scenery.

Their eyes were struck by the village stream;
Where pairs of ducks frolicked in the waves.
Their fellow students spoke to them as follows:
And said: "Brother Liang and Brother Zhu,

"Why don't we play a betting game today?
Each of us will try to hit the ducks with pebbles;
To those who hit the ducks
We will offer three cups of wine when we are back at school,
But those who cannot hit the ducks
Will promptly have to drink three cups of cold water!"

Everybody was excited and started throwing,
And everyone hit the ducks with their pebbles.
Only Zhu Yingtai, who didn't have the strength,
Could not manage to hit a duck and grew afraid.

Moreover, all the other boys made fun of her:
"Brother Zhu, you really look like a pretty girl!"
Upon these words Yingtai felt deeply ashamed.
Upon her return she somberly thought to herself:

"Eventually I'm bound to be found out by people,
I'd better go back home at the earliest opportunity!"
The next day she took her leave of teacher and students,
Ten ounces of silver she gave to the teacher as fee.

"This is because my father and mother told me
I was permitted to be a student for only three years.

So today I have to say good-bye to you, my teacher,
I'll remain grateful to you for the rest of my life."

The teacher noticed she had done well in her studies,
And, as it was her father's order, allowed her to leave.
After Yingtai had said good-bye to her fellow students,
She also said good-bye to Liang Shanbo, her sworn friend:

"Tonight you and I will still share the same room,
But tomorrow we will be separated far from each other.
I cannot bear to part from you, my dearest brother,
So Brother Liang,
Why don't you come along and leave tomorrow, too?

"Since ancient times the books give good advice:
'While parents are alive, one should not travel far.'
For three long years you have not seen your parents,
It's time that you go home and wait on them!"

Shanbo then spoke to her in the following words:
"My accomplishments still are only mediocre,
I should study here for yet another year, or a half.
By that time I can come along and leave with you."

"Brother Liang,
A full year or a half, that's not what is the problem,
It's only because of the instructions of my parents.
I really do not dare stay here any longer,
And so tomorrow I must say good-bye.

"But I have one thing that I want to ask you,
So listen carefully to what I have to say.
When once your studies are completed and you go home,
Make sure that you come to our mansion first!

"I have at home a darling little younger sister,
She has a thousand charms, a hundred beauties.
Because our friendship, Brother, is so intimate,
I want to see my little sister become your bride.

"If you arrive in time the marriage can be settled,
But if you come too late, I fear it may fall through.
And then I have this poem that I want to give you,

O Brother Liang,
To see this poem will be just like seeing me."

The poem went:
While both on the road, I remember, we swore friendship,
Three times the hundred flowers have blossomed in spring.
It's only the jade plum's heart that is able to endure the cold:
It will not because of spring desire furtively open its flowers.[68]

When Shanbo took the poem from her and had a look,
The poem turned out to be filled with a thousand feelings.

Thereupon he also wrote a poem in return for her,
And he said to Yingtai: "My dearest brother,
I've also written a poem to give to you,
To see that poem will be just like seeing me."

The poem went:
Three years we studied together, were united in feeling—
Our thoughts intense when writing of moon and breeze.
Now we have to part today, my heart is about to break,
But I promise to come and see you this coming fall.

When he had hastily given her his poem in return,
Yingtai accepted it—her eyes were filled with tears.
And she said: "Brother Liang, do not fail in your promise;
I hope to see you united in wedlock by next spring!"

The two of them kept talking well past midnight,
Holding hands they spoke intensely without stopping.
When the Golden Rooster cried thrice and heaven dawned,[69]
Yingtai got her luggage together and made ready to go.

Overcome by sadness, Shanbo accompanied her;
Master and servant together set out on the road.
Shanbo could not let go of his little brother Yingtai,
He accompanied her for the first stretch of the road.

After a while he had arrived with her at a garden,
And Yingtai cried out: "My dear elder brother,

68. The jade plum is the white-blossoming winter plum, which puts forth its flowers in the last month of winter (according to the traditional lunar calendar).

69. The Golden Rooster is the bird that announces daybreak in heaven.

During the first year we were roommates, sharing a deep attachment,
Just like a pair of mandarin ducks who never will be separated.

"Who'd have thought that today you and I have to part,
So let me discuss some 'past and present' with you.
We will not write poems or compose rhapsodies,
But I will only mention some animals and insects.

"Brother Liang,
Do you know who most resembles the butterfly?
Who most resembles the *tiansansao*?[70]
Who most resembles the frog with its croaking sound?

"Who most resembles the spider?
Who resembles the cricket that chirps in the shadow,
Who is as vicious as the golden scorpion?
Who most resembles the honey bee?"

Upon these words Shanbo replied as follows:
"Dear Brother, listen as I reply one by one.
Xi Shi best resembles the flowery butterfly,
With her demure posture she dances without end.[71]

"Concubine Plum conspired against Empress Su,
So she is a honeybee that lit the fire that burned herself![72]
It is Daji who best resembles the *tiansansao*,
She brought chaos to the realm, destroyed the peace.[73]

"The chirping cricket resembles the lute's lament:
Wang Zhaojun leaving the country to marry a barbarian.[74]

---

70. *Tiansansao* (third aunt fields) may refer to the dragonfly.

71. Xi Shi was the most beautiful girl in the ancient state of Yue. She was trained in all the arts of seduction and then given by the king of Yue to the king of the neighboring state of Wu. When the king of Wu, indeed, as hoped, neglected his duties because of Xi Shi, the king of Yue invaded the country and destroyed Wu.

72. Concubine Plum was, in legend and drama, a favorite concubine of Emperor Xuanzong. She was later replaced in his favor by the infamous Precious Consort Yang.

73. Daji was the evil concubine of King Zhou (r. 1075–1046 B.C.E.), the last king of the Shang dynasty (1600–1046 B.C.E.).

74. Wang Zhaojun was a palace lady during the reign of Emperor Yuan (r. 48–33 B.C.E.), of the Han dynasty. She was given as bride by the court to Huhanye, the ruler of the Southern Xiongnu at the time. The historical Wang Zhaojun volunteered to go, but later legend made her an innocent victim of court corruption.

The spider may be compared to Yan Boxi,
Spinning her net outside her door, waiting for her lover.[75]

"Fei Zhong and You Hun were like scorpions,
Filled with poison, wanting to harm loyal ministers.[76]
And the frog in the grass that croaks out its pain,
Resembles Meng Jiangnü, who by weeping brought down the
Great Wall."[77]

As he had mentioned all those animals and insects,
He had after a while accompanied her to the flower pavilion.
"Brother Liang,
During the second year we were roommates, sharing a deep
attachment,
Just like the cape jasmine that ties a common heart.

"Now you and I will have to part, my brother,
Let me talk once again of 'past and present.'
Again we'll not write poems or compose rhapsodies,
I will only mention a few names of birds.

"Brother Liang,
Do you know who most resembles the ladybird?
And whom would you say does the cuckoo [*zigui*] resemble?
Whom would you compare to the cormorant [*qinglu*]?
And whom would you compare to the egret [*lusi*]?

"Which person can be compared to the peacock?
Who is best compared to the thrush [*huamei*]?
Whom would you compare to the pigeon [*bogu*]?
To whom should the white-headed bird be compared?"

Shanbo promptly replied in the following words:
"Brother,
Now listen to each and every explanation.

---

75. Yan Boxi is the former prostitute and adulterous wife of Song Jiang in the sixteenth-century novel *Outlaws of the Marsh* (*Water Margin* [*Shuihu zhuan*]).

76. Fei Zhong and You Hun are evil councilors of King Zhou, the last king of the Shang dynasty in the Ming dynasty novel *The Creation of the Gods* (*Fengshen yanyi*).

77. Meng Jiangnü's husband had been drafted to work on the building of the Great Wall. When his wife traveled to the border to bring him his winter clothing, she learned that he had died of exhaustion and had been buried in the wall. She thereupon wept until the Great Wall collapsed on the spot where his bones had been buried.

It is Consort Yang, who, tipsy in Chaoyang Palace,
Most resembles a lady beneath a crab apple tree.[78]

"And once Jiaojilang had left and no news arrived,
Isn't it said that Li Sanniang wanted her son to return [*zigui*]?[79]
When Cui Yingying did not see Student Zhang return,
She waited till dusk for just a glimpse of her lover [*qinglü*].[80]

"When Cai Bojie went to the capital to seek an office,
Zhao Wuniang sought her husband, all along the road longing [*lusi*] [for him].[81]
The Monk of the Tang suffered no end of disasters,
Only because he wanted to fetch the *Peacock Sutra*.[82]

"Mu Suhui was filled with longing for Yu Shuye,
Isn't it said: 'Depressed, she sat in her room, too listless to paint her brows [*huamei*].'[83]

---

78. Consort Yang was the favorite concubine of Emperor Xuanzong during the last years of his reign. At one time, the emperor broke off their relationship, and Consort Yang one night consoled herself in her despair with drink. This scene was later popular on the stage.

79. These two lines refer to *The White Hare* (*Baituji*), the romance of Liu Zhiyuan and Li Sanniang. Liu Zhiyuan is a poor farmhand, but a local landlord, who is convinced of his future greatness, gives him his daughter Li Sanniang as wife. When the old man dies, her two elder brothers drive him from the farm, and he joins the army. His pregnant wife refuses to marry another man, and her brothers treat her as a maid. When she gives birth to her son, she is without any help, and so she bites off his umbilical cord. The boy, who is called Jiaojilang (The Boy Whose Umbilical Cord Was Bitten Off), is delivered to his father, who in the meantime has married the daughter of his commander and started on a dazzling military career. It will take another twelve years, however, before husband and wife, and mother and son, are reunited.

80. Cui Yingying and Student Zhang are the main characters of the drama *The Western Wing* (*Xixiang ji*), probably China's most popular love story ever. Cui Yingying and Student Zhang have an affair while both are staying at the same monastery. When her mother finds out, Student Zhang leaves to take part in the state examinations. The translation of this line is tentative.

81. Cai Bojie and Zhao Wuniang are the main protagonists in the drama *The Lute* (*Pipa ji*). Cai Bojie is ordered by his father to leave for the capital and take part in the examinations. His wife, Zhao Wuniang, stays behind to take care of her parents-in-law. Cai Bojie is detained in the capital after he has passed the examinations, and his home district is ravaged by a famine. His parents die, and after a destitute Zhao Wuniang has taken care of their burial, she sets out on the road to the capital to search for her husband.

82. The Monk of the Tang is better known as Xuanzang or Tripitaka. The sixteenth-century novel *Journey to the West* describes his pilgrimage to the Western Paradise in search of Buddhist sutras.

83. Mu Suhui and Yu Shuye (Juan) are the female and male protagonists of *The Western Loft* (*Xilou ji*), a play by Yuan Yuling (1592–1674).

Jinlian wanted to play the gold-embossed flute,
But she couldn't because of the old crones [*bogu*] all around.[84]
The old gardener Zhang Guo obtained for himself a wife:
Isn't it this: a young girl wedded to white-headed graybeard?"[85]

When he had explained the names of the birds one by one,
He had already accompanied her to the resting pavilion.

"Brother Liang,
During the third year we were roommates, sharing a deep attachment.
Who could have known that today we would have to part?
We are just like a pair of ducks that is beaten apart by a stick,
And that in their separate places are filled with anguish.

"Brother Liang,
I hope that you will go back home really soon,
And then you must come and visit our place!
In the inner rooms I have a darling younger sister,
Whom I want to see united in wedlock with you.

"Three years long we were united in friendship,
When you marry her, that will double our bond.
If you come early, the marriage can be arranged,
But if you are too late, there will be no wedding.

"No possibility then in 'The River's Water'
To roam like a fish in spring to one's heart's content;[86]
No possibility for 'The God's Second Son'
To express his love in the embroidery room.

"No possibility with 'The Winds in the Sails'
To consummate a marriage of intricate love,
No possibility then 'To Step out of the Crowd'
And have one's name listed on the Unicorn Tower.[87]

---

84. Pan Jinlian is a sexually insatiable female character in the sixteenth-century novel *Jin Ping Mei* (*Gold Vase Plum*). The translation of these two lines is mere guesswork.

85. Zhang Guo is an old gardener outside Yangzhou who marries the young daughter of his neighbor when he manages to pay the astronomical bride-price asked by her father. He later turns out to be an immortal and leaves with his bride for fairyland. The tale provides the plot for the play *Great-Peace Coin* (*Taiping qian*) by the Suzhou playwright Li Yu (1610–1680).

86. In this section, each couplet contains in the second part of the first line the name of a popular tune, in quotation marks, that is taken in its literal sense.

87. Emperor Wu (r. 141–87 B.C.E.), of the Han, had portraits of his most illustrious generals painted in the Unicorn Tower.

"No possibility 'To Assemble Fine Guests'
And have the lute plucked to move the heart,
No possibility for 'A Water Immortal'
To drink a few cups in Peony Pavilion.[88]

"No possibility with 'Dainty Steps'
To burn one's incense at Mount Putuo.[89]
No possibility under 'The Moon So High'
Together in the western room to talk of old love.

"No possibility for 'Little Miss Reddy'
To stir up romance in the western wing,[90]
No possibility then 'By Her Toilet Table'
To put her golden hairpins in her chignon.

"And no possibility to 'Please the Beauty [Yu Meiren]'[91]
And in the darkness of her room to tie hearts together."
Yingtai continued to speak in ambiguous words:
"I hope, Brother Liang, that fourth you'll accompany me to the flower pavilion.
The pomegranate's flowers are red like fire.
I'd like to pluck a flower and give it to you,
But you are not a girl with flowers in her hair.

"I hope, Brother Liang, that fifth you'll accompany me to the temple.
Just look inside and you'll see a pair of gods,
One of them is male and one of them female.
Two gods are sitting together day and night,
And all they need would be one matchmaker.

"I hope, Brother Liang, that sixth you'll accompany me to the riverbank.
Just look how that pair of mandarin ducks entwine their necks.
By the light of the moon male and female play in the stream,
They fly hither and thither, their hearts tied together.

---

88. Peony Pavilion is the site of a (dreamed) love tryst portrayed in *Peony Pavilion* (*Mudanting*), by the playwright Tang Xianzu (1550–1616).

89. Mount Putuo is the name of a small island off the Zhejiang coast, dedicated to the cult of the bodhisattva Guanyin, who is venerated there in female form.

90. Reddy (Hongniang) is the name of Cui Yingying's girl servant in *The Western Wing*, in which she serves as the *postillon d'amour* between the two lovers.

91. Yu Meiren (The Beauty Yu) refers to Lady Yu, the paramour of Xiang Yu. In order to make sense in context, the phrase here has to be read differently, according to one of the homophones of *yu*.

"I hope, Brother Liang, that seventh you'll accompany me to the peach garden.
I want to pick a peach of immortality for you to eat,
And hope you'll remember the taste, how sweet it was.

"I hope, Brother Liang, that eighth you'll accompany me to the riverside.
On the river we'll see a pair of white geese, united in spirit.
While the male goose goes on and swims ahead,
The female one follows behind, calling out 'Brother [*gege*]!'[92]

"I hope, Brother Liang, that ninth you'll accompany me to the side of the stream.
There we will see two boats for catching fish.
Look how the head of the boats rest on the bank,
But the bank will never move close to the boat."

Liang Shanbo never grasped Yingtai's intention,
So smilingly Yingtai continued still as follows:
"When Liu Chen and Ruan Zhao met with immortals,
They thought they had married only mere mortals.[93]

"Once they had left, they returned but could not find them:
To meet with an immortal maiden is rare indeed!
The bond of love between you and me cannot be broken,
Just as that of the two immortal swains Liu and Ruan.

"But I am afraid that as we go our separate ways today,
We may be compared to Buffalo Herder and Weaving Maid.[94]
The Qiantang River keeps us apart like the River of Heaven,
How can we in both locations not be filled with longing?"

Yingtai further addressed Shanbo in the following words:
"Now return to the school and work hard at your studies!

---

92. Traditionally in China, lovers address each other as Elder Brother (*gege*) and Sister (*meimei*).

93. Liu Chen and Ruan Zhao lost their way while searching for simples on Mount Tiantai. They then met with two girls who invited them into their homes and lived with them for a few months. When later they returned to their home village, centuries had passed. Only then did they realize that they had lived with the immortals. According to one version of the legend, they tried to find the location of the immortal maidens again, but were unable to do so.

94. The Buffalo Herder and the Weaving Maid are two stellar lovers who are separated by the Heavenly River (Milky Way). They can meet only once a year, on the night of the seventh day of the seventh month, when magpies form a bridge for them across the Heavenly River.

Go back home as soon as you are accomplished in study,
If you are too late, you'll not obtain that charming bride.

"Today the two of us have to part from each other,
In what year, in what month will we be reunited?"

In truth it is said:
"I may accompany you for a thousand miles, but in the end we must part,"
And:
"Once one has westward gone out through Yang Pass, one is without friends."
As soon as each of them had let go of the other's hand,
Their tears soaked their gowns as they went their own ways.
Let's not tell how Shanbo returned to the school,
Just let's show how Yingtai pursued her journey.

The two of them, master and servant, traveled on,
And they passed through one village after another.
The scenery along the road was beyond description,
Back in Xinghua village she arrived at her own home.

When her parents heard that their daughter was back,
They were overcome by joy and welcomed their child.
Yingtai came home to the house of her parents,
In front of the hall she greeted them with a bow:

"By being away from your care for three years
Your unfilial child has committed a serious crime!
I am grateful to my teacher for his words of wisdom,
And I have devoted all my energy to my studies.

"I've fooled them by a hundred kinds of clever tricks,
And with my virginity intact I arrive back home."
She greeted her brother and her sister-in-law,
And all relatives and relations came to visit.

The peony flower in its vase before the Buddha
Was still as fresh and green as when she left!
Everybody praised her: "This is truly rare!
This charming girl has proven her mettle!"

Yingtai went back to her own private room;
With a smile on her face she thought of Shanbo:
"A few times he suspected that I was a woman,
But I would get angry at him and hide the truth.

"By what I have seen of him, he's a true gentleman,
I'd be very happy indeed to have him for a husband!
I pray that high heaven will help and protect me,
Accomplish this marriage, this love of my life!"

She took off her male gown, changed into female attire,
And put up her raven-black hair into a new chignon.
Yingtai, Ninth Sister, was now nineteen years of age,
As beautiful as a lotus flower piercing through ice.
Seen by a hundred people, she was coveted by a hundred,
Seen by a thousand people, she was loved by a thousand.

In the neighboring village lived a powerful family,
Their son, named Ma Jun, was a dashing young man.
When he had been told how pretty Yingtai was,
He told his parents he wanted her as his bride.

Old Mr. Ma and his wife were filled with joy,
They asked a matchmaker to arrange the marriage.
Mr. Zhu and his wife agreed to the proposal,
Wrote out the date of her birth, and so settled the deal.
When Yingtai, Ninth Sister, came to learn of this,
It was as if she were hit by heaven, scared by thunder:

"I already gave my promise to Brother Liang!
I wanted to live with him for the rest of my life!
But now my parents have made the decision,
They promised me in marriage to the Ma family.

"So how will I be able to answer to Shanbo
When he in due time will pay me a visit?
Obviously I have betrayed Liang Shanbo,
His love and friendship of those three years!
O Brother Liang,
If we cannot become husband and wife in this life,
May you and I tie the knot in a future existence!"

Let's not sing of Yingtai's mental sufferings,
Let's resume the story now of Liang Shanbo.

He stayed in school for another six months,
But all by himself he felt bored and depressed.
All he could think of was his brother Yingtai,
Their attachment as roommates for three years.

So he desired to pack up and go back home,
And hastened to say good-bye to his teacher.
Two ingots of silver he added to the fee,
Then he said good-bye to his fellow students.

In a great hurry he left the city of Hangzhou.
He crossed the river and arrived at Xixing,
Where he hired a boat and departed that night,
And so he arrived the next morning in Shaoxing.

When he and his servant arrived in the Zhu family's
village,
All the houses belonged to people named Zhu;
But after he and his servant had made inquiries,
They went to his fellow student and roommate.

[*Speaks*:]

Shanbo said: "Is there anyone at the gate?"

"Who is it?"

"Dear Mr. Doorman, please inform your Ninth Young Master that his Hangzhou roommate of three years, Liang Shanbo, has come to pay him a visit."

The doorman answered: "Mr. Liang, you must be wrong. In this family there is only a Ninth Sister Yingtai; there is no Ninth Young Master!"

Shanbo thought to himself: "So my brother had left home in false attire!" And he said: "Mr. Doorman, I am not only the roommate of your Ninth Sister, we also became sworn brothers. You have to report me to her, this is no mistake!"

"If that's the case, just wait for a moment."

[*Sings*:]

The doorman went inside to report his arrival.
When Ninth Sister heard this, her tears coursed down.
She dispatched her servant girl Renxin to the gate
To invite the one surnamed Liang to come inside.

When his boy servant Four-Nine had seen her,
He came over to her, his heart filled with desire,
And he spoke to Renxin in the following words:
"So, Brother, you, too, went around in disguise:

"The master a fake and the servant also a fake,
It's time today for the two of us to get real!"
Renxin's only reaction to this was to spit
As she addressed the one surnamed Liang as follows:

[*Speaks*:]
"Our Ninth Sister invites Mr. Liang to meet with her in her study."

[*Sings*:]
Liang Shanbo followed behind the servant girl,
Passing through the front hall, he arrived at the rear hall.
Turning around corners, he went farther inside,
And then the inner study appeared before him.

When Liang Shanbo entered this study,
The study's features surpassed Penglai![95]
But as he lightly sat down on a bamboo chair,
He thought only of his roommate, his fellow student:

"When she was dressed as a man I called her Brother,
How to address her now that she is in female costume?

"I guess that I, Liang Shanbo, have been on her mind,
That's why she claimed to have a sister for me as bride.
If I indeed could succeed in becoming her husband,
I'd be happy in hundreds, in thousands of ways!"

Renxin served him a cup of fragrant tea—
But let's talk of the young lady inside.
"Brother Liang is verily a true gentleman,
There will be no harm in meeting with him."

Hurriedly she completed her toilette,
And with dainty steps entered the study!
When Shanbo lifted his head and had a look,
His soul immediately soared up to high heaven!

In female costume Yingtai looked like an immortal maiden,
Hairpins of turquoise and gold: exceedingly handsome.
Thousands and hundreds of charms: utterly perfect,
In this world without compare: a dazzling stunner!

Her cherry lips pouted with a bewitching smile
As she addressed Brother Liang, her fellow student:
"Thank you for gracing our house with a visit,
Forgive me for being so slow to welcome you."

---

95. In Chinese legend, Penglai is the floating island of the immortals in the Eastern Ocean.

The two of them greeted each other formally,
And sat down to left and right as host and guest.

[*Speaks*:]

Shanbo said: "So after all you were a girl dressed as a boy! I questioned you a few times about this, but each time you got angry and hid the truth. You truly are a chaste-minded maiden!" Yingtai replied with a smile: "Out of admiration for our teacher, I took on a disguise in order to be able to study with him, and you were so kind not to reject me but to become my sworn brother."

[*Sings*:]
She ordered her servant girl Renxin
To ask her father the squire to join them.
As soon as he got the message he quickly arrived,
And in the study they greeted each other as guest and host.

Yingtai informed her darling daddy:
"This is Brother Liang Shanbo,

"He is an utterly sincere true gentleman.
For three years he was my roommate and fellow student.
Our friendship surpassed the love between brothers,
We walked together and sat together, never parted."

Upon these words Squire Zhu was filled with joy:
"My child, please take care of your guest."
Following these words Squire Zhu went outside,
And Yingtai addressed her brother as follows:

"We two are understanding, lifelong friends,
Please come with me to the flower-garden hall."
Shanbo answered her he'd do her bidding gladly,
And the two of them went to the flower-garden hall.

Now the flower-garden hall actually was the place
In the inner apartments where Yingtai did her studies.

Just look at that six-paneled folding screen painted in red and powder,
A single *tianran* and a few *tieli*.
On top of that stood an ancient incense burner,
In it she burned in this study in each season *huangshu*.

To the left stood a Ding-ware vase, within it
Some brilliant and gorgeous flowers of the season.

To the right stood a bowl of transparent glass,
There goldfish darted through pure fresh water.

Twelve chairs of Xiang-goddess bamboo
And four bookcases were arrayed on both sides.
On the small desk for reading, made of red lacquer,
The Four Treasures of the Study were neatly laid out.

The hall was surrounded by a red balustrade,
And in the garden flowers spread their fragrance.
Behind the flower hall was a fine study,
And inside was found a small ivory bench.

Green gauze windows below red eaves,
The folding screen was painted in gold.
A small octagonal table was placed before the bench,
Chairs of eaglewood were arranged on both sides.

She invited Shanbo to take a seat on the left,
While she, that beauty, sat down on the right.
A hundred rare delicacies were spread out before him,
Wine was poured in golden cups from a silver pitcher.

During the first cup of wine not a word was said,
During the second cup of wine not a word was exchanged.
But as soon as the third cup of wine had been drained,
Yingtai became tipsy, her face flushed with wine.

Promptly her powdered face turned to peachlike pink,
And her pair of "autumn streams" had a hundred charms.[96]
At that sight, the soul of Liang Shanbo dissolved:
He would have liked to swallow her whole!

But alas, Four-Nine and Renxin were around,
Impossible to press the beauty to his breast!
With a smile on his lips he opened his mouth,
And spoke to her in the following words:

"Sometime ago you promised me you wanted
To entrust yourself to me for the rest of your life.
If indeed I can share with you blanket and pillow,
I'll be elated even if it might mean my death!"

---

96. "Autumn streams" is a common metaphor for eyes.

Upon these words Yingtai dissolved into tears,
And she told Brother Liang, her fellow student:
"Alas, my friend, you have arrived too late,
My parents have decided upon another match.

"Two days ago they promised me to young Ma,
And the engagement gifts have already arrived.
It's not that I, your sister, would be unwilling,
But to my regret I have been promised away."

Upon these words Shanbo was filled with remorse,
As if he had lost a rare treasure or jewel:

"Ah, my dear sister,
Even if your father may have promised you away,
You should remember our love of three years as roommates.
Far better you should marry me, this Liang Shanbo,
Don't marry that young Ma from the neighboring village.

"I will immediately return home and have a matchmaker
Come over here and ask for your hand in marriage!"

[*Speaks*:]

Yingtai replied: "Brother Liang, that is absolutely impossible! How can one girl receive the engagement gifts of two different families? Wouldn't that involve my father in a lawsuit, wouldn't he be punished?

[*Sings*:]
"How could I bear to see my parents transgress the law,
And become the object of gossip with the neighbors?"

Upon these words Shanbo did not know what to say,
Sorrow clouded his brow as he sank into depression.
Yingtai hastened to urge him to drink, and said,
"Dear Brother Liang, please, please listen to me.

"The ancient proverb goes:
'In books is found a maiden with a face as white as jade.'
Don't allow yourself to focus only on me alone.
If in this life we cannot become husband and wife,
We will try to tie the knot in a future existence.

"When we said good-bye, I made you a promise,
But I only said I had a sister fit to be your bride.

I compared my feelings to a thousand objects,
But you, Brother Liang, couldn't figure it out.

"You arrived too late, and my father gave me away—
It's not the case that I am not filled with love!"
But Shanbo replied: "Dear sister Yingtai,
I blame you for not speaking out more clearly!

"Now that it is impossible to become husband and wife,
I surely will take my plaint to the Yellow Springs.[97]
Your wine I'll not drink and your rice I'll not eat,
I will recite one poem and make my way home."

The poem went:
Filled with hope that the marriage might be accomplished—
But when I arrived you had been promised to another man.
In days bygone the winter plum in truth was wonderful,
But at the present time we lack the breeze to join in spring.

After he had handed the poem to Yingtai, she,
Awash in tears, also wrote a poem in reply.

The poem went:
Divided by the stream at Indigo Bridge: success denied[98]—
The winter plum silently grieves in the darkening dusk.
The one flowering sprig is tied up in spring sorrow,
As I sing to the easterly breeze this brokenhearted song.

When she had completed it, she handed it to Liang Shanbo,
Who was so wounded in his heart he found the pain unbearable.
He immediately said good-bye, and made ready to leave,
But Yingtai could not let go of him and saw him off.

Having swallowed *huanglian*, they felt all bitter inside,
Just as if their hearts and guts were cut to pieces with a knife:
One melting in tears looked at another melting in tears,
One with a broken heart accompanied another with a broken heart.

---

97. The Yellow Springs denotes the world of the dead, where impartial judges determine the fate of souls on the basis of their deeds during their lifetime. The courts of the underworld are headed by King Yama.

98. Indigo Bridge is the place where, according to a well-known Tang dynasty tale, a certain Pei Xing met with his predestined immortal lover, Yunying.

When she eventually had accompanied him out the gate,
They gazed upon each other, finding it impossible to part.
As each of them said the three words: "Fare thee well,"
Their tears streamed down as if gushing from a spring.

That pitiable Liangbo was overcome by sadness,
But he stiffened his face and went on his way.
We'll not tell how master and servant traveled on—
Crying and weeping, Yingtai went into her room.

She hated herself: she never should have left home to study,
Because of that, she had occasioned this unprecedented love,
And she had to fear that, after Shanbo got home,
There was little chance that he might survive.

Let's abandon the subject of Yingtai, awash in tears,
But let us tell of Shanbo as he traveled on:
When he traveled a mile, he wept for a mile,
As he traveled a stretch, and yet another stretch.

The only thought that filled his heart was of her,
That flowerlike girl with hundreds, thousands of charms!
He blamed himself: how could he have been so purblind
That all those three years he had not seen she was a girl!

Four-Nine also was filled with spite and remorse,
For not having engaged in an affair with Renxin.
Master and servant both were equally depressed,
But eventually they arrived at the gate of his home.

When his parents saw him, they were filled with joy,
And Shanbo knelt down to greet his father and mother.
He told them in detail of his teacher's instruction:
Now he was ready to go and sit for the examinations!

His overjoyed parents hastily arranged a banquet,
To welcome back home their son, this promising student!
Following the banquet Liang Shanbo retired to his study,
Depressed and dazed by the somber thoughts in his heart.

In the morning he longed for her, and so he did at night,
And soon that love longing turned into a bodily illness.
Because of the sorrow in his heart
He could not even swallow a sip of tea,

And as he continued to lose weight, he lost all strength.
When his father and mother learned of his condition,
They hurried to his room and questioned their son:

"Oh, our dear son,
You must have suffered too much there in school,
And become ill because of overexertion of body and mind.
Or is there something else that weighs on your heart?
Please tell your parents so we can find a solution."

Only after they had questioned him repeatedly,
Did Shanbo finally blurt out the truth.

[*Speaks*:]

He said: "Father and Mother, when I was on my way to Hangzhou, I met someone who was called Zhu Yingtai. We became sworn brothers, and together we went and studied with our teacher.

[*Sings*:]
"We walked together, we sat together, and we also slept together,
The attachment between us was more than two hundred
percent.
When after three years he had completed his studies in the arts,
He left earlier than I did in order to go home to his parents.

"As I, your son, could not bear to be parted from him,
I accompanied him till we came to the bank of the river.
Then he told me that he had a darling younger sister,
And that he wanted me to be married to her.

"For six months after our parting I constantly thought of him,
And so I took leave of my teacher and returned home.
As I passed through Guiji, I paid him a visit—
It happens he lives in Xinghua village.

"I was invited into his study to meet with him,
And then it turned out that he was a pretty girl!
She told me in detail that because she wanted to study,
She had disguised herself as a boy to enter the school.

"She set out wine in the flower hall to welcome me,
And then she even proceeded to blame me at length:
Three years we had been fellow students and brothers,
And she had wanted to entrust herself to me forever!

"She told me that I had arrived one month too late,
And that her parents had promised her to young Ma.
In this life we would not be able to become a couple,
So she hoped to tie the knot in a future existence.

"When your child heard her tell the full true story,
I felt as though hit by heaven, struck down by thunder!
It was not my fate to obtain that beautiful person,
Despite our three-year attachment as roommates!

"That's the reason for my depression since my return,
The sorrow turned into an illness that haunts my body.
Dear parents!
If you really want me to recover from this illness,
You'll have to find a way for me to marry that girl!"

Only then did Mr. and Mrs. Liang understand,
And they said to their son: "Dear Shanbo,
Please put your mind at rest for the time being,
We will see what we can do about this wedding.

"We'll send over a matchmaker to make sure
They will break the engagement and give her to you."
Upon these words Shanbo was filled with joy:
"Dear father and mother, please act quickly!"

Mr. and Mrs. Liang did not lose a moment
And invited a certain Mr. Li of their village:
He was an eloquent man with a honeyed tongue,
Bound as a matchmaker to make this succeed!

Because Mr. Li coveted the promised fee,
He immediately left to go and make the match.
In a light skiff he traveled fast—as if he flew!
Soon he had arrived at the gate of the Zhus.

Squire Zhu hastened to invite him in, greeted him,
Sat down with him as host and guest for a cup of tea.

[*Speaks*:]

Mr. Li said: "Dear friend, I have come here in connection with your daughter Yingtai, who three years ago became the roommate and sworn brother of Liang Shanbo.

[*Sings*:]
"That's why the love between them is without compare,
When she left, he accompanied her to the river's bank.
She promised him they would be linked by marriage,
Because at home she had a darling little sister.

"When Shanbo came by for a visit some days ago,
Your daughter confessed to him her long-standing love.
But alas, Shanbo had arrived one month too late,
As you had already promised her to young Ma!

"When Shanbo came back home, he was overcome by grief;
Because of that illness he's wasting away, on the verge of death.
Mr. and Mrs. Liang didn't know what else to do,
And asked me to come here and discuss their marriage.

"I hope, dear sir, that you will be so kind as to
Reverse your decision and give her to him!"

Squire Zhu immediately expressed his refusal:
"Dear Mr. Li, this is completely impossible!
I've already promised my daughter to young Mr. Ma,
So how can I promise her now to young Mr. Liang?

"Who doesn't fear the law of the king, hot as a furnace?
How could I act as a criminal and transgress the rule?
'In books there is a maiden with a face as white as jade.'
Please urge Mr. Liang to go and find someone elsewhere."

When tea had been served a second time as a sign,
Mr. Li could do little but return and go home.
When he had all this reported in great detail,
Mr. and Mrs. Liang were overcome by grief.

When Shanbo on his sickbed heard of this,
His sorrow grew and his illness increased even more.
The doctor's prescriptions were without any effect,
Oracles and prayers provided no solution whatsoever.

Upon seeing this, his parents grew even more distressed,
And they said to Shanbo: "Dear son, please listen.
Your mother will go in person to her house
And make sure that Yingtai will be your bride."

Upon hearing this, Shanbo wrote a letter: his mother
Came to ask for her hand, would they please consent.
Carrying this letter Mrs. Liang
Stepped in a boat and took off.

After a single stretch she arrived at the Zhus',
And Mrs. Zhu hastened to come out and welcome her.
After she had greeted her, they sat down as guest and host,
And Liang Shanbo's mother told the reason of her visit:

"It is all because of my little son Liang Shanbo,
And because of your daughter, demoiselle Yingtai.

"Three years as fellow students they were sworn brothers,
Their mutual attachment grew deeper than the sea.
When he came to your place for a visit,
He discovered that your daughter was a girl.

"Considering the old love of their shared life
When earlier she studied disguised as boy,
We hope you may give her to him as bride
And save our son from his wasting disease!"

Yingtai's mother also explained her side:
"She very much wanted to marry your son,
But because your son arrived here too late,
My husband had promised her to young Mr. Ma.

"Please tell your son not to be too distressed
And to find a fitting partner somewhere else."

She called for Yingtai to meet with Mrs. Liang,
Ninth Sister, fully costumed, came into the room.
Respectfully she greeted her brother's mother,
And Mrs. Liang lifted her head to look her over.

"Indeed she truly is a very pretty girl,
Her thousands of charms are hard to find!
No wonder my son cannot let go of her,
And longs for this beauty with all his heart."

At the front of the room a meal was set out for Mrs. Liang,
And Yingtai addressed to her the following question,

By saying to her: "Dear Mrs. Liang,
Has your son recovered from his illness?"

As her tears coursed down Mrs. Liang
Replied to Yingtai: "Demoiselle,

"Because of this impossible marriage,
His incessant love longing turned into an illness.
I came here on purpose to ask for your hand.
Please do not refuse and say only 'Yes!'"

She took the letter that Shanbo had written,
And handed it to Yingtai so she could read it.
It turned out the letter contained a poem, and
Each character and line had been written clearly.

The poem went:
  For three years we shared a bed but not the blanket,
  I did not know that you were a girl in male disguise.
  In truth, our two hearts bound by affection and love—
  If we are not married together, my life will be lost!

After Yingtai had read the poem's intentions,
She replied to Mrs. Liang, her brother's mother:

"Because I have accepted the presents of the Mas,
I am not capable of repaying him for his love,
So please tell your son this message of mine:
'Brother Liang, please, please let go and forget!'"

Having pronounced these words, she was overcome by grief,
And she returned to her room with a broken heart:
"I waited for you, Brother Liang, but you did not arrive,
And then I had already been promised to young Mr. Ma.

"If in this life I cannot be together with Liang Shanbo,
I wish to die so we may walk together in death.
Why was it impossible for us to become husband and wife?
It must be because we burned short sticks of incense!

"I will take off this sweatshirt I wear on my body,
I will cut off some tresses of hair, a few feet in length,

I will prick my fingers until I draw blood,
And write out my medicine for Brother Liang.

"First, you need the gall of the Eastern Ocean's black dragon,
Second, you need the gut of the five-colored phoenix.
Third, you need the blood from the silkworm's moth,
Fourth, you need the light from the eye of a mosquito.

"Fifth, you need a fingernail of one of the Eight Immortals,
Sixth, you need incense from the Queen Mother's palace,
Seventh, you need the leg claw of the Golden Rooster.
And eighth, you need a hair from the head of a housefly.

"Ninth, you need a raindrop from the thirty-third heaven.
And tenth, you need the flash of thunderstorm's lightning.
Once you have these ten kinds of priceless treasures,
Brother Liang, you will be able to recover completely."

The names of these ten medicines she all wrote down—
Yingtai, Ninth Sister, was awash in tears.
Her bright red breast cloths she hastened to take off,
Writing with bleeding fingers she wept her heart out.
She, oh so carefully wrapped the prescription up tightly, and then
Handed it over to Mrs. Liang, her brother's mother.

"Please, by all means tell Brother Liang, again and again,
Not to ruin his life out of love longing for me.
'In books there is a maiden with a face as white as jade.'
Let him choose a pretty girl from some other great family."

When Mrs. Liang saw that this wedding was not to be,
She took her leave and departed, tears coursing down.
All her trip she hastened on as fast as if she were flying,
To return home and see her son, to whom she handed

The sweatshirt, the breast cloth, and the recipe,
And, on the inside, the letter written in blood.
When Shanbo received these, his soul dissolved,
And he carefully read each character, and each line.

[*Speaks:*]

He read the following: "Three years we were roommates, for which I cherish your fine integrity. Your mother came to our house, but a marriage is impossible. Please take good care of yourself, and find yourself elsewhere a bride. I send you this letter written in blood in order to cut off our love and affection. My only wish is to die quickly, so I may repay once and for all your affection. Take care! What more can I say?"

[*Sings:*]
When Shanbo finished reading, he wept uncontrollably,
Wept till heaven was darkened and earth was darkened, too.
"Yingtai writes in blood to cut off all affection for me,
O Father and Mother,
The life of your son is bound to end soon!"

He wept in the morning, he wept till late at night,
And his disease became rapidly even more critical.
His father and mother were at a loss what to do,
And hurriedly tried to talk some sense into their son.

"On all accounts you must take good care of yourself,
We definitely will find you a smart handsome girl as your bride!
Why do you have to continue to cling to that Zhu Yingtai?
If something goes wrong, what can be done?

"You have no elder brother and no younger brother,
So, Son,
On whom do you want your old parents to rely?"
Shanbo nodded his head but said not a word in reply—
As tears coursed down, even more saddened!

But let's not tell of Shanbo and the Liang family,
Our story will take up the tale once more of the Mas.
Sending loads full of plates they came to the Zhus',
The wedding was set for the fifteenth of the eighth.

When Yingtai, Ninth Sister, heard about this,
Her tears coursed down without ever stopping.
She sat down and wrote a letter and note,
And dispatched a servant, a young serving boy.

She sent him to the Liang family in Zhuji,
To deliver the letter to Shanbo in his study.
As soon as Shanbo had seen the letter he received,
It scared him completely out of his wits!

"Dear sister!
How moved I am by your words and advice!
You want to tie the knot for a future existence.

How could I ever be able to abandon you—
Far better to die and find final peace!"

He spoke to the messenger in the following words:
"Report to the young lady when you return home,

"Tell her that it is my fate to die before my time,
Overcome by emotions my life cannot be preserved.
After my death I will be buried next to the road.
It kills a person not to be able to express his grief.

"So I hope you, Ninth Sister, will take pity on me,
For the sake of our love of three years as roommates.
Only if you will come to my grave in person to offer sacrifice,
Will I in the shades be able to put my mind at rest!"

Having uttered these words, his heart was about to break,
Then he stuffed her letter into his mouth and swallowed it.
As his breath stopped circulating in his throat,
His soul sped in darkness to the realm of the shades.

By his bedside his father and mother were grieved to death,
They stamped their feet, beat their breasts, pained by sadness.
The servant boy was also moved to tears,
And hastily took his leave to return home.

His father and mother encoffined Liang Shanbo,
And, remembering their son's last request,
They buried him outside town by the side of the road,
So Ninth Sister could come and offer sacrifice.

Now when the servant returned and reported,
Yingtai wept and fainted and came back to life.
Time and again she called out: "Liang Shanbo,
It is I, and I alone, who killed you!"

As Ninth Sister spent her days weeping and wailing,
The Ma family's party arrived to fetch the bride.
The colorful bridal chair was in tiptop order,
Music of drums shook the skies with its noise!

Mr. and Mrs. Zhu were in quite a hurry
To give their daughter away in marriage,

But Yingtai addressed her parents as follows:
"Please take my feelings into account.
Because I went to school in order to study,
Shanbo and I were fellow students for three years.

"I had hoped to be married to him as mandarin
ducks are,
But he arrived too late: I had been promised away.
Now Liang Shanbo has lost his life because of me—
In a lonely grave outside town, all desolate and cold.

"Now today I leave this house to be married off;
I want to be carried to the place of his grave.
This will enable me to offer sacrifice to his soul,
Finish off that three-year attachment as classmates.

"When afterward I'll arrive as bride at the Mas',
I'll have done away with that love for a roommate.
But if you, Father and Mother, don't grant me this
wish,
I, your daughter, will kill myself here in this house."

Mr. and Mrs. Zhu could do little else
But placate their young daughter:

"We will instruct the party that's here to fetch you,
To make a detour and take the road outside town,
So you may pass by the grave of Liang Shanbo,
And offer sacrifice to him to put your mind at rest."

Upon these words Ninth Sister was filled with joy,
Mr. Zhu gave his instructions to the bride fetchers.
All relatives of the Mas said they'd do as he wished,
And upon those words Yingtai called out to Renxin:

"Quickly prepare for me the soup and rice,
So I can offer sacrifice to my fellow student."

Upon these words Renxin prepared the foods,
And Yingtai said good-bye to her father and mother.
She also said good-bye to her brother and sister-in-law—
To the music of drums she was carried out of the hall.

Everybody praised her as the prettiest girl,
And said that she was the very image of Chang'e:[99]

Not too fat, not too slim: just the right measure,
Not too tall, not too short: an exceptional beauty!
Young Master Ma truly could be said to be lucky
As he would marry this girl like a flower, like jade.

Once Yingtai had ascended the colorful bridal chair,
Drums and fifes played: she went out of the gate,
And she went on her journey as fast as if flying,
Till, to the west of the town, she arrived at that road.

Before Shanbo's tomb the bridal chair was put down,
And all people looked on as that pretty girl
Lightly stepped out of that bridal chair, and,
Supported by Renxin, approached the grave.

After others had made the arrangements for her sacrifice,
Ninth Sister lifted her head to have a look.
She saw a single new grave in the overgrown fields,
A sight that wounded her innards, pierced her heart!

. . .[100]
With her slender white fingers she burned the incense,
And in front of the grave mound she deeply bowed.
Repeatedly, on and on, she called out: "Brother Liang,

"It is not the case that I, because of lack of feeling,
Today discard you and refuse to be your wife!"
She took out a sacrificial text, which she recited herself,
And, pouring out three cups of wine, she spoke her mind:

"I pray, Brother Liang, that your spirit will hear me,
As I show my respect with gifts of gold and silver.
But if, dearest Shanbo, your spirit can work a miracle,
Open your grave just one foot wide, let it bury my body!

"Because, dearest Shanbo, if you cannot work a miracle,
I will end up as the bride in Ma family village!"

---

99. Chang'e is the beautiful goddess of the moon.
100. One line of verse would seem to be missing here in the edited text.

Having spoken these words she wept piteously—
Suddenly a black cloud appeared above the grave.

In a moment a whirlwind arose from the ground,
Up in the sky the thunder continued to rumble.
All before one's eyes was darkness as at night,
Scaring the wits out of that bride-fetching party.

With the roar of an explosion the grave split open—
Ghosts wept, demons wailed, a terrible sight!
But Zhu Yingtai, the radiant bride,
Jumped into the fissure that had opened up.

The maids and serving women tried, of course,
To hold on to her by grasping her gauze skirt.
That embroidered gauze skirt was torn to pieces,
As Zhu Yingtai disappeared into that deep fissure.

That very moment the whirlwind entered the earth,
The sky was as clear as before, the sun was as bright.
No trace was left on the earth of that fissure,
But a pair of butterflies fluttered around the grave.

Black spots on white: that was Liang Shanbo,
White spots on yellow: that was Ninth Sister.
These are the transformations of their souls:
They fly hither and thither but always together.

The people who saw this were flabbergasted,
Such a miraculous event is really rare.
Having witnessed this event they could only
Carry the empty bridal chair back to the Ma family.

When this news reached the Ma family compound,
Master Ma Jun fell to weeping and wailing.
Having been cheated out of this beautiful person,
He hated the soul of that Liang Shanbo.

"How could he snatch away the soul of my wife?
This case of injustice demands retribution!"
In an instant his rage had the better of him,
And he swayed from a beam as a suicide!

Ma Jun had left to lay plaint in the shades,
Filling his weeping parents with sorrow.

They laid him in a coffin in the western hall,
But our story will turn to the Zhu family.

When they learned Yingtai had turned into a butterfly,
The whole family wept, overcome by grief.
Before Shanbo's grave they summoned her soul,
Set up a spirit tablet, and offered sacrifice.

But let's not narrate these doings of the Zhus,
But tell again of Ma Jun, that wronged soul.
Weeping, he entered King Yama's[101] hall, brandishing his complaint,
But horse-faced and buffalo-headed demons blocked his way.

[*Speaks*:]

"Hey! Where are you from, wronged ghost, coming here and laying plaint?"

Ma Jun answered: "Brother Demon, I have suffered a rare injustice. I have come on purpose to make a complaint and hope you will let me in."

"If that's the case, please state your case before His Majesty!"

[*Sings*:]
Horse-faced and buffalo-headed demons took him inside,
Where King Yama slapped his table and shouted to him:
"If you have suffered injustice, please tell the truth—
Unfounded accusations constitute a serious crime!"

Ma Jun told the whole story from the beginning,
And stated: "The solitary soul of Liang Shanbo
Snatched away the life and soul of my wedded wife,
And they turned into butterflies flitting around his grave."

Upon this report King Yama promptly gave orders
To his ghostly aides to check the relevant records.
The two of them had recently died, a few days ago,
If they were brought before the court, it would all be clear.

Ghostly runners were dispatched to go and arrest them,
And in a moment they led in the two apprehended souls.
King Yama in his hall raised his voice and shouted,
As he interrogated the solitary soul of Liang Shanbo:

"Why did you snatch away the soul of Miss Zhu,
And turn her into a butterfly in a display of magic?

---

101. King Yama is the king of the underworld.

If you do not tell the story here clear and straight,
The wolf-toothed iron cudgel will show no mercy!"

A weeping Shanbo told him the whole story:
"In male disguise Miss Zhu was my schoolmate.

"For three years we ate together and slept together,
And when she left, she promised me marriage.
But when I paid her a visit, I arrived too late,
As Yingtai had been promised to the Ma family.

"The disease of love longing ruined my body,
But luckily Yingtai offered sacrifice at my tomb.
I could not bear the thought she would marry Ma,
And snatched away her soul to be united in wedlock."

His Majesty ordered Liang Shanbo to one side,
And next he interrogated Zhu Yingtai:
"Student Liang snatched away your spirit and soul,
Is it indeed your wish to be married to him?"

A weeping Yingtai informed King Yama:
"It is indeed my wish to marry Liang Shanbo!

"I do not know that Ma Jun at all, and went only
Because one's father's orders cannot be disobeyed.
I cannot discard the love of our three years together,
I seek death so I may be reborn and marry my Liang!"

When His Majesty King Yama had heard their plea,
He declared that Yingtai should marry Liang Shanbo.
Ma Jun was to be reborn for another marriage,
In this way all aspects of the case were settled.

King Yama told the threesome his orders as follows:
"In this existence Liang Shanbo will be her lawful husband."

Then all of a sudden they woke and returned to life,
The corpse of Liang Shanbo was lying on top.
He opened the lid of his coffin and stepped outside,
Just as if he had woken from a long, long dream.

A smiling Yingtai stood in front of his grave,
Seeing each other, they were filled with joy.

Hand in hand they together started to walk,
And in just a while arrived at his house.

At this sight the doorman was struck dumb,
He believed he saw the apparition of a ghost!
Shanbo explained how he had returned to life,
Upon that news his happy parents welcomed him home.

Shanbo and Yingtai hastened to go inside
And showed his parents with a bow their respect.
His parents immediately asked their son:
"How could you return to life, become human again?

"How would the Ma family be willing to let matters rest,
If they found out anything about what has happened?"
Shanbo carefully explained to his parents:
"King Yama has given down a clear sentence:

"He set the three of us free to return to life,
Yingtai is set to become my lawful wife.
The Ma family is not going to dispute this,
So I pray you, my parents, put your minds at rest."

Mr. and Mrs. Liang were overcome with joy,
Palms pressed together, they thanked the gods.
They dispatched a servant to inform the Zhu family,
And once again they sent engagement presents.

Mr. and Mrs. Zhu thought this a miracle;
They thanked heaven and earth, and all the gods.
Immediately they sent gifts in return to the Liangs,
And husband and wife came to see their daughter.

Yingtai invited her father and mother inside,
It was as if they had found a lost treasure again

Our lovers were reunited, a wonderful joy!
In the bridal chamber the candles were lit.
Shanbo and Yingtai bowed to heaven and earth,
Husband and wife bowed to each other, tying the knot.

After they had bowed before her father and mother,
They also bowed before his father and mother.

All the relatives, one by one, came to greet them,
And to escort the couple to the bridal chamber!

Candles in the bridal chamber: they sat side by side,
And Shanbo, filled with joy, asked her with a smile:
"My wife,
In those days you refused to take off your clothes,
Would you perhaps tonight be willing to undress?"

Upon these words Yingtai replied with a smile:
"My husband, you really are not too smart!
If I had disrobed, I would have shown my body.

"Now you have returned from death to life,
Because of our three years of love as roommates."
The two of them talked and bantered and laughed,
Late that night they entered the bedstead hand in hand.

A thousand days of longing now were fulfilled:
The mandarin ducks entwined their necks for love.
Happy with joy they blamed the night for being too short,
At dawn the rooster crowed, and they had to get up.

After the couple had combed their hair and washed their faces,
And had dressed themselves, they emerged from their room.
Before their chamber they thanked all their relatives,
And they treated them to a banquet in a royal manner.

Yingtai raised the subject of her servant girl Renxin:
"In those days she followed me to the school.
She also shared three years of brotherly affection
With your servant boy, that Four-Nine.

"Why don't we have the two of them marry,
To bring to fruition their longtime desire?"
With a smile on his face Shanbo gave his assent,
And Four-Nine and Renxin then tied the knot.

Let's let go of this subject to talk of another—
Our tale will now turn to narrate that of the Ma family.
When Ma Jun in his coffin returned to life,
It scared the wits out of all those present!

They believed his ghost had come to haunt them,
So a weeping Mr. and Mrs. Ma asked him:
"Son,
Please don't act up in your coffin, since, of course,
We will invite monks to say masses for a speedy rebirth!"

When Ma Jun in his coffin heard these words,
He cried out: "Father and Mother, please listen!
Your son was not destined to die, so King Yama
Sent me off once again to come back to life!"

In detail he told them the whole tale of the verdict,
And upon his words his parents were filled with joy.
Immediately they opened the coffin to let him out,
And the whole family, all united, thanked the gods.

Mr. and Mrs. Ma made all possible haste
To find for their son another marriage partner.

Let's let go of this subject and talk of another—
Let me tell again about the Liang family.
After Mr. and Mrs. Zhu had stayed with the Liangs for over a month,
Young Mr. Zhu sent people over to take them back home.

He also invited his brother-in-law and his sister,
So they could talk things over back home at ease.

To return from death for a second life: truly a miracle!
So he hoped his parents would quickly come home.
Mr. and Mrs. Zhu were filled with joy,
And informed the in-laws of their intention.

The Liang family prepared fitting "gifts of return,"
And they hired a boat for Mr. and Mrs. Zhu.
Shanbo and his wife quickly dressed for the trip:
Like an immortal lad and an immortal maiden!

Together the couple bowed to his parents,
And then they left the house with Mr. and Mrs. Zhu.
Mr. and Mrs. Liang saw them off, as father-in-law and son-in-law,
Mother and daughter stepped in the boat to travel together.

They traveled quickly as if borne on the wind,
And soon arrived at the Xinghua village of the Zhus.

When the neighbors in the village heard about it,
They all called this return to life a rarely seen miracle.

Men and women crowded together to have a look,
In an excited throng they filled the village.
Young Mr. Zhu was busy no end
As he and his wife welcomed his parents back.

He also invited his brother-in-law and sister—
Sedan chairs from Xiaoshan waited for them as they got off the boat.
Mr. and Mrs. Zhu first took a seat in their sedan chairs,
And only then did Shanbo and Yingtai take a seat.

As they were carried up the hill to the mountain village,
They resembled the couple of Master Liu and the immortal maiden:[102]
Their clothes of embroidered brocade were exactly the same—
A brilliant student, a beautiful girl: without compare in this world!

When a thousand people saw them, a thousand loved them,
When ten thousand people saw them, ten thousand did.
All people praised this exceptional couple:
"Three years as roommates—their love was deep!

"Such a couple is rarely found in this world,
No wonder both man and wife loved each other so much they couldn't
bear to part!
Their souls together transformed into butterflies,
And together the two of them appealed to King Yama.

"Fortunately King Yama, pronouncing his verdict,
Set them free to return to life and get married.
Today both husband and wife arrive back home,
Isn't this a most wonderful sight to behold?"

Let's not go on about these people who were watching and talking,
But let's talk about the father-in-law and the others coming home.
In the hall they set out the incense table,
And again they thanked the heavenly gods.

The couple bowed before the father- and mother-in-law,
They greeted with a bow her brother and sister-in-law.

---

102. Master Liu here refers to Liu Chen.

Other members of the Zhu lineage came all to see them,
And a banquet was spread in the hall to feast them.

Her study was cleaned and properly furnished,
Just as if he had married into his wife's family.
Indescribable: each day was a party to host them well,
Each night was First Night with its celebrations.[103]

Husband and wife: a relation like that of fish and water,
Intoning verses and writing poems to their hearts' content.
But when suddenly it had been three months since they returned,
The Liang family made ready to hire a boat to bring them back.

His father- and mother-in-law were busily occupied
In preparing the trousseau to see their daughter off.
Indescribable the magnificence of her jewelry and furniture,
The servants and maids cannot all be mentioned.

No need to speak of the thousands of acres of dowry fields,
A banquet was spread in the hall to see the couple off.
At the end of the meal husband and wife made their bows,
As they were seen off through the gate and ascended the sedan chairs.

Very shortly they stepped on board their boat,
And within ten days they arrived back home.
When Mr. and Mrs. Liang saw how opulent the dowry gifts were,
The couple were extremely pleased and happy.

Husband and wife paid their respects to his parents,
Hand in hand, filled with joy, they retired to his room.
Spring passed, summer came, to be followed by fall,
Once the last month of winter was gone, spring again!

The king of Zhou, the Son of Heaven, held exams,
He widely invited all students of the realm to take part.
When the relevant edict arrived in Shaoxing prefecture,
The magistrate of Zhuji recommended his candidates.

Liang Shanbo combined in one person talent and study,
So prefecture and county summoned him to their offices.

---

103. First Night refers to the Lantern Festival, on the first night of the full moon in the first month.

Liang Shanbo found it impossible to part from Yingtai,
He had no desire to seek office and become a noble.

When the relevant offices had invited him repeatedly,
Yingtai urged her husband to go in the following words:
"When you studied with a teacher and sought wisdom,
It was for the sake of fame and glory, honor and wealth.
Now your fine talents are recommended by the officials,
So you rightly should go and sit for the examinations."

When Shanbo heard these words from his capable wife,
He could only take his leave of his father and mother.
Husband and wife said good-bye as tears coursed down,
Then he got on his horse and hastened on his journey.

Resting at night and leaving at dawn for many long days:
He arrived at the capital, that city of bright brocade.
On the third of the third he entered the examination grounds,
To be selected as one of the three hundred fine talents.

The king of Zhou, the Son of Heaven, was filled with joy,
From the golden vase his name was drawn as Top of the List.
And in the palace our Liang Shanbo was treated to
The Banquet of the Carnelian Forest—exceptional honor!

Parading the streets for three days he inspected the capital,
Then he asked the king to be allowed to inform his parents.
The Son of Heaven allowed his request and gave him a letter:
As a Hanlin Academy scholar he departed from the capital!

In his first attempt Liang Shanbo had achieved his fame,
Returning by way of the courier system he came home quickly.
In front of the hall he greeted and bowed to his parents,
And the gifts of the king of Zhou also arrived at the gate.

His parents received a patent of nobility from the king,
And Yingtai on this day was elevated to the rank of lady.

Before the hall a banquet was spread to celebrate this reunion,
And the strangest tale of all eternity reaches its conclusion.
Their undivided love and affection never diminished:
The gold-speckled butterflies remain united forever!

AN EXCERPT FROM A "WOMEN'S CHANTEFABLE"

Translated and introduced by Mark Bender

Chen Duansheng (1751–1796) was a native of the southern Chinese town of Qiantang in Zhejiang province, near present-day Hangzhou. She was only sixteen when she began to write *Love Reincarnate* (*Zaisheng yuan*), a fictional narrative of over six hundred thousand words composed in a prosimetric form (employing alternating passages of verse and prose) called *tanci* (literally, "plucking verses" or "plucking lyrics"). Many *tanci* were written by women, and a number have heroines who cross-dress as males. Circulating in both printed and handwritten forms among elite women in the late imperial period, a number of these works were written and edited by women in the Jiangnan region. As a group, these *tanci* by women sometimes have been called women's chantefable (*nü tanci*). Like most Chinese vernacular fiction, such texts feature many quasi-oral devices that in some ways mimic the style of an oral storyteller. Some of the written *tanci* were adapted into other genres for oral performance, though more research is needed on the relations between the written and the orally performed versions of these stories, especially in the early nineteenth century. The situation is complicated by the fact that the term *tanci* has been applied to a wide variety of written and oral forms. There is also evidence that some written chantefables, such as *Love Reincarnate*, were at times informally read aloud among small groups of women.

The main characters in Chen's work are reincarnations of those in an earlier *tanci*, *Jade Bracelet Romance* (*Yuchuan yuan*), which, though anonymous, may have been written by Chen's mother with Duansheng's help. *Love Reincarnate* begins in the southwestern city of Kunming, in Yunnan province, during the Yuan dynasty (1271–1368). The story concerns a talented and beautiful young woman named Meng Lijun; Lijun (Beautiful Gentleman) is known far and wide as the gifted maiden of Yunnan. Her father is a retired minister of the local military bureau. One day, go-betweens from two other powerful families, the Huangfus and the Lius, arrive to ask him for Lijun's hand in marriage to sons in their respective households.

Searching for a way out of an awkward situation, Minister Meng diplomatically suggests that the marriage be decided by a contest of arrows. Young Huangfu Shaohua and Liu Kuibi compete in an archery match held in the garden of the Meng mansion. The winner is the upright and dashing Shaohua. However, the rakish Liu Kuibi, whose sister happens to be the empress, is a sore loser, and he manages by various schemes to have the Huangfu family declared outlaws. In one episode, Shaohua escapes a murder plot with the aid of Liu Kuibi's compassionate half sister, Liu Yanyu. With Shaohua in hiding in the mountains, Liu manages to have an imperial order sent to the Meng household, and Lijun is betrothed to him.

Refusing this new engagement, Lijun dresses as a young male scholar to "save her purity" and runs off in the night with her maid, Ronglan. Lovely and learned Su Yingxue, another *qianjin* (a young lady figuratively worth a "thousand gold" pieces), has been Lijun's companion in the maidens' quarters since childhood. Yingxue (Reflecting Snow) had been taken in with her mother by the Mengs after the death of her father, an unaccomplished scholar. When the time comes to find a substitute for the vanished Lijun, Reflecting Snow is the natural choice. Because of a dream she had after viewing the archery match, Reflecting Snow feels that she, too, is engaged to Huangfu Shaohua.

The episode "Suitable Attire" describes the immediate events leading up to Reflecting Snow's short-lived masquerade as Meng Lijun. Particularly noteworthy are the intricate inner monologues, rare in other styles of Chinese vernacular narrative of this period.

After arriving at Liu Kuibi's home, Reflecting Snow tries to stab her groom to death in the wedding suite. Failing, she attempts to commit suicide by leaping out a window into a river. She is later rescued by the wife of a high-ranking court official, who takes her as a foster daughter. Meanwhile, Meng Lijun, under the name Li Mingtang, manages to pass the imperial examinations in the national capital, coming out number one on the list. "He" soon marries into the family of a powerful official, discovering on "his" wedding night that "his" bride is none other than Reflecting Snow, going under the name Liang Suhua. Li Mingtang becomes a powerful prime minister and manages to get the name of the Huangfu family cleared, though in the process raising the emperor's suspicions that "he" is not a man.

Chen Duansheng stopped writing at the end of the seventeenth chapter, leaving Meng Lijun debating as to whether she will reveal her true self and marry the emperor or continue as a successful man, living in fear of inevitable exposure. A less-open ending, comprising three chapters, was supplied to the story several decades later by another woman, Liang Desheng (1771–1847), who finished the story by having Huangfu Shaohua (who, with the disguised Meng Lijun's help, has become a high military minister) take Lijun, the virtuous Liu Yanyu, and Su Yingxue as his co-wives.

In all, Chen Duansheng had completed, by her early twenties, sixteen chapters of *Love Reincarnate*. As a result of a combination of factors that seem to have included the death of her mother, her marriage, and the exile of her husband to the northwest for his part in an examination scandal, Chen stopped writing for many years. Encouraged by relatives and friends, she completed chapter 17 sometime before her death in around 1796. Although records of other female members of her family survive, because of her husband's disgrace, little was recorded in the family histories about Chen herself.

Circulating for many years in handwritten form, the text was published in 1821, edited by Hou Zhi, a woman who wrote and edited a number of *tanci*. Several sequels or works with similar plots were written after the publication of *Love Reincarnate*, including *Heaven Re-created* (*Zai zao tian*) and *Elegant Words of the Brush* (*Bi sheng hua*), also written by women. Meng Lijun's "gender-bending" story has been adapted to many styles of local drama and professional storytelling, and it is especially popular in the Yangtze delta region of southeastern China. Although relatively undeveloped in Chen Duansheng's story, the character of Su Yingxue is elaborated considerably in orally performed versions of the tale popular since the mid-1940s, especially in the Suzhou chantefable (*Suzhou tanci*) tradition. (In the following text, the passages in italics are in prose. All the other passages represent lyric lines, which in the original may have three, seven, or ten syllables.)

SUITABLE ATTIRE

Written by Chen Duansheng

CHARACTERS

(in order of appearance or first mention)

PAN FA: The gardener
AUNTIE PAN: Pan Fa's wife
RONGLAN: Meng Lijun's maid, with whom she has escaped
SU REFLECTING SNOW (SU YINGXUE): Meng Lijun's maid and closest companion since childhood
XIUHUI: A new maid taken in with the intention of being sent with Meng Lijun to the Liu family
MENG LIJUN: The heroine of the story, a daughter in an elite household, originally engaged to Huangfu Shaohua, but later ordered by the emperor to marry Liu Kuibi
MADAME MENG (also termed GRAND MADAME or MADAME HAN, when using her own lineage name): Minister Meng's wife
ZHANG FAMILY: A servant's family living in the Meng household
AUNTIE LI: An older woman servant
MINISTER MENG SHIYUAN: A retired high minister of the military bureau; Meng Lijun's father
KUI: Grandson of the Mengs; Zhang Feifeng's child
ZHANG FEIFENG: Jialing's wife
JIALING: The son of Minister and Madame Meng; Zhang Feifeng's husband
HUANGFU SHAOHUA: Son of Commander Huangfu Jing; originally bested Liu Kuibi in an archery contest for Meng Lijun's hand
LIU KUIBI: A son of an imperial official, brother of the empress; by ill means received imperial sanction to marry Meng Lijun

Poem:

Date set, the six groom's gifts sent;
A red gown and scarlet sash donned to make merry.
Within the wedding suite sits Young Master Liu,
Expecting that eve the arrival of his fairy.

Let us speak of the garden keeper, Pan Fa. One day, arising as usual before dawn to sweep the garden, he discovered the rear gate thrown wide open and the lock lying on the ground. Shocked, he cried out that something was up: "There was certainly a thief afoot last night!" In the back of the garden a commotion arose, which he soon discovered concerned a missing yellow steed. Panicked, Pan Fa searched high and low for clues as to what had passed, and upon finding a series of doors all open, he ran to tell his wife: "Hurry inside to see. The way leads to Young Miss's chamber. I'm afraid if anything is missing, I'll get the blame!" Rushing off in a fluster, Auntie Pan declared that the situation was horrid!

Dashing into the maidens' quarters to investigate, Auntie Pan found the door slightly ajar and saw not a shadow moving within. She heard only the peeping of the birds in the treetops. Softly, she inquired if Sister Lan would rise to make her toilet; several times she called but received no reply. Boldly pushing on the door, she found only that the young lady's room was locked from within. The chamber was as silent as the dead—not a whisper could be heard. She cried out at once, asking where the maid Ronglan had gone, and why the double brass lock rings were secured so tightly. Reflecting Snow had just risen in the west chamber; Xiuhui opened the door to ask what the matter was. Auntie Pan described in detail the matter of the theft, and how she had come to investigate. Where on earth could Miss Lijun be? It was so silent behind the locked doors! Startled, Reflecting Snow hurried out of the room—the decorative pins in her hair nodding with her head, her pained flower face slightly wan, in her phoenix slippers urgent, yet bespeaking a gentle composure. Pushing open the east door, she looked carefully inside only to see the bed curtain still and the incense in ashes. Pushing aside the brocade curtains, she saw clearly that the pillow and coverlet were undisturbed. At this sight, Reflecting Snow was frightened. Her flower face paled as her eyebrows knit.

"Aiya! *How strange! Why has Young Miss disappeared? Auntie Pan, please hurry to the front hall. Might she be in Madame's chamber?"*

As Pan Fa's wife rushed off, the troubled Maiden Su turned to put on more clothing; in her chamber she donned her usual garb, and, tying on a white sash, she quickly and daintily moved away. Xinhui, new among the maids, hurried behind Reflecting Snow as they left the maidens' quarters. Zigzagging through the walkways, they finally arrived at Madame's chamber. At that moment, Auntie Pan flew out of the anteroom. In distress, she cried to the Zhang family and Auntie Li, asking whether Grand Madame had arisen that morning. It wasn't so serious that the garden gate had been found open and that the yellow steed was missing from its stall. And still no one was clear where Miss Lijun and Ronglan had gone. It was strange that the room in the maiden's chamber was so tightly locked. Thus, maids and servants shrieked out cries of alarm. In both wings of their quarters, maids and ladies were in a state, pulling on trousers in a frenzy and urgently donning their tunics—the entire courtyard was in an uproar! Stirred from their dreams, Master and Madame Meng cried out for the maids, asking what on earth was the matter. Maiden Su wended her way through the winding corridors to speak through the blinds, informing the couple as to the cause of the disturbance.

Madame and Master were told that: "This morning the rear garden gate was found wide open, and Miss's chamber door was ajar. At present, that is all that is known—no one knows the whereabouts of Miss and Ronglan."

Husband and wife were shocked and confused at this news. Again and again they spoke of how horrible it was and repeatedly opened the door to question Reflecting Snow. Miss had passed by Green Pine Hall with her maid—could they have gone to see Little Kui and not yet returned? Reflecting Snow said it might be possible—that she would look to make sure. Concerned and upset, she stepped with her three-inch feet precisely along the corridor as Madame and Minister sat foolishly in the hall, ignoring their toilet. Maids and ladies were called forth and the gardener questioned in detail. Just as Pan Fa was repeating the events one by one, news came that the missing persons were not in Green Pine Hall. Zhang Feifeng came forward, followed closely by Young Master Jialing. Reflecting Snow was frightened; weeping in despair, she declared it all unthinkable. Feifeng related that Young Miss had come to see Little Kui the night before; seemingly distressed and sorrowful, she had mentioned something about "parting from each other." She was unwilling to go through with the marriage, and now she had hidden herself who knew where?

Jialing stamped his foot and knit his brow: "There's no doubt she'd pull something like this! My sister is strongheaded. How could she be expected to simply follow the emperor's order and lose her purity?"

So it was: Miss had indeed been forced to escape; and in such a case, how did her parents feel? Madame Han at once wept bitterly, crying to heaven and earth, her tears falling in streams. The minister's heart seemed as though attacked by knives; he threw back his head and cried out to heaven. Stamping his boots on the ground, he cried out, "Horrible!" as he pitifully hobbled into the hall. Madame buried her face in her hands and sobbed loudly; Feifeng lowered her head in tears and sniffles, then left. Jialing sighed and followed his parents, along with a cluster of maids and servants. Together they all entered the maidens' quarters and proceeded to the middle chamber to inform Grand Madame, who tearfully asked the whereabouts of Young Miss all the way. They entered her chamber, finding it deserted, except for an empty bed. Turning their eyes to the desk before the window, they spied a letter of parting, written by the young lady herself.

On recognizing his daughter's script, Minister Meng knew the content was either of a secret escape or of a suicide. Thus, he sat beside the window to tear open the letter to look.

Reading it, he sighed, as innumerable tears of sorrow wet his face. Madame Han, together with her son and daughter-in-law, gathered before the green window. Seeing the words run away, Madame wept so sorrowfully that she fainted, her heart breaking in grief.

"Hai-yo! *My dear daughter, how could you desert your dear parents, running off this way?*

"This is your sixteenth year—all say you are a clever and wise girl with a future. Your father disagreed with your wish to marry Huangfu, and, indeed, at this moment, his family has brought disaster on ours. The affair of your marriage to Liu Kuibi was sanctioned by the Son of Heaven—such a fortunate occurrence for us, such an event of great happiness—a marriage arranged by a ruler! You needn't have defied the emperor's command out of mere infatuation; you needn't have risked death to follow a family of traitors—why didn't you consider the benefits we bestowed when raising you?

"Those debts cannot be deserted. How dare you sneak off into the twilight? You are just a girl—how, with your frail, pampered body, can you survive on your own? You've spent your whole life in the maidens' quarters—how can you find your way out there? How can you know the difficulties of surviving in a rough, tough world? Even though Ronglan accompanies you, what does she know? She, too, is just a girl, knowing nothing of the world. You ran off without knowing high from low—I fear you shall simply drift on till you become a ghost in some strange village. *Aiya!* My pet!

"Last night you had already agreed to the marriage—yet today, it must be thought of as if in a dream. A mother and daughter have parted halfway on the path of life! Why have you disappeared without a trace?" Madame sank to the floor in tears, her hair mussed, a scarlet blush rising on her powdered face. Jialing and his wife stood sobbing together. Minister Meng's heart seemed stirred by knives—his true feelings stood revealed. The opened letter seemed to be his daughter's face—tears of sorrow soaked his breast. "*Aiya!* Daughter, this letter reveals that you have donned a youth's clothing and escaped from the garden. This is an improper course of action! I fear that, wishing to retain your purity, indeed your dignity shall be lost. You are no coarse village girl lacking in looks—you are a budding beauty. Who can know, beneath heaven, the number of rakes who shall pursue your youth and beauty? One such as you shall find it hard to escape. You are totally ignorant of the ways of the world—how dare you let your precious body face life's vagaries? With a matchmaker and proper ceremony, you are still against the marriage—how can you fend off the opinions of boors and madmen? You feel you have acted to retain your purity—but I say, the future is hard to foretell. Though you disagreed, you should have told the truth—why have you hidden this from your parents? I thought we had your heartfelt agreement, and I was prepared to write the emperor—but you only pretended agreement; and now you have deserted your parents!" At these words, the minister became distraught. He wished to vent the sorrow in his breast, but instead his tears fell like springwater.

Jialing stamped his foot and, heaving a sigh, declared the matter was against his sister's will. "If father had allowed her to retain her purity, how could she ever have imagined escaping from the garden to avoid misfortune? But since this is the case, we have no choice but to do as the letter says." With these words, all eyes fell upon Reflecting Snow. They noticed the lovely girl was reading the letter. As her starry eyes traced up and down the sheet, two red clouds arose immediately upon her jade cheeks; she laid down the letter, as sorrow arose in her heart. Her eyes brimming with tears like dew-filled buds, a few words issued from her lips:

"Aiya, *Madame and Master—her order shall be difficult to obey.*

"Though foolish and lacking talent and ability, this servant does know something of retaining female virtue. Commander Huangfu Jing has turned against the dynasty—though in fact he is the victim of an evil minister's calumny. The emperor's relative, Liu Kuibi, attempted to destroy Master Huangfu by burning the gardens—but the plot was foiled and the culprit exposed. Thus, a calm sea was stirred by his scheming. Since his sister is the empress, is it unlikely that secret letters will be exchanged, begging for pardon and position? Now Young Miss has been forced to flee to retain her purity, and Liu Kuibi is the one I hate to his bones—if my rancor goes unrevenged, I shall remain forever indignant—how can I marry him in my lady's place? If I would do so for gain of wealth and position, my virtue would be sullied for a thousand years. Now must I not only transgress against protocol—I fear later to suffer even greater punishment for this deed. It has been said since ancient times that the influence of evil ministers is like ice and snow—swift to accrue but easy to melt away. Families destroyed by them may come to enjoy great reversals in fate and fortune; in such circumstances heaven pardons such behavior, not rescuing the oppressed from suffering. If today I wish to seek wealth and position—can't you see that I would be inviting disaster to destroy myself by such desires? Since Master and Madame know the truth of these old sayings, it will thus be my hardship that I must obey and join the Liu family. It would be best to inform the emperor directly of the case, and await his decision. Young Miss wished to keep her purity and not marry—it was the Liu family who forced her. Under such circumstances she had no choice but to escape secretly—we can find her nowhere under the sun. If the Liu family demands retribution, then this injustice can be righted. Though the Liu family has no power as great as that of the sea, it would still be difficult for the emperor to recognize the claim of his relatives in public. If asked to marry him on this coming day, I, Reflecting Snow, am more than willing to pass on to the netherworld." When the beauty spoke of this likely sorry consequence, she covered her face and sobbed sorrowfully, her painful tears falling like rain.

Before Master could say a word, Reflecting Snow's mother, Mother Su, by turns sorrowful, joyous, and angry, went forward to tug at her daughter's sleeve, giving her an earful of advice; accusing the girl of being unfilial:

"When your father died so young, we had no one to rely on; your mother became wet nurse for Young Miss. Had Master and Madame not pitied us, how could you have eaten or had proper clothes up till today? Don't speak of 'ifs'; think of with what feeling Young Miss has treated you. You sit together, walk together, with no pride between; you two share love and intimacy, unblemished by disdain. Though she is but several months your junior, she calls you Elder Sister. She is your unstinting teacher in painting and poetry—without her careful instruction, you'd be but a foolish, ignorant maid. This predicament should be solved with your help—why be a stumbling block? Why not just agree? You can't imply that a relative of the emperor's would bring you disgrace? You with your ragged gown and cheap baubles—a lowly maid. Now, you'd best do as I say—bow eight times before your stepparents. Should Master and Madame agree, you will join a family of wealth and position. If now you do not comply with them, it is really 'requiting kindness with enmity'—you seem a heartless ingrate—hurry forward before your masters!" As she finished her words, Mother Su grasped her daughter by the arm and drew her forward, urging her to quickly recognize her benefactors as stepparents. Breaking into tears, the minister and his wife queried the maid as to whether this path was suitable.

By this time, Reflecting Snow had nothing to say, and with eyes full of tears, silently pondered: "*Aiya!* Thousand Gold! I, this servant, imagined you had a change of heart, yielding to the emperor and your parents. Who would have known that each of your words was false. Now you have made off to parts unknown—Young Miss, you thought only of yourself in your flight—but how could you know that I, too, have feelings for Master Huangfu? This letter you left behind has brought me only disaster. Is there a way for me to escape as well? All right, all right, all right—since I am a red-cheeked beauty, it is just my fate to end up this way—it is natural. Su Reflecting Snow may go to the Liu family, but wealth and riches cannot taint my purity. I, this servant, can never forget that marriage in the dream—I shall simply sacrifice my little life and die; my ghost will search elsewhere for that talented young man. Though I may not have him when alive—after death, we shall be inseparable. Heaven bless Master Huangfu, that he attain great success, and that he take revenge to put my soul at ease. Miss Lijun may keep her dignity and purity—a woman of character with a handsome, talented scholar will become a couple—showing how loyal I, Reflecting Snow, have been from beginning to end. Today I am forced to fulfill her marriage vow, but I cannot say that I shall sacrifice my young life at this moment, today."

The beauty, Reflecting Snow, had made up her mind. Immediately, her expression altered, and she spoke to Master and Madame, saying, "I owe a great debt of gratitude to you. How dare I ignore it? At first I was unwilling to marry in Miss's stead, but since you have implored me in this way, how dare I object? I have no other choice, thus I dare recognize you as stepparents and beg you to excuse me. Madame and Master, please be seated; allow this servant to kneel and kowtow before you in the middle chamber."

Master's and Madame's hearts felt both pain and joy. Mother Su asked them to hurry—it was unnecessary to arrange an altar—all could be done in the maidens' chamber. Madame was forced to call this girl "Daughter," and weeping with infinite tears, she bid the girl by that name. Showing great pity for Reflecting Snow, the minister tried his best to solace the beauty. After Maiden Su had knelt and addressed them as her parents, Madame Meng wished to send a search party for the runaway. She suspected the missing girl had not gone far. "Go at once to search for Young Miss, then return as soon as possible." Disturbed by this idea, Jialing prevented his mother from issuing the order, saying: "If we send out a search party, ugly gossip will spread like wildfire—others won't regard you as high-minded, wanting to keep the girl's reputation clean—instead, it shall reveal the weak rule in this household. If the contents of this letter were known to the Liu family, how could we secretly marry Reflecting Snow to their son? My sister's mind is sharp—I'm sure she's not lacking in designs as to what to do—she disguised herself when she ran off—who will recognize her as a maiden? Besides, she's quite learned; I'm sure in one way or another she will succeed. If you did manage to find her and bring her back to marry, she would only end her life in the netherworld. Thinking of the long run, we'd better not dispatch a search party. Should the Liu family join the search, that would make it difficult for my sister to stay in hiding. After my new adopted sister marries, then we can execute a search for my sister."

Master and Madame both nodded their heads and, with great sighs, left the chamber. The scholar-official ordered that all persons were to keep the secret; receiving the order, the servants at once fell silent and went about their business. As it was an auspicious day, suited to a wedding, the first order of business was to pluck the bride's face. This region's customs may differ from others': here, when a bride marries, her face is plucked with silk thread,[104] and nothing but pearls are strung in her hair, with jade ornaments to complement the new gown.

Urgently they assembled a dowry and sent someone to ready the bridal suite. Madame Han glumly divided the dowry into two equal parts—with

104. Lengths of silk thread were manipulated between the fingers to form a kind of tweezers used to remove "peach fuzz" from a woman's face.

one for Mother Su. It is unnecessary to speak of the women's feelings, and unnecessary to describe the bustle in the house that day. No mention need be made of the events that night; thus, we shall speak of the events of the next day, when the red sun had broken over the horizon and was shining upon the mulberry trees, when the change in the household was so great that it may as well have been mythical Fusang Island.

Now let us speak of that next day, the second day of the lunar month, a fine day when it dawned. At sunrise, the Liu family hung the gateway with flowers and decked the halls with festoons and garlands. The bridal sedans were sent off to escort the bride home. The streets were crowded—the eyes of all were agog with envy at the wealth displayed by the rich family.

As the sedan chairs, enveloped in beautiful flowers, started on their way, household guards filed down both sides of the street. Hundreds of pairs of palace lanterns reflected on one another from high and low, thousands of white horses clopped on in droves. Fairy-sound music languidly flowed from reed trumpets; colorful banners fluttered all along the richly decked streets. In front of the procession of sedan chairs were two red plaques with gold characters, which read: "This marriage is sanctioned by the emperor." Arriving at the Meng mansion, the escorts asked that the bride be dressed quickly and mount the bridal sedan. Though unwilling, Minister Meng was forced to don his official attire; guests joined the celebration in swarms. Though downhearted, Madame Meng hid her true feelings, and to herself bewailed the heartrending matter. Though the sky was bright, she had yet to stir from bed. Her cloudlike hair was loose, tears streaked her cheeks. Her husband secretly entreated, "Why are you acting this way? You mustn't ignore your new daughter." It was clear that there were two sets of feelings over the daughter. Kneeling together before her, her daughter-in-law Feifeng and her son Jialing also entreated their mother. Madame Meng thus slowly arose, proceeded to her dressing stand, made her toilet, and dressed.

By the time she had finished, the women of the household had arrived and were received by her. Feifeng even held her own child that day. The bride's maids were all in the maidens' quarters, helping the bride to dress. Reflecting Snow had spent the night in her mother's bed, exchanging sorrowful words of parting. On her person was hidden a keen-edged knife—kept to revenge her hatred by murdering Master Liu. Facing the mirror, she dressed her hair and donned her bridal gown; a phoenix headdress and a colorful marriage cape were placed before her; lightly, she powdered her face and draped a string of pearls over her hair; a jade ring caught up her locks in a knot, stuck through with ornate pins; colorful sleeves draped her jadelike arms; her skirt allowed just the tips of her red slippers to peek out. With a graceful gait she departed from her chamber, the jade ornaments on her costume tinkling as she moved, like a fairy descended from the moon. Two maidens steadied her, one on each arm. It was heard that no further delays would be brooked—three times she had been summoned, and she could linger no longer.

Then, as she left the maidens' quarters, she wished to kneel and bid her farewells before mounting the bridal sedan. Maids spread a rug on the floor and helped her to kneel.

"Young Miss" daintily moved her feet across the red carpet, knelt down before her "parents," and silently wept. Sobbing painfully, she half covered her face, shedding tears. Master and Madame Meng spoke together; it is unnecessary to recount their advice. All the relatives met her one by one. Master Meng left his seat and called to the beauty: "Daughter, bid farewell to Mother Su, the mother at whose breast you suckled. You may kneel down and thank her for raising and caring for you." Mother Su was grateful for Master's kindness in urging the daughter to politely kowtow before her. In but a moment, mother and daughter would be parted forever. The beauty, full of hatred and sorrow, could not speak a word; her tears lined her cheeks like pearls, her sobs replacing dried tears with fresh ones. The true mother, she declared that she dared not accept the thanks—it was too hard to bear—"Young Miss" should arise. In name, they were now mistress and servant, and thus it was proper that the elder woman pay respects. Though they were truly mother and daughter, no longer could they enjoy such a relationship. Thus, they bowed halfway, pretending to have knelt, and hurriedly moved to adjust the bridal headdress. Thus, the rituals in the hall were complete.

Again and again the drumbeats urged them out. The ladies of the family departed; the bride's maids prepared to escort the beauty out of the rear hall. At that moment, a veil was made to cover her face. Relatives outside could not clearly distinguish the bride's appearance as Reflecting Snow was hurried into the decorated sedan. Three blasts of the fairy-sounding trumpets and three bright beats of the drum heralded the issuance of the sedan chairs from the mansion, amid a flurry of banners. The maids from three chambers followed behind; only the new maid, Xiuhui, kept to the household. The escort party of the Liu family turned toward home with the bridal sedan, the guards swaggering along in noisy laughter.

A SUZHOU CHANTEFABLE OPENING BALLAD

Translated and introduced by Stephanie Webster-Chang

In the tradition of Suzhou chantefable (*Suzhou tanci*), "Sighs from the Palace" is an opening ballad (*kaipian*), or musical prelude immediately preceding the storytelling proper. Such pieces, often in the form of short ballads or famous sections of longer works, help the storytellers to limber their voices and to settle the audience. The chantefable describes the legendary Yang Guifei, of the Tang dynasty (618–907), as she waits for the emperor in the Western Palace. The imperial consort's heart is broken when she discovers that the emperor has made other romantic plans for his evening. She contemplates her unhappy life as a concubine and muses about the joys of life lived outside the palace. This sentiment is captured in the last line, "A crape-myrtle flower for a crape-myrtle man," in which Yang imagines the happiness of a match between a common woman and man. The image of this common flowering tree is used here to symbolize an "ordinary" woman (flower) and man.

The ballad dates to the Qing dynasty (1644–1911), when it first appeared in the songbook *White Snow Posthumous Tunes* (*Bai xue yi yin*). It was made famous during the 1920s and 1930s through performances by the Suzhou artists Zhu Yaosheng and Zhu Jiasheng and later during the 1950s through performances by Yang Zhenxiong and Zhu Huizhen, of the Shanghai Pingtan Troupe. "Sighs from the Palace" is often performed in the style of the Yu school, a musical style distinguished by intricate embellishments and a wide vocal range.

SIGHS FROM THE PALACE

In the still of the night, the Western Palace is perfumed with the scent
of one hundred flowers,
Wanting to roll up the beaded curtain, but already dreading
the long spring.

Sitting alone on the fragrant bed,
Guifei waits for the emperor in the light of the red candle.

Eunuch Gao announces,
That tonight His Majesty has called on another.

Hearing this, her sorrow deepens;
Consort Yang listlessly removes her palace adornments.

She leans up against the dragon bed,
Sighing, with tears streaming down her face.

The coverlet is cold and the pillows cool,
  She watches the bright moon rise above the palace wall.

She wants to tell the world, "Do not marry the king,
  It is like being with a tiger or a wolf,
  The lord is a heartless man."

I'd rather marry a ladies' man,
  And enjoy life each day and night,
  A crape-myrtle flower for a crape-myrtle man.

A SUZHOU CHANTEFABLE CLASSIC FROM *PEARL PAGODA*

Edited by Zhou Liang and translated and introduced by Yu Li

Suzhou chantefable (*Suzhou tanci*) is a professional storytelling art that has been performed for centuries in cities of the lower Yangtze delta, particularly in its namesake, Suzhou. It is part of a dual storytelling tradition known as *pingtan* that is composed of a style of oral storytelling without music called *pinghua* (sometimes translated as "straight storytelling") and storytelling with music called *tanci* (literally, "plucking verses " or "plucking lyrics") or *tanchang* (literally, "pluck and sing"). Performances consist of an elegant mixture of narration, dialogue, and singing. Most performances today are presented by a pair of storytellers; one plays the three-stringed *sanxian* (banjolike instrument) and the other, the pear-shaped *pipa* (four-stringed lutelike instrument). Performances last for about two hours a session, many stories taking two weeks to tell (in the past, some stretched for as long as three months).

Pearl Pagoda (*Zhenzhu ta*) is one of the most popular stories in the Suzhou chantefable repertoire, which numbers over two hundred tales. One of the earliest recorded Suzhou chantefable stories, it can be traced back to the Daoguang reign period (1821–1850) in the Qing dynasty, when it was performed by Ma Chunfan (1795?–1835?). Throughout its long history, the story has undergone changes in the hands (and mouths) of various storytellers. The most famous storyteller associated with the story was Ma Rufei (late nineteenth century), the son of Ma Chunfan. His literary training helped him to refine the story and create the famous "Ma tune" (Madiao), which has been associated with *Pearl Pagoda* since his time.

Set in the fourth year of the reign of the Ming emperor Tianqi (r. 1620–1627), *Pearl Pagoda* concerns a poverty-stricken young scholar named Fang Qing, whose family once had several high officials in the imperial court. The tale begins when Fang Qing visits his aunt, Lady Chen, to borrow money so that his academic title will not be taken away by vicious local officials. Embarrassed by the appearance of her poor relative, snobbish Lady Chen greets him with contempt and ridicule. Feeling insulted, Fang Qing leaves the Chen household, swearing that he will not come back until he passes the imperial examinations. His elder cousin, Miss Chen Cui'e, hears about the incident and feels sorry for him. She apologizes to him and gives him a basket of food with a small pearl pagoda hidden inside. Her father, Master Chen Lian (who had been helped by the Fang family in the past), also goes after Fang Qing and betroths his only daughter to him. On his way back to his home, Fang Qing is robbed of the pearl pagoda and later is rescued by a high-ranking official, who asks him to stay at his house to study for the imperial examinations. Three years later, Fang Qing becomes the Number One Scholar[105] in the imperial

105. Number One Scholar (Zhuang Yuan) was the title given to the scholar who ranked highest on the imperial civil service examination.

examinations and is assigned a high position in the imperial court. He returns to the city of Xiangyang in the guise of a Daoist priest, planning to embarrass his scornful aunt and to look for his mother. Finally, he reveals his identity and marries Chen Cui'e, who has taken care of his mother during the time he was gone.

The episode "Descending the Stairs" is taken from the performance text of Wei Hanying (1911–1991), whose father, Wei Yuqing (1879–1946), was given the nickname Pagoda King in the 1920s when he performed the story in Shanghai. Wei Hanying started to learn Suzhou chantefable when he was only nine years old and began to perform as his father's partner when he was thirteen. During his fifty years of storytelling, he further developed the "Wei tune" (Weidiao) created by his father. The translation is based on a handwritten dictation made in the early 1980s, edited by the storytelling historian and cultural bureau official Zhou Liang. The text reflects Wei Hanying's storytelling style of the 1960s, since he (like many other storytellers) rarely performed during the political turmoil of the 1970s.

The scene is one of the most famous in the entire Suzhou chantefable tradition. Storytelling legend says that the scene once took days or even weeks to tell (in some performances, only one step a day), though in recent years the episode has taken at most a few hours (or even less) to relate, depending on the teller. One reason for the length is the convention of inner monologues, which reveal a character's thoughts. The scene takes place on the stairs outside Chen Cui'e's bedchamber. The maid Caiping is trying her best to persuade Miss Chen to go downstairs to meet her fiancé, Fang Qing, who has come to visit her after three years of separation. Although she has longed to see him for three years, Miss Chen feels too shy to meet him when the time comes. Each time she takes a step down the stairs, she thinks of another reason to refuse to walk any further. If not for the witty and clever maid Caiping, Miss Chen would not have descended the stairs to meet her future husband. This scene of persuasion constitutes the major part of the episode "Descending the Stairs."

If a pair is performing, one is the lead and the other is the assistant. The lead storyteller narrates and takes the major roles, and the assistant plays the minor parts. If performing alone, the lead performs all the roles. There are various ways of representing the intricate voicing of *pingtan* performances in print. In the selection, the speaking roles are presented in roman type, while the sung passages are in italics. The text begins with the storyteller as narrator and then shifts back and forth between dialogues (marked by double quotation marks) and inner monologues (marked by single quotation marks) of characters and narration in both speech and song.

DESCENDING THE STAIRS

Told by Wei Haiying (Han)

Chen Lian waited in the study near the Purple Rose Hall, ready to eavesdrop. Let's come back to Maid Caiping, who was upstairs. When she saw that the master had come upstairs by himself, she was relieved and said to herself: "Since Master has come, whether or not Miss goes downstairs will not be my responsibility. Who would have thought that when Master leaves, he would put the duty of asking Miss to go downstairs onto my shoulders? If I don't succeed in persuading Miss to go down, Young Master will certainly misunderstand. He will think: 'Young Miss will not come to see me despite my insistent requests. Father-in-law came and left. What can all this mean but contempt?' If he gets angry and leaves just as he did last time with no news at all about his whereabouts for three years, then Master will definitely put me under household penalty. Now all I can do is to try my best to persuade Miss to go downstairs."

The witty and clever maid Caiping, enthusiastically tries to persuade the Miss.
"Miss, please go downstairs!"
Miss did not have any choice but to stand up.
Young Miss is shy.
Without prodding, she walks reluctantly and helplessly.
"All right, Maid, let's go!"
Young Miss steps out the door and starts walking down the stairs.
No sooner has she descended the first stair
Than she stops herself and refuses to walk any further.

It took Caiping so much effort to persuade Young Miss to move that, she thought, as soon as she agreed to do so, she would go straight down to the Purple Rose Hall. Who would have thought that Miss would stop after only one step? She said to herself: 'Dear Miss, if you are so slow, Young Master will have nobody to accompany him. If he leaves, I cannot bear the responsibility.' She urged: "Dear Miss—

There is nobody to keep company with Master Fang.
He is alone in the garden.
I'm afraid he will leave without saying good-bye.
Master has gone to meet Mrs. Fang from Henan.
If he comes back and does not see Master Fang,
He will come up and blame you.

—Don't you think so, Miss?"

'That's right. If Cousin leaves, and Father comes back with Aunt and does not see him, not only will Father blame me but so will Aunt. Don't be shy, go downstairs.'

"Caiping, let's go!"
"Miss, watch your step!"

A few words from Caiping, and Miss happily descends the stairs.
While Maid holds her jadelike hand, both of them go downstairs.
No sooner has she descended the second stair
Than she stops herself and refuses to walk any further.

Resolved, you said, "Let's go!" But after only one step, you stopped again.
"Miss, why did you stop again?"
"There is a reason."
"What reason?"
"Dear Caiping—

It is difficult to meet Master Fang today.
After all, I cannot obey Father's order.
There is no good reason for me to meet him.
I will be embarrassed to death when we see each other."

Hearing this, Caiping thought that this was no reason at all.
"Miss, what you have said makes no sense at all."
"Why not?"
"Miss—

Why worry about embarrassment for this second meeting?
You have met each other before in the Green Autumn Pavilion.
Today, just meet and ask him quickly.
You can retire to your chamber in no time.
How come you are shy after three years?"

Last time you were meeting him for the first time but weren't embarrassed at all. Today is the second time. Why are you so shy? You might as well wear a mask if you are to meet him for the third time.
"Miss, we'd better hurry."
"That's right. Well, let's go."

The words of persuasion sound reasonable.
All of her shyness is gone without a trace.
With beautiful figure and elegant posture,
Young Miss steps down the stairs with her golden lotuses.[106]
No sooner has she descended the third stair
Than she stops herself and refuses to walk further.

---

106. The term "three-inch golden lotus" referred to women's bound feet in traditional times.

Again after only one step, she stopped for some unknown reason.
"Miss, why did you stop again?"
"There is an explanation."
"What explanation?"
"Here it is—

Although we met several years ago,
It was only a moment in the Green Autumn Pavilion.
I did that to fulfill my filial piety to Mother.
Today is different from last time.
Before, we were cousins, the closest relatives.
Now we have been engaged in the Pine Pavilion.

—So, I cannot go downstairs."

Oh, today's meeting would not be the same as the one in the Green Autumn Pavilion, because the cousins have already been engaged. Before, they were only cousins. Now they are engaged. How should she address him when she meets him? So, she cannot go downstairs. Caiping thinks: 'Your terms of address may suit whatever the guest likes. Your old relationship was cousins and your new one is couple-to-be. If you are shy, you can just use the old kinship terms. How easy this is!' "Miss—

Couples do not use couples' etiquette,
You can still treat each other as sister and brother.
Until now you have called your mother-in-law Aunt;
And he has called his father-in-law Uncle.
Do not talk about marriage when you meet.
Hold off the new relationship.
Address each other according to the old one.

—Miss, is this all right?" Wasn't this just a ruse?!

Upon hearing this, Chen Cui'e thought: 'That's correct. I can address him according to the old relationship instead of the new one. I can be bold enough to go downstairs and meet him as his cousin.' "In that case, let's go!" she agreed to go again.

Nodding slowly, she was quietly worried;
Yet the words of persuasion sound reasonable.
Moving her shoes and holding up her skirt,
She takes one step downward.
No sooner has she descended the fourth and fifth stairs
Than she stops herself and refuses to walk any further.

Seeing this, Caiping sighs. It took so much effort to persuade Miss to take one more step downward. Who would have expected that she would stop again? Looking at Young Miss, and turning to the stairs, Caiping is really sad. How long will it take to finish these stairs in this way? "Miss, why did you stop again?"

"There is a justification."

'There was a reason, then an explanation. Now it is a justification. No matter what you are going to say, I will persuade you to go downstairs.' "What justification?"

Chen Cui'e said: "Dear Caiping—

In the past, Mother was cold to him.
Today, they did not have a fight.
Last time I broke with etiquette to meet him in the Green Autumn Pavilion.
That was because Mother was snobbish and I went to intervene.
At present there is no reason for us to meet.
Why should I bother to go to the Purple Rose Study Garden,
Only to gain ridicule and contempt?

—Therefore, I . . . cannot go downstairs."

It all boiled down to this justification: in the past, the mother was snobbish toward the cousin. Young Miss went downstairs to apologize to her cousin for her mother's behavior. Today, the aunt and the nephew did not have a fight, so there was no good reason for her to go to the Purple Rose Hall to meet her cousin. Therefore, she could not rush downstairs. Caiping thinks: 'Then, Miss, according to your justification, relatives can meet only after they have a fight. They will not be able to meet if they are polite to one another. That way, all your relatives are bound to be lost, right? Plus, you said there is no reason to go downstairs today. I think there is not only a reason but a good and decent one.' Indeed, Miss wanted to meet Fang Qing. All that she said was simply excuses and could hardly be reasonable. "Miss, last time you—

. . . fulfilled your filial piety to Mother to act on her behalf.
Madame did not hear a word about that.
A while ago Master ascended the stairs to invite you.
Why can't you obey your father's order today?
You have always been known as a filial daughter.
How can you be filial not to your father but to your mother?
Who on the earth would treat her parents differently?

—Please reflect on this, Miss."

Hearing this, Miss agrees that what Caiping has just said is, again, correct. 'Last time, when I violated propriety to meet Cousin in the Green Autumn Pavilion, it was to act for Mother. Mother did not ask me to do that. Today, it was Father who came upstairs to invite me, and I will not go. Isn't this treating parents differently? Thus, how can I be lauded as a filial daughter?' Miss thought:

'How considerate Caiping is! I didn't think about this at all, which is really funny.' "Then, Caiping, let's go!"

"All right, Miss, please."

Miss smiles as she listens.
Parents should be treated the same, after all.
No longer shy and no longer embarrassed, both Miss and Maid step downstairs.
No sooner has she descended the sixth and seventh stairs
Than she stops herself and refuses to walk any further.

Caiping asks: "Why did you stop again, Miss?"

"Maid, I have a . . . "

"You have a what? Another reason?"

"Yes."

"What reason? Please say it."

"Dear Caiping—

It is fine to complete my betrothal without any gifts,
Yet criticism will follow if we meet while not yet married.
If I follow Father's order this time, both of us will be too embarrassed to talk.
What shall I do if we face each other speechless?
His secrets will remain secret, and I will be too embarrassed to open my mouth.
Will my visit to the garden be in vain?"

Caiping thinks: 'Dear Miss! You and Young Master have been apart for three years. How can you have nothing to say!' "Miss, I think you will have a lot of questions to ask your future husband when you meet him. If you don't know what to say, let me teach you."

Miss thinks: 'I think I will have nothing to say when I meet my cousin. But Caiping said there are many questions to ask him. She is afraid that I do not know what to say and is offering to teach me. Let me listen to what she has to say.' "Caiping, what shall I ask him?"

"Please listen to me, Miss! Ask him—

Why did you go back to your hometown last time?
Why did you fail to return?
Why is it that you encountered robbers on your way?
Why didn't you report it to the county court?
Why didn't we hear from you since then?
Why did you discard your old mother?
Why didn't you study the classics and statecraft?

Why didn't you intend to pursue an official career?
Why didn't you want to rebuild the fame of your family?
Why did you come to the city of Xiang today?
Why didn't you come through the gates to the front hall?
Why did you instead head toward the back garden?
Why don't you look like a scholar?
Why did you become a priest?
Why do you hold a drum and stick in hand?
Why did you fall into disgrace, singing daoqing[107] *for people?*
Why do you make a living wandering around?
Why do you bring shame on your ancestors? . . .

—Miss, there is so much to say. You just go ahead and ask. How can you claim there is nothing to say?"

Miss thinks: 'I felt there was nothing to say, but Caiping has enumerated a chain of eighteen[108] "whys." One "why" is one question. Eighteen "whys" is eighteen questions. Two or three "whys" should be enough for me. Eighteen is too many, and it will take more than three days and three nights to finish all of them. Since enough preparations for the talk have been made, let me go to meet him.' How was it possible that Young Miss would have nothing to say? Where have all her longings gone? "Then, Caiping, let's go!"

Hearing that Miss is ready to go again, Caiping steadies her to walk.

Hearing the words, she thinks silently,
She no longer cares about embarrassment.
Soft, jadelike hands held together, the golden lotuses step down the stairs.
No sooner has she descended the eighth and ninth stairs
Than she stops herself and refuses to walk any further.

"Hey!" Caiping asks: "Miss, why did you stop again?"

Chen Cui'e says: "Caiping—

I'm worried that when I meet Master Fang,
The gate to the West Garden will be too close.
If Mother also goes to the Purple Rose Hall,
I will hardly be able to escape her scolding.
She will blame me for my misbehavior
And for neglecting the teachings of the inner chambers.

---

107. The term *daoqing* (Daoist sentiments) signifies a group of songs that propagate the doctrines of Daoism.

108. "Eighteen" is commonly used in popular religion (especially Buddhism) to indicate a fairly large number.

—So, I . . . can't go downstairs."

Upon hearing this, Caiping thinks: 'What Miss has said is very correct. The Purple Rose Hall is only feet away from the West Garden. If Lady finds out, she will certainly blame Miss.' "But for the future of your husband-to-be and for your lifelong happiness, you must go downstairs. You cannot refuse to eat, fearing you may be choked by food. If you hurry to the Purple Rose Hall to meet Master Fang, inquire about his whereabouts during the past three years, give him some advice, then retire to the chamber, Madame will not find out.

"Miss, I think this will not be a problem, if you—

. . . Meet him, ask him for clear answers.
Why has the layman turned into a priest?
Why have you been away for more than two years,
Drifting in the world without sending any word?
Even though Mother has bullied you,
Father and daughter haven't mistreated you.
You should not have missed the date at Peach Blossom Garden.
Why is it that you wish to be a person with no feelings,
Becoming forever an unfilial person?
Do not quarrel, do not fight.
Aunt is elder, nephew is junior.
Better to reconcile than to make enemies.
Why go around building up more and more hostility?
The ancestors under the Nine Springs[109] *will not rest in peace;*
You can correct your misbehavior and start anew.
How can you be so slovenly and neglect your writing skills?
From now on you should pursue a career in officialdom.
Aunt is happy in her old years;
She has enjoyed the fame of having brought you up.
I advise you not to meet my mother;
I advise you to hurry to the Outer Flower Hall;
I advise you to change swiftly;
I advise you to study the classics diligently;
I advise you to take care of your white-haired mother.
Today there should be no quarrel between aunt and nephew;
The daughter is now good at mediation;
Your father and I will be grateful.
A few moments, only a while, not a long discussion about marriage;
Lady in the West Garden will not know it."

Miss heard these words and thought, 'What Caiping has said is absolutely correct. As soon as I meet Cousin in the Purple Rose Hall, I will ask him briefly

109. The Nine Springs is the netherworld of Chinese popular religion.

about everything and then go back to my chamber. There will be no way for Mother to find out. Thus, it is better to hurry than to delay!'

Hearing these words from Caiping, she no longer cares about taboos.
Nodding her head, she thinks silently.
Moving her shoes, she holds up her skirt.
Whenever she moves one step forward, there is a clink.
Gold bracelets and jade charms jingle and jangle.
Miss and Maid go downstairs, descending to the eighteenth stair.
Walking hurriedly, in haste, they run along the zigzagging corridor and path.
Fast, and soon enough, they arrive at the Purple Rose Hall.

Chen Cui'e has come downstairs. It took her quite a while to get to the ninth step. Now she has jumped from the ninth step and has already arrived at the Purple Rose Hall.

Wasn't this a little bit too fast? No. On the story of Chen Cui'e going down the eighteen-step stairs, Master Ma Rufei used to sing eighteen chapters. Each step down took one day. How come you haven't finished one chapter and the eighteen-step stairs have already been covered? To put it more simply, compared with Ma Rufei and lowering the standard by half, you should sing for at least nine days. In fact, that Master Ma Rufei took eighteen days to sing the plot of Chen Cui'e's going downstairs is an erroneous legend based on ungrounded fabrications.[110]

In the past, one chapter of a story was determined by the time it took for a two-*liang*[111] candle to burn out. When a two-*liang* candle burned out, one chapter had been completed. By today's reckoning, it was about one hour and fifteen minutes. Before the story started, the storyteller used to first play a three-six warm-up tune and sing an opening ballad. The actual time for storytelling was only one hour. From the point Fang Qing entered the garden for the second time and met Caiping at the Peony Platform until Caiping led Fang Qing out of the garden to visit his mother, Ma Rufei took eighteen days to perform the story, eighteen episodes altogether. It wasn't simply that "Descending the Stairs" took eighteen days. There is a saying about the rate of our storytelling: "When there is 'story,' you should relate it in detail; when there is no 'story,' you should just narrate." What that means is precisely this: the speed should be

---

110. The legend goes that once when Ma Rufei was telling the part about Chen Cui'e's meeting with Fang Qing, the weather was unpleasant, and the rain would not stop. Ma joked with the audience that if the rain did not stop, Chen Cui'e would not come downstairs in his story. The audience thought that Ma was too arrogant to keep such a promise. Therefore, they all came back to listen to him, even people who usually did not come so often came every day. With his talents in storytelling, Ma did not bore the audience. The rain stopped eighteen days later, and Chen Cui'e took her last step on the eighteen-step stairs.

111. One *liang* equals 1.75 ounces.

appropriate. If you tell a story fast when it should not be so, the story will not be attractive. For example, I can use only two minutes to complete singing the story from when Miss Chen Cui'e arrives at the Purple Rose Hall till they get married under imperial decree.

The young couple have an intimate talk.
He meets the aunt, sings the daoqing.
In the White Cloud Temple, he visits his mother.
Granted a marriage, the two ladies happily go back to Taiping village.
Such a hasty ending does not attract audiences . . .

This kind of storytelling is without interest and therefore is not worthy of listening to at all. When Chen Cui'e stops on her way downstairs, however, she has her reasons. Caiping, on the other hand, must refute all the reasons that Miss has in order for her to step downstairs. Within that process, the plot twists and turns. The audience will listen with an attentive ear. After they get to the ninth step, Chen Cui'e no longer has any reasons to stop walking. Then, of course, we can jump directly and sing of the story in the Purple Rose Hall.

Now, Miss and Maid have arrived at the back of the screen door in the Purple Rose Hall. Caiping says to herself: 'Since you have already arrived here, you can no longer behave the way you did on the stairs. If you do not want to go out, I can push you out by shouts and force. On the stairs, you were in control of the situation, and I couldn't do anything, because if I had dragged you, you might have fallen down the stairs. Now I am in charge of the situation, and you can't do anything about it. Whether you go out or not does not depend on you. Oh my goodness! What if as soon as I announce, "Here comes Young Miss," you get embarrassed and run away? What shall I do? Oh, I've got it.' She gently grabbed Miss's right sleeve with her left hand. With this "cable," she will have no way to run away or leave.

'I hasten to grab her sleeve gently.
I need to be careful about things that might be overlooked,
Just like attacking the strategic points in the game of Go.
As long as I am onstage and strike the gong,
I will not worry that you, the big star, will not come out.

This is like theatrical performance. As soon as the gong is struck on the stage, even a superstar will not dare not to come out. Now, if I announce it, you will certainly have to go out.' So, she announces loudly: "Young Master, our Miss is here. Please tidy your clothes and hat to receive her!"

As she came to the back of the screen door, Young Miss's heart wouldn't stop throbbing. Why would her heart throb? The reason was that she had been missing her cousin for a long time. But times had changed. Now he does not observe the proprieties and has become a Daoist priest. 'How can I face him?' Thinking about this, Chen Cui'e feels ashamed of herself. Her cheeks redden, and her heart beats more rapidly. Right at this moment, she hears Caiping's loud announcement: "Oh my!" She can't help turning away. *Step, step, step.* Only two steps away, and she can't move. She turns back and finds that her sleeve has been grabbed by Caiping. "My goodness!"

Caiping looks at Miss. 'Although you and I are Miss and Maid, we have been together for more than ten years and have become intimate. I know very well your temperament. I expected that you would make such a move, so I was already prepared. There is no way for you to run away.' She says: "Since you are already here, Miss, what need is there for you to feel shy?"

Chen Cui'e's face flushes: "Huh . . . , you're right."

'Caiping is right. Since I am already here, why feel shy? If I insist on not going out and dodge behind the screen, it is indeed inelegant.

Since we are to meet, why should I be shy?
I must take a good look at him.
In the past when we met as cousins, he looked gentle and scholarly.
Today he has come back but is no longer the same.
It is said that he is dressed like a priest.

A moment ago, because I thought that I could not bear the embarrassment of meeting a young priest, I wanted to leave. Now I think I should not have done that. I should go and take a look at him to see how absurd he is now.' Both Miss and Maid walk out from behind the door screen and go outside.

Elegant and graceful, Miss and Maid;
Quietly and softly, they come out from behind the screen.

Next door in the study, hearing Caiping's announcement that Miss had arrived, Chen Lian is very happy.

The imperial historian Chen is elated to death.
The young couple will meet and talk.
What they have to say will surely be true.

He thinks: 'The son-in-law did not tell the truth to me. When he meets my daughter, he will definitely tell the truth to her.' Therefore, he is waiting to hear the truth.

Caiping's announcement is also heard by Fang Qing. He only feels—

The warbling of orioles fills the courtyard;
Maid Cai's beautiful voice announces the coming of Miss from her chamber.

So, it is important to hide the priest's wooden fish and the bamboo clappers lest that cousin feel sorry for him upon seeing them.[112] Now he stands in front of the door screen, attentively waiting for Young Miss. Suddenly, a burst of rich fragrant scent floats in from behind the screen, accompanied by the clinking of jade bracelets and charms. 'How strange! Just now Caiping told me that Miss had become a nun, so why is there the fragrant scent and the clinking sound of jewelry? Is Caiping deceiving me again? Moreover, a while ago when she said that Miss would come, it turned out to be my father-in-law. Now again she says Miss is coming. What if it turns out to be my mother-in-law? Mother-in-law leads a contented life with her husband. Although she is around fifty, she doesn't look old. She still likes to decorate herself with flowers.' A second thought occurred: 'It must be my cousin, not my mother-in-law. Because this scent could be the fragrance of old sandalwood, and the clinking could be the copper cymbals that she carries.'[113] Finally Fang Qing thought: 'Why should I bother to guess right now. As soon as she steps out, I shall know.' So he keeps waiting.

Inside, as Caiping helps Young Miss step out from behind the screen door, she says: "Be careful!"

Soft-spoken and elegant, both Miss and Maid walk out from behind the screen door.
As if Saihuang were helping Chang'e come out,[114]
Both are like beauties from the Moon Palace.
Quietly and gracefully, Miss casts a sidelong glance and steals a glimpse of the young scholar.

Miss walks out from behind the screen door and glances at Fang Qing: he is indeed a young priest.

Wearing black shoes and cloth socks, he looks like an immortal;
Clad in feathery clothes and wearing a yellow hat, he appears to be a priest.

She thinks: 'Dear cousin, how could you become a priest? Why didn't you think of how many responsibilities you have? How many people have been let down by your action of becoming a priest now!

112. The wooden fish and bamboo clappers are attributes of mendicant Daoist priests. For a wealthy, high-ranking family, mendicancy is not to be admired, but is deserving of pity, if not censure.

113. Sandalwood incense for devotional services and bronze cymbals for chanting scriptures are the appurtenances of Buddhist and Daoist nuns.

114. Chang'e and Saihuang are, respectively, the goddess of the moon and her maid.

You have let down your ancestors, who started their careers with difficulty,
who had hoped that their descendants would carry out their will.
You have let down your grandfather, whose rancor is so vast that it would sink
to the bottom of the sea, whose injustice has not yet been corrected.
You have let down your mother, who guarded her chastity and brought you
up, who spent more than a decade educating you.
You have let down your father-in-law, who rushed to the Pine Pavilion on his
horse, who betrothed me to you.
You have let me down, who financed you with the pagoda,
With seven layers of pearls, which represented my sincerity.
You have let down Caiping, the maid who appreciated your talents.
You have let down Wang Ben, the white-haired servant who had been loyal
to his master.
You have let down your mother-in-law, who had forgotten her poor relatives
and insulted you, who has been polluted by snobbery.

If Fang Qing has indeed become a priest, he would have let down many people, but not his mother-in-law. No, what he let down was his mother-in-law's snobbery. Before, you hated your mother-in-law, who had been humble to the rich and arrogant to the poor. She was so snobbish that when you parted, she told you to come back to see her only after you had succeeded in the imperial examinations and become a high official. Then, you were supposed to win credit for yourself and come back to Xiangchu only after you had attained scholarly honor and official rank. This was what she meant by "letting down your mother-in-law with her snobbery." Today, you are even worse off than before: you have become a priest and earn your living by singing *daoqing* for people all over the place. Isn't this letting down your snobbish mother-in-law?' Thinking of these things, Miss lowers her head and doesn't want to see this slothful cousin again. There is good reason for Miss to be angry. At this moment, the young couple fall into silence.

Caiping, however, is never at rest. She has helped Young Miss to come to the Purple Rose Hall and now goes to the young priest and pulls his sleeve: "Young Master, come here!"

Fang Qing says: "Yes, yes, yes!"

Caiping pulls Fang Qing to the center of the Purple Rose Hall and says: "Young Master, please stand and wait in the 'upper-hand' place!"[115]

Fang Qing stands in the "upper-hand" place, on the left.

Caiping helps Miss to the "lower-hand" place, to the right, and says: "Miss, please stand here."

---

115. The original text has *shangshou* and *xiashou* to indicate the directions. *Shangshou* literally means "the upper hand," while *xiashou* means "the lower hand." This is an inside joke because, in *pingtan* storytelling, the lead, or "upper-hand," storyteller sits on the left of the storytelling platform, while the assistant, or "lower-hand," storyteller sits on the right.

Miss stands in the lower-hand place. Caiping herself stands beside Miss and asks the couple to pay respects to each other: "Young Master, our Miss is here, please pay your respects!"

How busy Caiping is! She has to be both the accompanying maid and the etiquette master, taking two roles at the same time.

Maid Cai is like the female master of ceremonies,
Standing beside and directing the ceremony in its proper course.

Fang Qing couldn't help but laugh to himself.

'These scenes are not unfamiliar to me;
I have paid my respects to His Majesty in the imperial court.
I have waited for the opening of court at the Wuchao Gate.
(With restrained jubilance)
Purple Rose Hall can be taken as the Soul Mountain Meeting.
Maid Cai looks like the Dragon Daughter.
My cousin is the kindhearted and merciful Avalokiteśvara[116] *Mercy Cloud.*

If Caiping is the Dragon Daughter, and my cousin is the Goddess of Mercy, then who am I?

I am the pious male believer—

I'm the pious boy. That said, today I'm not visiting my cousin or my fiancée but paying homage to Avalokiteśvara.'

It's clear that the boy is paying homage to Avalokiteśvara,
But, without incense or candles, sincerity is lacking.

Unexpectedly, the young priest is enjoying himself, regarding the meeting with his fiancée as paying homage to Avalokiteśvara. Now, he becomes more sincere.

Putting up his sleeves and tidying his scarf, he makes a deep bow.
Eagerly and attentively, he addresses the cousin.

"Elder Sister, I hereby show you my respect!"

Miss hears him address her; no one should refuse to respond to a salute. She should reply to him.

---

116. Avalokiteśvara is the Sanskrit name of Guanyin, the bodhisattva (savior) of compassion.

Pulling the lapels of her garment together carefully, Miss pays him her respects.
Opening her red cherrylike mouth, she addresses him.

She wants to call him "my dear brother" but can't do so. After a moment, when she can no longer hold it, she calls him "my dear brother" in an indistinct voice lower than the buzzing of a mosquito.

In a whispering voice, she calls him "my dear brother."

The greeting salutes are over. Caiping goes to Fang Qing and says: "Young Master, sit here."

Fang Qing says: "Yes, yes." He sits in the chair on the left side.

Then Caiping goes over to Miss and helps her to the chair on the right side. "Miss, you sit here."

Seeing her cousin as a young priest, Chen Cui'e could not wait to fly back to her chamber.[117] Thus, she does not even want to sit down. Caiping thinks: 'Dear Miss, what happened has already happened. Why must you behave this way? Now it's not up to you anymore. If you want to sit down, fine. If you don't want to sit down, you still have to sit down.' She pushes lightly on Miss's shoulders: "Please sit down!"

Miss is pushed by Caiping and does not have any choice but to sit down.

Caiping stands beside Young Miss.

Since you are meeting each other, why must the curtain be lowered?
High-ranking households should not be restrained by small details of etiquette.

According to etiquette, Caiping should have rolled down a curtain in front of Miss. Today, Caiping does not want to do this. 'For one thing, you cousins already have met once in the Green Autumn Pavilion. For another, you cousins were engaged in the Nine Pine Pavilion. You are now fiancé with fiancée, not like a meeting between common men and women.' Caiping glances at Fang Qing and thinks: 'Young priest, I'm doing you a favor today. You can take a good and thorough look at your fiancée now.' Now that the young couple have sat down, they face each other speechlessly. Caiping could presently mediate things, saying: "Young Master, greet your cousin. Miss, give a reply and greet him." But after all, Caiping is not a matchmaker, and she has already done her job by inviting Miss to come down to the Purple Rose Hall. Whether you speak

117. Her reasons for wanting to do so are numerous, but the main ones are the feelings about mendicancy and the fact that a priest would have no interest in finding true love with a woman or in domesticity.

or not does not have anything to do with her. That the couple do not open their mouths makes one person anxious to death.

The young couple meet yet do not say a word;
This drives the old scholar crazy in his study.

In his study, Chen Lian has begun to be anxious. He is old and has a lot of phlegm. Feeling that his throat is choked by phlegm and itching, he is on the brink of coughing. He says to himself: 'Now the Purple Rose Hall is so quiet. As soon as I cough, my daughter will run behind the screen, retreating to her chamber. The young priest will rush out the door. I won't be able to eavesdrop. Hurry up and speak so I can take the chance to cover my mouth with the hand, cough slightly, and get rid of my phlegm. If you continue to be silent, I won't be able to hold it anymore.' What an anxious Chen Lian!

Chen Cui'e is a miss "worth a thousand pounds of gold." A bit unhappy and embarrassed, she does not speak, with a flushed face and a lowered head.

How about Fang Qing? He was thinking: 'Caiping has told me that Cousin has been forced to become a nun by my furious mother-in-law. Now I want to see if she has told me the truth. Is it true or false that Cousin has become a nun? If Cousin has indeed become a nun, I will tell her all about my deeds in the past three years and ask her if my elderly mother is here or not. If Mother has not come to Xiangyang, then I will continue to be a priest and look for her all over the country from now on.[118] If Cousin has not become a nun and Caiping is deceiving me, then I will be rude and not say a word of truth. I will wait until I see my mother-in-law to vent my anger. But how shall I take a look at my cousin?

I must first take a good look, to see if Cousin has become a nun.
The situation now is that we have met but can hardly look at each other—'

He has an idea:

'If I want to take a look, there is no other way but to steal a glance.'

Unless he steals a glance, there is no other way out. So Fang Qing lowers his head and looks down. Before his eyes there is a seam between the bricks. His eyes slowly pore along the seam between the bricks.

Lowering his head, he first sees,
Under the long skirt, her three-inch golden lotuses.

---

118. This is the real reason for Fang Qing's adopting the guise of a Daoist priest, since it was expected that such a person would be an itinerant.

Fang Qing sees Miss's three-inch golden lotuses and thinks his cousin must not have become a nun, for if she had done so, her bound feet would have been loosened. On second thought, it was not necessarily so. Because Cousin has become a nun in her own household, it is possible that she did not have her feet loosened. But you may say that, in the past, during feudal times, there was a rule that a woman "should not show her feet when she walks." If her small feet were exposed to sight, then it was considered to be a breach of the rules. In that case, how did Fang Qing see his cousin's feet under the skirt? There is a reason. When Caiping asked the Young Miss to sit down, Chen Cui'e did not want to. She did so after being pushed slightly by Caiping. Thus, her skirt was forced open a little bit. She did not take notice of it and did not pull it together. Therefore Fang Qing could peek into the inside of the skirt and see Miss's three-inch golden lotuses. Now Fang Qing looks at the shoes his cousin is wearing: 'How beautiful these shoes are!'

The red-silk shoes are embellished with green silk;
The flowers all over them are just in fashion.

After studying Miss's golden lotuses, Fang Qing moves his eyes slightly upward—

What he sees is the sixteen-folded skirt like Xiang River[119] *waves,*
Scarlet-red skirt tassels dangle down.
Gold bracelets and jade charms hang low;
Whenever she moves, they make a jingling sound.

After studying the skirt, his eyes move further upward, to the upper body of his cousin.

Slim body with spotless silk blouse, shallow red with creamy gold.
Her bodice is fastened around her chest . . .

Is it that Fang Qing's eyesight is really so good that he can see the bodice next to her breasts? No, there is a reason—

It is only because Miss's breasts bulge outward even with her chest covered.

After looking at the upper blouse, now the most important thing to look at is Miss's head. 'Is it shaved, or is the hair still there with a beautiful luster?' Now, Fang Qing, you should go ahead and look! Strange! His eyelids seem to be pressed down by something. However hard he tries, they can't be raised. Why?

119. From antiquity, the Xiang River was associated with beautiful goddesses of the Chu culture (in south-central China).

Because he is doing all this secretly. While stealing a glance, he feels guilty. He thinks: 'That I have been peeking must have been noticed by Caiping, who has a pair of sharp eyes. Now, she doesn't utter a thing. If, as soon as I raise my eyes to check whether my cousin has hair or not, she should suddenly cough, how embarrassing that will be! So how can I take a look? Yes, I know. I will quickly direct my eyes toward Caiping.'

Only because of the inconvenience of looking directly,
He pretends to look at Caiping attentively.

Fang Qing stares at Caiping without a blink. Caiping does not notice that Fang has been peeking at Miss secretly. Now that she is being gazed at by Fang Qing attentively, she feels strange. Why am I worth looking at! Young Master continues the gaze and makes Caiping feel embarrassed. She says to herself: 'You look at me, I won't look at you.' She lowers her head.

Fang Qing thinks: 'Dear Caiping, you fell into my trap!' He soon moves his eyes toward Miss's head.

His gaze shoots toward her beautiful hair.
Gold and jade dazzle his eyes;
Gold phoenixes surrounded by green jade cover the black hair.

He sees that his cousin has a beautiful head of hair. Black and silky, it is not shaved at all. 'Goodness! I have been trapped by Caiping!

She said that it had been a while since I left,
That they worried I might want to break the marriage contract,
That Elder Sister had to be both filial and loyal,
That she had no choice but to become a nun.
Apparently I have fallen into Caiping's trap;
My great talents cannot be a match to her ingenuity.'

He looks at Caiping. 'How tough you are! A while ago, you deceived me and made me cry in the Lute House. I admire you!' Caiping is not stupid, either. As soon as she lowered her head, she realized something was up. The young priest was playing a trick. She raises her head and stares at Fang Qing. 'All right, I didn't expect you would play this trick. I admire you, too!' Both know clearly what is going on.

Finding that his cousin has not become a nun, Fang Qing makes up his mind. He cannot say: "Cousin, please go back to your chamber!" So he does not open his mouth. Moreover, he has his reasons. He thinks: 'Dear Cousin—

Because of the Pearl Pagoda, more things happened than I can tell.
Encountered by robbers in Nanyang, it was in the middle of the night.

The high official in the cabinet rescued me and I went to Beijing.
Assuming another person's name, I succeeded in the imperial examination.
Gold lotuses and precious torch, I married under imperial sponsorship.
You are supposed to be the wife of the canal inspector, the lady of the Number One Scholar.
I suffered my pains; you obtained your gains.
Today I came here, reentering the garden.
Although I'm your cousin, I'm still the guest.
Cousin, you should have addressed me first.'

Therefore, Fang Qing keeps silent. Then, Chen Cui'e, you should go ahead and address him first! She thinks: 'There is no need for me to call him first.' Why? Because she has her reasons, too. She thinks: 'Dear cousin—

Because of you, Fang Qing, more things happened than I can tell.
Countless sufferings, innumerable hardships.
The Pearl Pagoda revealed the case.
You did not come back, nor were there any messages.
I was seriously ill for more than a month.
Thanks to Wang Ben, who falsified a letter, I had a narrow escape.
In the White Cloud Temple, I went to fulfill my vows.
Aunt and niece met each other;
I invited Aunt to stay in the temple.
In front of my mother, I dared not say a word.
I preferred to accept the reputation of being unfilial.
All these things, for the sake of Fang Qing.
Gone for three years, no news at all.
Today you came here, reentering the garden.
After all I'm your cousin, older than you.
Cousin, you should address me first.'

One is complaining, which is reasonable. The other is proud, which is not fair.

Both have their own reasons, so neither is willing to address the other first. However, when it comes down to it, men are not as patient as women. In the end, Fang Qing opens his mouth first. The young couple are going to talk about his official career.

A SUZHOU CHANTEFABLE FROM THE 1950s

Translated by Mark Bender and Sun Jingyao and introduced by Mark Bender

Suzhou tanci—variously translated as "Suzhou chantefable," "Suzhou story singing," "Suzhou plucking verses," "Suzhou plucking lyrics," "Suzhou strum lyric," "Su-chou singing narrative," and "Soochow ballad"—is a sophisticated type of narrative performance employing instrumental music, singing, speech, and gestures to relate love stories concerning "gifted scholars and talented beauties" (*caizi jiaren*). Since at least the late eighteenth century, the art has been popular in the city of Suzhou, Jiangsu province, the ancient capital of the state of Wu. The city has been famous for centuries as a center for literature and the arts as well as for its canals, temples, and gardens. Presently, *Suzhou tanci* and similar forms of singing narrative are performed in Suzhou, Shanghai, and other cities and small towns in southeastern China.

Tanci performances are given daily in teahouses or storytellers' houses (*shuchang*), where patrons assemble to drink tea and enjoy snacks while they are entertained. Most performances are delivered by a pair of storytellers (mixed gender or same gender), both clad in traditional gowns or other formal attire. The lead (usually the man in a mixed-gender duo) strums the three-stringed *sanxian*, or *xianzi* (both referring to a banjolike instrument), and the assistant (usually a woman) plucks the lutelike *pipa*.

In the course of the narration, the performers utilize highly stylized gestures and facial movements (many borrowed from Kunqu opera) as they relate the narrative by shifting among a variety of voices, which include that of the narrator, spoken dialogues and monologues, and the inner speech of the characters.

Most of the narration and dialogue in the speaking roles is delivered in Suzhou dialect, though a formal register closer to Mandarin is used by high-class characters. Singing, along with instrumental accompaniment, is a powerful and enthralling dimension of any *tanci* performance. Songs are used to create emotional high points and are a powerful tool for manipulating feeling and moving audiences. Over a dozen major styles of *tanci* music are presently performed, the most famous being the Ma and Yu styles, named after their nineteenth-century founders: Ma Rufei and Yu Xiushan.

Unlike the actors in Chinese opera, performers wear only minimal makeup and no character costumes. Aside from their instruments, the only performance tools are a couple of folding fans, handkerchiefs, and the tea set that sits between the performers' chairs on a narrow table. Performances usually consist of a two-hour set (with a break after the first forty-five minutes), in which two episodes of the very lengthy and intricate stories are performed.

Before the main episodes are related, the performers warm up with an opening ballad (*kaipian*), which is often in the form of a short lyrical ballad. Some of the classic *tanci* works—such as *Pearl Pagoda* (*Zhenzhu ta*), *Romance of the Three Smiles* (*San xiao yin yuan*), *Legend of the White Snake* (*Bai she zhuan*),

Jade Dragonfly (*Yu qingting*), and *Pair of Pearl Phoenixes* (*Shuang zhu feng*)—traditionally took many weeks or months to tell. In the early 1950s, while the *tanci* performers were being formed into government troupes (the traditional guilds being dissolved), shorter narratives were promoted as being better suited to the work schedules of the "new society." Also, because of their often risqué elements, many of the older *tanci* were banned or censored.

"The Thrice-Draped Cape" (San gai yi), adapted by Qiu Xiaopeng, is among the many new shorter works written and performed by various storytellers in the 1950s. Like many *Suzhou tanci*, it was composed in a mixture of standard and nonstandard written characters to reflect the Suzhou dialect roles. Although based on a traditional opera, *The Jade Hair Clasp* (*Bi yu zhan*), the story was likely revived in the first decade of socialist China because of its concern with women's issues—in this case, the evils of wife abuse.

Much of the story's success in portraying traditional gender-role attitudes is the result of the sophisticated use of the "inner voices" of *tanci*, narrative conventions (actually written into the script of "The Thrice-Draped Cape") that allow the audience to hear what the characters are thinking. These conventions are particularly useful in a context where men and women by custom could not freely speak their true feelings to one another. In *tanci*, the voice of the narrator is flexible, jumping into and out of the dialogue and sometimes entering the characters' minds. Moreover, the narrator's role is often shared between the male and female performers (thus in some instances in the following selection, the voice of the narrator is subsumed under the roles of the characters). Performers are also capable of creating a vast range of paralinguistic utterances, such as the sound of the night gong or the wind, as in this text. Exclamations such as *oi-yo*, *ai-ya-ya*, *uh*, and *ah* pepper the characters' speeches and express a wide range of feelings. In places where the meaning can be understood by context, these expressions (represented for the most part in romanization, or, when close, in English) have been retained in the translation to give some idea of the texture of the original performance. Although in the same tradition as "Descending the Stairs," "The Thrice-Draped Cape" is presented in a different format that indicates the various roles of the storytellers as narrator and as different characters and their range of speaking voices. This reflects the diversity of styles used to represent Chinese performance traditions in print. Written around 1957, the text was performed by a number of different storytellers.

THE THRICE-DRAPED CAPE

Written by Qiu Xiaopeng (Han)

NARRATOR'S VOICE: This is an episode from the story *The Jade Hair Clasp* entitled "The Thrice-Draped Cape."

In the city of Jiaxing, in Zhejiang province, there lived the daughter of the minister of personnel affairs, named Li Xiuying. Talented and beautiful, she had just turned eighteen and was engaged to a gifted scholar of the East City named Wang Yulin. Wang had won first place in the provincial examinations and, although his family possessed only moderate means, his personality and talent were indeed worthy of Miss Li Xiuying. During the Midautumn Festival they married—but who would expect that on their wedding night Wang Yulin would pick up a love letter just outside the wedding suite?! The letter was from his bride to her cousin, and it related that she had been ordered by her father to marry Wang Yulin. It went on to say: "My love for you will never be forgotten. In accord with custom, I shall return to my family at the end of our honeymoon month to visit. Then we shall speak deeply of our love again. . . . Enclosed within the letter is a jade hair clasp, which I present to you as a token of remembrance." As Wang Yulin read, his eyes burned in anger. He imagined that the letter must have been given to the bridal escort by Li Xiuying to deliver to her cousin. As the escort was leaving, she must have dropped it carelessly on the doorstep.

Wang Yulin wished to speak out, but if he did, the face of each family would be lost—yet, if he kept silent, why, that would be abominable! Finally, he concluded that there was only one thing to do: completely ignore her. He said to himself: "Wait until next year when I become a high official through imperial examination; then I will go to her father and divorce her." Thereafter, he avoided his bride; if he should meet her, he wouldn't speak to her. From the first night on, he never once entered the wedding suite.

But in fact, the love letter was a false one; it was written by someone with the intention of driving these two apart. Who might that be? It was none other than Li Xiuying's cousin, Gu Wenyou, the wastrel son of an official! He had had his eye on Li Xiuying a long time, but she had married Wang Yulin instead of him. Thus he perpetrated the following evil scheme: he bribed an old woman who brokered wedding accessories named Qi who was often in and about his cousin's home and who, he learned, would be active in preparing his cousin's wedding. He ordered the old woman to borrow a jade hair clasp from Li Xiuying beforehand. He then wrote the false love letter, put the jade hair clasp inside, and instructed the old woman to place the letter outside the wedding suite when no one was looking.

Knowing that when Wang Yulin found the letter he would assume it as real and would abandon Li Xiuying, Gu calculated that he could then get his hands on his cousin. Sure enough, Wang Yulin walked right into his trap, and the newlyweds instantly became enemies.

Today is the fifteenth day of the ninth month. A month has passed since the wedding, and it is the day on which Li Xiuying should visit her family. Customarily, husband and wife return together to her home, but Wang Yulin complained of a headache and stayed behind. Therefore, Li Xiuying returned alone. Mother and daughter, however, had spoken but a few moments when a man dispatched by Wang Yulin arrived with a letter asking Li Xiuying to return immediately. The language of the letter was so harsh that the young woman could do nothing but return at once. Her mother was extremely dissatisfied, thinking that, having once found a husband, her daughter had forgotten her. Thus, mother and daughter parted very unhappily. Li Xiuying's heart was heavy, but not a word of her sorrow could escape her lips, and she returned with tears welling in her eyes. Entering the inner chamber she discovered her husband and mother-in-law sitting within.

LI YIUYING (*speaks*): This daughter-in-law must pay respects to her mother-in-law.

MOTHER WANG (*speaks*): *Ah!* (NARRATOR'S VOICE) Madame finds it highly peculiar that her daughter-in-law has returned home so early. (MOTHER WANG *speaks to herself*) When she was leaving, I enjoined her: "You are your mother's only daughter; it is only natural for you to stay several days." Why has she come back so soon? (*Speaks out loud*) Daughter-in-law! You and your mother have been parted a month; by your conversation and company you could have brought happiness to your family. It would have been perfectly all right for you to have stayed at your mother's home for several days. Why did you come back so soon?

LI XIUYING (*speaks*): Why, it's just because there is no one here to serve you, Mother-in-law. My master is studying, so there is no one to accompany you; your daughter-in-law felt uncomfortable about that, so she returned.

MOTHER WANG (*speaks*): *Ai-ya-ya!* You are so virtuous and filial—I really do not deserve it!

LI XIUYING (*speaks*): Mama overpraises me.

WANG YULIN (*speaks*): Humph! (NARRATOR'S VOICE) Wang Yulin regards his mother. (WANG *speaks to himself*) You see her great virtue, her high morality; who knows what immorality lurks beneath? If I had not ordered her back today, she and that shameless cousin of hers would be up to their old tricks again. (*Speaks out loud*) It is indeed overpraising.

LI XIUYING (*speaks, with tears*): Yes.

MOTHER WANG (*speaks*): *Ya!* (NARRATOR'S VOICE) Seeing this, the old lady realizes it's not right! (MOTHER WANG *speaks to herself*) My daughter-in-law's eyes are filled with tears, my son's face is so fierce—but why? From the very start I thought there was something strange. Since she came I have never seen my son speak even a word to her; he is always so cold. At first I thought it was because they were newlyweds: too embarrassed before me, their mother, to express their feelings. But now the more I observe, the more I see that's not the case. My daughter-in-law often laughs in front of me, but wipes away her tears behind me. Moreover, the two of them have both grown thinner. Today is their one-month anniversary, when they should go back to her family, but my son said he had a headache and didn't go. Yet when speaking with me later, he didn't seem to have a headache at all. My daughter-in-law went alone to her family, but then immediately returned. No, there must be a reason for all this; let me call my daughter-in-law over to greet my son.

(*Speaks out loud*) Why didn't you speak to each other when you met just now? Greet your husband!

LI XIUYING (*speaks*): Yes. Master, your wife pays you her respects.

WANG YULIN (*speaks*): Who is your . . . ?

MOTHER WANG (*speaks, wide-eyed*): *Ai!*

WANG YULIN (*speaks*): *Uh,* I was improperly returning my respects. (*Speaks to himself*) I said I would return my respects, but actually I haven't lifted a finger to do so.

MOTHER WANG (NARRATOR'S VOICE): Seeing her son's actions, she is unhappy. (MOTHER WANG *speaks*) My son, you don't behave with propriety; from your mouth come words of respect, but indeed, there is no action. Why is this?

WANG YULIN (*speaks*): This . . .

MOTHER WANG (*speaks*): When a husband and wife are paying respects, is it possible that they do not even greet each other?

WANG YULIN (*speaks*): *Uh,* yes . . .

MOTHER WANG (*speaks to* LI XIUYING): Pay respects again! Daughter-in-law, greet your master.

LI XIUYING (NARRATOR'S VOICE): Li Xiuying sighs. (LI *speaks to herself*) Mother-in-law, this is not the first time my husband has treated me so coldly—it's been this way a month! But I was afraid that if you knew this, you would be heartbroken. As a new bride, I'm embarrassed to speak of such a thing, so I've hidden it up to now. If you ask me to pay respects again, it's simply because you are good-hearted; but I know I will still be ignored by him. (*Speaks out loud*) Master, your wife pays respects to you.

MOTHER WANG (NARRATOR'S VOICE): Madame stares at her son. (MOTHER WANG *speaks to herself*) I'll see if you won't greet her! I'll see if you still won't return her respects!

WANG YULIN (*speaks*): This is impossible! (*Speaks to himself*) How can I call this slattern my wife?! When I lifted her veil on the wedding night, several times I called her "wife." But now I hate the fact that I cannot call back those words. By saying the word "wife" now, not only I but my mother also will lose face. Today, even if they should knock my teeth out, I wouldn't say that word! But if I don't say it, my mother will be angry! *Ah* Mother, *ah*! Do you know the difficulty? If you require me to do this, it puts me in very bad way. (*Speaks out loud*) Mother dear . . .

MOTHER WANG (*speaks*): Why should you address me instead of your wife?

WANG YULIN (*speaks*): It is . . .

MOTHER WANG (*speaks*): If you act this way toward my daughter-in-law, how can you two still be called husband and wife?

WANG YULIN (*speaks to himself*): I have never wanted to be husband and wife together with her. She is not my wife, she is my enemy. (*Speaks out loud*) Mother, . . .

MOTHER WANG (*speaks*): Before your mother's face you dare show such insolence; what is your mother to you, anyway?

WANG YULIN (*speaks*): Your son wouldn't dare do such a thing!

MOTHER WANG (*speaks*): Then if you don't dare, be quick and pay respects to my daughter-in-law.

WANG YULIN (*speaks*): Mother, dear, please forgive me, your child!

MOTHER WANG (*speaks*): *Oi-yo!* You anger me to death!

LI XIUYING (NARRATOR'S VOICE): Miss sees her mother-in-law is boiling with anger. She comes over with comfort in her eyes. (LI *speaks*) Mother, take care.

WANG YULIN (*speaks to himself*): Li Xiuying is hateful—who wants you to falsely comfort her? You are a culprit; you not only injure me but you injure my mother as well. (*Speaks out loud*) Who needs your comfort? Get out!

LI XIUYING (*speaks, weeping*): All right. Poor me! (NARRATOR'S VOICE) Li Xiuying turns and leaves at once.

MOTHER WANG (NARRATOR'S VOICE): Madame immediately calls to her to halt. (MOTHER WANG *speaks*) Daughter-in-law—Spring Fragrance, quick! Grab her! (NARRATOR'S VOICE) The maid, Spring Fragrance, immediately latches on to her.

LI XIUYING (NARRATOR'S VOICE): Li Xiuying simply lays her head onto Spring Fragrance's shoulder and weeps bitterly. (LI *speaks*) My fate is bitter.

MOTHER WANG (*speaks*): Daughter-in-law, please overlook everything for your mother-in-law's sake; let's not haggle with this beast.

LI XIUYING (*speaks, weeping*): Mother-in-law.

MOTHER WANG (*speaks*): Daughter-in-law, *ya*!

(*Sings*):

An unloving, rotten son, without virtue;
Each of his actions is absurd.
Newlyweds but just a month,
What causes such hatred of his wife
That he insults her to her face?
My daughter-in-law! So tolerant, you take no offense;
Whatever it is, you can forgive it for my sake—
But that he is so unfeeling is unbelievable,
He seems nothing like my son.
I raised him poorly, instilled too little righteousness;
And today, I am ashamed to face this lovely girl.

(*Speaks*): Please excuse your mother-in-law.

LI XIUYING (*speaks*): Mother-in-law, you mustn't say that. I am your daughter-in-law.

MOTHER WANG (*sings*):

Don't cry, don't be sad;
Your mother-in-law will stand by you—
I will beat him severely here and now!

(*Speaks*): Spring Fragrance, bring me the family paddle![120]

---

120. Heavy bamboo paddles were once used in some homes to administer family justice.

SPRING FRAGRANCE (*speaks*): Yes!

WANG YULIN (NARRATOR'S VOICE): Wang Yulin glares at Spring Fragrance, thinking, "Dare you get it?"

SPRING FRAGRANCE (NARRATOR'S VOICE): Spring Fragrance looks at him—of course she dares to get it! (SPRING FRAGRANCE *speaks to herself*) You have bullied Miss so brutally, well, today you can take a beating, and Miss will be avenged. (NARRATOR'S VOICE) She runs inside a room and brings out the family paddle. (SPRING FRAGRANCE *speaks out loud*) Madame, the bamboo is here.

MADAME WANG (*speaks*): Give it to me.

SPRING FRAGRANCE (*speaks*): Madame, let this maidservant tell you straight, from the first day Master and Miss married, their marriage has yet to be consummated. I've gone to invite Master, but I was driven out by his scolding. Because of this situation, Miss often cries. Today, Miss went to her family, originally planning to stay several days. Who would expect that Master would send a letter ordering her to return home, thus destroying the happiness between Miss and her mother? On her return home just now, Master was again very fierce to Miss, and what's the reason for all this? I simply don't know!

MOTHER WANG (*speaks*): Is this true?

SPRING FRAGRANCE (*speaks*): Madame, just ask Master if it isn't so.

MOTHER WANG (NARRATOR'S VOICE): Madame is shaking with anger—it's not strange that her daughter-in-law should cry so much with such unspoken bitterness in her heart! (MOTHER WANG *speaks to herself*) How can such a fine daughter-in-law as this deserve such shabby treatment from my son? I never knew you were so hard-hearted. Today, if you don't tell me the truth, I'll never forgive you. (*Speaks out loud*) You beast! Kneel!

WANG YULIN (*speaks, kneeling*): Yes.

MOTHER WANG (*speaks*): Every one of your actions is mistaken—yes or no?

WANG YULIN (NARRATOR'S VOICE): Wang Yulin says to himself: For your sake, I could concede to anything else, but I can't concede to this. If I admit I made a mistake, would her affair be excusable? I am willing to be beaten; even if my head is split, I won't concede that I am wrong. He lowers his head without a word.

MOTHER WANG (NARRATOR'S VOICE): Madame is now even angrier; her son has never been so disobedient. (MOTHER WANG *speaks to herself*) What is with him, has he really changed so much? (*Speaks out loud*) You beast, I'll rile myself to death over you!

WANG YULIN (NARRATOR'S VOICE): Seeing his mother angered to tears, Yulin feels unspeakable pain. (WANG *speaks to himself*) Mother, dear! If I tell you the truth, you'll be even more angry and hurt. I'd rather carry this suffering than make you suffer! If you wish to beat me, then do it—don't ruin your health with anger! (*Speaks out loud*) Mother, dear, you—you just go ahead and beat your child, then!

MOTHER WANG (NARRATOR'S VOICE): She thinks: The more you act this way, the more reluctant I am to beat you. (MOTHER WANG *speaks*) You bad boy— (*Sings*):

As a first-rank scholar, you know the meaning of principle;
Yet today you are so unwilling to be filial to Mother.
Because you have always complied with filial etiquette,
Been principled and proper,
Your father-in-law accepted you as a son-in-law.
Who would know your heart would change,
That your words would shift,
You would forget your father-in-law's kindness—
Why is it you have forgotten all etiquette and the goodwill of others?
When married, you made a pair;
But so soon you are like strangers.
Leaving your wife in the cold, making her suffer;
Why is it you are so ruthless?
When you meet, not a word is exchanged;
From dawn till dusk your face is frost and snow;
Why is it you have neither righteousness nor feeling?
Today is your one-month anniversary,
You two should have visited your mother-in-law together;
But you feigned a headache in your study—
Is that any way to act?
Daughter-in-law returned home but half a day,
But you immediately ordered her back;
The letter was too ridiculous—
Why is it you have these thoughts at heart?
Just now, she so gently called you "Master";
According to custom, you ought to respect each other as guests,
But you completely ignored her,
Forcing her tears to well.
What makes you bully your wife this way?
But your greatest breach of filial piety is your disregard of future generations;
Your marriage has yet to be consummated,
You two have yet to share a bed;
I see that from you I shall have no generations to follow me—
How can you be so lacking to your white-haired mother?
Since your ruthless heart is so unwilling to marry,
Why at first did you wish the phoenix to pair?
For nothing, you have wasted your wife's youth in an empty room;
You have harmed others and yourself—something you ought not to have done!
You are a great official's guest, a scholar;

You wished the first rank and its fame—
Such ingratitude is unthinkable.
How can such an ingrate place first in the examinations?
You have failed your wife, shown disrespect to your mother,
Forgotten the Five Constant Virtues and the Three Cardinal Guides.[121]
Why have you done all this?
Tell me the entire story—from the beginning!
If you do not, don't blame me if I beat you;
This family paddle has no feelings of its own;
I will beat the daylights out of this ungrateful rascal!

(*Speaks*): Tell me! If what you say makes sense, then we'll forget all this; but if what you say is nonsense, then the paddle will show no sympathy!

WANG YULIN (*speaks*): This child is willing to be beaten by his mother.

MOTHER WANG (*speaks*): And I certainly shall! (NARRATOR'S VOICE) Madame's hands shake as she lifts the paddle; she has yet to strike him, but her heart is already in pain. Seeing her son this way makes her hurt and upset. She sees that her son is keeping something to himself—(MOTHER WANG *speaks to herself*) Why is this happening? (NARRATOR'S VOICE) All things considered, she knows that her son is good, and that her daughter-in-law is good as well; so how can things be this way? (MOTHER WANG *speaks to herself*) Maybe it is because our ancestors' graves are positioned wrong, or maybe an ancestor's ghost has come to do mischief. If this situation continues, how can I be worthy of my daughter-in-law's family? How will I dare meet my husband in the capital? If I died and went to hell, my mouth and eyes wouldn't close! My dear son! Put yourself in your mother's place; if you act this way, how do you think I feel? (NARRATOR'S VOICE) So, there are tears in Madame's eyes, streaking her face to her chin. (MOTHER WANG *speaks out loud*) You, you unfilial . . .

LI XIUYING (NARRATOR'S VOICE): Li Xiuying sees that her mother-in-law intends to beat her husband; in her heart she, too, is suffering. Although he doesn't consider her his wife, she still considers him to be her husband. Suddenly she runs over, kneels, and raises both hands to stay the paddle. (LI *speaks*) Mother-in-law, for my sake, forgive Master, please.

MOTHER WANG (*speaks*): Daughter-in-law, this beast has bullied you so, but you still wish him to be forgiven? Why?

LI XIUYING (*speaks*): Mother, Master certainly is not without feelings; though he treats me this way, he must have a reason. Later, Master may tell it to me bit by bit, but if you beat him, my heart will not be at peace.

MOTHER WANG (*speaks*): Daughter-in-law, how can I be worthy of you?

LI XIUYING (*speaks*): My fate is bad, that's all. Since coming to the Wang family I have always thought: while alive I am a member of the Wang family, when

121. The Five Constant Virtues and Three Cardinal Guides are Confucian principles of filial piety and deference to superiors.

dead I will be a ghost of the Wang family. If Master has a change of heart, it will be my happiness; if he doesn't change, then it is predestined—I certainly would not blame you, my mother-in-law, nor my master.

MOTHER WANG (*speaks*): Such a daughter-in-law!

LI XIUYING (*speaks, weeping*): Mother-in-law!

WANG YULIN (NARRATOR'S VOICE): He sees her choking on her sobs, her tears like rain; hearing her words, which really seem from the heart—it doesn't seem to him like an act. (WANG *speaks to himself*) If she really were an immoral woman she would not care about me and wouldn't do this. Other things may be pretended, but crying like this is impossible to fake. Can it be that I wronged her? (*Speaks out loud*) This . . .

MOTHER WANG (*speaks*): Still "this and that"? Quick now, apologize to your wife.

WANG YULIN (*speaks*): *Uh*, yes. (*He begins to bow, but stops halfway, dumbstruck.*)

LI XIUYING (*speaks*): Master, I will return your respects.

MOTHER WANG (NARRATOR'S VOICE): Madame thinks that her son has shown evidence of a change of heart but now needs some leeway. (MOTHER WANG *speaks to herself*) If I force him to explain completely today, this might become a deadlock. For now, I shall lead them to their bridal suite. Only if the new pair spend time together can this knot be gently unraveled and things made gradually better between them. (*Speaks out loud*) Son, if you are filial to your mother, then you should love your virtuous wife. You see that my locks are already white. As old as I am, only a son or daughter begotten by you will allow me to live on much longer.

WANG YULIN (NARRATOR'S VOICE): Wang Yulin wishes to nod his head, but he feels it is wrong; he wishes to shake his head "no," but that would be wrong as well. So, he moves his head in a way that is neither a nod nor a shake. (WANG *speaks to himself*) In this world, only a mother has true love for her children; her love for them is really the deepest—not even a tiny bit false. If other persons' hearts were as fine as a mother's, how good things would be. But, a pity to say, it is not so! (NARRATOR'S VOICE) Realizing this, his eyes mist. (WANG *speaks out loud*) *Hai!*

MOTHER WANG (*speaks*): Son, you and your wife follow me upstairs.

WANG YULIN (*speaks*): *Uh*, no.

MOTHER WANG (*speaks*): *Ah?!*

WANG YULIN (*speaks*): Yes, I'll do as you say.

NARRATOR'S VOICE: Madame leads the pair upstairs into the wedding suite. When they have all sat down, she orders a maidservant to bring supper. Madame accompanies them in the meal. Afterward, just as the table is cleared, they notice that the moon has already brightened, for tonight is midmonth, and the moon is as round as can be.[122] Madame arises.

---

122. The moon, associated with the female, yin principle, is here a symbol of sexual consummation.

MOTHER WANG (*speaks*): Son, Daughter-in-law, do you see how round the moon is? You should be together tonight. It's getting late. I'd better leave.

WANG YULIN (*speaks*): Mother.

MOTHER WANG (*speaks*): You take good care of your wife; don't say too much.

WANG YULIN (*speaks*): Yes.

MOTHER WANG (*speaks*): Daughter-in-law, go to bed a bit early.

LI XIUYING (*speaks*): Let your daughter-in-law show you out.

MOTHER WANG (*speaks*): No, no, you needn't! Spring Fragrance, follow me. (NARRATOR'S VOICE) Spring Fragrance nods her head and follows Madame out. As soon as they go out, Madame shuts the door and instructs Spring Fragrance to bring the lock and secure it.

MOTHER WANG (*speaks*): In the name of the spirits of the Wang family and the blessings of Guanyin,[123] let them consummate their marriage tonight. (NARRATOR'S VOICE) With that she leaves with Spring Fragrance to go sleep.

LI XIUYING (NARRATOR'S VOICE): Li Xiuying turns back and sits opposite to Wang Yulin, thinking how good her mother-in-law is; she is so grateful to her, but when she thinks of the way she and her husband have become, she is very hurt. (LI *speaks to herself*) Since Mother-in-law has taken such good care of me this way, bringing my master into this room, I won't fail her good intentions. But if no one speaks a word, things will get even worse. As far as we two are concerned, one of us must speak first; so let me speak first to him. (NARRATOR'S VOICE) So she turns her head. (LI *speaks out loud*) *Ya.*

NARRATOR'S VOICE: After only a glimpse, Wang Yulin turns his back to her.

LI XIUYING (*speaks*): *Ai*— (NARRATOR'S VOICE) She is about to say, "Master," but she swallows the word. *Ai!* Mother-in-law, she cries, you locked him into this room, but you put only his body here—not his heart! (LI *speaks to herself*) If I can't speak with him, what can be done? I'm afraid your idea and plan are wasted, and this has only increased my suffering. (NARRATOR'S VOICE) She sighs lightly, slowly lowering her head. (*The first watch sounds.*) Her head nods lower and lower, but the moon above rises higher and higher. The moon's brightness enters through the window; the two persons' shadows are cast motionless on the floor. From within the room comes not a sound, almost as if no one were there. Miss's eyes have unconsciously brimmed full of tears.

(*Sings*):

A bright moon shines outside a maiden's chamber;
Seeing it, her sorrow only grows.
The wind carries the watchman's call;
I am full of sadness, and full of grief—
My broken heart can't stay the tears.
My master, I only hope we can love [each other] as fish do water,

---

123. Guanyin, a Buddhist bodhisattva, is regarded as a goddess of fertility. She is also known as the goddess of compassion.

Stuck together like glue;
When husband bids and wife complies—this till our heads grow gray.
Master, isn't it so that "The lovelier the maiden, the more bitter her fate"?
You treat me like a stranger,
Leave me desolate in the maiden's suite.
Master, your heart is like iron, without emotion;
So we face off like two enemies;
All my attempts to move you come to naught.
Master, if some say you are heartless, I still do not believe it;
For when you lifted my bridal veil, your words were so loving and gentle;
You ceaselessly called me "wife."
Then, you were so very gentle;
But Master, why did your manner change so in an instant?
In a rage you so quickly left the marriage suite;
So unexpectedly, you left for good.
I am so confused and hurt—
All this held inside;
I want to be brave and not so shy;
I want to ask my husband for his reasons.

(*Speaks to herself*): All right, I want to ask clearly why my master treats me this way. If I do not, then my pain shall be unaccounted for, and who knows when this injustice will be righted. (NARRATOR'S VOICE) Composing her thoughts, she raises her head.

(*Speaks*): Mas . . .

WANG YULIN (*speaks*): *Aiii!*

LI XIUYING (*speaks*): This . . . (NARRATOR'S VOICE) She spoke but half a word—it was cut short in her throat by her master's sigh; she steals a glance at him—his face is cold, as he slightly shakes his head. (LI *speaks to herself*) Even if I should ask him, he wouldn't answer me. I'd better not ask. (NARRATOR'S VOICE) She lowers her head in tears.

(*The second watch sounds.*)

WANG YULIN (*speaks*): Ah, it's the second watch. Mother! You hope so much for a grandson. Your love for your son is so deep that you have locked me into this room, hoping things could be well between my wife and me, and that we could begin our marriage again. Mother, it is not that your son lacks feelings or righteousness, indeed, it is that she . . . (*He stamps his foot.*) *Ai!*

LI XIUYING (NARRATOR'S VOICE): Miss is indeed unable to bear this; covering her face with her hands, she cries. (LI *speaks*) Daddy, you . . . you have destroyed my life.

WANG YULIN (*speaks*): *Ah!?* (*Speaks to himself*) I understand the meaning of her words. I hear her blame her father, though actually she is blaming me. She blames her father for blindly picking me as a son-in-law, thus destroying her life. That is to say, I am in the wrong!

LI XIUYING (*speaks, weeping*): So bitter . . .

WANG YULIN (*speaks*): This . . .

(*Sings to himself*):

I see her sorrowfully weeping, face hidden in her hands;
Each sound more heartrending than the last;
People are not made of wood, nor their hearts of iron.
I can't help stealing glimpses of her,
My heart is troubled, my mind is confused;
Could it be that you are not a slattern?
That you have been suffering from gratuitous wrongs?
Coldly treated by me in the maiden's suite, so sad;
Pain, sorrow, and hatred without end.
Because of her hurt, tears flow in streams,
If I chase the wind, clutch at shadows with no proof,
And give this cold face to this Lady Chan Juan,[124]
Then I am a heartless man, lacking feelings and righteousness.

(*Speaks to himself*): If I have been unjust to you without proof, treating you coldly, given you unspeakable pain and sorrow, then I am not human! But . . . I have proof! Yet, seeing her so hurt, I myself am beginning to have doubts. No! Let me directly ask her to clarify this. If she has done this thing, I will immediately divorce her; if she really has been unjustly accused, then I will be willing even to kowtow before her and ask forgiveness—yes! (*Speaks out loud*) *Ya*.

LI XIUYING (*speaks, lifting her head*): Master.

WANG YULIN (*speaks, pausing slightly*): A-*ya*, Wang Yulin, Wang Yulin, don't be taken in by her.

(*Sings to himself*):

A letter, a jade hair clasp—
I've looked them over many times.
The letter said, "I can't cross my father's word,
I must marry another;
But my love for you, Cousin, is tightly twined—
I'm unwilling to take another *pipa* to strum.[125]
After one month, we'll renew our love."
A shameless, illicit love affair like this
Brings disgrace to my Wang family's honor.
Her old love has been forced apart, yet her heart is with her lover;
The wild mandarin ducks cannot unite;
So word by word, sentence by sentence,
She complains, finding fault with her father and mother.

---

124. Lady Chan Juan was a famous beauty of the Warring States period (403–221 B.C.E.) and a friend of the poet Qu Yuan (ca. 340–278 B.C.E.).

125. This line paraphrases a common folk saying and implies that Li Xiuying does not want another lover.

(*Speaks to himself*): Her tears, of course, are because she is parted from her cousin. Yet why just now did she not wish Mother to beat me? And why did she say, "Alive, I am a member of the Wang family, when dead, I will be a ghost of the Wang family?" And furthermore, she said she would never blame me. What does it all mean? Ha! This is all just to humor me, because today I wrote a letter ordering her back; it must be clear to her now that I know of her illicit affair. Fear is in her heart, so she uses tears to move my heart, and crying to soften me, thus attempting to allay my suspicion. Crying is a woman's strongest weapon, especially for a woman like this, who is so good at pretending that her acting looks real.

(*Sings to himself*):

She knows she has been found out, her secret is known to me.
Knowing her illicit affair can no longer be hidden from me,
She is afraid that I'll abandon her and order her home;
Her bad name will circulate everywhere—
If her father knows of this affair, it will mean disaster,
So she thinks up these high-handed means to cover herself,
Putting on this little variety show to cheat everyone.
Her false heart has deceived my white-haired mother;
Her tears have put sorrow in my heart,
So that she can deceive us and protect herself.
She is a slattern, and acts accordingly.
Luckily, I've caught on to her early enough—
Had I wavered longer, all would be finished for me.

(*Speaks*): How dangerous, indeed! (*Speaks to himself*) If I had asked her for the truth, she would have certainly pretended, crying that she had been unjustly wronged; perhaps my heart would have softened, and I would have been misled by her, made confused, and thus made a laughingstock by others—to be laughed at by my future generations. Like that, how could I still be a man? You slattern, *ya* . . .

(*Sings to himself*):

Your act is complete deception, but to no avail;
If you cry your eyes dry,
It's nothing to me, I'll still look upon you coldly.
Yes, I gnash my teeth and clench my fists,
My heart like iron.
(*The third watch sounds.*)
I hear the gong tower; the third watch is past.
(*The wind comes up.*)
As the wind blows up, I feel cold;
In front and behind me lies difficulty,
Like arrows striking me;
Ai! In this, my life, I hate this bad marriage.

NARRATOR'S VOICE: After midnight a cold wind blows. He feels cold and is tired; his eyelids are drooping. This month he hasn't had even one good night's sleep; he can bear it no longer. Although there is a bed inside, he will not sleep in it, so he rests his head on the table to try to get some sleep, and after a moment, he is in slumber.

LI XIUYING (NARRATOR'S VOICE): Li Xiuying sobs until her mind is foggy. She doesn't realize that Wang Yulin has fallen asleep until she hears his snores. Raising her head and wiping her tears, she sees he is asleep on the table. (LI *speaks to herself*) He is really hard-hearted; I'm hurt this way, and he wasn't even moved a bit—in fact, he's fallen asleep! *Ai!* But asleep there, he will catch cold. Let me tell him to go to bed. (*Speaks out loud, timidly*) Master, Master . . . (*She shakes her head.*) *Ai!*

NARRATOR'S VOICE: She calls to him twice, but he doesn't stir, so she lets him sleep. Just as she thinks to enter the bedroom by herself, a draft flickers the candle's flame, making her chilly as well. (LI *speaks to herself*) If he sleeps here, he'll get a chill—*Ai!* He treated me so horribly, why should I care about him? Chilled or not, what has it to do with me? I am going to the bedroom! (NARRATOR'S VOICE) But who would guess that, although she told herself to go into the bedroom, her feet wouldn't follow; still standing there, she stares at him unblinking, her tears again flowing.

LI XIUYING (*sings*):

My tearful eyes look silently at my husband.
My heart and breast are full of sorrow and hatred.
You are like iron for not entering the wedding suite—
Despite the autumn cold, the lateness of the night,
With such unexpected soundness, you sleep upon a table;
Your body is thin, your clothes, too, are thin;
A draft blows icily,
You torture yourself.
If you are chilled and become ill—
I don't care—but do care,
Although you act like a stranger to me, your wife.
All maidens' hearts are good—
I want to have no love for you, but I do.
As hatred deepens, so, too, does love deepen;
I don't have the heart to see my master catch his death of cold,
So I shall remove my outer garment,
Lightly step to his side,
Bashful, fearful, shaking—
Jade hands, with pointed fingertips
Wipe away the tears.
Preparing to place the garment on his shoulders
To keep him from the cold and wind—

Who would guess that the sight would sorrow her so?
She pauses a moment,
Noiseless, wordless, silently grieving.

NARRATOR'S VOICE: Because today is the customary day to return to her home after a month of marriage, she is wearing her red bridal clothes, including her embroidered bridal cloak. Removing her cloak, she prepares to place it on his shoulders, but seeing the peonies and butterflies embroidered on the red silk, she becomes even more brokenhearted.[126]

LI XIUYING (*sings*):

Seeing the peonies, so fresh and bright,
The paired butterflies, so real;
These I embroidered as I waited to wed.
A thousand needles, ten thousand threads,
Countless hours.
Then I was happy, expectant,
With a beautiful face, but a heart full of joy;
This, just for marrying a good husband,
And the expectation of the wedding night.
Who would guess a good master would become heartless,
That the wonderful wedding night would turn into a nightmare?
Now such visceral sorrow, a heart broken by tears;
Teardrops soak my handkerchief,
My just-entered life, brought to an end.
He has no righteousness, I have no love;
Why should I cover him with my cloak and care for him?

NARRATOR'S VOICE: She wants to enter the wedding suite but hesitates, thinking of the words her mother spoke to her as she left home on her wedding day:

LI XIUYING (*sings*):

"You must be filial toward your in-laws,
And properly respect your master;
This way you shall be the precious daughter worthy of a court minister."
Thinking this over, considering it once more,
I exhort myself, I order myself that,
Although Master has been too unfeeling,
I won't take the matter to heart—
I shall play my role as a wife—
When respecting my husband, I am being filial to my mother as well.
Therefore, I turn my head and body,
To place the garment lightly on his shoulders.

---

126. Peonies and butterflies are popular symbols of love and marriage, usually appearing in pairs of symmetrical patterns in embroidery work.

NARRATOR'S VOICE: She wishes to place the garment on him.

LI XIUYING (*sings*):

In such anger, I cannot press down the hatred rising in my heart;
He is cold, fierce, and spiteful to me;
I cannot but be in a rage.

NARRATOR'S VOICE: Because she recalled her mother, she also recalls her visit home this day.

LI XIUYING (*sings*):

On the Returning Home Day, I saw my mother—
Mother and daughter met but a moment,
Before his letter was delivered at my home.
I had no choice but to leave right away;
My dear old mother was so hurt by this—
Should you have been so heartless to your mother-in-law?
When I returned to my new home, you were cold as ice,
You paid me no respects, nor gave a single word of greeting;
You gave only cold, icy words to humiliate me—
What is the meaning of such treatment?
You don't seem in the least like a scholar.

(*Speaks to herself*): Such thoughts! The more I think, the more painful it is; the more I think, the more hurt I become. Why should I show any more consideration for you? I'll go in now.

WANG YULIN (*speaks*): *Brrr!* (NARRATOR'S VOICE) A breeze blows in. Wang Yulin is dreaming, his back is cold as if freezing water were poured on it; he is very tired and chilly. (WANG *speaks*) *Oi-yo . . .*

LI XIUYING (*speaks*): *Ah!*

NARRATOR'S VOICE: Wang Yulin wraps his arms tightly about himself and buries his head in his arms, dropping off to sleep again.

LI XIUYING (*speaks, fondly, but with hatred*): My master—My Hated One!
(*Sings*):

I want to hate you wholeheartedly, but my heart won't let me hate;
When your body is cold, my heart is in pain.
I don't care for you; but still, I can't help caring for you—
I shake, shake my head and sigh.
Your breath goes *xuxu* as if you are dreaming,
But in your dreams, can you know my suffering?
I suffer to have married this unfeeling man;
This unfeeling man, as luck would have it, has met me, one with so much love;
So much love for you has wasted my heart,
Wasted my heart, as luck would have it, with my heartfelt care;
I hate the gentle, sweet love in this daughter's heart;
I'd rather have no righteousness at all

Than to have no love.
Although I have suffered one thousand injustices,
They cannot exclude ten thousand feelings;
So my tears obscure my sight, as my feet move lightly forward,
And I place this garment on my husband's body.

NARRATOR'S VOICE: She lightly places the garment upon him, but suddenly her nose begins to itch; indeed, she herself has caught cold. She tries to control it, but cannot, so she sneezes.

WANG YULIN (*speaks, startled*): *Ah!* (NARRATOR'S VOICE) Wang Yulin, awakened by the sneeze, opens his eyes to see Li Xiuying standing at his side, and an extra layer of clothing on his body. Removing the garment, he sees it is his wife's bridal cloak. (WANG *speaks to himself*) *Ya!* How did this slut's clothing get on my body? I know! She is, of course, plotting against me; she knows that I will go to the capital for the examinations next year; she wants to give me bad luck, so she put this filthy woman's garment on my body so I'll fail the examinations! *Hei!* Your heart is poison! (NARRATOR'S VOICE) He throws the cloak to the floor, tramps on it, then spits on it.[127] (WANG *speaks out loud*) *Pei!*

LI XIUYING (*speaks*): *Ah!?* (NARRATOR'S VOICE) How can Li Xiuying not help but be shocked? (LI *speaks*) Why Master . . . ?

WANG YULIN (*speaks*): I ask you—did you cover me with this cape?

LI XIUYING (*speaks, pausing*): Yes.

WANG YULIN (*speaks*): Good! Good! You placed it very well, so very well. Come here.

LI XIUYING (*goes to him, speaks*): Master, what do you want?

NARRATOR'S VOICE: In a hateful rage Wang Yulin slaps Li Xiuying on the cheek.

LI XIUYING (*speaks*): *Ah!* Master, you . . .

WANG YULIN (*speaks*): Nice little bitch; you put this filthy woman's garment on my body, thinking to destroy my chances of passing the examinations in this incarnation. You—you wicked-hearted creature!

LI XIUYING (*speaks, weeping*): Master, as your wife, I was afraid you would catch cold, so I placed the cloak on your body; I didn't expect that you would treat me this way. You—you are too cruel-hearted!

WANG YULIN (*speaks*): You harm me this way, and you call me cruel-hearted? (*He kicks her.*) Today, I shall beat this slut to death!

LI XIUYING (*speaks*): Father, Mother ! Your daughter's life is bitter, *ah* . . . (NARRATOR'S VOICE) Li Xiuying is filled with both anger and resentment. Breathless, her eyes waver, her body quakes, and she falls to the floor in a faint.

WANG YULIN (*speaks*): *Ah! A-ya!* What's to be done? Wretch! You are my enemy from a former life. *Ai!* Mother!

---

127. A common folk belief is that spitting will rob a bad-luck token of its power.

NARRATOR'S VOICE: The situation is simply a mess. Wang Yulin is wholly confused. From that time on Li Xiuying was ill. The situation had to await resolution until Li Xiuying's father returned. He threw her cousin, Gu Wenyou, and Qi, the broker of wedding accessories, into prison, and he severely criticized Wang Yulin. Admitting that he had made a mistake and had treated her shabbily, Wang Yulin begged Li Xiuying over and over to forgive him, until finally the husband and wife truly consummated their marriage.

A WOODEN-FISH SONG

Translated and introduced by Leo Shing-chi Yip

Wooden-fish songs (Cantonese, *muk'yu*; Mandarin, *muyu*) constitute an oral and oral-connected narrative tradition of the Cantonese local cultures in southern China. Their rich repertoire and popularity are similar to those of the drum songs (*guci*) in northern China and the chantefable (*tanci*) traditions in the lower Yangtze delta area. Wooden-fish songs have over three hundred years of history, flourishing in the late Ming dynasty (1368–1644) and gaining widespread popularity in the Qing (1644–1911), especially among women, who hired blind storytellers to perform the songs and stories in certain social gatherings.

The stories were a source of both entertainment and education, usually presenting models of good conduct and stressing the virtues of filial piety, righteousness, loyalty, and chastity. Although at times Chinese theater was banned because it attracted audiences of both sexes and touched on supposedly subversive, unsanctioned themes, blind storytellers were usually allowed to earn their living unhindered through street performances of the wooden-fish stories. Oral-connected texts, in both handwritten and printed versions, were circulated among friends or issued by regional and local publishing houses. The texts, often poorly printed, were sometimes read to groups of women by literate women. These printed versions were popular even among overseas Chinese, and many wooden-fish texts were exported to Southeast Asia and even North America.

More than four hundred different wooden-fish texts survive. A typical text is composed in verse, although, in the course of a storytelling session, the performer may spontaneously add passages of dialogue. The basic line length is seven syllables (each syllable corresponding to a Chinese character), though sometimes more are used. New passages, introducing a change in setting or character, sometimes use a six-syllable line. Each story consists of several chapterlike units that contain approximately a hundred verses. The first chapter provides the outline of the plot and introduces the setting and the characters.

Musical accompaniment (if any) can vary greatly, ranging from a pair of bamboo clappers to various stringed instruments, including the two-stringed fiddle (*erhu*), four-stringed lutelike *pipa*, and three-stringed *sanxian* (banjolike instrument). Some scholars believe that the percussion instrument called wooden fish (*muyu*), used by Buddhist monks and nuns in the recitation of Buddhist sutras, was the original instrument employed, possibly related to its use in traditions of precious volumes (*baojuan*) in northern China. Indeed, many of the performance aspects and contexts of *muk'yu* closely parallel those of *baojuan*.

Wooden-fish stories can be classified into five groups: (1) those derived from Buddhist stories or precious volumes, such as *Mulian Rescues His Mother* (*Mulian jiu mu*) and *The Birth of Guanyin* (*Guanyin chushi*); (2) retellings of military fiction, such as *Romance of the Three Kingdoms* (*Sanguo yanyi*); (3) stories derived from drama, Tang dynasty tales (*chuanqi*), and "romances" (*xiaoshuo*), such as *Legend of the White Snake* (*Baishe zhuan*); (4) adaptations of events and stories from society, such as "The Laments of a Chinese Worker" (Hua gong su hen); and (5) stories about the invasion of foreigners, such as "The Causes of the Nation's Demise" (Guo se su gan yuan). The best-known wooden-fish story is a romantic tale called "The Tale of the Flower" (Hua jian ji). Most of the names of authors marked on the texts are either nicknames or pen names, many presumably written by poor or unsuccessful scholars.

Two other Cantonese narrative traditions are also sometimes categorized as wooden fish, though they differ from those just described. These forms tend to be shorter ballads and differ from each other by structure and language. One is termed *nanyin* (Cantonese, *nam-yum* [southern tone]), and the other *longzhouge* (Cantonese, *long-chow* [dragon boat (song)]). The southern tone ballads tend to be longer than the dragon boat songs, adopting more poetic and less colloquial Cantonese. In contrast, the dragon boat songs tend to feature indigenous Cantonese idioms.

"Yingtai Returns Home" (Cantonese, Ying-toi wui heung) is an excerpt from the wooden-fish story *Liang Shanbo, the Tale of a Peony* (Cantonese, *Leung Shan-po maau daan gei*). The passage is the seventh of thirty-two chapters. The text is a version of a well-known folk story from Suzhou about a pair of star-crossed lovers named Liang Shanbo and Zhu Yingtai,[128] dating to the Tang dynasty (618–907). Zhu Yingtai, the daughter of a noble household, disguises herself as a boy in order to study in a classroom of young men. While at school, she meets and secretly falls in love with a classmate, Liang Shanbo. Shanbo later visits Yingtai after she has returned home. Only then does he realize Yingtai's true identity, and he proposes marriage. Unfortunately, Yingtai is already engaged to the son of the Ma family. Shanbo becomes a magistrate in the locality and dies.

On the day of her wedding, Yingtai is riding in a boat headed toward the Ma family's residence. As the travelers pass the tomb of Shanbo, a strong wind stops their journey. Yingtai then realizes that Shanbo is dead. Her moans cause the earth to rend and Shanbo's tomb to open. Yingtai jumps into the grave to join her true love, causing the tomb later to be renamed the Tomb of the Virtuous Woman. During the Song dynasty (960–1279), the story was retold with a new ending, in which the two lovers transform themselves into butterflies and fly together above the grave. The story has been adapted into many theater and storytelling pieces.

The following excerpt depicts Yingtai's journey home from school, during which Shanbo accompanies her. Much of this passage is in the form of an interior monologue on the part of Yingtai, in which, as in the original Chinese, the first-person pronoun is omitted. When Yingtai actually speaks, she hints, by using metaphors, that she is a woman, but Shanbo as yet does not fully understand

---

128. See "An Eighteenth-Century Version of 'Liang Shanbo and Zhu Yingtai.'"

the meaning behind the words. In the end, however, they make plans for Shanbo to visit Yingtai's home.

YINGTAI RETURNS HOME

Thinking to myself, returning home,
Saying good-bye to my fellow students.
Saying good-bye to the teacher Confucius,
And then to all the fellow classmates.
Three thousand classmates all seeing me off,
Brother Liang accompanying me for the longest way.
For three meals, sharing the same table,
At night, sharing the same bed;
Flower-embroidered quilt shared as a cover,
Not realizing that I, Yingtai, am a girl.

Upon departure, accompanying me through the Long Arbor Path,
Let me use words to make you realize it.
If he understands my words,
During the journey we will become a couple;
If he does not understand my words,
I'll tear up my heart and we'll go two separate ways.

He accompanies me down the street,
We see groups of men selling flowers;
Wishing to buy a beautiful flower for him,
Afraid he is not a man who likes flowers.
He accompanies me to the edge of the bridge,
At the edge of the bridge, there are branches of white pomegranates;
About to pick one and share the taste with him,
Afraid he will like the taste and want it again.
He accompanies me to the green pine,
At the green pine, the white cranes cry anxiously,
One is male, one is female,
Asking him which is male, which is female.
If he knows female from male,
We'll hold hands on the way home;
If he does not know female from male,
Farewell to you forever without a trace;
With affinity, a thousand miles apart we'll meet,
Without affinity, facing each other we'll not meet.
He accompanies me to the field,
In the field, there is a pair of toads;
Look! Animals also have feelings of love.

Today walking with you, I have no motivation.
He accompanies me to the edge of the pond,
At the pond's edge, there is a young lotus root;
About to pick one to ease our thirst,
Afraid he will like the taste and want it again.
He accompanies me to the seashore,
At the seashore, there is a fishing boat;
Hope the wind is right, no need for sails,
The fisherman is ignorant, he can't tell the weather;
He sees only the boat approaching the dock,
Doesn't see the dock approaching the boat.
He accompanies me to a well,
The two, holding hands, look at their faces reflecting;
After the faces separate today,
I don't know what day they will meet again.

He accompanies me to a temple;
In the temple is a statue of a male, not quite resembling a male;
Another statue looks like a Buddha sculpted of mud,
There lacks someone as a go-between;
Picking up and throwing the fortune-telling sticks,
One is yin, one is yang;
"If you know yin from yang,
We'll hold hands together on the way home;

"If you do not know yin from yang,
I worry one day you will realize it and be heartbroken!
You and I are like the sticks,
I am yin and you are yang."

Hearing this, Sanbo replies immediately,
"My dear brother Yingtai, listen to me,
You tease me for my ignorance,
Spelling out the reasons, it is clear;
Above there is heaven, below there is earth,
Heaven and earth, sun and moon, are yin-yang."
Hearing this, Yingtai's mind is vexed,
"How can you be such a dunce?
I am talking about the pairing of a couple,
You are talking about heaven and earth as yin-yang;
Exhausting thousands of words, you don't get it,
Praying to the moon to compose for you is vain;
Today is like swallowing a sharp knife into my stomach,
It either breaks my courage or breaks my heart!"

Hearing this, Scholar Liang delivers his words,
"My dear brother Yingtai, when you return home,
Let me come to your door and visit,
May I ask the location of your door?"

Hearing this, Yingtai replies,
Calling his name, "You have to know the details,
My home is located at Wang Shu Pass,
A place people call the White Sand River.
A tower higher than ten feet,
Pearl-braided nets aligned in rows,
An eight-sided room above the gate made of red camphorwood,
Surrounded by four walls all painted white,
Living rooms all covered with crystal tiles,
Four metal pillars embedded with gold,
Within there is a pond of pure water,
Treasured ducks fly from the four directions,
Both sides all planted with Guanyin[129] bamboo;
At the goldfish pond, fragrances of hundreds of flowers,
The flower garden as wide as the ocean;
There are tens of cute and lovely maids also.
If you have none, I will send one to marry you,
The maids are there, pick one for a concubine."
From the beginning, exhausting feelings of love,
The two say good-bye and separate,
Asking you to come in three or four days, if not, four, five, or six days,
My dear brother, better come to my door in seven or eight days at
the latest.

---

129. Guanyin is the bodhisattva (savior) of compassion.

AN EXCERPT FROM A GREAT VOLUMES SCRIPT OF THE BAI PEOPLE, YUNNAN

Collected, translated, and introduced by Beth E. Notar

Great volume songs (Chinese, *dabenqu*; Bai, *daoberzi ku*) are a form of prosimetric storytelling and ballad singing of the Bai people, who live in and around the Dali basin in the Himalayan foothills of Yunnan province. The Bai (who refer to themselves as *shua Bar ni gar* or *shua Bar ni* [people who speak Bar]) engage in trade, agriculture, fishing, and, increasingly, the tourism industry. Dali was once the capital of two Buddhist kingdoms, the Nanzhao (737–902) and Dali (937–1253), the latter of which fell to the Mongols. Bai is a tonal language classified as belonging to the Sino-Tibetan family by Chinese linguists, though further classification remains controversial. The great volume songs are written in a mixture of Chinese and Bai—the Bai language represented by selected Chinese characters chosen for their sound value. Thus to Chinese readers, the texts have many phrases and passages that are impossible to decode unless they also know Bai. Some scholars trace the roots of the great volumes story tradition to as early as the seventh to tenth centuries, while others see it as probably arising somewhat later, between the fourteenth and sixteenth centuries.

Great volumes stories are performed by a male storyteller who is accompanied by a man playing a three-stringed banjolike instrument called a *sanxian* (Bai, *xiezi*). Typical props include two chairs, a table, a cloth fan (often used when portraying female characters), and a wooden block (used to rap the table at dramatic moments for effect).

The content of the stories derives from two sources: Chinese legends and local Bai legends. The Chinese legends often tell of officials corrupted by power, such as "Chen Shimei Does Not Recognize His Former Wife" (Chen Shimei bu ren qian qi). The Bai legends often glorify former leaders or events of the ancient Dali kingdom, such as "The Story of the Bai King" (Bai wang de gushi) and the "Burning of the Songhua Pavilion" (Shaohua Songhua lou).

A performer sings and narrates from handwritten texts that are laid open on a table in front of him. When performing Chinese legends, the performer speaks some parts in Chinese prose and sings other parts in Bai rhyme. One story constitutes several volumes of handwritten text. The parts of the ballads sung in Bai correspond to four-line stanzas, the lines having syllable lengths of seven, seven, seven, and five, respectively. A number of different rhyming patterns are employed, the rhyme coming on the last syllable of a line (for example, *aaba*) or across several stanzas (for example, *aabc daea eaba*, or *abcb daeb*). There are three local styles of music: northern (*bei qiang*), southern (*nan qiang*), and eastern (*Haidong qiang*). The northern style has been described as "smooth and sweet," the southern as "unrestrained and proud," and the eastern as "easy and flowing." Sources elaborate most clearly on the differences between the northern and southern styles. The popular northern and southern styles both have nine basic rhythms (*ban*), though the southern style is faster and uses eighteen basic tunes (*diao*), while the northern style is slower and has thirteen basic tunes.

Before 1949, great volumes performances were given at temple festivals and family celebrations. During the former, the storytellers and musicians would sit on an outside stage under a tent, open for all to see. For the latter, they would sit inside someone's home, and male and female guests would sit in separate rooms to listen. Depending on the generosity of the patrons, performances might last for only one day or could extend for more than an entire month. Performances appealed to a wide audience of both young and old. After 1949, the government increasingly restricted performances of anything deemed to have "feudal" or "antirevolutionary" content. By the time of the Cultural Revolution (1966–1976), storytellers were prohibited from performing any of their old legends, and Red Guards had destroyed many song texts. Some texts were covertly preserved, and while storytellers were sometimes asked to sing revolutionary songs or those in praise of Chairman Mao, some continued to sing the old songs in secret.

By the mid-1980s and into the 1990s, as policies relaxed, the storytellers and musicians began once again performing freely, with some performances lasting from one to as many as seven days. As in the past, village patrons began to sponsor many of the performances. In recent years, such sponsors are often newly wealthy entrepreneurial families. Audiences are smaller than in the past, and fewer skilled storytellers are active. By the 1990s, balladeers and musicians were no longer performing at temple festivals. All performances were concentrated in the seventh lunar month, the time when, villagers say, ancestral spirits return to the village and wandering ghosts walk the land. Villagers explain that this is a good time to listen to great volumes songs and reflect on the relationship between the past and the present, and what it means to be a good person. After a late-night performance, a balladeer might also provide services as a spirit medium for those in the audience with questions for a particular ancestor. In some marketplaces, tape recordings of great volumes stories and tunes are sold. In certain tourist venues, shorter lyrical pieces, sung to great volumes tunes, are performed by young women accompanied by the *sanxian*.

The ballad "Wang Shipeng Sacrifices to the River" (Wang Shipeng jijiang) was performed by Zhao Peiding,[130] one of the most popular balladeers in the Dali basin, in the summer of 1994, during the seventh lunar month. Wang Shipeng (1112–1171) lived during the Southern Song dynasty (1127–1279), a man from Wenzhou (now in Zhejiang province) who passed the civil service examination and

130. Beth Notar extends many thanks to Zhao Peiding for letting her copy his ballad book and for explaining it. She also thanks Li Guo, who first introduced her to the ballad of Wang Shipeng; to Yang Dingzhu and Yang Zhou, who accompanied her on two different visits to Zhao Peiding; and to Professor Wang Ying for helping with aspects of the transcription and translation.

went on to become an official. He urged the reorganization of the court government and strove to restore it. "Wang Shipeng Sacrifices to the River" is a Chinese drama that describes Wang as a virtuous official who remained faithful to his first wife, despite others' attempts to arrange politically advantageous marriages for him. It is unclear when this drama reached Dali and at what point it started to be performed by balladeers.

During a performance, a balladeer shifts between speaking and singing, between Chinese and Bai, and between character voices and the narrator's voice. A multilinear comparison of the Chinese-character transcription, its Mandarin pronunciation, and the pronunciation as Zhao performed the ballad reveals several interesting phenomena. Zhao sometimes employed Chinese characters in his written texts to represent Bai sounds. (The parts sung in Bai are shown in italics.) For example, one line of Chinese characters reads:

Chinese: Sun San tigou deng ben bei. Yimian bei zi yimian mi . . .
Bai: Sun San *tigou dengben bei*. Yimian *beize* yimian *mi* . . .
English: Sun San now went. As he walked, he thought . . .

To a reader of Chinese, the latter phrase in the text appears nonsensical: "On one hand a cup self, on the other hand rice." When Zhao sings this, however, the Bai speaker hears "Yimian *beize* yimian *mi*" (As he walked, he thought). Similarly, Zhao played off the homophonous or near-homophonous nature of certain Chinese characters. For example, at the end of one stanza he wrote three characters that could mean "all fall down" or "all planted"; in his usage, however, the three characters are a shorthand for the homophonous phrase *youyou zai* (a life of leisure). This is only one example of various ways in which Chinese characters are employed in the texts to represent Bai sounds.

The brief excerpt from "Wang Shipeng Sacrifices to the River" comes from the beginning of the ballad, when the playboy-turned-lowlife narrator, Sun San, goes to the *yamen* (local administrative office) to find the official Wang Shipeng. As is typical of this storytelling style, passages of speaking alternate with those of singing.

WANG SHIPENG SACRIFICES TO THE RIVER

Written and performed by Zhao Peiding (Bai)

[*Speaks*:]
My family name is Sun, given name "Three."
When my parents were alive they treasured me,
From a young age I learned to play, gamble, and fool around.
Unfortunately, my parents passed away.
A good home, I frittered away.
I couldn't muddle along at home, so I drifted everywhere.

I grabbed quick meals and lounged.
For half a year I did not return home.
I wandered here and there, until I wandered into the capital city.

[*Sings*:]
Sun San now went. As he walked, he thought:
Since I was little, I have never worked.
I have never broken one stick of straw.
Now, without shoes or socks, I have traveled.

For years, months, and days, I wore silks.
Mornings I ate meat and evenings I ate fish.
Meal after meal I could not do without meat.
If there was a piece then I ate a piece.

Playing, gambling, fooling around, I did it all.
Now I have no money.
Days are difficult to get by.
Thirty-six trades, I can do none.
During the days I travel to the east and west.

I grab quick meals—I am most capable.
I trick people—
Where I can beat someone, I beat;
Where I can grab something, I grab.

I'm a hooligan and ruffian,
Drifting everywhere I go.
This time I have come out for half a year.
Home, I have not yet returned to.

I came to the capital city,
And found it lively.
Last night, after I checked into an inn,
The innkeeper, he said to me:

[A man] with the title Number One Scholar[131]
[named] Wang Shipeng,
I really like him.

---

131. Number One Scholar (Zhuang Yuan) was the title given to the scholar who ranked highest on the imperial civil service examination.

Shipeng is my old buddy,
He is also from my same village.

Why not go to find him
And relieve this poverty?
This is a good plan.
Happiness appeared in [Sun San's] eyebrows and smile;

Between old buddies it is easy to talk—
I'll find a way to bring out his money.
He walked down nine streets and eighteen alleys,
And took nine twists and eighteen turns.

The gate of the *yamen* was so high and fancy,
It hurt his eyes.
On the reflecting wall were written gold characters,
A pair of [stone] lions [guarded] each side,
Title: Number One Scholar Wang Shipeng,
Wen prefecture, Eight Li village.

AN EXCERPT FROM A GREAT VOLUMES SCRIPT OF THE BAI PEOPLE, YUNNAN

Collected and edited by Yang Liangcai (Bai), translated by Fu Wei, and introduced by Mark Bender

From the 1930s through the early decades of the People's Republic of China, traditional oral arts were often used as vehicles for political education in both rural and urban areas throughout China. Older stories involving class and gender conflicts, as well as other social ills or "backward" customs, were reworked, and new stories were written on old frameworks. Both forms were effectively utilized in a variety of ways to meet the political agenda of the moment. Such adaptations were often not difficult to make, since much of traditional narrative, either oral or written, has a didactic aspect, albeit Confucian or Buddhist. One traditional work from the Bai ethnic minority communities around Lake Erhai, Yunnan province, is "Singlet of Blood and Sweat" (Xue han shan), set in the ancient Dali kingdom (937–1253). It is in the great volumes storytelling tradition (Chinese, *dabenqu*; Bai, *daoberzi ku*) introduced in the preceding selection. The well-known narrative also goes by the names "Lan Jizi Meets Elder Brother" (Lan Jizi hui dage) and "The Millhouse Story" (Muofang ji). Some versions are as long as two thousand lines.

The general story line concerns a period during the Dali kingdom when the harvests were bad and the officials negligent. As time passes, the peasants begin to resist, and a pair of local scholar-officials of the Lan family decide to leave their parents and take up the cause. While they are away, the mother of the household, surnamed Qiao, takes the opportunity to try to get rid of a daughter-in-law she despises, surnamed Wang. She schemes to burn her alive in the millhouse, but the plot is ultimately foiled by her stepson, Lan Jizi. Unrelenting, Qiao devises a plot in which it appears that Wang has murdered her son, and the young woman is consequently arrested. Luckily for Wang, her husband and brother-in-law turn up just in the nick of time and save her from execution.

The theme of the cruel mother-in-law and the abused daughter-in-law is pervasive in the folklore and literature of East Asia. In this Bai version of the dynamic, the values of hard work and self-sacrifice are eulogized, but at the same time listeners are shown what life was like in China before the founding of the People's Republic in 1949 and the widespread women's reform movements that followed. For example, the weight of household chores is described in great detail, and both women have bound feet (though it is questionable whether foot-binding was a custom in Dali at the time of the story, notwithstanding that in later periods it was). Interestingly, there are several lines that refer to religion—such as Madame Qiao's crying out the Buddha's name, "Amituofu," and references to karmic consequences of previous lives—that implicitly acknowledge the strong Buddhist beliefs still common in the Dali area, especially among women.

The style of presentation is based on the traditional alternation between speaking and singing. The text, published in 1984, is drawn from a collection of great volumes stories and is an example of the politically didactic, yet entertaining, tradition-oriented narratives that were commonly published during the first decades of the People's Republic of China. The following passages are taken from a scene in the first part of "Singlet of Blood and Sweat" in which Madame Qiao physically and verbally abuses her daughter-in-law, Madame Wang, and schemes to send her to the millhouse. As is typical of the great volumes tradition (and many other storytelling traditions), the voices of individual characters (whether as direct song or speech, or as "silent" soliloquies) and the narrator sometimes mix or alternate within a single passage.

SINGLET OF BLOOD AND SWEAT

MADAME QIAO (*sings to herself*):

> Taking care of the household dawn to dusk;
> And speaking of the household—it's a mess;
> There are seven words for housekeeping:
> Oil, salt, firewood, rice, soy, vinegar, tea.

(NARRATOR'S VOICE): The more she thought about it, the angrier Old Woman Qiao became.

MADAME QIAO (*speaks to herself*): Since Zhonglin and Zhongxiu joined the army, there's been no news whether they live or die. Husband and Jizi went to East Village to collect debts, but still not a glimpse of them. That woman Wang didn't pay attention to me. I'll call her out, then beat her.

(*Speaks*): Wang! Come out here!

MADAME WANG: Gracious Mother-in-law, Daughter-in-law pays respect to you.

MADAME QIAO: I'm not a bodhisattva, to whom are you paying respects? Today I'm asking you, have you taken care of the housework, inside and out?

MADAME WANG: What do you mean "inside and out"?

MADAME QIAO: Inside work means taking care of cooking and entertaining guests; outside work means going to the mill and grinding flour.

MADAME WANG: I wish to obey Mother-in-law—it's just that Daughter-in-law has only a tiny pair of feet. It's hard to walk, and she can't turn the handle of the millstones.

MADAME QIAO: Little woman, you are really annoying.

(NARRATOR'S VOICE): Hearing this really annoys her.

MADAME QIAO (*sings to herself*):

> This woman dares to
> Lie and deceive me;
> Don't you think I don't know it?
>
> Big feet—you have bigger feet;
> Small feet, I have smaller feet.

Beating a donkey to scare a horse,
Clearly you were laughing at me.

Go ask everyone in every village.
We bind our feet so we can care for the household.

Now I'm getting old,
You have come to make things difficult for me.

I'm up by the time the cock crows at dawn.
By then how much work I've done:
Cleaning the house inside and out,
Stoking the cooking fire,
Making three pairs of shoes,
Mending and embroidery—I did them all.
Making meals in the morning,
Cutting grass for the horses at sunset.
Using my mouth to pod peas,
Using my hands to carry firewood;
The baby cried on the bed,
With no one to look after him.

Little woman can eat, but not do—
An open mouth talking about small feet;
You made me really angry today—
I'll beat you to death!
You useless woman, I'm going to beat you to death!

MADAME WANG (*sings to herself*):

Mother-in-law, please let me go!
I, Wang, am beaten to fainting;
My tears running like water,
Crying for my dear husband—
He shouldn't have gone to soldier.

Your wife suffers at home;
I'm afraid I won't see you in this lifetime—
Though evil people wouldn't agree with me,
And Mother-in-law won't forgive me.

(*Sings aloud*):

Mother-in-law, please excuse me,
I'm willing to go anywhere.

MADAME QIAO: If you intend to go, then get going. If you had accepted things earlier, would you have been beaten? Get up.

(*Sings to herself*):

I, Madame Qiao, must convince this daughter,
So don't take me calling her "daughter" as strange.

You've had a hot temper since youth;
You absolutely must not raise her suspicions.

(*Speaks*): Wang, today you must mill this bucket of wheat. One *dou* of wheat must equal three *dou* of flour—without the hulls. If you can't do that—don't let me set eyes on you again.

MADAME WANG (*sings to herself*):

She scares me, Wang, to death,
So tears of sorrow run like rivers.
One *dou* of wheat becomes three *dou*—
Whoever heard of that?

It has been said since ancient times,
That it is hard for in-laws to live together.
If a mother-in-law is offended, one can't survive.
Complaining about a mother-in-law is useless;
It's just that I have bad luck.

NARRATOR (*sings*):

Drying her face with both hands,
Wang would rather go to the mill.
Opening her mouth, she calls to her mother-in-law:
Please forgive your daughter-in-law.

MADAME QIAO (*speaks*): Yes, yes. As long as you go, I won't beat and curse you.

NARRATOR (*sings*):

Qiao is happy when she thinks about it:
Beat her once and gain control of the Wang woman—
To run a family you need a family cudgel,
A stick is the rule!

MADAME QIAO (*sings to herself*):

Beating makes me out of sorts,
My heart is fluttering and my limbs are sore;
I'll go to the kitchen for a break,
And eat a fried egg.

MADAME WANG (*speaks*): I'll shoulder this wheat, then leave.

NARRATOR (*sings*):

Madame Wang goes out the gate,
Her heart breaks as she mulls it over,
Wondering what she did in a former life
To deserve such a fate.

MADAME WANG (*sings to herself*):

There are countless women in the world,
But who compares to me, Wang Sanmei?
Just like a fritter fried in oil,
Such is the suffering of this world.

I have two feet but no place to go;
I have pain and sorrow, but there are no ears to listen.
I cry out for my husband,
But when can we meet again?

Without realizing it, I'm at the mill.
Let me look the place over,
Gently open the millhouse door,
And go inside the mill.

LAN JIZI (*sings to himself*):

Something is in my heart,
I'm restless day and night.
I'd best hurry back home,
And not tarry any longer.

(*Speaks to himself*): I, Lan Jizi, and my father went to the village for quite a few days. Last night I felt restless, afraid mother has ill-treated Sister-in-law at home. I must go home for a look.

(*Sings to himself*):

I, Lan Jizi, sigh,
Mama has treated people very strangely;
Trying to control everyone,
Including me.
She says that I'm another's son—
It cuts me to the heart.
Mama is venomous to one and all,
And the family is dissolving.

Now I head back home
To check on Sister-in-law,
Fearing that Mother will beat her,
And hoping to save her if I can.

(*Speaks to himself*): Arriving at home, I don't see a soul. Let me hide behind this door and listen.

MADAME QIAO (*sings to herself*):

Not even a three-eyed tiger scares me,
I fear only one with two hearts;
Whoever crosses this old lady,
Will have her skin peeled and nerves plucked.

(*Speaks*): Wang has gone to the millhouse and acted exactly according to my plan. Now it is midnight, and I'm gong to start a fire and burn her to death. Amituofu, I'd better leave right now. Otherwise, if Lan Jizi returns . . .

LAN JIZI (*speaks to himself*): This woman has planned such an evil thing—she wants to murder my sister-in-law! I have to find a way to save her.

FURTHER READINGS

BOOKS AND ARTICLES

Baiqu jingxuan [*The Best of Bai Songs*]. Recorded and translated by Duan Ling and Yang Yingxing. Kunming: Yunnan minzu chubanshe, 1994.

Bamo Qubumo. "Traditional Nuosu Origin Narratives: A Case of Ritualized Epos in *Bimo* Incantation Scriptures." *Oral Tradition* 16, no. 2 (2001): 453–79.

Bauman, Richard. *Verbal Art as Performance*. Prospect Heights, Ill.: Waveland, 1977.

Bender, Mark. "*Ashima* and *Gamo Anyo*: Aspects of Two 'Yi' Narrative Poems." *Chinoperl Papers* 27 (2008): 209–42.

——. *Butterfly Mother: Miao (Hmong) Creation Epics from Guizhou, China*. Indianapolis: Hackett, 2006.

——. "A Description of *Jiangjing* (Telling Scriptures) Services in Jingjiang, China." *Asian Folklore Studies* 60, no. 1 (2001): 101–33.

——. "Keys to Performance in Kunming *Pingshu*." *Chinoperl Papers* 19 (1996): 21–37.

——. *Plum and Bamboo: China's Suzhou Chantefable Tradition*. Urbana: University of Illinois Press, 2003.

——. "Shifting and Performance in Suzhou Chantefable." In *The Eternal Storyteller: Oral Literature in Modern China*, edited by Vibeke Børdahl, 181–96. Richmond: Curzon Press, 1999.

——. "'Tribes of Snow': Animals and Plants in the Nuosu *Book of Origins*." *Asian Ethnology* 67, no. 1 (2008): 5–42.

Bender, Mark, and Su Huana, trans. *Daur Folktales*. Beijing: New World Press, 1984.

Benson, Carleton. "The Manipulation of *Tanci* in Radio Shanghai During the 1930s." *Republican China* 20, no. 2 (1995): 116–46.

Blader, Susan. "Oral Narrative and Its Transformation into Print: The Case of *Baiyutang.*" In *The Eternal Storyteller: Oral Literature in Modern China*, edited by Vibeke Børdahl, 161–80. Richmond: Curzon Press, 1999.

Blake, C. Fred. "Death and Abuse in Marriage Laments: The Curse of Chinese Brides." *Asian Folklore Studies* 37, no. 1 (1978): 13–33.

Børdahl, Vibeke, ed. *The Eternal Storyteller: Oral Literature in Modern China*. Richmond, Surrey: Curzon Press, 1999.

——. "The Man-Hunting Tiger: From 'Wu Song Fights the Tiger' in Chinese Traditions." *Asian Folklore Studies* 66, nos. 1–2 (2007): 141–63.

——. *The Oral Tradition of Yangzhou Storytelling*. Richmond: Curzon Press, 1996.

——. "Professional Storytelling in Modern China: A Case Study of the 'Yangzhou Pinghua' Tradition." *Asian Folklore Studies* 56, no. 1 (1997): 7–32.

——. "The 'Storyteller's Manner' in Chinese Storytelling." *Asian Folklore Studies* 62, no. 1 (2003): 65–112.

——. "The Voice of Wang Shaotang." *Chinoperl Papers* 25 (2004): 1–34.

Børdahl, Vibeke, Fei Li, and Huang Ying, eds. *Four Masters of Chinese Storytelling: Full-Length Repertoires of Yangzhou Storytelling on Video* [*Yangzhou pinghua sijia yiren—quan shu biaoyan luxiang mulu*]. Bilingual ed. With DVD (60 minutes). Copenhagen: NIAS Press, 2004.

Børdahl, Vibeke, and Jette Ross. *Chinese Storytellers: Life and Art in the Yangzhou Tradition*. With VCD (60 minutes). Boston: Cheng and Tsui, 2002.

Børdahl, Vibeke, and Margaret Wan, eds. *Interplay of the Oral and the Written in Chinese Popular Literature*. Copenhagen: NIAS Press, 2010.

Bourgerie, Dana. "Eating the Mosquito: Transmission of a Chinese Children's Folksong." *Chinoperl Papers* 16 (1992–1993): 133–43.

Chao Gejin. "Mongolian Oral Epic Poetry: An Overview." *Oral Tradition* 12, no. 2 (1997): 322–36.

——. "The Oirat Epic Cycle of *Jangar*." *Oral Tradition* 16, no. 2 (2001): 402–35.

Chau, Adam Yuet. *Miraculous Response: Doing Popular Religion in Contemporary China*. Stanford, Calif.: Stanford University Press, 2006.

Che Xilun. "Jiangsu Jingjiangde *Jiangjing*" [The *Jiangjing* of Jingjiang]. *Minjian wenyi jikan* 3 (1988): 165–89.

Chen, Fan Pen Li. *Chinese Shadow Theatre: History, Popular Religion and Women Warriors*. Montreal: McGill–Queens University Press, 2007.

——. *Zhongguo baojuan congmu* [*A General Bibliography of "Precious Volumes"*]. Taipei: Academia Sinica, Institute of Literature and Philosophy, 1998.

Chen Wulou, Lucie Borotová, and Vibeke Børdahl. "Old Questions Discussed Anew on 'Huaben.'" *Asian Folklore Studies* 57, no. 1 (1998): 133–39.

Davis, Sara. *Songs and Silence: Ethnic Revival on China's Southwest Borders*. New York: Columbia University Press, 2005.

Deng, Minwen. "Dong Oral Poetry: Kuant Cix." *Oral Tradition* 16, no. 2 (2001): 436–52.

Dolby, William. "Early Chinese Plays and Theater." In *Chinese Theater: From Its Origins to the Present Day*, edited by Colin Mackerras, 7–31. Honolulu: University of Hawai'i Press, 1983.

Du, Shan Shan. *Chopsticks Only Work in Pairs: Gender Unity and Gender Equality Among the Lahu of Southwest China*. New York: Columbia University Press, 2002.

Duan Baolin. "The History and Prospects of Folk Tales and Storytelling in China." In *The Eternal Storyteller: Oral Literature in Modern China*, edited by Vibeke Børdahl, 53–61. Richmond: Curzon Press, 1999.

——. *Zhongguo mianjian wenxue gaiyao* [*Introduction to Chinese Folk Literature*]. Beijing: Wenhua yishu chubanshe, 2005.

Dudbridge, Glen. "The Goddess Hua-yüeh San-niang and the Cantonese Ballad *Ch'en-hsiang T'ai-tzu*." *Hanxue yanjiu* 8, no. 1 (1990): 627–46.

——. "The Worshippers of Mount Hua." In *Religious Experience and Lay Society in T'ang China: A Reading of Tai Fu's "Kuang-i chi,"* 86–116. Cambridge: Cambridge University Press, 1995.

Eliade, Mircea. *Shamanism: Archaic Techniques of Ecstasy*. Translated by Willard R. Trask. Princeton, N.J.: Princeton University Press, 1964.

Fine, Elizabeth. *The Folklore Text: From Performance to Print*. Bloomington: Indiana University Press, 1984.

Foley, John Miles. *How to Read an Oral Poem*. Urbana: University of Illinois Press, 2002.

Guo Jingrui and Gao Mobo. "*Che Wang fu* yu xiqu chaoben" [The Dramatic Texts in the *Tune Book of the Manor House of Lord Che*]. In *Che Wang fu quben yanjiu* [*Study on the "Book of the Manor House of Lord Che"*], edited by Liu Liemao et al. Guangzhou: Guangdong renmin chubanshe, 2000.

Guo Qitao. *Ritual Opera and Mercantile Lineage: The Confucian Transformation of Popular Culture in Late Imperial Huizhou*. Stanford, Calif.: Stanford University Press, 2005.

Hali, Awelkhan, Li Zengxiang, and Karl W. Luckert. *Kazakh Traditions of China*. Lanham, Md.: University Press of America, 1998.

Hanan, Patrick. "The Making of 'The Pearl-Sewn Shirt' and 'The Courtesan's Jewel Box.'" *Harvard Journal of Asiatic Studies* 33 (1973): 124–53.

Harrell, Stevan. *Ways of Being Ethnic in Southwest China: Studies on Ethnic Groups in China*. Seattle: University of Washington Press, 2002.

Heberer, Thomas. *China and Its National Minorities: Autonomy or Assimilation?* Armonk, N.Y.: Sharpe, 1989.

Heissig, Walter. "The Present State of the Mongolian Epic and Some Topics for Future Research." *Oral Tradition* 11, no. 1 (1996): 85–98.

Hensman, Bertha, and Mack Kwok-Ping. *Hong Kong Tale-Spinners: A Collection of Tales and Ballads Transcribed and Translated from Story-tellers in Hong Kong*. Hong Kong: Chinese University of Hong Kong, 1968.

Honko, Lauri. *Textualising the Siri Epic*. Folklore Fellows Communications, no. 264. Helsinki: Suomalainen Tiedeakatemia, Academia Scientiarum Fennica, 1998.

——. *Textualization of Oral Epics*. Berlin: Mouton de Gruyter, 2000.

Hrdličková, Vena. "The Professional Training of Chinese Storytelling and the Storyteller's Guilds." *Archiv Orientalni* 33 (1965): 225–49.

Huang Yongsha. *Zhuangzu geyao gailun* [*Introduction to Zhuang Songs*]. Nanning: Guangxi minzu chubanshe, 1983.

Humphrey, Caroline, with Urgunde Onon. *Elders and Shamans: Experience, Knowledge, and Power Among the Daur Mongols*. Oxford: Clarendon Press, 1996.

Idema, Wilt L., ed. and trans. *The Butterfly Lovers: The Legend of Liang Shanbo and Zhu Yingtai—Four Versions with Related Texts*. Indianapolis: Hackett, 2010.

——. "*Changben* Texts in the *Nushu* Repertoire of Southern Hunan." In *The Eternal Storyteller: Oral Literature in Modern China*, edited by Vibeke Børdahl, 95–114. Richmond: Curzon Press, 1999.

——. *Chinese Vernacular Fiction: The Formative Period.* Leiden: Brill, 1974.

——, ed. and trans. *Filial Piety and Its Divine Rewards: The Legend of Dong Yong and Weaving Maiden, with Related Texts.* Indianapolis: Hackett, 2009.

——. *Judge Bao and the Rule of Law: Eight Ballad-Stories from the Period 1250–1450.* Hackensack, N.J.: World Scientific, 2009.

——, trans. *Meng Jiangnu Brings Down the Great Wall: Ten Versions of a Chinese Legend.* Seattle: University of Washington Press, 2008.

——, trans. *The White Snake and Her Son: A Translation of "The Precious Scroll of Thunder Peak," with Related Texts.* Indianapolis: Hackett 2009.

Idema, Wilt, and Beata Grant. *The Red Brush: Writing Women of Imperial China.* Cambridge, Mass.: Harvard University Press, 2004.

Jiang, Jin. *Women Playing Men: Yue Opera and Social Change in Twentieth-Century Shanghai.* Seattle: University of Washington Press, 2009.

Jiangsu Sheng Minjian Wenxue Jicheng Bangongshi [Jiangsu Folk Literature Series Office] and Jingjiang Xian Minjian Wenxue Jicheng Bangongshi [Jingjiang County Folk Literature Series Office], eds. *San Mao baojuan* [*San Mao Precious Scrolls*]. Yangzhou, Jiangsu province: Zhongguo Minjian Wenxue Jicheng, 1988. [This is an internally circulating work. It was edited by Wu Genyuan, Guo Shouming, and Mou Binglin, based on the oral performances of Lu Manxiang, Zhu Mingchun, Chen Zixuan, and Wang Guofang.]

Johnson, David. "Actions Speak Louder than Words: The Cultural Significance of Chinese Ritual Opera." In *Ritual Opera, Operatic Ritual: "Mu-lien Rescues His Mother" in Chinese Popular Culture*, edited by David Johnson, 1–45. Publications of the Chinese Popular Culture Project 1. Berkeley: Institute of East Asian Studies, University of California, 1989.

——. "Communication, Class, and Consciousness in Late Imperial China." In *Popular Culture in Late Imperial China*, edited by David Johnson, Andrew J. Nathan, and Evelyn R. Rawski, 34–72. Berkeley: University of California Press, 1985.

——. "Mu-lien in *Pao-chuan*: The Performance Context and Religious Meaning of the *Yu-ming Pao-ch'uan.*" In *Ritual and Scripture in Chinese Popular Religion: Five Studies*, edited by David Johnson, 55–103. Publications of the Chinese Popular Culture Project 3. Berkeley: Institute of East Asian Studies, University of California, 1995.

Jones, Stephen. *Folk Music of China: Living Instrumental Traditions.* 2nd ed. With CD. Oxford: Clarendon Press, 1998.

——. "Turning a Blind Ear: Bards of Shaanbei." *Chinoperl Papers* 27 (2007): 173–208.

Ke Chi, ed. *Guangxi qing'ge* [*Guangxi Love Songs*]. Nanning: Guangxi renmin chubanshe, 1981.

Ke Yang, ed. "Flower Songs: Selected Works" [Hua'er zuopin xuan]. Unpublished, undated classroom material.

King, Gail Oman, trans. *The Story of Hua Guansuo.* Tempe, Ariz.: Center for Asian Studies, Arizona State University, 1989.

Krueger, John R., trans. *Mongolian Folktales, Stories, and Proverbs: In English Translation.* Mongolia Society Occasional Papers, no. 4. Bloomington, Ind.: Mongolia Society, 1967.

Leung, Pui-Chee. *Wooden-Fish Books: Critical Essays and an Annotated Catalogue Based on the Collections in the University of Hong Kong*. Hong Kong: University of Hong Kong, Centre of Asian Studies, 1978.

Li Bao and Yang Wenan, eds. *Lahu zu shi* [*A History of the Lahu Nationality*]. Kunming: Yunnan renmin chubanshe, 2003.

Li Yongxiang. "The Cold Funeral of the Nisu Yi." In *Perspectives on the Yi of Southwest China*, edited by Stevan Harrell, 135–43. Berkeley: University of California Press, 2000.

Link, Perry. "The Mum Sparrow: Non-vegetarian *Xiangsheng* in Action." *Chinoperl Papers* 16 (1992–1993): 1–27.

Link, Perry, Richard Madsen, and Paul G. Pickowicz. *Unofficial China: Popular Culture and Thought in the People's Republic of China*. Boulder, Colo.: Westview Press, 1989.

Lu Gong, ed. *Liang Zhu gushi shuochang ji* [*Prosimetric Versions of the Liang-Zhu Story*]. Shanghai: Shanghai guzhi chubanshe, 1985.

Mackerras, Colin. *China's Minority Cultures: Identities and Integration Since 1912*. New York: St. Martin's Press, 1995.

——. *The Performing Arts in Contemporary China*. London: Routledge and Kegan Paul, 1981.

Mair, Victor. "The Prosimetric Form in the Chinese Literary Tradition." In *Prosimetrum: Cross-Cultural Perspectives on Narrative in Prose and Verse*, edited by Joseph Harris and Karl Reichl, 365–85. Cambridge: Brewer, 1997.

——. *Tang Transformation Texts: A Study of the Buddhist Contribution to the Rise of Vernacular Fiction and Drama in China*. Harvard-Yenching Institute Monograph 28. Cambridge, Mass.: Council on East Asian Studies, Harvard University, 1989.

——. "What Is a Chinese 'Dialect/Topolect'? Reflections on Some Key Sino-English Linguistic Terms." *Sino-Platonic Papers* 29 (1991): 1–31.

Mair, Victor, Lowell Skar, Laura Hostetler, and Neil Schmid. "Three Contemporary Approaches to 'Oral Literature': Implications for the Study of Chinese Folklore." *Chinese Studies* 1, no. 8 (1990): 1–36.

McDougall, Bonnie. *Popular Chinese Literature and the Performing Arts in the People's Republic of China, 1949–1979*. Berkeley: University of California Press, 1984.

McLaren, Anne E. *Chinese Popular Culture and Ming Chantefables*. Leiden: Brill, 1998.

——. *Performing Grief: Bridal Laments in Rural China*. Honolulu: University of Hawai'i Press, 2008.

Metternich, Hilary Roe. *Mongolian Folktales*. Boulder, Colo.: Avery Press, 1996.

Mueggler, Eric. *The Age of Wild Ghosts: Memory, Violence, and Place in Southwest China*. Berkeley: University of California Press, 2001.

Notar, Beth E. *Displacing Desire: Travel and Popular Culture in China*. Honolulu: University of Hawai'i Press, 2006.

Olivova, Lucie, and Vibeke Børdahl, eds. *Lifestyle and Entertainment in Yangzhou*. Copenhagen: NIAS Press, 2009.

Oppitz, Michael, and Elizabeth Hsu, eds. *Naxi and Moso Ethnography: Kin, Rites, Pictographs*. Zurich: Völkerkundemuseum Zürich, 1998.

Overmyer, Daniel L. *Precious Volumes: An Introduction to Chinese Sectarian Scriptures from the Sixteenth and Seventeenth Centuries*. Cambridge, Mass.: Harvard University Press, 1999.

Park, Chan E. *Voices from the Straw Mat: Toward an Ethnography of Korean Story Singing*. Honolulu: University of Hawai'i Press, 2003.

Pian, Rulan Chao. "Text and Musical Transcription of a *Kaipian*, 'Birthday Wishes to the Eight Immortals.'" *Chinoperl Papers* 14 (1986): 15–25.

Ramsey, S. Robert. *The Languages of China*. Princeton, N.J.: Princeton University Press, 1987.

Rees, Helen. *Echoes of History: Naxi Music in Modern China*. Oxford: Oxford University Press, 2000.

Riftin, Boris. "'Three Kingdoms' in Chinese Storytelling: A Comparative Study." In *The Eternal Storyteller: Oral Literature in Modern China*, edited by Vibeke Børdahl, 137–60. Richmond: Curzon Press, 1999

Riley, Jo. *Chinese Theatre and the Actor in Performance*. Cambridge Studies in Modern Theatre. Cambridge: Cambridge University Press, 1997.

Schein, Louisa. *Minority Rules: The Miao and the Feminine in China's Cultural Politics*. Durham, N.C.: Duke University Press, 2000.

Sheng, Bright. "The Love Songs of Qinghai." *Asian Arts & Culture* (Arthur M. Sackler Gallery, Smithsonian Institution) 8, no. 3 (1995): 50–58.

Tan Zhengbi and Tan Xun. *Muyu ge, Chaozhou ge xulu* [*Bibliography of Wooden-Fish Songs and Chaozhou Songs*]. Beijing: Shumu wenxian chubanshe, 1982.

Tanaka Ichinari. "Guanyu *Che Wang fu quben*" [On the *Book of the Manor House of Lord Che*]. In *Che Wang fu quben yanjiu* [*Study on the "Book of the Manor House of Lord Che"*], edited by Liu Liemao et al. Guangzhou: Guangdong renmin chubanshe, 2000.

Teiser, Stephen F. *The Ghost Festival in Medieval China*. Princeton, N.J.: Princeton University Press, 1988.

Toelken, Barre. *The Dynamics of Folklore*. Logan: Utah State University Press, 1996.

Toon, Soon Lee. *Chinese Street Opera in Singapore*. Urbana: University of Illinois Press, 2008.

Tsao, Pen-yeh. *The Music of Su-chou T'an-tz'u: Elements of the Southern Chinese Singing Narrative*. Hong Kong: Chinese University Press, 1988.

Tuohy, Sue. "Cultural Metaphors and Ideology in Contemporary China." *Asian Folklore Studies* 50, no. 1 (1991): 189–220.

Walker, Anthony R. *Merit and the Millennium: Routine and Crisis in the Ritual Lives of the Lahu People*. New Delhi: Hindustan Publishing, 2003.

——, ed. *Mvuh Hpa Mi Hpa: Creating Heaven and Earth*. Bangkok: Silkworm Press, 1995.

Walls, Jan. "The Bamboo Clapper Tale." *Chinoperl Papers* 7 (1977): 60–91.

Wan, Margaret. "The Chantefable and the Novel: The Cases of Lü Mudan and Tianbao tu." *Harvard Journal of Asiatic Studies* 64, no. 2 (2004): 367–97.

——. *Green Peony and the Rise of the Chinese Martial Arts Novel*. Albany: State University of New York Press, 2009.

Wang Shaotang. "Wode xueyi jingguo he biaoyan jingyan" [My Education as an Artist and Experience of Performance]. *Shuo xin shu* (Shanghai) 2 (1979): 286–310.

——. *Wu Song*. Vols. 1–2. 1959. Reprint, Huaiyin: Jiangsu renmin chubanshe, 1984.

Wang Xiaotang. *Yi hai ku hang lu* [*Memoirs of the Difficult Navigation on the Sea of Art*]. Zhenjiang: Jiangsu wen shi ziliao bianjibu, 1992.

Wei Ren and Wei Minghua. *Yangzhou quyi shi hua* [*A History of Yangzhou Quyi*]. Beijing: Zhongguo quyi chubanshe, 1985.

Xu Lin and Zhao Yansun. *Baiyu jianzhi* [*A Concise Gazetteer of the Bai Language*]. Beijing: Renmin chubanshe, 1984.

Yang, Gladys, trans. *Ashima*. Beijing: Foreign Languages Press, 1981.

Yang Liangcai and Li Zuanxu, eds. *Baizu minjian xushi shiji* [*A Collection of Bai Nationality Folk Ballads*]. Beijing: Zhongguo minjian wenhua chubanshe, 1984.

Yang Lihui, An Deming, and Jessica Turner. *Handbook of Chinese Mythology*. Santa Barbara, Calif.: ABC-CLIO, 2005.

Yung, Bell. *A Blind Singer's Story: Fifty Years of Life and Work in Hong Kong*. DVD. Hong Kong: Hong Kong Museum of History, 2004.

——. "Popular Narrative in the Pleasure Houses of the South." *Chinoperl Papers* 11 (1982): 126–49.

——. "Reconstructing a Lost Performance Context: A Fieldwork Experiment." *Chinoperl Papers* 6 (1976): 120–43.

Zeitlin, Ida. *Gessar Khan*. New York: Doran, 1927.

Zhalgaa. "A Brief Account of Bensen Uliger and Uligeren Bense." *Oral Tradition* 16, no. 2 (2001): 264–79.

Zhang Dai [1597–1689]. *Tao'an meng yi* [*Recollections of Tao'an's Past Dreams*]. Shanghai: Shanghai guji chubanshe, 1982.

Zhang Xiaosong and Li Gen [Xiaogen]. *Lahu wenhua lun* [*A Discussion of Lahu Culture*]. Kunming: Yunnan da xue chubanshe, 1997.

——. *Lahu zu lusheng lian ge kouxian qing* [*The Lahu Nationality's Gourd Pipe Love Songs and Mouth Harp Feelings*]. Kunming: Yunnan jiaoyu chubanshe, 1995.

Zhang Yaxiong. *Collected Flower Songs* [*Hua'er ji*]. Beijing: National Peking University, 1938; Taipei: Dongfang wenhua shuju, 1972.

Zheng, Su De San. "From Toison to New York: *Muk'yu* Songs in Folk Tradition." *Chinoperl Papers* 16 (1992): 165–205.

Zhong Jingwen. "Liu Sanjie chuanshuo shilun" [Discussion of the Third Sister Liu Legend]. In *Zhong Jingwen minjian wenxue lunwen ji* [*Zhong Jingwen's Collected Works on Folk Literature*], 93–120. Shanghai: Shanghai wenyi chubanshe, 1982.

Zuo Xian. *Pingtan san lun* [*Random Essays on Pingtan*]. Shanghai: Shanghai wenyi chubanshe, 1982.

JOURNALS

Asian Folklore Studies (as of 2008, *Asian Ethnology*)

Asian Highlands Perspectives

Asian Theater Journal

CHIME: Journal of the European Foundation for Chinese Music Research

Chinoperl Papers

Oral Tradition, http://oraltradition.org., especially "Chinese Oral Traditions." Special issue, *Oral Tradition* 16, no. 2 (2001).

WEB SITE

Vibeke Børdahl. Chinese Storytelling. http/:shuoshu.org.

CONTRIBUTORS AND TRANSLATORS

Aku Wuwu (Luo Qingchun) is a professor in the Department of Yi Studies at the Southwest Nationalities University, Chengdu.

An Xiaoke teaches at the Yunnan Tourism School, Kunming, Yunnan.

E. N. Anderson is a professor emeritus of anthropology at the University of California–Riverside.

Awelkhan Hali is a researcher at the Xinjiang Education Institute, Ürümqi, Xinjiang.

Bamo Qubumo is a professor at the Institute for Minority Literature, Chinese Academy of Social Sciences, Beijing.

Mark Bender is an associate professor in the Department of East Asian Languages and Literatures at The Ohio State University.

Rostislav Berezkin is a doctoral candidate at the University of Pennsylvania.

Max L. Bohnenkamp is a graduate student at the University of Chicago.

Vibeke Børdahl is a senior researcher at the Nordic Institute of Asian Studies, Copenhagen.

Chao Gejin (Chogjin) is the director of the Institute for Minority Literature, Chinese Academy of Social Sciences, Beijing.

Fan Pen Li Chen is an associate professor of Chinese studies at the State University of New York–Albany.

Deng Minwen is a professor at the Institute for Minority Literature, Chinese Academy of Social Sciences, Beijing.

Charles Ettner teaches in the Department of Anthropology at California State University–Fresno.

Mareile Flitsch is a professor at the Institut für Philosophie, Wissenschaftstheorie, Wissenschafts und Technikgeschichte at the Technische Universität Berlin.

Fu Wei (Wei Fu Bender) is a consultant in Shawnee Hills, Ohio.

Wilt L. Idema is a professor of Chinese literature and the director of the Fairbank Center for East Asian Research at Harvard University.

Ngampit Jagacinski is a senior lecturer in Thai language at Cornell University.

Jihuwangjiu is a folklore researcher from Yunnan province.

Jimoreko is a folklore researcher from Yunnan province.

Jjiepa Ayi is a graduate of the Southwest Nationalities University, Chengdu.

Ellen R. Judd is a professor of anthropology at the University of Manitoba.

Ke Yang, a folklorist, is a professor emeritus of Chinese literature at Lanzhou University, Gansu province.

Frank Kouwenhoven is a founding member and the current secretary-treasurer of the European Foundation for Chinese Music Research (CHIME), Leiden.

Kun Shi is the director of the Confucius Institute at the University of South Florida.

Lamu Gatusa is an associate professor at the Yunnan Academy of Social Sciences, Kunming.

Lotan Dorje is at the University of Oslo.

Ok Joo Lee teaches at Ewha Womans University, Seoul, South Korea.

Peace Lee is a doctoral candidate in Chinese literature at The Ohio State University.

Zenxiang Li is a professor of Turkish language studies at the Central University for Nationalities, Beijing.

Libu Lakhi (Li Jianfu), from Dashui village, southern Sichuan province, is a student at Qinghai Normal University, Xining, Qinghai province.

Limusishiden, a professor at Qinghai Medical College, was born in Huzhu Mongghul (Tu) Autonomous County, Qinghai province.

Lorden, who teaches Tibetan and English at Qinghai Normal University, was born in Huangnan Tibetan Autonomous Prefecture, Qinghai province.

Kathryn Lowry teaches literature at Brown University and has been editor of the *Chinoperl Papers*.

Karl W. Luckert is a professor emeritus of religious studies at Southwest Missouri State University.

Ma Quanlin, a Qinghai native, graduated from Qinghai Education College and is an English teacher.

Victor Mair is a professor of Chinese language and literature at the University of Pennsylvania.

John McCoy (1924–2007) was for a period of his career a professor of linguistics at Cornell University.

Meng Zhidong (Mergendi) is a researcher on the folklore and culture of the Daur ethnic group and a resident of Hohhot, Inner Mongolia.

Na Xin is a graduate of the Department of East Asian Languages and Literatures at The Ohio State University.

Sonia Ng is an archivist at the Chinese Music Archives, Chinese University of Hong Kong.

Nienu Baxi is a researcher and translator of traditional Yi literature in Honghe, Yunnan province.

Jonathan Noble is an adviser to the provost for Asia at the University of Notre Dame.

Beth E. Notar is an associate professor of anthropology at Trinity College.

Rulan Chao Pian is a professor emerita of East Asian studies and music at Harvard University.

Qenf Dangk Hat Ged is a folklore researcher from southeastern Guizhou province.

Qu Liquan is a graduate of the Department of East Asian Languages and Literatures at The Ohio State University.

Antoinet Schimmelpenninck is a professor at the University of Leiden and a cofounder of the European Foundation for Chinese Music Research (CHIME), Leiden.

Sha Hong (1925–1985) was a poet and scholar from the Guangxi Zhuang Autonomous Region.

Eric Shepherd is an assistant professor of Chinese at the University of South Florida.

Richard VanNess Simmons is an associate professor of Chinese at Rutgers University.

Kate Stevens, a pioneer in the study of Chinese oral literature, is a professor emerita of Chinese literature at the University of Toronto.

Kevin Stuart has for many years been involved in English-language teaching and development projects for Tibetans and Mongols in Qinghai province.

Su Huana, from Hohhot, Inner Mongolia, is a teacher and translator living in Guangzhou, Guangdong province.

Sun Jingyao is a professor of comparative literature at East China Normal University, Shanghai.

Tian Zhongshan is a researcher in the Institute for the Study of Montagnard Languages and People, Central University for Nationalities, Beijing.

Anthony R. Walker is a professor in the Department of Sociology and Anthropology at the University of Brunei.

Wang Jiaxing is a folklore researcher from Yunnan province.

Stephanie Webster-Chang is a graduate of the Department of East Asian Languages and Literatures at the University of Pittsburgh.

Cuiyi Wei is the dean of Turkic studies at the Central University for Nationalities, Beijing.

Wen Xiangcheng is a graduate of Qinghai Normal University, Qinghai province.

Sue-Mei Wu is an associate professor of Chinese at Carnegie Mellon University.

Wu Yongshen is a folklore researcher from the Guangxi Zhuang Autonomous Region.

Xenx Jenb Eb Ghob is a folklore researcher from southeastern Guizhou province.

Yang Haixia is a graduate of the Central University for Nationalities, Beijing.

Yang Jizhong is a folklore researcher from Yunnan province.

Ye Jinyuan is a former employee of the district cultural office, Xining, Qinghai, and currently operates a restaurant in that city.

Leo Shing-Chi Yip is an assistant professor of Japanese studies at Gettysburg College.

Yu Li is a professor of Chinese literature and culture at Williams College.

Yu Lihang is a folklore researcher from Yunnan province.

Yu Ming is a researcher at the Yunnan Museum of Minority Nationalities (Minzu Bowuguan), Kunming, Yunnan province.

Yu Weiliang is a folklore researcher from Yunnan province.

Zeng Guopin is a researcher on Yi culture from Kunming, Yunnan province.

Delia Noble Zhang is a graduate of the Department of East Asian Languages and Literatures at The Ohio State University.

Juwen Zhang is the Luca Junior Professor of Chinese Language and Culture at Willamette University.

Qiguang Zhao is the Burton and Lily Levin Professor of Chinese at Carleton College.

Zhe Houpei is a folklore researcher from Yunnan province.

Su Zheng is a professor of Chinese music at Wesleyan University.

Zhou Liang researches the history of Suzhou storytelling in the Culture Bureau in Suzhou, Jiangsu province.

SOURCES OF PREVIOUSLY PUBLISHED SELECTIONS

FOLK STORIES AND OTHER SPOKEN TRADITIONS

"Mengongnenbo": Meng Zhidong, ed., *Dawo'erzu minjian gushi xuan* [*Selected Daur Folktales*] (Shanghai: Shanghai wenyi chubanshe, 1979); Mark Bender and Su Huana, trans., *Daur Folktales* (Beijing: New World Press, 1984), 110–25.

"February 2, the Dragon Raises His Head": Gu Xijia, *Long De Chuanshuo* [*Dragon Legends*] (Beijing: Zhongguo minjian wenyi, 1986), 156–58.

"Dragon-Print Stone of the West Mountains": Gu Xijia, *Long De Chuanshuo* [*Dragon Legends*] (Beijing: Zhongguo minjian wenyi, 1986), 58–61.

"The Egg Boy": Zhongyang Minzu Xueyuan Shaoshu Minzu Yuyan Wenxue San Xi Gaoshanzu Yuyan Wenxue Jiaoyanshi [Teaching and Research Department for the Languages and Literatures of the Mountain Aborigines, Section Three for Minority Nationalities, Languages, and Literatures of the Central Academy of Nationalities], ed., *Gaoshanzu yuyan wenxue* [*Languages and Literatures of the Mountain Aborigines*] (Beijing: Zhongyang Minzu Xueyuan chubanshe, 1988).

Folk Stories of the Uyghur: Wei Cuiyi and Karl W. Luckert, *Uighur Stories from Along the Silk Road* (Lanham, Md.: University Press of America, 1998). Reprinted by permission of the publisher.

FOLK SONG TRADITIONS

Flower Songs from Northwestern China: Ke Yang, ed., "Flower Songs: Selected Works" [Hua'er zuopin xuan] (unpublished, undated classroom material); Kathryn Lowry, "Flower Songs of Northwest China: Language, Music, and Ritual" (B.A.

thesis, Princeton University, 1985). [An appendix of songs was transcribed from the author's field recordings and other handwritten and mimeographed materials.]

Kazakh Marriage Songs of Lament and Sorrow: Awelkhan Hali, Sengxiang Li, and Karl W. Luckert, *Kazakh Traditions of China* (Lanham, Md.: University Press of America, 1998), 106–22. Reprinted by permission of the publisher.

FOLK RITUAL

"Sacrifice to the Python God": Shi Guangwei and Liu Housheng, eds., *Manzu shaman tiaoshen yanjiu* [*Study of Manchu Shamanism*] (Jilin: Jilin wenshi chubanshe, 1992), 235–36.

"A Song for the God of Sacrifices": Shi Guangwei and Liu Housheng, eds., *Manzu shaman tiaoshen yanjiu* [*Study of Manchu Shamanism*] (Jilin: Jilin wenshi chubanshe, 1992), 67.

Yi Chants from Chuxiong Prefecture, Yunnan: *Yunnan Yizu geyao jicheng* [*Collected Folk Songs of the Yunnan Yi*] (Kunming: Yunnan Nationalities Publishing House, 1986); Mark Bender and Fu Wei, "Calling Back a Child's Spirit," *Shaman's Drum* 13 (1988): 34; Mark Bender and Fu Wei, "'Closing the Coffin': Excerpt from a Bimo Funeral Chant," *Shaman's Drum* 10 (1987): 49; Mark Bender and Fu Wei, "'Cutting the New Year's Firewood': A Yi Folksong," *Chicago Review* 3 (1993): 256–57. Reprinted by permission of the publisher.

THE EPIC TRADITIONS

"The Twelve-Headed Monster": Pajie, *Yinxiong Gesi'er Kehan* [*The Hero Geser Khan*] (Beijing: Zuojia chubanshe, 1963), 51–60.

Introductory Cantos from the Mongol Epic *Jangar*: Sedorji, trans., *Jiangger'er, Mengguzu Minjian shishi* [*Jangar, a Mongolian Folk Epic*] (Beijing: Renmin wenxue chubanshe, 1983), 1–14.

"The *Mergen* and the Fox-Fairies": Fang Caifu, "Dawo'erzu wuqin merigen yu huli" [The *Mergen* and the Fox-Fairies Ballad], ed. and trans. Liu Xingye and Li Fuzhong, *Minjian wenxue* [*Folk Literature*] 9 (1981): 88–90.

The Palace Lamp of the Nanzhao Kingdom: Nienu Baxi, "Nanzhao guode gong deng" [The Palace Lamp of the Nanzhao Kingdom] (manuscript).

Miluotuo: Sha Hong, ed., *Miluotuo: Yaozu chuangshi guge* [*Miluotuo: Ancient Creation Song of the Yao Nationality*] (Nanning: Guangxi renmin chubanshe, 1981).

"How Much Do You Two Really Know?": Jin Dan, ed., *Bangx Hxak: Miaozu guge gehua* [*Song Flowers of the Miao Ancient Songs*] (Guiyang: Guizhou minzu chubanshe, 1998); Mark Bender, trans., "Hunting Nets and Butterflies: Ethnic Minority Songs from Southwest China," in *The Poem Behind the Poem: Translating Asian Poetry*, ed. Frank Stewart (Port Townsend, Wash.: Copper Canyon Press, 2004), 51.

"Don't Weave Cloth Without a Loom": Jin Dan, ed., *Bangx Hxak: Miaozu guge gehua* [*Song Flowers of the Miao Ancient Songs*] (Guiyang: Guizhou minzu chubanshe, 1998); Mark Bender, trans., "Hunting Nets and Butterflies: Ethnic Minority Songs from Southwest China," in *The Poem Behind the Poem: Translating Asian Poetry*, ed. Frank Stewart (Port Townsend, Wash.: Copper Canyon Press, 2004), 52.

FOLK DRAMA

A *Worthy Sister-in-Law*: Ellen R. Judd, "New *Yang'ge*: The Case of 'A Worthy Sister-in-Law,'" *Chinoperl Papers* 10 (1981): 167–86. Reprinted by permission of the publisher.

PROFESSIONAL STORYTELLING TRADITIONS OF THE NORTH AND SOUTH

Northern Prosimetric

"The Courtesan's Jewel Box": Performance recorded in 1962, China Records Company M-554.

"A Bannermen's Story of Hua Mulan": "Hua Mulan," in *Che wang fu qu ben xuan* ["*Tune Book of the Manor House of Lord Che*" *Anthology*], ed. Liu Liemao, Guo Jingrui, Chen Weiwu, Ouyang Shichang, Wu Chengxue, and Qiu Jiang (Guangzhou: Zhongshan daxue chubanshe, 1990), 493–507.

"The New Edition of the Manchu–Han Struggle": "Xin ke Man Han dou, juan yi" [The New Edition of the Manchu–Han Struggle, volume one], in *Che wang fu qu ben xuan* ["*Tune Book of the Manor House of Lord Che*" *Anthology*], ed. Liu Liemao, Guo Jingrui, Chen Weiwu, Ouyang Shichang, Wu Chengxue, and Qiu Jiang (Guangzhou: Zhongshan daxue chubanshe, 1990), 588–606

"The Precious Scroll of Chenxiang": Based on the typeset edition in Du Yingtao, ed., *Dong Yong Chenxiang heji* [*The Combined Collections of (Materials on) Dong Yong and on Chenxiang*] (Shanghai: Gudian wenxue chubanshe, 1957), 167–81. [This version is derived from a manuscript dated 1873 and claims, by its title, to belong to the genre of precious scrolls (*baojuan*).]

"On the Slopes of Changban": Kate Stevens, "'The Slopes of Changban': A Beijing Drumsong in the Liu Style," *Chinoperl Papers* 15 (1990): 27–44. Reprinted by permission of the publisher.

Southern Prosimetric

Hangzhou Storytelling and Songs: Richard VanNess Simmons, "Hangzhou Oral Performances," *Kai Pian: Chūgokugogaku kenkyū* [*Studies in Chinese Language*] 8 (1991): 34–37, and "Hangzhou Storytellers and Their Art," *Kai Pian: Chūgokugogaku kenkyū* 9 (1992): 1–25.

"The Newly Compiled Tale of the Golden Butterflies": Lu Gong, ed., *Liang Zhu gushi shuochang ji* [*The Collection of Narrative Ballads on the Story of Liang Shanbo and Zhu Yingtai*] (Shanghai: Shanghai chuban gongsi, 1955), 223–42. [This version was edited on the basis of a manuscript written by a popular professional artist from Suzhou in Jiangsu province in 1769.]

"Suitable Attire": Chen Duansheng, *Zaisheng yuan* [*Love Reincarnate*], ed. Zhao Jingsheng and Li Ping (Zhongzhou: Zhongzhou shuhuashe, 1982), 1:144–49.

"Sighs from the Palace": Wu Zongxi, ed., *Pingtan cidian* [*Pingtan Dictionary*] (Shanghai: Hanyu dacidian chubanshe, 1996), 119.

"Descending the Stairs": Zhou Liang, Jiang Kaihua, Ni Pingqian, and Xue Xiaofei, eds., *Zhenzhu ta: Wei Hanying yanchu ben*, xia ce ["*Pearl Pagoda*": *Wei Hanying's Performance Text*, volume two] (Shanghai: Shanghai wenyi chubanshe, 1988), 685–98.

"The Thrice-Draped Cape": Qiu Xiaopeng, "San gai yi" [The Thrice-Draped Cape], *Pingtan congkan* [*Pingtan Storytelling Series*] 8 (1962): 20–43.

"Singlet of Blood and Sweat": "Xue han shan" [Singlet of Blood and Sweat], in *Baizu minjian xushishi xuan* [*Narrative Poems of the Bai Nationality*], ed. Yang Liangcai and Li Zuanxu (Beijing: Zhongguo minjian wenyi chubanshe, 1984), 187–93.

TRANSLATIONS FROM THE ASIAN CLASSICS

Major Plays of Chikamatsu, tr. Donald Keene 1961

Four Major Plays of Chikamatsu, tr. Donald Keene. Paperback ed. only. 1961; rev. ed. 1997

Records of the Grand Historian of China, translated from the Shih chi of Ssu-ma Ch'ien, tr. Burton Watson, 2 vols. 1961

Instructions for Practical Living and Other Neo-Confucian Writings by Wang Yang-ming, tr. Wing-tsit Chan 1963

Hsün Tzu: Basic Writings, tr. Burton Watson, paperback ed. only. 1963; rev. ed. 1996

Chuang Tzu: Basic Writings, tr. Burton Watson, paperback ed. only. 1964; rev. ed. 1996

The Mahābhārata, tr. Chakravarthi V. Narasimhan. Also in paperback ed. 1965; rev. ed. 1997

The Manyōshū, Nippon Gakujutsu Shinkōkai edition 1965

Su Tung-p'o: Selections from a Sung Dynasty Poet, tr. Burton Watson. Also in paperback ed. 1965

Bhartrihari: Poems, tr. Barbara Stoler Miller. Also in paperback ed. 1967

Basic Writings of Mo Tzu, Hsün Tzu, and Han Fei Tzu, tr. Burton Watson. Also in separate paperback eds. 1967

The Awakening of Faith, Attributed to Aśvaghosha, tr. Yoshito S. Hakeda. Also in paperback ed. 1967

Reflections on Things at Hand: The Neo-Confucian Anthology, comp. Chu Hsi and Lü Tsu-ch'ien, tr. Wing-tsit Chan 1967

The Platform Sutra of the Sixth Patriarch, tr. Philip B. Yampolsky. Also in paperback ed. 1967

Essays in Idleness: The Tsurezuregusa of Kenkō, tr. Donald Keene. Also in paperback ed. 1967

The Pillow Book of Sei Shōnagon, tr. Ivan Morris, 2 vols. 1967

Two Plays of Ancient India: The Little Clay Cart and the Minister's Seal, tr. J. A. B. van Buitenen 1968

The Complete Works of Chuang Tzu, tr. Burton Watson 1968

The Romance of the Western Chamber (Hsi Hsiang chi), tr. S. I. Hsiung. Also in paperback ed. 1968

The Manyōshū, Nippon Gakujutsu Shinkōkai edition. Paperback ed. only. 1969

Records of the Historian: Chapters from the Shih chi of Ssu-ma Ch'ien, tr. Burton Watson. Paperback ed. only. 1969

Cold Mountain: 100 Poems by the T'ang Poet Han-shan, tr. Burton Watson. Also in paperback ed. 1970

Twenty Plays of the Nō Theatre, ed. Donald Keene. Also in paperback ed. 1970

Chūshingura: The Treasury of Loyal Retainers, tr. Donald Keene. Also in paperback ed. 1971; rev. ed. 1997

The Zen Master Hakuin: Selected Writings, tr. Philip B. Yampolsky 1971

Chinese Rhyme-Prose: Poems in the Fu Form from the Han and Six Dynasties Periods, tr. Burton Watson. Also in paperback ed. 1971

Kūkai: Major Works, tr. Yoshito S. Hakeda. Also in paperback ed. 1972

The Old Man Who Does as He Pleases: Selections from the Poetry and Prose of Lu Yu, tr. Burton Watson 1973

The Lion's Roar of Queen Śrīmālā, tr. Alex and Hideko Wayman 1974

Courtier and Commoner in Ancient China: Selections from the History of the Former Han by Pan Ku, tr. Burton Watson. Also in paperback ed. 1974

Japanese Literature in Chinese, vol. 1: *Poetry and Prose in Chinese by Japanese Writers of the Early Period*, tr. Burton Watson 1975

Japanese Literature in Chinese, vol. 2: *Poetry and Prose in Chinese by Japanese Writers of the Later Period*, tr. Burton Watson 1976

Love Song of the Dark Lord: Jayadeva's Gītagovinda, tr. Barbara Stoler Miller. Also in paperback ed. Cloth ed. includes critical text of the Sanskrit. 1977; rev. ed. 1997

Ryōkan: Zen Monk-Poet of Japan, tr. Burton Watson 1977

Calming the Mind and Discerning the Real: From the Lam rim chen mo of Tsoṇ-kha-pa, tr. Alex Wayman 1978

The Hermit and the Love-Thief: Sanskrit Poems of Bhartrihari and Bilhaṇa, tr. Barbara Stoler Miller 1978

The Lute: Kao Ming's P'i-p'a chi, tr. Jean Mulligan. Also in paperback ed. 1980

A Chronicle of Gods and Sovereigns: Jinnō Shōtōki of Kitabatake Chikafusa, tr. H. Paul Varley 1980

Among the Flowers: The Hua-chien chi, tr. Lois Fusek 1982

Grass Hill: Poems and Prose by the Japanese Monk Gensei, tr. Burton Watson 1983

Doctors, Diviners, and Magicians of Ancient China: Biographies of Fang-shih, tr. Kenneth J. DeWoskin. Also in paperback ed. 1983

Theater of Memory: The Plays of Kālidāsa, ed. Barbara Stoler Miller. Also in paperback ed. 1984

The Columbia Book of Chinese Poetry: From Early Times to the Thirteenth Century, ed. and tr. Burton Watson. Also in paperback ed. 1984

Poems of Love and War: From the Eight Anthologies and the Ten Long Poems of Classical Tamil, tr. A. K. Ramanujan. Also in paperback ed. 1985
The Bhagavad Gita: Krishna's Counsel in Time of War, tr. Barbara Stoler Miller 1986
The Columbia Book of Later Chinese Poetry, ed. and tr. Jonathan Chaves. Also in paperback ed. 1986
The Tso Chuan: Selections from China's Oldest Narrative History, tr. Burton Watson 1989
Waiting for the Wind: Thirty-six Poets of Japan's Late Medieval Age, tr. Steven Carter 1989
Selected Writings of Nichiren, ed. Philip B. Yampolsky 1990
Saigyō, Poems of a Mountain Home, tr. Burton Watson 1990
The Book of Lieh Tzu: A Classic of the Tao, tr. A. C. Graham. Morningside ed. 1990
The Tale of an Anklet: An Epic of South India—The Cilappatikāram of Iḷaṅkō Aṭikaḷ, tr. R. Parthasarathy 1993
Waiting for the Dawn: A Plan for the Prince, tr. with introduction by Wm. Theodore de Bary 1993
Yoshitsune and the Thousand Cherry Trees: A Masterpiece of the Eighteenth-Century Japanese Puppet Theater, tr., annotated, and with introduction by Stanleigh H. Jones, Jr. 1993
The Lotus Sutra, tr. Burton Watson. Also in paperback ed. 1993
The Classic of Changes: A New Translation of the I Ching *as Interpreted by Wang Bi*, tr. Richard John Lynn 1994
Beyond Spring: Tz'u Poems of the Sung Dynasty, tr. Julie Landau 1994
The Columbia Anthology of Traditional Chinese Literature, ed. Victor H. Mair 1994
Scenes for Mandarins: The Elite Theater of the Ming, tr. Cyril Birch 1995
Letters of Nichiren, ed. Philip B. Yampolsky; tr. Burton Watson et al. 1996
Unforgotten Dreams: Poems by the Zen Monk Shōtetsu, tr. Steven D. Carter 1997
The Vimalakirti Sutra, tr. Burton Watson 1997
Japanese and Chinese Poems to Sing: The Wakan rōei shū, tr. J. Thomas Rimer and Jonathan Chaves 1997
Breeze Through Bamboo: Kanshi of Ema Saikō, tr. Hiroaki Sato 1998
A Tower for the Summer Heat, by Li Yu, tr. Patrick Hanan 1998
Traditional Japanese Theater: An Anthology of Plays, by Karen Brazell 1998
The Original Analects: Sayings of Confucius and His Successors (0479–0249), by E. Bruce Brooks and A. Taeko Brooks 1998
The Classic of the Way and Virtue: A New Translation of the Tao-te ching *of Laozi as Interpreted by Wang Bi*, tr. Richard John Lynn 1999
The Four Hundred Songs of War and Wisdom: An Anthology of Poems from Classical Tamil, The Puṟanāṉūṟu, ed. and tr. George L. Hart and Hank Heifetz 1999
Original Tao: Inward Training (Nei-yeh) *and the Foundations of Taoist Mysticism*, by Harold D. Roth 1999
Po Chü-i: Selected Poems, tr. Burton Watson 2000
Lao Tzu's Tao Te Ching: *A Translation of the Startling New Documents Found at Guodian*, by Robert G. Henricks 2000
The Shorter Columbia Anthology of Traditional Chinese Literature, ed. Victor H. Mair 2000
Mistress and Maid (Jiaohongji), by Meng Chengshun, tr. Cyril Birch 2001

Chikamatsu: Five Late Plays, tr. and ed. C. Andrew Gerstle 2001
The Essential Lotus: Selections from the Lotus Sutra, tr. Burton Watson 2002
Early Modern Japanese Literature: An Anthology, 1600–1900, ed. Haruo Shirane 2002; abridged 2008
The Columbia Anthology of Traditional Korean Poetry, ed. Peter H. Lee 2002
The Sound of the Kiss, or The Story That Must Never Be Told: Pingali Suranna's Kalapurnodayamu, tr. Vecheru Narayana Rao and David Shulman 2003
The Selected Poems of Du Fu, tr. Burton Watson 2003
Far Beyond the Field: Haiku by Japanese Women, tr. Makoto Ueda 2003
Just Living: Poems and Prose by the Japanese Monk Tonna, ed. and tr. Steven D. Carter 2003
Han Feizi: Basic Writings, tr. Burton Watson 2003
Mozi: Basic Writings, tr. Burton Watson 2003
Xunzi: Basic Writings, tr. Burton Watson 2003
Zhuangzi: Basic Writings, tr. Burton Watson 2003
The Awakening of Faith, Attributed to Aśvaghosha, tr. Yoshito S. Hakeda, introduction by Ryuichi Abe 2005
The Tales of the Heike, tr. Burton Watson, ed. Haruo Shirane 2006
Tales of Moonlight and Rain, by Ueda Akinari, tr. with introduction by Anthony H. Chambers 2007
Traditional Japanese Literature: An Anthology, Beginnings to 1600, ed. Haruo Shirane 2007
The Philosophy of Qi, by Kaibara Ekken, tr. Mary Evelyn Tucker 2007
The Analects of Confucius, tr. Burton Watson 2007
The Art of War: Sun Zi's Military Methods, tr. Victor Mair 2007
One Hundred Poets, One Poem Each: A Translation of the Ogura Hyakunin Isshu, tr. Peter McMillan 2008
Zeami: Performance Notes, tr. Tom Hare 2008
Zongmi on Chan, tr. Jeffrey Lyle Broughton 2009
Scripture of the Lotus Blossom of the Fine Dharma, rev. ed., tr. Leon Hurvitz, preface and introduction by Stephen R. Teiser 2009
Mencius, tr. Irene Bloom, ed. with an introduction by Philip J. Ivanhoe 2009
Clouds Thick, Whereabouts Unknown: Poems by Zen Monks of China, tr. Charles Egan 2010
The Mozi: A Complete Translation, tr. Ian Johnston 2010
The Huainanzi: A Guide to the Theory and Practice of Government in Early Han China, by Liu An, tr. John S. Major, Sarah A. Queen, Andrew Seth Meyer, and Harold D. Roth, with Michael Puett and Judson Murray 2010
The Demon at Agi Bridge and Other Japanese Tales, tr. Burton Watson, ed. with introduction by Haruo Shirane 2011
Haiku Before Haiku: From the Renga Masters to Bashō, tr. with introduction by Steven D. Carter 2011
Tamil Love Poetry: The Five Hundred Short Poems of the Aiṅkuṟunūṟu, tr. and ed. Martha Ann Selby 2011
The Teachings of Master Wuzhu: Zen and Religion of No-Religion, by Wendi L. Adamek 2011